PENGUIN

THE FALL OF THE HOUSE OF USHER AND OTHER WRITINGS

EDGAR ALLAN POE was born in Boston in 1809, the son of itinerant actors. Both his parents died within two years of his birth. Edgar was taken into the home of a Richmond merchant, John Allan, although he was never legally adopted. Poe's relationship with his foster-father was not good and was further strained when he was forced to withdraw from the University of Virginia because Allan refused to finance him. After a reconciliation, Poe entered the Military Academy at West Point in 1830; he was dishonourably discharged in January 1831. It was a deliberate action on Poe's part and again was largely due to Allan's tight-fistedness. His early work as a writer went unrecognized and he was forced to earn his living on newspapers, working as an editor in Richmond, Philadelphia and New York. He achieved respect as a literary critic, but it was not until the publication of *The Raven and Other Poems* in 1845 that he gained success as a writer. And, despite his increasing fame, Poe remained in the same poverty which characterized most of his life. In 1836 he married his cousin, Virginia, who was then fourteen; she died eleven years later of tuberculosis.

Poe's life and personality have attracted almost as much attention as his writing, and he has been variously pictured as a sadomasochist, dipsomaniac, drug addict and manic depressive. There can be little doubt that Poe was a disturbed and tormented man and, like so many of his characters, often driven to the brink of madness. Writing of the effect of Virginia's death, Poe said: 'I became insane, with long intervals of horrible sanity. During these fits of absolute unconsciousness, I drank . . . my enemies referred the insanity to the drink, rather than the drink to the insanity.'

Poe died a few years later in 1849 and was buried in Baltimore beside his wife.

DAVID GALLOWAY is Ordinarius Professor for American Studies at the Ruhr University of Bochum, Germany, and an art critic whose writings appear regularly in *Art in America*, *ART news* and the *International Herald Tribune*. His critical works include *The Absurd Hero*, *Henry James: The Portrait of a Lady* and *Edward Lewis Wallant*; he is also the author of four novels – *Melody Jones*, *A Family Album*, *Lamaar Ransom: Private Eye* and *Tamsen*. He has also edited *Comedies and Satires* by Edgar Allan Poe for the Penguin Classics.

The Fall of the House of Usher and Other Writings

Poems, Tales, Essays and Reviews

Edited with an introduction by
David Galloway

Penguin Books

PENGUIN BOOKS

Published by the Penguin Group
Penguin Books Ltd, 27 Wrights Lane, London W8 5TZ, England
Penguin Putnam Inc., 375 Hudson Street, New York, New York 10014, USA
Penguin Books Australia Ltd, Ringwood, Victoria, Australia
Penguin Books Canada Ltd, 10 Alcorn Avenue, Toronto, Ontario, Canada M4V 3B2
Penguin Books India (P) Ltd, 11, Community Centre,
Panchsheel Park, New Delhi – 110 017, India
Penguin Books (NZ) Ltd, Private Bag 102902, NSMC, Auckland, New Zealand
Penguin Books (South Africa) (Pty) Ltd, 5 Watkins Street,
Denver Ext 4, Johannesburg 2094, South Africa

Penguin Books Ltd, Registered Offices: Harmondsworth, Middlesex, England

This collection first published as *Selected Writings of Edgar Allen Poe*, 1967
Reprinted in Penguin Classics as *The Fall of the House of Usher and Other Writings* 1986
22

Printed in England by Clays Ltd, St Ives plc
Set in Linotype Juliana

Contents

CONTENTS

3. ESSAYS AND REVIEWS

From childhood's hour I have not been
As others were – I have not seen
As others saw – I could not bring
My passions from a common spring –

Edgar Allan Poe, 'Alone'

Introduction

I

ON 16 May 1836 Edgar A. Poe and his friend Thomas Cleland filed a marriage bond with the Clerk of the Hustings Court in Richmond, Virginia, in preparation for Poe's marriage to his cousin Virginia Clemm. Mr Cleland added an affidavit that Virginia was 'of the full age of twenty-one years', though she was, in fact, only thirteen. Poe's marriage to a 'child bride' has taken its disproportionate place in the complex legend that has made of Poe's life a more baroque fiction than the author himself ever created, but the truth of his relationship with Virginia, so far as it can now be ascertained, is best seen later and in its proper context – that of Poe's life, and the work which Virginia directly inspired. At this point it is sufficient to note that in the spring of 1836 Poe seemed to have within reach two of his most persistent desires : the professional opportunity to put himself 'before the eye of the world', and the stable comforts of a well-ordered domestic life, provided not only by Virginia, but by her capable, devoted mother, Mrs Clemm.

In December 1835 Poe had become editor of the *Southern Literary Messenger*, and his fiction, essays, and reviews rapidly won the magazine a national audience. Life in a Richmond boarding house, with Poe's meagre salary supplemented by Mrs Clemm's industry as a seamstress, may seem a humdrum existence for an aesthetician who so persistently reiterated the principles of Beauty and Ideality, but for Poe as an artist it was a fruitful time, and in comparison with the desperate circumstances in which he had found himself in the years following his discharge from West Point and his appointment as editor of the *Messenger*, these months in Richmond could hardly have been an unpleasant interlude. Nonetheless, Poe resigned from the *Messenger* in January 1837, following a disagreement with the owner, T. W. White

White was uneasy about Poe's 'intemperance', and perhaps jealous of his success as an editor; but White was not an unreasonable man, and he seems to have been genuinely fond of Poe. To attribute Poe's resignation to professional disagreement alone is not sufficient: he was also tempted by the prospect of challenging more directly the literary hegemony of the North. While Richmond was the 'home' to which he repeatedly returned, it no doubt evoked baffling and painful memories; and he seems, further, to have been caught by that spirit of restlessness which marked so many periods of his life – one is tempted to use Poe's own term, 'perverseness'.

Following his resignation the *Southern Literary Messenger* began to serialize Poe's first attempt at a novel, *The Narrative of Arthur Gordon Pym*, but when Poe submitted a story entitled 'The Fall of the House of Usher', White promptly rejected it, for he doubted 'whether the readers of the *Messenger* have much relish for tales of the German school'. Poe eventually sold the story to *Burton's Gentleman's Magazine* for a fee of ten dollars. When 'The Fall of the House of Usher' appeared in the collected *Tales of the Grotesque and Arabesque*, Poe's sole remuneration consisted of a few complimentary copies of the volume; for a later and expanded edition he received payment in the form of twenty copies of the book; but when he subsequently offered the copyright of a two-volume collection of his stories on the same terms, the proposal was immediately rejected. Poe's brief letter to the Philadelphia publishers, Lea & Blanchard, in which he suggests that 'you receive all profits, and allow me twenty copies for distribution to friends', is a pathetic document in the life of a man who, even when greeted with wide popular acclaim, could do little more than maintain a genteel poverty – and often not even that. By one of those ironies which have by now become almost idiomatic to Poe's life, his six-sentence letter to Lea & Blanchard was auctioned less than a century after his death for $3,000.

Not only is 'The Fall of the House of Usher' one of Poe's finest tales, but one whose richness and totality of effect entitle it to unquestioned place among the short-fiction masterpieces of all time. Perhaps no other single story has exerted such profound influence on other artists as Poe's 'Germanic' tale. As a young man Debussy attempted to set the story in the form of a 'symphony on psychologically developed themes', and though the project was never realized in these terms, Poe's work continued to intrigue the composer, providing inspiration for his opera of *Pelléas*, as it had for Maeterlinck's drama with its over-refined hero 'so pale and feeble and overcome by destiny'. Later Debussy cherished the idea of composing an opera based on Poe's story, and although he died before the project was completed, during the last years of his life it haunted and inspired him; in letters he speaks of the 'obsession', the 'almost agonizing tyranny' which Poe exerts over him; his own phraseology begins to echo Poe's, and in a mood of depression he could write to André Caplet,

I have recently been living in the House of Usher which is not exactly the place where one can look after one's nerves – just the opposite. One develops the curious habit of listening to the stones as if they were in conversation with each other and of expecting houses to crumble to pieces as if this were not only natural but inevitable. Moreover, if you were to presume I should confess that I like these people more than many others. ... I have no confidence in the normal, well-balanced type of persons.

Film-makers, of course, have made wholesale use of Poe's fiction, and the House of Usher has had more than one cinematic fall; the most notable was the first, Jean Epstein's version of 1928. Despite improbable alterations in the plot, Epstein was able to use experimental camera techniques to capture the elusive mystery of the story, the unreal, dreamlike, baroque grandeur of the house itself, and the tormented soul of Roderick Usher. What is especially interesting is the degree to which the mood of Poe's story encouraged both Epstein and Debussy to seek new creative techniques in their respective arts. Yet this story – one of the most frequently anthologized pieces by Poe, and justifiably one of his most famous – was dismissed in the author's lifetime not only as too 'Germanic' for a popular audience, but, most damnably, as 'a juvenile production'.

Time, of course, has vindicated not just 'The Fall of the House of Usher', but Poe's reputation as well, and yet almost a century passed after his death before American critics began to treat his work with appropriate seriousness. European critics were far more astute in recognizing his significance, and the fact is hardly surprising. Poe's relationship to the European romantic tradition – to Coleridge and De Quincey, to Byron, Keats and Shelley, to the Gothic traditions of Germany and the critical theories of Schlegel – is more immediately recognizable than any American tradition, and his work marks him not simply as a precursor of the Symbolist school in France, but as a direct and major influence on Baudelaire, Mallarmé, Verlaine and Rimbaud. T. S. Eliot's suggestion that Poe's profound influence on the French resulted from improvements in the translation is of little worth. Baudelaire's translations of the tales, which comprise five of the twelve volumes of his collected works, are remarkable for their strict authenticity and adherence, wherever idiom permits, to Poe's phraseology.* Poe's poetry – which Baudelaire despaired of rendering accurately in French – received its most influential translation in Mallarmé's edition, where the form, that of the prose poem, made a direct and major contribution to the *vers libre* movement;† and yet Poe's theories of poetry – of beauty, inspiration, originality and imagination – almost certainly created a greater impact than his verse itself, and his criticism, like his fiction, was translated with literal exactitude.

While Poe's impact on the arts in France can hardly be overstressed, and while the French are entitled to full credit for critical recognition of his genius, Poe's influence outside France has also been considerable. Stevenson and Arthur Conan Doyle both acknowledged their debts to Poe's work, Conrad praised the authenticity of his descriptions of the sea, and Mann found in 'William Wilson' the classic example of the *Doppelgänger* theme. From

---

* Even idiomatic convention could be overlooked in order to preserve the flavour and rhythm of the original – as in Baudelaire's translation of the opening sentence in *The Narrative of Arthur Gordon Pym*. Poe's 'My name is Arthur Gordon Pym', Baudelaire translated as 'Mon nom est Arthur Gordon Pym'.

† Despite the 'freedom' of these translations, Mallarmé himself asserted that he had studied English 'the better to read Poe'.

Poe's tales we not only trace the growth of the detective story, but also the science-fiction genre (where one must again return to the French and to Jules Verne's acknowledgement in *Le Sphinx des Glaces*). Poe's influence on Hawthorne is verifiable, and the argument for influence on Melville has logic if not primary documentary evidence on its side. We can see in Poe an early elaboration of the grotesque tradition which underlies the work of William Faulkner, and in such neglected stories as 'The Man That Was Used Up' a significant foreshadowing of the Black Humourists. It is hardly necessary (or even reasonable) to claim that in each of these instances – and the score of others which might easily be cited – Poe acted as a direct influence, or, even when he did, as a strictly determining one. Without in any way distorting his work, we can see in it not only the origins of symbolism, but a crude statement of New Criticism, the stream-of-consciousness technique, ontological crises which defy any other description but 'existential', and methods which seem to foreshadow surrealism and abstract painting – even, indeed, in *Eureka*, theories of matter remarkably close to those of Einstein. To the sympathetic reader such variety and imaginative resourcefulness are intriguing, but it is tempting to overstress Poe's influence, and the critic must be particularly wary of committing *lèse-majesté*: like most men of genius, Poe was in many respects in advance of his time, and through the force of a profound creative intellect he could crystallize moods, techniques, ideas which seem to us peculiarly modern; but he was also of and for his time.

Just as Poe was once vilified by those who saw in him a prime example of diseased intellect, so too has his life been distorted by devotees who have pictured him as an exotic, trapped and finally destroyed by what Baudelaire described as 'a great barbarous realm equipped with gas fixtures'. It was a particularly gratifying image to the Decadents, and it persists as a popular misconception based on the fact that Poe made at best a precarious living as a writer and that he was, according to legend, driven to alcohol and drugs not only by the peculiar torments of his private life, but by a hostile and intolerant world which could not appreciate the rare light of his genius. Amid such elaborate romances there lurks, of course, some truth. There is a sense in which Poe was an exotic, an improbable product of his age, if we consider his work from the conventional viewpoints of intellectual history: in his lushness and sensuousness, his confirmed aestheticism, and his obsession with the grotesque and arabesque, he may well remind one more of exotics like Aubrey Beardsley, Oscar Wilde, Baudelaire or Rimbaud than he does of any American writer or artist. But as Poe's letters, essays, and reviews suggest, he maintained a real and varied interest in the world around him, not merely in literature, but in the theatre, in architecture, music, painting, commerce, education, theories of government, and particularly in science. His sonnet 'To Science' has been read as a conventional romantic cry of distress against a materialistic age, which in some measure it is; but such a reading denies the ambiguous tone of the poem and falsifies, somewhat, its intention, which is to establish, as a preface to 'Al Aaraaf', the distinction between man's power and responsibility as a rational creature and those of the intuitive, imaginative being. The contrast recurs throughout Poe's work – whether in the form of reason and imagination, or natural and supernatural, or matter and Ideality. Poe's ideal was a perfect synthesis of the two modes of intelligence. In his fiction the closest he came to this ideal was in the creation of the master detective Dupin, a poet who brings to commonplace reality the discriminating eye of the artist, but who weighs his evidence as a logician and is able to extrapolate from the raw materials of the *real* world the *ideal* solution. Art was, for Poe, the only method by which one could penetrate the shapeless empirical world in the search for order, and *Eureka* was his most elaborate attempt to reconcile the apparent split between imagination and fact. It is this ambitious intention which shapes all of Poe's best work, determining his use of image and symbol and underlying his insistence on the principle of unity in poetry and fiction. Science has its place in man's search for understanding, but science and the imagination have tended to bifurcate in the modern world; only the true poetic intellect can end this long-established dualism.

In his mingled fascination with and suspicion of scientific 'truth' Poe was clearly the child of the nineteenth century: what he feared was the dogmatism of science and the corrupting influence of materialism; but in an article entitled 'A Chapter on Science and Art' he could deal sympathetically with a variety of modern inventions and urge the establishment of a scientific foundation in Washington. He harshly ridiculed technological progress and obsessive materialism in 'The Man That Was Used Up', and yet his writing is studded with references to scientific treatises which clearly demonstrate a greater interest than the simple creation of mood or credibility. Poe's apparent ambiguity in this respect is not unique: Mark Twain could satirize the methods of geology in *Life on the Mississippi* and yet lose an enormous fortune through his investment in the Paige typesetting machine; at the Columbian Exhibition Henry Adams thrilled at the sight of the huge dynamos which were to transform American life, but feared that as a result of such technological progress men might become 'mere creatures of force round central power-houses'. Poe frequently paraded erudition which had come to him at second hand, and as a journalist he was occasionally compelled to write on subjects which could have held little real interest for him, but experience, reading, and a mind eagerly responsive to new ideas gave him a wide acquaintance with the world in which he lived.

Nonetheless, to many of his contemporaries and to succeeding generations of critics – even those who freely expressed their fascination with his fiction – Poe seemed peculiarly out of touch with his age. Vernon Parrington summarized the conventional critical response to Poe when he noted that:

An aesthete and a craftsman, the first American writer to be concerned with beauty alone, his ideals ran counter to every interest of the New England renaissance: the mystical, optimistic element in transcendentalism; the social conscience that would make the world over in accordance with French idealism, and that meddled with its neighbor's affairs in applying its equalitarianism to the Negro; the pervasive moralism that would accept no other criteria by which to judge life and letters – these things could not fail to irritate a nature too easily ruffled. ... Aside from his art he had no philosophy and no programs and no causes.

Though we can now recognize, in the mystical exaltation which often colours his work, some affinities with the transcendentalism of Emerson and Thoreau, it is nonetheless true that Poe stood apart from many of the social and political traditions of the nineteenth century. But with what a sardonic smile Poe would have read Parrington's lines, not simply because of his almost irrational dislike of 'New England', but because of the fervour with which he argued against provincialism (*not* nationalism) and urged that American writing must be seen in a world context. Furthermore, Poe, too, sought a transcendental experience, but one motivated and circumscribed by taste. In the search for a new vision of man, Poe took the route of aesthetics, while the major figures of the New England renaissance – Emerson, Thoreau, and Hawthorne – took that of ethics. In his definition of the 'Poetic Principle', Poe divided the world of mind into 'Pure Intellect, Taste, and the Moral Sense'. Taste was the most vital of these divisions because it could hold communion with both intellect and morality :

Just as the Intellect concerns itself with Truth, so Taste informs us of the Beautiful while the Moral Sense is regardful of Duty. Of this latter, while Conscience teaches the obligation, and Reason the expediency, Taste contents herself with displaying the charms : – waging war upon Vice solely on the ground of her deformity – her disproportion – her animosity to the fitting, to the appropriate, to the harmonious – in a word, to Beauty.

The aim of poetry for Poe was to put the reader in as direct a sensuous contact with this beauty as language would permit (and in describing the process by which such contact can be made in its highest and most enriched form, Poe is moving toward the concept of the 'objective correlative') : thus man could reach that elevated state of perception which he himself apothesized as 'the intoxication of the Heart'. Poe's debt to Coleridge is obvious; and yet whenever one speaks of influences and sources in Poe, it is well to remember the evolution which such suggestions underwent in his best work, leading him, in his late theories of poetry, to a conception of the creative process which seems distinctly modern – one which attempts to blend the Coleridgean aesthetic with a concept of mind as the formalistic and controlling force in composition.

In his early essays on poetry, Poe floundered about with the time-honoured bugbear of quantitative verse and rendered meaningless verdicts on 'bastard trochees'; if in theory he never comprehended the accentual basis of English poetry, in practice he could achieve remarkable effects. Happily, Poe abandoned these arguments in the later 'Poetic Principle', along with his carping attacks on individual poets. Style and idea have undergone extensive refinement, and his war on didacticism has been qualified, though hardly abandoned. Poe's own poetry has often been seen as poor evidence of the success of his theories of composition: Emerson dismissed him as 'the jingle man', and only recently have English or American critics begun to take serious issue with such a charge. Poe could describe poetry as the 'passion' of his life, and yet in fairness to his reputation the reader should be aware that most of his poetry was written before the age of twenty-two, and that personal anxiety and financial need prevented him from devoting his talents to verse with the consistency he desired. Nonetheless, one could cite few American poems written after the death of Edward Taylor in 1729 and before the early verse of Emily Dickinson to compare in richness or accomplishment with Poe's 'Helen', 'The Raven', 'Lenore', or 'Ulalume'. Furthermore, poetry was a far more comprehensive term for Poe than it was for his contemporaries, and when seeking the poetic in his work we must also look to critical statements like the following, in which Poe describes Man's aspiration toward Beauty:

It is the desire of the moth for the star. It is no mere appreciation of the Beauty before us – but a wild effort to reach the Beauty above. Inspired by an ecstatic prescience of the glories beyond the grave, we struggle, by multiform combinations among the things and thoughts of Time, to attain a portion of that Loveliness whose very elements, perhaps, appertain to eternity alone.

or to the opening sentence of 'Usher':

During the whole of a dull, dark, and soundless day in the autumn of the year, when the clouds hung oppressively low in the heavens,

17

I had been passing alone, on horseback, through a singularly dreary tract of country, and at length found myself, as the shades of the evening drew on, within view of the melancholy House of Usher.

It is unfortunate that in the small body of verse which he produced, Poe so often took as his models sentimentalists like Willis, Puckney, Moore, and Hood; but even at its worst, Poe's poetry suggests to us that quality of intensity and heightened consciousness which is the aim of all his work. He dismissed the representational style as commonplace and uninspiring, and cited music as the supreme art form, the one most suitable to 'the creation of supernal Beauty'. Poe would certainly have applauded Walter Pater's assertion that 'all art continuously aspires to the condition of music' – to that ideally abstract medium whose components are not distorted by material connotation, and are thus freed to create their own unique, transcendent relationships. It is not surprising, then, that music itself plays such a major role not only in the images and sounds of Poe's own poetry, but in his prose work as well. Thus Poe characterizes the temperament to be described in 'The Fall of the House of Usher' as a lute suspended in mid-air, and the 'wild fantasies' of Usher's own singing form a central image in the story. Poe's conviction of the musical properties of language as a necessary adjunct to the search for Beauty may threaten to overwhelm sense in 'The Bells' and justify his reputation as 'the jingle man'; it could also produce the memorable lines in 'To Helen', with their subtle overlaying of internal rhymes and assonance and richly evocative language:

> On desperate seas long wont to roam,
>   Thy hyacinth hair, thy classic face,
> Thy Naiad airs have brought me home
>   To the glory that was Greece,
>   And the grandeur that was Rome.

2

Poe's staunch opposition to didacticism, combined with the grotesque terror of his most memorable tales, did indeed seem to set him apart from what Parrington cited as the 'pervasive moralism' of his time; but without denying Poe's uniqueness, one can see numerous points of convergence between his work and that of other major American writers of the nineteenth century. Poe began his career as a writer of fiction with a series of satires on literary fashions: what we know of the early *Tales of the Folio Club* would be ample evidence of his familiarity with the popular fiction of his time, even if we did not have his reviews and articles as final substantiation. In parodying his contemporaries, Poe discovered his own particular gifts as a writer of fiction; that he did more than merely surpass many of them in the dramaturgy of death and decay is a point which can be dealt with later.

As a critic of literature Poe was fearless and often astute, the avowed enemy of the puffery which characterized so much of American literary life in the nineteenth century; but his criticisms often descended to the level of personalities, and not even the most sympathetic student of Poe can follow the history of his war with Longfellow or his own puffery of second-rate poetesses without acute embarrassment. James Russell Lowell described him as 'at once the most discriminating, philosophical, and fearless critic upon imaginative works ... in America', yet one who 'sometimes seems to mistake his phial of prussic acid for his inkstand'. But Poe's criticism was not simply directed against the literary foibles (and imagined plagiarisms) of his time. He was a harsh critic of democracy, sharing James Fenimore Cooper's distrust of a democratic audience as a great leveller of taste and literary standards. In 'Mallonta Tauta', a utopian projection into the year A.D. 2048, Poe derided the ruler of the 'ideal' Republic, King Mob:

This 'mob' (a foreigner, by the by) is said to have been the most odious of all men who ever encumbered the earth. He was a giant in stature – insolent, rapacious, filthy; had the gall of a bullock with the heart of a hyena and the brains of a peacock. He died, at length, by dint of his own energies, which exhausted him. ... As for Republicanism, no analogy could be found for it on the face of the earth – unless we except the case of the 'prairie dogs', an exception which seems to demonstrate, if anything, that democracy is a very admirable form of government – for dogs.

Such a viewpoint was far removed from the democratic idealism which Emerson and Thoreau asserted and which reached its supreme lyrical expression in Walt Whitman's *Leaves of Grass*. Yet Emerson himself was apprehensive of the excesses and abuses to which democracy might yield; and indeed there is a long conservative political tradition in American literature to which 'Mallonta Tauta' and several of Poe's other satirical pieces belong, the tradition which produced Hugh Henry Brackenridge's *Modern Chivalry*, Cooper's *The American Democrat*, *The Gilded Age* by Mark Twain and Charles Dudley Warner, and Henry Adams's *Esther*. Poe's image of the democratic mob – 'insolent, rapacious, filthy' – might easily be interpolated into Twain's description of the residents of Bricksville in *The Adventures of Huckleberry Finn*. Nonetheless, in suggesting Poe's links with this sceptical political tradition, one must add the important qualification that when Poe did turn his talent toward an evaluation of the political times in which he lived, he produced his crudest and least interesting work. On such contemporary subjects as architecture, landscape gardening, the theatre, and song-writing, the aesthetician was much more at home.

Placing Poe in the context of the American literary tradition, one does him greater justice in emphasizing his quest for transcendental experience, his repeated invocation of the voyage of the mind which conveys man out of the known world and into the ideal vision which rests beyond, even though the quest may often end in madness and death. In his symbolic presentation of this voyage, Poe has numerous affinities with Hawthorne and Melville, sharing with them what Melville identified as 'the power of Blackness', and what Poe himself described as 'the blackness of darkness'. Yet even on this common ground we are arrested as much by Poe's divergence from the methods of his contemporaries as by the similarities. Two lines from the poem which Poe inserts into 'Ligeia' could almost serve as an epigram for his most characteristic work:

And much of Madness and more of Sin
And Horror the soul of the plot.

Madness, to be sure, appears in the work of Hawthorne – in, for example, the distracted figure of Ethan Brand or the sinister intellect of Dr Rappaccini – but this madness is distanced from the reader; Hawthorne's primary concern is not with madness but with sin, in particular with the Unpardonable Sin which he identifies as 'the violation of a human heart'. While the pursuit of this self-destructive course and the realization of its consequences may drive his characters to something like madness, his primary concern is less with the madness itself than with madness as a reflection of alienation from the human community, as a symbol of the warping effect of sin on unrepentant consciousness. Poe's maddened heroes are closer to that arch monomaniac, Captain Ahab, than to any of Hawthorne's characters, and numerous parallels can be traced between Poe's *Narrative of Arthur Gordon Pym* and *Moby Dick* – not merely in their use of the voyage of consciousness motif, or the symbolism of black and white, but in the total movements of the two works – from the known to the unknown, from the natural to the supernatural.

Poe shares predominantly with Melville and Hawthorne the concept of the hero as a lonely and estranged figure, and in this respect Poe's 'The Man of the Crowd' bears close reading alongside Hawthorne's 'Wakefield' (as studies of the way in which creation often invokes parallel destruction, further and more subtle analogies are seen in Poe's 'The Oval Portrait' and Hawthorne's 'The Birthmark'). Like Hawthorne and Melville, Poe returned repeatedly to the theme of the outsider, and he shared with them a vision of the torment which threatened to engulf the character who stepped out of society. In Poe's most characteristic writing this withdrawal is, of course, more absolute than in the work of his contemporaries, so absolute that in the most memorable of his tales there is no attempt to invoke, except by the most minimal implication, the society which has moulded (and often warped) his characters. Poe's settings are mysterious, exotic, remote, and when he set his master detective, M. Dupin, the task of solving a real murder, that of Mary Cecilia Rogers, he transferred the crime to Paris. Poe's ultimate concern is less with society than with the individual mind driven to the brink of madness, and it is success ᴧtraying this ultimate agonized crisis of consciousness which ᴧks him as an original. But this does not deny him a place in American letters. This is a point worth emphasizing when as noted a critic as Joseph Wood Krutch has maintained in one of the most authoritative and frequently reprinted studies of Poe that his works 'have no place in the American literary tradition'. Perhaps we are better prepared today to recognize as 'real' the crisis of consciousness to which Poe's heroes are so often subjected, but even without this psychological (and existential) subtlety, a careful reading of Poe's complete work refutes such an assertion. Nor is it necessary to force the 'domestication' of Poe as one scholar has done by citing his allusions to 'cabbages, cucumbers, turnips, onions, celery, cauliflower, Irish potatoes, corn, parsley, pumpkins, water-melons, milkweed and purslain'.*

Elizabeth Barrett was far closer to an appreciation of the 'reality' of Poe's work than were either of these simplistic views when she remarked, with regard to 'The Facts in the Case of M. Valdemar', that 'The certain thing in the tale in question is the power of the writer, and the faculty he has of making horrible improbabilities seem near and familiar.' In the light not only of Poe's search for transcendental experience and his fascination with the estranged hero, but also of the frequently grotesque violence of frontier humour and the Negro folk tale, it would be possible to claim for Miss Barrett's concept a 'near' and 'familiar' place within that American tradition to which Krutch denies Poe access. But Miss Barrett had in mind the larger and more compelling 'reality' which is at the heart of Poe's most horrific tales and which accounts for the fact that while Poe can clearly be seen as a 'national' figure, his fiction has drawn a larger international audience than that of any other American writer. When we look to the work of Poe most frequently reprinted and translated, terror is the most distinctive quality. At times terror is produced by conventional means, and with conventional results, as in the description of the ruined English abbey, 'with its verdant decay', to which the narrator in 'Ligeia' takes his fair-haired bride, Lady

---

* Killis Campbell, *The Mind of Poe* (Cambridge, 1933), p. 220.

Rowena. Poe was a master of atmosphere, and here terror relies heavily on the unrelenting intensity of the picture he is able to construct from essentially 'Gothic' materials. But Poe attempted to go beyond the popular Gothic tradition, and deplored the meretricious use of terror and grotesquerie. In his preface to *Tales of the Grotesque and Arabesque*, he objected to being taxed by critics for

what they have pleased to term 'Germanism' and gloom. The charge is in bad taste, and the grounds of it have not been sufficiently considered. Let us admit, for the moment, that the 'phantasy pieces' now given *are* Germanic, or what not. Then Germanism is 'in the vein' for the time being. Tomorrow I may be anything but German, as yesterday I was everything else. These many pieces are yet one book. My friends would be quite as wise in taxing an astronomer with too much astronomy, or an ethical writer with treating too largely of morals. But the truth is that, with a single exception, there is no one of these stories in which the scholar would recognize the distinctive features of that species of pseudo-horror which we are taught to call Germanic. ... If in many of my productions terror has been the thesis, I maintain that terror is not of Germany, but of the soul – that I have deduced this terror only from its legitimate sources, and urged it only to its legitimate results.

All too often Poe's use of Gothic convention has served to obscure the real import of his work; it is not sufficient even to give him credit for the vividness with which he created such effects, unless we can also see the effects as evidence of the larger and more significant ontological struggle which underlies them.

Poe has been variously pictured as a sado-masochist, dypsomaniac, drug addict, manic depressive, sex pervert, and egomaniac. There can be little doubt that he was a disturbed, tormented man, like so many of his own characters, often driven to the perilous brink of madness. If his fiction were merely the product of disinterested fancy, his tales of horror could hardly produce their brooding, sinister intensity; and yet Poe's own mental state–while it may account for the tone and the themes to which he repeatedly returned – does not explain the work itself. The temptations to interpret Poe from a biographical point of view are numerous:

he gives Usher his own features and William Wilson his birth-date; he celebrates his life with Virginia Clemm in 'Eleanora', and would appear to be taking revenge on his critics in the allegorical 'Hop Frog'. The fiction demands that we look at the life that produced it, but the critic must approach such analysis with more than the usual caution; the temptation is to see Poe's work simply as the outpouring of a profoundly disturbed mind, denying, therefore, the conscious artistry in its composition. Poe meticulously revised what he regarded as his best work, and any study of those revisions is proof of his thorough control of his creative faculties. In *Le Génie d'Edgar Poe*, Camille Mauclair has pointedly asserted that Poe's work is 'constructed objectively by a will absolutely in control of itself', and that genius of the sort we see there is '*always sane*'. Nonetheless, Poe remains the perennial victim of the *idée fixe*, and of amateur psychoanalysis of the most blatant variety. Because it is the work not only of an expert in psychoanalysis but of a fine critic of literature, Marie Bonaparte's *Life and Works of Edgar Allan Poe* (a Freudian interpretation which enjoyed the prefatory blessing of Freud himself) is the most admirable effort of its kind. In one major sense, this pioneering study did Poe a great service – in suggesting the psychological complexity of the work itself and its underlying consistency; and yet too often it confuses the man with his narrators, and in so doing obscures the author's imaginative achievement. Perhaps Poe was a 'sadonecrophiliac', but when, in the climate created by such analysis, a critic like Leslie Fiedler is led to characterize 'Annabel Lee' as an example of 'child-love, necrophilia and incest', the mind of the sensitive reader may well boggle. If such impulses shape the mind of the poet, they do not constitute the substance of the poem: the contrast between material and immaterial love, the struggle to comprehend the destruction of innocence which accompanies human growth, the profound sense of loss which pervades every phrase in the poem, and the rigorously controlled structure which makes this poetry and not emotional or psycho-sexual self-indulgence. Modern psychiatry may greatly aid the critic of literature, but it cannot preempt the role of interpreter; it cannot thus far explain why other men, suffering from deprivations or fears or obsessions similar to Poe's, failed to demonstrate his particular creative talent. Though no doubt Marie Bonaparte was correct in seeing Poe's own art as a defence against madness, we must be wary of identifying the *necessity* for this defence, in terms of Poe's own life, with the *success* of the defence, which can only be measured in his art. How far, I wonder, has Freudian theory advanced our appreciation of Poe beyond that which Chauncey Burr demonstrated in his 'Memoir' of 1850:

I know that an attempt has been made by the enemies of Poe to show that he was 'without heart'; and even a contemporary [James Russell Lowell] whom we must acquit of any malice in the charge, has sung:

> 'But the heart somehow seems all squeezed out
> by the mind.'

Poe was undoubtedly the greatest *artist* among modern authors; and it is his consummate skill as an artist, that has led to these mistakes about the properties of his own heart. That perfection of horror which abounds in his writings, has been unjustly attributed to some moral defect in the man. But I perceive not why the competent critic should fall into this error. Of all authors, ancient or modern, Poe has given us the least of himself in his works. *He wrote as an artist.* He intuitively saw what Schiller has so well expressed, that it is an universal phenomenon of our nature that the mournful, the fearful, even the horrible, allures with irresistible enchantment. He probed this general psychological law, in its subtle windings through the mystic chambers of our being, as it was never probed before, until he stood in the very abyss of its center, the sole master of its effects.

Burr was reacting to the infamies of Rufus Griswold, that *'pédagogue vampire'* as Baudelaire called him, whom Poe had perversely selected as his official editor, and to the other commentators who attempted to seize a moment of glory by exposing the perverted debaucheries of Poe; but if we substitute 'psychological' for 'moral' in Burr's admonition not to attribute the peculiar horror of his work to 'some moral defect in the man', we also have a useful note of caution for the modern critic. If there is more of Poe's life in his work than Burr concedes, it remains true that Poe transcended the merely personal or biographical, and it seems best to approach the life itself – the major ascertainable facts and the more pervasive legends – with brevity and caution.

3

Although he later 'advanced' the date of his birth in order to stress his precocity, Edgar Poe was born on 19 January 1809, in Boston, Massachusetts. His parents, David and Elizabeth Arnold Poe, were professional actors, and Elizabeth Poe was so well received in Boston that on the back of a sketch which she had made of the city and left to Edgar she charged him to 'love Boston, the place of his birth, and where his mother found her best and most sympathetic friends'. David Poe had abandoned the study of law to become an actor, and his talents were indifferent; Elizabeth Poe, on the other hand, was not only a skilled actress, but a precocious and versatile one. Her first appearance as Ophelia was at the age of fourteen, and at the time of her death at the age of twenty-four, her repertory included more than two hundred roles, at least fourteen of them Shakespearian. But the Poes made a precarious living as actors: it was surely need more than devotion to the theatre which saw Elizabeth Poe on the stage of the Boston Theatre little more than a week before the birth of her second son, Edgar, and caused her to return less than a month later. All record of David Poe ends in July 1810: whether he died, or, like the father in *The Glass Menagerie*, merely 'fell in love with long distance', is uncertain. His first son, William Henry Poe, was in the care of his paternal grandparents, but Edgar was with his mother, who was pregnant with a third child and already well advanced in tuberculosis when she returned to the 'Southern circuit', where she had once been a favourite. In December 1811, Elizabeth Poe died in extreme poverty in a Richmond boarding house. William Henry was still with his grandparents, Edgar was taken into the home of the Scottish tobacco merchant John Allan, and the infant Rosalie into that of another Richmond family, the William Mackenzies.

Biographers have made eloquent drama of the contrast between the stern, unimaginative Scottish merchant and his loving, childless wife, but Poe's childhood and his later insecurity can hardly be accounted for by quite such a dramatic dichotomy. Poe's early letters, addressed to 'My dear Pa', are evidence of deep and real affection; in Richmond, Allan procured for the boy the best education available, and even when his own financial circumstances approached bankruptcy during the family's years in England (1815–20), he transferred Edgar from a respectable boarding school to the more expensive and academically more distinguished Manor House School at Stoke Newington. Allan was not, furthermore, the puritanical enemy of art which Poe's early biographers thrilled at excoriating, as his correspondence amply suggests; a typical letter concludes with the observation that

these things called privations – starvations – taxations – and, lastly, vexations, show the very age and figure of the times – their form and pressure, as Shakespeare says, – and he was a tolerable judge. Gods! what would I not give, if I had his talent for writing, and what use would I not make of the raw material at my command!

While in his boyhood Poe may have suffered occasionally from his schoolmates' knowledge that he was the son of strolling players, these early years would seem to have been essentially untroubled. His schoolmasters remembered him as 'charming', a boy of 'very sweet disposition', and one with a 'tender and sensitive heart'. They noted occasional but not extraordinary wilfulness, and he was an enthusiastic, imaginative friend. Allan's refusal to adopt the boy legally placed him in an ambiguous and awkward situation, but the omission was not so strange in nineteenth-century America as it seems today: adoption was not such a common proceeding, and since John Allan's illegitimate children were proof that he might one day have a legal heir of his own blood (as he did by his second wife), the omission may have been tactical as well. It was not until Poe was seventeen, however, that the rift with Allan made itself strongly apparent. In 1826 Poe entered the University of Virginia, leaving behind him in Richmond his childhood sweetheart, Sarah Elmira Royster, to whom he had recently become engaged. According to Griswold's charges, Poe was expelled from the University, but in fact he was compelled to withdraw because of debt; his scholastic record was outstanding, and is hardly consistent with the myths of continuous debaucheries. The simple fact is that Allan declined to send Poe enough money to cover his basic university expenses and then berated him for not attending an additional lecture course which would further have extended his debts. Poe gambled in the hope of bettering his financial position, and his chronic bad luck resulted in 'debts of honour' which Allan refused to discharge; not only did he thus make the boy aware that his sense of obligation was waning, but Poe returned to Richmond to learn that his letters to Sarah had been intercepted, and that she was being forced to marry another man. Perhaps Allan had told the Roysters that Poe could expect nothing from his estate; perhaps, too, Allan was jealous of the tireless affection which his wife showed for Edgar; and by this time Poe almost certainly knew that Allan was being unfaithful to his wife. In any event, the temporary reconciliation which was effected after Poe's return from the University of Virginia ended three months later in a violent quarrel, and Poe left Allan's house. In a letter to Allan in which he first expresses despair over the frustration of his ambitions to achieve a good education, Poe continues,

> ... I have heard you say (when you little thought I was
> listening and therefore must have said it in earnest) that
> you had no affection for me –
> You have moreover ordered me to quit your house, and are
> continually upbraiding me with eating the bread of idleness,
> when you yourself were the only person to remedy the evil by
> placing me to some business –
> You take delight in exposing me before those whom you think
> likely to advance my interest in this world –
> You suffer me to be subjected to the whims & caprice, not only
> of your white family, but the complete authority of the blacks –
> these grievances I could not submit to; and I am gone –

Understandably, Poe was destined for Boston, 'where his mother had found her best and most sympathetic friends', and there he found a publisher for his earliest work, *Tamerlane and Other Poems*, setting forth in clear if crude form the themes that were to preoccupy him for the remainder of his life, and announcing his intended vocation. But before the book was published, Poe had enlisted in the army under the name of Edgar A. Perry; if there seems some 'perverseness' in his decision, it is well to remember that his training had hardly fitted a young man of eighteen to support himself in a trade or profession. Poe's army record was in every way distinguished: at the time of his discharge he had risen to the highest non-commissioned rank, and his superiors gave him outstanding references, even for sobriety; as an enlisted man Poe demonstrated the determination and responsibility which were to make him an outstanding editor. Even for the artist the years were not wholly lost: Poe's stay at Fort Moultrie on Sullivan's Island provided the vivid setting for 'The Gold Bug', and its beaches were to welcome the travellers in 'The Balloon-Hoax'; there must have been opportunity to cultivate his 'passion' as well, since shortly after being discharged Poe published his second volume of poems, which included 'To Science', 'Romance', and 'Fairy Land'.

In 1829 Poe accomplished what was to prove his final reconciliation with John Allan, and through his assistance obtained an honourable discharge from the army with the idea of entering the United States Military Academy at West Point – perhaps because the education there was commensurate with his notions of a 'gentleman', perhaps in the misguided hope that his previous military experience would allow him to breeze through the course there and devote most of his time to writing. Allan, in turn, may have felt that this was a painless method of terminating whatever responsibility he owed to Poe, and he would certainly have been softened somewhat by the death of Mrs Allan; Poe, then still an enlisted man, had arrived in Richmond the day after her funeral.

Edgar Poe entered West Point in June 1830, and was dishonourably discharged in January 1831: it was a deliberate action on Poe's part. In letters he complains of ill health and fatigue as well as Allan's continued tight-fistedness, which created the same embarrassments he had endured at university. When Allan refused to sign his release papers, Poe intentionally neglected his duties and at his court martial pleaded guilty to all charges *except* those which could be proved conclusively. Once more, and despite this calculated insubordination, Poe's superiors thought highly of him, and he left West Point with a subscription list made up by his fellow cadets, which guaranteed publication of his third volume of poetry. The volume was dedicated to the U.S. Corps of Cadets, linking one of the most colourless events in Poe's life to one of the most important steps in his literary development – the preface, 'Letter to B—', in which he made the first statement of his poetic principle.

The years from 1831 to 1835, when Poe returned to Richmond to edit the *Messenger*, are particularly obscure. He lived all or most of this time in extreme poverty in Baltimore and was a frequent boarder at the home of Mrs Clemm, where he helped to nurse his brother William, who was dying of tuberculosis, and his widowed grandmother. It would seem, from all evidence, to have been a time of sobriety and industry in the face of great hardship – but, more importantly, the period in which he came to love his young cousin Virginia, and in which he began to write fiction. Five grotesques and farces were published in 1832, and in 1833 'MS. Found in a Bottle' won the *Baltimore Saturday Visitor* short story competition. The judges were enthusiastically unanimous in their choice of Poe's story, especially when they compared it with the other namby-pamby entries of 'the *Laura Matilda* school'; it would appear that the committee then decided against awarding the poetry prize to Poe's 'The Coliseum' only to escape the appearance of favouritism. As soon as the prize was announced, Poe called on the judges to tell them of his appreciation, and from one of them comes a description of Poe worth quoting at length :

He was if anything, below the middle size, and yet could not be described as a small man. His figure was remarkably good, and he carried himself erect and well, as one who had been trained to it. He was dressed in black, and his frock coat was buttoned to the throat, where it met the black stock, then almost universally worn. Not a particle of white was visible. Coat, hat, boots, and gloves had evidently seen their best days, but so far as mending and brushing go, everything had been done apparently to make them presentable. On most men his clothes would have looked shabby and seedy, but there was something about this man that prevented one from criticizing his garments. ... Gentleman was written all over him. His manner was easy and quiet, and although he came to return thanks for what he regarded as deserving them, there was nothing obsequious in what he said or did. ... The expression of his face was grave, almost sad, except when he became engaged in conversation, when it became animated and changeable.

Although descriptions of Poe vary enormously, and the impressions he created were by no means consistent, Latrobe's description rings true when compared to what seem the most trustworthy of other accounts.

Despite the fact that he was now favourably launched as a writer of fiction, Poe was unable to find a publisher for his collected tales, and in the face of mounting financial anxiety, he eagerly accepted the editorship of the *Southern Literary Messenger* in 1835. His reception in Richmond was a cordial one – except from the Allan household : John Allan had died the year before, and the second Mrs Allan was occupied with preserving the inheritance rights of her children and idealizing the memory of her husband. During the obscure Baltimore years, Poe had tried to effect a reconciliation with Allan, and had certainly paid one – if not two – visits to Richmond, but all hope of reconciliation had been lost through Poe's own bad taste and indiscretion. In 1830, while he was awaiting the West Point appointment, Poe wrote a letter to his army substitute, 'Bully Graves', in which he explained his failure to discharge a debt by observing that 'Mr Allan is not very often sober – which accounts for it'. John Allan eventually saw Poe's letter, and while there may well have been truth in Poe's accusation ('I leave it', he observed to Allan, 'to God, and your conscience'), the damage was irreparable.

While Poe eventually assumed full editorial responsibility at the *Messenger*, he was never granted the unqualified title of editor, though this clearly troubled him less than the news that his cousin Neilson Poe in Baltimore had proposed taking Virginia into his family and providing for her education and support. In one of the most revealing letters he ever wrote, Poe explained to Mrs Clemm his situation in Richmond and pleaded with her to come there with his cousin, adding a postcript, 'For Virginia' : 'My love, my own sweetest Sissy, my darling little wifey, think well before you break the heart of your cousin Eddy.' Poe returned briefly to Baltimore following a disagreement with White, but in October he was reinstated as 'editor' of the *Messenger*, and arrived in Richmond accompanied by Mrs Clemm and Virginia. The following spring Poe and his young cousin were married.

Much has been made by biographers and Freudian critics of the 'unnaturalness' of Poe's marriage, its probable celibacy, and his repeated references to Virginia as 'Sis' or 'Sissy'. (The nickname itself hardly seems suspect if we remember that when Poe first met Virginia she was only eight years old.) Speculation about Poe's relationship with Virginia – clouded in an obscurity not entirely inappropriate – would hardly seem worth pursuing if it had not already been so persistently exercised in interpreting his fiction, and were it not for statements like that of Joseph Wood Krutch that 'however full the tales may be of sex disguised and perverted, there is never from the first to the last any recognition of the existence of natural amorousness. ...' Little fiction of the period, of course, dwelt in detail on 'natural amorousness', and yet, ironically enough, one of the most 'amorous' tales written in nineteenth-century America was written by Edgar Allan Poe; it is one in which the autobiographical allusions appear so intentional that it seems pointless to ignore them. 'Eleonora' describes the love of a man 'noted for vigor of fancy and ardor of passion' and his youthful cousin. 'I, and my cousin, and her mother', the narrator tells us, dwell together in 'the Valley of the Many-Colored Grass' :

Hand in hand about this valley, for fifteen years, roamed I with Eleonora before Love entered within our hearts. It was one evening at the close of the third lustrum of her life, and of the fourth of my own, that we sat, locked in each other's embrace, beneath the serpent-like trees, and looked down within the waters of the River of Silence at our images therein. We spoke no words during the rest of that sweet day; and our words even upon the morrow were tremulous and few. We had drawn the god Eros from that wave, and now we felt that we had enkindled within us the fiery souls of our forefathers. ... A change fell upon all things. Strange brilliant flowers, star-shaped, burst out upon the trees where no flowers had been known before. The tints of the green carpet deepened; and when, one by one, the white daisies shrank away, there sprang up, in place of them, ten by ten of the ruby-red asphodel. And life arose in our paths; for the tall flamingo, hitherto unseen, with all flowing birds, flaunted his scarlet plumage before us.

'Eleonora' has particular interest in Poe's treatment of the imaginative escape from the world of reality, but since evidence of his relationship with Virginia is so slim, and so much theory – both critical and biographical – has been woven from it, the reader of Poe would be well advised to keep this tender and moving story in mind. Nor is it surprising that the idyllic love pictured here should end in death, for the death or loss of the women he loved was one of the most constant factors of Poe's life : first the death of his mother; then the madness and death of Mrs Jane Stith Stannard, who befriended Poe as a boy and became immortal as the first of his idealized Helens; the loss of his sweetheart Sarah Elmira Royster to another man; and the death of Mrs Allan. At the time Poe composed 'Eleonora', Virginia had, on more than one occasion, been in ill health; shortly after its publication she suffered a violent haemorrhage, the first unmistakable sign of the tuberculosis that was to end in her death five years later.

After his break with White, Poe went first to New York for a brief period, and then to Philadelphia, where for a year he served as editor of *Burton's Gentleman's Magazine* and then as editor of *Graham's*. From the work for which he is most widely remembered today, Poe made practically nothing, as we have seen, and it was as an editor that he hoped to achieve financial independence to pursue his creative work, although he also applied unsuccessfully for the kind of customs-house post with which Hawthorne's career began and Melville's obscurely ended. Poe's own ambitions were distinctly unmaterialistic : 'Depend upon it,' he wrote to a friend, 'Literature is the most noble of all professions. In fact, it is about the only one fit for a man. . . . I shall be a *littérateur* at least all my life; nor would I abandon the hopes which lead me on for all the gold in California.' In keeping with this disregard for material reward, Poe was careless about his financial affairs, and frequently had to call upon friends and relatives for assistance, but it is hardly surprising that Poe's creative writing should have done so little to relieve his poverty : American publishers were reluctant to pay a native author for a copyright when it was much more profitable to pirate works printed in England. The novelist had some commercial advantage over the writer of short stories or poetry, who was compelled to seek his living through the magazines and newspapers, but neither Poe's temperament nor his theories of composition permitted him more than one successful attempt at a long prose work. Nonetheless, had Poe ever received appropriate compensation for his editorial work, he could have been freed from financial worry. During the two years he edited the *Southern Literary Messenger* its circulation increased from 500 to 3,500, while his salary only inched beyond the ten dollars a week, plus occasional extras, at which he had originally been hired. Poe's work for *Graham's* produced even more dramatic results : the magazine's profits during the first year of his editorship were $25,000, but Poe never received more than $800 a year. Despite rumours of 'intemperance' and the fact that Poe's own cherished ideals about magazine publication often clashed with those of the owner for whom he worked, the real index of his success and dependability as an editor rests in the verifiable facts of the subscription lists and in Poe's correspondence with contributors and rivals : the inescapable conclusion is that one of America's most brilliant and imaginative editors was one of its most grossly underpaid.

Thus the Philadelphia interlude was marked by the usual frustrations and disappointments, but it was also one of the most fecund periods of Poe's life : he had published thirty-one of his short stories, his *Tales of the Grotesque and Arabesque* had been a critical if not a financial success, and 'The Gold-Bug' had won him a large popular audience. In 1844 the family moved to New York, and while their early months there were even more troubled and impoverished than before, Edgar Allan Poe was about to enter the most significant year of his life.

In January 1845, 'The Raven' appeared in the New York *Evening Mirror*, and as Poe remarked, 'the bird beat the bug all hollow': he was now, without question, a famous man. This was the year in which Poe entered New York literary society, initiated his first 'poetic' flirtation, and began to augment his meagre income with lecturing. More importantly, in 1845 he wrote 'The Philosophy of Composition' and supervised the Wiley & Putnam editions of both the *Tales* and *The Raven and Other Poems*. This was the year of the Longfellow war, of Lowell's critical article on Poe in *Graham's*, and of Poe's first recognition in France. In March of 1845 Poe became an editor of the *Broadway Journal*, and in November its sole proprietor; his experience with the *Journal*, which ceased publication early in 1846, was sadly unlike his dream of his own publication, but even before he assumed control the magazine was in severe financial difficulty, and Poe was unable to raise sufficient funds in order to keep it alive until he might shape it to his ideals. If the year thus ended badly for Poe, it was nonetheless his *annus mirabilis*.

Despite his ever-increasing fame, Poe remained in the same grim poverty which characterized most of his adult life. When Mrs Mary Gove visited the little cottage at Fordham where Virginia was dying, she found that Mrs Poe had only her husband's old army cloak and a large tortoiseshell cat to keep her warm. Poe's own life during these years must have been a nightmare: the contrast between public recognition and private suffering might have wrought damaging effects in men of far less sensitive temperament. We know enough about Poe's life to be certain that for long periods of time he was abstemious, but that at moments he yielded to alcohol (to which he seems to have had a very low resistance) is obviously true. While we must always keep in mind Poe's inclination for self-dramatization and the adroitness with which he could mask the facts of his own life, his letter written to an admirer in 1848 has, I think, the ring of absolute candour:

You say, 'Can you *hint* to me what was the "terrible evil" which caused the "irregularities" so profoundly lamented?' Yes, I can do more than hint. This 'evil' was the greatest which can befall a man. Six years ago, a wife, whom I loved as no man ever loved before, ruptured a blood-vessel in singing. Her life was despaired of. I took leave of her forever, and underwent all the agonies of her death. She recovered partially, and I again hoped. At the end of a year, the vessel broke again. I went through precisely the same scene. Again in about a year afterward. Then again – again – again – and even once again, at varying intervals. Each time I felt all the agonies of her death – and at each accession of the disorder I loved her more dearly and clung to her life with more desperate pertinacity. But I am constitutionally sensitive – nervous in a very unusual degree. I became insane, with long intervals of horrible sanity. During these fits of absolute unconsciousness, I drank – God only knows how often or how much. As a matter of course, my enemies referred the insanity to the drink, rather than the drink to the insanity.

A friend with some medical experience observed that Poe's heartbeat was irregular, and Dr Valentine Mott concurred that Poe had a physiological disorder which made him particularly susceptible to stimulants. Literary enemies and sensationalists made much of Poe's bouts of intemperance: at the time, of course, it was far more fashionable to attribute such incidents to Vice than to anxiety or physiology, and for Dr J. E. Snodgrass, one of the doctors attendant on Poe at the time of his death, the lustre of the story of Poe's destruction by the demon rum became the dramatic core of a series of temperance lectures.

Poe's productivity is simply not commensurate with the idea of *chronic* alcoholism or of drug addiction; when he did drink, the effect on his body and his mind was highly deleterious. He may, on occasion, have become violent, but the most frank and trustworthy contemporary accounts indicate that he was basically a gentle comrade, a conscientious editor, and a solicitous husband. He could be caustic when he saw the cause of literature cheapened and was often indiscreet in his critical pronouncements; he could be swayed in his judgements by friendship as well as by the code of the vendetta, and earned himself a reputation as 'The Tomahawk Man', but such aberrations – unfortunate, even embarrassing as they may seem to us – are insufficient to negate the fact that Poe raised popular criticism in America to new levels of perception, exactitude, and discrimination. A critic of Poe's integrity laboured under enormous difficulties, especially when he challenged such powerful cliques as the *Knickerbocker* group, and some of Poe's own critical indiscretions must be seen in light of the vicious attacks he received in his battle against what Mrs Trollope deplored as the 'immense exaltation of periodical trash' in America. Longfellow himself, the victim of Poe's most inexcusably personal abuse, helps further to account for the critic's excesses: 'The harshness of his criticisms, I have never attributed to anything but the irritation of a sensitive nature, chafed by some indefinite sense of wrong.' Longfellow's generosity in such a remark cannot be overvalued, though today we realize that the 'wrongs' done Poe – in the literary world as well as in his private life – were anything but 'indefinite'.

Such wrongs would be sufficient, in a man of far less sensitive temperament, to account for erratic opinion and behaviour; certainly we do not have to call upon alcoholism in order to understand this aspect of the writer's career. If, however, the stories of Poe's drunken debauches were sensational exaggerations, the charge that he was a drug addict can almost certainly be dismissed as total fabrication. Their major substantiation has relied on Poe's references to opium in the short stories (where the source is as likely to be literary as personal), on the testimony of a cousin made nearly half a century after Poe's death, and on his own retarded sister's observation that he once 'begged for morphine'. Against this doubtful evidence we must set two facts: first of all, while Poe could easily have known opium in the form of laudanum, since that drug was at the time dispensed almost as freely as aspirin is today, his own story of an attempt to commit suicide with laudanum indicates his unfamiliarity with its potency and general physiological effects. Secondly, we have an expert medical opinion available from Dr Thomas Dunn English, who knew Poe well and had some reason to dislike him: 'Had Poe had the opium habit when I knew him (before 1846) I should both as a physician and a man of observation, have discovered it during his frequent visits to my rooms, my visits to his house, and our meetings elsewhere – I saw no signs of it and believe the charge to be a baseless slander.'

If the grief and deprivation of his own life ever led him to such excesses, the period between Virginia's death in 1847 and his own death in 1849 must have offered the greatest temptations, but he continued (with increasing success) to lecture, to write fiction, poetry, and criticism, was hard at work on his most ambitious work, *Eureka*, and carried on an extraordinary succession of flirtations. The first of these began before Virginia's death, when Mrs Frances Sargent Osgood became enraptured with the 'weird, unearthly music' of 'The Raven' – and later with the 'dark flashing eyes' of the poet himself. But it was, like most of Poe's later relationships with women, the meeting of minds and poetic spirits. In the final years of his life Poe – like so many of his own heroes – sought a transcendent love experience with an idealized woman whose spirit could blend with his own in the quest for beauty, but he continued to crave the comforts and stability of a conventional domestic life. Three women play particularly significant roles in this drama. One of them, the widow Sarah Helen Whitman, had addressed the poet in a Valentine verse inspired by 'The Raven' and read at a New York literary party; through Mrs Osgood the tribute reached Poe, and their 'courtship' began in the pages of national magazines even before they had met. Eventually, Poe and Mrs Whitman became engaged, but in the face of her family's disapproval, rumours about her fiancé's dissipation, and a drinking bout on Poe's part, the engagement was broken off. With Mrs Whitman Poe had hoped to establish an exalted literary aristocracy in America, and he may well have hoped that her money could finance the magazine which was his recurrent dream. Certainly there is every indication that it was intellect and aestheticism and to some degree loneliness which drew him to the eccentric poetess, for during their courtship he continued to express his love for Mrs Nancy Lock ('Annie') Richmond – a simpler and far more domesticated woman whom Poe addressed as 'my own sweet *sister* Annie, my *pure* beautiful angel – *wife* of my soul – to be mine hereafter & forever in the Heavens'.

Poe was still sending such impassioned letters to Annie when he left on a lecture tour which took him to Richmond, where he began to pay court to the sweetheart of his youth, Sarah Elmira Royster, now the widowed Mrs Shelton. They became engaged, Poe joined a temperance society, revelled in the cordial welcome which Richmond offered him, and yet could still write to Mrs Clemm, 'I want to live *near Annie*.' Several of the friends who saw Poe during his last days in Richmond noted that he seemed ill and feverish, but he continued with his plans to visit New York, settle his affairs there, and return to marry Mrs Shelton. Elmira was so concerned about him that she felt the journey should be postponed, but when she called to inquire about him on 27 September, he had already taken the boat for Baltimore. Nearly a week later Dr J. E. Snodgrass received the following note:

Baltimore City, Oct. 3, 1849

Dear Sir, –

There is a gentleman, rather the worse for wear, at Ryan's 4th ward polls, who goes under the cognomen of Edgar A. Poe, and who appears in great distress & he says he is acquainted with you, and I assure you, he is in need of immediate assistance.

Yours, in haste,

Jos. W. Walker.

Walker, a compositor on the *Baltimore Sun*, had found Poe, lying in a semi-conscious state and dressed in clothes obviously not his own, outside of Ryan's Fourth Ward polls. He was taken to Washington College Hospital, where he remained unconscious until the following morning; he was unable to account for his condition, evidenced acute despair, and was delirious from Thursday until Saturday evening, when he began to call for 'Reynolds!' – perhaps Jeremiah Reynolds, whose projected voyages to the South Seas had inspired *Arthur Gordon Pym*. The following morning Poe ceased to fight whatever daemons were tormenting his mind, and died at approximately 5 o'clock in the afternoon of 7 October 1849. Various theories have been advanced to account for this fatal attack: Poe may have suffered from epilepsy, brain tumour, or heart disease, and may have indulged in alcohol to a degree that fatally aggravated this condition. What actually happened during the final days of Poe's life can never be known; it was election time in Baltimore, and he may have been rounded up with other derelicts and kept in one of the party 'coops', whose alcohol-blurred occupants were sent out to the polls to vote as often as they were able to put their X in the proper box. Only one thing is certain – that few men of genius have had to endure such squalor in the final days of their lives.

I find it difficult to agree with Edward H. Davidson that Poe's life was 'one of the dullest any figure of literary importance has lived in the past two hundred years', though certainly it was one of the most tragic and pitiable. But Poe's chronic bad luck was not to end with his own death; through one of his characteristically 'perverse' decisions, Poe had assigned Rufus Griswold as his official editor, and on the day of Poe's funeral Griswold published an article in the New York *Tribune* beginning,

Edgar Allan Poe is dead. He died in Baltimore the day before yesterday. This announcement will startle many, but few will be grieved by it. The poet was well known, personally or by reputation, in all this country; he had readers in England, and in several of the states of Continental Europe, but he had no friends.

It was the first of many steps in that campaign of *infamie immortelle*, as Baudelaire was to describe it. Years before, Poe had levelled one of his critical attacks against Griswold and there had, perhaps, been other grievances, but Poe clearly imagined that their disagreement had been righted. Griswold, however, now took advantage of this trust in order to advance his own literary reputation by slandering Poe. He forged some letters, altered others, and perhaps destroyed more, and in the memoir which he wrote for the third volume of Poe's collected works he put forward so many myths and laid so many false trails that even those contemporaries who rose to Poe's defence found it impossible to dispel the illusion created by the 'official' editor.

Poe himself did not aid later biographers. During his own lifetime he circulated a variety of legends about his adventurous life, including visits to Greece and Russia, which were obviously intended as 'cover' for his ungentlemanly years as an enlisted man in the army. He also claimed to have spent some time in France and Spain, and to have published a novel under the name of Eugène Sue; Alexandre Dumas obliged by leaving an improbable description of Poe's visit with him near Paris in 1832, but all available evidence points to Poe's never having left America after his return from England in 1820. We need not, therefore, conclude that Poe was simply a pathological liar: to some degree he sought, in such fancies, the illusion of Byronic romance which he wanted his life to be, as a defence against the grim and often drab reality which it was. Furthermore, it is important not to overlook Poe's own great fondness for a practical joke: according to one contemporary, who claimed Mrs Clemm's authority, 'Poe allowed the error [of the St Petersburg episode] to continue from motives of delicacy, in that it was a rather *rum affair*'. Nonetheless, Poe himself began the legend that continues to enshroud his life, Griswold aggravated and severely distorted it, and Poe inspired in many of his contemporaries the American passion for anecdote and tall tale. The mysteries can never all be dispelled, and the temptation to use Poe's writing as a source of biographical illumination will no doubt persist – along with the effort to catalogue the peculiar hallmarks of his work by reference to his tragic life. Poe, the man who enjoyed a practical joke and took delight in contriving biographical smoke-screens, would perhaps not be entirely displeased at the sight of such acrobatics, but Poe the critic would, I think, take many of his own biographically oriented critics to task, for it was Poe who argued, in a manner which uncannily foreshadows the theories of New Criticism, that the work of art is an integral and self-contained *fact*, embodying 'everything necessary for its understanding'. If only to accord Poe the justice he was so frequently denied in his own lifetime, and which has been repeatedly withheld since his death, we should heed as far as possible his admonitions against seeking personal, introspective revelations in his art.

4

The best of Poe's creative work demands to be taken symbolically; its roots are in his desire to avoid the mundane, to break through the conventional frontiers of consciousness into 'the elevating excitement of the Soul'. The real clue to Poe's writing is thus to be found in his own criticism – in the aesthetic ideals put forward in his essay on 'The Poetic Principle' and the preface to *Tales of the Grotesque and Arabesque*. Here we find the two most persistent determinants of Poe's art, the imaginative quest for Beauty and what he termed 'the terror of the soul'; together they form the writer's *Weltanschauung*. The poetry and prose are thus linked not only by recurrent images and themes, but as studies of what Edward Davidson has termed the 'stages of consciousness when the real world slipped away or disintegrated and the mind found itself fronting the "horror" of its own loneliness and loss'. In 'MS. Found in a Bottle', the narrator describes himself as 'hurrying onwards to some exciting knowledge – some never-to-be-imparted secret, whose attainment is destruction'. A similar image occurs at the conclusion of *Arthur Gordon Pym*, as Pym and his companion vanish into a chasm dominated by 'a shrouded human figure' whose skin 'was of the perfect whiteness of the snow'. The lesson is the same: the voyage of the mind out of the real world ends in a blinding vision that is at once revelation and destruction.

All of Poe's most memorable characters withdraw from life in its conventional aspects, into heavily draped rooms with artificial lighting (as in his own description of the ideal room in 'The Philosophy of Furniture'), and there they cultivate a life of their own, so distinct and cut apart from the world that they lose all touch with reality. In this condition, they can develop an acuteness of sense (even, at times, synaesthesia) and an almost mystical perception in keeping with Poe's own aesthetic principles. When Hawthorne's characters step out of life they often develop a kind of clairvoyance, and they dabble in witchcraft, but they pay for their vision the Faustian price: they lose their souls. Poe's outsiders lose their sanity and often their lives as a result of expanded consciousness. In 'The Masque of the Red Death' Poe makes the lesson unmistakably clear: under Prince Prospero (a figure totally lacking the redemptive magic of Shakespeare's Prospero), a thousand knights and ladies take refuge in a castellated abbey, sealing themselves away from the plague which stalks the land, and there they cultivate Beauty in its most elaborately artificial forms. But they cannot elude death, and it finally stalks through the exotic chambers of the abbey, infecting all the revellers : the ebony clock stops, the torches expire, and 'Darkness and Decay and the Red Death held illimitable dominion over all'.

'The Masque of the Red Death' forms an interesting corollary to the more complex 'Fall of the House of Usher', where the central character has actually approached that acute sensitivity in which beauty can be perceived in its ideal forms, but the concomitant of this mystical transcendence is madness, as well as the inability to bear the conventional ingredients of reality :

He suffered much from a morbid acuteness of the senses; the most insipid food was alone endurable; he could wear only garments of certain texture; the odors of all flowers were oppressive; his eyes were tortured by even a faint light; and there were but peculiar sounds, and these from stringed instruments, which did not inspire him with horror.

Usher's malady is described as 'a constitutional and a family evil', and because the Usher line is without collateral issue, his deterioration is the deterioration of a family – of a 'house', and perhaps of a culture as well. Whether Usher's acute sensitivity is a product of madness, or madness the result of extreme cultivation of the senses, matters less than the realization that the two states merge in Poe into a single image of terror. Their relationship is fully explored in 'The Haunted Palace', the song which Usher sings for his guest. In mood and even in phrasing, it echoes Coleridge's 'Kubla Khan', with its description of the creation of a fair and stately palace in the centre of a lush green valley; in this ideal and exotic setting, art flourishes : through 'two luminous windows' passers by see spirits moving to 'a lute's well-tuned law', and through the palace door flow

> A troop of Echoes whose sweet duty
> Was but to sing,
> In voices of surpassing beauty,
> The wit and wisdom of their King.

Sorrow, despair, and death come to this pleasure dome, as they come to the sealed abbey in 'The Masque of the Red Death': 'evil things, in robes of sorrow' which assail 'the monarch's high estate'.

> And travellers now within that valley,
>> Through the red-litten windows, see
> Vast forms that move fantastically
>> To a discordant melody;
> While, like a rapid ghastly river,
>> Through the pale door,
> A hideous throng rush out forever,
>> And laugh – but smile no more.

As numerous commentators have noted, the palace is Usher's own mind, the windows the wild eyes which reflect his madness. But the real import of the poem is surely more complex, for it reiterates a theme so often encountered in Poe's work: the retreat from the world, the attempt to create an ideal state of perception, ends, at last, in madness and despair, in the insane laugh without a smile with which the poem concludes. The danger of the departure from the mundane is that the individual will be engulfed by his experience, for such a retreat is, finally, a retreat into the self. The ultimate danger is that man will be trapped there, that the quest for new and more fulfilling levels of consciousness will prove destructive: hence the repeated obsession in Poe's fiction with being buried alive, with the maelstrom, with the claustrophobic chamber, and the fusing of creation and destruction seen in 'The Oval Portrait'. It is only in grasping the full implications of Poe's *Weltanschauung* that we appreciate the implications of the sinister 'encrimsoned light' which penetrates Usher's study, the latently incestuous relationship with his sister, and the grotesque unreality of the house they occupy. Usher's library indicates the degree to which he has cultivated the mystical, and yet with all his knowledge he is overwhelmed by 'the grim phantasm, FEAR'.

Usher's crisis is two-fold: there is a split in his own personality, and there is also a total disruption of his relationship with the world outside himself; the result, as in so many of Poe's stories, is remarkably like what Kierkegaard described as the Concept of Dread:

a desire for what one dreads, a sympathetic antipathy. Dread is an alien power which lays hold of an individual, and yet one cannot tear oneself away, nor has a will to do so; for one fears, but what one fears one desires. Dread then makes the individual impotent, and the first sin always occurs in impotence. Apparently, therefore, the man lacks accountability, but this lack is what ensnares him.

How often Poe has been berated for the 'motiveless malignity' which his characters display. We never know the specific motive which impels Montresor to wall Fortunato up in the damp catacombs; although the murderer refers to 'a thousand injuries' and to 'insult', what concerns us in 'The Cask of Amontillado' is not any specific motive but the gross and terrifying consequences of this 'unaccountable' action. All of Poe's murderers are obsessive in this degree: even in 'The Black Cat', where murder is impulsive rather than premeditated, we have few glimpses into the circumstances which create the exacerbated state of mind which leads so readily to violence; those of his characters who are tormented rather than tormenting suffer, like Kafka's Joseph K., for unnamed wrongs.

I am not attempting to recruit Poe to the existential movement (so voracious in the acquisition of ancestors), but only to suggest that his work has particular interest at a time in which individualism seems increasingly threatened by a depersonalized computer age and in which, therefore, the rent in man's relation with his environment, and hence the disruption of his relation with himself, so often seems an unavoidable fact. In mirroring the extreme tensions produced by this crisis of consciousness, in evoking the horrors that result when the individual allows himself to be transported too far beyond the limits of reality, Poe created a body of work that bears particular relevance for our time. How aptly Poe summarized, in the conclusion to *Eureka*, what has become the repeated theme of modern literature, philosophy, and theology:

We walk about, amid the destinies of our world-existence, encompassed by dim but ever present *Memories* of a Destiny more vast – very distant in the bygone time, and infinitely more awful.

We live out a Youth peculiarly haunted by such dreams; yet never mistaking them for dreams. ...

So long as this Youth endures, the feeling *that we exist*, is the most natural of all feelings. We understand it *thoroughly*. That there was a period at which we did *not* exist – or, that it might so have happened that we never had existed at all – are the considerations, indeed, which *during this youth*, we find difficulty in understanding. Why we should *not* exist, is *up to the epoch of our Manhood*, of all queries the most unanswerable. Existence – existence from all Time and to all Eternity – seems, up to the Epoch of Manhood, of all queries the most unanswerable. Existence – self-existence – existence from all Time and to all Eternity – seems, up to the epoch of Manhood, a normal and unquestionable condition : *seems, because it is.*

But now comes the period at which a conventional World-Reason awakens us from the truth of our dream. Doubt, Surprise and Incomprehensibility arrive at the same moment.

The rent in consciousness, the feeling of ontological insecurity called forth here, does not always end in madness or despair, though horror is the quality which will always most distinctly characterize Poe's work. Against it, however, one must set lyrics like 'To Helen', the pastoral exaltation of 'Eleonora', the tales of ratiocination in which intellect is triumphant, and the elaborate synthesis which Poe attempted in *Eureka*.

For more than a century Poe's work has been among the most popular in the world, cherished by the kind of readers who gave Sterne such pleasure – even though 'they know not why, and care not wherefore'. But it is to be hoped that readers in increasing numbers will see beyond the skill and efficiency with which Poe has created his effects, for even those tales and poems which seem to depend almost entirely on the conventional devices of horror – metempsychosis, the influence of supernatural agencies, premature burial, physical torture and murder – produce a terror which demands to be taken at something more than its face value; and in its most complex forms, this terror represents a profound disruption of man's mind and soul, a spiritual agony which transcends the age in which it was written, as well as the agonized life which created it.

University of Sussex   *David Galloway*

Note on the Text

THE definitive edition of Poe's work is still that prepared by James A. Harrison and originally published by Thomas Y. Crowell & Co., New York. The seventeen-volume 'Virginia' edition has recently been reprinted by the AMS Press, Inc. (New York), and I am grateful to them for permission to draw on it as the basic text for this volume. In some instances I have favoured earlier versions of individual works to those selected by Harrison, but the precise source of each entry is indicated in the notes.

The order of entries under each of the three major divisions is chronological; as it is often impossible to establish dates of composition for Poe's work, chronology must be determined by the earliest known date of publication. Much of Poe's best work was extensively revised for subsequent publication, and therefore such a system is clearly deficient in representing the development of his literary technique. Nonetheless, it avoids the rather arbitrary groupings – like that of the tales into 'grotesques' and 'arabesques' – to which Poe objected on more than one occasion during his own lifetime as failing to represent the variety of technique and subject matter in his work.

Poe's own spelling and punctuation have been retained throughout, but his notes – some of which call for editorial comment – have been printed at the end of this volume.

D.G.

1. Poems

Stanzas

How often we forget all time, when lone
Admiring Nature's universal throne;
Her woods – her wilds – her mountains – the intense
Reply of HERS to our intelligence!

1

In youth have I known one with whom the Earth
In secret communing held – as he with it,
In daylight, and in beauty from his birth:
Whose fervid, flickering torch of life was lit
From the sun and stars, whence he had drawn forth
A passionate light – such for his spirit was fit –
And yet that spirit knew not, in the hour
Of its own fervour, what had o'er it power.

2

Perhaps it may be that my mind is wrought
To a fever by the moonbeam that hangs o'er,
But I will half believe that wild light fraught
With more of sovereignty than ancient lore
Hath ever told; – or is it of a thought
The unembodied essence, and no more,
That with a quickening spell doth o'er us pass
As dew of the night-time o'er the summer grass?

3

Doth o'er us pass, when, as th' expanding eye
To the loved object, – so the tear to the lid
Will start, which lately slept in apathy?
And yet it need not be – (that object) hid

From us in life – but common – which doth lie
Each hour before us – but *then* only, bid
With a strange sound, as of a harp-string broken,
To awake us – 'T is a symbol and a token

4

Of what in other worlds shall be – and given
In beauty by our God, to those alone
Who otherwise would fall from life and Heaven
Drawn by their heart's passion, and that tone,
That high tone of the spirit which hath striven,
Tho' not with Faith – with godliness – whose throne
With desperate energy 't hath beaten down;
Wearing its own deep feeling as a crown.

Sonnet – to Science

Science! true daughter of Old Time thou art!
  Who alterest all things with thy peering eyes.
Why preyest thou thus upon the poet's heart,
  Vulture, whose wings are dull realities?
How should he love thee? or how deem thee wise,
  Who wouldst not leave him in his wandering
To seek for treasure in the jewelled skies,
  Albeit he soared with an undaunted wing?
Hast thou not dragged Diana from her car?
  And driven the Hamadryad[1] from the wood
To seek a shelter in some happier star?
  Hast thou not torn the Naiad[2] from her flood,
The Elfin from the green grass, and from me
The summer dream beneath the tamarind tree?

Al Aaraaf[1]

PART I

O ! nothing earthly save the ray
(Thrown back from flowers) of Beauty's eye,
As in those gardens where the day
Springs from the gems of Circassy –
O ! nothing earthly save the thrill
Of melody in woodland rill –
Or (music of the passion-hearted)
Joy's voice so peacefully departed
That like the murmur in the shell,
Its echo dwelleth and will dwell –
Oh, nothing of the dross of ours –
Yet all the beauty – all the flowers
That list our Love, and deck our bowers –
Adorn yon world afar, afar –
The wandering star.

'T was a sweet time for Nesace[2] – for there
Her world lay lolling on the golden air,
Near four bright suns – a temporary rest –
An oasis in desert of the blest.
Away – away – 'mid seas of rays that roll
Empyrean splendor o'er th' unchained soul –
The soul that scarce (the billows are so dense)
Can struggle to its destin'd eminence –
To distant spheres, from time to time, she rode,
And late to ours, the favour'd one of God –
But, now, the ruler of an anchor'd realm,
She throws aside the sceptre – leaves the helm,
And, amid incense and high spiritual hymns,
Laves in quadruple light her angel limbs.

Now happiest, loveliest in yon lovely Earth,
Whence sprang the 'Idea of Beauty' into birth,

(Falling in wreaths thro' many a startled star,
Like woman's hair 'mid pearls, until, afar,
It lit on hills Achaian, and there dwelt)
She look'd into Infinity – and knelt.
Rich clouds, for canopies, about her curled –
Fit emblems of the model of her world –
Seen but in beauty – not impeding sight
Of other beauty glittering thro' the light –
A wreath that twined each starry form around,
And all the opal'd air in color bound.

    All hurriedly she knelt upon a bed
Of flowers: of lilies such as rear'd the head
On the fair Capo Deucato,[3] and sprang
So eagerly around about to hang
Upon the flying footsteps of — deep pride –
Of her who lov'd a mortal – and so died.[4]
The Sephalica, budding with young bees,
Uprear'd its purple stem around her knees:
And gemmy flower, of Trebizond misnam'd[5] –
Inmate of highest stars, where erst it sham'd
All other loveliness: its honied dew
(The fabled nectar that the heathen knew)
Deliriously sweet, was dropp'd from Heaven,
And fell on gardens of the unforgiven
In Trebizond – and on a sunny flower
So like its own above that, to this hour,
It still remaineth, torturing the bee
With madness, and unwonted reverie:
In Heaven, and all its environs, the leaf
And blossom of the fairy plant, in grief
Disconsolate linger – grief that hangs her head,
Repenting follies that full long have fled,
Heaving her white breast to the balmy air,
Like guilty beauty, chasten'd, and more fair:
Nyctanthes too, as sacred as the light
She fears to perfume, perfuming the night:

And Clytia[6] pondering between many a sun,
While pettish tears adown her petals run :
And that aspiring flower that sprang on earth –
And died, ere scarce exalted into birth,
Bursting its odorous heart in spirit to wing
Its way to Heaven, from garden of a king :[7]
And Valisnerian lotus thither flown
From struggling with the waters of the Rhone :[8]
And thy most lovely purple perfume, Zante ![9]
Isola d'oro ! – Fior di Levante !
And the Nelumbo bud that floats for ever[10]
With Indian Cupid down the holy river –
Fair flowers, and fairy ! to whose care is given
To bear the Goddess' song, in odors, up to Heaven :[11]

  'Spirit ! that dwellest where,
   In the deep sky,
  The terrible and fair,
   In beauty vie !
  Beyond the line of blue –
   The boundary of the star
  Which turneth at the view
   Of thy barrier and thy bar –
  Of the barrier overgone
   By the comets who were cast
  From their pride, and from their throne
   To be drudges till the last –
  To be carriers of fire
   (The red fire of their heart)
  With speed that may not tire
   And with pain that shall not part –
  Who livest – *that* we know –
   In Eternity – we feel –
  But the shadow of whose brow
   What spirit shall reveal ?
  Tho' the beings whom thy Nesace,
   Thy messenger hath known

Have dream'd for thy Infinity
   A model of their own –[12]
Thy will is done, Oh, God!
   The star hath ridden high
Thro' many a tempest, but she rode
   Beneath thy burning eye;
And here, in thought, to thee –
   In thought that can alone
Ascend thy empire and so be
   A partner of thy throne –
By winged Fantasy,[13]
   My embassy is given,
Till secrecy shall knowledge be
   In the environs of Heaven.'

She ceas'd – and buried then her burning cheek
Abash'd, amid the lilies there, to seek
A shelter from the fervour of His eye;
For the stars trembled at the Deity.
She stirr'd not – breath'd not – for a voice was there
How solemnly pervading the calm air!
A sound of silence on the startled ear
Which dreamy poets name 'the music of the sphere.'
Ours is a world of words: Quiet we call
'Silence' – which is the merest word of all.
All Nature speaks, and ev'n ideal things
Flap shadowy sounds from visionary wings –
But ah! not so when, thus, in realms on high
The eternal voice of God is passing by,
And the red winds are withering in the sky!

'What tho' in worlds which sightless cycles run,[14]
Link'd to a little system, and one sun –
Where all my love is folly and the crowd
Still think my terrors but the thunder cloud,
The storm, the earthquake, and the ocean-wrath –
(Ah! will they cross me in my angrier path?)

What tho' in worlds which own a single sun
The sands of Time grow dimmer as they run,
Yet thine is my resplendency, so given
To bear my secrets thro' the upper Heaven.
Leave tenantless thy crystal home, and fly,
With all thy train, athwart the moony sky –
Apart – like fire-flies in Sicilian night,[15]
And wing to other worlds another light !
Divulge the secrets of thy embassy
To the proud orbs that twinkle – and so be
To ev'ry heart a barrier and a ban
Lest the stars totter in the guilt of man !'

Up rose the maiden in the yellow night,
The single-mooned eve ! – on Earth we plight
Our faith to one love – and one moon adore –
The birthplace of young Beauty had no more.
As sprang that yellow star from downy hours
Up rose the maiden from her shrine of flowers,
And bent o'er sheeny mountain and dim plain
Her way – but left not yet her Therasæan reign.[16]

PART II

High on a mountain of enamell'd head –
Such as the drowsy shepherd on his bed
Of giant pasturage lying at his ease,
Raising his heavy eyelid, starts and sees
With many a mutter'd 'hope to be forgiven'
What time the moon is quadrated in Heaven –
Of rosy head, that towering far away
Into the sunlit ether, caught the ray
Of sunken suns at eve – at noon of night,
While the moon danc'd with the fair stranger light –
Uprear'd upon such height arose a pile
Of gorgeous columns on th' unburthen'd air,
Flashing from Parian marble that twin smile

Far down upon the wave that sparkled there,
And nursled the young mountain in its lair.
Of molten stars their pavement,[1] such as fall
Thro' the ebon air, besilvering the pall
Of their own dissolution, while they die –
Adorning then the dwellings of the sky.
A dome, by linked light from Heaven let down,
Sat gently on these columns as a crown –
A window of one circular diamond, there,
Look'd out above into the purple air,
And rays from God shot down that meteor chain
And hallow'd all the beauty twice again,
Save when, between th' Empyrean and that ring,
Some eager spirit flapp'd his dusky wing.
But on the pillars Seraph eyes have seen
The dimness of this world : that greyish green
That Nature loves the best for Beauty's grave
Lurk'd in each cornice, round each architrave –
And every sculptur'd cherub thereabout
That from his marble dwelling peeréd out,
Seem'd earthly in the shadow of his niche –
Achaian statues in a world so rich?
Friezes from Tadmor and Persepolis –[2]
From Balbec, and the stilly, clear abyss
Of beautiful Gomorrah ! Oh, the wave
Is now upon thee – but too late to save ![3]

Sound loves to revel in a summer night :
Witness the murmur of the grey twilight
That stole upon the ear, in Eyraco,[4]
Of many a wild star-gazer long ago –
That stealeth ever on the ear of him
Who, musing, gazeth on the distance dim,
And sees the darkness coming as a cloud –
Is not its form – its voice – most palpable and loud?[5]

But what is this? – it cometh – and it brings
A music with it – 't is the rush of wings –
A pause – and then a sweeping, falling strain
And Nesace is in her halls again.
From the wild energy of wanton haste
　Her cheeks were flushing, and her lips apart;
And zone that clung around her gentle waist
　Had burst beneath the heaving of her heart.
Within the centre of that hall to breathe
She paus'd and panted, Zanthe ! all beneath,
The fairy light that kiss'd her golden hair
And long'd to rest, yet could but sparkle there !

Young flowers were whispering in melody[6]
To happy flowers that night – and tree to tree;
Fountains were gushing music as they fell
In many a star-lit grove, or moon-lit dell;
Yet silence came upon material things –
Fair flowers, bright waterfalls and angel wings –
And sound alone that from the spirit sprang
Bore burthen to the charm the maiden sang:

　　　' 'Neath blue-bell or streamer –
　　　　Or tufted wild spray
　　　That keeps, from the dreamer,
　　　　The moonbeam away –[7]
　　　Bright beings ! that ponder,
　　　　With half closing eyes,
　　　On the stars which your wonder
　　　　Hath drawn from the skies,
　　　'Till they glance thro' the shade, and
　　　　Come down to your brow
　　　Like — eyes of the maiden
　　　　Who calls on you now –
　　　Arise ! from your dreaming
　　　　In violet bowers,
　　　To duty beseeming
　　　　These star-litten hours –

And shake from your tresses
  Encumber'd with dew
The breath of those kisses
  That cumber them too –
(O ! how, without you, Love !
  Could angels be blest ?)
Those kisses of true love
  That lull'd ye to rest !
Up ! – shake from your wing
  Each hindering thing :
The dew of the night –
  It would weigh down your flight;
And true love caresses –
  O ! leave them apart !
They are light on the tresses,
  But lead on the heart.

Ligeia ! Ligeia ![8]
  My beautiful one !
Whose harshest idea
  Will to melody run,
O ! is it thy will
  On the breezes to toss ?
Or, capriciously still,
  Like the lone Albatross,
Incumbent on night[9]
  ´(As she on the air)
To keep watch with delight
  On the harmony there ?
Ligeia ! wherever
  Thy image may be,
No magic shall sever
  Thy music from thee.
Thou hast bound many eyes
  In a dreamy sleep –
But the strains still arise
  Which *thy* vigilance keep –

The sound of the rain
  Which leaps down to the flower,
And dances again
  In the rhythm of the shower –
The murmur that springs
  From the growing of grass[10]
Are the music of things –
  But are modell'd, alas ! –
Away, then my dearest,
  O ! hie thee away
To springs that lie clearest
  Beneath the moon-ray –
To lone lake that smiles,
  In its dream of deep rest,
At the many star-isles
  That enjewel its breast –
Where wild flowers, creeping,
  Have mingled their shade,
On its margin is sleeping
  Full many a maid –
Some have left the cool glade, and
  Have slept with the bee –[11]
Arouse them my maiden,
  On moorland and lea –
Go ! breathe on their slumber,
  All softly in ear,
The musical number
  They slumber'd to hear –
For what can awaken
  An angel so soon
Whose sleep hath been taken
  Beneath the cold moon,
As the spell which no slumber
  Of witchery may test,
The rhythmical number
  Which lull'd him to rest?'

Spirits in wing, and angels to the view,
A thousand seraphs burst th' Empyrean thro',
Young dreams still hovering on their drowsy flight –
Seraphs in all but 'Knowledge,' the keen light
That fell, refracted, thro' thy bounds, afar
O Death! from eye of God upon that star:
Sweet was that error – sweeter still that death –
Sweet was that error – ev'n with *us* the breath
Of Science dims the mirror of our joy –
To them 't were the Simoom, and would destroy –
For what (to them) availeth it to know
That Truth is Falsehood – or that Bliss is Woe?
Sweet was their death – with them to die was rife
With the last ecstasy of satiate life –
Beyond that death no immortality –
But sleep that pondereth and is not 'to be' –
And there – oh! may my weary spirit dwell –
Apart from Heaven's Eternity – and yet how far from Hell![12]
What guilty spirit, in what shrubbery dim,
Heard not the stirring summons of that hymn?
But two: they fell: for Heaven no grace imparts
To those who hear not for their beating hearts.
A maiden-angel and her seraph-lover –
O! where (and ye may seek the wide skies over)
Was Love, the blind, near sober Duty known?
Unguided Love hath fallen – 'mid 'tears of perfect moan.'[13]
He was a goodly spirit – he who fell:
A wanderer by moss-y-mantled well –
A gazer on the lights that shine above –
A dreamer in the moonbeam by his love:
What wonder? for each star is eye-like there,
And looks so sweetly down on Beauty's hair –
And they, and ev'ry mossy spring were holy
To his love-haunted heart and melancholy.
The night had found (to him a night of wo)
Upon a mountain crag, young Angelo –[14]

Beetling it bends athwart the solemn sky,
And scowls on starry worlds that down beneath it lie.
Here sate he with his love – his dark eye bent
With eagle gaze along the firmament :
Now turn'd it upon her – but ever then
It trembled to the orb of EARTH again.

'Ianthe, dearest, see ! how dim that ray !
How lovely 't is to look so far away !
She seem'd not thus upon that autumn eve
I left her gorgeous halls – nor mourn'd to leave.
That eve – that eve – I should remember well –
The sun-ray dropp'd, in Lemnos, with a spell
On th' Arabesque carving of a gilded hall
Wherein I sate, and on the draperied wall –
And on my eye-lids – O the heavy light !
How drowsily it weigh'd them into night !
On flowers, before, and mist, and love they ran
With Persian Saadi in his Gulistan :
But O that light ! – I slumber'd – Death, the while,
Stole o'er my senses in that lovely isle
So softly that no single silken hair
Awoke that slept – or knew that he was there.
The last spot of Earth's orb I trod upon
Was a proud temple call'd the Parthenon –[15]
More beauty clung around her column'd wall
Than ev'n thy glowing bosom beats withal,[16]
And when old Time my wing did disenthral
Thence sprang I – as the eagle from his tower,
And years I left behind me in an hour.
What time upon her airy bounds I hung
One half the garden of her globe was flung
Unrolling as a chart unto my view –
Tenantless cities of the desert too !
Ianthe, beauty crowded on me then,
And half I wish'd to be again of men.'

'My Angelo ! and why of them to be?
A brighter dwelling-place is there for thee –
And greener fields than in yon world above,
And woman's loveliness – and passionate love.'

'But, list, Ianthe ! when the air so soft
Fail'd, as my pennon'd[17] spirit leapt aloft,
Perhaps my brain grew dizzy – but the world
I left so late was into chaos hurl'd –
Sprang from her station, on the winds apart,
And roll'd, a flame, the fiery Heaven athwart.
Methought, my sweet one, then I ceased to soar
And fell – not swiftly as I rose before,
But with a downward, tremulous motion thro'
Light, brazen rays, this golden star unto !
Nor long the measure of my falling hours,
For nearest of all stars was thine to ours –
Dread star ! that came, amid a night of mirth,
A red Dædalion on the timid Earth.'

'We came – and to thy Earth – but not to us
Be given our lady's bidding to discuss :
We came, my love; around, above, below,
Gay fire-fly of the night we come and go,
Nor ask a reason save the angel-nod
She grants to us, as granted by her God –
But, Angelo, than thine grey Time unfurl'd
Never his fairy wing o'er fairier world !
Dim was its little disk, and angel eyes
Alone could see the phantom in the skies,
When first Al Aaraaf knew her course to be
Headlong thitherward o'er the starry sea –
But when its glory swell'd upon the sky,
As glowing Beauty's bust beneath man's eye,
We paus'd before the heritage of men,
And thy star trembled – as doth Beauty then !'

Thus, in discourse, the lovers whiled away
The night that waned and waned and brought no day.
They fell : for Heaven to them no hope imparts
Who hear not for the beating of their hearts.

Romance

Romance, who loves to nod and sing,
With drowsy head and folded wing,
Among the green leaves as they shake
Far down within some shadowy lake,
To me a painted paroquet
Hath been – a most familiar bird –
Taught me my alphabet to say –
To lisp my very earliest word
While in the wild wood I did lie,
A child – with a most knowing eye.

Of late, eternal Condor years
So shake the very Heaven on high
With tumult as they thunder by,
I have no time for idle cares
Through gazing on the unquiet sky.
And when an hour with calmer wings
Its down upon my spirit flings –
That little time with lyre and rhyme
To while away – forbidden things !
My heart would feel to be a crime
Unless it trembled with the strings.

To Helen

Helen, thy beauty is to me
  Like those Nicéan[1] barks of yore,
That gently, o'er a perfumed sea,
  The weary, way-worn wanderer bore
  To his own native shore.

On desperate seas long wont to roam,
  Thy hyacinth hair, thy classic face,
Thy Naiad airs have brought me home
  To the glory that was Greece,
  And the grandeur that was Rome.

Lo ! in yon brilliant window-niche
  How statue-like I see thee stand,
The agate lamp within thy hand !
  Ah, Psyche, from the regions which
  Are Holy-Land !

Israfel[1]

In Heaven a spirit doth dwell
  'Whose heart-strings are a lute;'
None sing so wildly well
As the angel Israfel,
And the giddy stars (so legends tell)
Ceasing their hymns, attend the spell
  Of his voice, all mute.

Tottering above
  In her highest noon,
  The enamoured moon
Blushes with love,
  While, to listen, the red levin
  (With the rapid Pleiads,[2] even,
  Which were seven,)
  Pauses in Heaven.

And they say (the starry choir
  And the other listening things)
That Israfeli's fire
Is owing to that lyre
  By which he sits and sings –
The trembling living wire
Of those unusual strings.

But the skies that angel trod,
  Where deep thoughts are a duty –
Where Love's a grown-up God –
  Where the Houri[3] glances are
Imbued with all the beauty
  Which we worship in a star.

Therefore, thou art not wrong,
   Israfeli, who despisest
An unimpassioned song;
To thee the laurels belong,
   Best bard, because the wisest !
Merrily live, and long !

The ecstasies above
   With thy burning measures suit –
Thy grief, thy joy, thy hate, thy love,
   With the fervour of thy lute –
   Well may the stars be mute !

Yes, Heaven is thine; but this
   Is a world of sweets and sours;
   Our flowers are merely – flowers,
And the shadow of thy perfect bliss
   Is the sunshine of ours.

If I could dwell
Where Israfel
   Hath dwelt, and he where I,
He might not sing so wildly well
   A mortal melody,
While a bolder note than this might swell
   From my lyre within the sky.

The City in the Sea

Lo ! Death has reared himself a throne
In a strange city lying alone
Far down within the dim West,
Where the good and the bad and the worst and the best
Have gone to their eternal rest.
There shrines and palaces and towers
(Time-eaten towers that tremble not !)
Resemble nothing that is ours.
Around, by lifting winds forgot,
Resignedly beneath the sky
The melancholy waters lie.

No rays from the holy heaven come down
On the long night-time of that town;
But light from out the lurid sea
Streams up the turrets silently –
Gleams up the pinnacles far and free –
Up domes – up spires – up kingly halls –
Up fanes – up Babylon-like walls –
Up shadowy long-forgotten bowers
Of sculptured ivy and stone flowers –
Up many and many a marvellous shrine
Whose wreathéd friezes intertwine
The viol, the violet, and the vine.
Resignedly beneath the sky
The melancholy waters lie.
So blend the turrets and shadows there
That all seem pendulous in air,
While from a proud tower in the town
Death looks gigantically down.

There open fanes and gaping graves
Yawn level with the luminous waves

But not the riches there that lie
In each idol's diamond eye –

Not the gaily-jewelled dead
Tempt the waters from their bed;
For no ripples curl, alas !
Along that wilderness of glass –
No swellings tell that winds may be
Upon some far-off happier sea –
No heavings hint that winds have been
On seas less hideously serene.

But lo, a stir is in the air !
The wave – there is a movement there !
As if the towers had thrust aside,
In slightly sinking, the dull tide –
As if their tops had feebly given
A void within the filmy Heaven.
The waves have now a redder glow –
The hours are breathing faint and low –
And when, amid no earthly moans,
Down, down that town shall settle hence,
Hell, rising from a thousand thrones,
Shall do it reverence.

The Sleeper

At midnight, in the month of June,
I stand beneath the mystic moon.
An opiate vapour, dewy, dim,
Exhales from out her golden rim,
And, softly dripping, drop by drop,
Upon the quiet mountain top,
Steals drowsily and musically
Into the universal valley.
The rosemary nods upon the grave;
The lily lolls upon the wave;
Wrapping the fog about its breast,
The ruin moulders into rest;
Looking like Lethe, see ! the lake
A conscious slumber seems to take,
And would not, for the world, awake.
All Beauty sleeps ! – and lo ! where lies
Irene, with her Destinies !

Oh, lady bright ! can it be right –
This window open to the night ?
The wanton airs, from the tree-top,
Laughingly through the lattice drop –
The bodiless airs, a wizard rout,
Flit through thy chamber in and out,
And wave the curtain canopy
So fitfully – so fearfully –
Above the closed and fringéd lid
'Neath which thy slumb'ring soul lies hid,
That, o'er the floor and down the wall,
Like ghosts the shadows rise and fall !
Oh, lady dear, hast thou no fear ?
Why and what art thou dreaming here ?

Sure thou art come o'er far-off seas,
A wonder to these garden trees !
Strange is thy pallor ! strange thy dress !
Strange, above all, thy length of tress,
And this all solemn silentness !

The lady sleeps ! Oh, may her sleep,
Which is enduring, so be deep !
Heaven have her in its sacred keep !
This chamber changed for one more holy,
This bed for one more melancholy,
I pray to God that she may lie
Forever with unopened eye,
While the pale sheeted ghosts go by !

My love, she sleeps ! Oh, may her sleep,
As it is lasting, so be deep !
Soft may the worms about her creep !
Far in the forest, dim and old,
For her may some tall vault unfold –
Some vault that oft hath flung its black
And wingéd panels fluttering back,
Triumphant, o'er the crested palls,
Of her grand family funerals –
Some sepulchre, remote, alone,
Against whose portal she hath thrown,
In childhood, many an idle stone –
Some tomb from out whose sounding door
She ne'er shall force an echo more,
Thrilling to think, poor child of sin !
It was the dead who groaned within.

Lenore

Ah, broken is the golden bowl ! the spirit flown forever !
Let the bell toll ! – a saintly soul floats on the Stygian river;
And, Guy De Vere, hast *thou* no tear? – weep now or never more !
See ! on yon drear and rigid bier low lies thy love, Lenore !
Come ! let the burial rite be read – the funeral song be sung ! –
An anthem for the queenliest dead that ever died so young –
A dirge for her the doubly dead in that she died so young.

'Wretches ! ye loved her for her wealth and hated her for her pride,
'And when she fell in feeble health, ye blessed her – that she died !
'How *shall* the ritual, then, be read? – the requiem how be sung
'By you – by yours, the evil eye, – by yours, the slanderous tongue
'That did to death the innocence that died, and died so young?'

Peccavimus; but rave not thus ! and let a Sabbath song
Go up to God so solemnly the dead may feel no wrong !
The sweet Lenore hath 'gone before,' with Hope, that flew beside,
Leaving thee wild for the dear child that should have been thy
    bride –
For her, the fair and *debonair*, that now so lowly lies,
The life upon her yellow hair but not within her eyes –
The life still there, upon her hair – the death upon her eyes.

'Avaunt ! – avaunt ! from fiends below, the indignant ghost is
    riven –
'From Hell unto a high estate far up within the Heaven –
'From grief and groan, to a golden throne, beside the King of
    Heaven.'
Let no bell toll then ! – lest her soul, amid its hallowed mirth,
Should catch the note as it doth float up from the damnéd Earth ! –
And I ! – to-night my heart is light ! No dirge will I upraise,
But waft the angel on her flight with a Pæan of old days !

The Valley of Unrest

Once it smiled a silent dell
Where the people did not dwell;
They had gone unto the wars,
Trusting to the mild-eyed stars,
Nightly, from their azure towers,
To keep watch above the flowers,
In the midst of which all day
The red sun-light lazily lay.
Now each visiter shall confess
The sad valley's restlessness.
Nothing there is motionless –
Nothing save the airs that brood
Over the magic solitude.
Ah, by no wind are stirred those trees
That palpitate like the chill seas
Around the misty Hebrides !
Ah, by no wind those clouds are driven
That rustle through the unquiet Heaven
Uneasily, from morn till even,
Over the violets there that lie
In myriad types of the human eye –
Over the lilies three that wave
And weep above a nameless grave !
They wave : – from out their fragrant tops
Eternal dews come down in drops.
They weep : – from off their delicate stems
Perennial tears descend in gems.

The Raven

Once upon a midnight dreary, while I pondered, weak and weary,
Over many a quaint and curious volume of forgotten lore –
While I nodded, nearly napping, suddenly there came a tapping,
As of some one gently rapping, rapping at my chamber door.
' 'T is some visiter,' I muttered, 'tapping at my chamber door –
Only this and nothing more.'

Ah, distinctly I remember it was in the bleak December;
And each separate dying ember wrought its ghost upon the floor.
Eagerly I wished the morrow; – vainly I had sought to borrow
From my books surcease of sorrow – sorrow for the lost Lenore –
For the rare and radiant maiden whom the angels name Lenore –
Nameless *here* for evermore.

And the silken, sad, uncertain rustling of each purple curtain
Thrilled me – filled me with fantastic terrors never felt before;
So that now, to still the beating of my heart, I stood repeating
' 'T is some visiter entreating entrance at my chamber door –
Some late visiter entreating entrance at my chamber door; –
This it is and nothing more.'

Presently my soul grew stronger; hesitating then no longer,
'Sir,' said I, 'or Madam, truly your forgiveness I implore;
But the fact is I was napping, and so gently you came rapping,
And so faintly you came tapping, tapping at my chamber door,
That I scarce was sure I heard you' – here I opened wide the door; –
Darkness there and nothing more.

Deep into that darkness peering, long I stood there wondering,
fearing,
Doubting, dreaming dreams no mortal ever dared to dream before;
But the silence was unbroken, and the stillness gave no token,
And the only word there spoken was the whispered word, 'Lenore!'
This I whispered, and an echo murmured back the word 'Lenore!'
Merely this and nothing more.

Back into the chamber turning, all my soul within me burning,
Soon again I heard a tapping somewhat louder than before.
'Surely,' said I, 'surely that is something at my window lattice;
Let me see, then, what thereat is, and this mystery explore –
Let my heart be still a moment and this mystery explore; –
      'T is the wind and nothing more!'

Open here I flung the shutter, when, with many a flirt and flutter
In there stepped a stately Raven of the saintly days of yore.
Not the least obeisance made he; not a minute stopped or stayed he;
But, with mien of lord or lady, perched above my chamber door –
Perched upon a bust of Pallas just above my chamber door –
      Perched, and sat, and nothing more.

Then this ebony bird beguiling my sad fancy into smiling,
By the grave and stern decorum of the countenance it wore,
'Though thy crest be shorn and shaven, thou,' I said, 'are sure no
  craven,
Ghastly grim and ancient Raven wandering from the Nightly
  shore –
Tell me what thy lordly name is on the Night's Plutonian shore!'
      Quoth the Raven, 'Nevermore.'

Much I marvelled this ungainly fowl to hear discourse so plainly,
Though its answer little meaning – little relevancy bore;
For we cannot help agreeing that no living human being
Ever yet was blessed with seeing bird above his chamber door –
Bird or beast upon the sculptured bust above his chamber door,
      With such name as 'Nevermore.'

But the Raven, sitting lonely on the placid bust, spoke only
That one word, as if his soul in that one word he did outpour.
Nothing farther then he uttered – not a feather then he fluttered –
Till I scarcely more than muttered 'Other friends have flown be-
  fore –
On the morrow *he* will leave me, as my hopes have flown before.'
      Then the bird said 'Nevermore.'

Startled at the stillness broken by reply so aptly spoken,
'Doubtless,' said I, 'what it utters is its only stock and store
Caught from some unhappy master whom unmerciful Disaster
Followed fast and followed faster till his songs one burden bore –
Till the dirges of his Hope that melancholy burden bore
        Of "Never – nevermore." '

But the Raven still beguiling all my fancy into smiling,
Straight I wheeled a cushioned seat in front of bird, and bust and
   door;
Then, upon the velvet sinking, I betook myself to linking
Fancy unto fancy, thinking what this ominous bird of yore –
What this grim, ungainly, ghastly, gaunt, and ominous bird of
   yore
        Meant in croaking 'Nevermore.'

This I sat engaged in guessing, but no syllable expressing
To the fowl whose fiery eyes now burned into my bosom's core;
This and more I sat divining, with my head at ease reclining
On the cushion's velvet lining that the lamp-light gloated[1] o'er,
But whose velvet violet lining with the lamp-light gloating o'er,
       She shall press, ah, nevermore !

Then, methought, the air grew denser, perfumed from an unseen
   censer
Swung by Seraphim whose foot-falls tinkled on the tufted floor.
'Wretch,' I cried, 'thy God hath lent thee – by these angels he hath
   sent thee
Respite – respite and nepenthe[2] from thy memories of Lenore;
Quaff, oh quaff this kind nepenthe and forget this lost Lenore !'
       Quoth the Raven 'Nevermore.'

'Prophet !' said I, 'thing of evil ! prophet still, if bird or devil ! –
Whether Tempter sent, or whether tempest tossed thee here ashore,
Desolate yet all undaunted, on this desert land enchanted –
On this home by Horror haunted – tell me truly, I implore –
Is there – *is* there balm in Gilead ? – tell me – tell me, I implore !'
       Quoth the Raven 'Nevermore.'

'Prophet !' said I, 'thing of evil ! – prophet still, if bird or devil !
By that Heaven that bends above us – by that God we both adore –
Tell this soul with sorrow laden if, within the distant Aidenn,
It shall clasp a sainted maiden whom the angels name Lenore –
Clasp a rare and radiant maiden whom the angels name Lenore.'
Quoth the Raven 'Nevermore.'

'Be that word our sign of parting, bird or fiend !' I shrieked, up-
starting –
'Get thee back into the tempest and the Night's Plutonian shore !
Leave no black plume as a token of that lie thy soul hath spoken !
Leave my loneliness unbroken ! – quit the bust above my door !
Take thy beak from out my heart, and take thy form from off my
door !'
Quoth the Raven 'Nevermore.'

And the Raven, never flitting, still is sitting, *still* is sitting
On the pallid bust of Pallas just above my chamber door;
And his eyes have all the seeming of a demon's that is dreaming,
And the lamp-light o'er him streaming throws his shadow on the
floor;
And my soul from out that shadow that lies floating on the floor
Shall be lifted – nevermore !

Ulalume

The skies they were ashen and sober;
    The leaves they were crisped and sere –
    The leaves they were withering and sere;
It was night in the lonesome October
    Of my most immemorial year;
It was hard by the dim lake of Auber,[1]
    In the misty mid region of Weir –[2]
It was down by the dank tarn of Auber,
    In the ghoul-haunted woodland of Weir.

Here once, through an alley Titanic,
    Of cypress, I roamed with my Soul –
    Of cypress, with Psyche, my Soul.
These were days when my heart was volcanic
    As the scoriac rivers that roll –
    As the lavas that restlessly roll
Their sulphurous currents down Yaanek[3]
    In the ultimate climes of the pole –
That groan as they roll down Mount Yaanek
    In the realms of the boreal pole.

Our talk had been serious and sober,
    But our thoughts they were palsied and sere –
    Our memories were treacherous and sere –
For we knew not the month was October,
    And we marked not the night of the year –
    (Ah, night of all nights in the year !)
We noted not the dim lake of Auber –
    (Though once we had journeyed down here) –
Remembered not the dank tarn of Auber,
    Nor the ghoul-haunted woodland of Weir.

And now, as the night was senescent
    And star-dials pointed to morn –

As the star-dials hinted of morn –
At the end of our path a liquescent
    And nebulous lustre was born,
Out of which a miraculous crescent
    Arose with a duplicate horn –
Astarte's bediamonded crescent
    Distinct with its duplicate horn.

And I said – 'She is warmer than Dian:
    She rolls through an ether of sighs –
    She revels in a region of sighs:
She has seen that the tears are not dry on
    These cheeks, where the worm never dies
And has come past the stars of the Lion
    To point us the path to the skies –
    To the Lethean peace of the skies –
Come up, in despite of the Lion,
    To shine on us with her bright eyes –
Come up through the lair of the Lion,
    With love in her luminous eyes.'

But Psyche, uplifting her finger,
    Said – 'Sadly this star I mistrust –
    Her pallor I strangely mistrust: –
Oh, hasten ! – oh, let us not linger !
    Oh, fly ! – let us fly ! – for we must.'
In terror she spoke, letting sink her
    Wings until they trailed in the dust –
In agony sobbed, letting sink her
    Plumes till they trailed in the dust –
    Till they sorrowfully trailed in the dust.

I replied – 'This is nothing but dreaming:
    Let us on by this tremulous light !
    Let us bathe in this crystalline light !
Its Sibyllic splendor is beaming

With Hope and in Beauty to-night : –
    See ! – it flickers up the sky through the night !
Ah, we safely may trust to its gleaming,
    And be sure it will lead us aright –
We safely may trust to a gleaming
    That cannot but guide us aright,
    Since it flickers up to Heaven through the night.'

Thus I pacified Psyche and kissed her,
    And tempted her out of her gloom –
    And conquered her scruples and gloom ;
And we passed to the end of the vista,
    But were stopped by the door of a tomb –
    By the door of a legended tomb ;
And I said – 'What is written, sweet sister,
    On the door of this legended tomb ?'
    She replied – 'Ulalume – Ulalume –
    'T is the vault of thy lost Ulalume !'

Then my heart it grew ashen and sober
    As the leaves that were crisped and sere –
    As the leaves that were withering and sere,
And I cried – 'It was surely October
    On *this* very night of last year
    That I journeyed – I journeyed down here –
    That I brought a dread burden down here –
    On this night of all nights in the year,
    Ah, what demon has tempted me here ?
Well I know, now, this dim lake of Auber –
    This misty mid region of Weir –
Well I know, now, this dank tarn of Auber,
    This ghoul-haunted woodland of Weir.'

For Annie

Thank Heaven ! the crisis –
   The danger is past,
And the lingering illness
   Is over at last –
And the fever called 'Living'
   Is conquered at last.

Sadly, I know
   I am shorn of my strength,
And no muscle I move
   As I lie at full length –
But no matter ! – I feel
   I am better at length.

And I rest so composedly
   Now, in my bed,
That any beholder
   Might fancy me dead –
Might start at beholding me,
   Thinking me dead.

The moaning and groaning,
   The sighing and sobbing,
Are quieted now,
   With that horrible throbbing
At heart : – ah that horrible,
   Horrible throbbing !

The sickness – the nausea –
   The pitiless pain –
Have ceased with the fever
   That maddened my brain –
With the fever called 'Living'
   That burned in my brain.

And oh ! of all tortures
   That torture the worst
Has abated – the terrible
   Torture of thirst
For the napthaline river
   Of Passion accurst : –
I have drank of a water
   That quenches all thirst : –

Of a water that flows,
   With a lullaby sound,
From a spring but a very few
   Feet under ground –
From a cavern not very far
   Down under ground.

And ah ! let it never
   Be foolishly said
That my room it is gloomy
   And narrow my bed;
For man never slept
   In a different bed –
And, to sleep, you must slumber
   In just such a bed.

My tantalized spirit
   Here blandly reposes,
Forgetting, or never
   Regretting, its roses –
Its old agitations
   Of myrtles and roses :

For now, while so quietly
   Lying, it fancies
A holier odor
   About it, of pansies –
A rosemary odor,

Commingled with pansies –
With rue and the beautiful
Puritan pansies.

And so it lies happily,
Bathing in many
A dream of the truth
And the beauty of Annie –
Drowned in a bath
Of the tresses of Annie.

She tenderly kissed me,
She fondly caressed,
And then I fell gently
To sleep on her breast –
Deeply to sleep
From the heaven of her breast.

When the light was extinguished,
She covered me warm,
And she prayed to the angels
To keep me from harm –
To the queen of the angels
To shield me from harm.

And I lie so composedly,
Now, in my bed,
(Knowing her love)
That you fancy me dead –
And I rest so contentedly,
Now, in my bed,
(With her love at my breast)
That you fancy me dead –
That you shudder to look at me,
Thinking me dead : –

But my heart it is brighter
    Than all of the many
Stars of the sky,
    For it sparkles with Annie –
It glows with the light
    Of the love of my Annie –
With the thought of the light
    Of the eyes of my Annie.

A Valentine

To — — —

For her this rhyme is penned, whose luminous eyes,
    Brightly expressive as the twins of Leda,
Shall find her own sweet name, that, nestling lies
    Upon the page, enwrapped from every reader
Search narrowly the lines ! – they hold a treasure
    Divine – a talisman – an amulet
That must be worn *at heart*. Search well the measure –
    The words – the syllables ! Do not forget
The trivialest point, or you may lose your labor !
    And yet there is in this no Gordian knot
Which one might not undo without a sabre,
    If one could merely comprehend the plot.
Enwritten upon the leaf where now are peering
    Eyes scintillating soul, there lie *perdus*
Three eloquent words oft uttered in the hearing
    Of poets, by poets – as the name is a poet's, too.
Its letters, although naturally lying
    Like the knight Pinto – Mendez Ferdinando –
Still form a synonym for Truth. – Cease trying !
    You will not read the riddle, though you do the best you *can* do.

Annabel Lee

It was many and many a year ago,
      In a kingdom by the sea
That a maiden there lived whom you may know
      By the name of ANNABEL LEE;
And this maiden she lived with no other thought
      Than to love and be loved by me.

I was a child and *she* was a child,
      In this kingdom by the sea,
But we loved with a love that was more than love –
      I and my ANNABEL LEE –
With a love that the winged seraphs of heaven
      Coveted her and me.

And this was the reason that, long ago,
      In this kingdom by the sea,
A wind blew out of a cloud, chilling
      My beautiful ANNABEL LEE;
So that her highborn kinsmen came
      And bore her away from me,
To shut her up in a sepulchre
      In this kingdom by the sea.

The angels, not half so happy in heaven,
      Went envying her and me –
Yes ! – that was the reason (as all men know,
      In this kingdom by the sea)
That the wind came out of the cloud by night,
      Chilling and killing my ANNABEL LEE.

But our love it was stronger by far than the love
      Of those who were older than we –
      Of many far wiser than we –

And neither the angels in heaven above,
          Nor the demons down under the sea,
Can ever dissever my soul from the soul
          Of the beautiful ANNABEL LEE:

For the moon never beams, without bringing me dreams
          Of the beautiful ANNABEL LEE;
And the stars never rise, but I feel the bright eyes
          Of the beautiful ANNABEL LEE:
And so, all the night-tide, I lie down by the side
Of my darling – my darling – my life and my bride,
          In the sepulchre there by the sea –
          In her tomb by the sounding sea.

The Bells

I

Hear the sledges with the bells —
           Silver bells !
What a world of merriment their melody foretells !
      How they tinkle, tinkle, tinkle,
           In the icy air of night !
      While the stars that oversprinkle
      All the heavens, seem to twinkle
           With a crystalline delight;
           Keeping time, time, time,
           In a sort of Runic rhyme,
To the tintinnabulation that so musically wells
      From the bells, bells, bells, bells,
           Bells, bells, bells —
From the jingling and the tinkling of the bells.

II

      Hear the mellow wedding bells
           Golden bells !
What a world of happiness their harmony foretells !
      Through the balmy air of night
      How they ring out their delight ! —
           From the molten-golden notes,
                And all in tune,
           What a liquid ditty floats
To the turtle-dove that listens, while she gloats
                On the moon !
      Oh, from out the sounding cells,
What a gush of euphony voluminously wells !
                How it swells !
                How it dwells

On the Future ! – how it tells
Of the rapture that impels
To the swinging and the ringing
Of the bells, bells, bells –
Of the bells, bells, bells, bells,
Bells, bells, bells –
To the rhyming and the chiming of the bells !

III

Hear the loud alarum bells –
Brazen bells !
What a tale of terror, now their turbulency tells !
In the startled ear of night
How they scream out their affright !
Too much horrified to speak,
They can only shriek, shriek,
Out of tune,
In a clamorous appealing to the mercy of the fire,
In a mad expostulation with the deaf and frantic fire,
Leaping higher, higher, higher,
With a desperate desire,
And a resolute endeavour
Now – now to sit, or never,
By the side of the pale-faced moon.
Oh, the bells, bells, bells !
What a tale their terror tells
Of Despair !
How they clang, and clash, and roar !
What a horror they outpour
On the bosom of the palpitating air !
Yet the ear, it fully knows,
By the twanging,
And the clanging,
How the danger ebbs and flows;
Yet the ear distinctly tells,

In the jangling,
And the wrangling,
How the danger sinks and swells,
By the sinking or the swelling in the anger of the bells –
Of the bells –
Of the bells, bells, bells, bells,
Bells, bells, bells –
In the clamor and the clanging of the bells !

IV

Hear the tolling of the bells –
Iron bells !
What a world of solemn thought their monody compels !
In the silence of the night,
How we shiver with affright
At the melancholy menace of their tone !
For every sound that floats
From the rust within their throats
Is a groan.
And the people – ah, the people –
They that dwell up in the steeple,
All alone,
And who, tolling, tolling, tolling,
In that muffled monotone,
Feel a glory in so rolling
On the human heart a stone –
They are neither man nor woman –
They are neither brute nor human –
They are Ghouls : –
And their king it is who tolls : –
And he rolls, rolls, rolls,
Rolls
A pæan from the bells !
And his merry bosom swells
With the pæan of the bells !
And he dances, and he yells;

Keeping time, time, time,
In a sort of Runic rhyme,
  To the pæan of the bells: –
    Of the bells:
Keeping time, time, time
In a sort of Runic rhyme,
  To the throbbing of the bells –
Of the bells, bells, bells –
  To the sobbing of the bells: –
Keeping time, time, time,
  As he knells, knells, knells,
In a happy Runic rhyme,
  To the rolling of the bells –
Of the bells, bells, bells: –
  To the tolling of the bells –
Of the bells, bells, bells, bells,
  Bells, bells, bells –
To the moaning and the groaning of the bells.

Eldorado

Gaily bedight,
A gallant knight,
In sunshine and in shadow,
Had journeyed long,
Singing a song,
In search of Eldorado.

But he grew old –
This knight so bold –
And o'er his heart a shadow
Fell as he found
No spot of ground
That looked like Eldorado.

And, as his strength
Failed him at length,
He met a pilgrim shadow –
'Shadow,' said he,
'Where can it be –
This land of Eldorado?'

'Over the Mountains
Of the Moon,
Down the Valley of the Shadow,
Ride, boldly ride,'
The shade replied, –
'If you seek for Eldorado.'

2. Tales

Manuscript Found in a Bottle

Qui n'a plus qu'un moment à vivre
N'a plus rien à dissimuler.

QUINAULT – *Atys* [1]

OF my country and of my family I have little to say. Ill usage and length of years have driven me from the one, and estranged me from the other. Hereditary wealth afforded me an education of no common order, and a contemplative turn of mind enabled me to methodize the stores which early study very diligently garnered up. – Beyond all things, the study of the German moralists gave me great delight; not from any ill-advised admiration of their eloquent madness, but from the ease with which my habits of rigid thought enabled me to detect their falsities. I have often been reproached with the aridity of my genius; a deficiency of imagination has been imputed to me as a crime; and the Pyrrhonism of my opinions has at all times rendered me notorious. Indeed, a strong relish for physical philosophy has, I fear, tinctured my mind with a very common error of this age – I mean the habit of referring occurrences, even the least susceptible of such reference, to the principles of that science. Upon the whole, no person could be less liable than myself to be led away from the severe precincts of truth by the *ignes fatui* of superstition. I have thought proper to premise thus much, lest the incredible tale I have to tell should be considered rather the raving of a crude imagination, than the positive experience of a mind to which the reveries of fancy have been a dead letter and a nullity.

After many years spent in foreign travel, I sailed in the year 18—, from the port of Batavia, in the rich and populous island of Java, on a voyage to the Archipelago of the Sunda islands. I went as passenger – having no other inducement than a kind of nervous restlessness which haunted me as a fiend.

Our vessel was a beautiful ship of about four hundred tons, copper-fastened, and built at Bombay of Malabar teak. She was freighted with cotton-wool and oil, from the Lachadive islands. We had also on board coir, jaggeree, ghee, cocoa-nuts, and a few cases of opium. The stowage was clumsily done, and the vessel consequently crank.

We got under way with a mere breath of wind, and for many days stood along the eastern coast of Java, without any other incident to beguile the monotony of our course than the occasional meeting with some of the small grabs of the Archipelago to which we were bound.

One evening, leaning over the taffrail, I observed a very singular, isolated cloud, to the N. W. It was remarkable, as well for its color, as from its being the first we had seen since our departure from Batavia. I watched it attentively until sunset, when it spread all at once to the eastward and westward, girting in the horizon with a narrow strip of vapor, and looking like a long line of low beach. My notice was soon afterwards attracted by the dusky-red appearance of the moon, and the peculiar character of the sea. The latter was undergoing a rapid change, and the water seemed more than usually transparent. Although I could distinctly see the bottom, yet, heaving the lead, I found the ship in fifteen fathoms. The air now became intolerably hot, and was loaded with spiral exhalations similar to those arising from heated iron. As night came on, every breath of wind died away, and a more entire calm it is impossible to conceive. The flame of a candle burned upon the poop without the least perceptible motion, and a long hair, held between the finger and thumb, hung without the possibility of detecting a vibration. However, as the captain said he could perceive no indication of danger, and as we were drifting in bodily to shore, he ordered the sails to be furled, and the anchor let go. No watch was set, and the crew, consisting principally of Malays, stretched themselves deliberately upon deck. I went below – not without a full presentiment of evil. Indeed, every appearance warranted me in apprehending a simoom. I told the captain my fears, but he paid no attention to what I said, and left me without deigning to give a reply. My uneasiness, however, prevented me from sleeping, and about midnight I went upon deck. – As I placed my foot upon the upper step of the companion-ladder, I was startled by a loud, humming noise, like that occasioned by the rapid revolution of a mill-wheel, and before I could ascertain its meaning, I found the ship quivering to its centre. In the next instant, a wilderness of foam hurled us upon our beam-ends, and, rushing over us fore and aft, swept the entire decks from stem to stern.

The extreme fury of the blast proved, in a great measure, the salvation of the ship. Although completely water-logged, yet, as her masts had gone by the board, she rose, after a minute, heavily from the sea, and, staggering awhile beneath the immense pressure of the tempest, finally righted.

By what miracle I escaped destruction, it is impossible to say. Stunned by the shock of the water, I found myself, upon recovery, jammed in between the stern-post and rudder. With great difficulty I gained my feet and looking dizzily around, was, at first, struck with the idea of our being among breakers so terrific, beyond the wildest imagination, was the whirlpool of mountainous and foaming ocean within which we were engulfed. After a while, I heard the voice of an old Swede, who had shipped with us at the moment of our leaving port. I hallooed to him with all my strength, and presently he came reeling aft. We soon discovered that we were the sole survivors of the accident. All on deck, with the exception of ourselves, had been swept overboard; – the captain and mates must have perished as they slept, for the cabins were deluged with water. Without assistance, we could expect to do little for the security of the ship, and our exertions were at first paralyzed by the momentary expectation of going down. Our cable had, of course, parted like pack-thread, at the first breath of the hurricane, or we should have been instantaneously overwhelmed. We scudded with frightful velocity before the sea, and the water made clear breaches over us. The frame-work of our stern was shattered excessively, and, in almost every respect, we had received considerable injury; but to our extreme joy we found the pumps unchoked, and that we had made no great shifting of our ballast. The main fury of the blast had already blown over, and we apprehended little danger from the violence of the wind; but we looked forward to its total cessation with dismay; well believing, that, in our shattered condition, we should inevitably perish in the tremendous swell which would ensue. But this very just apprehension seemed by no means likely to be soon verified. For five entire days and nights – during which our only subsistence was a small quantity of jaggeree, procured with great difficulty from the forecastle – the hulk flew at a rate defying computation, before rapidly succeeding flaws of wind, which, without equalling the first violence of the Simoom, were still more terrific than any tempest I had before encountered. Our course for the first four days was, with trifling variations, S. E. and by S.; and we must have run down the coast of New Holland. – On the fifth day the cold became extreme, although the wind had hauled round a point more to the northward. – The sun arose with a sickly yellow lustre, and clambered a very few degrees above the horizon – emitting no decisive light. – There were no clouds apparent, yet the wind was upon the increase, and blew with a fitful and unsteady fury. About noon, as nearly as we could guess, our attention was again arrested by the appearance of the sun. It gave out no light, properly so called, but a dull and sullen glow without reflection, as if all its rays were polarized. Just before sinking within the turgid sea, its central fires suddenly went out, as if hurriedly extinguished by some unaccountable power. It was a dim, silver-like rim, alone, as it rushed down the unfathomable ocean.

We waited in vain for the arrival of the sixth day – that day to me has not arrived – to the Swede, never did arrive. Thenceforward we were enshrouded in pitchy darkness, so that we could not have seen an object at twenty paces from the ship. Eternal night continued to envelop us, all unrelieved by the phosphoric sea-brilliancy to which we had been accustomed in the tropics. We observed too, that, although the tempest continued to rage with unabated violence, there was no longer to be discovered the usual appearance of surf, or foam, which had hitherto attended us. All around were horror, and thick gloom, and a black sweltering desert of ebony. – Superstitious terror crept by degrees into the spirit of the old Swede, and my own soul was wrapped up in silent wonder. We neglected all care of the ship, as worse than useless, and securing ourselves, as well as possible, to the stump of the mizen-mast, looked out bitterly into the world of ocean. We had no means of calculating time, nor could we form any guess of our situation. We were, however, well aware of having made farther to the southward than any previous navigators, and felt great amazement at not meeting with the usual impediments of ice. In the meantime every moment threatened to be our last – every mountainous billow hurried to overwhelm us. The swell surpassed anything I had imagined possible, and that we were not instantly buried is a miracle. My companion spoke of the lightness of our cargo, and reminded me of the excellent qualities of our ship; but I could not help feeling the utter hopelessness of hope itself, and prepared myself gloomily for that death which I thought nothing could defer beyond an hour, as, with every knot of way the ship made, the swelling of the black stupendous seas became more dismally appalling. At times we gasped for breath at an elevation beyond the albatross – at times became dizzy with the velocity of our descent into some watery hell, where the air grew stagnant, and no sound disturbed the slumbers of the kraken.

We were at the bottom of one of these abysses, when a quick scream from my companion broke fearfully upon the night. 'See! see!' cried he, shrieking in my ears, 'Almighty God! see! see!' As he spoke, I became aware of a dull, sullen glare of red light which streamed down the sides of the vast chasm where we lay, and threw a fitful brilliancy upon our deck. Casting my eyes upwards, I beheld a spectacle which froze the current of my blood. At a terrific height directly above us, and upon the very verge of the precipitous descent, hovered a gigantic ship of, perhaps, four thousand tons. Although upreared upon the summit of a wave more than a hundred times her own altitude, her apparent size still exceeded that of any ship of the line or East Indiaman in existence. Her huge hull was of a deep dingy black, unrelieved by any of the customary carvings of a ship. A single row of brass cannon protruded from her open ports, and dashed from their polished surfaces the fires of innumerable battle-lanterns, which swung to and fro about her rigging. But what mainly inspired us with horror and astonishment, was that she bore up under a press of sail in the very teeth of that super-natural sea, and of that ungovernable hurricane. When we first discovered her, her bows were alone to be seen, as she rose slowly from the dim and horrible gulf beyond her. For a moment of intense terror she paused upon the giddy pinnacle, as if in con-templation of her own sublimity, then trembled and tottered, and – came down.

At this instant, I know not what sudden self-possession came over my spirit. Staggering as far aft as I could, I awaited fear-lessly the ruin that was to overwhelm. Our own vessel was at length ceasing from her struggles, and sinking with her head to the sea. The shock of the descending mass struck her, conse-quently, in that portion of her frame which was already under water, and the inevitable result was to hurl me, with irresistible violence, upon the rigging of the stranger.

As I fell, the ship hove in stays, and went about; and to the confusion ensuing I attributed my escape from the notice of the crew. With little difficulty I made my way unperceived to the main hatchway, which was partially open, and soon found an opportunity of secreting myself in the hold. Why I did so I can hardly tell. An indefinite sense of awe, which at first sight of the navigators of the ship had taken hold of my mind, was perhaps the principle of my concealment. I was unwilling to trust myself with a race of people who had offered, to the cursory glance I had taken, so many points of vague novelty, doubt, and apprehension. I therefore thought proper to contrive a hiding-place in the hold. This I did by removing a small portion of the shifting-boards, in such a manner as to afford me a convenient retreat between the huge timbers of the ship.

I had scarcely completed my work, when a footstep in the hold forced me to make use of it. A man passed by my place of concealment with a feeble and unsteady gait. I could not see his face, but had an opportunity of observing his general appearance. There was about it an evidence of great age and infirmity. His knees tottered beneath a load of years, and his entire frame quivered under the burthen. He muttered to himself, in a low broken tone, some words of a language which I could not understand, and groped in a corner among a pile of singular-looking instruments, and decayed charts of navigation. His manner was a wild mixture of the peevishness of second childhood, and the solemn dignity of a God. He at length went on deck, and I saw him no more.

*

A feeling, for which I have no name, has taken possession of my soul – a sensation which will admit of no analysis, to which the lessons of by-gone times are inadequate, and for which I fear futurity itself will offer me no key. To a mind constituted like my own, the latter consideration is an evil. I shall never – I know that I shall never – be satisfied with regard to the nature of my conceptions. Yet it is not wonderful that these conceptions are indefinite, since they have their origin in sources so utterly novel. A new sense – a new entity is added to my soul.

*

It is long since I first trod the deck of this terrible ship, and the rays of my destiny are, I think, gathering to a focus. Incomprehensible men! Wrapped up in meditations of a kind which I cannot divine, they pass me by unnoticed. Concealment is utter folly on my part, for the people *will not* see. It was but just now that I passed directly before the eyes of the mate – it was no long while ago that I ventured into the captain's own private cabin, and took thence the materials with which I write, and have written. I shall from time to time continue this journal. It is true that I may not find an opportunity of transmitting it to the world, but I will not fail to make the endeavour. At the last moment I will enclose the MS. in a bottle, and cast it within the sea.

*

An incident has occurred which has given me new room for meditation. Are such things the operation of ungoverned Chance? I had ventured upon deck and thrown myself down, without attracting any notice, among a pile of ratlin-stuff and old sails, in the bottom of the yawl. While musing upon the singularity of my fate, I unwittingly daubed with a tar-brush the edges of a neatly-folded studding-sail which lay near me on a barrel. The studding-sail is now bent upon the ship, and the thoughtless touches of the brush are spread out into the word DISCOVERY. * * *

I have made many observations lately upon the structure of the vessel. Although well armed, she is not, I think, a ship of war. Her rigging, build, and general equipment, all negative a supposition of this kind. What she is *not*, I can easily perceive – what she *is* I fear it is impossible to say. I know not how it is, but in scrutinizing her strange model and singular cast of spars, her huge size and overgrown suits of canvass, her severely simple bow and antiquated stern, there will occasionally flash across my mind a sensation of familiar things, and there is always mixed up with such indistinct shadows of recollection, an unaccountable memory of old foreign chronicles and ages long ago. * * *

I have been looking at the timbers of the ship. She is built of a material to which I am a stranger. There is a peculiar character about the wood which strikes me as rendering it unfit for the purpose to which it has been applied. I mean its extreme *porousness*, considered independently of the worm-eaten condition which is a consequence of navigation in these seas, and apart from the rottenness attendant upon age. It will appear perhaps an observation somewhat over-curious, but this wood would have every characteristic of Spanish oak, if Spanish oak were distended by any unnatural means.

In reading the above sentence a curious apothegm of an old

weather-beaten Dutch navigator comes full upon my recollection. 'It is as sure,' he was wont to say, when any doubt was entertained of his veracity, 'as sure as there is a sea where the ship itself will grow in bulk like the living body of the seaman.' * * *

About an hour ago, I made bold to thrust myself among a group of the crew. They paid me no manner of attention, and, although I stood in the very midst of them all, seemed utterly unconscious of my presence. Like the one I had at first seen in the hold, they all bore about them the marks of a hoary old age. Their knees trembled with infirmity; their shoulders were bent double with decrepitude; their shrivelled skins rattled in the wind; their voices were low, tremulous and broken; their eyes glistened with the rheum of years; and their gray hairs streamed terribly in the tempest. Around them, on every part of the deck, lay scattered mathematical instruments of the most quaint and obsolete construction. * * *

I mentioned some time ago the bending of a studding-sail. From that period the ship, being thrown dead off the wind, has continued her terrific course due south, with every rag of canvas packed upon her, from her trucks to her lower studding-sail booms, and rolling every moment her top-gallant yard-arms into the most appalling hell of water which it can enter into the mind of man to imagine. I have just left the deck, where I find it impossible to maintain a footing, although the crew seem to experience little inconvenience. It appears to me a miracle of miracles that our enormous bulk is not swallowed up at once and forever. We are surely doomed to hover continually upon the brink of Eternity, without taking a final plunge into the abyss. From billows a thousand times more stupendous than any I have ever seen, we glide away with the facility of the arrowy sea-gull; and the colossal waters rear their heads above us like demons of the deep, but like demons confined to simple threats and forbidden to destroy. I am led to attribute these frequent escapes to the only natural cause which can account for such effect. – I must suppose the ship to be within the influence of some strong current, or impetuous under-tow. * * *

I have seen the captain face to face, and in his own cabin – but, as I expected, he paid me no attention. Although in his appearance there is, to a casual observer, nothing which might bespeak him more or less than man – still a feeling of irrepressible reverence and awe mingled with the sensation of wonder with which I regarded him. In stature he is nearly my own height; that is, about five feet eight inches. He is of a well-knit and compact frame of body, neither robust nor remarkably otherwise. But it is the singularity of the expression which reigns upon the face – it is the intense, the wonderful, the thrilling evidence of old age, so utter, so extreme, which excites within my spirit a sense – a sentiment ineffable. His forehead, although little wrinkled, seems to bear upon it the stamp of a myriad of years. – His gray hairs are records of the past, and his grayer eyes are Sybils of the future. The cabin floor was thickly strewn with strange, iron-clasped folios, and mouldering instruments of science, and obsolete long-forgotten charts. His head was bowed down upon his hands, and he pored, with a fiery unquiet eye, over a paper which I took to be a commission, and which, at all events, bore the signature of a monarch. He muttered to himself, as did the first seaman whom I saw in the hold, some low peevish syllables of a foreign tongue, and although the speaker was close at my elbow, his voice seemed to reach my ears from the distance of a mile. * * *

The ship and all in it are imbued with the spirit of Eld. The crew glide to and fro like the ghosts of buried centuries; their eyes have an eager and uneasy meaning; and when their fingers fall athwart my path in the wild glare of the battle-lanterns, I feel as I have never felt before, although I have been all my life a dealer in antiquities, and have imbibed the shadows of fallen columns at Balbec, and Tadmor, and Persepolis, until my very soul has become a ruin. * * *

When I look around me I feel ashamed of my former apprehensions. If I trembled at the blast which has hitherto attended us, shall I not stand aghast at a warring of wind and ocean, to convey any idea of which the words tornado and simoom are trivial and ineffective? All in the immediate vicinity of the ship is the blackness of eternal night, and a chaos of foamless water;

but, about a league on either side of us, may be seen, indistinctly and at intervals, stupendous ramparts of ice, towering away into the desolate sky, and looking like the walls of the universe. * * *

As I imagined, the ship proves to be in a current; if that appellation can properly be given to a tide which, howling and shrieking by the white ice, thunders on to the southward with a velocity like the headlong dashing of a cataract. * * *

To conceive the horror of my sensations is, I presume, utterly impossible; yet a curiosity to penetrate the mysteries of these awful regions, predominates even over my despair, and will reconcile me to the most hideous aspect of death. It is evident that we are hurrying onwards to some exciting knowledge – some never-to-be-imparted secret, whose attainment is destruction. Perhaps this current leads us to the southern pole itself. It must be confessed that a supposition apparently so wild has every probability in its favor. * * *

The crew pace the deck with unquiet and tremulous step; but there is upon their countenances an expression more of the eagerness of hope than of the apathy of despair.

In the meantime the wind is still in our poop, and, as we carry a crowd of canvass, the ship is at times lifted bodily from out the sea – Oh, horror upon horror! the ice opens suddenly to the right, and to the left, and we are whirling dizzily, in immense concentric circles, round and round the borders of a gigantic amphitheatre, the summit of whose walls is lost in the darkness and the distance. But little time will be left me to ponder upon my destiny – the circles rapidly grow small – we are plunging madly within the grasp of the whirlpool – and amid a roaring, and bellowing, and thundering of ocean and of tempest, the ship is quivering, oh God! and – going down.[2]

Ligeia

And the will therein lieth, which dieth not. Who
knoweth the mysteries of the will, with its vigor?
For God is but a great will pervading all things by
nature of its intentness. Man doth not yield himself
to the angels, nor unto death utterly, save only
through the weakness of his feeble will.

JOSEPH GLANVILL[1]

I CANNOT, for my soul, remember how, when, or even precisely
where, I first became acquainted with the lady Ligeia. Long years
have since elapsed, and my memory is feeble through much suffering. Or, perhaps, I cannot *now* bring these points to mind, because, in truth, the character of my beloved, her rare learning, her
singular yet placid cast of beauty, and the thrilling and enthral-
ling eloquence of her low musical language, made their way into
my heart by paces so steadily and stealthily progressive that they
have been unnoticed and unknown. Yet I believe that I met her
first and most frequently in some large, old, decaying city near
the Rhine. Of her family – I have surely heard her speak. That it
is of a remotely ancient date cannot be doubted. Ligeia! Ligeia!
Buried in studies of a nature more than all else adapted to deaden
impressions of the outward world, it is by that sweet word alone
– by Ligeia – that I bring before mine eyes in fancy the image of
her who is no more. And now, while I write, a recollection flashes
upon me that I have *never known* the paternal name of her who
was my friend and my betrothed, and who became the partner of
my studies, and finally the wife of my bosom. Was it a playful
charge on the part of my Ligeia? or was it a test of my strength
of affection, that I should institute no inquiries upon this point?
or was it rather a caprice of my own – a wildly romantic offering
on the shrine of the most passionate devotion? I but indistinctly
recall the fact itself – what wonder that I have utterly forgotten
the circumstances which originated or attended it? And, indeed,

if ever that spirit which is entitled *Romance* – if ever she, the wan and the misty-winged *Ashtophet*[2] of idolatrous Egypt, presided, as they tell, over marriages ill-omened, then most surely she presided over mine.

There is one dear topic, however, on which my memory fails me not. It is the *person* of Ligeia. In stature she was tall, somewhat slender, and, in her latter days, even emaciated. I would in vain attempt to portray the majesty, the quiet ease, of her demeanor, or the incomprehensible lightness and elasticity of her footfall. She came and departed as a shadow. I was never made aware of her entrance into my closed study save by the dear music of her low sweet voice, as she placed her marble hand upon my shoulder. In beauty of face no maiden ever equalled her. It was the radiance of an opium-dream – an airy and spirit-lifting vision more wildly divine than the phantasies which hovered about the slumbering souls of the daughters of Delos. Yet her features were not of that regular mould which we have been falsely taught to worship in the classical labors of the heathen. 'There is no exquisite beauty,' says Bacon, Lord Verulam, speaking truly of all the forms and *genera* of beauty, 'without some *strangeness* in the proportion.' Yet, although I saw that the features of Ligeia were not of a classic regularity – although I perceived that her loveliness was indeed 'exquisite,' and felt that there was much of 'strangeness' pervading it, yet I have tried in vain to detect the irregularity and to trace home my own perception of 'the strange.' I examined the contour of the lofty and pale forehead – it was faultless – how cold indeed that word when applied to a majesty so divine ! – the skin rivalling the purest ivory, the commanding extent and repose, the gentle prominence of the regions above the temples; and then the raven-black, the glossy, the luxuriant and naturally-curling tresses, setting forth the full force of the Homeric epithet, 'hyacinthine !' I looked at the delicate outlines of the nose – and nowhere but in the graceful medallions of the Hebrews had I beheld a similar perfection. There were the same luxurious smoothness of surface, the same scarcely perceptible tendency to the aquiline, the same harmoniously curved nostrils speaking the free spirit. I regarded the sweet mouth. Here was indeed the triumph of all things heavenly – the magnificent turn of the short upper lip – the soft, voluptuous slumber of the under – the dimples which sported, and the color which spoke – the teeth glancing back, with a brilliancy almost startling, every ray of the holy light which fell upon them in her serene and placid, yet most exultingly radiant of all smiles. I scrutinized the formation of the chin – and here, too, I found the gentleness of breadth, the softness and the majesty, the fullness and the spirituality, of the Greek – the contour which the god Apollo revealed but in a dream, to Cleomenes, the son of the Athenian. And then I peered into the large eyes of Ligeia.

–For eyes we have no models in the remotely antique. It might have been, too, that in these eyes of my beloved lay the secret to which Lord Verulam alludes. They were, I must believe, far larger than the ordinary eyes of our own race. They were even fuller than the fullest of the gazelle eyes of the tribe of the valley of Nourjahad.[3] Yet it was only at intervals – in moments of intense excitement – that this peculiarity became more than slightly noticeable in Ligeia. And at such moments was her beauty – in my heated fancy thus it appeared perhaps – the beauty of beings either above or apart from the earth – the beauty of the fabulous Houri of the Turk. The hue of the orbs was the most brilliant of black, and, far over them, hung jetty lashes of great length. The brows, slightly irregular in outline, had the same tint. The 'strangeness,' however, which I found in the eyes, was of a nature distinct from the formation, or the color, or the brilliancy of the features, and must, after all, be referred to the *expression*. Ah, word of no meaning! behind whose vast latitude of mere sound we intrench our ignorance of so much of the spiritual. The expression of the eyes of Ligeia! How for long hours have I pondered upon it! How have I, through the whole of a midsummer night, struggled to fathom it! What was it – that something more profound than the well of Democritus – which lay far within the pupils of my beloved? What *was* it? I was possessed with a passion to discover. Those eyes! those large, those shining, those divine orbs! they became to me twin stars of Leda, and I to them devoutest of astrologers.

There is no point, among the many incomprehensible anomalies of the science of mind, more thrillingly exciting than the fact – never, I believe, noticed in the schools – that, in our endeavors to recall to memory something long forgotten, we often find ourselves *upon the very verge* of remembrance, without being able, in the end, to remember. And thus how frequently, in my intense scrutiny of Ligeia's eyes, have I felt approaching the full knowledge of their expression – felt it approaching – yet not quite be mine – and so at length entirely depart! And (strange, oh strangest mystery of all!) I found, in the commonest objects of the universe, a circle of analogies to that expression. I mean to say that, subsequently to the period when Ligeia's beauty passed into my spirit, there dwelling as in a shrine, I derived, from many existences in the material world, a sentiment such as I felt always aroused within me by her large and luminous orbs. Yet not the more could I define that sentiment, or analyze, or even steadily view it. I recognized it, let me repeat, sometimes in the survey of a rapidly-growing vine – in the contemplation of a moth, a butterfly, a chrysalis, a stream of running water. I have felt it in the ocean; in the falling of a meteor. I have felt it in the glances of unusually aged people. And there are one or two stars in heaven – (one especially, a star of the sixth magnitude, double and changeable, to be found near the large star in Lyra) in a telescopic scrutiny of which I have been made aware of the feeling. I have been filled with it by certain sounds from stringed instruments, and not unfrequently by passages from books. Among innumerable other instances, I well remember something in a volume of Joseph Glanvill, which (perhaps merely from its quaintness – who shall say?) never failed to inspire me with the sentiment; – 'And the will therein lieth, which dieth not. Who knoweth the mysteries of the will, with its vigor? For God is but a great will pervading all things by nature of its intentness. Man doth not yield him to the angels, nor unto death utterly, save only through the weakness of his feeble will.' –

Length of years, and subsequent reflection, have enabled me to trace, indeed, some remote connection between this passage in the English moralist and a portion of the character of Ligeia.

An *intensity* in thought, action, or speech, was possibly, in her, a result, or at least an index, of that gigantic volition which, during our long intercourse, failed to give other and more immediate evidence of its existence. Of all the women whom I have ever known, she, the outwardly calm, the ever-placid Ligeia, was the most violently a prey to the tumultuous vultures of stern passion. And of such passion I could form no estimate, save by the miraculous expansion of those eyes which at once so delighted and appalled me – by the almost magical melody, modulation, distinctness and placidity of her very low voice – and by the fierce energy (rendered doubly effective by contrast with her manner of utterance) of the wild words which she habitually uttered.

I have spoken of the learning of Ligeia: it was immense – such as I have never known in woman. In the classical tongues was she deeply proficient, and as far as my own acquaintance extended in regard to the modern dialects of Europe, I have never known her at fault. Indeed upon any theme of the most admired, because simply the most abstruse of the boasted erudition of the academy, have I *ever* found Ligeia at fault? How singularly – how thrillingly, this one point in the nature of my wife has forced itself, at this late period only, upon my attention! I said her knowledge was such as I have never known in woman – but where breathes the man who has traversed, and successfully, *all* the wide areas of moral, physical, and mathematical science? I saw not then what I now clearly perceive, that the acquisitions of Ligeia were gigantic, were astounding; yet I was sufficiently aware of her infinite supremacy to resign myself, with a childlike confidence, to her guidance through the chaotic world of metaphysical investigation at which I was most busily occupied during the earlier years of our marriage. With how vast a triumph – with how vivid a delight – with how much of all that is ethereal in hope – did I *feel*, as she bent over me in studies but little sought – but less known – that delicious vista by slow degrees expanding before me, down whose long, gorgeous, and all untrodden path, I might at length pass onward to the goal of a wisdom too divinely precious not to be forbidden!

How poignant, then, must have been the grief with which, after some years, I beheld my well-grounded expectations take wings to themselves and fly away! Without Ligeia I was but as a child groping benighted. Her presence, her readings alone, rendered vividly luminous the many mysteries of the transcendentalism in which we were immersed. Wanting the radiant lustre of her eyes, letters, lambent and golden, grew duller than Saturnian lead. And now those eyes shone less and less frequently upon the pages over which I pored. Ligeia grew ill. The wild eyes blazed with a too – too glorious effulgence; the pale fingers became of the transparent waxen hue of the grave, and the blue veins upon the lofty forehead swelled and sank impetuously with the tides of the most gentle emotion. I saw that she must die – and I struggled desperately in spirit with the grim Azrael. And the struggles of the passionate wife were, to my astonishment, even more energetic than my own. There had been much in her stern nature to impress me with the belief that, to her, death would have come without its terrors; – but not so. Words are impotent to convey any just idea of the fierceness of resistance with which she wrestled with the Shadow. I groaned in anguish at the pitiable spectacle. I would have soothed – I would have reasoned; but, in the intensity of her wild desire for life, – for life – but for life – solace and reason were alike the uttermost of folly. Yet not until the last instance, amid the most convulsive writhings of her fierce spirit, was shaken the external placidity of her demeanor. Her voice grew more gentle – grew more low – yet I would not wish to dwell upon the wild meaning of the quietly uttered words. My brain reeled as I hearkened entranced, to a melody more than mortal – to assumptions and aspirations which mortality had never before known.

That she loved me I should not have doubted; and I might have been easily aware that, in a bosom such as hers, love would have reigned no ordinary passion. But in death only, was I fully impressed with the strength of her affection. For long hours, detaining my hand, would she pour out before me the overflowing of a heart whose more than passionate devotion amounted to idolatry. How had I deserved to be so blessed by such confessions?

– how had I deserved to be so cursed with the removal of my beloved in the hour of her making them? But upon this subject I cannot bear to dilate. Let me say only, that in Ligeia's more than womanly abandonment to a love, alas! all unmerited, all unworthily bestowed, I at length recognized the principle of her longing with so wildly earnest a desire for the life which was now fleeing so rapidly away. It is this wild longing – it is this eager vehemence of desire for life – but for life – that I have no power to portray – no utterance capable of expressing.

At high noon of the night in which she departed, beckoning me, peremptorily, to her side, she bade me repeat certain verses composed by herself not many days before. I obeyed her. – They were these:[4]

> Lo! 't is a gala night
>   Within the lonesome latter years!
> An angel throng, bewinged, bedight
>   In veils, and drowned in tears,
> Sit in a theatre, to see
>   A play of hopes and fears,
> While the orchestra breathes fitfully
>   The music of the spheres.
>
> Mimes, in the form of God on high,
>   Mutter and mumble low,
> And hither and thither fly –
>   Mere puppets they, who come and go
> At bidding of vast formless things
>   That shift the scenery to and fro,
> Flapping from out their Condor wings
>   Invisible Wo!
>
> That motley drama! – oh, be sure
>   It shall not be forgot!
> With its Phantom chased forever more,
>   By a crowd that seize it not,

Through a circle that ever returneth in
    To the self-same spot,
And much of Madness and more of Sin
    And Horror the soul of the plot.

But see, amid the mimic rout,
    A crawling shape intrude!
A blood-red thing that writhes from out
    The scenic solitude!
It writhes! – it writhes! – with mortal pangs
    The mimes become its food,
And the seraphs sob at vermin fangs
    In human gore imbued.

[handwritten marginal note: Worm crawling in & out of corpses]

Out – out are the lights – out all!
    And over each quivering form,
The curtain, a funeral pall,
    Comes down with the rush of a storm,
And the angels, all pallid and wan,
    Uprising, unveiling, affirm
That the play is the tragedy, 'Man,'
    And its hero the Conqueror Worm.

[handwritten marginal note: → death]

'O God!' half shrieked Ligeia, leaping to her feet and extending her arms aloft with a spasmodic movement, as I made an end of these lines – 'O God! O Divine Father! – shall these things be undeviatingly so? – shall this Conqueror be not once conquered? Are we not part and parcel in Thee? Who – who knoweth the mysteries of the will with its vigor? Man doth not yield him to the angels, *nor unto death utterly*, save only through the weakness of his feeble will.'

And now, as if exhausted with emotion, she suffered her white arms to fall, and returned solemnly to her bed of death. And as she breathed her last sighs, there came mingled with them a low murmur from her lips. I bent to them my ear and distinguished, again, the concluding words of the passage in Glanvill – '*Man doth not yield him to the angels, nor unto death utterly, save only through the weakness of his feeble will.'*

She died; – and I, crushed into the very dust with sorrow, could no longer endure the lonely desolation of my dwelling in the dim and decaying city by the Rhine. I had no lack of what the world calls wealth. Ligeia had brought me far more, very far more than ordinarily falls to the lot of mortals. After a few months, therefore, of weary and aimless wandering, I purchased, and put in some repair, an abbey, which I shall not name, in one of the wildest and least frequented portions of fair England. The gloomy and dreary grandeur of the building, the almost savage aspect of the domain, the many melancholy and time-honored memories connected with both, had much in unison with the feelings of utter abandonment which had driven me into that remote and unsocial region of the country. Yet although the external abbey, with its verdant decay hanging about it, suffered but little alteration, I gave way, with a child-like perversity, and perchance with a faint hope of alleviating my sorrows, to a display of more than regal magnificence within. – For such follies, even in childhood, I had imbibed a taste and now they came back to me as if in the dotage of grief. Alas, I feel how much even of incipient madness might have been discovered in the gorgeous and fantastic draperies, in the solemn carvings of Egypt, in the wild cornices and furniture, in the Bedlam patterns of the carpets of tufted gold! I had become a bounden slave in the trammels of opium, and my labors and my orders had taken a coloring from my dreams. But these absurdities I must not pause to detail. Let me speak only of that one chamber, ever accursed, whither in a moment of mental alienation, I led from the altar as my bride – as the successor of the unforgotten Ligeia – the fair-haired and blue-eyed Lady Rowena Trevanion, of Tremaine.

There is no individual portion of the architecture and decoration of that bridal chamber which is not now visibly before me. Where were the souls of the haughty family of the bride, when, through thirst of gold, they permitted to pass the threshold of an apartment so bedecked, a maiden and a daughter so beloved? I have said that I minutely remember the details of the chamber –

yet I am sadly forgetful on topics of deep moment – and here there was no system, no keeping, in the fantastic display, to take hold upon the memory. The room lay in a high turret of the castellated abbey, was pentagonal in shape, and of capacious size. Occupying the whole southern face of the pentagon was the sole window – an immense sheet of unbroken glass from Venice – a single pane, and tinted of a leaden hue, so that the rays of either the sun or moon, passing through it, fell with a ghastly lustre on the objects within. Over the upper portion of this huge window, extended the trellice-work of an aged vine, which clambered up the massy walls of the turret. The ceiling, of gloomy-looking oak, was excessively lofty, vaulted, and elaborately fretted with the wildest and most grotesque specimens of a semi-Gothic, semi-Druidical device. From out the most central recess of this melancholy vaulting, depended, by a single chain of gold with long links, a huge censer of the same metal, Saracenic in pattern, and with many perforations so contrived that there writhed in and out of them, as if endued with a serpent vitality, a continual succession of parti-colored fires.

Some few ottomans and golden candelabra, of Eastern figure, were in various stations about – and there was the couch, too – the bridal couch – of an Indian model, and low, and sculptured of solid ebony, with a pall-like canopy above. In each of the angles of the chamber stood on end a gigantic sarcophagus of black granite, from the tombs of the kings over against Luxor, with their aged lids full of immemorial sculpture. But in the draping of the apartment lay, alas! the chief phantasy of all. The lofty walls, gigantic in height – even unproportionably so – were hung from summit to foot, in vast folds, with a heavy and massive-looking tapestry – tapestry of a material which was found alike as a carpet on the floor, as a covering for the ottomans and the ebony bed, as a canopy for the bed, and as the gorgeous volutes of the curtains which partially shaded the window. The material was the richest cloth of gold. It was spotted all over, at irregular intervals, with arabesque figures, about a foot in diameter, and wrought upon the cloth in patterns of the most jetty black. But these figures partook of the true character of the arabesque only when regarded from a single point of view. By a contrivance now common, and indeed traceable to a very remote period of antiquity, they were made changeable in aspect. To one entering the room, they bore the appearance of simple monstrosities; but upon a farther advance, this appearance gradually departed; and step by step, as the visiter moved his station in the chamber, he saw himself surrounded by an endless succession of the ghastly forms which belong to the superstition of the Norman, or arise in the guilty slumbers of the monk. The phantasmagoric effect was vastly heightened by the artificial introduction of a strong continual current of wind behind the draperies – giving a hideous and uneasy animation to the whole.

In halls such as these – in a bridal chamber such as this – I passed, with the Lady of Tremaine, the unhallowed hours of the first month of our marriage – passed them with but little disquietude. That my wife dreaded the fierce moodiness of my temper – that she shunned me and loved me but little – I could not help perceiving; but it gave me rather pleasure than otherwise. I loathed her with a hatred belonging more to demon than to man. My memory flew back, (oh, with what intensity of regret!) to Ligeia, the beloved, the august, the beautiful, the entombed. I revelled in recollections of her purity, of her wisdom, of her lofty, her ethereal nature, of her passionate, her idolatrous love. Now, then, did my spirit fully and freely burn with more than all the fires of her own. In the excitement of my opium dreams (for I was habitually fettered in the shackles of the drug) I would call aloud upon her name, during the silence of the night, or among the sheltered recesses of the glens by day, as if, through the wild eagerness, the solemn passion, the consuming ardor of my longing for the departed, I could restore her to the pathway she had abandoned – ah, *could* it be forever? – upon the earth.

About the commencement of the second month of the marriage, the Lady Rowena was attacked with sudden illness, from which her recovery was slow. The fever which consumed her rendered her nights uneasy; and in her perturbed state of half-slumber, she spoke of sounds, and of motions, in and about the chamber of the turret, which I concluded had no origin save in the distemper of her fancy, or perhaps in the phantasmagoric influences of the chamber itself. She became at length convalescent – finally well. Yet but a brief period elapsed, ere a second more violent disorder again threw her upon a bed of suffering; and from this attack her frame, at all times feeble, never altogether recovered. Her illnesses were, after this epoch, of alarming character, and of more alarming recurrence, defying alike the knowledge and the great exertions of her physicians. With the increase of the chronic disease which had thus, apparently, taken too sure hold upon her constitution to be eradicated by human means, I could not fail to observe a similar increase in the nervous irritation of her temperament, and in her excitability by trivial causes of fear. She spoke again, and now more frequently and pertinaciously, of the sounds – of the slight sounds – and of the unusual motions among the tapestries, to which she had formerly alluded.

One night, near the closing in of September, she pressed this distressing subject with more than usual emphasis upon my attention. She had just awakened from an unquiet slumber, and I had been watching, with feelings half of anxiety, half of vague terror, the workings of her emaciated countenance. I sat by the side of her ebony bed, upon one of the ottomans of India. She partly arose, and spoke, in an earnest low whisper, of sounds which she *then* heard, but which I could not hear – of motions which she *then* saw, but which I could not perceive. The wind was rushing hurriedly behind the tapestries, and I wished to show her (what, let me confess it, I could not *all* believe) that those almost inarticulate breathings, and those very gentle variations of the figures upon the wall, were but the natural effects of that customary rushing of the wind. But a deadly pallor, overspreading her face, had proved to me that my exertions to reassure her would be fruitless. She appeared to be fainting, and no attendants were within call. I remembered where was deposited a decanter of light wine which had been ordered by her physicians, and hastened across the chamber to procure it. But, as I stepped beneath the light of the censer, two circumstances of a startling nature attracted my attention. I had felt that some palpable although invisible object had passed lightly by my person; and I saw that there lay upon the golden carpet, in the very middle of the rich lustre thrown from the censer, a shadow – a faint, indefinite shadow of angelic aspect – such as might be fancied for the shadow of a shade. But I was wild with the excitement of an immoderate dose of opium, and heeded these things but little, nor spoke of them to Rowena. Having found the wine, I recrossed the chamber, and poured out a goblet-ful, which I held to the lips of the fainting lady. She had now partially recovered, however, and took the vessel herself, while I sank upon an ottoman near me, with my eyes fastened upon her person. It was then that I became distinctly aware of a gentle foot-fall upon the carpet, and near the couch; and in a second thereafter, as Rowena was in the act of raising the wine to her lips, I saw, or may have dreamed that I saw, fall within the goblet, as if from some invisible spring in the atmosphere of the room, three or four large drops of a brilliant and ruby colored fluid. If this I saw – not so Rowena. She swallowed the wine unhesitatingly, and I forbore to speak to her of a circumstance which must, after all, I considered, have been but the suggestion of a vivid imagination, rendered morbidly active by the terror of the lady, by the opium, and by the hour.

Yet I cannot conceal it from my own perception that, immediately subsequent to the fall of the ruby-drops, a rapid change for the worse took place in the disorder of my wife; so that, on the third subsequent night, the hands of her menials prepared her for the tomb, and on the fourth, I sat alone, with her shrouded body, in that fantastic chamber which had received her as my bride. – Wild visions, opium-engendered, flitted, shadow-like, before me. I gazed with unquiet eye upon the sarcophagi in the angles of the room, upon the varying figures of the drapery, and upon the writhing of the parti-colored fires in the censer overhead. My eyes then fell, as I called to mind the circumstances of a former night, to the spot beneath the glare of the censer where I had seen the faint traces of the shadow. It was there, however, no longer; and breathing with greater freedom, I turned my glances to the pallid and rigid figure upon the bed. Then rushed upon me a thousand memories of Ligeia — and then came back upon my heart, with the turbulent violence of a flood, the whole of that unutterable wo with which I had regarded *her* thus enshrouded. The night waned; and still, with a bosom full of bitter thoughts of the one only and supremely beloved, I remained gazing upon the body of Rowena.

It might have been midnight, or perhaps earlier, or later, for I had taken no note of time, when a sob, low, gentle, but very distinct, startled me from my revery. – I *felt* that it came from the bed of ebony – the bed of death. I listened in an agony of superstitious terror – but there was no repetition of the sound. I strained my vision to detect any motion in the corpse – but there was not the slightest perceptible. Yet I could not have been deceived. I *had* heard the noise, however faint, and my soul was awakened within me. I resolutely and perseveringly kept my attention riveted upon the body. Many minutes elapsed before any circumstance occurred tending to throw light upon the mystery. At length it became evident that a slight, a very feeble, and barely noticeable tinge of color had flushed up within the cheeks, and along the sunken small veins of the eyelids. Through a species of unutterable horror and awe, for which the language of mortality has no sufficiently energetic expression, I felt my heart cease to beat, my limbs grow rigid where I sat. Yet a sense of duty finally operated to restore my self-possession. I could no longer doubt that we had been precipitate in our preparations – that Rowena still lived. It was necessary that some immediate exertion be made; yet the turret was altogether apart from the portion of the abbey tenanted by the servants – there were none within call – I had no means of summoning them to my aid without leaving the room for many minutes – and this I could not venture to do. I therefore struggled alone in my endeavors to call back the spirit still hovering. In a short period it was certain, however, that a relapse had taken place; the color disappeared from both eyelid and cheek, leaving a wanness even more than that of marble; the lips became doubly shrivelled and pinched up in the ghastly expression of death; a repulsive clamminess and coldness overspread rapidly the surface of the body; and all the usual rigorous stiffness immediately supervened. I fell back with a shudder upon the couch from which I had been so startlingly aroused, and again gave myself up to passionate waking visions of Ligeia.

An hour thus elapsed when (could it be possible?) I was a second time aware of some vague sound issuing from the region of the bed. I listened – in extremity of horror. The sound came again – it was a sigh. Rushing to the corpse, I saw – distinctly saw – a tremor upon the lips. In a minute afterward they relaxed, disclosing a bright line of the pearly teeth. Amazement now struggled in my bosom with the profound awe which had hitherto reigned there alone. I felt that my vision grew dim, that my reason wandered; and it was only by a violent effort that I at length succeeded in nerving myself to the task which duty thus once more had pointed out. There was now a partial glow upon the forehead and upon the cheek and throat; a perceptible warmth pervaded the whole frame; there was even a slight pulsation at the heart. The lady *lived*; and with redoubled ardor I betook myself to the task of restoration. I chafed and bathed the temples and the hands, and used every exertion which experience, and no little medical reading, could suggest. But in vain. Suddenly, the color fled, the pulsation ceased, the lips resumed the expression of the dead, and, in an instant afterward, the whole body took upon itself the icy chilliness, the livid hue, the intense rigidity, the sunken outline, and all the loathsome peculiarities of that which has been, for many days, a tenant of the tomb.

And again I sunk into visions of Ligeia – and again, (what marvel that I shudder while I write?) *again* there reached my ears a low sob from the region of the ebony bed. But why shall I minutely detail the unspeakable horrors of that night? Why shall I pause to relate how, time after time, until near the period of the gray dawn, this hideous drama of revification was repeated; how each terrific relapse was only into a sterner and apparently more irredeemable death; how each agony wore the aspect of a struggle with some invisible foe; and how each struggle was succeeded by I know not what of wild change in the personal appearance of the corpse? Let me hurry to a conclusion.

The greater part of the fearful night had worn away, and she who had been dead, once again stirred – and now more vigorously than hitherto, although arousing from a dissolution more appalling in its utter hopelessness than any. I had long ceased to struggle or to move, and remained sitting rigidly upon the ottoman, a helpless prey to a whirl of violent emotions, of which extreme awe was perhaps the least terrible, the least consuming. The corpse, I repeat, stirred, and now more vigorously than before. The hues of life flushed up with unwonted energy into the countenance – the limbs relaxed – and, save that the eyelids were yet pressed heavily together, and that the bandages and draperies of the grave still imparted their charnel character to the figure, I might have dreamed that Rowena had indeed shaken off, utterly, the fetters of Death. But if this idea was not, even then, altogether adopted, I could at least doubt no longer, when, arising from the bed, tottering, with feeble steps, with closed eyes, and with the manner of one bewildered in a dream, the thing that was enshrouded advanced boldly and palpably into the middle of the apartment.

I trembled not – I stirred not – for a crowd of unutterable fancies connected with the air, the stature, the demeanor of the figure, rushing hurriedly through my brain, had paralyzed – had chilled me into stone. I stirred not – but gazed upon the apparition. There was a mad disorder in my thoughts – a tumult unappeasable. Could it, indeed, be the *living* Rowena who confronted me? Could it indeed be Rowena *at all* – the fair-haired, the blue-eyed Lady Rowena Trevanion of Tremaine? Why, *why* should I doubt it? The bandage lay heavily about the mouth – but then might it not be the mouth of the breathing Lady of Tremaine? And the cheeks – there were the roses as in her noon of life – yes, these might indeed be the fair cheeks of the living Lady of Tremaine. And the chin, with its dimples, as in health, might it not be hers? – but *had she then grown taller since her malady?* What inexpressible madness seized me with that thought? One bound, and I had reached her feet! Shrinking from my touch, she let fall from her head, unloosened, the ghastly cerements which had confined it, and there streamed forth, into the rushing atmosphere of the chamber, huge masses of long and dishevelled hair; *it was blacker than the raven wings of the midnight!* And now slowly opened *the eyes* of the figure which stood before me. 'Here then, at least,' I shrieked aloud, 'can I never – can I never be mistaken – these are the full, and the black, and the wild eyes – of my lost love – of the lady – of the LADY LIGEIA.'

The Man that was Used Up

A Tale of the Late Bugaboo and Kickapoo
Campaign

Pleurez, pleurez, mes yeux, et fondez-vous en eau!
La moitié de ma vie a mis l' autre au tombeau.
CORNEILLE[1]

I CANNOT just now remember when or where I first made the acquaintance of that truly fine-looking fellow, Brevet Brigadier General John A. B. C. Smith. Some one *did* introduce me to the gentleman, I am sure – at some public meeting, I know very well – held about something of great importance, no doubt – at some place or other, I feel convinced, – whose name I have unaccountably forgotten. The truth is – that the introduction was attended, upon my part, with a degree of anxious embarrassment which operated to prevent any definite impressions of either time or place. I am constitutionally nervous – this, with me, is a family failing, and I can't help it. In especial, the slightest appearance of mystery – of any point I cannot exactly comprehend – puts me at once into a pitiable state of agitation.

There was something, as it were, remarkable – yes, *remarkable,* although this is but a feeble term to express my full meaning – about the entire individuality of the personage in question. He was, perhaps, six feet in height, and of a presence singularly commanding. There was an *air distingué* pervading the whole man, which spoke of high breeding, and hinted at high birth. Upon this topic – the topic of Smith's personal appearance – I have a kind of melancholy satisfaction in being minute. His head of hair would have done honor to a Brutus; – nothing could be more richly flowing, or possess a brighter gloss. It was of a jetty black; – which was also the color, or more properly the no color, of his unimaginable whiskers. You perceive I cannot speak of these latter without enthusiasm; it is not too much to say that they were the handsomest pair of whiskers under the sun. At all events, they encircled, and at times partially overshadowed, a mouth utterly unequalled. Here were the most entirely even, and the most brilliantly white of all conceivable teeth. From between them, upon every proper occasion, issued a voice of surpassing clearness, melody, and strength. In the matter of eyes, also, my acquaintance was pre-eminently endowed. Either one of such a pair was worth a couple of the ordinary ocular organs. They were of a deep hazel, exceedingly large and lustrous; and there was perceptible about them, ever and anon, just that amount of interesting obliquity which gives pregnancy to expression.

The bust of the General was unquestionably the finest bust I ever saw. For your life you could not have found a fault with its wonderful proportion. This rare peculiarity set off to great advantage a pair of shoulders which would have called up a blush of conscious inferiority into the countenance of the marble Apollo. I have a passion for fine shoulders, and may say that I never beheld them in perfection before. The arms altogether were admirably modelled. Nor were the lower limbs less superb. These were, indeed, the *ne plus ultra* of good legs. Every connoisseur in such matters admitted the legs to be good. There was neither too much flesh, nor too little, – neither rudeness nor fragility. I could not imagine a more graceful curve than that of the *os femoris*, and there was just that due gentle prominence in the rear of the *fibula* which goes to the conformation of a properly proportioned calf. I wish to God my young and talented friend Chiponchipino, the sculptor, had but seen the legs of Brevet Brigadier General John A. B. C. Smith.

But although men so absolutely fine-looking are neither as plenty as reasons or blackberries, still I could not bring myself to believe that *the remarkable* something to which I alluded just now, – that the odd air of *je ne sais quoi* which hung about my new acquaintance, – lay altogether, or indeed at all, in the supreme excellence of his bodily endowments. Perhaps it might be traced to the *manner*; – yet here again I could not pretend to be positive. There *was* a primness, not to say stiffness, in his carriage – a degree of measured, and, if I may so express it, of rectangular precision, attending his every movement, which, observed in a more diminutive figure, would have had the least little savor in the world, of affectation, pomposity or constraint, but which, noticed in a gentleman of his undoubted dimension, was readily placed to the account of reserve, *hauteur* – of a commendable sense, in short, of what is due to the dignity of colossal proportion.

The kind friend who presented me to General Smith whispered in my ear some few words of comment upon the man. He was a *remarkable* man – a *very* remarkable man – indeed one of the *most* remarkable men of the age. He was an especial favorite, too, with the ladies – chiefly on account of his high reputation for courage.

'In *that* point he is unrivalled – indeed he is a perfect desperado – a down-right fire-eater, and no mistake,' said my friend, here dropping his voice excessively low, and thrilling me with the mystery of his tone.

'A down-right fire-eater, and *no* mistake. Showed *that*, I should say, to some purpose, in the late tremendous swamp-fight away down South, with the Bugaboo and Kickapoo Indians.' [Here my friend opened his eyes to some extent.] 'Bless my soul! – blood and thunder, and all that! – *prodigies* of valor! – heard of him of course? – you know he's the man' –

'Man alive, how *do* you do? why how *are* ye? *very* glad to see ye, indeed!' here interrupted the General himself, seizing my companion by the hand as he drew near, and bowing stiffly, but profoundly, as I was presented. I then thought, (and I think so still), that I never heard a clearer nor a stronger voice, nor beheld a finer set of teeth: but I *must* say that I was sorry for the interruption just at that moment, as, owing to the whispers and insinuations aforesaid, my interest had been greatly excited in the hero of the Bugaboo and Kickapoo campaign.

However, the delightfully luminous conversation of Brevet Brigadier General John A. B. C. Smith soon completely dissipated this chagrin. My friend leaving us immediately, we had quite a long *tête-à-tête*, and I was not only pleased but *really* – instructed. I never heard a more fluent talker, or a man of greater general information. With becoming modesty, he forebore, nevertheless, to touch upon the theme I had just then most at heart – I mean the mysterious circumstances attending the Bugaboo war – and, on my own part, what I conceive to be a proper sense of delicacy forbade me to broach the subject; although, in truth, I was exceedingly tempted to do so. I perceived, too, that the gallant soldier preferred topics of philosophical interest, and that he delighted, especially, in commenting upon the rapid march of mechanical invention. Indeed, lead him where I would, this was a point to which he invariably came back.

'There is nothing at all like it,' he would say; 'we are a wonderful people, and live in a wonderful age. Parachutes and rail-roads – man-traps and spring-guns! Our steam-boats are upon every sea, and the Nassau balloon packet is about to run regular trips (fare either way only twenty pounds sterling) between London and Timbuctoo. And who shall calculate the immense influence upon social life – upon arts – upon commerce – upon literature – which will be the immediate result of the great principles of electro-magnetics! Nor is this all, let me assure you! There is really no end to the march of invention. The most wonderful – the most ingenious – and let me add, Mr – Mr – Thompson, I believe, is your name – let me add, I say, the most *useful* – the most truly *useful* mechanical contrivances, are daily springing up like mushrooms, if I may so express myself, or, more figuratively, like – ah – grasshoppers – like grasshoppers, Mr Thompson – about us and ah – ah – ah – around us!'

Thompson, to be sure, is not my name; but it is needless to say that I left General Smith with a heightened interest in the man, with an exalted opinion of his conversational powers, and a deep sense of the valuable privileges we enjoy in living in this age of mechanical invention. My curiosity, however, had not been altogether satisfied, and I resolved to prosecute immediate inquiry among my acquaintances touching the Brevet Brigadier General himself, and particularly respecting the tremendous

events *quorum pars magna fuit*, during the Bugaboo and Kickapoo campaign.

The first opportunity which presented itself, and which (*hor-
resco referens*) I did not in the least scruple to seize, occurred
at the Church of the Reverend Doctor Drummummupp, where
I found myself established, one Sunday just at sermon time,
not only in the pew, but by the side, of that worthy and com-
municative little friend of mine, Miss Tabitha T. Thus seated,
I congratulated myself, and with much reason, upon the very
flattering state of affairs. If any person knew anything about
Brevet Brigadier General John A. B. C. Smith, that person, it
was clear to me, was Miss Tabitha T. We telegraphed a few
signals, and then commenced, *sotto voce*, a brisk *tête-à-tête*.

'Smith!' said she, in reply to my very earnest inquiry; 'Smith!
– why, not General John A. B. C.? Bless me, I thought you
knew all about *him!* This is a wonderfully inventive age! Horrid
affair that! – a bloody set of wretches, those Kickapoos! –
fought like a hero – prodigies of valor – immortal renown.
Smith! – Brevet Brigadier General John A. B. C.! – why, you
know he's the man –'

'Man,' here broke in Doctor Drummummupp, at the top of
his voice, and with a thump that came near knocking the pulpit
about our ears; 'man that is born of a woman hath but a short
time to live; he cometh up and is cut down like a flower!' I
started to the extremity of the pew, and perceived by the
animated looks of the divine, that the wrath which had
nearly proved fatal to the pulpit had been excited by the whispers of the lady and myself. There was no help for it; so I
submitted with a good grace, and listened, in all the martyr-
dom of dignified silence, to the balance of that very capital
discourse.

Next evening found me a somewhat late visitor at the Rantipole theatre, where I felt sure of satisfying my curiosity at once,
by merely stepping into the box of those exquisite specimens of
affability and omniscience, the Misses Arabella and Miranda
Cognoscenti. That fine tragedian, Climax, was doing Iago to a
very crowded house, and I experienced some little difficulty in

making my wishes understood; especially as our box was next the slips, and completely overlooked the stage.

'Smith?' said Miss Arabella, as she at length comprehended the purport of my query; 'Smith? – why, not General John A. B. C.?'

'Smith?' inquired Miranda, musingly, 'God bless me, did you ever behold a finer figure?'

'Never, madam, but do tell me –'

'Or so inimitable grace?'

'Never, upon my word! – but pray inform me –'

'Or so just an appreciation of stage effect?'

'Madam!'

'Or a more delicate sense of the true beauties of Shakespeare? Be so good as to look at that leg!'

'The devil!' and I turned again to her sister.

'Smith?' said she, 'why, not General John A. B. C.? Horrid affair that, wasn't it? – great wretches, those Bugaboos – savage and so on – but we live in a wonderfully inventive age! – Smith! – O yes! great man! – perfect desperado – immortal renown – prodigies of valor! *Never heard!*" [This was given in a scream.] 'Bless my soul! – why, he's the man –'

> ' – mandragora
> Nor all the drowsy syrups of the world
> Shall ever medicine thee to that sweet sleep
> Which thou owd'st yesterday!'

here roared out Climax just in my ear, and shaking his fist in my face all the time, in a way that I *couldn't* stand, and I *wouldn't*. I left the Misses Cognoscenti immediately, went behind the scenes forthwith, and gave the beggarly scoundrel such a thrashing as I trust he will remember to the day of his death.

At the *soirée* of the lovely widow, Mrs Kathleen O'Trump, I was confident that I should meet with no similar disappointment. Accordingly, I was no sooner seated at the card table, with my pretty hostess for a *vis-à-vis*, than I propounded those questions the solution of which had become a matter so essential to my peace.

'Smith?' said my partner, 'why, not General John A. B. C.? Horrid affair that, wasn't it? – diamonds, did you say? – terrible wretches those Kickapoos! – we are playing *whist*, if you please, Mr Tattle – however, this is the age of invention, most certainly *the* age, one may say – *the age par excellence* – speak French? – oh, quite a hero – perfect desperado – *no hearts*, Mr Tattle? I don't believe it! – immortal renown and all that – prodigies of valor! *Never heard!!* – why, bless me, he's the man –'

'Mann? – *Captain* Mann?' here screamed some little feminine interloper from the farthest corner of the room. 'Are you talking about Captain Mann and the duel? – oh, I *must* hear – do tell – go on, Mrs O'Trump! – do now go on!' And go on Mrs O'Trump did – all about a certain Captain Mann who was either shot or hung, or should have been both shot and hung. Yes! Mrs O'Trump, she went on, and I – I went off. There was no chance of hearing anything farther that evening in regard to Brevet Brigadier General John A. B. C. Smith.

Still I consoled myself with the reflection that the tide of ill luck would not run against me forever, and so determined to make a bold push for information at the rout of that bewitching little angel, the graceful Mrs Pirouette.

'Smith?' said Mrs P., as we twirled about together in a *pas de zéphyr*, 'Smith? – why not General John A. B. C.? Dreadful business that of the Bugaboos, wasn't it? – terrible creatures, those Indians! – *do* turn out your toes! I really am ashamed of you – man of great courage, poor fellow! – but this is a wonderful age for invention – O dear me, I'm out of breath – quite a desperado – prodigies of valor – *never heard!!* – can't believe it – I shall have to sit down and enlighten you – Smith! why he's the man –'

'Man-*Fred*, I tell you!' here bawled out Miss Bas-Bleu, as I led Mrs Pirouette to a seat. 'Did ever anybody hear the like? It's Man-*Fred*, I say, and not at all by any means Man-*Friday*.' Here Miss Bas-Bleu beckoned to me in a very peremptory manner; and I was obliged, will I nill I, to leave Mrs P. for the purpose of deciding a dispute touching the title of a certain poetical drama of Lord Byron's. Although I pronounced, with great promptness,

that the true title was Man-*Friday*, and not by any means
Man-*Fred*, yet when I returned to seek Mrs Pirouette she was
not to be discovered, and I made my retreat from the house in
a very bitter spirit of animosity against the whole race of the
Bas-Bleus.

Matters had now assumed a really serious aspect, and I resolved to call at once upon my particular friend, Mr Theodore
Sinivate; for I knew that here at least I should get something
like definite information.

'Smith?' said he, in his well-known peculiar way of drawling
out his syllables; 'Smith? – why, not General John A – B – C.?
Savage affair that with the Kickapo-o-o-os, wasn't it? Say! don't
you think so? – perfect despera-a-ado – great pity, pon my
honor! – wonderfully inventive age! – pro-o-odigies of valor!
By the by, did you ever hear about Captain Ma-a-a-a-n?'

'Captain Mann be d—d!' said I, 'please to go on with your
story.'

'Hem! – oh well! – quite *la même cho-o-ose*, as we say in
France. Smith, eh? Brigadier General John A – B – C.? I say' –
[here Mr S. thought proper to put his finger to the side of his
nose] – 'I say, you don't mean to insinuate now, really, and truly,
and conscientiously, that you don't know all about that affair of
Smith's, as well as I do, eh? Smith? John A – B – C.? Why bless
me, he's the ma-a-an –'

'*Mr* Sinivate,' said I, imploringly, '*is* he the man in the mask?'

'No-o-o!' said he, looking wise, 'nor the man in the
mo-o-o-on.'

This reply I considered a pointed and positive insult, and so
left the house at once in high dudgeon, with a firm resolve to call
my friend, Mr Sinivate, to a speedy account for his ungentlemanly conduct and ill-breeding.

In the meantime, however, I had no notion of being thwarted
touching the information I desired. There was one resource left
me yet. I would go to the fountain head. I would call forthwith
upon the General himself, and demand, in explicit terms, a
solution of this abominable piece of mystery. Here at least, there
should be no chance for equivocation. I would be plain, positive,

peremptory – as short as pie-crust – as concise as Tacitus or Montesquieu.

It was early when I called, and the General was dressing; but I pleaded urgent business, and was shown at once into his bedroom by an old negro valet, who remained in attendance during my visit. As I entered the chamber, I looked about, of course, for the occupant, but did not immediately perceive him. There was a large and exceedingly odd looking bundle of something which lay close by my feet on the floor, and, as I was not in the best humor in the world, I gave it a kick out of the way.

'Hem! ahem! rather civil that, I should say!' said the bundle, in one of the smallest, and altogether the funniest little voices, between a squeak and a whistle, that I ever heard in all the days of my existence.

'Ahem! rather civil that, I should observe.'

I fairly shouted with terror, and made off, at a tangent, into the farthest extremity of the room.

'God bless me! my dear fellow,' here again whistled the bundle, 'what – what – what – why, what *is* the matter? I really believe you don't know me at all.'

What *could* I say to all this – what *could* I? I staggered into an arm-chair, and, with staring eyes and open mouth, awaited the solution of the wonder.

'Strange you shouldn't know me though, isn't it?' presently re-squeaked the nondescript, which I now perceived was performing, upon the floor, some inexplicable evolution, very analogous to the drawing on of a stocking. There was only a single leg, however, apparent.

'Strange you shouldn't know me, though, isn't it? Pompey, bring me that leg!' Here Pompey handed the bundle a very capital cork leg, already dressed, which it screwed on in a trice; and then it stood upright before my eyes.

'And a bloody action it *was*,' continued the thing, as if in a soliloquy; 'but then one mustn't fight with the Bugaboos and Kickapoos, and think of coming off with a mere scratch. Pompey, I'll thank you now for that arm. Thomas' [turning to me] 'is decidedly the best hand at a cork leg; but if you should ever want an arm, my dear fellow, you must really let me recommend you to Bishop.' Here Pompey screwed on an arm.

'We had rather hot work of it, that you may say. Now, you dog, slip on my shoulders and bosom! Pettitt makes the best shoulders, but for a bosom you will have to go to Ducrow.'

'Bosom!' said I.

'Pompey, will you *never* be ready with that wig? Scalping is a rough process after all; but then you can procure such a capital scratch at De L'Orme's.'

'Scratch!'

'Now, you nigger, my teeth! For a *good* set of these you had better go to Parmly's at once; high prices, but excellent work. I swallowed some very capital articles, though, when the big Bugaboo rammed me down with the butt end of his rifle.'

'Butt end! ram down!! my eye!!!'

'Oh yes, by the by, my eye – here, Pompey, you scamp, screw it in! Those Kickapoos are not so very slow at a gouge; but he's a belied man, that Dr Williams, after all; you can't imagine how well I see with the eyes of his make.'

I now began very clearly to perceive that the object before me was nothing more nor less than my new acquaintance, Brevet Brigadier General John A. B. C. Smith. The manipulations of Pompey had made, I must confess, a very striking difference in the appearance of the personal man. The voice, however, still puzzled me no little; but even this apparent mystery was speedily cleared up.

'Pompey, you black rascal,' squeaked the General, 'I really do believe you would let me go out without my palate.'

Hereupon the negro, grumbling out an apology, went up to his master, opened his mouth with the knowing air of a horse-jockey, and adjusted therein a somewhat singular-looking machine, in a very dexterous manner, that I could not altogether comprehend. The alteration, however, in the entire expression of the General's countenance was instantaneous and surprising. When he again spoke, his voice had resumed all that rich melody and strength which I had noticed upon our original introduction.

'D—n the vagabonds!' said he, in so clear a tone that I positively started at the change, 'D—n the vagabonds! they not only knocked in the roof of my mouth, but took the trouble to cut off at least seven-eighths of my tongue. There isn't Bonfanti's equal, however, in America, for really good articles of this description. I can recommend you to him with confidence,' [here the General bowed,] 'and assure you that I have the greatest pleasure in so doing.'

I acknowledged his kindness in my best manner, and took leave of him at once, with a perfect understanding of the true state of affairs, with a full comprehension of the mystery which had troubled me so long. It was evident. It was a clear case. Brevet Brigadier General John A. B. C. Smith was the man – was *the man that was used up*.

The Fall of the House of Usher

Son coeur est un luth suspendu;
Sitôt qu'on le touche il résonne.

DE BÉRANGER[1]

DURING the whole of a dull, dark, and soundless day in the autumn of the year, when the clouds hung oppressively low in the heavens, I had been passing alone, on horseback, through a singularly dreary tract of country; and at length found myself, as the shades of the evening drew on, within view of the melancholy House of Usher. I know not how it was – but, with the first glimpse of the building, a sense of insufferable gloom pervaded my spirit. I say insufferable; for the feeling was unrelieved by any of that half-pleasurable, because poetic, sentiment, with which the mind usually receives even the sternest natural images of the desolate or terrible. I looked upon the scene before me – upon the mere house, and the simple landscape features of the domain – upon the bleak walls – upon the vacant eye-like windows – upon a few rank sedges – and upon a few white trunks of decayed trees – with an utter depression of soul which I can compare to no earthly sensation more properly than to the after-dream of the reveller upon opium – the bitter lapse into everyday life – the hideous dropping off of the veil. There was an iciness, a sinking, a sickening of the heart – an unredeemed dreariness of thought which no goading of the imagination could torture into aught of the sublime. What was it – I paused to think – what was it that so unnerved me in the contemplation of the House of Usher? It was a mystery all insoluble; nor could I grapple with the shadowy fancies that crowded upon me as I pondered. I was forced to fall back upon the unsatisfactory conclusion, that while, beyond doubt, there *are* combinations of very simple natural objects which have the power of thus affecting us, still the analysis of this power lies among considerations beyond our depth. It was possible, I reflected, that a mere different arrangement of the particulars of the scene, of the details of the picture, would be sufficient to modify, or perhaps to annihilate its capacity for sorrowful impression; and, acting upon this idea, I reined my horse to the precipitous brink of a black and lurid tarn that lay in unruffled lustre by the dwelling, and gazed down – but with a shudder even more thrilling than before – upon the remodelled and inverted images of the gray sedge, and the ghastly tree-stems, and the vacant and eye-like windows.

Nevertheless, in this mansion of gloom I now proposed to myself a sojourn of some weeks. Its proprietor, Roderick Usher, had been one of my boon companions in boyhood; but many years had elapsed since our last meeting. A letter, however, had lately reached me in a distant part of the country – a letter from him – which, in its wildly importunate nature, had admitted of no other than a personal reply. The MS. gave evidence of nervous agitation. The writer spoke of acute bodily illness – of a mental disorder which oppressed him – and of an earnest desire to see me, as his best, and indeed his only personal friend, with a view of attempting, by the cheerfulness of my society, some alleviation of his malady. It was the manner in which all this, and much more, was said – it was the apparent *heart* that went with his request – which allowed me no room for hesitation; and I accordingly obeyed forthwith what I still considered a very singular summons.

Although, as boys, we had been even intimate associates, yet I really knew little of my friend. His reserve had been always excessive and habitual. I was aware, however, that his very ancient family had been noted, time out of mind, for a peculiar sensibility of temperament, displaying itself, through long ages, in many works of exalted art, and manifested, of late, in repeated deeds of munificent yet unobtrusive charity, as well as in a passionate devotion to the intricacies, perhaps even more than to the orthodox and easily recognisable beauties, of musical science. I had learned, too, the very remarkable fact, that the stem of the Usher race, all time-honoured as it was, had put forth, at no period, any enduring branch; in other words, that the entire family lay in the direct line of descent, and had always, with very trifling and very temporary variation, so lain. It was this deficiency, I considered, while running over in thought the perfect keeping of the character of the premises with the accredited character of the people, and while speculating upon the possible influence which the one, in the long lapse of centuries, might have exercised upon the other – it was this deficiency, perhaps, of collateral issue, and the consequent undeviating transmission, from sire to son, of the patrimony with the name, which had, at length, so identified the two as to merge the original title of the estate in the quaint and equivocal appellation of the 'House of Usher' – an appellation which seemed to include, in the minds of the peasantry who used it, both the family and the family mansion.

I have said that the sole effect of my somewhat childish experiment – that of looking down within the tarn – had been to deepen the first singular impression. There can be no doubt that the consciousness of the rapid increase of my superstition – for why should I not so term it? – served mainly to accelerate the increase itself. Such, I have long known, is the paradoxical law of all sentiments having terror as a basis. And it might have been for this reason only, that, when I again uplifted my eyes to the house itself, from its image in the pool, there grew in my mind a strange fancy – a fancy so ridiculous, indeed, that I but mention it to show the vivid force of the sensations which oppressed me. I had so worked upon my imagination as really to believe that about the whole mansion and domain there hung an atmosphere peculiar to themselves and their immediate vicinity – an atmosphere which had no affinity with the air of heaven, but which had reeked up from the decayed trees, and the gray wall, and the silent tarn – a pestilent and mystic vapour, dull, sluggish, faintly discernible, and leaden-hued.

Shaking off from my spirit what *must* have been a dream, I scanned more narrowly the real aspect of the building. Its principal feature seemed to be that of an excessive antiquity. The discoloration of ages had been great. Minute fungi overspread the whole exterior, hanging in a fine tangled web-work from the eaves. Yet all this was apart from any extraordinary dilapidatiōn. No portion of the masonry had fallen; and there appeared to be a wild inconsistency between its still perfect adaptation of parts, and the crumbling condition of the individual stones. In this there was much that reminded me of the specious totality of old wood-work which has rotted for long years in some neglected vault, with no disturbance from the breath of the external air. Beyond this indication of extensive decay, however, the fabric gave little token of instability. Perhaps the eye of a scrutinising observer might have discovered a barely perceptible fissure, which, extending from the roof of the building in front, made its way down the wall in a zigzag direction, until it became lost in the sullen waters of the tarn.

Noticing these things, I rode over a short causeway to the house. A servant in waiting took my horse and I entered the Gothic archway of the hall. A valet, of stealthy step, thence conducted me, in silence, through many dark and intricate passages in my progress to the *studio* of his master. Much that I encountered on the way contributed, I know not how, to heighten the vague sentiments of which I have already spoken. While the objects around me – while the carvings of the ceilings, the sombre tapestries of the walls, the ebon blackness of the floors, and the phantasmagoric armorial trophies which rattled as I strode, were but matters to which, or to such as which, I had been accustomed from my infancy – while I hesitated not to acknowledge how familiar was all this – I still wondered to find how unfamiliar were the fancies which ordinary images were stirring up. On one of the staircases, I met the physician of the family. His countenance, I thought, wore a mingled expression of low cunning and perplexity. He accosted me with trepidation and passed on. The valet now threw open a door and ushered me into the presence of his master.

The room in which I found myself was very large and lofty. The windows were long, narrow, and pointed, and at so vast a distance from the black oaken floor as to be altogether inaccessible from within. Feeble gleams of encrimsoned light made their way through the trellised panes, and served to render sufficiently distinct the more prominent objects around; the eye, however, struggled in vain to reach the remoter angles of the chamber, or the recesses of the vaulted and fretted ceiling. Dark draperies hung upon the walls. The general furniture was profuse, comfortless, antique, and tattered. Many books and musical instruments lay scattered about, but failed to give any vitality to the scene. I felt that I breathed an atmosphere of sorrow. An air of stern, deep, and irredeemable gloom hung over and pervaded all.

Upon my entrance, Usher arose from a sofa on which he had been lying at full length, and greeted me with a vivacious warmth which had much in it, I at first thought, of an overdone cordiality – of the constrained effort of the *ennuyé* man of the world. A glance, however, at his countenance, convinced me of his perfect sincerity. We sat down; and for some moments, while he spoke not, I gazed upon him with a feeling half of pity, half of awe. Surely, man had never before so terribly altered, in so brief a period, as had Roderick Usher! It was with difficulty that I could bring myself to admit the identity of the wan being before me with the companion of my early boyhood. Yet the character of his face had been at all times remarkable. A cadaverousness of complexion; an eye large, liquid, and luminous beyond comparison; lips somewhat thin and very pallid, but of a surpassingly beautiful curve; a nose of a delicate Hebrew model, but with a breadth of nostril unusual in similar formations; a finely moulded chin, speaking, in its want of prominence, of a want of moral energy; hair of a more than web-like softness and tenuity; these features, with an inordinate expansion above the regions of the temple, made up altogether a countenance not easily to be forgotten. And now in the mere exaggeration of the prevailing character of these features, and of the expression they were wont to convey, lay so much of change that I doubted to whom I spoke. The now ghastly pallor of the skin, and the now miraculous lustre of the eye, above all things startled and even awed me. The silken hair, too, had been suffered to grow all unheeded, and as, in its wild gossamer texture, it floated rather than fell about the face, I could not, even with effort, connect its Arabesque expression with any idea of simple humanity.

In the manner of my friend I was at once struck with an incoherence – an inconsistency; and I soon found this to arise from a series of feeble and futile struggles to overcome an habitual trepidancy – an excessive nervous agitation. For something of this nature I had indeed been prepared, no less by his letter, than by reminiscences of certain boyish traits, and by conclusions deduced from his peculiar physical conformation and temperament. His action was alternately vivacious and sullen. His voice varied rapidly from a tremulous indecision (when the animal spirits seemed utterly in abeyance) to that species of energetic concision – that abrupt, weighty, unhurried, and hollow-sounding enunciation – that leaden, self-balanced and perfectly modulated guttural utterance, which may be observed in the lost drunkard, or the irreclaimable eater of opium, during the periods of his most intense excitement.

It was thus that he spoke of the object of my visit, of his earnest desire to see me, and of the solace he expected me to afford him. He entered, at some length, into what he conceived to be the nature of his malady. It was, he said, a constitutional and a family evil, and one for which he despaired to find a remedy – a mere nervous affection, he immediately added, which would undoubtedly soon pass off. It displayed itself in a host of unnatural sensations. Some of these, as he detailed them, interested and bewildered me; although, perhaps, the terms, and the general manner of the narration had their weight. He suffered much from a morbid acuteness of the senses; the most insipid food was alone endurable; he could wear only garments of certain texture; the odours of all flowers were oppressive; his eyes were tortured by even a faint light; and there were but peculiar sounds, and these from stringed instruments, which did not inspire him with horror.

To an anomalous species of terror I found him a bounden slave. 'I shall perish,' said he, 'I *must* perish in this deplorable folly. Thus, thus, and not otherwise, shall I be lost. I dread the events of the future, not in themselves, but in their results. I shudder at the thought of any, even the most trivial, incident, which may operate upon this intolerable agitation of soul. I have, indeed, no abhorrence of danger, except in its absolute effect – in terror. In this unnerved – in this pitiable condition – I feel that the period will sooner or later arrive when I must abandon life and reason together, in some struggle with the grim phantasm, FEAR.'

I learned, moreover, at intervals, and through broken and equivocal hints, another singular feature of his mental condition. He was enchained by certain superstitious impressions in regard to the dwelling which he tenanted, and whence, for many years, he had never ventured forth – in regard to an influence whose supposititious force was conveyed in terms too shadowy here to be re-stated – an influence which some peculiarities in the mere form and substance of his family mansion, had, by dint of long sufferance, he said, obtained over his spirit – an effect which the *physique* of the gray walls and turrets, and of the dim tarn into which they all looked down, had, at length, brought about upon the *morale* of his existence.

He admitted, however, although with hesitation, that much of the peculiar gloom which thus afflicted him could be traced to a more natural and far more palpable origin – to the severe and long-continued illness – indeed to the evidently approaching dissolution – of a tenderly beloved sister – his sole companion for long years – his last and only relative on earth. 'Her decease,' he said, with a bitterness which I can never forget, 'would leave him (him the hopeless and the frail) the last of the ancient race of the Ushers.' While he spoke, the lady Madeline (for so was she called) passed slowly through a remote portion of the apartment, and, without having noticed my presence, disappeared. I regarded her with an utter astonishment not unmingled with dread – and yet I found it impossible to account for such feelings. A sensation of stupor oppressed me, as my eyes followed her retreating steps. When a door, at length, closed upon her, my glance sought instinctively and eagerly the countenance of the brother – but he had buried his face in his hands, and I could only perceive that a far more than ordinary wanness had overspread the emaciated fingers through which trickled many passionate tears.

The disease of the lady Madeline had long baffled the skill of her physicians. A settled apathy, a gradual wasting away of the person, and frequent although transient affections of a partially cataleptical character, were the unusual diagnosis. Hitherto she had steadily borne up against the pressure of her malady, and had not betaken herself finally to bed; but, on the closing in of the evening of my arrival at the house, she succumbed (as her brother told me at night with inexpressible agitation) to the prostrating power of the destroyer; and I learned that the glimpse I had obtained of her person would thus probably be the last I should obtain – that the lady, at least while living, would be seen by me no more.

For several days ensuing, her name was unmentioned by either Usher or myself : and during this period I was busied in earnest endeavours to alleviate the melancholy of my friend. We painted and read together; or I listened, as if in a dream, to the wild improvisations of his speaking guitar. And thus, as a closer and still closer intimacy admitted me more unreservedly into the recesses of his spirit, the more bitterly did I perceive the futility of all attempt at cheering a mind from which darkness, as if an inherent positive quality, poured forth upon all objects of the moral and physical universe, in one unceasing radiation of gloom.

I shall ever bear about me a memory of the many solemn hours I thus spent alone with the master of the House of Usher. Yet I should fail in any attempt to convey an idea of the exact character of the studies, or of the occupations, in which he involved me, or led me the way. An excited and highly distempered ideality threw a sulphureous lustre over all. His long improvised dirges will ring forever in my ears. Among other things, I hold painfully in mind a certain singular perversion and amplification of the wild air of the last waltz of Von Weber. From the paintings over which his elaborate fancy brooded, and which grew, touch by touch, into vaguenesses at which I shuddered the more thrillingly, because I shuddered knowing not why; – from these paintings (vivid as their images now are before me) I would in vain endeavour to educe more than a small portion which should lie within the compass of merely written words. By the utter simplicity, by the nakedness of his designs, he arrested and over-awed attention. If ever mortal painted an idea, that mortal was Roderick Usher. For me at least – in the circumstances then surrounding me – there arose out of the pure abstractions which the hypochondriac contrived to throw upon his canvas, an intensity of intolerable awe, no shadow of which felt I ever yet in the contemplation of the certainly glowing yet too concrete reveries of Fuseli.

One of the phantasmagoric conceptions of my friend, partaking not so rigidly of the spirit of abstraction, may be shadowed forth, although feebly, in words. A small picture presented the interior of an immensely long and rectangular vault or tunnel, with low walls, smooth, white, and without interruption or device. Certain accessory points of the design served well to convey the idea that this excavation lay at an exceeding depth below the surface of the earth. No outlet was observed in any portion of its vast extent, and no torch, or other artificial source of light was discernible; yet a flood of intense rays rolled throughout, and bathed the whole in a ghastly and inappropriate splendour.

I have just spoken of that morbid condition of the auditory nerve which rendered all music intolerable to the sufferer, with the exception of certain effects of stringed instruments. It was, perhaps, the narrow limits to which he thus confined himself upon the guitar, which gave birth, in great measure, to the fantastic character of his performances. But the fervid *facility* of his *impromptus* could not be so accounted for. They must have been, and were, in the notes, as well as in the words of his wild fantasias (for he not unfrequently accompanied himself with rhymed verbal improvisations), the result of that intense mental collectedness and concentration to which I have previously alluded as observable only in particular moments of the highest artificial excitement. The words of one of these rhapsodies I have easily remembered. I was, perhaps, the more forcibly impressed with it, as he gave it, because, in the under or mystic current of its meaning, I fancied that I perceived, and for the first time, a full consciousness on the part of Usher, of the tottering of his lofty reason upon her throne. The verses, which were entitled 'The Haunted Palace,'[2] ran very nearly, if not accurately, thus:

I

In the greenest of our valleys,
  By good angels tenanted,
Once a fair and stately palace –
  Radiant palace – reared its head.
In the monarch Thought's dominion –
  It stood there!
Never seraph spread a pinion
  Over fabric half so fair.

II

Banners yellow, glorious, golden,
  On its roof did float and flow;
(This – all this – was in the olden
  Time long ago)
And every gentle air that dallied,
  In that sweet day,
Along the ramparts plumed and pallid,
  A winged odour went away.

III

Wanderers in that happy valley
  Through two luminous windows saw
Spirits moving musically
  To a lute's well-tunèd law,
Round about a throne, where sitting
  (Porphyrogene!)
In state his glory well befitting,
  The ruler of the realm was seen.

IV

And all with pearl and ruby glowing
   Was the fair palace door,
Through which came flowing, flowing, flowing
   And sparkling evermore,
A troop of Echoes whose sweet duty
   Was but to sing,
In voices of surpassing beauty,
   The wit and wisdom of their king.

V

But evil things, in robes of sorrow,
   Assailed the monarch's high estate;
(Ah, let us mourn, for never morrow
   Shall dawn upon him, desolate!)
And, round about his home, the glory
   That blushed and bloomed
Is but a dim-remembered story
   Of the old time entombed.

VI

And travellers now within that valley,
   Through the red-litten windows, see
Vast forms that move fantastically
   To a discordant melody;
While, like a rapid ghastly river,
   Through the pale door,
A hideous throng rush out forever,
   And laugh – but smile no more.

I well remember that suggestions arising from this ballad, led us into a train of thought wherein there became manifest an opinion of Usher's which I mention not so much on account of its novelty, (for other men have thought thus,) as on account of the pertinacity with which he maintained it. This opinion, in its general form, was that of the sentience of all vegetable things. But, in his disordered fancy, the idea had assumed a more daring character, and trespassed, under certain conditions, upon the kingdom of inorganization. I lack words to express the full extent, or the earnest *abandon* of his persuasion. The belief, however, was connected (as I have previously hinted) with the gray stones of the home of his forefathers. The conditions of the sentience had been here, he imagined, fulfilled in the method of collocation of these stones – in the order of their arrangement, as well as in that of the many *fungi* which overspread them, and of the decayed trees which stood around – above all, in the long undisturbed endurance of this arrangement, and in its reduplication in the still waters of the tarn. Its evidence – the evidence of the sentience – was to be seen, he said, (and I here started as he spoke,) in the gradual yet certain condensation of an atmosphere of their own about the waters and the walls. The result was discoverable, he added, in that silent, yet importunate and terrible influence which for centuries had moulded the destinies of his family, and which made *him* what I now saw him – what he was. Such opinions need no comment, and I will make none.

Our books – the books which, for years, had formed no small portion of the mental existence of the invalid – were, as might be supposed, in strict keeping with this character of phantasm. We pored together over such works as the Ververt et Chartreuse of Gresset; the Belphegor of Machiavelli; the Heaven and Hell of Swedenborg; the Subterranean Voyage of Nicholas Klimm by Holberg; the Chiromancy of Robert Flud, of Jean D'Indaginé, and of De la Chambre; the Journey into the Blue Distance of Tieck; and the City of the Sun of Campanella. One favourite volume was a small octavo edition of the *Directorium Inquisitorum*, by the Dominican Eymeric de Gironne; and there were passages in Pomponius Mela, about the old African Satyrs and Ægipans, over which Usher would sit dreaming for hours. His chief delight, however, was found in the perusal of an exceedingly rare and curious book in quarto Gothic – the manual of a forgotten church – the *Vigiliæ Mortuorum secundum Chorum Ecclesiæ Maguntinæ*.[3]

I could not help thinking of the wild ritual of this work, and of its probable influence upon the hypochondriac, when, one evening, having informed me abruptly that the lady Madeline was no more, he stated his intention of preserving her corpse for a fortnight, (previously to its final interment,) in one of the numerous vaults within the main walls of the building. The worldly reason, however, assigned for this singular proceeding, was one which I did not feel at liberty to dispute. The brother had been led to his resolution (so he told me) by consideration of the unusual character of the malady of the deceased, of certain obtrusive and eager inquiries on the part of her medical men, and of the remote and exposed situation of the burial-ground of the family. I will not deny that when I called to mind the sinister countenance of the person whom I met upon the staircase, on the day of my arrival at the house, I had no desire to oppose what I regarded as at best but a harmless, and by no means an unnatural, precaution.

At the request of Usher, I personally aided him in the arrangements for the temporary entombment. The body having been encoffined, we two alone bore it to its rest. The vault in which we placed it (and which had been so long unopened that our torches, half smothered in its oppressive atmosphere, gave us little opportunity for investigation) was small, damp, and entirely without means of admission for light; lying, at great depth, immediately beneath that portion of the building in which was my own sleeping apartment. It had been used, apparently, in remote feudal times, for the worst purposes of a donjon-keep, and, in later days, as a place of deposit for powder, or some other highly combustible substance, as a portion of its floor, and the whole interior of a long archway through which we reached it, were carefully sheathed with copper. The door, of massive iron, had been, also, similarly protected. Its immense weight caused an unusually sharp grating sound, as it moved upon its hinges.

Having deposited our mournful burden upon tressels within this region of horror, we partially turned aside the yet unscrewed lid of the coffin, and looked upon the face of the tenant. A striking similitude between the brother and sister now first arrested my attention; and Usher, divining, perhaps, my thoughts, murmured out some few words from which I learned that the deceased and himself had been twins, and that sympathies of a scarcely intelligible nature had always existed between them. Our glances, however, rested not long upon the dead – for we could not regard her unawed. The disease which had thus entombed the lady in the maturity of youth, had left, as usual in all maladies of a strictly cataleptical character, the mockery of a faint blush upon the bosom and the face, and that suspiciously lingering smile upon the lip which is so terrible in death. We replaced and screwed down the lid, and, having secured the door of iron, made our way, with toil, into the scarcely less gloomy apartments of the upper portion of the house.

And now, some days of bitter grief having elapsed, an observable change came over the features of the mental disorder of my friend. His ordinary manner had vanished. His ordinary occupations were neglected or forgotten. He roamed from chamber to chamber with hurried, unequal, and objectless step. The pallor of his countenance had assumed, if possible, a more ghastly hue – but the luminousness of his eye had utterly gone out. The once occasional huskiness of his tone was heard no more; and a tremulous quaver, as if of extreme terror, habitually characterized his utterance. There were times, indeed, when I thought his unceasingly agitated mind was labouring with some oppressive secret, to divulge which he struggled for the necessary courage. At times, again, I was obliged to resolve all into the mere inexplicable vagaries of madness, for I beheld him gazing upon vacancy for long hours, in an attitude of the profoundest attention, as if listening to some imaginary sound. It was no wonder that his condition terrified – that it infected me. I felt creeping upon me, by slow yet certain degrees, the wild influences of his own fantastic yet impressive superstitions.

It was, especially, upon retiring to bed late in the night of the seventh or eighth day after the placing of the lady Madeline within the donjon, that I experienced the full power of such feelings. Sleep came not near my couch – while the hours waned and waned away. I struggled to reason off the nervousness which had dominion over me. I endeavoured to believe that much, if not all of what I felt, was due to the bewildering influence of the gloomy furniture of the room – of the dark and tattered draperies, which, tortured into motion by the breath of a rising tempest, swayed fitfully to and fro upon the walls, and rustled uneasily about the decorations of the bed. But my efforts were fruitless. An irrepressible tremour gradually pervaded my frame; and, at length, there sat upon my very heart an incubus of utterly causeless alarm. Shaking this off with a gasp and a struggle, I uplifted myself upon the pillows, and, peering earnestly within the intense darkness of the chamber, hearkened – I know not why, except that an instinctive spirit prompted me – to certain low and indefinite sounds which came, through the pauses of the storm, at long intervals, I knew not whence. Overpowered by an intense sentiment of horror, unaccountable yet unendurable, I threw on my clothes with haste (for I felt that I should sleep no more during the night), and endeavoured to arouse myself from the pitiable condition into which I had fallen, by pacing rapidly to and fro through the apartment.

I had taken but few turns in this manner, when a light step on an adjoining staircase arrested my attention. I presently recognised it as that of Usher. In an instant afterward he rapped, with a gentle touch, at my door, and entered, bearing a lamp. His countenance was, as usual, cadaverously wan – but, moreover, there was a species of mad hilarity in his eyes – an evidently restrained *hysteria* in his whole demeanour. His air appalled me – but anything was preferable to the solitude which I had so long endured, and I even welcomed his presence as a relief.

'And you have not seen it?' he said abruptly, after having stared about him for some moments in silence – 'you have not then seen it? – but, stay! you shall.' Thus speaking, and having carefully shaded his lamp, he hurried to one of the casements, and threw it freely open to the storm.

The impetuous fury of the entering gust nearly lifted us from our feet. It was, indeed, a tempestuous yet sternly beautiful night, and one wildly singular in its terror and its beauty. A whirlwind had apparently collected its force in our vicinity; for there were frequent and violent alterations in the direction of the wind; and the exceeding density of the clouds (which hung so low as to press upon the turrets of the house) did not prevent our perceiving the life-like velocity with which they flew careering from all points against each other, without passing away into the distance. I say that even their exceeding density did not prevent our perceiving this – yet we had no glimpse of the moon or stars – nor was there any flashing forth of the lightning. But the under surfaces of the huge masses of agitated vapour, as well as all terrestrial objects immediately around us, were glowing in the unnatural light of a faintly luminous and distinctly visible gaseous exhalation which hung about and enshrouded the mansion.

'You must not – you shall not behold this!' said I, shudderingly, to Usher, as I led him, with a gentle violence, from the window to a seat. 'These appearances, which bewilder you, are merely electrical phenomena not uncommon – or it may be that they have their ghastly origin in the rank miasma of the tarn. Let us close this casement; – the air is chilling and dangerous to your frame. Here is one of your favourite romances. I will read, and you shall listen; – and so we will pass away this terrible night together.'

The antique volume which I had taken up was the 'Mad Trist' of Sir Launcelot Canning; [4] but I had called it a favourite of Usher's more in sad jest than in earnest; for, in truth, there is little in its uncouth and unimaginative prolixity which could have had interest for the lofty and spiritual ideality of my friend. It was, however, the only book immediately at hand; and I indulged a vague hope that the excitement which now agitated the hypochondriac, might find relief (for the history of mental disorder is full of similar anomalies) even in the extremeness of the folly which I should read. Could I have judged, indeed, by the wild overstrained air of vivacity with which he hearkened, or apparently hearkened, to the words of the tale, I might well have congratulated myself upon the success of my design.

I had arrived at that well-known portion of the story where Ethelred, the hero of the Trist, having sought in vain for peaceable admission into the dwelling of the hermit, proceeds to make good an entrance by force. Here, it will be remembered, the words of the narrative run thus:

'And Ethelred, who was by nature of a doughty heart, and who was now mighty withal, on account of the powerfulness of the wine which he had drunken, waited no longer to hold parley with the hermit, who, in sooth, was of an obstinate and maliceful turn, but, feeling the rain upon his shoulders, and fearing the rising of the tempest, uplifted his mace outright, and, with blows, made quickly room in the plankings of the door for his gauntleted hand; and now pulling therewith sturdily, he so cracked, and ripped, and tore all asunder, that the noise of the dry and hollow-sounding wood alarumed and reverberated throughout the forest.'

At the termination of this sentence I started, and for a moment, paused; for it appeared to me (although I at once concluded that my excited fancy had deceived me) – it appeared to me that, from some very remote portion of the mansion, there came, indistinctly, to my ears, what might have been, in its exact similarity of character, the echo (but a stifled and dull one certainly) of the very cracking and ripping sound which Sir Launcelot had so particularly described. It was, beyond doubt, the coincidence alone which had arrested my attention; for, amid the rattling of the sashes of the casements, and the ordinary commingled noises of the still increasing storm, the sound, in itself, had nothing, surely, which should have interested or disturbed me. I continued the story:

'But the good champion Ethelred, now entering within the door, was sore enraged and amazed to perceive no signal of the maliceful hermit; but, in the stead thereof, a dragon of a scaly and prodigious demeanour, and of a fiery tongue, which sate in guard before a palace of gold, with a floor of silver; and upon the wall there hung a shield of shining brass with this legend enwritten –

Who entereth herein, a conqueror hath bin;
Who slayeth the dragon, the shield he shall win;

And Ethelred uplifted his mace, and struck upon the head of the dragon, which fell before him, and gave up his pesty breath, with a shriek so horrid and harsh, and withal so piercing, that Ethelred had fain to close his ears with his hands against the dreadful noise of it, the like whereof was never before heard.'

Here again I paused abruptly, and now with a feeling of wild amazement – for there could be no doubt whatever that, in this instance, I did actually hear (although from what direction it proceeded I found it impossible to say) a low and apparently distant, but harsh, protracted, and most unusual screaming or grating sound – the exact counterpart of what my fancy had already conjured up for the dragon's unnatural shriek as described by the romancer.

Oppressed, as I certainly was, upon the occurrence of the second and most extraordinary coincidence, by a thousand conflicting sensations, in which wonder and extreme terror were predominant, I still retained sufficient presence of mind to avoid exciting, by any observation, the sensitive nervousness of my companion. I was by no means certain that he had noticed the sounds in question; although, assuredly, a strange alteration had, during the last few minutes, taken place in his demeanour. From a position fronting my own, he had gradually brought round his chair, so as to sit with his face to the door of the chamber; and thus I could but partially perceive his features, although I saw that his lips trembled as if he were murmuring inaudibly. His head had dropped upon his breast – yet I knew that he was not asleep, from the wide and rigid opening of the eye as I caught a glance of it in profile. The motion of his body, too, was at variance with this idea – for he rocked from side to side with a gentle yet constant and uniform sway. Having rapidly taken notice of all this, I resumed the narrative of Sir Launcelot, which thus proceeded:

'And now, the champion, having escaped from the terrible fury of the dragon, bethinking himself of the brazen shield, and of the breaking up of the enchantment which was upon it, removed the carcass from out of the way before him, and approached valorously over the silver pavement of the castle to where the shield was upon the wall; which in sooth tarried not for his full coming, but fell down at his feet upon the silver floor, with a mighty great and terrible ringing sound.'

No sooner had these syllables passed my lips, than – as if a shield of brass had indeed, at the moment, fallen heavily upon a floor of silver – I became aware of a distinct, hollow, metallic, and clangorous, yet apparently muffled reverberation. Completely unnerved, I leaped to my feet; but the measured rocking movement of Usher was undisturbed. I rushed to the chair in which he sat. His eyes were bent fixedly before him, and throughout his whole countenance there reigned a stony rigidity. But, as I placed my hand upon his shoulder, there came a strong shudder over his whole person; a sickly smile quivered about his lips; and I saw that he spoke in a low, hurried, and gibbering murmur, as if unconscious of my presence. Bending closely over him, I at length drank in the hideous import of his words.

'Not hear it? – yes, I hear it, and *have* heard it. Long – long – long – many minutes, many hours, many days, have I heard it – yet I dared not – oh, pity me, miserable wretch that I am! – I dared not – I *dared* not speak! *We have put her living in the tomb!* Said I not that my senses were acute? I *now* tell you that I heard her first feeble movements in the hollow coffin. I heard them – many, many days ago – yet I dared not – I *dared not speak!* And now – to-night – Ethelred – ha! ha! – the breaking of the hermit's door, and the death-cry of the dragon, and the clangour of the shield! – say, rather, the rending of her coffin, and the grating of the iron hinges of her prison, and her struggles within the coppered archway of the vault! Oh whither shall I fly? Will she not be here anon? Is she not hurrying to upbraid me for my haste? Have I not heard her footstep on the stair? Do I not distinguish that heavy and horrible beating of her heart? MADMAN!' – here he sprang furiously to his feet, and shrieked out his syllables, as if in the effort he were giving up his soul – 'MADMAN! I TELL YOU THAT SHE NOW STANDS WITHOUT THE DOOR!'

As if in the superhuman energy of his utterance there had been found the potency of a spell – the huge antique panels to which the speaker pointed, threw slowly back, upon the instant, their ponderous and ebony jaws. It was the work of the rushing gust – but then without those doors there DID stand the lofty and enshrouded figure of the lady Madeline of Usher. There was blood upon her white robes, and the evidence of some bitter struggle upon every portion of her emaciated frame. For a moment she remained trembling and reeling to and fro upon the threshold, then, with a low moaning cry, fell heavily inward upon the person of her brother, and in her violent and now final death-agonies, bore him to the floor a corpse, and a victim to the terrors he had anticipated.

From that chamber, and from that mansion, I fled aghast. The storm was still abroad in all its wrath as I found myself crossing the old causeway. Suddenly there shot along the path a wild light, and I turned to see whence a gleam so unusual could have issued; for the vast house and its shadows were alone behind me. The radiance was that of the full, setting, and blood-red moon which now shone vividly through that once barely-discernible fissure of which I have before spoken as extending from the roof of the building, in a zigzag direction, to the base. While I gazed, this fissure rapidly widened – there came a fierce breath of the whirlwind – the entire orb of the satellite burst at once upon my sight – my brain reeled as I saw the mighty walls rushing asunder – there was a long tumultuous shouting sound like the voice of a thousand waters – and the deep and dank tarn at my feet closed sullenly and silently over the fragments of the 'HOUSE OF USHER.'

William Wilson

What say of it? what say [of] CONSCIENCE grim,
That spectre in my path?
                              CHAMBERLAYNE'S *Pharronida*[1]

LET me call myself, for the present, William Wilson. The fair page now lying before me need not be sullied with my real appellation. This has been already too much an object for the scorn – for the horror – for the detestation of my race. To the uttermost regions of the globe have not the indignant winds bruited its unparalleled infamy? Oh, outcast of all outcasts most abandoned! – to the earth art thou not forever dead? to its honors, to its flowers, to its golden aspirations? – and a cloud, dense, dismal, and limitless, does it not hang eternally between thy hopes and heaven?

I would not, if I could, here or to-day, embody a record of my later years of unspeakable misery, and unpardonable crime. This epoch – these later years – took unto themselves a sudden elevation in turpitude, whose origin alone it is my present purpose to assign. Men usually grow base by degrees. From me, in an instant, all virtue dropped bodily as a mantle. From comparatively trivial wickedness I passed, with the stride of a giant, into more than the enormities of an Elah-Gabalus. What chance – what one event brought this evil thing to pass, bear with me while I relate. Death approaches; and the shadow which foreruns him has thrown a softening influence over my spirit. I long, in passing through the dim valley, for the sympathy – I had nearly said for the pity – of my fellow men. I would fain have them believe that I have been, in some measure, the slave of circumstances beyond human control. I would wish them to seek out for me, in the details I am about to give, some little oasis of *fatality* amid a wilderness of error. I would have them allow –

what they cannot refrain from allowing – that, although temptation may have erewhile existed as great, man was never *thus*, at least, tempted before – certainly, never *thus* fell. And is it therefore that he has never thus suffered? Have I not indeed been living in a dream? And am I not now dying a victim to the horror and the mystery of the wildest of all sublunary visions?

I am the descendant of a race whose imaginative and easily excitable temperament has at all times rendered them remarkable; and, in my earliest infancy, I gave evidence of having fully inherited the family character. As I advanced in years it was more strongly developed; becoming, for many reasons, a cause of serious disquietude to my friends, and of positive injury to myself. I grew self-willed, addicted to the wildest caprices, and a prey to the most ungovernable passions. Weak-minded, and beset with constitutional infirmities akin to my own, my parents could do but little to check the evil propensities which distinguished me. Some feeble and ill-directed efforts resulted in complete failure on their part, and, of course, in total triumph on mine. Thenceforward my voice was a household law; and at an age when few children have abandoned their leading-strings, I was left to the guidance of my own will, and became, in all but name, the master of my own actions.

My earliest recollections of a school-life, are connected with a large, rambling, Elizabethan house, in a misty-looking village of England, where were a vast number of gigantic and gnarled trees, and where all the houses were excessively ancient. In truth, it was a dream-like and spirit-soothing place, that venerable old town. At this moment, in fancy, I feel the refreshing chilliness of its deeply-shadowed avenues, inhale the fragrance of its thousand shrubberies, and thrill anew with undefinable delight, at the deep hollow note of the church-bell, breaking, each hour, with sullen and sudden roar, upon the stillness of the dusky atmosphere in which the fretted Gothic steeple lay imbedded and asleep.

It gives me, perhaps, as much of pleasure as I can now in any manner experience, to dwell upon minute recollections of the school and its concerns. Steeped in misery as I am – misery, alas! only too real – I shall be pardoned for seeking relief, however slight and temporary, in the weakness of a few rambling details. These, moreover, utterly trivial, and even ridiculous in themselves, assume, to my fancy, adventitious importance, as connected with a period and a locality when and where I recognise the first ambiguous monitions of the destiny which afterwards so fully overshadowed me. Let me then remember.

The house, I have said, was old and irregular. The grounds were extensive, and a high and solid brick wall, topped with a bed of mortar and broken glass, encompassed the whole. This prison-like rampart formed the limit of our domain; beyond it we saw but thrice a week – once every Saturday afternoon, when, attended by two ushers, we were permitted to take brief walks in a body through some of the neighbouring fields – and twice during Sunday, when we were paraded in the same formal manner to the morning and evening service in the one church of the village. Of this church the principal of our school was pastor. With how deep a spirit of wonder and perplexity was I wont to regard him from our remote pew in the gallery, as, with step solemn and slow, he ascended the pulpit! This reverend man, with countenance so demurely benign, with robes so glossy and so clerically flowing, with wig so minutely powdered, so rigid and so vast, – could this be he who, of late, with sour visage, and in snuffy habiliments, administered, ferule in hand, the Draconian laws of the academy? Oh, gigantic paradox, too utterly monstrous for solution!

At an angle of the ponderous wall frowned a more ponderous gate. It was riveted and studded with iron bolts, and surmounted with jagged iron spikes. What impressions of deep awe did it inspire! It was never opened save for the three periodical egressions and ingressions already mentioned; then, in every creak of its mighty hinges, we found a plenitude of mystery – a world of matter for solemn remark, or for more solemn meditation.

The extensive enclosure was irregular in form, having many capacious recesses. Of these, three or four of the largest constituted the play-ground. It was level, and covered with fine hard gravel. I well remember it had no trees, nor benches, nor anything similar within it. Of course it was in the rear of the house. In front lay a small parterre, planted with box and other shrubs; but through this sacred division we passed only upon rare occasions indeed – such as a first advent to school or final departure thence, or perhaps, when a parent or friend having called for us, we joyfully took our way home for the Christmas or Midsummer holy-days.

But the house! – how quaint an old building was this! – to me how veritably a palace of enchantment! There was really no end to its windings – to its incomprehensible subdivisions. It was difficult, at any given time, to say with certainty upon which of its two stories one happened to be. From each room to every other there were sure to be found three or four steps either in ascent or descent. Then the lateral branches were innumerable – inconceivable – and so returning in upon themselves, that our most exact ideas in regard to the whole mansion were not very far different from those with which we pondered upon infinity. During the five years of my residence here, I was never able to ascertain with precision, in what remote locality lay the little sleeping apartment assigned to myself and some eighteen or twenty other scholars.

The school-room was the largest in the house – I could not help thinking, in the world. It was very long, narrow, and dismally low, with pointed Gothic windows and a ceiling of oak. In a remote and terror-inspiring angle was a square enclosure of eight or ten feet, comprising the *sanctum*, 'during hours,' of our principal, the Reverend Dr Bransby. It was a solid structure, with massy door, sooner than open which in the absence of the 'Dominie,' we would all have willingly perished by the *peine forte et dure*. In other angles were two other similar boxes, far less reverenced, indeed, but still greatly matters of awe. One of these was the pulpit of the 'classical' usher, one of the 'English and mathematical.' Interspersed about the room, crossing and recrossing in endless irregularity, were innumerable benches and desks, black, ancient, and time-worn, piled desperately with much-bethumbed books, and so beseamed with initial letters, names at full length, grotesque figures, and other multiplied efforts of the knife, as to have entirely lost what little of original form might have been their portion in days long departed. A huge bucket with water stood at one extremity of the room, and a clock of stupendous dimensions at the other.

Encompassed by the massy walls of this venerable academy, I passed, yet not in tedium or disgust, the years of the third lustrum of my life. The teeming brain of childhood requires no external world of incident to occupy or amuse it; and the apparently dismal monotony of a school was replete with more intense excitement than my riper youth has derived from luxury, or my full manhood from crime. Yet I must believe that my first mental development had in it much of the uncommon – even much of the *outré*. Upon mankind at large the events of very early existence rarely leave in mature age any definite impression. All is gray shadow – a weak and irregular remembrance – an indistinct regathering of feeble pleasures and phantasmagoric pains. With me this is not so. In childhood I must have felt with the energy of a man what I now find stamped upon memory in lines as vivid, as deep, and as durable as the *exergues* of the Carthaginian medals.

Yet in fact – in the fact of the world's view – how little was there to remember! The morning's awakening, the nightly summons to bed; the connings, the recitations; the periodical half-holidays, and perambulations; the play-ground, with its broils, its pastimes, its intrigues; – these, by a mental sorcery long forgotten, were made to involve a wilderness of sensation, a world of rich incident, an universe of varied emotion, of excitement of the most passionate and spirit-stirring. 'Oh, *le bon temps, que ce siècle de fer!*'

In truth, the ardor, the enthusiasm, and the imperiousness of my disposition, soon rendered me a marked character among my schoolmates, and by slow, but natural gradations, gave me an ascendancy over all not greatly older than myself; – over all with a single exception. This exception was found in the person of a scholar, who, although no relation, bore the same Christian and surname as myself; – a circumstance, in fact, little remarkable; for, notwithstanding a noble descent, mine was one of those everyday appellations which seem, by prescriptive right, to have been, time out of mind, the common property of the mob. In this narrative I have therefore designated myself as William Wilson, – a fictitious title not very dissimilar to the real. My namesake alone, of those who in school phraseology constituted 'our set,' presumed to compete with me in the studies of the class – in the sports and broils of the play-ground – to refuse implicit belief in my assertions, and submission to my will – indeed, to interfere with my arbitrary dictation in any respect whatsoever. If there is on earth a supreme and unqualified despotism, it is the despotism of a master mind in boyhood over the less energetic spirits of its companions.

Wilson's rebellion was to me a source of the greatest embarrassment; – the more so as, in spite of the bravado with which in public I made a point of treating him and his pretensions, I secretly felt that I feared him, and could not help thinking the equality which he maintained so easily with myself, a proof of his true superiority; since not to be overcome cost me a perpetual struggle. Yet this superiority – even this equality – was in truth acknowledged by no one but myself; our associates, by some unaccountable blindness, seemed not even to suspect it. Indeed, his competition, his resistance, and especially his impertinent and dogged interference with my purposes, were not more pointed than private. He appeared to be destitute alike of the ambition which urged, and of the passionate energy of mind which enabled me to excel. In his rivalry he might have been supposed actuated solely by a whimsical desire to thwart, astonish, or mortify myself; although there were times when I could not help observing, with a feeling made up of wonder, abasement, and pique, that he mingled with his injuries, his insults, or his contradictions, a certain most inappropriate, and assuredly most unwelcome *affectionateness* of manner. I could only conceive this singular behavior to arise from a consummate self-conceit assuming the vulgar airs of patronage and protection.

Perhaps it was this latter trait in Wilson's conduct, conjoined with our identity of name, and the mere accident of our having entered the school upon the same day, which set afloat the notion that we were brothers, among the senior classes in the academy. These do not usually inquire with much strictness into the affairs of their juniors. I have before said, or should have said, that Wilson was not, in the most remote degree, connected with my family. But assuredly if we *had* been brothers we must have been twins; for, after leaving Dr Bransby's, I casually learned that my namesake was born on the nineteenth of January, 1813 – and this is a somewhat remarkable coincidence; for the day is precisely that of my own nativity.

It may seem strange that in spite of the continual anxiety occasioned me by the rivalry of Wilson, and his intolerable spirit of contradiction, I could not bring myself to hate him altogether. We had, to be sure, nearly every day a quarrel in which, yielding me publicly the palm of victory, he, in some manner, contrived to make me feel that it was he who had deserved it; yet a sense of pride on my part, and a veritable dignity on his own, kept us always upon what are called 'speaking terms,' while there were many points of strong congeniality in our tempers, operating to awake in me a sentiment which our position alone, perhaps, prevented from ripening into friendship. It is difficult, indeed, to define, or even to describe, my real feelings towards him. They formed a motley and heterogeneous admixture; – some petulant animosity, which was not yet hatred, some esteem, more respect, much fear, with a world of uneasy curiosity. To the moralist it will be unnecessary to say, in addition, that Wilson and myself were the most inseparable of companions.

It was no doubt the anomalous state of affairs existing between us, which turned all my attacks upon him, (and they were many, either open or covert) into the channel of banter or practical joke (giving pain while assuming the aspect of mere fun) rather than into a more serious and determined hostility. But my endeavours on this head were by no means uniformly successful, even when my plans were the most wittily concocted; for my namesake had much about him, in character, of that unassuming and quiet austerity which, while enjoying the poignancy of its own jokes, has no heel of Achilles in itself, and absolutely refuses to be laughed at. I could find, indeed, but one vulnerable point, and that, lying in a personal peculiarity, arising, perhaps, from constitutional disease, would have been spared by any antagonist less at his wit's end than myself; – my rival had a weakness in the faucial or guttural organs, which precluded him from raising his voice at any time *above a very low whisper*. Of this defect I did not fail to take what poor advantage lay in my power.

Wilson's retaliations in kind were many; and there was one form of his practical wit that disturbed me beyond measure. How his sagacity first discovered at all that so petty a thing would vex me, is a question I never could solve; but, having discovered, he habitually practised the annoyance. I had always felt aversion to my uncourtly patronymic, and its very common, if not plebeian prænomen. The words were venom in my ears; and when, upon the day of my arrival, a second William Wilson came also to the academy, I felt angry with him for bearing the name, and doubly disgusted with the name because a stranger bore it, who would be the cause of its twofold repetition, who would be constantly in my presence, and whose concerns, in the ordinary routine of the school business, must inevitably, on account of the detestable coincidence, be often confounded with my own.

The feeling of vexation thus engendered grew stronger with every circumstance tending to show resemblance, moral or physical, between my rival and myself. I had not then discovered the remarkable fact that we were of the same age; but I saw that we were of the same height, and I perceived that we were even singularly alike in general contour of person and outline of feature. I was galled, too, by the rumor touching a relationship, which had grown current in the upper forms. In a word, nothing could more seriously disturb me, (although I scrupulously concealed such disturbance,) than any allusion to a similarity of mind, person, or condition existing between us. But, in truth, I had no reason to believe that (with the exception of the matter of relationship, and in the case of Wilson himself,) this similarity had ever been made a subject of comment, or even observed at all by our schoolfellows. That *he* observed it in all its bearings, and as fixedly as I, was apparent; but that he could discover in such circumstances so fruitful a field of annoyance, can only be attributed, as I said before, to his more than ordinary penetration.

His cue, which was to perfect an imitation of myself, lay both in words and in actions; and most admirably did he play his part. My dress it was an easy matter to copy; my gait and general manner were, without difficulty, appropriated; in spite of his constitutional defect, even my voice did not escape him. My louder tones were, of course, unattempted, but then the key, it was identical; *and his singular whisper, it grew the very echo of my own.*

How greatly this most exquisite portraiture harassed me, (for it could not justly be termed a caricature,) I will not now venture to describe. I had but one consolation – in the fact that the imitation, apparently, was noticed by myself alone, and that I had to endure only the knowing and strangely sarcastic smiles of my namesake himself. Satisfied with having produced in my bosom the intended effect, he seemed to chuckle in secret over the sting he had inflicted, and was characteristically disregardful of the public applause which the success of his witty endeavours might have so easily elicited. That the school, indeed, did not feel his design, perceive its accomplishment, and participate in his sneer, was, for many anxious months, a riddle I could not resolve. Perhaps the *gradation* of his copy rendered it not so readily perceptible; or, more possibly, I owed my security to the masterly air of the copyist, who, disdaining the letter, (which in a painting is all the obtuse can see,) gave but the full spirit of his original for my individual contemplation and chagrin.

I have already more than once spoken of the disgusting air of patronage which he assumed toward me, and of his frequent officious interference with my will. This interference often took the ungracious character of advice; advice not openly given, but hinted or insinuated. I received it with a repugnance which gained strength as I grew in years. Yet, at this distant day, let me do him the simple justice to acknowledge that I can recall no occasion when the suggestions of my rival were on the side of those errors or follies so usual to his immature age and seeming inexperience; that his moral sense, at least, if not his general talents and worldly wisdom, was far keener than my own; and that I might, to-day, have been a better, and thus a happier man, had I less frequently rejected the counsels embodied in those meaning whispers which I then but too cordially hated and too bitterly despised.

As it was, I at length grew restive in the extreme under his distasteful supervision, and daily resented more and more openly what I considered his intolerable arrogance. I have said that, in the first years of our connexion as schoolmates, my feelings in regard to him might have been easily ripened into friendship: but, in the latter months of my residence at the academy, although the intrusion of his ordinary manner had, beyond doubt, in some measure, abated, my sentiments, in nearly similar proportion, partook very much of positive hatred. Upon one occasion he saw this, I think, and afterwards avoided, or made a show of avoiding me.

It was about the same period, if I remember aright, that, in an altercation of violence with him, in which he was more than usually thrown off his guard, and spoke and acted with an openness of demeanor rather foreign to his nature, I discovered, or fancied I discovered, in his accent, his air, and general appearance, a something which first startled, and then deeply interested me, by bringing to mind dim visions of my earliest infancy – wild, confused and thronging memories of a time when memory herself was yet unborn. I cannot better describe the sensation which oppressed me than by saying that I could with difficulty shake off the belief of my having been acquainted with the being who stood before me, at some epoch very long ago – some point of the past even infinitely remote. The delusion, however, faded rapidly as it came; and I mention it at all but to define the day of the last conversation I there held with my singular namesake.

The huge old house, with its countless subdivisions, had several large chambers communicating with each other, where slept the greater number of the students. There were, however, (as must necessarily happen in a building so awkwardly planned,) many little nooks or recesses, the odds and ends of the structure; and these the economic ingenuity of Dr Bransby had also fitted up as dormitories; although, being the merest closets, they were capable of accommodating but a single individual. One of these small apartments was occupied by Wilson.

One night, about the close of my fifth year at the school, and immediately after the altercation just mentioned, finding every one wrapped in sleep, I arose from bed, and, lamp in hand, stole through a wilderness of narrow passages from my own bedroom to that of my rival. I had long been plotting one of those ill-natured pieces of practical wit at his expense in which I had hitherto been so uniformly unsuccessful. It was my intention, now, to put my scheme in operation, and I resolved to make him feel the whole extent of the malice with which I was imbued. Having reached his closet, I noiselessly entered, leaving the lamp, with a shade over it, on the outside. I advanced a step, and listened to the sound of his tranquil breathing. Assured of his being asleep, I returned, took the light, and with it again approached the bed. Close curtains were around it, which, in the prosecution of my plan, I slowly and quietly withdrew, when the bright rays fell vividly upon the sleeper, and my eyes, at the same moment, upon his countenance. I looked; – and a numbness, an iciness of feeling instantly pervaded my frame. My breast heaved, my knees tottered, my whole spirit became possessed with an objectless yet intolerable horror. Gasping for breath, I lowered the lamp in still nearer proximity to the face. Were these – *these* the lineaments of William Wilson? I saw, indeed, that they were his, but I shook as if with a fit of the ague in fancying they were not. What *was* there about them to confound me in this manner? I gazed; – while my brain reeled with a multitude of incoherent thoughts. Not thus he appeared – assuredly not *thus* – in the vivacity of his waking hours. The same name! the same contour of person! the same day of arrival at the academy! And then his dogged and meaningless imitation of my gait, my voice, my habits, and my manner! Was it, in truth, within the bounds of human possibility, that *what I now saw* was the result, merely, of the habitual practice of this sarcastic imitation? Awestricken, and with a creeping shudder, I extinguished the lamp, passed silently from the chamber, and left, at once, the halls of that old academy, never to enter them again.

After a lapse of some months, spent at home in mere idleness, I found myself a student at Eton. The brief interval had been sufficient to enfeeble my remembrance of the events at Dr Bransby's, or at least to effect a material change in the nature of the feelings with which I remembered them. The truth – the tragedy – of the drama was no more. I could now find room to doubt the evidence of my senses; and seldom called up the subject at all but with wonder at the extent of human credulity, and a smile at the vivid force of the imagination which I hereditarily possessed. Neither was this species of scepticism likely to be diminished by the character of the life I led at Eton. The vortex of thoughtless folly into which I there so immediately and so recklessly plunged, washed away all but the froth of my past hours, engulfed at once every solid or serious impression, and left to memory only the veriest levities of a former existence.

I do not wish, however, to trace the course of my miserable profligacy here – a profligacy which set at defiance the laws, while it eluded the vigilance of the institution. Three years of folly, passed without profit, had but given me rooted habits of vice, and added, in a somewhat unusual degree, to my bodily stature, when, after a week of soulless dissipation, I invited a small party of the most dissolute students to a secret carousal in my chambers. We met at a late hour of the night; for our debaucheries were to be faithfully protracted until morning. The wine flowed freely, and there were not wanting other and perhaps more dangerous seductions; so that the grey dawn had already faintly appeared in the east, while our delirious extravagance was at its height. Madly flushed with cards and intoxication, I was in the act of insisting upon a toast of more than wonted profanity, when my attention was suddenly diverted by the violent, although partial unclosing of the door of the apartment, and by the eager voice of a servant from without. He said that some person, apparently in great haste, demanded to speak with me in the hall.

Wildly excited with wine, the unexpected interruption rather delighted than surprised me. I staggered forward at once, and a few steps brought me to the vestibule of the building. In this low and small room there hung no lamp; and now no light at all was admitted, save that of the exceedingly feeble dawn which made its way through the semi-circular window. As I put my foot over the threshold, I became aware of the figure of a youth about my own height, and habited in a white kerseymere morning frock, cut in the novel fashion of the one I myself wore at the moment. This the faint light enabled me to perceive; but the features of his face I could not distinguish. Upon my entering he strode hurriedly up to me, and, seizing me by the arm with a gesture of petulant impatience, whispered the words 'William Wilson!' in my ear.

I grew perfectly sober in an instant.

There was that in the manner of the stranger, and in the tremulous shake of his uplifted finger, as he held it between my eyes and the light, which filled me with unqualified amazement; but it was not this which had so violently moved me. It was the pregnancy of solemn admonition in the singular, low, hissing utterance; and, above all, it was the character, the tone, *the key*, of those few, simple, and familiar, yet *whispered* syllables, which came with a thousand thronging memories of by-gone days, and struck upon my soul with the shock of a galvanic battery. Ere I could recover the use of my senses he was gone.

Although this event failed not of a vivid effect upon my disordered imagination, yet was it evanescent as vivid. For some weeks, indeed, I busied myself in earnest inquiry, or was wrapped in a cloud of morbid speculation. I did not pretend to disguise from my perception the identity of the singular individual who thus perseveringly interfered with my affairs, and harassed me with his insinuated counsel. But who and what was this Wilson? – and whence came he? – and what were his purposes? Upon neither of these points could I be satisfied; merely ascertaining, in regard to him, that a sudden accident in his family had caused his removal from Dr Bransby's academy on the afternoon of the day in which I myself had eloped. But in a brief period I ceased to think upon the subject; my attention being all absorbed in a contemplated departure for Oxford. Thither I soon went; the uncalculating vanity of my parents furnishing me with an outfit and annual establishment, which would enable me to indulge at will in the luxury already so dear to my heart, – to vie in profuseness of expenditure with the haughtiest heirs of the wealthiest earldoms in Great Britain.

Excited by such appliances to vice, my constitutional temperament broke forth with redoubled ardor, and I spurned even the common restraints of decency in the mad infatuation of my revels. But it were absurd to pause in the detail of my extravagance. Let it suffice, that among spendthrifts I out-Heroded Herod, and that, giving name to a multitude of novel follies, I added no brief appendix to the long catalogue of vices then usual in the most dissolute university of Europe.

It could hardly be credited, however, that I had, even here, so utterly fallen from the gentlemanly estate, as to speak acquaintance with the vilest arts of the gambler by profession, and, having become an adept in his despicable science, to practise it habitually as a means of increasing my already enormous income at the expense of the weak-minded among my fellow-collegians. Such, nevertheless, was the fact. And the very enormity of this offence against all manly and honourable sentiment proved, beyond doubt, the main if not the sole reason of the impunity with which it was committed. Who, indeed, among my most abandoned associates, would not rather have disputed the clearest evidence of his senses, than have suspected of such courses, the gay, the frank, the generous William Wilson – the noblest and most liberal commoner at Oxford – him whose follies (said his parasites) were but the follies of youth and unbridled fancy – whose errors but inimitable whim – whose darkest vice but a careless and dashing extravagance?

I had been now two years successfully busied in this way, when there came to the university a young *parvenu* nobleman, Glendinning – rich, said report, as Herodes Atticus – his riches, too, as easily acquired. I soon found him of weak intellect, and, of course, marked him as a fitting subject for my skill. I frequently engaged him in play, and contrived, with the gambler's usual art, to let him win considerable sums, the more effectually to entangle him in my snares. At length, my schemes being ripe, I met him (with the full intention that this meeting should be final and decisive) at the chambers of a fellow-commoner, (Mr Preston,) equally intimate with both, but who, to do him justice, entertained not even a remote suspicion of my design. To give to this a better colouring, I had contrived to have assembled a party of some eight or ten, and was solicitously careful that the introduction of cards should appear accidental, and originate in the proposal of my contemplated dupe himself. To be brief upon a vile topic, none of the low finesse was omitted, so customary upon similar occasions that it is a just matter for wonder how any are still found so besotted as to fall its victim.

We had protracted our sitting far into the night, and I had at length effected the manœuvre of getting Glendinning as my sole antagonist. The game, too, was my favorite *écarté*. The rest of the company, interested in the extent of our play, had abandoned their own cards, and were standing around us as spectators. The *parvenu*, who had been induced by my artifices in the early part of the evening, to drink deeply, now shuffled, dealt, or played, with a wild nervousness of manner for which his intoxication, I thought, might partially, but could not altogether account. In a very short period he had become my debtor to a large amount, when, having taken a long draught of port, he did precisely what I had been coolly anticipating – he proposed to double our already extravagant stakes. With a well-feigned show of reluctance, and not until after my repeated refusal had seduced him into some angry words which gave a color of *pique* to my compliance, did I finally comply. The result, of course, did but prove how entirely the prey was in my toils; in less than an hour he had quadrupled his debt. For some time his countenance had been losing the florid tinge lent it by the wine; but now, to my astonishment, I perceived that it had grown to a pallor truly fearful. I say to my astonishment. Glendinning had been represented to my eager inquiries as immeasurably wealthy; and the sums which he had as yet lost, although in themselves vast, could not, I supposed, very seriously annoy, much less so violently affect him. That he was overcome by the wine just swallowed, was the idea which most readily presented itself; and, rather with a view to the preservation of my own character in the eyes of my associates, than from any less interested motive, I was about to insist, peremptorily, upon a discontinuance of the play, when some expressions at my elbow from among the company, and an ejaculation evincing utter despair on the part of Glendinning, gave me to understand that I had effected his total ruin under circumstances which, rendering him an object for the pity of all, should have protected him from the ill offices even of a fiend.

What now might have been my conduct it is difficult to say. The pitiable condition of my dupe had thrown an air of embarrassed gloom over all; and, for some moments, a profound silence was maintained, during which I could not help feeling my cheeks tingle with the many burning glances of scorn or reproach cast upon me by the less abandoned of the party. I will even own that an intolerable weight of anxiety was for a brief instant lifted from my bosom by the sudden and extraordinary interruption which ensued. The wide, heavy folding doors of the apartment were all at once thrown open, to their full extent, with a vigorous and rushing impetuosity that extinguished, as if by magic, every candle in the room. Their light, in dying, enabled us just to perceive that a stranger had entered, about my own height, and closely muffled in a cloak. The darkness, however, was now total; and we could only *feel* that he was standing in our midst. Before any one of us could recover from the extreme astonishment into which this rudeness had thrown all, we heard the voice of the intruder.

'Gentlemen,' he said, in a low, distinct, and never-to-be-forgotten *whisper* which thrilled to the very marrow of my bones, 'Gentlemen, I make no apology for this behaviour, because in thus behaving, I am but fulfilling a duty. You are, beyond doubt, uninformed of the true character of the person who has to-night won at *écarté* a large sum of money from Lord Glendinning. I will therefore put you upon an expeditious and decisive plan of obtaining this very necessary information. Please to examine, at your leisure, the inner linings of the cuff of his left sleeve, and the several little packages which may be found in the some-what capacious pockets of his embroidered morning wrapper.'

While he spoke, so profound was the stillness that one might have heard a pin drop upon the floor. In ceasing, he departed at once, and as abruptly as he had entered. Can I – shall I describe my sensations? – must I say that I felt all the horrors of the damned? Most assuredly I had little time given for reflection. Many hands roughly seized me upon the spot, and lights were immediately reprocured. A search ensued. In the lining of my sleeve were found all the court cards essential in *écarté*, and, in the pockets of my wrapper, a number of packs, fac-similes of those used at our sittings, with the single exception that mine were of the species called, technically, *arrondées*; the honours being slightly convex at the ends, the lower cards slightly convex at the sides. In this disposition, the dupe who cuts, as customary, at the length of the pack, will invariably find that he cuts his antagonist an honor; while the gambler, cutting at the breadth, will, as certainly, cut nothing for his victim which may count in the records of the game.

Any burst of indignation upon this discovery would have affected me less than the silent contempt, or the sarcastic composure, with which it was received.

'Mr Wilson,' said our host, stooping to remove from beneath his feet an exceedingly luxurious cloak of rare furs, 'Mr Wilson, this is your property.' (The weather was cold; and, upon quitting my own room, I had thrown a cloak over my dressing wrapper, putting it off upon reaching the scene of play.) 'I presume it is supererogatory to seek here (eyeing the folds of the garment with a bitter smile) for any farther evidence of your skill. Indeed, we have had enough. You will see the necessity, I hope, of quitting Oxford – at all events, of quitting instantly my chambers.'

Abased, humbled to the dust as I then was, it is probable that I should have resented this galling language by immediate personal violence, had not my whole attention been at the moment arrested by a fact of the most startling character. The cloak which I had worn was of a rare description of fur; how rare, how extravagantly costly, I shall not venture to say. Its fashion, too, was of my own fantastic invention; for I was fastidious to an absurd degree of coxcombry, in matters of this frivolous nature. When, therefore, Mr Preston reached me that which he had picked up upon the floor, and near the folding doors of the apartment, it was with an astonishment nearly bordering upon terror, that I perceived my own already hanging on my arm, (where I had no doubt unwittingly placed it,) and that the one presented me was but its exact counterpart in every, in even the minutest possible particular. The singular being who had so disastrously exposed me, had been muffled, I remembered, in a cloak; and none had been worn at all by any of the members of our party with the exception of myself. Retaining some presence of mind, I took the one offered me by Preston; placed it, unnoticed, over my own; left the apartment with a resolute scowl of defiance; and, next morning ere dawn of day, commenced a hurried journey from Oxford to the continent, in a perfect agony of horror and of shame.

I *fled in vain*. My evil destiny pursued me as if in exultation, and proved, indeed, that the exercise of its mysterious dominion had as yet only begun. Scarcely had I set foot in Paris ere I had fresh evidence of the detestable interest taken by this Wilson in my concerns. Years flew, while I experienced no relief. Villain! – at Rome, with how untimely, yet with how spectral an officiousness, stepped he in between me and my ambition! At Vienna, too – at Berlin – and at Moscow! Where, in truth, had I *not* bitter cause to curse him within my heart? From his inscrutable tyranny did I at length flee, panic-stricken, as from a pestilence; and to the very ends of the earth I *fled in vain*.

And again, and again, in secret communion with my own spirit, would I demand the questions 'Who is he? – whence came he? – and what are his objects?' But no answer was there found. And then I scrutinized, with a minute scrutiny, the forms, and the methods, and the leading traits of his impertinent supervision. But even here there was very little upon which to base a conjecture. It was noticeable, indeed, that, in no one of the multiplied instances in which he had of late crossed my path, had he so crossed it except to frustrate those schemes, or to disturb those actions, which, if fully carried out, might have resulted in bitter mischief. Poor justification this, in truth, for an authority so imperiously assumed! Poor indemnity for natural rights of self-agency so pertinaciously, so insultingly denied!

I had also been forced to notice that my tormentor, for a very long period of time, (while scrupulously and with miraculous dexterity maintaining his whim of and identity of apparel with myself,) had so contrived it, in the execution of his varied interference with my will, that I saw not, at any moment, the features of his face. Be Wilson what he might, *this*, at least, was but the veriest of affectation, or of folly. Could he, for an instant, have supposed that, in my admonisher at Eton – in the destroyer of my honour at Oxford, – in him who thwarted my ambition at Rome, my revenge at Paris, my passionate love at Naples, or what he falsely termed my avarice in Egypt, – that in this, my arch-enemy and evil genius, I could fail to recognise the William Wilson of my school boy days, – the namesake, the companion, the rival, – the hated and dreaded rival at Dr Bransby's? Impossible! – But let me hasten to the last eventful scene of the drama.

Thus far I had succumbed supinely to this imperious domination. The sentiment of deep awe with which I habitually regarded the elevated character, the majestic wisdom, the apparent omnipresence and omnipotence of Wilson, added to a feeling of even terror, with which certain other traits in his nature and assumptions inspired me, had operated, hitherto, to impress me with an idea of my own utter weakness and helplessness, and to suggest an implicit, although bitterly reluctant submission to his arbitrary will. But, of late days, I had given myself up entirely to wine; and its maddening influence upon my hereditary temper rendered me more and more impatient of control. I began to murmur, – to hesitate, – to resist. And was it only fancy which induced me to believe that, with the increase of my own firmness, that of my tormentor underwent a proportional diminution? Be this as it may, I now began to feel the inspiration of a burning hope, and at length nurtured in my secret thoughts a stern and desperate resolution that I would submit no longer to be enslaved.

It was at Rome, during the Carnival of 18–, that I attended a masquerade in the palazzo of the Neapolitan Duke Di Broglio. I had indulged more freely than usual in the excesses of the wine-table; and now the suffocating atmosphere of the crowded rooms irritated me beyond endurance. The difficulty, too, of forcing my way through the mazes of the company contributed not a little to the ruffling of my temper; for I was anxiously seeking, (let me not say with what unworthy motive) the young, the gay, the beautiful wife of the aged and doting Di Broglio. With a too unscrupulous confidence she had previously communicated to me the secret of the costume in which she would be habited, and now, having caught a glimpse of her person, I was hurrying to make my way into her presence. – At this moment I felt a light hand placed upon my shoulder, and that ever-remembered, low, damnable *whisper* within my ear.

In an absolute phrenzy of wrath, I turned at once upon him who had thus interrupted me, and seized him violently by the collar. He was attired, as I had expected, in a costume altogether similar to my own; wearing a Spanish cloak of blue velvet, begirt about the waist with a crimson belt sustaining a rapier. A mask of black silk entirely covered his face.

'Scoundrel!' I said, in a voice husky with rage, while every syllable I uttered seemed as new fuel to my fury, 'scoundrel! impostor! accursed villain! you shall not – you *shall not* dog me unto death! Follow me, or I stab you where you stand!' – and I broke my way from the ball-room into a small ante-chamber adjoining – dragging him unresistingly with me as I went.

Upon entering, I thrust him furiously from me. He staggered against the wall, while I closed the door with an oath, and commanded him to draw. He hesitated but for an instant; then, with a slight sigh, drew in silence, and put himself upon his defence.

The contest was brief indeed. I was frantic with every species of wild excitement, and felt within my single arm the energy and power of a multitude. In a few seconds I forced him by sheer strength against the wainscoting, and thus, getting him at mercy, plunged my sword, with brute ferocity, repeatedly through and through his bosom.

At that instant some person tried the latch of the door. I hastened to prevent an intrusion, and then immediately returned to my dying antagonist. But what human language can adequately portray *that* astonishment, *that* horror which possessed me at the spectacle then presented to view? The brief moment in which I averted my eyes had been sufficient to produce, apparently, a material change in the arrangements at the upper or farther end of the room. A large mirror, – so at first it seemed to me in my confusion – now stood where none had been perceptible before; and, as I stepped up to it in extremity of terror, mine own image, but with features all pale and dabbled in blood, advanced to meet me with a feeble and tottering gait.

Thus it appeared, I say, but was not. It was my antagonist – it was Wilson, who then stood before me in the agonies of his dissolution. His mask and cloak lay, where he had thrown them, upon the floor. Not a thread in all his raiment – not a line in all the marked and singular lineaments of his face which was not, even in the most absolute identity, *mine own!*

It was Wilson; but he spoke no longer in a whisper, and I could have fancied that I myself was speaking while he said:

'You have conquered, and I yield. Yet, henceforward art thou also dead – dead to the World, to Heaven and to Hope! In me didst thou exist – and, in my death, see by this image, which is thine own, how utterly thou hast murdered thyself.'

The Man of the Crowd

Ce grand malheur, de ne pouvoir être seul.
LA BRUYÈRE[1]

IT was well said of a certain German book that '*es lässt sich nicht lesen*' – it does not permit itself to be read. There are some secrets which do not permit themselves to be told. Men die nightly in their beds, wringing the hands of ghostly confessors, and looking them piteously in the eyes – die with despair of heart and convulsion of throat, on account of the hideousness of mysteries which will not *suffer themselves* to be revealed. Now and then, alas, the conscience of man takes up a burthen so heavy in horror that it can be thrown down only into the grave. And thus the essence of all crime is undivulged.

Not long ago, about the closing in of an evening in autumn, I sat at the large bow window of the D— Coffee-House in London. For some months I had been ill in health, but was now convalescent, and, with returning strength, found myself in one of those happy moods which are so precisely the converse of *ennui* – moods of the keenest appetency, when the film from the mental vision departs – the ἀχλὺς ἣ πρὶν ἐπῆεν – and the intellect, electrified, surpasses as greatly its everyday condition, as does the vivid yet candid reason of Leibnitz, the mad and flimsy rhetoric of Gorgias. Merely to breathe was enjoyment; and I derived positive pleasure even from many of the legitimate sources of pain. I felt a calm but inquisitive interest in every thing. With a cigar in my mouth and a newspaper in my lap, I had been amusing myself for the greater part of the afternoon, now in poring over advertisements, now in observing the promiscuous company in the room, and now in peering through the smoky panes into the street.

This latter is one of the principal thoroughfares of the city,

179

and had been very much crowded during the whole day. But, as the darkness came on, the throng momently increased; and, by the time the lamps were well lighted, two dense and continuous tides of population were rushing past the door. At this particular period of the evening I had never before been in a similar situation, and the tumultuous sea of human heads filled me, therefore, with a delicious novelty of emotion. I gave up, at length, all care of things within the hotel, and became absorbed in contemplation of the scene without.

At first my observations took an abstract and generalizing turn. I looked at the passengers in masses, and thought of them in their aggregate relations. Soon, however, I descended to details, and regarded with minute interest the innumerable varieties of figure, dress, air, gait, visage, and expression of countenance.

By far the greater number of those who went by had a satisfied business-like demeanor, and seemed to be thinking only of making their way through the press. Their brows were knit, and their eyes rolled quickly; when pushed against by fellow-wayfarers they evinced no symptom of impatience, but adjusted their clothes and hurried on. Others, still a numerous class, were restless in their movements, had flushed faces, and talked and gesticulated to themselves, as if feeling in solitude on account of the very denseness of the company around. When impeded in their progress, these people suddenly ceased muttering, but redoubled their gesticulations, and awaited, with an absent and overdone smile upon the lips, the course of the persons impeding them. If jostled, they bowed profusely to the jostlers, and appeared overwhelmed with confusion. – There was nothing very distinctive about these two large classes beyond what I have noted. Their habiliments belonged to that order which is pointedly termed the decent. They were undoubtedly noblemen, merchants, attorneys, tradesmen, stock-jobbers – the Eupatrids and the common-places of society – men of leisure and men actively engaged in affairs of their own – conducting business upon their own responsibility. They did not greatly excite my attention.

The tribe of clerks was an obvious one; and here I discerned two remarkable divisions. There were the junior clerks of flash houses – young gentlemen with tight coats, bright boots, well-oiled hair, and supercilious lips. Setting aside a certain dapperness of carriage, which may be termed *deskism* for want of a better word, the manner of these persons seemed to me an exact fac-simile of what had been the perfection of *bon ton* about twelve or eighteen months before. They wore the cast-off graces of the gentry; – and this, I believe, involves the best definition of the class.

The division of the upper clerks of staunch firms, or of the 'steady old fellows,' it was not possible to mistake. These were known by their coats and pantaloons of black or brown, made to sit comfortably, with white cravats and waistcoats, broad solid-looking shoes, and thick hose or gaiters. – They had all slightly bald heads, from which the right ears, long used to pen-holding, had an odd habit of standing off on end. I observed that they always removed or settled their hats with both hands, and wore watches, with short gold chains of a substantial and ancient pattern. Theirs was the affectation of respectability; – if indeed there be an affectation so honorable.

There were many individuals of dashing appearance, whom I easily understood as belonging to the race of swell pick-pockets, with which all great cities are infested. I watched these gentry with much inquisitiveness, and found it difficult to imagine how they should ever be mistaken for gentlemen by gentlemen themselves. Their voluminousness of wristband, with an air of excessive frankness, should betray them at once.

The gamblers, of whom I descried not a few, were still more easily recognisable. They wore every variety of dress, from that of the desperate thimble-rig bully, with velvet waistcoat, fancy neckerchief, gilt chains, and filagreed buttons, to that of the scrupulously inornate clergyman than which nothing could be less liable to suspicion. Still all were distinguished by a certain sodden swarthiness of complexion, a filmy dimness of eye, and pallor and compression of lip. There were two other traits, moreover, by which I could always detect them; – a guarded lowness of tone in conversation, and a more than ordinary extension of the thumb in a direction at right angles with the fingers. – Very often, in company with these sharpers, I observed an order of men somewhat different in habits, but still birds of a kindred feather. They may be defined as the gentlemen who live by their wits. They seem to prey upon the public in two battalions – that of the dandies and that of the military men. Of the first grade the leading features are long locks and smiles; of the second frogged coats and frowns.

Descending in the scale of what is termed gentility, I found darker and deeper themes for speculation. I saw Jew pedlars, with hawk eyes flashing from countenances whose every other feature wore only an expression of abject humility; sturdy professional street beggars scowling upon mendicants of a better stamp, whom despair alone had driven forth into the night for charity; feeble and ghastly invalids, upon whom death had placed a sure hand, and who sidled and tottered through the mob, looking every one beseechingly in the face, as if in search of some chance consolation, some lost hope; modest young girls returning from long and late labor to a cheerless home, and shrinking more tearfully than indignantly from the glances of ruffians, whose direct contact, even, could not be avoided; women of the town of all kinds and of all ages – the unequivocal beauty in the prime of her womanhood, putting one in mind of the statue in Lucian, with the surface of Parian marble, and the interior filled with filth – the loathsome and utterly lost leper in rags – the wrinkled, bejewelled and paint-begrimed beldame, making a last effort at youth – the mere child of immature form, yet, from long association, an adept in the dreadful coquetries of her trade, and burning with a rabid ambition to be ranked the equal of her elders in vice; drunkards innumerable and indescribable – some in shreds and patches, reeling, inarticulate, with bruised visage and lack-lustre eyes – some in whole although filthy garments, with a slightly unsteady swagger, thick sensual lips, and hearty-looking rubicund faces – others clothed in materials which had once been good, and which even now were scrupulously well brushed – men who walked with a more than naturally firm and springy step, but whose countenances were fearfully pale, whose eyes hideously wild and red, and who clutched with quivering fingers, as they strode through the crowd, at every object which came within their reach; beside these, pie-men, porters, coal-heavers, sweeps; organ-grinders, monkey-exhibiters and ballad mongers, those who vended with those who sang; ragged artizans and exhausted laborers of every description, and all full of a noisy and inordinate vivacity which jarred discordantly upon the ear, and gave an aching sensation to the eye.

As the night deepened, so deepened to me the interest of the scene; for not only did the general character of the crowd materially alter (its gentler features retiring in the gradual withdrawal of the more orderly portion of the people, and its harsher ones coming out into bolder relief, as the late hour brought forth every species of infamy from its den,) but the rays of the gas-lamps, feeble at first in their struggle with the dying day, had now at length gained ascendancy, and threw over every thing a fitful and garish lustre. All was dark yet splendid – as that ebony to which has been likened the style of Tertullian.

The wild effects of the light enchained me to an examination of individual faces; and although the rapidity with which the world of light flitted before the window, prevented me from casting more than a glance upon each visage, still it seemed that, in my then peculiar mental state, I could frequently read, even in that brief interval of a glance, the history of long years.

With my brow to the glass, I was thus occupied in scrutinizing the mob, when suddenly there came into view a countenance (that of a decrepid old man, some sixty-five or seventy years of age,) – a countenance which at once arrested and absorbed my whole attention, on account of the absolute idiosyncrasy of its expression. Any thing even remotely resembling that expression I had never seen before. I well remember that my first thought, upon beholding it, was that Retzsch, had he viewed it, would have greatly preferred it to his own pictural incarnations of the fiend. As I endeavored, during the brief minute of my original survey, to form some analysis of the meaning conveyed, there arose confusedly and paradoxically within my mind, the ideas of vast mental power, of caution, of penuriousness, of avarice, of coolness, of malice, of blood-thirstiness, of triumph, of merriment, of excessive terror, of intense – of extreme despair. I felt singularly aroused, startled, fascinated. 'How wild a history,' I said to myself, 'is written within that bosom!' Then came a craving desire to keep the man in view – to know more of him. Hurriedly putting on an overcoat, and seizing my hat and cane, I made my way into the street, and pushed through the crowd in the direction which I had seen him take; for he had already disappeared. With some little difficulty I at length came within sight of him, approached, and followed him closely, yet cautiously, so as not to attract his attention.

I had now a good opportunity of examining his person. He was short in stature, very thin, and apparently very feeble. His clothes, generally, were filthy and ragged; but as he came, now and then, within the strong glare of a lamp, I perceived that his linen, although dirty, was of beautiful texture; and my vision deceived me, or, through a rent in a closely-buttoned and evidently second-handed *roquelaire* which enveloped him, I caught a glimpse both of a diamond and of a dagger. These observations heightened my curiosity, and I resolved to follow the stranger whithersoever he should go.

It was now fully night-fall, and a thick humid fog hung over the city, soon ending in a settled and heavy rain. This change of weather had an odd effect upon the crowd, the whole of which was at once put into new commotion, and overshadowed by a world of umbrellas. The waver, the jostle, and the hum increased in a tenfold degree. For my own part I did not much regard the rain – the lurking of an old fever in my system rendering the moisture somewhat too dangerously pleasant. Tying a handkerchief about my mouth, I kept on. For half an hour the old man held his way with difficulty along the great thoroughfare; and I here walked close at his elbow through fear of losing sight of him. Never once turning his head to look back, he did not observe me. By and bye he passed into a cross street, which, although densely filled with people, was not quite so much thronged as the main one he had quitted. Here a change in his demeanor became evident. He walked more slowly and with less object than before –

more hesitatingly. He crossed and re-crossed the way repeatedly without apparent aim; and the press was still so thick, that, at every such movement, I was obliged to follow him closely. The street was a narrow and long one, and his course lay within it for nearly an hour, during which the passengers had gradually diminished to about that number which is ordinarily seen at noon in Broadway near the Park – so vast a difference is there between a London populace and that of the most frequented American city. A second turn brought us into a square, brilliantly lighted, and overflowing with life. The old manner of the stranger re-appeared. His chin fell upon his breast, while his eyes rolled wildly from under his knit brows, in every direction, upon those who hemmed him in. He urged his way steadily and perseveringly. I was surprised, however, to find, upon his having made the circuit of the square, that he turned and retraced his steps. Still more was I astonished to see him repeat the same walk several times – once nearly detecting me as he came round with a sudden movement.

In this exercise he spent another hour, at the end of which we met with far less interruption from passengers than at first. The rain fell fast; the air grew cool; and the people were retiring to their homes. With a gesture of impatience, the wanderer passed into a by-street comparatively deserted. Down this, some quarter of a mile long, he rushed with an activity I could not have dreamed of seeing in one so aged, and which put me to much trouble in pursuit. A few minutes brought us to a large and busy bazaar, with the localities of which the stranger appeared well acquainted, and where his original demeanor again became apparent, as he forced his way to and fro, without aim, among the host of buyers and sellers.

During the hour and a half, or thereabouts, which we passed in this place, it required much caution on my part to keep him within reach without attracting his observation. Luckily I wore a pair of caoutchouc over-shoes, and could move about in perfect silence. At no moment did he see that I watched him. He entered shop after shop, priced nothing, spoke no word, and looked at all objects with a wild and vacant stare. I was now utterly amazed at his behaviour, and firmly resolved that we should not part until I had satisfied myself in some measure respecting him.

A loud-toned clock struck eleven, and the company were fast deserting the bazaar. A shop-keeper, in putting up a shutter, jostled the old man, and at the instant I saw a strong shudder come over his frame. He hurried into the street, looked anxiously around him for an instant, and then ran with incredible swiftness through many crooked and people-less lanes, until we emerged once more upon the great thoroughfare whence we had started – the street of the D— Hotel. It no longer wore, however, the same aspect. It was still brilliant with gas; but the rain fell fiercely, and there were few persons to be seen. The stranger grew pale. He walked moodily some paces up the once populous avenue, then, with a heavy sigh, turned in the direction of the river, and, plunging through a great variety of devious ways, came out, at length, in view of one of the principal theatres. It was about being closed, and the audience were thronging from the doors. I saw the old man gasp as if for breath while he threw himself amid the crowd; but I thought that the intense agony of his countenance had, in some measure, abated. His head again fell upon his breast; he appeared as I had seen him at first. I observed that he now took the course in which had gone the greater number of the audience – but, upon the whole, I was at a loss to comprehend the waywardness of his actions.

As he proceeded, the company grew more scattered, and his old uneasiness and vacillation were resumed. For some time he followed closely a party of some ten or twelve roisterers; but from this number one by one dropped off, until three only remained together, in a narrow and gloomy lane little frequented. The stranger paused, and, for a moment, seemed lost in thought; then, with every mark of agitation, pursued rapidly a route which brought us to the verge of the city, amid regions very different from those we had hitherto traversed. It was the most noisome quarter of London, where everything wore the worst impress of the most deplorable poverty, and of the most desperate crime. By the dim light of an accidental lamp, tall, antique, worm-eaten, wooden tenements were seen tottering to their fall, in directions so many and capricious that scarce the semblance of a passage was discernible between them. The paving-stones lay at random, displaced from their beds by the rankly growing grass. Horrible filth festered in the dammed-up gutters. The whole atmosphere teemed with desolation. Yet, as we proceeded, the sounds of human life revived by sure degrees, and at length large bands of the most abandoned of a London populace were seen reeling to and fro. The spirits of the old man again flickered up, as a lamp which is near its death-hour. Once more he strode onward with elastic tread. Suddenly a corner was turned, a blaze of light burst upon our sight, and we stood before one of the huge suburban temples of Intemperance – one of the palaces of the fiend, Gin.

It was now nearly day-break; but a number of wretched inebriates still pressed in and out of the flaunting entrance. With a half shriek of joy the old man forced a passage within, resumed at once his original bearing, and stalked backward and forward, without apparent object, among the throng. He had not been thus long occupied, however, before a rush to the doors gave token that the host was closing them for the night. It was something even more intense than despair that I then observed upon the countenance of the singular being whom I had watched so pertinaciously. Yet he did not hesitate in his career, but, with a mad energy, retraced his steps at once, to the heart of the mighty London. Long and swiftly he fled, while I followed him in the wildest amazement, resolute not to abandon a scrutiny in which I now felt an interest all-absorbing. The sun arose while we proceeded, and, when we had once again reached that most thronged mart of the populous town, the street of the D— Hotel, it presented an appearance of human bustle and activity scarcely inferior to what I had seen on the evening before. And here, long, amid the momently increasing confusion, did I persist in my pursuit of the stranger. But, as usual, he walked to and fro, and during the day did not pass from out the turmoil of that street. And, as the shades of the second evening came on, I grew wearied unto death, and, stopping fully in front of the wanderer, gazed at him steadfastly in the face. He noticed me not, but resumed his solemn walk, while I, ceasing to follow, remained absorbed in contemplation. 'This old man,' I said at length, 'is the type and the genius of deep crime. He refuses to be alone. *He is the man of the crowd.* It will be in vain to follow; for I shall learn no more of him, nor of his deeds. The worst heart of the world is a grosser book than the "Hortulus Animæ,"[2] and perhaps it is but one of the great mercies of God that *es lässt sich nicht lesen.*'

The Murders in the Rue Morgue

What song the Syrens sang, or what name Achilles
assumed when he hid himself among women, although puzzling questions are not beyond *all*
conjecture.

SIR THOMAS BROWNE, *Urn-Burial*

THE mental features discoursed of as the analytical, are, in
themselves, but little susceptible of analysis. We appreciate them
only in their effects. We know of them, among other things, that
they are always to their possessor, when inordinately possessed, a
source of the liveliest enjoyment. As the strong man exults in his
physical ability, delighting in such exercises as call his muscles
into action, so glories the analyst in that moral activity which
disentangles. He derives pleasure from even the most trivial
occupations bringing his talents into play. He is fond of enigmas,
of conundrums, of hieroglyphics; exhibiting in his solutions of
each a degree of *acumen* which appears to the ordinary apprehension preternatural. His results, brought about by the very
soul and essence of method, have, in truth, the whole air of
intuition. The faculty of re-solution is possibly much invigorated
by mathematical study, and especially by that highest branch of
it which, unjustly, and merely on account of its retrograde operations, has been called, as if *par excellence*, analysis. Yet to calculate is not in itself to analyze. A chess-player, for example,
does the one without effort at the other. It follows that the game
of chess, in its effects upon mental character, is greatly misunderstood. I am not now writing a treatise, but simply prefac-
ing a somewhat peculiar narrative by observations very much at
random; I will, therefore, take occasion to assert that the higher
powers of the reflective intellect are more decidedly and more
usefully tasked by the unostentatious game of draughts than by
all the elaborate frivolity of chess. In this latter, where the pieces

have different and *bizarre* motions, with various and variable values, what is only complex is mistaken (a not unusual error) for what is profound. The *attention* is here called powerfully into play. If it flag for an instant, an oversight is committed, resulting in injury or defeat. The possible moves being not only manifold but involute, the chances of such oversights are multiplied; and in nine cases out of ten it is the more concentrative rather than the more acute player who conquers. In draughts, on the contrary, where the moves are *unique* and have but little variation, the probabilities of inadvertence are diminished, and the mere attention being left comparatively unemployed, what advantages are obtained by either party are obtained by superior *acumen*. To be less abstract – Let us suppose a game of draughts where the pieces are reduced to four kings, and where, of course, no oversight is to be expected. It is obvious that here the victory can be decided (the players being at all equal) only by some *recherché* movement, the result of some strong exertion of the intellect. Deprived of ordinary resources, the analyst throws himself into the spirit of his opponent, identifies himself therewith, and not unfrequently sees thus, at a glance, the sole methods (sometimes indeed absurdly simple ones) by which he may seduce into error or hurry into miscalculation.

Whist has long been noted for its influence upon what is termed the calculating power; and men of the highest order of intellect have been known to take an apparently unaccountable delight in it, while eschewing chess as frivolous. Beyond doubt there is nothing of a similar nature so greatly tasking the faculty of analysis. The best chess-player in Christendom *may* be little more than the best player of chess; but proficiency in whist implies capacity for success in all these more important undertakings where mind struggles with mind. When I say proficiency, I mean that perfection in the game which includes a comprehension of *all* the sources whence legitimate advantage may be derived. These are not only manifold but multiform, and lie frequently among recesses of thought altogether inaccessible to the ordinary understanding. To observe attentively is to remember distinctly;

and, so far, the concentrative chess-player will do very well at whist; while the rules of Hoyle (themselves based upon the mere mechanism of the game) are sufficiently and generally comprehensible. Thus to have a retentive memory, and to proceed by 'the book,' are points commonly regarded as the sum total of good playing. But it is in matters beyond the limits of mere rule that the skill of the analyst is evinced. He makes, in silence, a host of observations and inferences. So, perhaps, do his companions; and the difference in the extent of the information obtained, lies not so much in the validity of the inference as in the quality of the observation. The necessary knowledge is that of *what* to observe. Our player confines himself not at all; nor, because the game is the object, does he reject deductions from things external to the game. He examines the countenance of his partner, comparing it carefully with that of each of his opponents. He considers the mode of assorting the cards in each hand; often counting trump by trump, and honor by honor, through the glances bestowed by their holders upon each. He notes every variation of face as the play progresses, gathering a fund of thought from the differences in the expression of certainty, of surprise, of triumph, or chagrin. From the manner of gathering up a trick he judges whether the person taking it can make another in the suit. He recognizes what is played through feint, by the air with which it is thrown upon the table. A casual or inadvertent word; the accidental dropping or turning of a card, with the accompanying anxiety or carelessness in regard to its concealment; the counting of the tricks, with the order of their arrangement; embarrassment, hesitation, eagerness or trepidation – all afford, to his apparently intuitive perception, indications of the true state of affairs. The first two or three rounds having been played, he is in full possession of the contents of each hand, and thenceforward puts down his cards with as absolute a precision of purpose as if the rest of the party had turned outward the faces of their own.

The analytical power should not be confounded with simple ingenuity; for while the analyst is necessarily ingenious, the ingenious man is often remarkably incapable of analysis. The constructive or combining power, by which ingenuity is usually manifested, and to which the phrenologists (I believe erroneously) have assigned a separate organ, supposing it a primitive faculty, has been so frequently seen in those whose intellect bordered otherwise upon idiocy, as to have attracted general observation among writers on morals. Between ingenuity and the analytic ability there exists a difference far greater, indeed, than that between the fancy and the imagination, but of a character very strictly analogous. It will be found, in fact, that the ingenious are always fanciful, and the *truly* imaginative never otherwise than analytic.

The narrative which follows will appear to the reader somewhat in the light of a commentary upon the propositions just advanced.

Residing in Paris during the spring and part of the summer of 18—, I there became acquainted with a Monsieur C. Auguste Dupin. This young gentleman was of an excellent – indeed of an illustrious family, but, by a variety of untoward events, had been reduced to such poverty that the energy of his character succumbed beneath it, and he ceased to bestir himself in the world, or to care for the retrieval of his fortunes. By courtesy of his creditors, there still remained in his possession a small remnant of his patrimony; and, upon the income arising from this, he managed, by means of a rigorous economy, to procure the necessaries of life, without troubling himself about its superfluities. Books, indeed, were his sole luxuries, and in Paris these are easily obtained.

Our first meeting was at an obscure library in the Rue Montmartre, where the accident of our both being in search of the same very rare and very remarkable volume, brought us into closer communion. We saw each other again and again. I was deeply interested in the little family history which he detailed to me with all that candor which a Frenchman indulges whenever mere self is the theme. I was astonished, too, at the vast extent of his reading; and, above all, I felt my soul enkindled within me by the wild fervor, and the vivid freshness of his imagination. Seeking in Paris the objects I then sought, I felt that the society of such a man would be to me a treasure beyond price; and this feeling I frankly confided to him. It was at length arranged that we should live together during my stay in the city; and as my worldly circumstances were somewhat less embarrassed than his own, I was permitted to be at the expense of renting, and furnishing in a style which suited the rather fantastic gloom of our common temper, a time-eaten and grotesque mansion, long deserted through superstitions into which we did not inquire, and tottering to its fall in a retired and desolate portion of the Faubourg St Germain.

Had the routine of our life at this place been known to the world, we should have been regarded as madmen – although, perhaps, as madmen of a harmless nature. Our seclusion was perfect. We admitted no visitors. Indeed the locality of our retirement had been carefully kept a secret from my own former associates; and it had been many years since Dupin had ceased to know or be known in Paris. We existed within ourselves alone.

It was a freak of fancy in my friend (for what else shall I call it?) to be enamored of the Night for her own sake; and into this *bizarrerie*, as into all his others, I quietly fell; giving myself up to his wild whims with a perfect *abandon*. The sable divinity would not herself dwell with us always; but we could counterfeit her presence. At the first dawn of the morning we closed all the massy shutters of our old building; lighted a couple of tapers which, strongly perfumed, threw out only the ghastliest and feeblest of rays. By the aid of these we then busied our souls in dreams – reading, writing, or conversing, until warned by the clock of the advent of the true Darkness. Then we sallied forth into the streets, arm and arm, continuing the topics of the day, or roaming far and wide until a late hour, seeking, amid the wild lights and shadows of the populous city, that infinity of mental excitement which quiet observation can afford.

At such times I could not help remarking and admiring (although from his rich ideality I had been prepared to expect it) a peculiar analytical ability in Dupin. He seemed, too, to take an eager delight in its exercise – if not exactly in its display – and did not hesitate to confess the pleasure thus derived. He boasted to me, with a low chuckling laugh, that most men, in respect to himself, wore windows in their bosoms, and was wont to follow up such assertions by direct and very startling proofs of his intimate knowledge of my own. His manner at these moments was frigid and abstract; his eyes were vacant in expression; while his voice, usually a rich tenor, rose into a treble which would have sounded petulantly but for the deliberateness and entire distinctness of the enunciation. Observing him in these moods, I often dwelt meditatively upon the old philosophy of the Bi-Part Soul, and amused myself with the fancy of a double Dupin – the creative and the resolvent.

Let it not be supposed, from what I have just said, that I am detailing any mystery, or penning any romance. What I have described in the Frenchman, was merely the result of an excited, or perhaps of a diseased intelligence. But of the character of his remarks at the periods in question an example will best convey the idea.

We were strolling one night down a long dirty street, in the vicinity of the Palais Royal Being both, apparently, occupied with thought, neither of us had spoken a syllable for fifteen minutes at least. All at once Dupin broke forth with these words : –

'He is a very little fellow, that's true, and would do better for the *Théâtre des Variétés.*'

'There can be no doubt of that,' I replied unwittingly, and not at first observing (so much had I been absorbed in reflection) the extraordinary manner in which the speaker had chimed in with my meditations. In an instant afterward I recollected myself, and my astonishment was profound.

'Dupin,' said I, gravely, 'this is beyond my comprehension. I do not hesitate to say that I am amazed, and can scarcely credit my senses. How was it possible you should know I was thinking of – ?' Here I paused, to ascertain beyond a doubt whether he really knew of whom I thought.

– 'of Chantilly,' said he, 'why do you pause? You were remarking to yourself that his diminutive figure unfitted him for tragedy.'

This was precisely what had formed the subject of my reflections. Chantilly was a *quondam* cobbler of the Rue St Denis, who, becoming stage-mad, had attempted the *rôle* of Xerxes, in Crébillon's tragedy so called, and been notoriously Pasquinaded for his pains.

'Tell me, for Heaven's sake,' I exclaimed, 'the method – if method there is – by which you have been enabled to fathom my soul in this matter.' In fact I was even more startled than I would have been willing to express.

'It was the fruiterer,' replied my friend, 'who brought you to the conclusion that the mender of soles was not of sufficient height for Xerxes *et id genus omne.*'

'The fruiterer ! – you astonish me – I know no fruiterer whomsoever.'

'The man who ran up against you as we entered the street – it may have been fifteen minutes ago.'

I now remembered that, in fact, a fruiterer, carrying upon his head a large basket of apples, had nearly thrown me down, by accident, as we passed from the Rue C— into the thoroughfare where we stood; but what this had to do with Chantilly I could not possibly understand.

There was not a particle of *charlatanerie* about Dupin. 'I will explain,' he said, 'and that you may comprehend all clearly, we will first retrace the course of your meditations, from the moment in which I spoke to you until that of the *rencontre* with the fruiterer in question. The larger links of the chain run thus – Chantilly, Orion, Dr Nichols, Epicurus, Stereotomy, the street stones, the fruiterer.'

There are few persons who have not, at some period of their lives, amused themselves in retracing the steps by which particular conclusions of their own minds have been attained. The occupation is often full of interest; and he who attempts it for the first time is astonished by the apparently illimitable distance and incoherence between the starting-point and the goal. What, then, must have been my amazement when I heard the Frenchman speak what he had just spoken, and when I could not help acknowledging that he had spoken the truth. He continued :

'We had been talking of horses, if I remember aright, just before leaving the Rue C—. This was the last subject we discussed. As we crossed into this street, a fruiterer, with a large basket upon his head, brushing quickly past us, thrust you upon a pile of paving-stones collected at a spot where the causeway is undergoing repair. You stepped upon one of the loose fragments, slipped, slightly strained your ankle, appeared vexed or sulky, muttered a few words, turned to look at the pile, and then proceeded in silence. I was not particularly attentive to what you did; but observation has become with me, of late, a species of necessity.

'You kept your eyes upon the ground – glancing, with a petulant expression, at the holes and ruts in the pavement, (so that I saw you were still thinking of the stones,) until we reached the little alley called Lamartine, which has been paved, by way of experiment, with the overlapping and riveted blocks. Here your countenance brightened up, and, perceiving your lips move, I could not doubt that you murmured the word 'stereotomy,' a term very affectedly applied to this species of pavement. I knew that you could not say to yourself 'stereotomy' without being brought to think of atomies, and thus of the theories of Epicurus; and since, when we discussed this subject not very long ago, I mentioned to you how singularly, yet with how little notice, the vague guesses of that noble Greek had met with confirmation in the late nebular cosmogony, I felt that you could not avoid casting your eyes upward to the great *nebula* in Orion, and I certainly expected that you would do so. You did look up; and I was now assured that I had correctly followed your steps. But in that bitter *tirade* upon Chantilly, which appeared in yesterday's '*Musée*,' the satirist, making some disgraceful allusions to the cobbler's change of name upon assuming the buskin, quoted a Latin line about which we have often conversed. I mean the line

Perdidit antiquum litera prima sonum.[1]

I had told you that this was in reference to Orion, formerly written Urion; and, from certain pungencies connected with this explanation, I was aware that you could not have forgotten it. It was clear, therefore, that you would not fail to combine the two ideas of Orion and Chantilly. That you did combine them I saw by the character of the smile which passed over your lips. You thought of the poor cobbler's immolation. So far, you had been stooping in your gait; but now I saw you draw yourself up to your full height. I was then sure that you reflected upon the diminutive figure of Chantilly. At this point I interrupted your meditations to remark that as, in fact, he *was* a very little fellow – that Chantilly – he would do better at the *Théâtre des Variétés*.'

Not long after this, we were looking over an evening edition of the 'Gazette des Tribunaux,' when the following paragraphs arrested our attention.

'EXTRAORDINARY MURDERS. – This morning, about three o'clock, the inhabitants of the Quartier St Roch were aroused from sleep by a succession of terrific shrieks, issuing, apparently, from the fourth story of a house in the Rue Morgue, known to be in the sole occupancy of one Madame L'Espanaye, and her daughter, Mademoiselle Camille L'Espanaye. After some delay, occasioned by a fruitless attempt to procure admission in the usual manner, the gateway was broken in with a crowbar, and eight or ten of the neighbors entered, accompanied by two *gendarmes*. By this time the cries had ceased; but, as the party rushed up the first flight of stairs, two or more rough voices, in angry contention, were distinguished, and seemed to proceed from the upper part of the house. As the second landing was reached, these sounds, also, had ceased, and everything remained perfectly quiet. The party spread themselves, and hurried from room to room. Upon arriving at a large back chamber in the fourth story, (the door of which, being found locked, with the key inside, was forced open,) a spectacle presented itself which struck every one present not less with horror than with astonishment.

'The apartment was in the wildest disorder – the furniture broken and thrown about in all directions. There was only one bedstead; and from this the bed had been removed, and thrown into the middle of the floor. On a chair lay a razor, besmeared with blood. On the hearth were two or three long and thick tresses of grey human hair, also dabbled in blood, and seeming to have been pulled out by the roots. Upon the floor were found four Napoleons, an ear-ring of topaz, three large silver spoons, three smaller of *métal d'Alger*, and two bags, containing nearly four thousand francs in gold. The drawers of a *bureau*, which stood in one corner, were open, and had been, apparently, rifled, although many articles still remained in them. A small iron safe was discovered under the *bed* (not under the bedstead). It was open, with the key still in the door. It had no contents beyond a few old letters, and other papers of little consequence.

'Of Madame L'Espanaye no traces were here seen; but an unusual quantity of soot being observed in the fire-place, a search was made in the chimney, and (horrible to relate!) the corpse of the daughter, head downward, was dragged therefrom; it having been thus forced up the narrow aperture for a considerable distance. The body was quite warm. Upon examining it, many excoriations were perceived, no doubt occasioned by the violence with which it had been thrust up and disengaged. Upon the face were many severe scratches, and, upon the throat, dark bruises, and deep indentations of finger nails, as if the deceased had been throttled to death.

'After a thorough investigation of every portion of the house, without farther discovery, the party made its way into a small paved yard in the rear of the building, where lay the corpse of the old lady, with her throat so entirely cut that, upon an attempt to raise her, the head fell off. The body, as well as the head, was fearfully mutilated – the former so much so as scarcely to retain any semblance of humanity.

'To this horrible mystery there is not as yet, we believe, the slightest clew.'

The next day's paper had these additional particulars.

'*The Tragedy of the Rue Morgue*. Many individuals have been examined in relation to this most extraordinary and frightful affair.' [The word *'affaire'* has not yet, in France, that levity of import which it conveys with us,] 'but nothing whatever has transpired to throw light upon it. We give below all the material testimony elicited.

'*Pauline Dubourg*, laundress, deposes that she has known both the deceased for three years, having washed for them during that period. The old lady and her daughter seemed on good terms – very affectionate towards each other. They were excellent pay. Could not speak in regard to their mode or means of living. Believed that Madame L. told fortunes for a living. Was reputed to have money put by. Never met any persons in the house when she called for the clothes or took them home. Was sure that they had no servant in employ. There appeared to be no furniture in any part of the building except in the fourth story.

'*Pierre Moreau*, tobacconist, deposes that he has been in the habit of selling small quantities of tobacco and snuff to Madame L'Espanaye for nearly four years. Was born in the neighborhood, and has always resided there. The deceased and her daughter had occupied the house in which the corpses were found, for more than six years. It was formerly occupied by a jeweller, who underlet the upper rooms to various persons. The house was the property of Madame L. She became dissatisfied with the abuse of the premises by her tenant, and moved into them herself, refusing to let any portion. The old lady was childish. Witness had seen the daughter some five or six times during the six years. The two lived an exceedingly retired life – were reputed to have money. Had heard it said among the neighbors that Madame L. told fortunes – did not believe it. Had never seen any person enter the door except the old lady and her daughter, a porter once or twice, and a physician some eight or ten times.

'Many other persons, neighbors, gave evidence to the same effect. No one was spoken of as frequenting the house. It was not known whether there were any living connexions of Madame L. and her daughter. The shutters of the front windows were seldom opened. Those in the rear were always closed, with the exception of the large back room, fourth story. The house was a good house – not very old.

'*Isidore Muset*, *gendarme*, deposes that he was called to the house about three o'clock in the morning, and found some twenty or thirty persons at the gateway, endeavoring to gain admittance. Forced it open, at length, with a bayonet – not with a crowbar. Had but little difficulty in getting it open, on account of its being a double or folding gate, and bolted neither at bottom nor top. The shrieks were continued until the gate was forced – and then suddenly ceased. They seemed to be screams of some person (or persons) in great agony – were loud and drawn out, not short and quick. Witness led the way up stairs. Upon reaching the first landing, heard two voices in loud and angry contention – the one a gruff voice, the other much shriller – a very strange voice. Could distinguish some words of the former, which was that of a Frenchman. Was positive that it was not a woman's voice. Could distinguish the words 'sacré' and 'diable.' The shrill voice was that of a foreigner. Could not be sure whether it was the voice of a man or of a woman. Could not make out what was said, but believed the language to be Spanish. The state of the room and of the bodies was described by this witness as we described them yesterday.

'Henri Duval, a neighbor, and by trade a silversmith, deposes that he was one of the party who first entered the house. Corroborates the testimony of Musèt in general. As soon as they forced an entrance, they reclosed the door, to keep out the crowd, which collected very fast, notwithstanding the lateness of the hour. The shrill voice, the witness thinks, was that of an Italian. Was certain it was not French. Could not be sure that it was a man's voice. It might have been a woman's. Was not acquainted with the Italian language. Could not distinguish the words, but was convinced by the intonation that the speaker was an Italian. Knew Madame L. and her daughter. Had conversed with both frequently. Was sure that the shrill voice was not that of either of the deceased.

'— Odenheimer, restaurateur. This witness volunteered his testimony. Not speaking French, was examined through an interpreter. Is a native of Amsterdam. Was passing the house at the time of the shrieks. They lasted for several minutes – probably ten. They were long and loud – very awful and distressing. Was one of those who entered the building. Corroborated the previous evidence in every respect but one. Was sure that the shrill voice was that of a man – of a Frenchman. Could not distinguish the words uttered. They were loud and quick – unequal – spoken apparently in fear as well as in anger. The voice was harsh – not so much shrill as harsh. Could not call it a shrill voice. The gruff voice said repeatedly 'sacré,' 'diablé' and once 'mon Dieu.'

'Jules Mignaud, banker, of the firm of Mignaud et Fils, Rue Deloraine. Is the elder Mignaud. Madame L'Espanaye had some property. Had opened an account with his banking house in the spring of the year — (eight years previously). Made frequent deposits in small sums. Had checked for nothing until the third day before her death, when she took out in person the sum of 4,000 francs. This sum was paid in gold, and a clerk sent home with the money.

'Adolphe Le Bon, clerk to Mignaud et Fils, deposes that on the day in question, about noon, he accompanied Madame L'Espanaye to her residence with the 4,000 francs, put up in two bags. Upon the door being opened, Mademoiselle L. appeared and took from his hands one of the bags, while the old lady relieved him of the other. He then bowed and departed. Did not see any person in the street at the time. It is a bye-street – very lonely.

'William Bird, tailor, deposes that he was one of the party who entered the house. Is an Englishman. Has lived in Paris two years. Was one of the first to ascend the stairs. Heard the voices in contention. The gruff voice was that of a Frenchman. Could make out several words, but cannot now remember all. Heard distinctly 'sacré' and 'mon Dieu.' There was a sound at the moment as if of several persons struggling – a scraping and scuffling sound. The shrill voice was very loud – louder than the gruff one. Is sure that it was not the voice of an Englishman. Appeared to be that of a German. Might have been a woman's voice. Does not understand German.

'Four of the above-named witnesses, being recalled, deposed that the door of the chamber in which was found the body of Mademoiselle L. was locked on the inside when the party reached it. Every thing was perfectly silent – no groans or noises of any kind. Upon forcing the door no person was seen. The windows, both of the back and front room, were down and firmly fastened from within. A door between the two rooms was closed, but not locked. The door leading from the front room into the passage was locked, with the key on the inside. A small room in the front of the house, on the fourth story, at the head of the passage, was open, the door being ajar. This room was crowded with old beds, boxes, and so forth. These were carefully removed and searched. There was not an inch of any portion of the house which was not carefully searched. Sweeps were sent up and down the chimneys. The house was a four story one, with garrets (*mansardes*). A trapdoor on the roof was nailed down very securely – did not appear to have been opened for years. The time elapsing between the hearing of the voices in contention and the breaking open of the room door, was variously stated by the witnesses. Some made it as short as three minutes – some as long as five. The door was opened with difficulty.

'*Alfonzo Garcio*, undertaker, deposes that he resides in the Rue Morgue. Is a native of Spain. Was one of the party who entered the house. Did not proceed up stairs. Is nervous, and was apprehensive of the consequences of agitation. Heard the voices in contention. The gruff voice was that of a Frenchman. Could not distinguish what was said. The shrill voice was that of an Englishman – is sure of this. Does not understand the English language, but judges by the intonation.

'*Alberto Montani*, confectioner, deposes that he was among the first to ascend the stairs. Heard the voices in question. The gruff voice was that of a Frenchman. Distinguished several words. The speaker appeared to be expostulating. Could not make out the words of the shrill voice. Spoke quick and unevenly. Thinks it the voice of a Russian. Corroborates the general testimony. Is an Italian. Never conversed with a native of Russia.

'Several witnesses, recalled, here testified that the chimneys of all the rooms on the fourth story were too narrow to admit the passage of a human being. By "sweeps" were meant cylindrical sweeping-brushes, such as are employed by those who clean chimneys. These brushes were passed up and down every flue in the house. There is no back passage by which any one could have descended while the party proceeded up stairs. The body of Mademoiselle L'Espanaye was so firmly wedged in the chimney that it could not be got down until four or five of the party united their strength.

'*Paul Dumas*, physician, deposes that he was called to view the bodies about day-break. They were both then lying on the sacking of the bedstead in the chamber where Mademoiselle L. was found. The corpse of the young lady was much bruised and excoriated. The fact that it had been thrust up the chimney would sufficiently account for these appearances. The throat was greatly chafed. There were several deep scratches just below the chin, together with a series of livid spots which were evidently the impression of fingers. The face was fearfully discolored, and the eye-balls protruded. The tongue had been partially bitten through. A large bruise was discovered upon the pit of the stomach, produced, apparently, by the pressure of a knee. In the opinion of M. Dumas, Mademoiselle L'Espanaye had been throttled to death by some person or persons unknown. The corpse of the mother was horribly mutilated. All the bones of the right leg and arm were more or less shattered. The left *tibia* much splintered, as well as all the ribs of the left side. Whole body dreadfully bruised and discolored. It was not possible to say how the injuries had been inflicted. A heavy club of wood, or a broad bar of iron – a chair – any large, heavy, and obtuse weapon would have produced such results, if wielded by the hands of a very powerful man. No woman could have inflicted the blows with any weapon. The head of the deceased, when seen by witness, was entirely separated from the body, and was also greatly shattered. The throat had evidently been cut with some very sharp instrument – probably with a razor.

'*Alexandre Etienne*, surgeon, was called with M. Dumas to view the bodies. Corroborated the testimony, and the opinions of M. Dumas.

'Nothing farther of importance was elicited, although several other persons were examined. A murder so mysterious, and so perplexing in all its particulars, was never before committed in Paris – if indeed a murder has been committed at all. The police are entirely at fault – an unusual occurrence in affairs of this nature. There is not, however, the shadow of a clew apparent.'

The evening edition of the paper stated that the greatest excitement still continued in the Quartier St Roch – that the premises in question had been carefully re-searched, and fresh examinations of witnesses instituted, but all to no purpose. A postscript, however mentioned that Adolphe Le Bon had been arrested and imprisoned – although nothing appeared to criminate him, beyond the facts already detailed.

Dupin seemed singularly interested in the progress of this affair – at least so I judged from his manner, for he made no comments. It was only after the announcement that Le Bon had been imprisoned, that he asked me my opinion respecting the murders.

I could merely agree with all Paris in considering them an insoluble mystery. I saw no means by which it would be possible to trace the murderer.

'We must not judge of the means,' said Dupin, 'by this shell of an examination. The Parisian police, so much extolled for *acumen*, are cunning, but no more. There is no method in their proceedings, beyond the method of the moment. They make a vast parade of measures; but, not unfrequently, these are so ill adapted to the objects proposed, as to put us in mind of Monsieur Jourdain's calling for his *robe-de-chambre – pour mieux entendre la musique*. The results attained by them are not unfrequently surprising, but, for the most part, are brought about by simple diligence and activity. When these qualities are unavailing, their schemes fail. Vidocq, for example, was a good guesser, and a persevering man. But, without educated thought, he erred continually by the very intensity of his investigations. He impaired his vision by holding the object too close. He might see, perhaps, one or two points with unusual clearness, but in so doing he, necessarily, lost sight of the matter as a whole. Thus there is such a thing as being too profound. Truth is not always in a well. In fact, as regards the more important knowledge, I do believe that she is invariably superficial. The depth lies in the valleys where we seek her, and not upon the mountain-tops where she is found. The modes and sources of this kind of error are well typified in the contemplation of the heavenly bodies. To look at a star by glances – to view it in a side-long way, by turning toward it the exterior portions of the *retina* (more susceptible of feeble impressions of light than the interior), is to behold the star distinctly – is to have the best appreciation of its lustre – a lustre which grows dim just in proportion as we turn our vision *fully* upon it. A greater number of rays actually fall upon the eye in the latter case, but, in the former, there is the more refined capacity for comprehension. By undue profundity we perplex and enfeeble thought; and it is possible to make even Venus herself vanish from the firmament by a scrutiny too sustained, too concentrated, or too direct.

'As for these murders, let us enter into some examinations for ourselves, before we make up an opinion respecting them. An inquiry will afford us amusement,' [I thought this an odd term, so applied, but said nothing] 'and, besides, Le Bon once rendered me a service for which I am not ungrateful. We will go and see the premises with our own eyes. I know G—, the Prefect of Police, and shall have no difficulty in obtaining the necessary permission.'

The permission was obtained, and we proceeded at once to the Rue Morgue. This is one of those miserable thoroughfares which intervene between the Rue Richelieu and the Rue St Roch. It was late in the afternoon when we reached it; as this quarter is at a great distance from that in which we resided. The house was readily found; for there were still many persons gazing up at the closed shutters, with an objectless curiosity, from the opposite side of the way. It was an ordinary Parisian house, with a gateway, on one side of which was a glazed watch-box, with a sliding panel in the window, indicating a *loge de concierge*. Before going in we walked up the street, turned down an alley, and then, again turning, passed in the rear of the building – Dupin, meanwhile, examining the whole neighborhood, as well as the house, with a minuteness of attention for which I could see no possible object.

Retracing our steps, we came again to the front of the dwelling, rang, and, having shown our credentials, were admitted by the agents in charge. We went up stairs – into the chamber where the body of Mademoiselle L'Espanaye had been found, and where both the deceased still lay. The disorders of the room had, as usual, been suffered to exist. I saw nothing beyond what had been stated in the 'Gazette des Tribunaux.' Dupin scrutinized every thing – not excepting the bodies of the victims. We then went into the other rooms, and into the yard; a *gendarme* accompanying us throughout. The examination occupied us until dark, when we took our departure. On our way home my companion stopped in for a moment at the office of one of the daily papers.

I have said that the whims of my friend were manifold, and that *Je les menageais* : – for this phrase there is no English equivalent. It was his humor, now, to decline all conversation on the subject of the murder, until about noon the next day. He then asked me, suddenly, if I had observed any thing *peculiar* at the scene of the atrocity.

There was something in his manner of emphasizing the word 'peculiar,' which caused me to shudder, without knowing why.

'No, nothing *peculiar*,' I said; 'nothing more, at least, than we both saw stated in the paper.'

'The "Gazette,"' he replied, 'has not entered, I fear, into the unusual horror of the thing. But dismiss the idle opinions of this print. It appears to me that this mystery is considered insoluble, for the very reason which should cause it to be regarded as easy of solution – I mean for the *outré* character of its features. The police are confounded by the seeming absence of motive – not for the murder itself – but for the atrocity of the murder. They are puzzled, too, by the seeming impossibility of reconciling the voices heard in contention, with the facts that no one was discovered up stairs but the assassinated Mademoiselle L'Espanaye, and that there were no means of egress without the notice of the party ascending. The wild disorder of the room; the corpse thrust, with the head downward, up the chimney; the frightful mutilation of the body of the old lady; these considerations, with those just mentioned, and others which I need not mention, have sufficed to paralyze the powers, by putting completely at fault the boasted *acumen*, of the government agents. They have fallen into the gross but common error of confounding the unusual with the abstruse. But it is by these deviations from the plane of the ordinary, that reason feels its way, if at all, in its search for the true. In investigations such as we are now pursuing, it should not be so much asked "what has occurred," as "what has occurred that has never occurred before." In fact, the facility with which I shall arrive, or have arrived, at the solution of this mystery, is in the direct ratio of its apparent insolubility in the eyes of the police.'

I stared at the speaker in mute astonishment.

'I am now awaiting,' continued he, looking toward the door of our apartment – 'I am now awaiting a person who, although perhaps not the perpetrator of these butcheries, must have been in some measure implicated in their perpetration. Of the worst portion of the crimes committed, it is probable that he is inno-cent. I hope that I am right in this supposition; for upon it I build my expectation of reading the entire riddle. I look for the man here – in this room – every moment. It is true that he may not arrive; but the probability is that he will. Should he come, it will be necessary to detain him. Here are pistols; and we both know how to use them when occasion demands their use.'

I took the pistols, scarcely knowing what I did, or believing what I heard, while Dupin went on, very much as if in a soliloquy. I have already spoken of his abstract manner at such times. His discourse was addressed to myself; but his voice, although by no means loud, had that intonation which is commonly employed in speaking to some one at a great distance. His eyes, vacant in expression, regarded only the wall.

'That the voices heard in contention,' he said, 'by the party upon the stairs, were not the voices of the women themselves, was fully proved by the evidence. This relieves us of all doubt upon the question whether the old lady could have first destroyed the daughter, and afterward have committed suicide. I speak of this point chiefly for the sake of method; for the strength of Madame L'Espanaye would have been utterly unequal to the task of thrusting her daughter's corpse up the chimney as it was found; and the nature of the wounds upon her own person entirely preclude the idea of self-destruction. Murder, then, has been committed by some third party; and the voices of this third party were those heard in contention. Let me now advert – not to the whole testimony respecting these voices – but to what was *peculiar* in that testimony. Did you observe anything peculiar about it?'

I remarked that, while all the witnesses agreed in supposing the gruff voice to be that of a Frenchman, there was much disagreement in regard to the shrill, or, as one individual termed it, the harsh voice.

'That was the evidence itself,' said Dupin, 'but it was not the peculiarity of the evidence. You have observed nothing distinctive. Yet there *was* something to be observed. The witnesses, as you remark, agreed about the gruff voice; they were here unanimous. But in regard to the shrill voice, the peculiarity is – not that they disagreed – but that, while an Italian, an Englishman, a Spaniard, a Hollander, and a Frenchman attempted to describe it, each one spoke of it as that *of a foreigner*. Each is sure that it was not the voice of one of his own countrymen. Each likens it – not to the voice of an individual of any nation with whose language he is conversant – but the converse. The Frenchman supposes it the voice of a Spaniard, and "might have distinguished some words *had he been acquainted with the Spanish.*" The Dutchman maintains it to have been that of a Frenchman; but we find it stated that "*not understanding French this witness was examined through an interpreter.*" The Englishman thinks it the voice of a German, and "*does not understand German.*" The Spaniard "is sure" that it was that of an Englishman, but "judges by the intonation" altogether, "*as he has no knowledge of the English.*" The Italian believes it the voice of a Russian, but "*has never conversed with a native of Russia.*" A second Frenchman differs, moreover, with the first, and is positive that the voice was that of an Italian; but, *not being cognizant of that tongue*, is, like the Spaniard, "convinced by the intonation." Now, how strangely unusual must that voice have really been, about which such testimony as this *could* have been elicited! – in whose *tones*, even, denizens of the five great divisions of Europe could recognise nothing familiar! You will say that it might have been the voice of an Asiatic – of an African. Neither Asiatics nor Africans abound in Paris; but, without denying the inference, I will now merely call your attention to three points. The voice is termed by one witness "harsh rather than shrill." It is represented by two others to have been "quick and *unequal*." No words – no sounds resembling words – were by any witness mentioned as distinguishable.

'I know not,' continued Dupin, 'what impression I may have made, so far, upon your own understanding; but I do not hesitate to say that legitimate deductions even from this portion of the testimony – the portion respecting the gruff and shrill voices – are in themselves sufficient to engender a suspicion which should give direction to all farther progress in the investigation of the mystery. I said "legitimate deductions;" but my meaning is not thus fully expressed. I designed to imply that the deductions are the *sole* proper ones, and that the suspicion arises *inevitably* from them as the single result. What the suspicion is, however, I will not say just yet. I merely wish you to bear in mind that, with myself, it was sufficiently forcible to give a definite form – a certain tendency – to my inquiries in the chamber.

'Let us now transport ourselves, in fancy, to this chamber. What shall we first seek here? The means of egress employed by the murderers. It is not too much to say that neither of us believe in præternatural events. Madame and Mademoiselle L'Espanaye were not destroyed by spirits. The doers of the deed were material, and escaped materially. Then how? Fortunately, there is but one mode of reasoning upon the point, and that mode *must* lead us to a definite decision. – Let us examine, each by each, the possible means of egress. It is clear that the assassins were in the room where Mademoiselle L'Espanaye was found, or at least in the room adjoining, when the party ascended the stairs. It is then only from these two apartments that we have to seek issues. The police have laid bare the floors, the ceilings, and the masonry of the walls, in every direction. No *secret* issues could have escaped their vigilance. But, not trusting to *their* eyes, I examined with my own. There were, then, *no* secret issues. Both doors leading from the rooms into the passage were securely locked, with the keys inside. Let us turn to the chimneys. These, although of ordinary width for some eight or ten feet above the hearths, will not admit, throughout their extent, the body of a large cat. The impossibility of egress, by means already stated, being thus absolute, we are reduced to the windows. Through those of the front room no one could have escaped without notice from the crowd in the street. The murderers *must* have passed, then, through those of the back room. Now, brought to this conclusion in so unequivocal a manner as we are, it is not our part, as reasoners, to reject it on account of apparent impossibilities. It is only left for us to prove that these apparent "impossibilities" are, in reality, not such.

'There are two windows in the chamber. One of them is unobstructed by furniture, and is wholly visible. The lower portion of the other is hidden from view by the head of the unwieldy bedstead which is thrust close up against it. The former was found securely fastened from within. It resisted the utmost force of those who endeavored to raise it. A large gimlet-hole had been pierced in its frame to the left, and a very stout nail was found fitted therein, nearly to the head. Upon examining the other window, a similar nail was seen similarly fitted in it; and a vigorous attempt to raise this sash, failed also. The police were now entirely satisfied that egress had not been in these directions. And, *therefore*, it was thought a matter of supererogation to withdraw the nails and open the windows.

'My own examination was somewhat more particular, and was so for the reason I have just given – because here it was, I knew, that all apparent impossibilities *must* be proved to be not such in reality.

'I proceeded to think thus – *à posteriori*. The murderers *did* escape from one of these windows. This being so, they could not have re-fastened the sashes from the inside, as they were found fastened; – the consideration which put a stop, through its obviousness, to the scrutiny of the police in this quarter. Yet the sashes *were* fastened. They *must*, then, have the power of fastening themselves. There was no escape from this conclusion. I stepped to the unobstructed casement, withdrew the nail with some difficulty, and attempted to raise the sash. It resisted all my efforts, as I had anticipated. A concealed spring must, I now knew, exist; and this corroboration of my idea convinced me that my premises, at least, were correct, however mysterious still appeared the circumstances attending the nails. A careful search soon brought to light the hidden spring. I pressed it, and, satisfied with the discovery, forebore to upraise the sash.

'I now replaced the nail and regarded it attentively. A person passing out through this window might have reclosed it, and the spring would have caught – but the nail could not have been replaced. The conclusion was plain, and again narrowed in the field of my investigations. The assassins *must* have escaped through the other window. Supposing, then, the springs upon each sash to be the same, as was probable, there *must* be found a difference between the nails, or at least between the modes of their fixture. Getting upon the sacking of the bedstead, I looked over the head-board minutely at the second casement. Passing my hand down behind the board, I readily discovered and pressed the spring, which was, as I had supposed, identical in character with its neighbor. I now looked at the nail. It was as stout as the other, and apparently fitted in the same manner – driven in nearly up to the head.

'You will say that I was puzzled; but, if you think so, you must have misunderstood the nature of the inductions. To use a sporting phrase, I had not been once "at fault." The scent had never for an instant been lost. There was no flaw in any link of the chain. I had traced the secret to its ultimate result, – and that result was *the nail*. It had, I say, in every respect, the appearance of its fellow in the other window; but this fact was an absolute nullity (conclusive as it might seem to be) when compared with the consideration that here, at this point, terminated the clew. "There *must* be something wrong," I said, "about the nail." I touched it; and the head, with about a quarter of an inch of the shank, came off in my fingers. The rest of the shank was in the gimlet-hole, where it had been broken off. The fracture was an old one (for its edges were incrusted with rust), and had apparently been accomplished by the blow of a hammer, which had partially imbedded, in the top of the bottom sash, the head portion of the nail. I now carefully replaced this head portion in the indentation whence I had taken it, and the resemblance to a perfect nail was complete – the fissure was invisible. Pressing the spring, I gently raised the sash for a few inches; the head went up with it, remaining firm in its bed. I closed the window, and the semblance of the whole nail was again perfect.

'The riddle, so far, was now unriddled. The assassin had escaped through the window which looked upon the bed. Dropping of its own accord upon his exit (or perhaps purposely closed), it had become fastened by the spring; and it was the retention of this spring which had been mistaken by the police for that of the nail, – farther inquiry being thus considered unnecessary.

'The next question is that of the mode of descent. Upon this point I had been satisfied in my walk with you around the building. About five feet and a half from the casement in question there runs a lightning-rod. From this rod it would have been impossible for any one to reach the window itself, to say nothing of entering it. I observed, however, that the shutters of the fourth story were of the peculiar kind called by Parisian carpenters *ferrades* – a kind rarely employed at the present day, but frequently seen upon very old mansions at Lyons and Bordeaux. They are in the form of an ordinary door, (a single, not a folding door) except that the upper half is latticed or worked in open trellis – thus affording an excellent hold for the hands. In the present instance these shutters are fully three feet and a half broad. When we saw them from the rear of the house, they were both about half open – that is to say, they stood off at right angles from the wall. It is probable that the police, as well as myself, examined the back of the tenement; but, if so, in looking at these *ferrades* in the line of their breadth (as they must have done), they did not perceive this great breadth itself, or, at all events, failed to take it into due consideration. In fact, having once satisfied themselves that no egress could have been made in this quarter, they would naturally bestow here a very cursory examination. It was clear to me, however, that the shutter belonging to the window at the head of the bed, would, if swung fully back to the wall, reach to within two feet of the lightning-rod. It was also evident that, by exertion of a very unusual degree of activity and courage, an entrance into the window, from the rod, might have been thus effected. – By reaching to the distance of two feet and a half (we now suppose the shutter open to its whole extent) a robber might have taken a firm grasp upon the trellis-work. Letting go, then, his hold upon the rod, placing his feet securely against the wall, and springing boldly from it, he might have swung the shutter so as to close it, and, if we imagine the window open at the time, might even have swung himself into the room.

'I wish you to bear especially in mind that I have spoken of a *very* unusual degree of activity as requisite to success in so hazardous and so difficult a feat. It is my design to show you, first, that the thing might possibly have been accomplished: – but, secondly and *chiefly*, I wish to impress upon your understanding the *very extraordinary* – the almost præternatural character of that agility which could have accomplished it.

'You will say, no doubt, using the language of the law, that "to make out my case" I should rather undervalue, than insist upon a full estimation of the activity required in this matter. This may be the practice in law, but it is not the usage of reason. My ultimate object is only the truth. My immediate purpose is to lead you to place in juxta-position that *very unusual* activity of which I have just spoken, with that *very peculiar* shrill (or harsh) and *unequal* voice, about whose nationality no two persons could be found to agree, and in whose utterance no syllabification could be detected.'

At these words a vague and half-formed conception of the meaning of Dupin flitted over my mind. I seemed to be upon the verge of comprehension, without power to comprehend – as men, at times, find themselves upon the brink of remembrance, without being able, in the end, to remember. My friend went on with his discourse.

'You will see,' he said, 'that I have shifted the question from the mode of egress to that of ingress. It was my design to suggest that both were effected in the same manner, at the same point. Let us now revert to the interior of the room. Let us survey the appearances here. The drawers of the bureau, it is said, had been rifled, although many articles of apparel still remained within them. The conclusion here is absurd. It is a mere guess – a very silly one – and no more. How are we to know that the articles found in the drawers were not all these drawers had originally contained? Madame L'Espanaye and her daughter lived an exceedingly retired life – saw no company – seldom went out – had little use for numerous changes of habiliment. Those found were at least of as good quality as any likely to be possessed by these ladies. If a thief had taken any, why did he not take the best – why did he not take all? In a word, why did he abandon four thousand francs in gold to encumber himself with a bundle of linen? The gold *was* abandoned. Nearly the whole sum mentioned by Monsieur Mignaud, the banker, was discovered, in bags, upon the floor. I wish you, therefore, to discard from your thoughts the blundering idea of *motive*, engendered in the brains of the police by that portion of the evidence which speaks of money delivered at the door of the house. Coincidences ten times as remarkable as this (the delivery of the money, and murder committed within three days upon the party receiving it), happen to all of us every hour of our lives, without attracting even momentary notice. Coincidences, in general, are great stumbling-blocks in the way of that class of thinkers who have been educated to know nothing of the theory of probabilities – that theory to which the most glorious objects of human research are indebted for the most glorious of illustration. In the present instance, had the gold been gone, the fact of its delivery three days before would have formed something more than a coincidence. It would have been corroborative of this idea of motive. But, under the real circumstances of the case, if we are to suppose gold the motive of this outrage, we must also imagine the perpetrator so vacillating an idiot as to have abandoned his gold and his motive altogether.

'Keeping now steadily in mind the points to which I have drawn your attention – that peculiar voice, that unusual agility, and that startling absence of motive in a murder so singularly atrocious as this – let us glance at the butchery itself. Here is a woman strangled to death by manual strength, and thrust up a chimney, head downward. Ordinary assassins employ no such modes of murder as this. Least of all, do they thus dispose of the murdered. In the manner of thrusting the corpse up the chimney, you will admit that there was something *excessively outré* – something altogether irreconcilable with our common notions of human action, even when we suppose the actors the most depraved of men. Think, too, how great must have been that strength which could have thrust the body *up* such an aperture so forcibly that the united vigor of several persons was found barely sufficient to drag it *down*!

'Turn, now, to other indications of the employment of a vigor most marvellous. On the hearth were thick tresses – very thick tresses – of grey human hair. These had been torn out by the roots. You are aware of the great force necessary in tearing thus from the head even twenty or thirty hairs together. You saw the locks in question as well as myself. Their roots (a hideous sight!) were clotted with fragments of the flesh of the scalp – sure token of the prodigious power which had been exerted in uprooting perhaps half a million of hairs at a time. The throat of the old lady was not merely cut, but the head absolutely severed from the body: the instrument was a mere razor. I wish you also to look at the *brutal* ferocity of these deeds. Of the bruises upon the body of Madame L'Espanaye I do not speak. Monsieur Dumas, and his worthy coadjutor Monsieur Etienne, have pronounced that they were inflicted by some obtuse instrument; and so far these gentlemen are very correct. The obtuse instrument was clearly the stone pavement in the yard, upon which the victim had fallen from the window which looked in upon the bed. This idea, however simple it may now seem, escaped the police for the same reason that the breadth of the shutters escaped them – because, by the affair of the nails, their perceptions had been hermetically sealed against the possibility of the windows having been opened at all.

'If now, in addition to all these things, you have properly

reflected upon the odd disorder of the chamber, we have gone so far as to combine the ideas of an agility astounding, a strength superhuman, a ferocity brutal, a butchery without motive, a *grotesquerie* in horror absolutely alien from humanity, and a voice foreign in tone to the ears of men of many nations, and devoid of all distinct or intelligible syllabification. What result, then, has ensued? What impression have I made upon your fancy?'

I felt a creeping of the flesh as Dupin asked me the question. 'A madman,' I said, 'has done this deed – some raving maniac, escaped from a neighboring *Maison de Santé.*'

'In some respects,' he replied, 'your idea is not irrelevant. But the voices of madmen, even in their wildest paroxysms, are never found to tally with that peculiar voice heard upon the stairs. Madmen are of some nation, and their language, however incoherent in its words, has always the coherence of syllabification. Besides, the hair of a madman is not such as I now hold in my hand. I disentangled this little tuft from the rigidly clutched fingers of Madame L'Espanaye. Tell me what you can make of it.'

'Dupin!' I said, completely unnerved; 'this hair is most unusual – this is no *human* hair.'

'I have not asserted that it is,' said he; 'but, before we decide this point, I wish you to glance at the little sketch I have here traced upon this paper. It is a *fac-simile* drawing of what has been described in one portion of the testimony as "dark bruises, and deep indentations of finger nails," upon the throat of Mademoiselle L'Espanaye, and in another, (by Messrs Dumas and Etienne,) as a "series of livid spots, evidently the impression of fingers."

'You will perceive,' continued my friend, spreading out the paper upon the table before us, 'that this drawing gives the idea of a firm and fixed hold. There is no *slipping* apparent. Each finger has retained – possibly until the death of the victim – the fearful grasp by which it originally imbedded itself. Attempt, now, to place all your fingers, at the same time, in the respective impressions as you see them.'

I made the attempt in vain.

'We are possibly not giving this matter a fair trial,' he said. 'The paper is spread out upon a plane surface; but the human throat is cylindrical. Here is a billet of wood, the circumference of which is about that of the throat. Wrap the drawing around it, and try the experiment again.'

I did so; but the difficulty was even more obvious than before. 'This,' I said, 'is the mark of no human hand.'

'Read now,' replied Dupin, 'this passage from Cuvier.'

It was a minute anatomical and generally descriptive account of the large fulvous Ourang-Outang of the East Indian Islands. The gigantic stature, the prodigious strength and activity, the wild ferocity, and the imitative propensities of these mammalia are sufficiently well known to all. I understood the full horrors of the murder at once.

'The description of the digits,' said I, as I made an end of reading, 'is in exact accordance with this drawing. I see that no animal but an Ourang-Outang, of the species here mentioned, could have impressed the indentations as you have traced them. This tuft of tawny hair, too, is identical in character with that of the beast of Cuvier. But I cannot possibly comprehend the particulars of this frightful mystery. Besides there were *two* voices heard in contention, and one of them was unquestionably the voice of a Frenchman.'

'True; and you will remember an expression attributed almost unanimously, by the evidence, to this voice, – the expression, "*mon Dieu!*" This, under the circumstances, has been justly characterized by one of the witnesses (Montani, the confectioner,) as an expression of remonstrance or expostulation. Upon these two words, therefore, I have mainly built my hopes of a full solution of the riddle. A Frenchman was cognizant of the murder. It is possible – indeed it is far more than probable – that he was innocent of all participation in the bloody transactions which took place. The Ourang-Outang may have escaped from him. He may have traced it to the chamber; but, under the agitating circumstances which ensued, he could never have recaptured it. It is still at large. I will not pursue these guesses – for

I have no right to call them more – since the shades of reflection upon which they are based are scarcely of sufficient depth to be appreciable by my own intellect, and since I could not pretend to make them intelligible to the understanding of another. We will call them guesses then, and speak of them as such. If the Frenchman in question is indeed, as I suppose, innocent of this atrocity, this advertisement, which I left last night, upon our return home, at the office of "Le Monde," (a paper devoted to the shipping interest, and much sought by sailors,) will bring him to our residence.'

He handed me a paper, and I read thus :

CAUGHT – *In the Bois de Boulogne, early in the morning of the — inst.,* (the morning of the murder,) *a very large, tawny Ourang-Outang of the Bornese species. The owner,* (*who is ascertained to be a sailor, belonging to a Maltese vessel,*) *may have the animal again, upon identifying it satisfactorily, and paying a few charges arising from its capture and keeping. Call at No. —, Rue —, Faubourg St Germain – au troisième.*

'How was it possible,' I asked, 'that you should know the man to be a sailor, and belonging to a Maltese vessel?'

'I do *not* know it,' said Dupin. 'I am not *sure* of it. Here, however, is a small piece of ribbon, which from its form, and from its greasy appearance, has evidently been used in tying the hair in one of those long *queues* of which sailors are so fond. Moreover, this knot is one which few besides sailors can tie, and is peculiar to the Maltese. I picked the ribbon up at the foot of the lightning-rod. It could not have belonged to either of the deceased. Now if, after all, I am wrong in my induction from this ribbon, that the Frenchman was a sailor belonging to a Maltese vessel, still I can have done no harm in saying what I did in the advertisement. If I am in error, he will merely suppose that I have been misled by some circumstance into which he will not take the trouble to inquire. But if I am right, a great point is gained. Cognizant although innocent of the murder, the Frenchman will naturally hesitate about replying to the advertisement

– about demanding the Ourang-Outang. He will reason thus:
– "I am innocent; I am poor; my Ourang-Outang is of great
value – to one in my circumstances a fortune of itself – why
should I lose it through idle apprehensions of danger? Here it
is, within my grasp. It was found in the Bois de Boulogne – at
a vast distance from the scene of that butchery. How can it ever
be suspected that a brute beast should have done the deed? The
police are at fault – they have failed to procure the slightest
clew. Should they even trace the animal, it would be impossible
to prove me cognizant of the murder, or to implicate me in guilt
on account of that cognizance. Above all, I *am known*. The
advertiser designates me as the possessor of the beast. I am not
sure to what limit his knowledge may extend. Should I avoid
claiming a property of so great value, which it is known that I
possess, I will render the animal, at least, liable to suspicion. It is
not my policy to attract attention either to myself or to the
beast. I will answer the advertisement, get the Ourang-Outang,
and keep it close until this matter has blown over." '

At this moment we heard a step upon the stairs.

'Be ready,' said Dupin, 'with your pistols, but neither use them
nor show them until at a signal from myself.'

The front door of the house had been left open, and the
visitor had entered, without ringing, and advanced several steps
upon the staircase. Now, however, he seemed to hesitate.
Presently we heard him descending. Dupin was moving quickly
to the door, when we again heard him coming up. He did not
turn back a second time, but stepped up with decision and
rapped at the door of our chamber.

'Come in,' said Dupin, in a cheerful and hearty tone.

A man entered. He was a sailor, evidently, – a tall, stout, and
muscular-looking person, with a certain dare-devil expression
of countenance, not altogether unprepossessing. His face, greatly
sunburnt, was more than half hidden by whisker and *mustachio*.
He had with him a huge oaken cudgel, but appeared to be otherwise unarmed. He bowed awkwardly, and bade us 'good evening,'
in French accents, which, although somewhat Neufchatelish,
were still sufficiently indicative of a Parisian origin.

'Sit down, my friend,' said Dupin. 'I suppose you have called about the Ourang-Outang. Upon my word, I almost envy you the possession of him; a remarkably fine, and no doubt a very valuable animal. How old do you suppose him to be?'

The sailor drew a long breath, with the air of a man relieved of some intolerable burden, and then replied, in an assured tone:

'I have no way of telling – but he can't be more than four or five years old. Have you got him here?'

'Oh no; we had no conveniences for keeping him here. He is at a livery stable in the Rue Dubourg, just by. You can get him in the morning. Of course you are prepared to identify the property?'

'To be sure I am, sir.'

'I shall be sorry to part with him,' said Dupin.

'I don't mean that you should be at all this trouble for nothing, sir,' said the man. 'Couldn't expect it. Am very willing to pay a reward for the finding of the animal – that is to say, any thing in reason.'

'Well,' replied my friend, 'that is all very fair, to be sure. Let me think! – what should I have? Oh! I will tell you. My reward shall be this. You shall give me all the information in your power about these murders in the Rue Morgue.'

Dupin said the last words in a very low tone, and very quietly. Just as quietly, too, he walked toward the door, locked it, and put the key in his pocket. He then drew a pistol from his bosom and placed it, without the least flurry, upon the table.

The sailor's face flushed up as if he were struggling with suffocation. He started to his feet and grasped his cudgel; but the next moment he fell back into his seat, trembling violently, and with the countenance of death itself. He spoke not a word. I pitied him from the bottom of my heart.

'My friend,' said Dupin, in a kind tone, 'you are alarming yourself unnecessarily – you are indeed. We mean you no harm whatever. I pledge you the honor of a gentleman, and of a Frenchman, that we intend you no injury. I perfectly well know that you are innocent of the atrocities in the Rue Morgue. It will not do, however, to deny that you are in some measure implicated in them. From what I have already said, you must know that I have had means of information about this matter – means of which you could never have dreamed. Now the thing stands thus. You have done nothing which you could have avoided – nothing, certainly, which renders you culpable. You were not even guilty of robbery, when you might have robbed with impunity. You have nothing to conceal. You have no reason for concealment. On the other hand, you are bound by every principle of honor to confess all you know. An innocent man is now imprisoned, charged with that crime of which you can point out the perpetrator.'

The sailor had recovered his presence of mind, in a great measure, while Dupin uttered these words; but his original boldness of bearing was all gone.

'So help me God,' said he, after a brief pause, 'I *will* tell you all I know about this affair; – but I do not expect you to believe one half I say – I would be a fool indeed if I did. Still, I *am* innocent, and I will make a clean breast if I die for it.'

What he stated was, in substance, this. He had lately made a voyage to the Indian Archipelago. A party, of which he formed one, landed at Borneo, and passed into the interior on an excursion of pleasure. Himself and a companion had captured the Ourang-Outang. This companion dying, the animal fell into his own exclusive possession. After great trouble, occasioned by the intractable ferocity of his captive during the home voyage, he at length succeeded in lodging it safely at his own residence in Paris, where, not to attract toward himself the unpleasant curiosity of his neighbors, he kept it carefully secluded, until such time as it should recover from a wound in the foot, received from a splinter on board ship. His ultimate design was to sell it.

Returning home from some sailors' frolic on the night, or rather in the morning of the murder, he found the beast occupying his own bed-room, into which it had broken from a closet adjoining, where it had been, as was thought, securely confined. Razor in hand, and fully lathered, it was sitting before a looking-glass, attempting the operation of shaving, in which it had no doubt previously watched its master through the key-hole of the closet. Terrified at the sight of so dangerous a weapon in the possession of an animal so ferocious, and so well able to use it, the man, for some moments, was at a loss what to do. He had been accustomed, however, to quiet the creature, even in its fiercest moods, by the use of a whip, and to this he now resorted. Upon sight of it, the Ourang-Outang sprang at once through the door of the chamber, down the stairs, and thence, through a window, unfortunately open, into the street.

The Frenchman followed in despair; the ape, razor still in hand, occasionally stopping to look back and gesticulate at its pursuer, until the latter had nearly come up with it. It then again made off. In this manner the chase continued for a long time. The streets were profoundly quiet, as it was nearly three o'clock in the morning. In passing down an alley in the rear of the Rue Morgue, the fugitive's attention was arrested by a light gleaming from the open window of Madame L'Espanaye's chamber, in the fourth story of her house. Rushing to the building, it perceived the lightning-rod, clambered up with inconceivable agility, grasped the shutter, which was thrown fully back against the wall, and, by its means, swung itself directly upon the headboard of the bed. The whole feat did not occupy a minute. The shutter was kicked open again by the Ourang-Outang as it entered the room.

The sailor, in the meantime, was both rejoiced and perplexed. He had strong hopes of now recapturing the brute, as it could scarcely escape from the trap into which it had ventured, except by the rod, where it might be intercepted as it came down. On the other hand, there was much cause for anxiety as to what it might do in the house. This latter reflection urged the man still to follow the fugitive. A lightning-rod is ascended without difficulty, especially by a sailor; but, when he had arrived as high as the window, which lay far to his left, his career was stopped; the most that he could accomplish was to reach over so as to obtain a glimpse of the interior of the room. At this glimpse he nearly fell from his hold through excess of horror. Now it was that those hideous shrieks arose upon the night, which had startled from slumber the inmates of the Rue Morgue. Madame L'Espanaye and her daughter, habited in their night clothes, had apparently been arranging some papers in the iron chest already mentioned, which had been wheeled into the middle of the room. It was open, and its contents lay beside it on the floor. The victims must have been sitting with their backs toward the window; and, from the time elapsing between the ingress of the beast and the screams, it seems probable that it was not immediately perceived. The flapping-to of the shutter would naturally have been attributed to the wind.

As the sailor looked in, the gigantic animal had seized Madame L'Espanaye by the hair, (which was loose, as she had been combing it,) and was flourishing the razor about her face, in imitation of the motions of a barber. The daughter lay prostrate and motionless; she had swooned. The screams and struggles of the old lady (during which the hair was torn from her head) had the effect of changing the probably pacific purposes of the Ourang-Outang into those of wrath. With one determined sweep of its muscular arm it nearly severed her head from her body. The sight of blood inflamed its anger into phrenzy. Gnashing its teeth, and flashing fire from its eyes, it flew upon the body of the girl, and imbedded its fearful talons in her throat, retaining its grasp until she expired. Its wandering and wild glances fell at this moment upon the head of the bed, over which the face of its master, rigid with horror, was just discernible. The fury of the beast, who no doubt bore still in mind the dreaded whip, was instantly converted into fear. Conscious of having deserved punishment, it seemed desirous of concealing its bloody deeds, and skipped about the chamber in an agony of nervous agitation; throwing down and breaking the furniture as it moved, and dragging the bed from the bedstead. In conclusion, it seized first the corpse of the daughter, and thrust it up the chimney, as it was found; then that of the old lady, which it immediately hurled through the window headlong.

As the ape approached the casement with its mutilated burden, the sailor shrank aghast to the rod, and, rather gliding than clambering down it, hurried at once home – dreading the consequences of the butchery, and gladly abandoning, in his terror, all solicitude about the fate of the Ourang-Outang. The words heard by the party upon the staircase were the Frenchman's exclamations of horror and affright, commingled with the fiendish jabberings of the brute.

I have scarcely anything to add. The Ourang-Outang must have escaped from the chamber, by the rod, just before the breaking of the door. It must have closed the window as it passed through it. It was subsequently caught by the owner himself, who obtained for it a very large sum at the *Jardin des Plantes.* Le Bon was instantly released, upon our narration of the circumstances (with some comments from Dupin) at the *bureau* of the Prefect of Police. This functionary, however well disposed to my friend, could not altogether conceal his chagrin at the turn which affairs had taken, and was fain to indulge in a sarcasm or two, about the propriety of every person minding his own business.

'Let them talk,' said Dupin, who had not thought it necessary to reply. 'Let him discourse; it will ease his conscience. I am satisfied with having defeated him in his own castle. Nevertheless, that he failed in the solution of this mystery, is by no means that matter for wonder which he supposes it; for, in truth, our friend the Prefect is somewhat too cunning to be profound. In his wisdom is no *stamen.* It is all head and no body, like the pictures of the Goddess Laverna, – or, at best, all head and shoulders, like a codfish. But he is a good creature after all. I like him especially for one master stroke of cant, by which he has attained his reputation for ingenuity. I mean the way he has *"de nier ce qui est, et d'expliquer ce qui n'est pas."* '[2]

A Descent into the Maelström

The ways of God in Nature, as in Providence, are
not as *our* ways; nor are the models that we frame
any way commensurate to the vastness, profundity,
and unsearchableness of His works, *which have a
depth in them greater than the well of Democritus.*
JOSEPH GLANVILLE[1]

WE had now reached the summit of the loftiest crag. For some
minutes the old man seemed too much exhausted to speak.

'Not long ago,' said he at length, 'and I could have guided
you on this route as well as the youngest of my sons; but, about
three years past, there happened to me an event such as never
happened before to mortal man – or at least such as no man ever
survived to tell of – and the six hours of deadly terror which I
then endured have broken me up body and soul. You suppose
me a *very* old man – but I am not. It took less than a single day
to change these hairs from a jetty black to white, to weaken my
limbs, and to unstring my nerves, so that I tremble at the least
exertion, and am frightened at a shadow. Do you know I can
scarcely look over this little cliff without getting giddy?'

The 'little cliff,' upon whose edge he had so carelessly thrown
himself down to rest that the weightier portion of his body hung
over it, while he was only kept from falling by the tenure of his
elbow on its extreme and slippery edge – this 'little cliff' arose, a
sheer unobstructed precipice of black shining rock, some fifteen
or sixteen hundred feet from the world of crags beneath us.
Nothing would have tempted me to within half a dozen yards
of its brink. In truth so deeply was I excited by the perilous
position of my companion, that I fell at full length upon the
ground, clung to the shrubs around me, and dared not even
glance upward at the sky – while I struggled in vain to divest

myself of the idea that the very foundations of the mountain were in danger from the fury of the winds. It was long before I could reason myself into sufficient courage to sit up and look out into the distance.

'You must get over these fancies,' said the guide, 'for I have brought you here that you might have the best possible view of the scene of that event I mentioned – and to tell you the whole story with the spot just under your eye.'

'We are now,' he continued, in that particularizing manner which distinguished him – 'we are now close upon the Norwegian coast – in the sixty-eighth degree of latitude – in the great province of Nordland – and in the dreary district of Lofoden.[2] The mountain upon whose top we sit is Helseggen, the Cloudy. Now raise yourself up a little higher – hold on to the grass if you feel giddy – so – and look out beyond the belt of vapor beneath us, into the sea.'

I looked dizzily, and beheld a wide expanse of ocean, whose waters wore so inky a hue as to bring at once to my mind the Nubian geographer's account of the *Mare Tenebrarum*. A panorama more deplorably desolate no human imagination can conceive. To the right and left, as far as the eye could reach, there lay outstretched, like ramparts of the world, lines of horridly black and beetling cliff, whose character of gloom was but the more forcibly illustrated by the surf which reared high up against it its white and ghastly crest, howling and shrieking for ever. Just opposite the promontory upon whose apex we were placed, and at a distance of some five or six miles out at sea, there was visible a small, bleak-looking island; or, more properly, its position was discernible through the wilderness of surge in which it was enveloped. About two miles nearer the land, arose another of smaller size, hideously craggy and barren, and encompassed at various intervals by a cluster of dark rocks.

The appearance of the ocean, in the space between the more distant island and the shore, had something very unusual about it. Although, at the time, so strong a gale was blowing landward that a brig in the remote offing lay to under a double-reefed trysail, and constantly plunged her whole hull out of sight, still there was here nothing like a regular swell, but only a short, quick, angry cross dashing of water in every direction – as well in the teeth of the wind as otherwise. Of foam there was little except in the immediate vicinity of the rocks.

'The island in the distance,' resumed the old man, 'is called by the Norwegians Vurrgh. The one midway is Moskoe. That a mile to the northward is Ambaaren. Yonder are Iflesen, Hoeyholm, Kieldholm, Suarven, and Buckholm. Farther off – between Moskoe and Vurrgh – are Otterholm, Flimen, Sandflesen, and Skarholm. These are the true names of the places – but why it has been thought necessary to name them at all, is more than either you or I can understand. Do you hear any thing? Do you see any change in the water?'

We had now been about ten minutes upon the top of Helseggen, to which we had ascended from the interior of Lofoden, so that we had caught no glimpse of the sea until it had burst upon us from the summit. As the old man spoke, I became aware of a loud and gradually increasing sound, like the moaning of a vast herd of buffaloes upon an American prairie; and at the same moment I perceived that what seamen term the *chopping* character of the ocean beneath us, was rapidly changing into a current which set to the eastward. Even while I gazed, this current acquired a monstrous velocity. Each moment added to its speed – to its headlong impetuosity. In five minutes the whole sea, as far as Vurrgh, was lashed into ungovernable fury; but it was between Moskoe and the coast that the main uproar held its sway. Here the vast bed of the waters, seamed and scarred into a thousand conflicting channels, burst suddenly into phrensied convulsion – heaving, boiling, hissing – gyrating in gigantic and innumerable vortices, and all whirling and plunging on to the eastward with a rapidity which water never elsewhere assumes except in precipitous descents.

In a few minutes more, there came over the scene another radical alteration. The general surface grew somewhat more smooth, and the whirlpools, one by one, disappeared, while prodigious streaks of foam became apparent where none had been seen before. These streaks, at length, spreading out to a great distance, and entering into combination, took unto themselves the gyratory motion of the subsided vortices, and seemed to form the germ of another more vast. Suddenly – very suddenly – this assumed a distinct and definite existence, in a circle of more than half a mile in diameter. The edge of the whirl was represented by a broad belt of gleaming spray; but no particle of this slipped into the mouth of the terrific funnel, whose interior, as far as the eye could fathom it, was a smooth, shining, and jet-black wall of water, inclined to the horizon at an angle of some forty-five degrees, speeding dizzily round and round with a swaying and sweltering motion, and sending forth to the winds an appalling voice, half shriek, half roar, such as not even the mighty cataract of Niagara ever lifts up in its agony to Heaven.

The mountain trembled to its very base, and the rock rocked. I threw myself upon my face, and clung to the scant herbage in an excess of nervous agitation.

'This,' said I at length, to the old man – 'this *can* be nothing else than the great whirlpool of the Maelström.'

'So it is sometimes termed,' said he. 'We Norwegians call it the Moskoe-ström, from the island of Moskoe in the midway.'

The ordinary accounts of this vortex had by no means prepared me for what I saw. That of Jonas Ramus, which is perhaps the most circumstantial of any, cannot impart the faintest conception either of the magnificence, or of the horror of the scene – or of the wild bewildering sense of *the novel* which confounds the beholder. I am not sure from what point of view the writer in question surveyed it, nor at what time; but it could neither have been from the summit of Helseggen, nor during a storm. There are some passages of his description, nevertheless, which may be quoted for their details, although their effect is exceedingly feeble in conveying an impression of the spectacle.

'Between Lofoden and Moskoe,' he says, 'the depth of the water is between thirty-six and forty fathoms; but on the other side, toward Ver (Vurrgh) this depth decreases so as not to afford a convenient passage for a vessel, without the risk of splitting on the rocks, which happens even in the calmest weather. When it is flood, the stream runs up the country between Lofoden and Moskoe with a boisterous rapidity; but the roar of its impetuous ebb to the sea is scarce equalled by the loudest and most dreadful cataracts; the noise being heard several leagues off, and the vortices or pits are of such an extent and depth, that if a ship comes within its attraction, it is inevitably absorbed and carried down to the bottom, and there beat to pieces against the rocks; and when the water relaxes, the fragments thereof are thrown up again. But these intervals of tranquillity are only at the turn of the ebb and flood, and in calm weather, and last but a quarter of an hour, its violence gradually returning. When the stream is most boisterous, and its fury heightened by a storm, it is dangerous to come within a Norway mile of it. Boats, yachts, and ships have been carried away by not guarding against it before they were within its reach. It likewise happens frequently, that whales come too near the stream, and are overpowered by its violence; and then it is impossible to describe their howlings and bellowings in their fruitless struggles to disengage themselves. A bear once, attempting to swim from Lofoden to Moskoe, was caught by the stream and borne down, while he roared terribly, so as to be heard on shore. Large stocks of firs and pine trees, after being absorbed by the current, rise again broken and torn to such a degree as if bristles grew upon them. This plainly shows the bottom to consist of craggy rocks, among which they are whirled to and fro. This stream is regulated by the flux and reflux of the sea – it being constantly high and low water every six hours. In the year 1645, early in the morning of Sexagesima Sunday, it raged with such noise and impetuosity that the very stones of the houses on the coast fell to the ground.'

In regard to the depth of the water, I could not see how this could have been ascertained at all in the immediate vicinity of the vortex. The 'forty fathoms' must have reference only to portions of the channel close upon the shore either of Moskoe or Lofoden. The depth in the centre of the Moskoe-ström must be immeasurably greater; and no better proof of this fact is necessary than can be obtained from even the side-long glance into the abyss of the whirl which may be had from the highest crag of

Helseggen. Looking down from this pinnacle upon the howling Phlegethon below, I could not help smiling at the simplicity with which the honest Jonas Ramus records, as a matter difficult of belief, the anecdotes of the whales and the bears; for it appeared to me, in fact, a self-evident thing, that the largest ships of the line in existence, coming within the influence of that deadly attraction, could resist it as little as a feather the hurricane, and must disappear bodily and at once.

The attempts to account for the phenomenon – some of which, I remember, seemed to me sufficiently plausible in perusal – now wore a very different and unsatisfactory aspect. The idea generally received is that this, as well as three smaller vortices among the Feroe islands, 'have no other cause than the collision of waves rising and falling, at flux and reflux, against a ridge of rocks and shelves, which confines the water so that it precipitates itself like a cataract; and thus the higher the flood rises, the deeper must the fall be, and the natural result of all is a whirlpool or vortex, the prodigious suction of which is sufficiently known by lesser experiments.' – These are the words of the Encyclopædia Britannica. Kircher and others imagine that in the centre of the channel of the Maelström is an abyss penetrating the globe, and issuing in some very remote part – the Gulf of Bothnia being somewhat decidedly named in one instance. This opinion, idle in itself, was the one to which, as I gazed, my imagination most readily assented; and, mentioning it to the guide, I was rather surprised to hear him say that, although it was the view almost universally entertained of the subject by the Norwegians, it nevertheless was not his own. As to the former notion he confessed his inability to comprehend it; and here I agreed with him – for, however conclusive on paper, it becomes altogether unintelligible, and even absurd, amid the thunder of the abyss.

'You have had a good look at the whirl now,' said the old man, 'and if you will creep round this crag, so as to get in its lee, and deaden the roar of the water, I will tell you a story that will convince you I ought to know something of the Moskoeström.'

I placed myself as desired, and he proceeded.

'Myself and my two brothers once owned a schooner-rigged smack of about seventy tons burthen, with which we were in the habit of fishing among the islands beyond Moskoe, nearly to Vurrgh. In all violent eddies at sea there is good fishing, at proper opportunities, if one has only the courage to attempt it; but among the whole of the Lofoden coastmen, we three were the only ones who made a regular business of going out to the islands, as I tell you. The usual grounds are a great way lower down to the southward. There fish can be got at all hours, without much risk, and therefore these places are preferred. The choice spots over here among the rocks, however, not only yield the finest variety, but in far greater abundance; so that we often got in a single day, what the more timid of the craft could not scrape together in a week. In fact, we made it a matter of desperate speculation – the risk of life standing instead of labor, and courage answering for capital.

'We kept the smack in a cove about five miles higher up the coast than this; and it was our practice, in fine weather, to take advantage of the fifteen minutes' slack to push across the main channel of the Moskoe-ström, far above the pool, and then drop down upon anchorage somewhere near Otterholm, or Sandflesen, where the eddies are not so violent as elsewhere. Here we used to remain until nearly time for slack-water again, when we weighed and made for home. We never set out upon this expedition without a steady side wind for going and coming – one that we felt sure would not fail us before our return – and we seldom made a mis-calculation upon this point. Twice, during six years, we were forced to stay all night at anchor on account of a dead calm, which is a rare thing indeed just about here; and once we had to remain on the grounds nearly a week, starving to death, owing to a gale which blew up shortly after our arrival, and made the channel too boisterous to be thought of. Upon this occasion we should have been driven out to sea in spite of everything, (for the whirlpools threw us round and round so violently, that, at length, we fouled our anchor and dragged it) if it had not been that we drifted into one of the innumerable cross currents

– here to-day and gone to-morrow – which drove us under the lee of Flimen, where, by good luck, we brought up.

'I could not tell you the twentieth part of the difficulties we encountered "on the ground" – it is a bad spot to be in, even in good weather – but we made shift always to run the gauntlet of the Moskoe-ström itself without accident; although at times my heart has been in my mouth when we happened to be a minute or so behind or before the slack. The wind sometimes was not as strong as we thought it at starting, and then we made rather less way than we could wish, while the current rendered the smack unmanageable. My eldest brother had a son eighteen years old, and I had two stout boys of my own. These would have been of great assistance at such times, in using the sweeps, as well as afterward in fishing – but, somehow, although we ran the risk ourselves, we had not the heart to let the young ones get into the danger – for, after all said and done, it *was* a horrible danger, and that is the truth.

'It is now within a few days of three years since what I am going to tell you occurred. It was on the tenth of July, 18—, a day which the people of this part of the world will never forget – for it was one in which blew the most terrible hurricane that ever came out of the heavens. And yet all the morning, and indeed until late in the afternoon, there was a gentle and steady breeze from the south-west, while the sun shone brightly, so that the oldest seaman among us could not have foreseen what was to follow.

'The three of us – my two brothers and myself – had crossed over to the islands about two o'clock P. M., and soon nearly loaded the smack with fine fish, which, we all remarked, were more plenty that day than we had ever known them. It was just seven, *by my watch*, when we weighed and started for home, so as to make the worst of the Ström at slack water, which we knew would be at eight.

'We set out with a fresh wind on our starboard quarter, and for some time spanked along at a great rate, never dreaming of danger, for indeed we saw not the slightest reason to apprehend it. All at once we were taken aback by a breeze from over Helseggen. This was most unusual – something that had never happened to us before – and I began to feel a little uneasy, without exactly knowing why. We put the boat on the wind, but could make no headway at all for the eddies, and I was upon the point of proposing to return to the anchorage, when, looking astern, we saw the whole horizon covered with a singular copper-colored cloud that rose with the most amazing velocity.

'In the meantime the breeze that had headed us off fell away, and we were dead becalmed, drifting about in every direction. This state of things, however, did not last long enough to give us time to think about it. In less than a minute the storm was upon us – in less than two the sky was entirely overcast – and what with this and the driving spray, it became suddenly so dark that we could not see each other in the smack.

'Such a hurricane as then blew it is folly to attempt describing. The oldest seaman in Norway never experienced any thing like it. We had let our sails go by the run before it cleverly took us; but, at the first puff, both our masts went by the board as if they had been sawed off – the mainmast taking with it my youngest brother, who had lashed himself to it for safety.

'Our boat was the lightest feather of a thing that ever sat upon water. It had a complete flush deck, with only a small hatch near the bow, and this hatch it had always been our custom to batten down when about to cross the Ström, by way of precaution against the chopping seas. But for this circumstance we should have foundered at once – for we lay entirely buried for some moments. How my elder brother escaped destruction I cannot say, for I never had an opportunity of ascertaining. For my part, as soon as I had let the foresail run, I threw myself flat on deck, with my feet against the narrow gunwale of the bow, and with my hands grasping a ring-bolt near the foot of the foremast. It was mere instinct that prompted me to do this – which was undoubtedly the very best thing I could have done – for I was too much flurried to think.

'For some moments we were completely deluged, as I say, and all this time I held my breath, and clung to the bolt. When I could stand it no longer I raised myself upon my knees, still keeping hold with my hands, and thus got my head clear. Presently our little boat gave herself a shake, just as a dog does in coming out of the water, and thus rid herself, in some measure, of the seas. I was now trying to get the better of the stupor that had come over me, and to collect my senses so as to see what was to be done, when I felt somebody grasp my arm. It was my elder brother, and my heart leaped for joy, for I had made sure that he was overboard – but the next moment all this joy was turned into horror – for he put his mouth close to my ear, and screamed out the word "*Moskoe-ström!*"

'No one ever will know what my feelings were at that moment. I shook from head to foot as if I had had the most violent fit of the ague. I knew what he meant by that one word well enough – I knew what he wished to make me understand. With the wind that now drove us on, we were bound for the whirl of the Ström, and nothing could save us!

'You perceive that in crossing the Ström *channel*, we always went a long way up above the whirl, even in the calmest weather, and then had to wait and watch carefully for the slack – but now we were driving right upon the pool itself, and in such a hurricane as this! "To be sure," I thought, "we shall get there just about the slack – there is some little hope in that" – but in the next moment I cursed myself for being so great a fool as to dream of hope at all. I knew very well that we were doomed, had we been ten times a ninety-gun ship.

'By this time the first fury of the tempest had spent itself, or perhaps we did not feel it so much, as we scudded before it, but at all events the seas, which at first had been kept down by the wind, and lay flat and frothing, now got up into absolute mountains. A singular change, too, had come over the heavens. Around in every direction it was still as black as pitch, but nearly overhead there burst out, all at once, a circular rift of clear sky – as clear as I ever saw – and of a deep bright blue – and through it there blazed forth the full moon with a lustre that I never before knew her to wear. She lit up every thing about us with the greatest distinctness – but, oh God, what a scene it was to light up!

'I now made one or two attempts to speak to my brother – but in some manner which I could not understand, the din had so increased that I could not make him hear a single word, although I screamed at the top of my voice in his ear. Presently he shook his head, looking as pale as death, and held up one of his fingers, as if to say "listen !"

'At first I could not make out what he meant – but soon a hideous thought flashed upon me. I dragged my watch from its fob. It was not going. I glanced at its face by the moonlight, and then burst into tears as I flung it far away into the ocean. It had run down at seven o'clock! We were behind the time of the slack, and the whirl of the Ström was in full fury!

'When a boat is well built, properly trimmed, and not deep laden, the waves in a strong gale, when she is going large, seem always to slip from beneath her – which appears very strange to a landsman – and this is what is called riding, in sea phrase.

'Well, so far we had ridden the swells very cleverly; but presently a gigantic sea happened to take us right under the counter, and bore us with it as it rose – up – up – as if into the sky. I would not have believed that any wave could rise so high. And then down we came with a sweep, a slide, and a plunge, that made me feel sick and dizzy, as if I was falling from some lofty mountain-top in a dream. But while we were up I had thrown a quick glance around – and that one glance was all sufficient. I saw our exact position in an instant. The Moskoe-ström whirl-pool was about a quarter of a mile dead ahead – but no more like the every-day Moskoe-ström, than the whirl as you now see it, is like a mill-race. If I had not known where we were, and what we had to expect, I should not have recognised the place at all. As it was, I involuntarily closed my eyes in horror. The lids clenched themselves together as if in a spasm.

'It could not have been more than two minutes afterwards until we suddenly felt the waves subside, and were enveloped in foam. The boat made a sharp half turn to larboard, and then shot off in its new direction like a thunderbolt. At the same moment the roaring noise of the water was completely drowned in a kind of shrill shriek – such a sound as you might imagine given out by the water-pipes of many thousand steam-vessels, letting off their steam all together. We were now in the belt of surf that always surrounds the whirl; and I thought, of course, that another moment would plunge us into the abyss – down which we could only see indistinctly on account of the amazing velocity with which we were borne along. The boat did not seem to sink into the water at all, but to skim like an air-bubble upon the surface of the surge. Her starboard side was next the whirl, and on the larboard arose the world of ocean we had left. It stood like a huge writhing wall between us and the horizon.

'It may appear strange, but now, when we were in the very jaws of the gulf, I felt more composed than when we were only approaching it. Having made up my mind to hope no more, I got rid of a great deal of that terror which unmanned me at first. I suppose it was despair that strung my nerves.

'It may look like boasting – but what I tell you is truth – I began to reflect how magnificent a thing it was to die in such a manner, and how foolish it was in me to think of so paltry a consideration as my own individual life, in view of so wonderful a manifestation of God's power. I do believe that I blushed with shame when this idea crossed my mind. After a little while I became possessed with the keenest curiosity about the whirl itself. I positively felt a *wish* to explore its depths, even at the sacrifice I was going to make; and my principal grief was that I should never be able to tell my old companions on shore about the mysteries I should see. These, no doubt, were singular fancies to occupy a man's mind in such extremity – and I have often thought since, that the revolutions of the boat around the pool might have rendered me a little light-headed.

'There was another circumstance which tended to restore my self-possession; and this was the cessation of the wind, which could not reach us in our present situation – for, as you saw yourself, the belt of surf is considerably lower than the general bed of the ocean, and this latter now towered above us, a high, black, mountainous ridge. If you have never been at sea in a heavy gale, you can form no idea of the confusion of mind occasioned by the wind and spray together. They blind, deafen and strangle you, and take away all power of action or reflection. But we were now, in a great measure, rid of these annoyances – just as death-condemned felons in prison are allowed petty indulgences, forbidden them while their doom is yet uncertain.

'How often we made the circuit of the belt it is impossible to say. We careered round and round for perhaps an hour, flying rather than floating, getting gradually more and more into the middle of the surge, and then nearer and nearer to its horrible inner edge. All this time I had never let go of the ring-bolt. My brother was at the stern, holding on to a large empty water-cask which had been securely lashed under the coop of the counter, and was the only thing on deck that had not been swept overboard when the gale first took us. As we approached the brink of the pit he let go his hold upon this, and made for the ring, from which, in the agony of his terror, he endeavored to force my hands, as it was not large enough to afford us both a secure grasp. I never felt deeper grief than when I saw him attempt this act – although I knew he was a madman when he did it – a raving maniac through sheer fright. I did not care, however, to contest the point with him. I thought it could make no difference whether either of us held on at all; so I let him have the bolt, and went astern to the cask. This there was no great difficulty in doing; for the smack flew round steadily enough, and upon an even keel – only swaying to and fro, with the immense sweeps and swelters of the whirl. Scarcely had I secured myself in my new position, when we gave a wild lurch to starboard, and rushed headlong into the abyss. I muttered a hurried prayer to God, and thought all was over.

'As I felt the sickening sweep of the descent, I had instinctively tightened my hold upon the barrel, and closed my eyes. For some seconds I dared not open them – while I expected instant destruction, and wondered that I was not already in my death-struggles with the water. But moment after moment elapsed. I still lived. The sense of falling had ceased; and the motion of the vessel seemed much as it had been before while in the belt of foam, with the exception that she now lay more along. I took courage and looked once again upon the scene.

'Never shall I forget the sensations of awe, horror, and admiration with which I gazed about me. The boat appeared to be hanging, as if by magic, midway down, upon the interior surface of a funnel vast in circumference, prodigious in depth, and whose perfectly smooth sides might have been mistaken for ebony, but for the bewildering rapidity with which they spun around, and for the gleaming and ghastly radiance they shot forth, as the rays of the full moon, from that circular rift amid the clouds which I have already described, streamed in a flood of golden glory along the black walls, and far away down into the inmost recesses of the abyss.

'At first I was too much confused to observe anything accurately. The general burst of terrific grandeur was all that I beheld. When I recovered myself a little, however, my gaze fell instinctively downward. In this direction I was able to obtain an unobstructed view, from the manner in which the smack hung on the inclined surface of the pool. She was quite upon an even keel – that is to say, her deck lay in a plane parallel with that of the water – but this latter sloped at an angle of more than forty-five degrees, so that we seemed to be lying upon our beam-ends. I could not help observing, nevertheless, that I had scarcely more difficulty in maintaining my hold and footing in this situation, than if we had been upon a deal level; and this, I suppose, was owing to the speed at which we revolved.

'The rays of the moon seemed to search the very bottom of the profound gulf; but still I could make out nothing distinctly, on account of a thick mist in which everything there was enveloped, and over which there hung a magnificent rainbow, like that narrow and tottering bridge which Mussulmen say is the only pathway between Time and Eternity. This mist, or spray, was no doubt occasioned by the clashing of the great walls of the funnel, as they all met together at the bottom – but the yell that went up to the Heavens from out of that mist, I dare not attempt to describe.

'Our first slide into the abyss itself, from the belt of foam above, had carried us to a great distance down the slope; but our farther descent was by no means proportionate. Round and round we swept – not with any uniform movement – but in dizzying swings and jerks, that sent us sometimes only a few hundred feet – sometimes nearly the complete circuit of the whirl. Our progress downward, at each revolution, was slow, but very perceptible.

'Looking about me upon the wide waste of liquid ebony on which we were thus borne, I perceived that our boat was not the only object in the embrace of the whirl. Both above and below us were visible fragments of vessels, large masses of building timber and trunks of trees, with many smaller articles, such as pieces of house furniture, broken boxes, barrels and staves. I have already described the unnatural curiosity which had taken the place of my original terrors. It appeared to grow upon me as I drew nearer and nearer to my dreadful doom. I now began to watch, with a strange interest, the numerous things that floated in our company. I *must* have been delirious – for I even sought *amusement* in speculating upon the relative velocities of their several descents toward the foam below. "This fir tree," I found myself at one time saying, "will certainly be the next thing that takes the awful plunge and disappears," – and then I was disappointed to find that the wreck of a Dutch merchant ship overtook it and went down before. At length, after making several guesses of this nature, and being deceived in all – this fact – of my invariable miscalculation, set me upon a train of reflection that made my limbs again tremble, and my heart beat heavily once more.

'It was not a new terror that thus affected me, but the dawn of a more exciting *hope*. This hope arose partly from memory, and partly from present observation. I called to mind the great variety of buoyant matter that strewed the coast of Lofoden, having been absorbed and then thrown forth by the Moskoeström. By far the greater number of the articles were shattered in the most extraordinary way – so chafed and roughened as to have the appearance of being stuck full of splinters – but then I distinctly recollected that there were *some* of them which were not disfigured at all. Now I could not account for this difference except by supposing that the roughened fragments were the only ones which had been *completely absorbed* – that the others had entered the whirl at so late a period of the tide, or, from some reason, had descended so slowly after entering, that they did not reach the bottom before the turn of the flood came, or of the ebb, as the case might be. I conceived it possible, in either instance, that they might thus be whirled up again to the level of the ocean, without undergoing the fate of those which had been drawn in more early or absorbed more rapidly. I made, also, three important observations. The first was, that as a general rule, the larger the bodies were, the more rapid their descent; – the second, that, between two masses of equal extent, the one spherical, and the other of *any other shape*, the superiority in speed of descent was with the sphere; – the third, that, between two masses of equal size, the one cylindrical, and the other of any other shape, the cylinder was absorbed the more slowly.

'Since my escape, I have had several conversations on this subject with an old school-master of the district; and it was from him that I learned the use of the words "cylinder" and "sphere." He explained to me – although I have forgotten the explanation – how what I observed was, in fact, the natural consequence of the forms of the floating fragments – and showed me how it happened that a cylinder, swimming in a vortex, offered more resistance to its suction, and was drawn in with greater difficulty than an equally bulky body, of any form whatever.[3]

'There was one startling circumstance which went a great way in enforcing these observations, and rendering me anxious to turn them to account, and this was that, at every revolution, we passed something like a barrel, or else the broken yard or the mast of a vessel, while many of these things, which had been on our level when I first opened my eyes upon the wonders of the whirlpool, were now high up above us, and seemed to have moved but little from their original station.

'I no longer hesitated what to do. I resolved to lash myself securely to the water cask upon which I now held, to cut it loose from the counter, and to throw myself with it into the water. I attracted my brother's attention by signs, pointed to the floating barrels that came near us, and did everything in my power to make him understand what I was about to do. I thought at length that he comprehended my design – but, whether this was the case or not, he shook his head despairingly, and refused to move from his station by the ring-bolt. It was impossible to force him; the emergency admitted no delay; and so, with a bitter struggle, I resigned him to his fate, fastened myself to the cask by means of the lashings which secured it to the counter, and precipitated myself with it into the sea, without another moment's hesitation.

'The result was precisely what I had hoped it might be. As it is myself who now tell you this tale – as you see that I *did* escape – and as you are already in possession of the mode in which this escape was effected, and must therefore anticipate all that I have farther to say – I will bring my story quickly to conclusion. It might have been an hour, or thereabout, after my quitting the smack, when, having descended to a vast distance beneath me, it made three or four wild gyrations in rapid succession, and, bearing my loved brother with it, plunged headlong, at once and forever, into the chaos of foam below. The barrel to which I was attached sunk very little farther than half the distance between the bottom of the gulf and the spot at which I leaped overboard, before a great change took place in the character of the whirlpool. The slope of the sides of the vast funnel became momently less and less steep. The gyrations of the whirl grew, gradually, less and less violent. By degrees, the froth and the rainbow disappeared, and the bottom of the gulf seemed slowly to uprise. The sky was clear, the winds had gone down, and the full moon was setting radiantly in the west, when I found myself on the surface of the ocean, in full view of the shores of Lofoden, and above the spot where the pool of the Moskoe-ström *had been*. It was the hour of the slack – but the sea still heaved in mountainous waves from the effects of the hurricane. I was borne violently into the channel of the Ström, and in a few minutes, was hurried down the coast into the "grounds" of the fishermen. A boat picked me up – exhausted from fatigue – and (now that the danger was removed) speechless from the memory of its horror. Those who drew me on board were my old mates and daily companions – but they knew me no more than they would have known a traveller from the spirit-land. My hair, which had been raven-black the day before, was as white as you see it now. They say too that the whole expression of my countenance had changed. I told them my story – they did not believe it. I now tell it to *you* – and I can scarcely expect you to put more faith in it than did the merry fishermen of Lofoden.'

Eleonora

Sub conservatione formæ specificæ salva anima.
RAYMOND LULLY [1]

I AM come of a race noted for vigor of fancy and ardor of passion. Men have called me mad; but the question is not yet settled, whether madness is or is not the loftiest intelligence – whether much that is glorious – whether all that is profound – does not spring from disease of thought – from *moods* of mind exalted at the expense of the general intellect. They who dream by day are cognizant of many things which escape those who dream only by night. In their grey visions they obtain glimpses of eternity, and thrill, in awaking, to find that they have been upon the verge of the great secret. In snatches, they learn something of the wisdom which is of good, and more of the mere knowledge which is of evil. They penetrate, however rudderless or compassless, into the vast ocean of the 'light ineffable' and again, like the adventurers of the Nubian geographer, *'agressi sunt mare tenebrarum, quid in eo esset exploraturi.'* [2]

We will say, then, that I am mad. I grant, at least, that there are two distinct conditions of my mental existence – the condition of a lucid reason, not to be disputed, and belonging to the memory of events forming the first epoch of my life – and a condition of shadow and doubt, appertaining to the present, and to the recollection of what constitutes the second great era of my being. Therefore, what I shall tell of the earlier period, believe; and to what I may relate of the later time, give only such credit as may seem due; or doubt it altogether; or, if doubt it ye cannot, then play unto its riddle the Oedipus.

She whom I loved in youth, and of whom I now pen calmly and distinctly these remembrances, was the sole daughter of the only sister of my mother long departed. Eleonora was the na···

of my cousin. We had always dwelled together, beneath a tropical sun, in the Valley of the Many-Colored Grass. No unguided footstep ever came upon that vale; for it lay far away up among a range of giant hills that hung beetling around about it, shutting out the sunlight from its sweetest recesses. No path was trodden in its vicinity; and, to reach our happy home, there was need of putting back, with force, the foliage of many thousands of forest trees, and of crushing to death the glories of many millions of fragrant flowers. Thus it was that we lived all alone, knowing nothing of the world without the valley, – I, and my cousin, and her mother.

From the dim regions beyond the mountains at the upper end of our encircled domain, there crept out a narrow and deep river, brighter than all save the eyes of Eleonora; and, winding stealthily about in mazy courses, it passed away, at length, through a shadowy gorge, among hills still dimmer than those whence it had issued. We called it the 'River of Silence;' for there seemed to be a hushing influence in its flow. No murmur arose from its bed, and so gently it wandered along, that the pearly pebbles upon which we loved to gaze, far down within its bosom, stirred not at all, but lay in a motionless content, each in its own old station, shining on gloriously forever.

The margin of the river, and of the many dazzling rivulets that glided, through devious ways, into its channel, as well as the spaces that extended from the margins away down into the depths of the streams until they reached the bed of pebbles at the bottom, – these spots, not less than the whole surface of the valley, from the river to the mountains that girdled it in, were carpeted all by a soft green grass, thick, short, perfectly even, and vanilla-perfumed, but so besprinkled throughout with the yellow buttercup, the white daisy, the purple violet, and the ruby-red asphodel, that its exceeding beauty spoke to our hearts, in loud tones, of the love and of the glory of God.

And, here and there, in groves about this grass, like wildernesses of dreams, sprang up fantastic trees, whose tall slender stems stood not upright, but slanted gracefully towards the light that peered at noon-day into the centre of the valley. Their bark was speckled with the vivid alternate splendor of ebony and silver, and was smoother than all save the cheeks of Eleonora; so that but for the brilliant green of the huge leaves that spread from their summits in long tremulous lines, dallying with the Zephyrs, one might have fancied them giant serpents of Syria doing homage to their Sovereign the Sun.

Hand in hand about this valley, for fifteen years, roamed I with Eleonora before Love entered within our hearts. It was one evening at the close of the third lustrum of her life, and of the fourth of my own, that we sat, locked in each other's embrace, beneath the serpent-like trees, and looked down within the waters of the River of Silence at our images therein. We spoke no words during the rest of that sweet day; and our words even upon the morrow were tremulous and few. We had drawn the god Eros from that wave, and now we felt that he had enkindled within us the fiery souls of our forefathers. The passions which had for centuries distinguished our race, came thronging with the fancies for which they had been equally noted, and together breathed a delirious bliss over the Valley of the Many-Colored Grass. A change fell upon all things. Strange brilliant flowers, star-shaped, burst out upon the trees where no flowers had been known before. The tints of the green carpet deepened; and when, one by one, the white daisies shrank away, there sprang up, in place of them, ten·by ten of the ruby-red asphodel. And life arose in our paths; for the tall flamingo, hitherto unseen, with all gay glowing birds, flaunted his scarlet plumage before us. The golden and silver fish haunted the river, out of the bosom of which issued, little by little, a murmur that swelled, at length, into a lulling melody more divine than that of the harp of Æolus – sweeter than all save the voice of Eleonora. And now, too, a voluminous cloud, which we had long watched in the regions of Hesper, floated out thence, all gorgeous in crimson and gold, and settling in peace above us, sank, day by day, lower and lower, until its edges rested upon the tops of the mountains, turning all their dimness into magnificence, and shutting us up, as if forever, within a magic prison-house of grandeur and of glory.

The loveliness of Eleonora was that of the Seraphim; but she was a maiden artless and innocent as the brief life she had led among the flowers. No guile disguised the fervor of love which animated her heart, and she examined with me its inmost recesses as we walked together in the Valley of the Many-Colored Grass, and discoursed of the mighty changes which had lately taken place therein.

At length, having spoken one day, in tears, of the last sad change which must befall Humanity, she thence forward dwelt only upon this one sorrowful theme, interweaving it into all our converse, as, in the songs of the bard of Schiraz, the same images are found occurring, again and again, in every impressive variation of phrase.

She had seen that the finger of Death was upon her bosom – that, like the ephemeron, she had been made perfect in loveliness only to die; but the terrors of the grave, to her, lay solely in a consideration which she revealed to me, one evening at twilight, by the banks of the River of Silence. She grieved to think that, having entombed her in the Valley of the Many-Colored Grass, I would quit forever its happy recesses, transferring the love which now was so passionately her own to some maiden of the outer and every-day world. And, then and there, I threw myself hurriedly at the feet of Eleonora, and offered up a vow, to herself and to Heaven, that I would never bind myself in marriage to any daughter of Earth – that I would in no manner prove recreant to her dear memory, or to the memory of the devout affection with which she had blessed me. And I called the Mighty Ruler of the Universe to witness the pious solemnity of my vow. And the curse which I invoked of Him and of her, a saint in Helusion, should I prove traitorous to that promise, involved a penalty the exceeding great horror of which will not permit me to make record of it here. And the bright eyes of Eleonora grew brighter at my words; and she sighed as if a deadly burthen had been taken from her breast; and she trembled and very bitterly wept; but she made acceptance of the vow, (for what was she but a child?) and it made easy to her the bed of her death. And she said to me, not many days afterwards, tranquilly dying, that, because of what I had done for the comfort of her spirit, she would watch over me in that spirit when departed, and, if so it were permitted her, return to me visibly in the watches of the night; but, if this thing were, indeed, beyond the power of the souls in Paradise, that she would, at least, give me frequent indications of her presence; sighing upon me in the evening winds, or filling the air which I breathed with perfume from the censers of the angels. And, with these words upon her lips, she yielded up her innocent life, putting an end to the first epoch of my own.

Thus far I have faithfully said. But as I pass the barrier in Time's path formed by the death of my beloved, and proceed with the second era of my existence, I feel that a shadow gathers over my brain, and I mistrust the perfect sanity of the record. But let me on. – Years dragged themselves along heavily, and still I dwelled within the Valley of the Many-Colored Grass; – but a second change had come upon all things. The star-shaped flowers shrank into the stems of the trees, and appeared no more. The tints of the green carpet faded; and, one by one, the ruby-red asphodels withered away; and there sprang up, in place of them, ten by ten, dark eye-like violets that writhed uneasily and were ever encumbered with dew. And Life departed from our paths; for the tall flamingo flaunted no longer his scarlet plumage before us, but flew sadly from the vale into the hills, with all the gay glowing birds that had arrived in his company. And the golden and silver fish swam down through the gorge at the lower end of our domain and bedecked the sweet river never again. And the lulling melody that had been softer than the wind-harp of Æolus and more divine than all save the voice of Eleonora, it died little by little away, in murmurs growing lower and lower, until the stream returned, at length, utterly, into the solemnity of its original silence. And then, lastly the voluminous cloud uprose, and, abandoning the tops of the mountains to the dimness of old, fell back into the regions of Hesper, and took away all its manifold golden and gorgeous glories from the Valley of the Many-Colored Grass.

Yet the promises of Eleonora were not forgotten; for I heard the sounds of the swinging of the censers of the angels; and streams of a holy perfume floated ever and ever about the valley; and at lone hours, when my heart beat heavily, the winds that bathed my brow came unto me laden with soft sighs; and indistinct murmurs filled often the night air; and once – oh, but once only! I was awakened from a slumber like the slumber of death by the pressing of spiritual lips upon my own.

But the void within my heart refused, even thus, to be filled. I longed for the love which had before filled it to overflowing. At length the valley *pained* me through its memories of Eleonora, and I left it forever for the vanities and the turbulent triumphs of the world.

*

I found myself within a strange city, where all things might have served to blot from recollection the sweet dreams I had dreamed so long in the Valley of the Many-Colored Grass. The pomps and pageantries of a stately court, and the mad clangor of arms, and the radiant loveliness of woman, bewildered and intoxicated my brain. But as yet my soul had proved true to its vows, and the indications of the presence of Eleonora were still given me in the silent hours of the night. Suddenly, these manifestations they ceased; and the world grew dark before mine eyes; and I stood aghast at the burning thoughts which possessed – at the terrible temptations which beset me; for there came from some far, far distant and unknown land, into the gay court of the king I served, a maiden to whose beauty my whole recreant heart yielded at once – at whose footstool I bowed down without a struggle, in the most ardent, in the most abject worship of love. What indeed was my passion for the young girl of the valley in comparison with the fervor, and the delirium, and the spirit-lifting ecstasy of adoration with which I poured out my whole soul in tears at the feet of the ethereal Ermengarde? – Oh bright was the seraph Ermengarde! and in that knowledge I had room for none other. – Oh divine was the angel Ermengarde! and as I looked down into the depths of her memorial eyes I thought only of them – and *of her.*

I wedded; – nor dreaded the curse I had invoked; and its bitterness was not visited upon me. And once – but once again in the silence of the night, there came through my lattice the soft sighs which had forsaken me; and they modelled themselves into familiar and sweet voice, saying:

'Sleep in peace! – for the Spirit of Love reigneth and ruleth, and, in taking to thy passionate heart her who is Ermengarde, thou art absolved, for reasons which shall be made known to thee in Heaven, of thy vows unto Eleonora.'

The Oval Portrait

THE chateau into which my valet had ventured to make forcible entrance, rather than permit me, in my desperately wounded condition, to pass a night in the open air, was one of those piles of commingled gloom and grandeur which have so long frowned among the Apennines, not less in fact than in the fancy of Mrs Radcliffe. To all appearance it had been temporarily and very lately abandoned. We established ourselves in one of the smallest and least sumptuously furnished apartments. It lay in a remote turret of the building. Its decorations were rich, yet tattered and antique. Its walls were hung with tapestry and bedecked with manifold and multiform armorial trophies, together with an unusually great number of very spirited modern paintings in frames of rich golden arabesque. In these paintings, which depended from the walls not only in their main surfaces, but in very many nooks which the bizarre architecture of the chateau rendered necessary – in these paintings my incipient delirium, perhaps, had caused me to take deep interest; so that I bade Pedro to close the heavy shutters of the room – since it was already night – to light the tongues of a tall candelabrum which stood by the head of my bed – and to throw open far and wide the fringed curtains of black velvet which enveloped the bed itself. I wished all this done that I might resign myself, if not to sleep, at least alternately to the contemplation of these pictures, and the perusal of a small volume which had been found upon the pillow, and which purported to criticise and describe them.

Long – long I read – and devoutly, devotedly I gazed. Rapidly and gloriously the hours flew by, and the deep midnight came. The position of the candelabrum displeased me, and outreaching my hand with difficulty, rather than disturb my slumbering valet, I placed it so as to throw its rays more fully upon the book.

But the action produced an effect altogether unanticipated. The rays of the numerous candles (for there were many) now fell within a niche of the room which had hitherto been thrown into deep shade by one of the bed-posts. I thus saw in vivid light a picture all unnoticed before. It was the portrait of a young girl just ripening into womanhood. I glanced at the painting hurriedly, and then closed my eyes. Why I did this was not at first apparent even to my own perception. But while my lids remained thus shut, I ran over in mind my reason for so shutting them. It was an impulsive movement to gain time for thought – to make sure that my vision had not deceived me – to calm and subdue my fancy for a more sober and more certain gaze. In a very few moments I again looked fixedly at the painting.

That I now saw aright I could not and would not doubt; for the first flashing of the candles upon that canvas had seemed to dissipate the dreamy stupor which was stealing over my senses, and to startle me at once into waking life.

The portrait, I have already said, was that of a young girl. It was a mere head and shoulders, done in what is technically termed a *vignette* manner; much in the style of the favorite heads of Sully. The arms, the bosom and even the ends of the radiant hair, melted imperceptibly into the vague yet deep shadow which formed the back-ground of the whole. The frame was oval, richly gilded and filagreed in *Moresque*. As a thing of art nothing could be more admirable than the painting itself. But it could have been neither the execution of the work, nor the immortal beauty of the countenance, which had so suddenly and so vehemently moved me. Least of all, could it have been that my fancy, shaken from its half slumber, had mistaken the head for that of a living person. I saw at once that the peculiarities of the design, of the *vignetting*, and of the frame, must have instantly dispelled such idea – must have prevented even its momentary entertainment. Thinking earnestly upon these points, I remained, for an hour perhaps, half sitting, half re-clining, with my vision riveted upon the portrait. At length, satisfied with the true secret of its effect, I fell back within the bed. I had found the spell of the picture in an absolute *life-likeliness* of expression, which at first startling, finally confounded, sub-dued and appalled me. With deep and reverent awe I replaced the candelabrum in its former position. The cause of my deep agitation being thus shut from view, I sought eagerly the volume which discussed the paintings and their histories. Turning to the number which designated the oval portrait, I there read the vague and quaint words which follow:

'She was a maiden of rarest beauty, and not more lovely than full of glee. And evil was the hour when she saw, and loved, and wedded the painter. He, passionate, studious, austere, and having already a bride in his Art; she a maiden of rarest beauty, and not more lovely than full of glee: all light and smiles, and frolicksome as the young fawn: loving and cherishing all things: hating only the Art which was her rival: dreading only the pallet and brushes and other untoward instruments which deprived her of the countenance of her lover. It was thus a terrible thing for this lady to hear the painter speak of his desire to pourtray even his young bride. But she was humble and obedient, and sat meekly for many weeks in the dark high turret-chamber where the light dripped upon the pale canvas only from overhead. But he, the painter, took glory in his work, which went on from hour to hour and from day to day. And he was a passionate, and wild and moody man, who became lost in reveries; so that he would not see that the light which fell so ghastlily in that lone turret withered the health and the spirits of his bride, who pined visibly to all but him. Yet she smiled on and still on, uncomplainingly, because she saw that the painter, (who had high renown,) took a fervid and burning pleasure in his task, and wrought day and night to depict her who so loved him, yet who grew daily more dispirited and weak. And in sooth some who beheld the portrait spoke of its resemblance in low words, as of a mighty marvel, and a proof not less of the power of the painter than of his deep love for her whom he depicted so surpassingly well. But at length, as the labor drew nearer to its conclusion, there were admitted none into the turret; for the painter had grown wild with the ardor of his work, and turned his eyes from the canvas rarely, even to regard the countenance of his wife. And he would not see that the tints which he spread upon the canvas were drawn from the cheeks of her who sate beside him. And when many weeks had passed, and but little remained to do, save one brush upon the mouth and one tint upon the eye, the spirit of the lady again flickered up as the flame within the socket of the lamp. And then the brush was given, and then the tint was placed; and, for one moment, the painter stood entranced before the work which he had wrought; but in the next, while he yet gazed, he grew tremulous and very pallid, and aghast, and crying with a loud voice, "This is indeed *Life* itself!" turned suddenly to regard his beloved: – *She was dead!*

The Masque of the Red Death

THE 'Red Death' had long devastated the country. No pestilence had ever been so fatal, or so hideous. Blood was its Avatar and its seal – the redness and the horror of blood. There were sharp pains, and sudden dizziness, and then profuse bleeding at the pores, with dissolution. The scarlet stains upon the body and especially upon the face of the victim, were the pest ban which shut him out from the aid and from the sympathy of his fellow-men. And the whole seizure, progress and termination of the disease, were the incidents of half an hour.

But the Prince Prospero was happy and dauntless and sagacious. When his dominions were half depopulated, he summoned to his presence a thousand hale and light-hearted friends from among the knights and dames of his court, and with these retired to the deep seclusion of one of his castellated abbeys. This was an extensive and magnificent structure, the creation of the prince's own eccentric yet august taste. A strong and lofty wall girdled it in. This wall had gates of iron. The courtiers, having entered, brought furnaces and massy hammers and welded the bolts. They resolved to leave means neither of ingress or egress to the sudden impulses of despair or of frenzy from within. The abbey was amply provisioned. With such precautions the courtiers might bid defiance to contagion. The external world could take care of itself. In the meantime it was folly to grieve, or to think. The prince had provided all the appliances of pleasure. There were buffoons, there were improvisatori, there were ballet-dancers, there were musicians, there was Beauty, there was wine. All these and security were within. Without was the 'Red Death.'

It was toward the close of the fifth or sixth month of his seclusion, and while the pestilence raged most furiously abroad, that the Prince Prospero entertained his thousand friends at a masked ball of the most unusual magnificence.

It was a voluptuous scene, that masquerade. But first let me tell of the rooms in which it was held. There were seven – an imperial suite. In many palaces, however, such suites form a long and straight vista, while the folding doors slide back nearly to the walls on either hand, so that the view of the whole extent is scarcely impeded. Here the case was very different; as might have been expected from the duke's love of the *bizarre*. The apartments were so irregularly disposed that the vision embraced but little more than one at a time. There was a sharp turn at every twenty or thirty yards, and at each turn a novel effect. To the right and left, in the middle of each wall, a tall and narrow Gothic window looked out upon a closed corridor which pursued the windings of the suite. These windows were of stained glass whose color varied in accordance with the prevailing hue of the decorations of the chamber into which it opened. That at the eastern extremity was hung, for example, in blue – and vividly blue were its windows. The second chamber was purple in its ornaments and tapestries, and here the panes were purple. The third was green throughout, and so were the casements. The fourth was furnished and lighted with orange – the fifth with white – the sixth with violet. The seventh apartment was closely shrouded in black velvet tapestries that hung all over the ceiling and down the walls, falling in heavy folds upon a carpet of the same material and hue. But in this chamber only, the color of the windows failed to correspond with the decorations. The panes here were scarlet – a deep blood color. Now in no one of the seven apartments was there any lamp or candelabrum, amid the profusion of golden ornaments that lay scattered to and fro or depended from the roof. There was no light of any kind emanating from lamp or candle within the suite of chambers. But in the corridors that followed the suite, there stood, opposite to each window, a heavy tripod, bearing a brazier of fire that projected its rays through the tinted glass and so glaringly illumined the room. And thus were produced a multitude of gaudy and fantastic appearances. But in the western or black chamber the effect of the fire-light that streamed upon the dark hangings through the blood-tinted panes, was ghastly in the extreme, and produced so wild a look upon the countenances of those who entered, that there were few of the company bold enough to set foot within its precincts at all.

It was in this apartment, also, that there stood against the western wall, a gigantic clock of ebony. Its pendulum swung to and fro with a dull, heavy, monotonous clang; and when the minute-hand made the circuit of the face, and the hour was to be stricken, there came from the brazen lungs of the clock a sound which was clear and loud and deep and exceedingly musical, but of so peculiar a note and emphasis that, at each lapse of an hour, the musicians of the orchestra were constrained to pause, momentarily, in their performance, to hearken to the sound; and thus the waltzers perforce ceased their evolutions; and there was a brief disconcert of the whole gay company; and, while the chimes of the clock yet rang, it was observed that the giddiest grew pale, and the more aged and sedate passed their hands over their brows as if in confused reverie or meditation. But when the echoes had fully ceased, a light laughter at once pervaded the assembly; the musicians looked at each other and smiled as if at their own nervousness and folly, and made whispering vows, each to the other, that the next chiming of the clock should produce in them no similar emotion; and then, after the lapse of sixty minutes, (which embrace three thousand and six hundred seconds of the Time that flies,) there came yet another chiming of the clock, and then were the same disconcert and tremulousness and meditation as before.

But, in spite of these things, it was a gay and magnificent revel. The tastes of the duke were peculiar. He had a fine eye for colors and effects. He disregarded the *decora* of mere fashion. His plans were bold and fiery, and his conceptions glowed with barbaric lustre.—There are some who would have thought him mad. His followers felt that he was not. It was necessary to hear and see and touch him to be *sure* that he was not.

He had directed, in great part, the moveable embellishments of the seven chambers, upon occasion of this great *fête*; and it was his own guiding taste which had given character to the masqueraders. Be sure they were grotesque. There were much glare and glitter and piquancy and phantasm – much of what has been since seen in 'Hernani.'—There were arabesque figures with un-suited limbs and appointments. There were delirious fancies such as the madman fashions. There was much of the beautiful, much of the wanton, much of the *bizarre*, something of the terrible, and not a little of that which might have excited disgust.—To and fro in the seven chambers there stalked, in fact, a multitude of dreams. And these – the dreams – writhed in and about, taking hue from the rooms, and causing the wild music of the orchestra to seem as the echo of their steps. And, anon, there strikes the ebony clock which stands in the hall of the velvet. And then, for a moment, all is still, and all is silent save the voice of the clock. The dreams are stiff-frozen as they stand. But the echoes of the chime die away – they have endured but an instant – and a light, half-subdued laughter floats after them as they depart. And now again the music swells, and the dreams live, and writhe to and fro more merrily than ever, taking hue from the many-tinted windows through which stream the rays from the tripods. But to the chamber which lies most westwardly of the seven, there are now none of the maskers who venture; for the night is waning away; and there flows a ruddier light through the blood-colored panes; and the blackness of the sable drapery appals; and to him whose foot falls upon the sable carpet, there comes from the near clock of ebony a muffled peal more solemnly emphatic than any which reaches *their* ears who indulge in the more remote gaieties of the other apartments.

But these other apartments were densely crowded, and in them beat feverishly the heart of life. And the revel went whirlingly on, until at length there commenced the sounding of midnight upon the clock. And then the music ceased, as I have told; and the evolutions of the waltzers were quieted; and there was an uneasy cessation of all things as before. But now there were twelve strokes to be sounded by the bell of the clock; and thus it hap-pened, perhaps, that more of thought crept, with more of time, into the meditations of the thoughtful among those who revelled. And thus, too, it happened, perhaps, that before the last echoes of the last chime had utterly sunk into silence, there were many individuals in the crowd who had found leisure to become aware of the presence of a masked figure which had arrested the attention of no single individual before. And the rumor of this new presence having spread itself whisperingly around, there arose at length from the whole company a buzz, or murmur, expressive of disapprobation and surprise – then, finally, of terror, of horror, and of disgust.

In an assembly of phantasms such as I have painted it, it may well be supposed that no ordinary appearance could have excited such sensation. In truth the masquerade license of the night was nearly unlimited; but the figure in question had out-Heroded Herod, and gone beyond the bounds of even the prince's indefinite decorum. There are chords in the hearts of the most reckless which cannot be touched without emotion. Even with the utterly lost, to whom life and death are equally jests, there are matters of which no jest can be made. The whole company, indeed, seemed now deeply to feel that in the costume and bearing of the stranger neither wit nor propriety existed. The figure was tall and gaunt, and shrouded from head to foot in the habiliments of the grave. The mask which concealed the visage was made so nearly to resemble the countenance of a stiffened corpse that the closest scrutiny must have had difficulty in detecting the cheat. And yet all this might have been endured, if not approved, by the mad revellers around. But the mummer had gone so far as to assume the type of the Red Death. His vesture was dabbled in blood – and his broad brow, with all the features of the face, was besprinkled with the scarlet horror.

When the eyes of Prince Prospero fell upon this spectral image (which with a slow and solemn movement, as if more fully to sustain its rôle, stalked to and fro among the waltzers) he was seen to be convulsed, in the first moment with a strong shudder either of terror or distaste; but, in the next, his brow reddened with rage.

'Who dares?' he demanded hoarsely of the courtiers who stood near him – 'who dares insult us with this blasphemous mockery? Seize him and unmask him – that we may know whom we have to hang at sunrise, from the battlements!'

It was in the eastern or blue chamber in which stood the Prince

Prospero as he uttered these words. They rang throughout the seven rooms loudly and clearly – for the prince was a bold and robust man, and the music had become hushed at the waving of his hand.

It was in the blue room where stood the prince, with a group of pale courtiers by his side. At first, as he spoke, there was a slight rushing movement of this group in the direction of the intruder, who at the moment was also near at hand, and now, with deliberate and stately step, made closer approach to the speaker. But from a certain nameless awe with which the mad assumptions of the mummer had inspired the whole party, there were found none who put forth hand to seize him; so that, unimpeded, he passed within a yard of the prince's person; and, while the vast assembly, as if with one impulse, shrank from the centres of the rooms to the walls, he made his way uninterruptedly, but with the same solemn and measured step which had distinguished him from the first, through the blue chamber to the purple – through the purple to the green – through the green to the orange – through this again to the white – and even thence to the violet, ere a decided movement had been made to arrest him. It was then, however, that the Prince Prospero, maddening with rage and the shame of his own momentary cowardice, rushed hurriedly through the six chambers, while none followed him on account of a deadly terror that had seized upon all. He bore aloft a drawn dagger, and had approached, in rapid impetuosity, to within three or four feet of the retreating figure, when the latter, having attained the extremity of the velvet apartment, turned suddenly and confronted his pursuer. There was a sharp cry – and the dagger dropped gleaming upon the sable carpet, upon which, instantly afterwards, fell prostrate in death the Prince Prospero. Then, summoning the wild courage of despair, a throng of the revellers at once threw themselves into the black apartment, and, seizing the mummer, whose tall figure stood erect and motionless within the shadow of the ebony clock, gasped in unutterable horror at finding the grave-cerements and corpse-like mask which they handled with so violent a rudeness, untenanted by any tangible form.

—And now was acknowledged the presence of the Red Death. He had come like a thief in the night. And one by one dropped the revellers in the blood-bedewed halls of their revel, and died each in the despairing posture of his fall. And the life of the ebony clock went out with that of the last of the gay. And the flames of the tripods expired. And Darkness and Decay and the Red Death held illimitable dominion over all. —

The Pit and the Pendulum

Impia tortorum longos hic turba furores
Sanguinis innocui, non satiata, aluit.
Sospite nunc patriâ, fracto nunc funeris antro,
Mors ubi dira fuit vita salusque patent.[1]

I WAS sick – sick unto death with that long agony; and when they at length unbound me, and I was permitted to sit, I felt that my senses were leaving me. The sentence – the dread sentence of death – was the last of distinct accentuation which reached my ears. After that, the sound of the inquisitorial voices seemed merged in one dreamy indeterminate hum. It conveyed to my soul the idea of *revolution* – perhaps from its association in fancy with the burr of a mill-wheel. This only for a brief period; for presently I heard no more. Yet, for a while, I saw; but with how terrible an exaggeration! I saw the lips of the black-robed judges. They appeared to me white – whiter than the sheet upon which I trace these words – and thin even to grotesqueness; thin with the intensity of their expression of firmness – of immoveable resolution – of stern contempt of human torture. I saw that the decrees of what to me was Fate, were still issuing from those lips. I saw them writhe with a deadly locution. I saw them fashion the syllables of my name; and I shuddered because no sound succeeded. I saw, too, for a few moments of delirious horror, the soft and nearly imperceptible waving of the sable draperies which enwrapped the walls of the apartment. And then my vision fell upon the seven tall candles upon the table. At first they wore the aspect of charity, and seemed white slender angels who would save me; but then, all at once, there came a most deadly nausea over my spirit, and I felt every fibre in my frame thrill as if I had touched the wire of a galvanic battery, while the angel forms became meaningless spectres, with heads of flame, and I saw that from them there would be no help. And then there stole into my fancy, like a rich musical note, the thought of what sweet rest there must be in the grave. The thought came gently and stealthily, and it seemed long before it attained full appreciation; but just as my spirit came at length properly to feel and entertain it, the figures of the judges vanished, as if magically, from before me; the tall candles sank into nothingness; their flames went out utterly; the blackness of darkness supervened; all sensations appeared swallowed up in a mad rushing descent as of the soul into Hades. Then silence, and stillness, and night were the universe.

I had swooned but still will not say that all of consciousness was lost. What of it there remained I will not attempt to define, or even to describe; yet all was not lost. In the deepest slumber – no! In delirium – no! In a swoon – no! In death – no! even in the grave all is not lost. Else there is no immortality for man. Arousing from the most profound of slumbers, we break the gossamer web of some dream. Yet in a second afterward, (so frail may that web have been) we remember not that we have dreamed. In the return to life from the swoon there are two stages; first, that of the sense of mental or spiritual; secondly, that of the sense of physical, existence. It seems probable that if, upon reaching the second stage, we could recall the impressions of the first, we should find these impressions eloquent in memories of the gulf beyond. And that gulf is – what? How at least shall we distinguish its shadows from those of the tomb? But if the impressions of what I have termed the first stage, are not, at will, recalled, yet, after long interval, do they not come unbidden, while we marvel whence they come? He who has never swooned, is not he who finds strange palaces and wildly familiar faces in coals that glow; is not he who beholds floating in mid-air the sad visions that the many may not view; is not he who ponders over the perfume of some novel flower – is not he whose brain grows bewildered with the meaning of some musical cadence which has never before arrested his attention.

Amid frequent and thoughtful endeavors to remember; amid earnest struggles to regather some token of the state of seeming nothingness into which my soul had lapsed, there have been moments when I have dreamed of success; there have been brief, very brief periods when I have conjured up remembrances which the lucid reason of a later epoch assures me could have had reference only to that condition of seeming unconsciousness. These shadows of memory tell, indistinctly, of tall figures that lifted and bore me in silence down – down – still down – till a hideous dizziness oppressed me at the mere idea of the interminableness of the descent. They tell also of a vague horror at my heart, on account of that heart's unnatural stillness. Then comes a sense of sudden motionlessness throughout all things; as if those who bore me (a ghastly train !) had outrun, in their descent, the limits of the limitless, and paused from the wearisomeness of their toil. After this I call to mind flatness and dampness; and then all is *madness* – the madness of a memory which busies itself among forbidden things.

Very suddenly there came back to my soul motion and sound – the tumultuous motion of the heart, and, in my ears, the sound of its beating. Then a pause in which all is blank. Then again sound, and motion, and touch – a tingling sensation pervading my frame. Then the mere consciousness of existence, without thought – a condition which lasted long. Then, very suddenly, *thought*, and shuddering terror, and earnest endeavor to comprehend my true state. Then a strong desire to lapse into insensibility. Then a rushing revival of soul and a successful effort to move. And now a full memory of the trial, of the judges, of the sable draperies, of the sentence, of the sickness, of the swoon. Then entire forgetfulness of all that followed; of all that a later day and much earnestness of endeavor have enabled me vaguely to recall.

So far, I had not opened my eyes. I felt that I lay upon my back, unbound. I reached out my hand, and it fell heavily upon something damp and hard. There I suffered it to remain for many minutes, while I strove to imagine where and *what* I could be. I longed, yet dared not to employ my vision. I dreaded the first glance at objects around me. It was not that I feared to look upon things horrible, but that I grew aghast lest there should be *nothing* to see. At length, with a wild desperation at heart, I quickly unclosed my eyes. My worst thoughts, then, were confirmed. The blackness of eternal night encompassed me. I struggled for breath. The intensity of the darkness seemed to oppress and stifle me. The atmosphere was intolerably close. I still lay quietly, and made effort to exercise my reason. I brought to mind the inquisitorial proceedings, and attempted from that point to deduce my real condition. The sentence had passed; and it appeared to me that a very long interval of time had since elapsed. Yet not for a moment did I suppose myself actually dead. Such a supposition, notwithstanding what we read in fiction, is altogether inconsistent with real existence; – but where and in what state was I? The condemned to death, I knew, perished usually at the *autos-da-fé*, and one of these had been held on the very night of the day of my trial. Had I been remanded to my dungeon, to await the next sacrifice, which would not take place for many months? This I at once saw could not be. Victims had been in immediate demand. Moreover, my dungeon, as well as all the condemned cells at Toledo, had stone floors, and light was not altogether excluded.

A fearful idea now suddenly drove the blood in torrents upon my heart, and for a brief period, I once more relapsed into insensibility. Upon recovering, I at once started to my feet, trembling convulsively in every fibre. I thrust my arms wildly above and around me in all directions. I felt nothing; yet dreaded to move a step, lest I should be impeded by the walls of a *tomb*. Perspiration burst from every pore, and stood in cold big beads upon my forehead. The agony of suspense grew at length intolerable, and I cautiously moved forward, with my arms extended, and my eyes straining from their sockets, in the hope of catching some faint ray of light. I proceeded for many paces; but still all was blackness and vacancy. I breathed more freely. It seemed evident that mine was not, at least, the most hideous of fates.

And now, as I still continued to step cautiously onward, there came thronging upon my recollection a thousand vague rumors of the horrors of Toledo. Of the dungeons there had been strange things narrated – fables I had always deemed them – but yet strange, and too ghastly to repeat, save in a whisper. Was I left to perish of starvation in this subterranean world of darkness; or what fate, perhaps even more fearful, awaited me? That the result would be death, and a death of more than customary bitterness, I knew too well the character of my judges to doubt. The mode and the hour were all that occupied or distracted me.

My outstretched hands at length encountered some solid obstruction. It was a wall, seemingly of stone masonry – very smooth, slimy, and cold. I followed it up; stepping with all the careful distrust with which certain antique narratives had inspired me. This process, however, afforded me no means of ascertaining the dimensions of my dungeon; as I might make its circuit, and return to the point whence I set out, without being aware of the fact; so perfectly uniform seemed the wall. I therefore sought the knife which had been in my pocket, when led into the inquisitorial chamber; but it was gone; my clothes had been exchanged for a wrapper of coarse serge. I had thought of forcing the blade in some minute crevice of the masonry, so as to identify my point of departure. The difficulty, nevertheless, was but trivial; although, in the disorder of my fancy, it seemed at first insuperable. I tore a part of the hem from the robe and placed the fragment at full length, and at right angles to the wall. In groping my way around the prison, I could not fail to encounter this rag upon completing the circuit. So, at least I thought: but I had not counted upon the extent of the dungeon, or upon my own weakness. The ground was moist and slippery. I staggered onward for some time, when I stumbled and fell. My excessive fatigue induced me to remain prostrate; and sleep soon overtook me as I lay.

Upon awaking, and stretching forth an arm, I found beside me a loaf and a pitcher with water. I was too much exhausted to reflect upon this circumstance, but ate and drank with avidity. Shortly afterward, I resumed my tour around the prison, and with much toil, came at last upon the fragment of the serge. Up to the period when I fell I had counted fifty-two paces, and upon resuming my walk, I had counted forty-eight more; –

when I arrived at the rag. There were in all, then, a hundred paces; and, admitting two paces to the yard, I presumed the dungeon to be fifty yards in circuit. I had met, however, with many angles in the wall, and thus I could form no guess at the shape of the vault; for vault I could not help supposing it to be.

I had little object – certainly no hope – in these researches; but a vague curiosity prompted me to continue them. Quitting the wall, I resolved to cross the area of the enclosure. At first I proceeded with extreme caution, for the floor, although seemingly of solid material, was treacherous with slime. At length, however, I took courage, and did not hesitate to step firmly; endeavoring to cross in as direct a line as possible. I had advanced some ten or twelve paces in this manner, when the remnant of the torn hem of my robe became entangled between my legs. I stepped on it, and fell violently on my face.

In the confusion attending my fall, I did not immediately apprehend a somewhat startling circumstance, which yet, in a few seconds afterward, and while I still lay prostrate, arrested my attention. It was this – my chin rested upon the floor of the prison, but my lips and the upper portion of my head, although seemingly at a less elevation than the chin, touched nothing. At the same time my forehead seemed bathed in a clammy vapor, and the peculiar smell of decayed fungus arose to my nostrils. I put forward my arm, and shuddered to find that I had fallen at the very brink of a circular pit, whose extent, of course, I had no means of ascertaining at the moment. Groping about the masonry just below the margin, I succeeded in dislodging a small fragment, and let it fall into the abyss. For many seconds I hearkened to its reverberations as it dashed against the sides of the chasm in its descent; at length there was a sullen plunge into water, succeeded by loud echoes. At the same moment there came a sound resembling the quick opening, and as rapid closing of a door overhead, while a faint gleam of light flashed suddenly through the gloom, and as suddenly faded away.

I saw clearly the doom which had been prepared for me, and congratulated myself upon the timely accident by which I had escaped. Another step before my fall, and the world had seen me no more. And the death just avoided, was of that very character which I had regarded as fabulous and frivolous in the tales respecting the Inquisition. To the victims of its tyranny, there was the choice of death with its direst physical agonies, or death with its most hideous moral horrors. I had been reserved for the latter. By long suffering my nerves had been unstrung, until I trembled at the sound of my own voice, and had become in every respect a fitting subject for the species of torture which awaited me.

Shaking in every limb, I groped my way back to the wall; resolving there to perish rather than risk the terrors of the wells, of which my imagination now pictured many in various positions about the dungeon. In other conditions of mind I might have had courage to end my misery at once by a plunge into one of these abysses; but now I was the veriest of cowards. Neither could I forget what I had read of these pits – that the *sudden* extinction of life formed no part of their most horrible plan.

Agitation of spirit kept me awake for many long hours; but at length I again slumbered. Upon arousing, I found by my side, as before, a loaf and a pitcher of water. A burning thirst consumed me, and I emptied the vessel at a draught. It must have been drugged; for scarcely had I drunk, before I became irresistibly drowsy. A deep sleep fell upon me – a sleep like that of death. How long it lasted of course, I know not; but when, once again, I unclosed my eyes, the objects around me were visible. By a wild sulphurous lustre, the origin of which I could not at first determine, I was enabled to see the extent and aspect of the prison.

In its size I had been greatly mistaken. The whole circuit of its walls did not exceed twenty-five yards. For some minutes this fact occasioned me a world of vain trouble; vain indeed! for what could be of less importance, under the terrible circumstances which environed me, than the mere dimensions of my dungeon? But my soul took a wild interest in trifles, and I busied myself in endeavors to account for the error I had committed in my measurement. The truth at length flashed upon me. In my first attempt at exploration I had counted fifty-two paces, up to the period when I fell; I must then have been within a pace or two of the fragment of serge; in fact, I had nearly performed the circuit of the vault. I then slept, and upon awaking, I must have returned upon my steps – thus supposing the circuit nearly double what it actually was. My confusion of mind prevented me from observing that I began my tour with the wall to the left, and ended it with the wall to the right.

I had been deceived, too, in respect to the shape of the enclosure. In feeling my way I had found many angles, and thus deduced an idea of great irregularity; so potent is the effect of total darkness upon one arousing from lethargy or sleep! The angles were simply those of a few slight depressions, or niches, at odd intervals. The general shape of the prison was square. What I had taken for masonry seemed now to be iron, or some other metal, in huge plates, whose sutures or joints occasioned the depression. The entire surface of this metallic enclosure was rudely daubed in all the hideous and repulsive devices to which the charnel superstition of the monks has given rise. The figures of fiends in aspects of menace, with skeleton forms, and other more really fearful images, overspread and disfigured the walls. I observed that the outlines of these monstrosities were sufficiently distinct, but that the colors seemed faded and blurred, as if from the effects of a damp atmosphere. I now noticed the floor, too, which was of stone. In the centre yawned the circular pit from whose jaws I had escaped; but it was the only one in the dungeon.

All this I saw indistinctly and by much effort: for my personal condition had been greatly changed during slumber. I now lay upon my back, and at full length, on a species of low framework of wood. To this I was securely bound by a long strap resembling a surcingle. It passed in many convolutions about my limbs and body, leaving at liberty only my head, and my left arm to such extent that I could, by dint of much exertion, supply myself with food from an earthen dish which lay by my side on the floor. I saw, to my horror, that the pitcher had been removed. I say to my horror; for I was consumed with intolerable thirst. This thirst it appeared to be the design of my persecutors to stimulate: for the food in the dish was meat pungently seasoned.

Looking upward, I surveyed the ceiling of my prison. It was some thirty or forty feet overhead, and constructed much as the side walls. In one of its panels a very singular figure riveted my whole attention. It was the painted figure of Time as he is commonly represented, save that, in lieu of a scythe, he held what, at a casual glance, I supposed to be the pictured image of a huge pendulum such as we see on antique clocks. There was something, however, in the appearance of this machine which caused me to regard it more attentively. While I gazed directly upward at it (for its position was immediately over my own) I fancied that I saw it in motion. In an instant afterward the fancy was confirmed. Its sweep was brief, and of course slow. I watched it for some minutes, somewhat in fear, but more in wonder. Wearied at length with observing its dull movement, I turned my eyes upon the other objects in the cell.

A slight noise attracted my notice, and, looking to the floor, I saw several enormous rats traversing it. They had issued from the well, which lay just within view to my right. Even then, while I gazed, they came up in troops, hurriedly, with ravenous eyes, allured by the scent of the meat. From this it required much effort and attention to scare them away.

It might have been half an hour, perhaps even an hour, (for I could take but imperfect note of time) before I again cast my eyes upward. What I then saw confounded and amazed me. The sweep of the pendulum had increased in extent by nearly a yard. As a natural consequence, its velocity was also much greater. But what mainly disturbed me was the idea that it had perceptibly *descended*. I now observed – with what horror it is needless to say – that its nether extremity was formed of a crescent of glittering steel, about a foot in length from horn to horn; the horns upward, and the under edge evidently as keen as that of a razor. Like a razor also, it seemed massy and heavy, tapering from the edge into a solid and broad structure above. It was appended to a weighty rod of brass, and the whole *hissed* as it swung through the air.

I could no longer doubt the doom prepared for me by monkish ingenuity in torture. My cognizance of the pit had become known to the inquisitorial agents – *the pit* whose horrors had been destined for so bold a recusant as myself – *the pit*, typical of hell, and regarded by rumor as the Ultima Thule of all their punishments. The plunge into this pit I had avoided by the merest of accidents, and I knew that surprise, or entrapment into torment, formed an important portion of all the grotesquerie of these dungeon deaths. Having failed to fall, it was no part of the demon plan to hurl me into the abyss; and thus (there being no alternative) a different and a milder destruction awaited me. Milder! I half smiled in my agony as I thought of such application of such a term.

What boots it to tell of the long, long hours of horror more than mortal, during which I counted the rushing vibrations of the steel! Inch by inch – line by line – with a descent only appreciable at intervals that seemed ages – down and still down it came! Days passed – it might have been that many days passed – ere it swept so closely over me as to fan me with its acrid breath. The odor of the sharp steel forced itself into my nostrils. I prayed – I wearied heaven with my prayer for its more speedy descent. I grew frantically mad, and struggled to force myself upward against the sweep of the fearful scimitar. And then I fell suddenly calm, and lay smiling at the glittering death, as a child at some rare bauble.

There was another interval of utter insensibility; it was brief; for, upon again lapsing into life there had been no perceptible descent in the pendulum. But it might have been long; for I knew there were demons who took note of my swoon, and who could have arrested the vibration at pleasure. Upon my recovery, too, I felt very – oh, inexpressibly sick and weak, as if through long inanition. Even amid the agonies of that period, the human nature craved food. With painful effort I outstretched my left arm as far as my bonds permitted, and took possession of the small remnant which had been spared me by the rats. As I put a portion of it within my lips, there rushed to my mind a half formed thought of joy – of hope. Yet what business had I with hope? It was, as I say, a half formed thought – man has many such which are never completed. I felt that it was of joy – of hope; but I felt also that it had perished in its formation. In vain I struggled to perfect – to regain it. Long suffering had nearly annihilated all my ordinary powers of mind. I was an imbecile – an idiot.

The vibration of the pendulum was at right angles to my length. I saw that the crescent was designed to cross the region of the heart. It would fray the serge of my robe – it would return and repeat its operations – again – and again. Notwithstanding its terrifically wide sweep (some thirty feet or more) and the hissing vigor of its descent, sufficient to sunder these very walls of iron, still the fraying of my robe would be all that, for several minutes, it would accomplish. And at this thought I paused. I dared not go farther than this reflection. I dwelt upon it with a pertinacity of attention – as if, in so dwelling, I could arrest *here* the descent of the steel. I forced myself to ponder upon the sound of the crescent as it should pass across the garment – upon the peculiar thrilling sensation which the friction of cloth produces on the nerves. I pondered upon all this frivolity until my teeth were on edge.

Down – steadily down it crept. I took a frenzied pleasure in contrasting its downward with its lateral velocity. To the right – to the left – far and wide – with the shriek of a damned spirit; to my heart with the stealthy pace of the tiger! I alternately laughed and howled as the one or the other idea grew predominant.

Down – certainly, relentlessly down! It vibrated within three inches of my bosom! I struggled violently, furiously, to free my left arm. This was free only from the elbow to the hand. I could reach the latter, from the platter beside me, to my mouth, with great effort, but no farther. Could I have broken the fastenings above the elbow, I would have seized and attempted to arrest the pendulum. I might as well have attempted to arrest an avalanche!

Down – still unceasingly – still inevitably down! I gasped and struggled at each vibration. I shrunk convulsively at its every sweep. My eyes followed its outward or upward whirls with the eagerness of the most unmeaning despair; they closed themselves spasmodically at the descent, although death would have been a relief, oh! how unspeakable! Still I quivered in every nerve to think how slight a sinking of the machinery would precipitate that keen, glistening axe upon my bosom. It was *hope* that prompted the nerve to quiver – the frame to shrink. It was *hope* – the hope that triumphs on the rack – that whispers to the death-condemned even in the dungeons of the Inquisition.

I saw that some ten or twelve vibrations would bring the steel in actual contact with my robe, and with this observation there suddenly came over my spirit all the keen, collected calmness of despair. For the first time during many hours – or perhaps days – I *thought*. It now occurred to me that the bandage, or surcingle, which enveloped me, was *unique*. I was tied by no separate cord. The first stroke of the razor-like crescent athwart any portion of the band, would so detach it that it might be unwound from my person by means of my left hand. But how fearful, in that case, the proximity of the steel! The result of the slightest struggle how deadly! Was it likely, moreover, that the minions of the torturer had not foreseen and provided for this possibility! Was it probable that the bandage crossed my bosom in the track of the pendulum? Dreading to find my faint, and, as it seemed, my last hope frustrated, I so far elevated my head as to obtain a distinct view of my breast. The surcingle enveloped my limbs and body close in all directions – *save in the path of the destroying crescent.*

Scarcely had I dropped my head back into its orginal position, when there flashed upon my mind what I cannot better describe than as the unformed half of that idea of deliverance to which I have previously alluded, and of which a moiety only floated indeterminately through my brain when I raised food to my burning lips. The whole thought was now present – feeble, scarcely sane, scarcely definite, – but still entire. I proceeded at once, with the nervous energy of despair, to attempt its execution.

For many hours the immediate vicinity of the low framework

upon which I lay, had been literally swarming with rats. They were wild, bold, ravenous; their red eyes glaring upon me as if they waited but for motionlessness on my part to make me their prey. 'To what food,' I thought, 'have they been accustomed in the well?'

They had devoured, in spite of all my efforts to prevent them, all but a small remnant of the contents of the dish. I had fallen into an habitual see-saw, or wave of the hand about the platter: and, at length, the unconscious uniformity of the movement deprived it of effect. In their voracity the vermin frequently fastened their sharp fangs in my fingers. With the particles of the oily and spicy viand which now remained, I thoroughly rubbed the bandage wherever I could reach it; then, raising my hand from the floor, I lay breathlessly still.

At first the ravenous animals were startled and terrified at the change – at the cessation of movement. They shrank alarmedly back; many sought the well. But this was only for a moment. I had not counted in vain upon their voracity. Observing that I remained without motion, one or two of the boldest leaped upon the frame-work, and smelt at the surcingle. This seemed the signal for a general rush. Forth from the well they hurried in fresh troops. They clung to the wood – they overran it, and leaped in hundreds upon my person. The measured movement of the pendulum disturbed them not at all. Avoiding its strokes they busied themselves with the anointed bandage. They pressed – they swarmed upon me in ever accumulating heaps. They writhed upon my throat; their cold lips sought my own; I was half stifled by their thronging pressure; disgust, for which the world has no name, swelled my bosom, and chilled, with a heavy clamminess, my heart. Yet one minute, and I felt that the struggle would be over. Plainly I perceived the loosening of the bandage. I knew that in more than one place it must be already severed. With a more than human resolution I lay *still*.

Nor had I erred in my calculations – nor had I endured in vain. I at length felt that I was *free*. The surcingle hung in ribands from my body. But the stroke of the pendulum already pressed upon my bosom. It had divided the serge of the robe. It had cut through the linen beneath. Twice again it swung, and a sharp sense of pain shot through every nerve. But the moment of escape had arrived. At a wave of my hand my deliverers hurried tumultuously away. With a steady movement – cautious, sidelong, shrinking, and slow – I slid from the embrace of the bandage and beyond the reach of the scimitar. For the moment, at least, I was free.

Free ! – and in the grasp of the Inquisition ! I had scarcely stepped from my wooden bed of horror upon the stone floor of the prison, when the motion of the hellish machine ceased and I beheld it drawn up, by some invisible force, through the ceiling. This was a lesson which I took desperately to heart. My every motion was undoubtedly watched. Free ! – I had but escaped death in one form of agony, to be delivered unto worse than death in some other. With that thought I rolled my eyes nervously around on the barriers of iron that hemmed me in. Something unusual – some change which, at first, I could not appreciate distinctly – it was obvious, had taken place in the apartment. For many minutes of a dreamy and trembling abstraction, I busied myself in vain, unconnected conjecture. During this period, I became aware, for the first time, of the origin of the sulphurous light which illuminated the cell. It proceeded from a fissure, about half an inch in width, extending entirely around the prison at the base of the walls, which thus appeared, and were, completely separated from the floor. I endeavored, but of course in vain, to look through the aperture.

As I arose from the attempt, the mystery of the alteration in the chamber broke at once upon my understanding. I have observed that, although the outlines of the figures upon the walls were sufficiently distinct, yet the colours seemed blurred and indefinite. These colors had now assumed, and were momentarily assuming, a startling and most intense brilliancy, that gave to the spectral and fiendish portraitures an aspect that might have thrilled even firmer nerves than my own. Demon eyes, of a wild and ghastly vivacity, glared upon me in a thousand directions, where none had been visible before, and gleamed with the lurid lustre of a fire that I could not force my imagination to regard as unreal.

Unreal! – Even while I breathed there came to my nostrils the breath of the vapour of heated iron ! A suffocating odour pervaded the prison ! A deeper glow settled each moment in the eyes that glared at my agonies ! A richer tint of crimson diffused itself over the pictured horrors of blood. I panted ! I gasped for breath ! There could be no doubt of the design of my tormentors – oh ! most unrelenting ! oh ! most demoniac of men ! I shrank from the glowing metal to the centre of the cell. Amid the thought of the fiery destruction that impended, the idea of the coolness of the well came over my soul like balm. I rushed to its deadly brink. I threw my straining vision below. The glare from the enkindled roof illumined its inmost recesses. Yet, for a wild moment, did my spirit refuse to comprehend the meaning of what I saw. At length it forced – it wrestled its way into my soul – it burned itself in upon my shuddering reason. – Oh ! for a voice to speak ! – oh ! horror ! – oh ! any horror but this ! With a shriek, I rushed from the margin, and buried my face in my hands – weeping bitterly.

The heat rapidly increased, and once again I looked up, shuddering as with a fit of the ague. There had been a second change in the cell – and now the change was obviously in the *form*. As before, it was in vain that I, at first, endeavoured to appreciate or understand what was taking place. But not long was I left in doubt. The Inquisitorial vengeance had been hurried by my twofold escape, and there was to be no more dallying with the King of Terrors. The room had been square. I saw that two of its iron angles were now acute – two, consequently, obtuse. The fearful difference quickly increased with a low rumbling or moaning sound. In an instant the apartment had shifted its form into that of a lozenge. But the alteration stopped not here – I neither hoped nor desired it to stop. I could have clasped the red walls to my bosom as a garment of eternal peace. 'Death,' I said, 'any death but that of the pit !' Fool ! might I have not known that *into the pit* it was the object of the burning iron to urge me? Could I resist its glow? or, if even that, could I withstand its pressure? And now, flatter and flatter grew the lozenge, with a rapidity that left me no time for contemplation. Its centre, and of course, its greatest width, came just over the yawning gulf. I shrank back – but the closing walls pressed me resistlessly onward. At length for my seared and writhing body there was no longer an inch of foothold on the firm floor of the prison. I struggled no more, but the agony of my soul found vent in one loud, long, and final scream of despair. I felt that I tottered upon the brink – I averted my eyes –

There was a discordant hum of human voices! There was a loud blast as of many trumpets! There was a harsh grating as of a thousand thunders! The fiery walls rushed back! An outstretched arm caught my own as I fell, fainting, into the abyss. It was that of General Lasalle. The French army had entered Toledo. The Inquisition was in the hands of its enemies.

The Tell-Tale Heart

TRUE! – nervous – very, very dreadfully nervous I had been and am; but why will you say that I am mad? The disease had sharpened my senses – not destroyed – not dulled them. Above all was the sense of hearing acute. I heard all things in the heaven and in the earth. I heard many things in hell. How, then, am I mad? Hearken! and observe how healthily – how calmly I can tell you the whole story.

It is impossible to say how first the idea entered my brain; but once conceived, it haunted me day and night. Object there was none. Passion there was none. I loved the old man. He had never wronged me. He had never given me insult. For his gold I had no desire. I think it was his eye! yes, it was this! He had the eye of a vulture – a pale blue eye, with a film over it. Whenever it fell upon me, my blood ran cold; and so by degrees – very gradually – I made up my mind to take the life of the old man, and thus rid myself of the eye forever.

Now this is the point. You fancy me mad. Madmen know nothing. But you should have seen me. You should have seen how wisely I proceeded – with what caution – with what foresight – with what dissimulation I went to work! I was never kinder to the old man than during the whole week before I killed him. And every night, about midnight, I turned the latch of his door and opened it – oh so gently! And then, when I had made an opening sufficient for my head, I put in a dark lantern, all closed, closed, so that no light shone out, and then I thrust in my head. Oh, you would have laughed to see how cunningly I thrust it in! I moved it slowly – very, very slowly, so that I might not disturb the old man's sleep. It took me an hour to place my whole head within the opening so far that I could see him as he lay upon his bed. Ha! – would a madman have been so wise as this? And then, when my head was well in the room, I undid the lantern cautiously – oh, so cautiously – cautiously (for the hinges creaked) – I undid it just so much that a single thin ray fell upon the vulture eye. And this I did for seven long nights – every night just at midnight – but I found the eye always closed; and so it was impossible to do the work; for it was not the old man who vexed me, but his Evil Eye. And every morning, when the day broke, I went boldly into the chamber, and spoke courageously to him, calling him by name in a hearty tone, and inquiring how he had passed the night. So you see he would have been a very profound old man, indeed, to suspect that every night, just at twelve, I looked in upon him while he slept.

Upon the eighth night I was more than usually cautious in opening the door. A watch's minute hand moves more quickly than did mine. Never before that night, had I *felt* the extent of my own powers – of my sagacity. I could scarcely contain my feelings of triumph. To think that there I was, opening the door, little by little, and he not even to dream of my secret deeds or thoughts. I fairly chuckled at the idea; and perhaps he heard me; for he moved on the bed suddenly, as if startled. Now you may think that I drew back – but no. His room was as black as pitch with the thick darkness, (for the shutters were close fastened, through fear of robbers,) and so I knew that he could not see the opening of the door, and I kept pushing it on steadily, steadily.

I had my head in, and was about to open the lantern, when my thumb slipped upon the tin fastening, and the old man sprang up in bed, crying out – 'Who's there?'

I kept quite still and said nothing. For a whole hour I did not move a muscle, and in the meantime I did not hear him lie down. He was still sitting up in the bed listening; – just as I have done, night after night, hearkening to the death watches in the wall.

Presently I heard a slight groan, and I knew it was the groan of mortal terror. It was not a groan of pain or of grief – oh, no! – it was the low stifled sound that arises from the bottom of the soul when overcharged with awe. I knew the sound well. Many a night, just at midnight, when all the world slept, it has welled up from my own bosom, deepening, with its dreadful echo, the terrors that distracted me. I say I knew it well. I knew what the old man felt, and pitied him, although I chuckled at heart. I knew that he had been lying awake ever since the first slight noise, when he had turned in the bed. His fears had been ever since growing upon him. He had been trying to fancy them causeless, but could not. He had been saying to himself – 'It is nothing but the wind in the chimney – it is only a mouse crossing the floor,' or 'it is merely a cricket which has made a single chirp.' Yes, he had been trying to comfort himself with these suppositions: but he had found all in vain. *All in vain;* because Death, in approaching him had stalked with his black shadow before him, and enveloped the victim. And it was the mournful influence of the unperceived shadow that caused him to feel – although he neither saw nor heard – to *feel* the presence of my head within the room.

When I had waited a long time, very patiently, without hearing him lie down, I resolved to open a little – a very, very little crevice in the lantern. So I opened it – you cannot imagine how stealthily, stealthily – until, at length a simple dim ray, like the thread of the spider, shot from out the crevice and fell full upon the vulture eye.

It was open – wide, wide open – and I grew furious as I gazed upon it. I saw it with perfect distinctness – all a dull blue, with a hideous veil over it that chilled the very marrow in my bones; but I could see nothing else of the old man's face or person: for I had directed the ray as if by instinct, precisely upon the damned spot.

And have I not told you that what you mistake for madness is but over acuteness of the senses? – now, I say, there came to my ears a low, dull, quick sound, such as a watch makes when enveloped in cotton. I knew *that* sound well, too. It was the beating of the old man's heart. It increased my fury, as the beating of a drum stimulates the soldier into courage.

But even yet I refrained and kept still. I scarcely breathed. I held the lantern motionless. I tried how steadily I could maintain the ray upon the eye. Meantime the hellish tattoo of the heart increased. It grew quicker and quicker, and louder and louder every instant. The old man's terror *must* have been extreme! It grew louder, I say, louder every moment! – do you mark me well? I have told you that I am nervous: so I am. And now at the dead hour of the night, amid the dreadful silence of that old house, so strange a noise as this excited me to uncontrollable terror. Yet, for some minutes longer I refrained and stood still. But the beating grew louder, louder! I thought the heart must burst. And now a new anxiety seized me – the sound would be heard by a neighbour! The old man's hour had come! With a loud yell, I threw open the lantern and leaped into the room. He shrieked once – once only. In an instant I dragged him to the floor, and pulled the heavy bed over him. I then smiled gaily, to find the deed so far done. But, for many minutes, the heart beat on with a muffled sound. This, however, did not vex me; it would not be heard through the wall. At length it ceased. The old man was dead. I removed the bed and examined the corpse. Yes, he was stone, stone dead. I placed my hand upon the heart and held it there many minutes. There was no pulsation. He was stone dead. His eye would trouble me no more.

If still you think me mad, you will think so no longer when I describe the wise precautions I took for the concealment of the body. The night waned; and I worked hastily, but in silence. First of all I dismembered the corpse. I cut off the head and the arms and the legs.

I then took up three planks from the flooring of the chamber, and deposited all between the scantlings. I then replaced the boards so cleverly, so cunningly, that no human eye – not even *his* – could have detected any thing wrong. There was nothing to wash out – no stain of any kind – no blood-spot whatever. I had been too wary for that. A tub had caught all – ha! ha!

When I had made an end of these labors, it was four o'clock – still dark as midnight. As the bell sounded the hour, there came a knocking at the street door. I went down to open it with a light heart, – for what had I *now* to fear? There entered three men, who introduced themselves, with perfect suavity, as officers of the police. A shriek had been heard by a neighbour during the night; suspicion of foul play had been aroused; information had been lodged at the police office, and they (the officers) had been deputed to search the premises.

I smiled, – for what had I to fear? I bade the gentlemen welcome. The shriek, I said, was my own in a dream. The old man, I mentioned, was absent in the country. I took my visitors all over the house. I bade them search – search well. I led them, at length, to his chamber. I showed them his treasures, secure, undisturbed. In the enthusiasm of my confidence, I brought chairs into the room, and desired them here to rest from their fatigues, while I myself, in the wild audacity of my perfect triumph, placed my own seat upon the very spot beneath which reposed the corpse of the victim.

The officers were satisfied. My manner had convinced them. I was singularly at ease. They sat, and while I answered cheerily, they chatted of familiar things. But, ere long, I felt myself getting pale and wished them gone. My head ached, and I fancied a ringing in my ears: but still they sat and still chatted. The ringing became more distinct: – it continued and became more distinct: I talked more freely to get rid of the feeling: but it continued and gained definiteness – until, at length, I found that the noise was not within my ears.

No doubt I now grew very pale; – but I talked more fluently, and with a heightened voice. Yet the sound increased – and what could I do? It was a low, dull, quick sound – much such a sound as a watch makes when enveloped in cotton. I gasped for breath – and yet the officers heard it not. I talked more quickly – more vehemently; but the noise steadily increased. I arose and argued about trifles, in a high key and with violent gesticulations; but the noise steadily increased. Why would they not be gone? I paced the floor to and fro with heavy strides, as if excited to fury by the observations of the men – but the noise steadily increased. Oh God! what could I do? I foamed – I raved – I swore! I swung the chair upon which I had been sitting, and grated it upon the boards, but the noise arose over all and continually increased. It grew louder – louder – louder! And still the men chatted pleasantly, and smiled. Was it possible they heard not? Almighty God! – no, no! They heard! – they suspected! – they *knew!* – they were making a mockery of my horror! – this I thought, and this I think. But anything was better than this agony! Anything was more tolerable than this derision! I could bear those hypocritical smiles no longer! I felt that I must scream or die! and now – again! – hark! louder! louder! louder! *louder!*

'Villains!' I shrieked, 'dissemble no more! I admit the deed! – tear up the planks! here, here! – it is the beating of his hideous heart!'

The Gold-Bug

What ho! what ho! this fellow is dancing mad!
He hath been bitten by the Tarantula.
All in the Wrong [1]

MANY years ago, I contracted an intimacy with a Mr William
Legrand. He was of an ancient Huguenot family, and had once
been wealthy; but a series of misfortunes had reduced him to
want. To avoid the mortification consequent upon his disasters,
he left New Orleans, the city of his forefathers, and took up his
residence at Sullivan's Island, near Charleston, South Carolina.

This Island is a very singular one. It consists of little else
than the sea sand, and is about three miles long. Its breadth at no
point exceeds a quarter of a mile. It is separated from the main
land by a scarcely perceptible creek, oozing its way through a
wilderness of reeds and slime, a favorite resort of the marsh-hen.
The vegetation, as might be supposed, is scant, or at least
dwarfish. No trees of any magnitude are to be seen. Near the
western extremity, where Fort Moultrie stands, and where are
some miserable frame buildings, tenanted, during summer, by the
fugitives from Charleston dust and fever, may be found, indeed,
the bristly palmetto; but the whole island, with the exception of
this western point, and a line of hard, white beach on the sea-
coast, is covered with a dense undergrowth of the sweet myrtle,
so much prized by the horticulturists of England. The shrub here
often attains the height of fifteen or twenty feet, and forms an
almost impenetrable coppice, burthening the air with its
fragrance.

In the inmost recesses of this coppice, not far from the eastern
or more remote end of the island, Legrand had built himself a
small hut, which he occupied when I first, by mere accident,
made his acquaintance. This soon ripened into friendship – for

there was much in the recluse to excite interest and esteem. I found him well educated, with unusual powers of mind, but infected with misanthropy, and subject to perverse moods of alternate enthusiasm and melancholy. He had with him many books, but rarely employed them. His chief amusements were gunning and fishing, or sauntering along the beach and through the myrtles, in quest of shells or entomological specimens; – his collection of the latter might have been envied by a Swammerdamm. In these excursions he was usually accompanied by an old negro, called Jupiter, who had been manumitted before the reverses of the family, but who could be induced, neither by threats nor by promises, to abandon what he considered his right of attendance upon the footsteps of his young 'Massa Will.' It is not improbable that the relatives of Legrand, conceiving him to be somewhat unsettled in intellect, had contrived to instil this obstinacy into Jupiter, with a view to the supervision and guardianship of the wanderer.

The winters in the latitude of Sullivan's Island are seldom very severe, and in the fall of the year it is a rare event indeed when a fire is considered necessary. About the middle of October, 18—, there occurred, however, a day of remarkable chilliness. Just before sunset I scrambled my way through the evergreens to the hut of my friend, whom I had not visited for several weeks – my residence being, at that time, in Charleston, a distance of nine miles from the Island, while the facilities of passage and repassage were very far behind those of the present day. Upon reaching the hut I rapped, as was my custom, and getting no reply, sought for the key where I knew it was secreted, unlocked the door and went in. A fine fire was blazing upon the hearth. It was a novelty, and by no means an ungrateful one. I threw off an overcoat, took an arm-chair by the crackling logs, and awaited patiently the arrival of my hosts.

Soon after dark they arrived, and gave me a most cordial welcome. Jupiter, grinning from ear to ear, bustled about to prepare some marsh-hens for supper. Legrand was in one of his fits – how else shall I term them? – of enthusiasm. He had found an unknown bivalve, forming a new genus, and, more than this, he had hunted down and secured, with Jupiter's assistance, a *scarabæus* which he believed to be totally new, but in respect to which he wished to have my opinion on the morrow.

'And why not to-night?' I asked, rubbing my hands over the blaze, and wishing the whole tribe of *scarabæi* at the devil.

'Ah, if I had only known you were here!' said Legrand, 'but it's so long since I saw you; and how could I foresee that you would pay me a visit this very night of all others? As I was coming home I met Lieutenant G—, from the fort, and, very foolishly, I lent him the bug; so it will be impossible for you to see it until morning. Stay here to-night, and I will send Jup down for it at sunrise. It is the loveliest thing in creation!'

'What? – sunrise?'

'Nonsense! no! – the bug. It is of a brilliant gold color – about the size of a large hickory-nut – with two jet black spots near one extremity of the back, and another, somewhat longer, at the other. The *antennæ* are –'

'Dey aint *no* tin in him, Massa Will, I keep a tellin on you,' here interrupted Jupiter; 'de bug is a goole bug, solid, ebery bit of him, inside and all, sep him wing – neber feel half so hebby a bug in my life.'

'Well, suppose it is, Jup,' replied Legrand, somewhat more earnestly, it seemed to me, than the case demanded, 'is that any reason for your letting the birds burn? The color' – here he turned to me – 'is really almost enough to warrant Jupiter's idea. You never saw a more brilliant metallic lustre than the scales emit – but of this you cannot judge till to-morrow. In the mean time I can give you some idea of the shape.' Saying this, he seated himself at a small table, on which were a pen and ink, but no paper. He looked for some in a drawer, but found none.

'Never mind,' said he at length, 'this will answer;' and he drew from his waistcoat pocket a scrap of what I took to be very dirty foolscap, and made upon it a rough drawing with the pen. While he did this, I retained my seat by the fire, for I was still chilly. When the design was complete, he handed it to me without rising. As I received it, a loud growl was heard, succeeded by a scratching at the door. Jupiter opened it, and a large Newfoundland, belonging to Legrand, rushed in, leaped upon my shoulders, and loaded me with caresses; for I had shown him much attention during previous visits. When his gambols were over, I looked at the paper, and, to speak the truth, found myself not a little puzzled at what my friend had depicted.

'Well!' I said, after contemplating it for some minutes, 'this is a strange *scarabæus*, I must confess: new to me: never saw anything like it before – unless it was a skull, or a death's-head – which it more nearly resembles than anything else that has come under *my* observation.'

'A death's-head!' echoed Legrand – 'Oh – yes – well, it has something of that appearance upon paper, no doubt. The two upper black spots look like eyes, eh? and the longer one at the bottom like a mouth – and then the shape of the whole is oval.'

'Perhaps so,' said I; 'but, Legrand, I fear you are no artist. I must wait until I see the beetle itself, if I am to form any idea of its personal appearance.'

'Well, I don't know,' said he, a little nettled, 'I draw tolerably – *should* do it at least – have had good masters, and flatter myself that I am not quite a blockhead.'

'But, my dear fellow, you are joking then,' said I, 'this is a very passable *skull* – indeed, I may say that it is a very *excellent* skull, according to the vulgar notions about such specimens of physiology – and your *scarabæus* must be the queerest *scarabæus* in the world if it resembles it. Why, we may get up a very thrilling bit of superstition upon this hint. I presume you will call the bug *scarabæus caput hominis*, or something of that kind – there are many similar titles in the Natural Histories. But where are the antennæ you spoke of?'

'The *antennæ*!' said Legrand, who seemed to be getting unaccountably warm upon the subject; 'I am sure you must see the *antennæ*. I made them as distinct as they are in the original insect, and I presume that is sufficient.'

'Well, well,' I said, 'perhaps you have – still I don't see them;' and I handed him the paper without additional remark, not wishing to ruffle his temper; but I was much surprised at the turn affairs had taken; his ill humor puzzled me – and, as for the drawing of the beetle, there were positively *no antennæ* visible, and the whole *did* bear a very close resemblance to the ordinary cuts of a death's-head.

He received the paper very peevishly, and was about to crumple it, apparently to throw it in the fire, when a casual glance at the design seemed suddenly to rivet his attention. In an instant his face grew violently red – in another as excessively pale. For some minutes he continued to scrutinize the drawing minutely where he sat. At length he arose, took a candle from the table, and proceeded to seat himself upon a sea-chest in the farthest corner of the room. Here again he made an anxious examination of the paper; turning it in all directions. He said nothing, however, and his conduct greatly astonished me; yet I thought it prudent not to exacerbate the growing moodiness of his temper by any comment. Presently he took from his coat pocket a wallet, placed the paper carefully in it, and deposited both in a writing-desk, which he locked. He now grew more composed in his demeanor; but his original air of enthusiasm had quite disappeared. Yet he seemed not so much sulky as abstracted. As the evening wore away he became more and more absorbed in reverie, from which no sallies of mine could arouse him. It had been my intention to pass the night at the hut, as I had frequently done before, but, seeing my host in this mood, I deemed it proper to take leave. He did not press me to remain, but, as I departed, he shook my hand with even more than his usual cordiality.

It was about a month after this (and during the interval I had seen nothing of Legrand) when I received a visit, at Charleston, from his man, Jupiter. I had never seen the good old negro look so dispirited, and I feared that some serious disaster had befallen my friend.

'Well, Jup,' said I, 'what is the matter now? – how is your master?'

'Why, to speak de troof, massa, him not so berry well as mought be.'

'Not well! I am truly sorry to hear it. What does he complain of?'

'Dar! dat 's it! – him neber plain of notin – but him berry sick for all dat.'

'Very sick, Jupiter! – why did n't you say so at once? Is he confined to bed?'

'No, dat he aint! – he aint find nowhar – dat's just whar de shoe pinch – my mind is got to be berry hebby bout poor Massa Will.'

'Jupiter, I should like to understand what it is you are talking about. You say your master is sick. Has n't he told you what ails him?'

'Why, massa, taint worf while for to git mad bout de matter – Massa Will say noffin at all aint de matter wid him – but den what make him go about looking dis here way, wid he head down and he soldiers up, and as white as a gose? And den he keep a syphon all de time –'

'Keeps a what, Jupiter?'

'Keeps a syphon wid de figgurs on de slate – de queerest figgurs I ebber did see. Ise gittin to be skeered, I tell you. Hab for to keep mighty tight eye pon him noovers. Todder day he gib me slip fore de sun up and was gone de whole ob de blessed day. I had a big stick ready cut for to gib him d—d good beating when he did come – but Ise sich a fool dat I had n't de heart arter all – he look so berry poorly.'

'Eh? – what? – ah yes! – upon the whole I think you had better not be too severe with the poor fellow – don't flog him, Jupiter – he can't very well stand it – but can you form no idea of what has occasioned this illness, or rather this change of conduct? Has anything unpleasant happened since I saw you?'

'No, massa, dey aint bin noffin onpleasant since den – 't was fore den I 'm feared – 't was de berry day you was dare.'

'How? what do you mean?'

'Why, massa, I mean de bug – dare now.'

'The what?'

'De bug – I 'm berry sartain dat Massa Will bin bit somewhere bout de head by dat goole-bug.'

'And what cause have you, Jupiter, for such a supposition?'

'Claws enuff, massa, and mouff too. I nebber did see sich a d—d bug – he kick and he bite ebery ting what cum near him. Massa Will cotch him fuss, but had for to let him go gin mighty quick, I tell you – den was de time he must ha got de bite. I did n't like de look ob de bug mouff, myself, no how, so I would n't take hold ob him wid my finger, but I cotch him wid a piece ob paper dat I found. I rap him up in de paper and stuff piece ob it in he mouff – dat was de way.'

'And you think, then, that your master was really bitten by the beetle, and that the bite made him sick?'

'I don't tink noffin about it – I nose it. What make him dream bout de goole so much, if taint cause he bit by de goole-bug? Ise heerd bout dem goole-bugs fore dis.'

'But how do you know he dreams about gold?'

'How I know? why cause he talk about it in he sleep – dat 's how I nose.'

'Well, Jup, perhaps you are right; but to what fortunate circumstance am I to attribute the honor of a visit from you to-day?'

'What de matter, massa?'

'Did you bring any message from Mr Legrand?'

'No, massa, I bring dis here pissel;' and here Jupiter handed me a note which ran thus:

My Dear —

Why have I not seen you for so long a time? I hope you have not been so foolish as to take offence at any little *brusquerie* of mine; but no, that is improbable.

Since I saw you I have had great cause for anxiety. I have something to tell you, yet scarcely know how to tell it, or whether I should tell it at all.

I have not been quite well for some days past, and poor old Jup annoys me, almost beyond endurance, by his well-meant attentions. Would you believe it? – he had prepared a huge stick, the other day, with which to chastise me for giving him the slip, and spending the day, *solus*, among the hills on the main land. I verily believe that my ill looks alone saved me a flogging.

I have made no addition to my cabinet since we met.

If you can, in any way, make it convenient, come over with Jupiter. Do come. I wish to see you *tonight*, upon business of importance. I assure you that it is of the *highest* importance.

Ever yours,
WILLIAM LEGRAND

There was something in the tone of this note which gave me great uneasiness. Its whole style differed materially from that of Legrand. What could he be dreaming of? What new crotchet possessed his excitable brain? What 'business of the highest importance' could *he* possibly have to transact? Jupiter's account of him boded no good. I dreaded lest the continued pressure of misfortune had, at length, fairly unsettled the reason of my friend. Without a moment's hesitation, therefore, I prepared to accompany the negro.

Upon reaching the wharf, I noticed a scythe and three spades, all apparently new, lying in the bottom of the boat in which we were to embark.

'What is the meaning of all this, Jup?' I inquired.

'Him syfe, massa, and spade.'

'Very true; but what are they doing here?'

'Him de syfe and de spade what Massa Will sis pon my buying for him in de town, and de debbil's own lot of money I had to gib for em.'

'But what, in the name of all that is mysterious, is your "Massa Will" going to do with scythes and spades?'

'Dat 's more dan I know, and debbil take me if I don't blieve 't is more dan he know, too. But it 's all cum ob de bug.'

Finding that no satisfaction was to be obtained of Jupiter, whose whole intellect seemed to be absorbed by 'de bug,' I now stepped into the boat and made sail. With a fair and strong breeze we soon ran into the little cove to the northward of Fort Moultrie, and a walk of some two miles brought us to the hut. It was about three in the afternoon when we arrived. Legrand had been awaiting us in eager expectation. He grasped my hand with a nervous *empressement* which alarmed me and strengthened the suspicions already entertained. His countenance was pale even to ghastliness, and his deep-set eyes glared with unnatural lustre. After some inquiries respecting his health, I asked him, not knowing what better to say, if he had yet obtained the *scarabæus* from Lieutenant G—.

'Oh, yes,' he replied, coloring violently, 'I got it from him the next morning. Nothing should tempt me to part with that *scarabæus*. Do you know that Jupiter is quite right about it?'

'In what way?' I asked, with a sad foreboding at heart.

'In supposing it to be a bug of *real gold*.' He said this with an air of profound seriousness, and I felt inexpressibly shocked.

'This bug is to make my fortune,' he continued, with a triumphant smile, 'to reinstate me in my family possessions. Is it any wonder, then, that I prize it? Since Fortune has thought fit to bestow it upon me, I have only to use it properly and I shall arrive at the gold of which it is the index. Jupiter, bring me that *scarabæus* !'

'What ! de bug, massa? I 'd rudder not go fer trubble dat bug – you mus git him for your own self.' Hereupon Legrand arose, with a grave and stately air, and brought me the beetle from a glass case in which it was enclosed. It was a beautiful *scarabæus*, and, at that time, unknown to naturalists – of course a great prize in a scientific point of view. There were two round, black spots near one extremity of the back, and a long one near the other. The scales were exceedingly hard and glossy, with all the appearance of burnished gold. The weight of the insect was very remarkable, and, taking all things into consideration, I could hardly blame Jupiter for his opinion respecting it; but what to make of Legrand's agreement with that opinion, I could not, for the life of me, tell.

'I sent for you,' said he, in a grandiloquent tone, when I had completed my examination of the beetle, 'I sent for you, that I might have your counsel and assistance in furthering the views of Fate and of the bug' –

'My dear Legrand,' I cried, interrupting him, 'you are certainly unwell, and had better use some little precautions. You shall go to bed, and I will remain with you a few days, until you get over this. You are feverish and ' –

'Feel my pulse,' said he.

I felt it, and, to say the truth, found not the slightest indication of fever.

'But you may be ill and yet have no fever. Allow me this once to prescribe for you. In the first place, go to bed. In the next' –

'You are mistaken,' he interposed, 'I am as well as I can expect to be under the excitement which I suffer. If you really wish me well, you will relieve this excitement.'

'And how is this to be done?'

'Very easily. Jupiter and myself are going upon an expedition into the hills, upon the main land, and, in this expedition, we shall need the aid of some person in whom we can confide. You are the only one we can trust. Whether we succeed or fail, the excitement which you now perceive in me will be equally allayed.'

'I am anxious to oblige you in any way,' I replied; 'but do you mean to say that this infernal beetle has any connection with your expedition into the hills?'

'It has.'

'Then, Legrand, I can become a party to no such absurd proceeding.'

'I am sorry – very sorry – for we shall have to try it by ourselves.'

'Try it by yourselves! The man is surely mad! – but stay! – how long do you propose to be absent?'

'Probably all night. We shall start immediately, and be back, at all events, by sunrise.'

'And will you promise me, upon your honor, that when this freak of yours is over, and the bug business (good God!) settled to your satisfaction, you will then return home and follow my advice implicitly, as that of your physician?'

'Yes; I promise; and now let us be off, for we have no time to lose.'

With a heavy heart I accompanied my friend. We started about four o'clock – Legrand, Jupiter, the dog, and myself. Jupiter had with him the scythe and spades – the whole of which he insisted upon carrying – more through fear, it seemed to me, of trusting either of the implements within reach of his master, than from any excess of industry or complaisance. His demeanor was dogged in the extreme, and 'dat d—d bug' were the sole words which escaped his lips during the journey. For my own part, I had charge of a couple of dark lanterns, while Legrand contented himself with the *scarabæus*, which he carried attached to the end of a bit of whip-cord; twirling it to and fro, with the air of a conjuror, as he went. When I observed this last, plain evidence of my friend's aberration of mind, I could scarcely refrain from tears. I thought it best, however, to humor his fancy, at least for the present, or until I could adopt some more energetic measures with a chance of success. In the mean time I endeavored, but all in vain, to sound him in regard to the object of the expedition. Having succeeded in inducing me to accompany him, he seemed unwilling to hold conversation upon any topic of minor importance, and to all my questions vouchsafed no other reply than 'we shall see !'

We crossed the creek at the head of the island by means of a skiff, and, ascending the high grounds on the shore of the main land, proceeded in a northwesterly direction, through a tract of country excessively wild and desolate, where no trace of a human footstep was to be seen. Legrand led the way with decision; pausing only for an instant, here and there, to consult what appeared to be certain landmarks of his own contrivance upon a former occasion.

In this manner we journeyed for about two hours, and the sun was just setting when we entered a region infinitely more dreary than any yet seen. It was a species of table land, near the summit of an almost inaccessible hill, densely wooded from base to pinnacle, and interspersed with huge crags that appeared to lie loosely upon the soil, and in many cases were prevented from precipitating themselves into the valleys below, merely by the support of the trees against which they reclined. Deep ravines, in various directions, gave an air of still sterner solemnity to the scene.

The natural platform to which we had clambered was thickly overgrown with brambles, through which we soon discovered that it would have been impossible to force our way but for the scythe; and Jupiter, by direction of his master, proceeded to clear for us a path to the foot of an enormously tall tulip-tree, which stood, with some eight or ten oaks, upon the level, and far surpassed them all, and all other trees which I had then ever seen, in the beauty of its foliage and form, in the wide spread of its branches, and in the general majesty of its appearance. When we reached this tree, Legrand turned to Jupiter, and asked him if he thought he could climb it. The old man seemed a little staggered by the question, and for some moments made no reply. At length he approached the huge trunk, walked slowly around it, and examined it with minute attention. When he had completed his scrutiny, he merely said,

'Yes, massa, Jup climb any tree he ebber see in he life.'

'Then up with you as soon as possible, for it will soon be too dark to see what we are about.'

'How far mus go up, massa?' inquired Jupiter.

'Get up the main trunk first, and then I will tell you which way to go – and here – stop! take this beetle with you.'

'De bug, Massa Will! – de goole bug!' cried the negro, drawing back in dismay – 'what for mus tote de bug way up de tree? – d—n if I do!'

'If you are afraid, Jup, a great big negro like you, to take hold of a harmless little dead beetle, why you can carry it up by this string – but, if you do not take it up with you in some way, I shall be under the necessity of breaking your head with this shovel.'

'What de matter now, massa?' said Jup, evidently shamed into compliance; 'always want for to raise fuss wid old nigger. Was only funnin any how. Me feered de bug! what I keer for de bug?' Here he took cautiously hold of the extreme end of the string, and, maintaining the insect as far from his person as circumstances would permit, prepared to ascend the tree.

In youth, the tulip-tree, or *Liriodendron Tulipiferum*, the most magnificent of American foresters, has a trunk peculiarly smooth, and often rises to a great height without lateral branches; but, in its riper age, the bark becomes gnarled and uneven, while many short limbs make their appearance on the stem. Thus the difficulty of ascension, in the present case, lay more in semblance than in reality. Embracing the huge cylinder, as closely as possible, with his arms and knees, seizing with his hands some projections, and resting his naked toes upon others, Jupiter, after one or two narrow escapes from falling, at length wriggled himself into the first great fork, and seemed to consider the whole business as virtually accomplished. The *risk* of the achievement was, in fact, now over, although the climber was some sixty or seventy feet from the ground.

'Which way mus go now, Massa Will?' he asked.

'Keep up the largest branch – the one on this side,' said Legrand. The negro obeyed him promptly, and apparently with but little trouble; ascending higher and higher, until no glimpse of his squat figure could be obtained through the dense foliage which enveloped it. Presently his voice was heard in a sort of halloo.

'How much fudder is got for go?'

'How high up are you?' asked Legrand.

'Ebber so fur,' replied the negro; 'can see de sky fru de top ob de tree.'

'Never mind the sky, but attend to what I say. Look down the trunk and count the limbs below you on this side. How many limbs have you passed?'

'One, two, tree, four, fibe – I done pass fibe big limb, massa, pon dis side.'

'Then go one limb higher.'

In a few minutes the voice was heard again, announcing that the seventh limb was attained.

'Now, Jup,' cried Legrand, evidently much excited, 'I want you to work your way out upon that limb as far as you can. If you see anything strange, let me know.'

By this time what little doubt I might have entertained of my poor friend's insanity, was put finally at rest. I had no alternative but to conclude him stricken with lunacy, and I became seriously anxious about getting him home. While I was pondering upon what was best to be done, Jupiter's voice was again heard.

'Mos feerd for to ventur pon dis limb berry far – tis dead limb putty much all de way.'

'Did you say it was a *dead* limb, Jupiter?' cried Legrand in a quavering voice.

'Yes, massa, him dead as de door-nail – done up for sartain – done departed dis here life.'

'What in the name of heaven shall I do?' asked Legrand, seemingly in the greatest distress.

'Do!' said I, glad of an opportunity to interpose a word, 'why come home and go to bed. Come now! – that's a fine fellow. It's getting late, and, besides, you remember your promise.'

'Jupiter,' cried he, without heeding me in the least, 'do you hear me?'

'Yes, Massa Will, hear you ebber so plain.'

'Try the wood well, then, with your knife, and see if you think it *very* rotten.'

'Him rotten, massa, sure nuff,' replied the negro in a few moments, 'but not so berry rotten as mought be. Mought ventur out leetle way pon de limb by myself, dat's true.'

'By yourself! – what do you mean?'

'Why I mean de bug. 'T is *berry* hebby bug. Spose I drop him down fuss, and den de limb won't break wid just de weight ob one nigger.'

'You infernal scoundrel!' cried Legrand, apparently much relieved, 'what do you mean by telling me such nonsense as that? As sure as you let that beetle fall! – I'll break your neck. Look here, Jupiter! do you hear me?'

'Yes, massa, need n't hollo at poor nigger dat style.'

'Well! now listen! – if you will venture out on the limb as far as you think safe, and not let go the beetle, I'll make you a present of a silver dollar as soon as you get down.'

'I'm gwine, Massa Will – deed I is,' replied the negro very promptly – 'mos out to the eend now.'

'*Out to the end!*' here fairly screamed Legrand, 'do you say you are out to the end of that limb?'

'Soon be to de eend, massa, – o-o-o-o-oh! Lorgol-a-marcy! what is dis here pon de tree?'

'Well!' cried Legrand, highly delighted, 'what is it?'

'Why taint noffin but a skull – somebody bin lef him head up de tree, and de crows done gobble ebery bit ob de meat off.'

'A skull, you say! – very well! – how is it fastened to the limb? – what holds it on?'

'Sure nuff, massa; mus look. Why dis berry curous sarcumstance, pon my word – dare's a great big nail in de skull, what fastens ob it on to de tree.'

'Well now, Jupiter, do exactly as I tell you – do you hear?'

'Yes, massa.'

'Pay attention, then! – find the left eye of the skull.'

'Hum! hoo! dat's good? why dar aint no eye lef at all.'

'Curse your stupidity! do you know your right hand from your left?'

'Yes, I nose dat – nose all bout dat – tis my left hand what I chops de wood wid.'

'To be sure! you are left-handed; and your left eye is on the same side as your left hand. Now, I suppose, you can find the left eye of the skull, or the place where the left eye has been. Have you found it?'

Here was a long pause. At length the negro asked,

'Is de lef eye of de skull pon de same side as de lef hand of de skull, too? – cause de skull aint got not a bit ob a hand at all – nebber mind! I got de lef eye now – here the lef eye! what mus do wid it?'

'Let the beetle drop through it, as far as the string will reach – but be careful and not let go your hold of the string.'

'All dat done, Massa Will; mighty easy ting for to put de bug fru de hole – look out for him dar below!'

During this colloquy no portion of Jupiter's person could be seen; but the beetle, which he had suffered to descend, was now visible at the end of the string, and glistened, like a globe of burnished gold, in the last rays of the setting sun, some of which still faintly illumined the eminence upon which we stood. The *scarabæus* hung quite clear of any branches, and, if allowed to fall, would have fallen at our feet. Legrand immediately took the scythe, and cleared with it a circular space, three or four yards in diameter, just beneath the insect, and, having accomplished this, ordered Jupiter to let go the string and come down from the tree.

Driving a peg, with great nicety, into the ground, at the precise spot where the beetle fell, my friend now produced from his pocket a tape-measure. Fastening one end of this at that point of the trunk of the tree which was nearest the peg, he unrolled it till it reached the peg, and thence farther unrolled it, in the direction already established by the two points of the tree and the peg, for the distance of fifty feet – Jupiter clearing away the brambles with the scythe. At the spot thus attained a second peg was driven, and about this, as a centre, a rude circle, about four feet in diameter, described. Taking now a spade himself, and giving one to Jupiter and one to me, Legrand begged us to set about digging as quickly as possible.

To speak the truth, I had no especial relish for such amusement at any time, and, at that particular moment, would most willingly have declined it; for the night was coming on, and I felt much fatigued with the exercise already taken; but I saw no mode of escape, and was fearful of disturbing my poor friend's equanimity by a refusal. Could I have depended, indeed, upon Jupiter's aid, I would have had no hesitation in attempting to get the lunatic home by force; but I was too well assured of the old negro's disposition, to hope that he would assist me, under any circumstances, in a personal contest with his master. I made no doubt that the latter had been infected with some of the innumerable Southern superstitions about money buried, and that his phantasy had received confirmation by the finding of the *scarabæus*, or, perhaps, by Jupiter's obstinacy in maintaining it to be 'a bug of real gold.' A mind disposed to lunacy would readily be led away by such suggestions – especially if chiming in with favorite preconceived ideas – and then I called to mind the poor fellow's speech about the beetle's being 'the index of his fortune.' Upon the whole, I was sadly vexed and puzzled, but, at length, I concluded to make a virtue of necessity – to dig with a good will, and thus the sooner to convince the visionary, by ocular demonstration, of the fallacy of the opinions he entertained.

The lanterns having been lit, we all fell to work with a zeal worthy a more rational cause; and, as the glare fell upon our persons and implements, I could not help thinking how picturesque a group we composed, and how strange and suspicious our labors must have appeared to any interloper who, by chance, might have stumbled upon our whereabouts.

We dug very steadily for two hours. Little was said; and our chief embarrassment lay in the yelpings of the dog, who took exceeding interest in our proceedings. He, at length, became so obstreperous that we grew fearful of his giving the alarm to some stragglers in the vicinity; – or, rather, this was the apprehension of Legrand; – for myself, I should have rejoiced at any interruption which might have enabled me to get the wanderer home. The noise was, at length, very effectually silenced by Jupiter, who, getting out of the hole with a dogged air of deliberation, tied the brute's mouth up with one of his suspenders, and then returned, with a grave chuckle, to his task.

When the time mentioned had expired, we had reached a depth of five feet, and yet no signs of any treasure became manifest. A general pause ensued, and I began to hope that the farce was at an end. Legrand, however, although evidently much disconcerted, wiped his brow thoughtfully and recommenced. We had excavated the entire circle of four feet diameter, and now we slightly enlarged the limit, and went to the farther depth of two feet. Still nothing appeared. The gold-seeker, whom I sincerely pitied, at length clambered from the pit, with the bitterest disappointment imprinted upon every feature, and proceeded, slowly and reluctantly, to put on his coat, which he had thrown off at the beginning of his labor. In the mean time I made no remark. Jupiter, at a signal from his master, began to gather up his tools. This done, and the dog having been unmuzzled, we turned in profound silence towards home.

We had taken, perhaps, a dozen steps in this direction, when, with a loud oath, Legrand strode up to Jupiter, and seized him by the collar. The astonished negro opened his eyes and mouth to the fullest extent, let fall the spades, and fell upon his knees.

'You scoundrel,' said Legrand, hissing out the syllables from between his clenched teeth – 'you infernal black villain! – speak, I tell you! – answer me this instant, without prevarication! – which – which is your left eye?'

'Oh, my golly, Massa Will! aint dis here my lef eye for sartain?' roared the terrified Jupiter, placing his hand upon his *right* organ of vision, and holding it there with a desperate pertinacity, as if in immediate dread of his master's attempt at a gouge.

'I thought so! – I knew it! – hurrah!' vociferated Legrand, letting the negro go, and executing a series of curvets and caracols, much to the astonishment of his valet, who, arising from his knees, looked, mutely, from his master to myself, and then from myself to his master.

'Come! we must go back,' said the latter, 'the game's not up yet;' and he again led the way to the tulip-tree.

'Jupiter,' said he, when we reached its foot, 'come here! was the skull nailed to the limb with the face outward, or with the face to the limb?'

'De face was out, massa, so dat de crows could get at de eyes good, widout any trouble.'

'Well, then, was it this eye or that through which you let the beetle fall?' – here Legrand touched each of Jupiter's eyes.

'T was dis eye, massa – de lef eye – jis as you tell me,' and here it was his right eye that the negro indicated.

'That will do – we must try it again.'

Here my friend, about whose madness I now saw, or fancied that I saw, certain indications of method, removed the peg which marked the spot where the beetle fell, to a spot about three inches to the westward of its former position. Taking, now, the tape-measure from the nearest point of the trunk to the peg, as before, and continuing the extension in a straight line to the distance of fifty feet, a spot was indicated, removed, by several yards, from the point at which we had been digging.

Around the new position a circle, somewhat larger than in the former instance, was now described, and we again set to work with the spades. I was dreadfully weary, but, scarcely understanding what had occasioned the change in my thoughts, I felt no longer any great aversion from the labor imposed. I had become most unaccountably interested – nay, even excited. Perhaps there was something, amid all the extravagant demeanor of Legrand – some air of forethought, or of deliberation, which impressed me. I dug eagerly, and now and then caught myself actually looking, with something that very much resembled expectation, for the fancied treasure, the vision of which had demented my unfortunate companion. At a period when such vagaries of thought most fully possessed me, and when we had been at work perhaps an hour and a half, we were again interrupted by the violent howlings of the dog. His uneasiness, in the first instance, had been, evidently, but the result of playfulness or caprice, but he now assumed a bitter and serious tone. Upon Jupiter's again attempting to muzzle him, he made furious resistance, and, leaping into the hole, tore up the mould frantically with his claws. In a few seconds he had uncovered a mass of human bones, forming two complete skeletons, intermingled with several buttons of metal, and what appeared to be the dust of decayed woollen. One or two strokes of a spade upturned the blade of a large Spanish knife, and, as we dug farther, three or four loose pieces of gold and silver coin came to light.

At sight of these the joy of Jupiter could scarcely be restrained, but the countenance of his master wore an air of extreme disappointment. He urged us, however, to continue our exertions, and the words were hardly uttered when I stumbled and fell forward, having caught the toe of my boot in a large ring of iron that lay half buried in the loose earth.

We now worked in earnest, and never did I pass ten minutes of more intense excitement. During this interval we had fairly unearthed an oblong chest of wood, which, from its perfect preservation, and wonderful hardness, had plainly been subjected to some mineralizing process – perhaps that of the Bi-chloride of Mercury. This box was three feet and a half long, three feet broad, and two and a half feet deep. It was firmly secured by bands of wrought iron, riveted, and forming a kind of trellis-work over the whole. On each side of the chest, near the top, were three rings of iron – six in all – by means of which a firm hold could be obtained by six persons. Our utmost united endeavors served only to disturb the coffer very slightly in its bed. We at once saw the impossibility of removing so great a weight. Luckily, the sole fastenings of the lid consisted of two sliding bolts. These we drew back – trembling and panting with anxiety. In an instant, a treasure of incalculable value lay gleaming before us. As the rays of the lanterns fell within the pit, there flashed upwards, from a confused heap of gold and of jewels, a glow and a glare that absolutely dazzled our eyes.

I shall not pretend to describe the feelings with which I gazed. Amazement was, of course, predominant. Legrand appeared exhausted with excitement, and spoke very few words. Jupiter's countenance wore, for some minutes, as deadly a pallor as it is possible, in the nature of things, for any negro's visage to assume. He seemed stupified – thunder-stricken. Presently he fell upon his knees in the pit, and, burying his naked arms up to the elbows in gold, let them there remain, as if enjoying the luxury of a bath. At length, with a deep sigh, he exclaimed, as if in a soliloquy,

'And dis all cum ob de goole-bug! de putty goole-bug! de poor little goole-bug, what I boosed in dat sabage kind ob style! Aint you shamed ob yourself, nigger? – answer me dat!'

It became necessary, at last, that I should arouse both master and valet to the expediency of removing the treasure. It was growing late, and it behooved us to make exertion, that we might get every thing housed before daylight. It was difficult to say what should be done; and much time was spent in deliberation – so confused were the ideas of all. We, finally, lightened the box by removing two thirds of its contents, when we were enabled, with some trouble, to raise it from the hole. The articles taken out were deposited among the brambles, and the dog left to guard them, with strict orders from Jupiter neither, upon any pretence, to stir from the spot, nor to open his mouth until our return. We then hurriedly made for home with the chest; reaching the hut in safety, but after excessive toil, at one o'clock in the morning. Worn out as we were, it was not in human nature to do more just then. We rested until two, and had supper; starting for the hills immediately afterwards, armed with three stout sacks, which, by good

luck, were upon the premises. A little before four we arrived at
the pit, divided the remainder of the booty, as equally as might
be, among us, and, leaving the holes unfilled, again set out for the
hut, at which, for the second time, we deposited our golden bur-
thens, just as the first streaks of the dawn gleamed from over the
tree-tops in the East.

We were now thoroughly broken down; but the intense excitement of the time denied us repose. After an unquiet slumber of
some three or four hours' duration, we arose, as if by preconcert,
to make examination of our treasure.

The chest had been full to the brim, and we spent the whole
day, and the greater part of the next night, in a scrutiny of its
contents. There had been nothing like order or arrangement.
Every thing had been heaped in promiscuously. Having assorted
all with care, we found ourselves possessed of even vaster wealth
than we had at first supposed. In coin there was rather more
than four hundred and fifty thousand dollars – estimating the
value of the pieces, as accurately as we could, by the tables of the
period. There was not a particle of silver. All was gold of antique
date and of great variety – French, Spanish, and German money,
with a few English guineas, and some counters, of which we had
never seen specimens before. There were several very large and
heavy coins, so worn that we could make nothing of their inscrip-
tions. There was no American money. The value of the jewels we
found more difficulty in estimating. There were diamonds – some
of them exceedingly large and fine – a hundred and ten in all, and
not one of them small; eighteen rubies of remarkable brilliancy; –
three hundred and ten emeralds, all very beautiful; and twenty-
one sapphires, with an opal. These stones had all been broken
from their settings and thrown loose in the chest. The settings
themselves, which we picked out from among the other gold,
appeared to have been beaten up with hammers, as if to prevent
identification. Besides all this, there was a vast quantity of solid
gold ornaments; – nearly two hundred massive finger and ear
rings; – rich chains – thirty of these, if I remember; – eighty-
three very large and heavy crucifixes; – five gold censers of great
value; – a prodigious golden punch-bowl, ornamented with richly

chased vine-leaves and Bacchanalian figures; with two sword-handles exquisitely embossed, and many other smaller articles which I cannot recollect. The weight of these valuables exceeded three hundred and fifty pounds avoirdupois; and in this estimate I have not included one hundred and ninety-seven superb gold watches; three of the number being worth each five hundred dollars, if one. Many of them were very old, and as time keepers valueless; the works having suffered, more or less, from corrosion – but all were richly jewelled and in cases of great worth. We estimated the entire contents of the chest, that night, at a million and a half of dollars; and, upon the subsequent disposal of the trinkets and jewels (a few being retained for our own use), it was found that we had greatly undervalued the treasure.

When, at length, we had concluded our examination, and the intense excitement of the time had, in some measure, subsided, Legrand, who saw that I was dying with impatience for a solution of this most extraordinary riddle, entered into a full detail of all the circumstances connected with it.

'You remember,' said he, 'the night when I handed you the rough sketch I had made of the *scarabæus*. You recollect also, that I became quite vexed at you for insisting that my drawing resembled a death's-head. When you first made this assertion I thought you were jesting; but afterwards I called to mind the peculiar spots on the back of the insect, and admitted to myself that your remark had some little foundation in fact. Still, the sneer at my graphic powers irritated me – for I am considered a good artist – and, therefore, when you handed me the scrap of parchment, I was about to crumple it up and throw it angrily into the fire.'

'The scrap of paper, you mean,' said I.

'No; it had much of the appearance of paper, and at first I supposed it to be such, but when I came to draw upon it, I discovered it, at once, to be a piece of very thin parchment. It was quite dirty, you remember. Well, as I was in the very act of crumpling it up, my glance fell upon the sketch at which you had been looking, and you may imagine my astonishment when I perceived, in fact, the figure of a death's-head just where, it seemed to me, I had made the drawing of the beetle. For a moment I was too much amazed to think with accuracy. I knew that my design was very different in detail from this – although there was a certain similarity in general outline. Presently I took a candle, and seating myself at the other end of the room, proceeded to scrutinize the parchment more closely. Upon turning it over, I saw my own sketch upon the reverse, just as I had made it. My first idea, now, was mere surprise at the really remarkable similarity of outline – at the singular coincidence involved in the fact, that unknown to me, there should have been a skull upon the other side of the parchment, immediately beneath my figure of the *scarabæus*, and that this skull, not only in outline, but in size, should so closely resemble my drawing. I say the singularity of this coincidence absolutely stupified me for a time. This is the usual effect of such coincidences. The mind struggles to establish a connection – a sequence of cause and effect – and, being unable to do so, suffers a species of temporary paralysis. But, when I recovered from this stupor, there dawned upon me gradually a conviction which startled me even far more than the coincidence. I began distinctly, positively, to remember that there had been *no* drawing on the parchment when I made my sketch of the *scarabæus*. I became perfectly certain of this; for I recollected turning up first one side and then the other, in search of the cleanest spot. Had the skull been then there, of course I could not have failed to notice it. Here was indeed a mystery which I felt it impossible to explain; but, even at that early moment, there seemed to glimmer, faintly, within the most remote and secret chambers of my intellect, a glow-wormlike conception of that truth which last night's adventure brought to so magnificent a demonstration. I arose at once, and putting the parchment securely away, dismissed all farther reflection until I should be alone.

'When you had gone, and when Jupiter was fast asleep, I betook myself to a more methodical investigation of the affair. In the first place I considered the manner in which the parchment had come into my possession. The spot where we discovered the *scarabæus* was on the coast of the main land, about a mile eastward of the island, and but a short distance above high water mark. Upon my taking hold of it, it gave me a sharp bite, which caused me to let it drop. Jupiter, with his accustomed caution, before seizing the insect, which had flown towards him, looked about him for a leaf, or something of that nature, by which to take hold of it. It was at this moment that his eyes, and mine also, fell upon the scrap of parchment, which I then supposed to be paper. It was lying half buried in the sand, a corner sticking up. Near the spot where we found it, I observed the remnants of the hull of what appeared to have been a ship's long boat. The wreck seemed to have been there for a very great while; for the resemblance to boat timbers could scarcely be traced.

'Well, Jupiter picked up the parchment, wrapped the beetle in it, and gave it to me. Soon afterwards we turned to go home, and on the way met Lieutenant G—. I showed him the insect, and he begged me to let him take it to the fort. On my consenting, he thrust it forthwith into his waistcoat pocket, without the parchment in which it had been wrapped, and which I had continued to hold in my hand during his inspection. Perhaps he dreaded my changing my mind, and thought it best to make sure of the prize at once – you know how enthusiastic he is on all subjects connected with Natural History. At the same time, without being conscious of it, I must have deposited the parchment in my own pocket.

'You remember that when I went to the table, for the purpose of making a sketch of the beetle, I found no paper where it was usually kept. I looked in the drawer, and found none there. I searched my pockets, hoping to find an old letter – and then my hand fell upon the parchment. I thus detail the precise mode in which it came into my possession; for the circumstances impressed me with peculiar force.

'No doubt you will think me fanciful – but I had already established a kind of *connection*. I had put together two links of a great chain. There was a boat lying on a sea-coast, and not far from the boat was a parchment – *not a paper* – with a skull depicted on it. You will, of course, ask "where is the connection?" I reply that the skull, or death's-head, is the well-known emblem of the pirate. The flag of the death's-head is hoisted in all engagements.

'I have said that the scrap was parchment, and not paper. Parchment is durable – almost imperishable. Matters of little moment are rarely consigned to parchment; since, for the mere ordinary purposes of drawing or writing, it is not nearly so well adapted as paper. This reflection suggested some meaning – some relevancy – in the death's-head. I did not fail to observe, also, the *form* of the parchment. Although one of its corners had been, by some accident, destroyed, it could be seen that the original form was oblong. It was just such a slip, indeed, as might have been chosen for a memorandum – for a record of something to be long remembered and carefully preserved.'

'But,' I interposed, 'you say that the skull was *not* upon the parchment when you made the drawing of the beetle. How then do you trace any connection between the boat and the skull – since this latter, according to your own admission, must have been designed (God only knows how or by whom) at some period subsequent to your sketching the *scarabæus*?'

'Ah, hereupon turns the whole mystery; although the secret, at this point, I had comparatively little difficulty in solving. My steps were sure, and could afford but a single result. I reasoned, for example, thus: When I drew the *scarabæus*, there was no skull apparent on the parchment. When I had completed the drawing, I gave it to you, and observed you narrowly until you returned it. *You*, therefore, did not design the skull, and no one else was present to do it. Then it was not done by human agency. And nevertheless it was done.

'At this stage of my reflections I endeavored to remember, and *did* remember, with entire distinctness, every incident which occurred about the period in question. The weather was chilly (oh rare and happy accident!), and a fire was blazing on the hearth. I was heated with exercise and sat near the table. You, however, had drawn a chair close to the chimney. Just as I placed the parchment in your hand, and as you were in the act of inspecting it, Wolf, the Newfoundland, entered, and leaped upon your shoulders. With your left hand you caressed him and kept him off, while your right, holding the parchment, was permitted to fall listlessly between your knees, and in close proximity to the fire.

At one moment I thought the blaze had caught it, and was about to caution you, but, before I could speak, you had withdrawn it, and were engaged in its examination. When I considered all these particulars, I doubted not for a moment that *heat* had been the agent in bringing to light, on the parchment, the skull which I saw designed on it. You are well aware that chemical preparations exist, and have existed time out of mind, by means of which it is possible to write on either paper or vellum, so that the characters shall become visible only when subjected to the action of fire. Zaffre, digested in *aqua regia*, and diluted with four times its weight of water, is sometimes employed; a green tint results. The regulus of cobalt, dissolved in spirit of nitre, gives a red. These colors disappear at longer or shorter intervals after the material written on cools, but again become apparent upon the re-application of heat.

'I now scrutinized the death's-head with care. Its outer edges – the edges of the drawing nearest the edge of the vellum – were far more *distinct* than the others. It was clear that the action of the caloric had been imperfect or unequal. I immediately kindled a fire, and subjected every portion of the parchment to a glowing heat. At first, the only effect was the strengthening of the faint lines in the skull; but, on persevering in the experiment, there became visible, at the corner of the slip, diagonally opposite to the spot in which the death's-head was delineated, the figure of what I at first supposed to be a goat. A closer scrutiny, however, satisfied me that it was intended for a kid.'

'Ha! ha!' said I, 'to be sure I have no right to laugh at you – a million and a half of money is too serious a matter for mirth – but you are not about to establish a third link in your chain – you will not find any especial connexion between your pirates and a goat – pirates, you know, have nothing to do with goats; they appertain to the farming interest.'

'But I have just said that the figure was *not* that of a goat.'

'Well, a kid then – pretty much the same thing.'

'Pretty much, but not altogether,' said Legrand. 'You may have heard of one *Captain* Kidd. I at once looked on the figure of the animal as a kind of punning or hieroglyphical signature. I say signature; because its position on the vellum suggested this idea. The death's-head at the corner diagonally opposite, had, in the same manner, the air of a stamp, or seal. But I was sorely put out by the absence of all else – of the body to my imagined instrument – of the text for my context.'

'I presume you expected to find a letter between the stamp and the signature.'

'Something of that kind. The fact is, I felt irresistibly impressed with a presentiment of some vast good fortune impending. I can scarcely say why. Perhaps, after all, it was rather a desire than an actual belief; – but do you know that Jupiter's silly words, about the bug being of solid gold, had a remarkable effect on my fancy? And then the series of accidents and coincidences – these were so *very* extraordinary. Do you observe how mere an accident it was that these events should have occurred on the *sole* day of all the year in which it has been, or may be, sufficiently cool for fire, and that without the fire, or without the intervention of the dog at the precise moment in which he appeared, I should never have become aware of the death's-head, and so never the possessor of the treasure?'

'But proceed – I am all impatience.'

'Well; you have heard, of course, the many stories current – the thousand vague rumors afloat about money buried, somewhere on the Atlantic coast, by Kidd and his associates. These rumors must have had some foundation in fact. And that the rumors have existed so long and so continuously could have resulted, it appeared to me, only from the circumstance of the buried treasure still *remaining* entombed. Had Kidd concealed his plunder for a time, and afterwards reclaimed it, the rumors would scarcely have reached us in their present unvarying form. You will observe that the stories told are all about money-seekers, not about money-finders. Had the pirate recovered his money, there the affair would have dropped. It seemed to me that some accident – say the loss of a memorandum indicating its locality – had deprived him of the means of recovering it, and that this accident had become known to his followers, who otherwise might never have heard that treasure had been concealed at all, and who, busying themselves

in vain, because unguided attempts, to regain it, had given first
birth, and then universal currency, to the reports which are now
so common. Have you ever heard of any important treasure being
unearthed along the coast?'

'Never.'

'But that Kidd's accumulations were immense, is well known.
I took it for granted, therefore, that the earth still held them; and
you will scarcely be surprised when I tell you that I felt a hope,
nearly amounting to certainty, that the parchment so strangely
found, involved a lost record of the place of deposit.'

'But how did you proceed?'

'I held the vellum again to the fire, after increasing the heat;
but nothing appeared. I now thought it possible that the coating
of dirt might have something to do with the failure; so I carefully
rinsed the parchment by pouring warm water over it, and, having
done this, I placed it in a tin pan, with the skull downwards, and
put the pan upon a furnace of lighted charcoal. In a few minutes,
the pan having become thoroughly heated, I removed the slip, and,
to my inexpressible joy, found it spotted, in several places, with
what appeared to be figures arranged in lines. Again I placed it in
the pan, and suffered it to remain another minute. On taking it
off, the whole was just as you see it now.'

Here Legrand, having re-heated the parchment, submitted it to
my inspection. The following characters were rudely traced, in a
red tint, between the death's-head and the goat:

53‡‡†305))6*;4826)4‡.)4‡);806*;48†8¶60))85;]8*:‡*8†83(88)5*†;
46(;88*96*?;8)*‡(;485);5*†2:*‡(;4956*2(5*—4)8¶8*;4069285);)6†8)
4‡‡;1(‡9;48081;8:8‡1;48†85;4)485†528806*81(‡9;48;(88;4(‡?34;48)
4‡;161;:188;‡?;

'But,' said I, returning him the slip, 'I am as much in the dark
as ever. Were all the jewels of Golconda awaiting me on my solution of this enigma, I am quite sure that I should be unable to
earn them.'

'And yet,' said Legrand, 'the solution is by no means so difficult
as you might be led to imagine from the first hasty inspection of
the characters. These characters, as any one might readily guess,

form a cipher – that is to say, they convey a meaning; but then, from what is known of Kidd, I could not suppose him capable of constructing any of the more abstruse cryptographs. I made up my mind, at once, that this was of a simple species – such, however, as would appear, to the crude intellect of the sailor, absolutely insoluble without the key.'

'And you really solved it?'

'Readily; I have solved others of an abstruseness ten thousand times greater. Circumstances, and a certain bias of mind, have led me to take interest in such riddles, and it may well be doubted whether human ingenuity can construct an enigma of the kind which human ingenuity may not, by proper application, resolve. In fact, having once established connected and legible characters, I scarcely gave a thought to the mere difficulty of developing their import.

'In the present case – indeed in all cases of secret writing – the first question regards the *language* of the cipher; for the principles of solution, so far, especially, as the more simple ciphers are concerned, depend on, and are varied by, the genius of the particular idiom. In general, there is no alternative but experiment (directed by probabilities) of every tongue known to him who attempts the solution, until the true one be attained. But, with the cipher now before us, all difficulty is removed by the signature. The pun on the word "Kidd" is appreciable in no other language than the English. But for this consideration I should have begun my attempts with the Spanish and French, as the tongues in which a secret of this kind would most naturally have been written by a pirate of the Spanish main. As it was, I assumed the cryptograph to be English.

'You observe there are no divisions between the words. Had there been divisions, the task would have been comparatively easy. In such case I should have commenced with a collation and analysis of the shorter words, and, had a word of a single letter occurred, as is most likely, (*a* or *I*, for example,) I should have considered the solution as assured. But, there being no division, my first step was to ascertain the predominant letters, as well as the least frequent. Counting all, I constructed a table, thus:

Of the character 8 there are 33.

;	"	26.
4	"	19.
‡)	"	16.
*	"	13.
5	"	12.
6	"	11.
† 1	"	8.
0	"	6.
9 2	"	5.
: 3	"	4.
?	"	3.
¶	"	2.
] —	'	

'Now, in English, the letter which most frequently occurs is *e*. Afterwards, the succession runs thus: *a o i d h n r s t u y c f g l m w b k p q x z*. E however predominates so remarkably that an individual sentence of any length is rarely seen, in which it is not the prevailing character.

'Here, then, we have, in the very beginning, the groundwork for something more than a mere guess. The general use which may be made of the table is obvious – but, in this particular cipher, we shall only very partially require its aid. As our predominant character is 8, we will commence by assuming it as the *e* of the natural alphabet. To verify the supposition, let us observe if the 8 be seen often in couples – for *e* is doubled with great frequency in English – in such words, for example, as "meet," "fleet," "speed," "seen," "been," "agree," &c. In the present instance we see it doubled no less than five times, although the cryptograph is brief.

'Let us assume 8, then, as *e*. Now, of all *words* in the language, "the" is most usual; let us see, therefore, whether there are not repetitions of any three characters, in the same order of collocation, the last of them being 8. If we discover repetitions of such letters, so arranged, they will most probably represent the word "the." On inspection, we find no less than seven such arrangements, the characters being ;48. We may, therefore, assume that the semicolon represents *t*, that 4 represents *h*, and that 8 represents *e* – the last being now well confirmed. Thus a great step has been taken.

'But, having established a single word, we are enabled to establish a vastly important point; that is to say, several commencements and terminations of other words. Let us refer, for example, to the last instance but one, in which the combination ;48 occurs – not far from the end of the cipher. We know that the semicolon immediately ensuing is the commencement of a word, and, of the six characters succeeding this "the," we are cognizant of no less than five. Let us set these characters down, thus, by the letters we know them to represent, leaving a space for the unknown –

t eeth.

'Here we are enabled, at once, to discard the "*th*," as forming no portion of the word commencing with the first *t*; since, by experiment of the entire alphabet for a letter adapted to the vacancy we perceive that no word can be formed of which this *th* can be a part. We are thus narrowed into

t ee,

and, going through the alphabet, if necessary, as before, we arrive at the word "tree," as the sole possible reading. We thus gain another letter, *r*, represented by (, with the words "the tree" in juxtaposition.

'Looking beyond these words, for a short distance, we again see the combination ;48, and employ it by way of *termination* to what immediately precedes. We have thus this arrangement:

the tree ;4(‡?34 the,

or, substituting the natural letters, where known, it reads thus:

the tree thr‡?3h the.

'Now, if, in place of the unknown characters, we leave blank spaces, or substitute dots, we read thus:

the tree thr…h the,

when the word "*through*" makes itself evident at once. But this discovery gives us three new letters, *o*, *u* and *g*, represented by ‡ ? and 3.

'Looking now, narrowly, through the cipher for combinations

313

of known characters, we find, not very far from the beginning, this arrangement,

83(88, or egree,

which, plainly, is the conclusion of the word "degree," and gives us another letter, d, represented by †.

'Four letters beyond the word "degree," we perceive the combination

;46(;88*.

'Translating the known characters, and representing the unknown by dots, as before, we read thus:

th.rtee.

an arrangement immediately suggestive of the word "thirteen," and again furnishing us with two new characters, i and n, represented by 6 and *.

'Referring, now, to the beginning of the cryptograph, we find the combination,

53‡‡†.

'Translating, as before, we obtain

.good,

which assures us that the first letter is A, and that the first two words are "A good."

'To avoid confusion, it is now time that we arrange our key, as far as discovered, in a tabular form. It will stand thus:

5	represents	a
†	"	d
8	"	e
3	"	g
4	"	h
6	"	i
*	"	n
‡	"	o
(	"	r
;	"	t

'We have, therefore, no less than ten of the most important letters represented, and it will be unnecessary to proceed with the details of the solution. I have said enough to convince you that ciphers of this nature are readily soluble, and to give you some insight into the *rationale* of their development. But be assured that the specimen before us appertains to the very simplest species of cryptograph. It now only remains to give you the full translation of the characters upon the parchment, as unriddled. Here it is:

' "A good glass in the bishop's hostel in the devil's seat twenty-one degrees and thirteen minutes northeast and by north main branch seventh limb east side shoot from the left eye of the death's-head a bee-line from the tree through the shot fifty feet out." '

'But,' said I, 'the enigma seems still in as bad a condition as ever. How is it possible to extort a meaning from all this jargon about "devil's seats," "death's-heads," and "bishop's hostels?" '

'I confess,' replied Legrand, 'that the matter still wears a serious aspect, when regarded with a casual glance. My first endeavor was to divide the sentence into the natural division intended by the cryptographist.'

'You mean, to punctuate it?'

'Something of that kind.'

'But how was it possible to effect this?'

'I reflected that it had been a *point* with the writer to run his words together without division, so as to increase the difficulty of solution. Now, a not over-acute man, in pursuing such an object, would be nearly certain to overdo the matter. When, in the course of his composition, he arrived at a break in his subject which would naturally require a pause, or a point, he would be exceedingly apt to run his characters, at this place, more than usually close together. If you will observe the MS., in the present instance, you will easily detect five such cases of unusual crowding. Acting on this hint, I made the division thus:

' "A good glass in the Bishop's hostel in the Devil's seat — twenty-one degrees and thirteen minutes — northeast and by north — main branch seventh limb east side — shoot from the left eye of the death's-head — a bee-line from the tree through the shot fifty feet out." '

'Even this division,' said I, 'leaves me still in the dark.'

'It left me also in the dark,' replied Legrand, 'for a few days; during which I made diligent inquiry, in the neighborhood of

Sullivan's Island, for any building which went by the name of the "Bishop's Hotel;" for, of course, I dropped the obsolete word "hostel." Gaining no information on the subject, I was on the point of extending my sphere of search, and proceeding in a more systematic manner, when, one morning, it entered into my head, quite suddenly, that this "Bishop's Hostel" might have some reference to an old family, of the name of Bessop, which, time out of mind, had held possession of an ancient manor-house, about four miles to the northward of the Island. I accordingly went over to the plantation, and reinstituted my inquiries among the older negroes of the place. At length one of the most aged of the women said that she had heard of such a place as *Bessop's Castle*, and thought that she could guide me to it, but that it was not a castle, nor a tavern, but a high rock.

'I offered to pay her well for her trouble, and, after some demur, she consented to accompany me to the spot. We found it without much difficulty, when, dismissing her, I proceeded to examine the place. The "castle" consisted of an irregular assemblage of cliffs and rocks – one of the latter being quite remarkable for its height as well as for its insulated and artificial appearance. I clambered to its apex, and then felt much at a loss as to what should be next done.

'While I was busied in reflection, my eyes fell upon a narrow ledge in the eastern face of the rock, perhaps a yard below the summit on which I stood. This ledge projected about eighteen inches, and was not more than a foot wide, while a niche in the cliff just above it, gave it a rude resemblance to one of the hollow-backed chairs used by our ancestors. I made no doubt that here was the "devil's-seat" alluded to in the MS., and now I seemed to grasp the full secret of the riddle.

'The "good glass," I knew, could have reference to nothing but a telescope; for the word "glass" is rarely employed in any other sense by seamen. Now here, I at once saw, was a telescope to be used, and a definite point of view, *admitting no variation*, from which to use it. Nor did I hesitate to believe that the phrases, "twenty-one degrees and thirteen minutes," and "northeast and by north," were intended as directions for the levelling of the

glass. Greatly excited by these discoveries, I hurried home, procured a telescope, and returned to the rock.

'I let myself down to the ledge, and found that it was impossible
to retain a seat on it unless in one particular position. This fact
confirmed my preconceived idea. I proceeded to use the glass. Of
course, the "twenty-one degrees and thirteen minutes" could
allude to nothing but elevation above the visible horizon, since
the horizontal direction was clearly indicated by the words,
"northeast and by north." This latter direction I at once established by means of a pocket-compass; then, pointing the glass as
nearly at an angle of twenty-one degrees of elevation as I could
do it by guess, I moved it cautiously up or down, until my attention was arrested by a circular rift or opening in the foliage of a
large tree that overtopped its fellows in the distance. In the centre
of this rift I perceived a white spot, but could not, at first, distinguish what it was. Adjusting the focus of the telescope, I again
looked, and now made it out to be a human skull.

'On this discovery I was so sanguine as to consider the enigma
solved; for the phrase "main branch, seventh limb, east side,"
could refer only to the position of the skull on the tree, while
"shoot from the left eye of the death's head" admitted, also, of
but one interpretation, in regard to a search for buried treasure.
I perceived that the design was to drop a bullet from the left eye
of the skull, and that a bee-line, or, in other words, a straight line,
drawn from the nearest point of the trunk through "the shot,"
(or the spot where the bullet fell,) and thence extended to a distance of fifty feet, would indicate a definite point – and beneath
this point I thought it at least *possible* that a deposit of value lay
concealed.'

'All this,' I said, 'is exceedingly clear, and, although ingenious,
still simple and explicit. When you left the Bishop's Hotel, what
then?'

'Why, having carefully taken the bearings of the tree, I turned
homewards. The instant that I left "the devil's seat," however, the
circular rift vanished; nor could I get a glimpse of it afterwards,
turn as I would. What seems to me the chief ingenuity in this
whole business, is the fact (for repeated experiment has convinced

me it is a fact) that the circular opening in question is visible from no other attainable point of view than that afforded by the narrow ledge on the face of the rock.

'In this expedition to the "Bishop's Hotel" I had been attended by Jupiter, who had, no doubt, observed, for some weeks past, the abstraction of my demeanor, and took especial care not to leave me alone. But, on the next day, getting up very early, I contrived to give him the slip, and went into the hills in search of the tree. After much toil I found it. When I came home at night my valet proposed to give me a flogging. With the rest of the adventure I believe you are as well acquainted as myself.'

'I suppose,' said I, 'you missed the spot, in the first attempt at digging, through Jupiter's stupidity in letting the bug fall through the right instead of through the left eye of the skull.'

'Precisely. This mistake made a difference of about two inches and a half in the "shot" – that is to say, in the position of the peg nearest the tree; and had the treasure been *beneath* the "shot," the error would have been of little moment; but "the shot," together with the nearest point of the tree, were merely two points for the establishment of a line of direction; of course the error, however trivial in the beginning, increased as we proceeded with the line, and by the time we had gone fifty feet, threw us quite off the scent. But for my deep-seated convictions that treasure was here somewhere actually buried, we might have had all our labor in vain.'

'I presume the fancy of *the skull*, of letting fall a bullet through the skull's eye – was suggested to Kidd by the piratical flag. No doubt he felt a kind of poetical consistency in recovering his money through this ominous insignium.'

'Perhaps so; still I cannot help thinking that common-sense had quite as much to do with the matter as poetical consistency. To be visible from the devil's-seat, it was necessary that the object, if small, should be white; and there is nothing like your human skull for retaining and even increasing its whiteness under exposure to all vicissitudes of weather.'

'But your grandiloquence, and your conduct in swinging the beetle – how excessively odd! I was sure you were mad. And why did you insist on letting fall the bug, instead of a bullet, from the skull?'

'Why, to be frank, I felt somewhat annoyed by your evident suspicions touching my sanity, and so resolved to punish you quietly, in my own way, by a little bit of sober mystification. For this reason I swung the beetle, and for this reason I let it fall from the tree. An observation of yours about its great weight suggested the latter idea.'

'Yes, I perceive; and now there is only one point which puzzles me. What are we to make of the skeletons found in the hole?'

'That is a question I am no more able to answer than yourself. There seems, however, only one plausible way of accounting for them – and yet it is dreadful to believe in such atrocity as my suggestion would imply. It is clear that Kidd – if Kidd indeed secreted this treasure, which I doubt not – it is clear that he must have had assistance in the labor. But, the worst of this labor concluded, he may have thought it expedient to remove all participants in his secret. Perhaps a couple of blows with a mattock were sufficient, while his coadjutors were busy in the pit; perhaps it required a dozen – who shall tell?'

The Black Cat

FOR the most wild, yet most homely narrative which I am about to pen, I neither expect nor solicit belief. Mad indeed would I be to expect it, in a case where my very senses reject their own evidence. Yet, mad am I not – and very surely do I not dream. But to-morrow I die, and to-day I would unburthen my soul. My immediate purpose is to place before the world, plainly, succinctly, and without comment, a series of mere household events. In their consequences, these events have terrified – have tortured – have destroyed me. Yet I will not attempt to expound them. To me, they have presented little but Horror – to many they will seem less terrible than *baroques*. Hereafter, perhaps, some intellect may be found which will reduce my phantasm to the common-place – some intellect more calm, more logical, and far less excitable than my own, which will perceive, in the circumstances I detail with awe, nothing more than an ordinary succession of very natural causes and effects.

From my infancy I was noted for the docility and humanity of my disposition. My tenderness of heart was even so conspicuous as to make me the jest of my companions. I was especially fond of animals, and was indulged by my parents with a great variety of pets. With these I spent most of my time, and never was so happy as when feeding and caressing them. This peculiarity of character grew with my growth, and, in my manhood, I derived from it one of my principal sources of pleasure. To those who have cherished an affection for a faithful and sagacious dog, I need hardly be at the trouble of explaining the nature or the intensity of the gratification thus derivable. There is something in the unselfish and self-sacrificing love of a brute, which goes directly to the heart of him who has had frequent occasion to test the paltry friendship and gossamer fidelity of mere *Man*.

I married early, and was happy to find in my wife a disposition not uncongenial with my own. Observing my partiality for domestic pets, she lost no opportunity of procuring those of the most agreeable kind. We had birds, gold fish, a fine dog, rabbits, a small monkey, and *a cat*.

This latter was a remarkably large and beautiful animal, entirely black, and sagacious to an astonishing degree. In speaking of his intelligence, my wife, who at heart was not a little tinctured with superstition, made frequent allusion to the ancient popular notion, which regarded all black cats as witches in disguise. Not that she was ever *serious* upon this point – and I mention the matter at all for no better reason than that it happens, just now, to be remembered.

Pluto – this was the cat's name – was my favourite pet and playmate. I alone fed him, and he attended me wherever I went about the house. It was even with difficulty that I could prevent him from following me through the streets.

Our friendship lasted, in this manner, for several years, during which my general temperament and character ⸺ through the instrumentality of the Fiend Intemperance – had (I blush to confess it) experienced a radical alteration for the worse. I grew, day by day, more moody, more irritable, more regardless of the feelings of others. I suffered myself to use intemperate language to my wife. At length, I even offered her personal violence. My pets, of course, were made to feel the change in my disposition. I not only neglected, but ill-used them. For Pluto, however, I still retained sufficient regard to restrain me from maltreating him, as I made no scruple of maltreating the rabbits, the monkey, or even the dog, when by accident, or through affection, they came in my way. But my disease grew upon me – for what disease is like Alcohol ! – and at length even Pluto, who was now becoming old, and consequently somewhat peevish – even Pluto began to experience the effects of my ill temper.

One night, returning home, much intoxicated, from one of my haunts about town, I fancied that the cat avoided my presence. I seized him; when, in his fright at my violence, he inflicted a slight wound upon my hand with his teeth. The fury of a demon instantly possessed me. I knew myself no longer. My original soul seemed, at once, to take its flight from my body; and a more than

sees his double

fiendish malevolence, gin-nurtured, thrilled every fibre of my frame. I took from my waistcoat-pocket a pen-knife, opened it, grasped the poor beast by the throat, and deliberately cut one of its eyes from the socket! I blush, I burn, I shudder, while I pen the damnable atrocity.

When reason returned with the morning – when I had slept off the fumes of the night's debauch – I experienced a sentiment half of horror, half of remorse, for the crime of which I had been guilty; but it was, at best, a feeble and equivocal feeling, and the soul remained untouched. I again plunged into excess, and soon drowned in wine all memory of the deed.

In the meantime the cat slowly recovered. The socket of the lost eye presented, it is true, a frightful appearance, but he no longer appeared to suffer any pain. He went about the house as usual, but, as might be expected, fled in extreme terror at my approach. I had so much of my old heart left, as to be at first grieved by this evident dislike on the part of a creature which had once so loved me. But this feeling soon gave place to irritation. And then came, as if to my final and irrevocable overthrow, the spirit of PER-VERSENESS. Of this spirit philosophy takes no account. Yet I am not more sure that my soul lives, than I am that perverseness is one of the primitive impulses of the human heart – one of the indivisible primary faculties, or sentiments, which give direction to the character of Man. Who has not, a hundred times, found himself committing a vile or a silly action, for no other reason than because he knows he should *not*? Have we not a perpetual inclination, in the teeth of our best judgment, to violate that which is *Law*, merely because we understand it to be such? This spirit of perverseness, I say, came to my final overthrow. It was this unfathomable longing of the soul *to vex itself* – to offer violence to its own nature – to do wrong for the wrong's sake only – that urged me to continue and finally to consummate the injury I had inflicted upon the unoffending brute. One morning, in cool blood, I slipped a noose about its neck and hung it to the limb of a tree; – hung it with the tears streaming from my eyes, and with the bitterest remorse at my heart; – hung it *because* I knew that it had loved me, and *because* I felt it had given me no reason of offence; – hung it *because* I knew that in so doing I was committing a sin – a deadly sin that would so jeopardize my immortal soul as to place it – if such a thing were possible – even beyond the reach of the infinite mercy of the Most Merciful and Most Terrible God.

On the night of the day on which this cruel deed was done, I was aroused from sleep by the cry of fire. The curtains of my bed were in flames. The whole house was blazing. It was with great difficulty that my wife, a servant, and myself, made our escape from the conflagration. The destruction was complete. My entire worldly wealth was swallowed up, and I resigned myself thenceforward to despair.

I am above the weakness of seeking to establish a sequence of cause and effect, between the disaster and the atrocity. But I am detailing a chain of facts – and wish not to leave even a possible link imperfect. On the day succeeding the fire, I visited the ruins. The walls, with one exception, had fallen in. This exception was found in a compartment wall, not very thick, which stood about the middle of the house, and against which had rested the head of my bed. The plastering had here, in great measure, resisted the action of the fire – a fact which I attributed to its having been recently spread. About this wall a dense crowd were collected, and many persons seemed to be examining a particular portion of it with very minute and eager attention. The words 'strange!' 'singular!' and other similar expressions, excited my curiosity. I approached and saw, as if graven in *bas relief* upon the white surface, the figure of a gigantic *cat*. The impression was given with an accuracy truly marvellous. There was a rope about the animal's neck.

When I first beheld this apparition – for I could scarcely regard it as less – my wonder and my terror were extreme. But at length reflection came to my aid. The cat, I remembered, had been hung in a garden adjacent to the house. Upon the alarm of fire, this garden had been immediately filled by the crowd – by some one of whom the animal must have been cut from the tree and thrown, through an open window, into my chamber. This had probably been done with the view of arousing me from sleep. The falling of other walls had compressed the victim of my cruelty into the substance of the freshly-spread plaster; the lime of which, with the flames, and the *ammonia* from the carcass, had then accomplished the portraiture as I saw it.

Although I thus readily accounted to my reason, if not altogether to my conscience, for the startling fact just detailed, it did not the less fail to make a deep impression upon my fancy. For months I could not rid myself of the phantasm of the cat; and, during this period, there came back into my spirit a half-sentiment that seemed, but was not, remorse. I went so far as to regret the loss of the animal, and to look about me, among the vile haunts which I now habitually frequented, for another pet of the same species, and of somewhat similar appearance, with which to supply its place.

One night as I sat, half stupified, in a den of more than infamy, my attention was suddenly drawn to some black object, reposing upon the head of one of the immense hogsheads of Gin, or of Rum, which constituted the chief furniture of the apartment. I had been looking steadily at the top of this hogshead for some minutes, and what now caused me surprise was the fact that I had not sooner perceived the object thereupon. I approached it, and touched it with my hand. It was a black cat – a very large one – fully as large as Pluto, and closely resembling him in every respect but one. Pluto had not a white hair upon any portion of his body; but this cat had a large, although indefinite splotch of white, covering nearly the whole region of the breast.

Upon my touching him, he immediately arose, purred loudly, rubbed against my hand, and appeared delighted with my notice. This, then, was the very creature of which I was in search. I at once offered to purchase it of the landlord; but this person made no claim to it – knew nothing of it – had never seen it before.

I continued my caresses, and, when I prepared to go home, the animal evinced a disposition to accompany me. I permitted it to do so; occasionally stooping and patting it as I proceeded. When it reached the house it domesticated itself at once, and became immediately a great favorite with my wife.

For my own part, I soon found a dislike to it arising within me.

This was just the reverse of what I had anticipated; but I know not how or why it was – its evident fondness for myself rather disgusted and annoyed. By slow degrees, these feelings of disgust and annoyance rose into the bitterness of hatred. I avoided the creature; a certain sense of shame, and the remembrance of my former deed of cruelty, preventing me from physically abusing it. I did not, for some weeks, strike, or otherwise violently ill use it; but gradually – very gradually – I came to look upon it with un-utterable loathing, and to flee silently from its odious presence, as from the breath of a pestilence.

What added, no doubt, to my hatred of the beast, was the dis-covery, on the morning after I brought it home, that, like Pluto, it also had been deprived of one of its eyes. This circumstance, however, only endeared it to my wife, who, as I have already said, possessed, in a high degree, that humanity of feeling which had once been my distinguishing trait, and the source of many of my simplest and purest pleasures.

With my aversion to this cat, however, its partiality for myself seemed to increase. It followed my footsteps with a pertinacity which it would be difficult to make the reader comprehend. When-ever I sat, it would crouch beneath my chair, or spring upon my knees, covering me with its loathsome caresses. If I arose to walk it would get between my feet and thus nearly throw me down, or, fastening its long and sharp claws in my dress, clamber, in this manner, to my breast. At such times, although I longed to destroy it with a blow, I was yet withheld from so doing, partly by a memory of my former crime, but chiefly – let me confess it at once – by absolute *dread* of the beast.

This dread was not exactly a dread of physical evil – and yet I should be at a loss how otherwise to define it. I am almost ashamed to own – yes, even in this felon's cell, I am almost ashamed to own – that the terror and horror with which the animal inspired me, had been heightened by one of the merest chimæras it would be possible to conceive. My wife had called my attention, more than once, to the character of the mark of white hair, of which I have spoken, and which constituted the sole visible difference between the strange beast and the one I had destroyed. The reader will remember that this mark, although large, had been originally very indefinite; but, by slow degrees – degrees nearly imperceptible, and which for a long time my reason struggled to reject as fanciful – it had, at length, assumed a rigorous distinctness of outline. It was now the representation of an object that I shudder to name – and for this, above all, I loathed, and dreaded, and would have rid myself of the monster *had I dared* – it was now, I say, the image of a hideous – of a ghastly thing – of the GALLOWS ! – oh, mournful and terrible engine of Horror and of Crime – of Agony and of Death !

And now was I indeed wretched beyond the wretchedness of mere Humanity. And *a brute beast* – whose fellow I had contemptuously destroyed – *a brute beast* to work out for *me* – for me a man, fashioned in the image of the High God – so much of insufferable wo ! Alas ! neither by day nor by night knew I the blessing of Rest any more ! During the former the creature left me no moment alone; and, in the latter, I started, hourly, from dreams of unutterable fear, to find the hot breath of *the thing* upon my face, and its vast weight – an incarnate Night-Mare that I had no power to shake off – incumbent eternally upon my *heart* !

Beneath the pressure of torments such as these, the feeble remnant of the good within me succumbed. Evil thoughts became my sole intimates – the darkest and most evil of thoughts. The moodiness of my usual temper increased to hatred of all things and of all mankind; while, from the sudden, frequent, and ungovernable outbursts of a fury to which I now blindly abandoned myself, my uncomplaining wife, alas ! was the most usual and the most patient of sufferers.

One day she accompanied me, upon some household errand, into the cellar of the old building which our poverty compelled us to inhabit. The cat followed me down the steep stairs, and, nearly throwing me headlong, exasperated me to madness. Uplifting an axe, and forgetting, in my wrath, the childish dread which had hitherto stayed my hand, I aimed a blow at the animal which, of course, would have proved instantly fatal had it descended as I wished. But this blow was arrested by the hand of my wife. Goaded, by the interference, into a rage more than demoniacal,

I withdrew my arm from her grasp and buried the axe in her brain. She fell dead upon the spot, without a groan.

This hideous murder accomplished, I set myself forthwith, and with entire deliberation, to the task of concealing the body. I knew that I could not remove it from the house, either by day or by night, without the risk of being observed by the neighbors. Many projects entered my mind. At one period I thought of cutting the corpse into minute fragments, and destroying them by fire. At another, I resolved to dig a grave for it in the floor of the cellar. Again, I deliberated about casting it in the well in the yard – about packing it in a box, as if merchandize, with the usual arrangements, and so getting a porter to take it from the house. Finally I hit upon what I considered a far better expedient than either of these. I determined to wall it up in the cellar – as the monks of the middle ages are recorded to have walled up their victims.

For a purpose such as this the cellar was well adapted. Its walls were loosely constructed, and had lately been plastered throughout with a rough plaster, which the dampness of the atmosphere had prevented from hardening. Moreover, in one of the walls was a projection, caused by a false chimney, or fireplace, that had been filled up, and made to resemble the rest of the cellar. I made no doubt that I could readily displace the bricks at this point, insert the corpse, and wall the whole up as before, so that no eye could detect anything suspicious.

And in this calculation I was not deceived. By means of a crow-bar I easily dislodged the bricks, and, having carefully deposited the body against the inner wall, I propped it in that position, while, with little trouble, I re-laid the whole structure as it originally stood. Having procured mortar, sand, and hair, with every possible precaution, I prepared a plaster which could not be distinguished from the old, and with this I very carefully went over the new brick-work. When I had finished, I felt satisfied that all was right. The wall did not present the slightest appearance of having been disturbed. The rubbish on the floor was picked up with the minutest care. I looked around triumphantly, and said to myself – 'Here at least, then, my labor has not been in vain.'

My next step was to look for the beast which had been the cause of so much wretchedness; for I had, at length, firmly resolved to put it to death. Had I been able to meet with it, at the moment, there could have been no doubt of its fate; but it appeared that the crafty animal had been alarmed at the violence of my previous anger, and forebore to present itself in my present mood. It is impossible to describe, or to imagine, the deep, the blissful sense of relief which the absence of the detested creature occasioned in my bosom. It did not make its appearance during the night – and thus for one night at least, since its introduction into the house, I soundly and tranquilly slept; aye, *slept* even with the burden of murder upon my soul !

The second and the third day passed, and still my tormentor came not. Once again I breathed as a free-man. The monster, in terror, had fled the premises forever ! I should behold it no more ! My happiness was supreme ! The guilt of my dark deed disturbed me but little. Some few inquiries had been made, but these had been readily answered. Even a search had been instituted – but of course nothing was to be discovered. I looked upon my future felicity as secured.

Upon the fourth day of the assassination, a party of the police came, very unexpectedly, into the house, and proceeded again to make rigorous investigation of the premises. Secure, however, in the inscrutability of my place of concealment, I felt no embarrassment whatever. The officers bade me accompany them in their search. They left no nook or corner unexplored. At length, for the third or fourth time, they descended into the cellar. I quivered not in a muscle. My heart beat calmly as that of one who slumbers in innocence. I walked the cellar from end to end. I folded my arms upon my bosom, and roamed easily to and fro. The police were thoroughly satisfied and prepared to depart. The glee at my heart was too strong to be restrained. I burned to say if but one word, by way of triumph, and to render doubly sure their assurance of my guiltlessness.

'Gentlemen,' I said at last, as the party ascended the steps, 'I delight to have allayed your suspicions. I wish you all health, and a little more courtesy. By the bye, gentlemen, this – this is a very well constructed house.' [In the rabid desire to say something easily, I scarcely knew what I uttered at all.] – 'I may say an *excellently* well constructed house. These walls – are you going, gentlemen? – these walls are solidly put together;' and here, through the mere phrenzy of bravado, I rapped heavily, with a cane which I held in my hand, upon that very portion of the brick-work behind which stood the corpse of the wife of my bosom.

But may God shield and deliver me from the fangs of the Arch-Fiend! No sooner had the reverberation of my blows sunk into silence, than I was answered by a voice from within the tomb! – by a cry, at first muffled and broken, like the sobbing of a child, and then quickly swelling into one long, loud, and continuous scream, utterly anomalous and inhuman – a howl – a wailing shriek, half of horror and half of triumph, such as might have arisen only out of hell, conjointly from the throats of the damned in their agony and of the demons that exult in the damnation.

Of my own thoughts it is folly to speak. Swooning, I staggered to the opposite wall. For one instant the party upon the stairs remained motionless, through extremity of terror and of awe. In the next, a dozen stout arms were toiling at the wall. It fell bodily. The corpse, already greatly decayed and clotted with gore, stood erect before the eyes of the spectators. Upon its head, with red extended mouth and solitary eye of fire, sat the hideous beast whose craft had seduced me into murder, and whose informing voice had consigned me to the hangman. I had walled the monster up within the tomb!

The Purloined Letter

Nil sapientiae odiosius acumine nimio.
SENECA[1]

AT Paris, just after dark one gusty evening in the autumn of 18—,
I was enjoying the twofold luxury of meditation and a meerschaum, in company with my friend C. Auguste Dupin, in his
little back library, or book-closet, *au troisième*, No. 33, *Rue
Dunôt, Faubourg St Germain*. For one hour at least we had
maintained a profound silence; while each, to any casual observer, might have seemed intently and exclusively occupied with
the curling eddies of smoke that oppressed the atmosphere of
the chamber. For myself, however, I was mentally discussing certain topics which had formed matter for conversation between us
at an earlier period of the evening; I mean the affair of the Rue
Morgue, and the mystery attending the murder of Marie Rogêt.
I looked upon it, therefore, as something of a coincidence, when
the door of our apartment was thrown open and admitted our
old acquaintance, Monsieur G—, the Prefect of the Parisian
police.

We gave him a hearty welcome; for there was nearly half as
much of the entertaining as of the contemptible about the man,
and we had not seen him for several years. We had been sitting in
the dark, and Dupin now arose for the purpose of lighting a
lamp, but sat down again, without doing so, upon G.'s saying
that he had called to consult us, or rather to ask the opinion of
my friend, about some official business which had occasioned a
great deal of trouble.

'If it is any point requiring reflection,' observed Dupin, as he
forbore to enkindle the wick, 'we shall examine it to better purpose in the dark.'

'That is another of your odd notions,' said the Prefect, who
had a fashion of calling every thing 'odd' that was beyond his

comprehension, and thus lived amid an absolute legion of 'oddities.'

'Very true,' said Dupin, as he supplied his visiter with a pipe, and rolled towards him a comfortable chair.

'And what is the difficulty now?' I asked. 'Nothing more in the assassination way, I hope?'

'Oh no; nothing of that nature. The fact is, the business is *very* simple indeed, and I make no doubt that we can manage it sufficiently well ourselves; but then I thought Dupin would like to hear the details of it, because it is so excessively *odd*.'

'Simple and odd,' said Dupin.

'Why, yes; and not exactly that, either. The fact is, we have all been a good deal puzzled because the affair *is* so simple, and yet baffles us altogether.'

'Perhaps it is the very simplicity of the thing which puts you at fault,' said my friend.

'What nonsense you *do* talk!' replied the Prefect, laughing heartily.

'Perhaps the mystery is a little *too* plain,' said Dupin.

'Oh, good heavens! who ever heard of such an idea?'

'A little *too* self-evident.'

'Ha! ha! ha! – ha! ha! ha! – ho! ho! ho!' – roared our visiter, profoundly amused, 'oh, Dupin, you will be the death of me yet!'

'And what, after all, *is* the matter on hand?' I asked.

'Why, I will tell you,' replied the Prefect, as he gave a long, steady, and contemplative puff, and settled himself in his chair. 'I will tell you in a few words; but, before I begin, let me caution you that this is an affair demanding the greatest secrecy, and that I should most probably lose the position I now hold, were it known that I confided it to any one.'

'Proceed,' said I.

'Or not,' said Dupin.

'Well, then; I have received personal information, from a very high quarter, that a certain document of the last importance, has been purloined from the royal apartments. The individual who purloined it is known; this beyond a doubt; he was seen to take it. It is known, also, that it still remains in his possession.'

'How is this known?' asked Dupin.

'It is clearly inferred,' replied the Prefect, 'from the nature of the document, and from the non-appearance of certain results which would at once arise from its passing *out* of the robber's possession; – that is to say, from his employing it as he must design in the end to employ it.'

'Be a little more explicit,' I said.

'Well, I may venture so far as to say that the paper gives its holder a certain power in a certain quarter where such power is immensely valuable.' The Prefect was fond of the cant of diplomacy.

'Still I do not quite understand,' said Dupin.

'No? Well; the disclosure of the document to a third person, who shall be nameless, would bring in question the honor of a personage of most exalted station; and this fact gives the holder of the document an ascendancy over the illustrious personage whose honor and peace are so jeopardized.'

'But this ascendancy,' I interposed, 'would depend upon the robber's knowledge of the loser's knowledge of the robber. Who would dare –'

'The thief,' said G., 'is the Minister D—, who dares all things, those unbecoming as well as those becoming a man. The method of the theft was not less ingenious than bold. The document in question – a letter, to be frank – had been received by the personage robbed while alone in the royal *boudoir*. During its perusal she was suddenly interrupted by the entrance of the other exalted personage from whom especially it was her wish to conceal it. After a hurried and vain endeavour to thrust it in a drawer, she was forced to place it, open as it was, upon a table. The address, however, was uppermost, and, the contents thus unexposed, the letter escaped notice. At this juncture enters the Minister D—. His lynx eye immediately perceives the paper, recognises the handwriting of the address, observes the confusion of the personage addressed, and fathoms her secret. After some business transactions, hurried through in his ordinary manner, he produces a letter somewhat similar to the one in question, opens it, pretends to read it, and then places it in close juxtaposition to the other. Again he converses, for some fifteen minutes, upon the public affairs. At length, in taking leave, he takes also from the table the letter to which he had no claim. Its rightful owner saw, but, of course, dared not call attention to the act, in the presence of the third personage who stood at her elbow. The minister decamped; leaving his own letter – one of no importance – upon the table.'

'Here, then,' said Dupin to me, 'you have precisely what you demand to make the ascendancy complete – the robber's knowledge of the loser's knowledge of the robber.'

'Yes,' replied the Prefect; 'and the power thus attained has, for some months past, been wielded, for political purposes, to a very dangerous extent. The personage robbed is more thoroughly convinced, every day, of the necessity of reclaiming her letter. But this, of course, cannot be done openly. In fine, driven to despair, she has committed the matter to me.'

'Than whom,' said Dupin, amid a perfect whirlwind of smoke, 'no more sagacious agent could, I suppose, be desired, or even imagined.'

'You flatter me,' replied the Prefect; 'but it is possible that some such opinion may have been entertained.'

'It is clear,' said I, 'as you observe, that the letter is still in possession of the minister; since it is this possession, and not any employment of the letter, which bestows the power. With the employment the power departs.'

'True,' said G.; 'and upon this conviction I proceeded. My first care was to make thorough search of the minister's hotel; and here my chief embarrassment lay in the necessity of searching without his knowledge. Beyond all things, I have been warned of the danger which would result from giving him reason to suspect our design.'

'But,' said I, 'you are quite *au fait* in these investigations. The Parisian police have done this thing often before.'

'O yes; and for this reason I did not despair. The habits of the minister gave me, too, a great advantage. He is frequently absent from home all night. His servants are by no means numerous. They sleep at a distance from their master's apartment, and, being chiefly Neapolitans, are readily made drunk. I have keys, as you know, with which I can open any chamber or cabinet in Paris. For three months a night has not passed, during the greater part of which I have not been engaged, personally, in ransacking the D— Hôtel. My honor is interested, and, to mention a great secret, the reward is enormous. So I did not abandon the search until I had become fully satisfied that the thief is a more astute man than myself. I fancy that I have investigated every nook and corner of the premises in which it is possible that the paper can be concealed.'

'But is it not possible,' I suggested, 'that although the letter may be in possession of the minister, as it unquestionably is, he may have concealed it elsewhere than upon his own premises?'

'This is barely possible,' said Dupin. 'The present peculiar condition of affairs at court, and especially of those intrigues in which D— is known to be involved, would render the instant availability of the document – its susceptibility of being produced at a moment's notice – a point of nearly equal importance with its possession.'

'Its susceptibility of being produced?' said I.

'That is to say, of being *destroyed*,' said Dupin.

'True,' I observed; 'the paper is clearly then upon the premises. As for its being upon the person of the minister, we may consider that as out of the question.'

'Entirely,' said the Prefect. 'He has been twice waylaid, as if by footpads, and his person rigorously searched under my own inspection.'

'You might have spared yourself this trouble,' said Dupin. 'D—, I presume, is not altogether a fool, and, if not, must have anticipated these waylayings, as a matter of course.'

'Not *altogether* a fool,' said G., 'but then he's a poet, which I take to be only one remove from a fool.'

'True,' said Dupin, after a long and thoughtful whiff from his meerschaum, 'although I have been guilty of certain doggerel myself.'

'Suppose you detail,' said I, 'the particulars of your search.'

'Why the fact is, we took our time, and we searched *every where*. I have had long experience in these affairs. I took the entire building, room by room; devoting the nights of a whole week to each. We examined, first, the furniture of each apartment. We opened every possible drawer; and I presume you know that, to a properly trained police agent, such a thing as a *secret* drawer is impossible. Any man is a dolt who permits a "secret" drawer to escape him in a search of this kind. The thing is so plain. There is a certain amount of bulk – of space – to be accounted for in every cabinet. Then we have accurate rules. The fiftieth part of a line could not escape us. After the cabinets we took the chairs. The cushions we probed with the fine long needles you have seen me employ. From the tables we removed the tops.'

'Why so?'

'Sometimes the top of a table, or other similarly arranged piece of furniture, is removed by the person wishing to conceal an article; then the leg is excavated, the article deposited within the cavity, and the top replaced. The bottoms and tops of bed-posts are employed in the same way.'

'But could not the cavity be detected by sounding?' I asked.

'By no means, if, when the article is deposited, a sufficient wadding of cotton be placed around it. Besides, in our case, we were obliged to proceed without noise.'

'But you could not have removed – you could not have taken to pieces *all* articles of furniture in which it would have been possible to make a deposit in the manner you mention. A letter may be compressed into a thin spiral roll, not differing much in shape or bulk from a large knitting-needle, and in this form it might be inserted into the rung of a chair, for example. You did not take to pieces all the chairs?'

'Certainly not; But we did better – we examined the rungs of every chair in the hotel, and, indeed, the jointings of every description of furniture, by the aid of a most powerful microscope. Had there been any traces of recent disturbance we should not have failed to detect it instantly. A single grain of gimlet-dust, for example, would have been as obvious as an apple. Any disorder in the glueing – any unusual gaping in the joints – would have sufficed to insure detection.'

'I presume you looked to the mirrors, between the boards and the plates, and you probed the beds and the bed-clothes, as well as the curtains and carpets.'

'That of course; and when we had absolutely completed every particle of the furniture in this way, then we examined the house itself. We divided its entire surface into compartments, which we numbered, so that none might be missed; then we scrutinized each individual square inch throughout the premises, including the two houses immediately adjoining, with the microscope, as before.'

'The two houses adjoining!' I exclaimed; 'you must have had a great deal of trouble.'

'We had; but the reward offered is prodigious.'

'You include the *grounds* about the houses?'

'All the grounds are paved with brick. They gave us comparatively little trouble. We examined the moss between the bricks, and found it undisturbed.'

'You looked among D—'s papers, of course, and into the books of the library?'

'Certainly: we opened every package and parcel; we not only opened every book, but we turned over every leaf in each volume, not contenting ourselves with a mere shake, according to the fashion of some of our police officers. We also measured the thickness of every book-*cover*, with the most accurate admeasurement, and applied to each the most jealous scrutiny of the microscope. Had any of the bindings been recently meddled with it would have been utterly impossible that the fact should have escaped observation. Some five or six volumes, just from the hands of the binder, we carefully probed, longitudinally, with the needles.'

'You explored the floors beneath the carpets?'

'Beyond doubt. We removed every carpet, and examined the boards with the microscope.'

'And the paper on the walls?'

'Yes.'

'You looked into the cellars?'

'We did.'

'Then,' I said, 'you have been making a miscalculation, and the letter is *not* upon the premises, as you suppose.'

'I fear you are right there,' said the Prefect. 'And now, Dupin, what would you advise me to do?'

'To make a thorough re-search of the premises.'

'That is absolutely needless,' replied G——. 'I am not more sure that I breathe than I am that the letter is not at the Hôtel.'

'I have no better advice to give you,' said Dupin. 'You have, of course, an accurate description of the letter?'

'Oh yes!' – And here the Prefect, producing a memorandum-book, proceeded to read aloud a minute account of the internal, and especially of the external appearance of the missing document. Soon after finishing the perusal of this description, he took his departure, more entirely depressed in spirits than I had ever known the good gentleman before.

In about a month afterwards he paid us another visit, and found us occupied very nearly as before. He took a pipe and a chair and entered into some ordinary conversation. At length I said, –

'Well, but G——, what of the purloined letter? I presume you have at last made up your mind that there is no such thing as overreaching the Minister?'

'Confound him, say I – yes; I made the re-examination, however, as Dupin suggested – but it was all labor lost, as I knew it would be.'

'How much was the reward offered, did you say?' asked Dupin.

'Why, a very great deal – a *very* liberal reward – I don't like to say how much, precisely; but one thing I *will* say, that I wouldn't mind giving my individual check for fifty thousand francs to any one who could obtain me that letter. The fact is, it is becoming of more and more importance every day; and the reward has been lately doubled. If it were trebled, however, I could do no more than I have done.'

'Why, yes,' said Dupin, drawlingly, between the whiffs of his meerschaum, 'I really – think, G——, you have not exerted your-self – to the utmost in this matter. You might – do a little more, I think, eh?'

'How? – in what way?'

'Why – puff, puff – you might – puff, puff – employ counsel in the matter, eh? – puff, puff, puff. Do you remember the story they tell of Abernethy?'

'No; hang Abernethy!'

'To be sure! hang him and welcome. But, once upon a time, a certain rich miser conceived the design of spunging upon this Abernethy for a medical opinion. Getting up, for this purpose, an ordinary conversation in a private company, he insinuated his case to the physician, as that of an imaginary individual.

'"We will suppose," said the miser, "that his symptoms are such and such; now, doctor, what would *you* have directed him to take?"

'"Take!" said Abernethy, "why, take *advice*, to be sure."'

'But,' said the Prefect, a little discomposed, 'I am *perfectly* willing to take advice, and to pay for it. I would *really* give fifty thousand francs to any one who would aid me in the matter.'

'In that case,' replied Dupin, opening a drawer, and producing a check-book, 'you may as well fill me up a check for the amount mentioned. When you have signed it, I will hand you the letter.'

I was astounded. The Prefect appeared absolutely thunder-stricken. For some minutes he remained speechless and motion-less, looking incredulously at my friend with open mouth, and eyes that seemed starting from their sockets; then, apparently recovering himself in some measure, he seized a pen, and after several pauses and vacant stares, finally filled up and signed a check for fifty thousand francs, and handed it across the table to Dupin. The latter examined it carefully and deposited it in his pocket-book; then, unlocking an *escritoire*, took thence a letter and gave it to the Prefect. This functionary grasped it in a per-fect agony of joy, opened it with a trembling hand, cast a rapid glance at its contents, and then, scrambling and struggling to the door, rushed at length unceremoniously from the room and from the house, without having uttered a syllable since Dupin had requested him to fill up the check.

When he had gone, my friend entered into some explanations.

'The Parisian police,' he said, 'are exceedingly able in their way. They are persevering, ingenious, cunning, and thoroughly versed in the knowledge which their duties seem chiefly to demand. Thus, when G— detailed to us his mode of searching the premises at the Hôtel D—, I felt entire confidence in his having made a satisfactory investigation – so far as his labors extended.'

'So far as his labors extended?' said I.

'Yes,' said Dupin. 'The measures adopted were not only the best of their kind, but carried out to absolute perfection. Had the letter been deposited within the range of their search, these fellows would, beyond a question, have found it.'

I merely laughed – but he seemed quite serious in all that he said.

'The measures, then,' he continued, 'were good in their kind, and well executed; their defect lay in their being inapplicable to the case, and to the man. A certain set of highly ingenious resources are, with the Prefect, a sort of Procrustean bed, to which he forcibly adapts his designs. But he perpetually errs by being too deep or too shallow, for the matter in hand; and many a schoolboy is a better reasoner than he. I knew one about eight years of age, whose success at guessing in the game of "even and odd" attracted universal admiration. This game is simple, and is played with marbles. One player holds in his hand a number of these toys, and demands of another whether that number is even or odd. If the guess is right, the guesser wins one; if wrong, he loses one. The boy to whom I allude won all the marbles of the school. Of course he had some principle of guessing; and this lay in mere observation and admeasurement of the astuteness of his opponents. For example, an arrant simpleton is his opponent, and, holding up his closed hand, asks, "are they even or odd?" Our schoolboy replies, "odd," and loses; but upon the second trial he wins, for he then says to himself, "the simpleton had them even upon the first trial, and his amount of cunning is just sufficient to make him have them odd upon the second; I will therefore guess odd;" – he guesses odd, and wins. Now, with a simpleton a degree above the first, he would have reasoned thus: "This fellow finds that in the first instance I guessed odd, and, in the second, he will propose to himself upon the first impulse, a simple variation from even to odd, as did the first simpleton; but then a second thought will suggest that this is too simple a variation, and finally he will decide upon putting it even as before. I will therefore guess even" – he guesses even, and wins. Now this mode of reasoning in the schoolboy, whom his fellows termed "lucky," – what, in its last analysis, is it?'

'It is merely,' I said, 'an identification of the reasoner's intellect with that of his opponent.'

'It is,' said Dupin; 'and, upon inquiring of the boy by what means he effected the *thorough* identification in which his success consisted, I received answer as follows: "When I wish to find out how wise, or how stupid, or how good, or how wicked is any one, or what are his thoughts at the moment, I fashion the expression of my face, as accurately as possible, in accordance with the expression of his, and then wait to see what thoughts or sentiments arise in my mind or heart, as if to match or correspond with the expression." This response of the schoolboy lies at the bottom of all the spurious profundity which has been attributed to Rochefoucauld, to La Bougive, to Machiavelli, and to Campanella.'

'And the identification,' I said, 'of the reasoner's intellect with that of his opponent, depends, if I understand you aright, upon the accuracy with which the opponent's intellect is admeasured.'

'For its practical value it depends upon this,' replied Dupin; 'and the Prefect and his cohort fail so frequently, first, by default of this identification, and, secondly, by ill-admeasurement, or rather through non-admeasurement, of the intellect with which they are engaged. They consider only their *own* ideas of ingenuity; and, in searching for anything hidden, advert only to the modes in which *they* would have hidden it. They are right in this much – that their own ingenuity is a faithful representative of that of the *mass*; but when the cunning of the individual felon is diverse in character from their own, the felon foils them, of course. This always happens when it is above their own, and very usually when it is below. They have no variation of principle in their investigations; at best, when urged by some unusual emergency – by some extraordinary reward – they extend or exaggerate their old modes of *practice*, without touching their principles. What, for example, in this case of D—, has been done to vary the principle of action? What is all this boring, and probing, and sounding, and scrutinizing with the microscope, and dividing the surface of the building into registered square inches – what is it all but an exaggeration *of the application* of the one principle or set of principles of search, which are based upon the one set of notions regarding human ingenuity, to which the Prefect, in the long routine of his duty, has been accustomed? Do you not see he has taken it for granted that *all* men proceed to conceal a letter, – not exactly in a gimlet-hole bored in a chair-leg – but, at least, in *some* out-of-the-way hole or corner suggested by the same tenor of thought which would urge a man to secrete a letter in a gimlet-hole bored in a chair-leg? And do you not see also, that such *recherchés* nooks for concealment are adapted only for ordinary occasions, and would be adopted only by ordinary intellects; for, in all cases of concealment, a disposal of the article concealed – a disposal of it in this *recherché* manner, – is, in the very first instance, presumable and presumed; and thus its discovery depends, not at all upon the acumen, but altogether upon the mere care, patience, and determination of the seekers; and where the case is of importance – or, what amounts to the same thing in the policial eyes, when the reward is of magnitude, – the qualities in question have *never* been known to fail. You will now understand what I meant in suggesting that, had the purloined letter been hidden any where within the limits of the Prefect's examination – in other words, had the principle of its concealment been comprehended within the principles of the Prefect – its discovery would have been a matter altogether beyond question. This functionary, however, has been thoroughly mystified; and the remote source of his defeat lies in the supposition that the Minister is a fool, because he has acquired renown as a poet. All fools are poets; this the Prefect *feels*; and he is merely guilty of a *non distributio medii* in thence inferring that all poets are fools.'

'But is this really the poet?' I asked. 'There are two brothers, I know; and both have attained reputation in letters. The Minister I believe has written learnedly on the Differential Calculus. He is a mathematician, and no poet.'

'You are mistaken; I know him well; he is both. As poet *and* mathematician, he would reason well; as mere mathematician, he could not have reasoned at all, and thus would have been at the mercy of the Prefect.'

'You surprise me,' I said, 'by these opinions, which have been contradicted by the voice of the world. You do not mean to set at naught the well-digested idea of centuries. The mathematical reason has long been regarded as *the* reason *par excellence*.'

' "Il y a à parier," ' replied Dupin, quoting from Chamfort, ' "que toute idée publique, toute convention reçue, est une sottise, car elle a convenu au plus grand nombre." The mathematicians, I grant you, have done their best to promulgate the popular error to which you allude, and which is none the less an error for its promulgation as truth. With an art worthy a better cause, for example, they have insinuated the term "analysis" into application to algebra. The French are the originators of this particular deception; but if a term is of any importance – if words derive any value from applicability – then "analysis" conveys "algebra" about as much as, in Latin, "*ambitus*" implies "ambition," "*religio*," "religion," or "*homines honesti*," a set of *honorable* men.'

'You have a quarrel on hand, I see,' said I, 'with some of the algebraists of Paris; but proceed.'

'I dispute the availability, and thus the value, of that reason which is cultivated in any especial form other than the abstractly logical. I dispute, in particular, the reason educed by mathematical study. The mathematics are the science of form and quantity; mathematical reasoning is merely logic applied to observation upon form and quantity. The great error lies in supposing that even the truths of what is called *pure* algebra, are abstract or general truths. And this error is so egregious that I am confounded at the universality with which it has been received. Mathematical axioms are *not* axioms of general truth. What is true of *relation* – of form and quantity – is often grossly false in regard to morals, for example. In this latter science it is very usually *un*true that the aggregated parts are equal to the whole. In chemistry also the axiom fails. In the consideration of motive it fails; for two motives, each of a given value, have not, necessarily, a value when united, equal to the sum of their values apart. There are numerous other mathematical truths which are only truths within the limits of *relation*. But the mathematician argues, from his *finite truths*, through habit, as if they were of an absolutely general applicability – as the world indeed imagines them to be. Bryant, in his very learned "Mythology," mentions an analogous source of error, when he says that "although the Pagan fables are not believed, yet we forget ourselves continually, and make inferences from them as existing realities." With the algebraists, however, who are Pagans themselves, the "Pagan fables" *are* believed, and the inferences are made, not so much through lapse of memory, as through an unaccountable addling of the brains. In short, I never yet encountered the mere mathematician who could be trusted out of equal roots, or one who did not clandestinely hold it as a point of his faith that x^2+px was absolutely and unconditionally equal to q. Say to one of these gentlemen, by way of experiment, if you please, that you believe occasions may occur where x^2+px is *not* altogether equal to q, and, having made him understand what you mean, to get out of his reach as speedily as convenient, for, beyond doubt, he will endeavor to knock you down.

'I mean to say,' continued Dupin, while I merely laughed at his last observations, 'that if the Minister had been no more than a mathematician, the Prefect would have been under no necessity of giving me this check. I knew him, however, as both mathematician and poet, and my measures were adapted to his capacity, with reference to the circumstances by which he was surrounded. I knew him as a courtier, too, and as a bold *intriguant*. Such a man, I considered, could not fail to be aware of the ordinary political modes of action. He could not have failed to anticipate – and events have proved that he did not fail to anticipate – the waylayings to which he was subjected. He must have foreseen, I reflected, the secret investigations of his premises. His frequent absences from home at night, which were hailed by the Prefect as certain aids to his success, I regarded only as *ruses*, to afford opportunity for thorough search to the police, and thus the sooner to impress them with the conviction to which G—, in fact, did finally arrive – the conviction that the letter was not upon the premises. I felt, also, that the whole train of thought, which I was at some pains in detailing to you just now, concerning the invariable principle of policial action in searches for articles concealed – I felt that this whole train of thought would necessarily pass through the mind of the Minister. It would imperatively lead him to despise all the ordinary *nooks* of concealment. *He* could not, I reflected, be so weak as not to see that the most intricate and remote recess of his hotel would be as open as his commonest closets to the eyes, to the probes, to the gimlets, and to the microscopes of the Prefect. I saw, in fine, that he would be driven, as a matter of course, to *simplicity*, if not deliberately induced to it as a matter of choice. You will remember, perhaps, how desperately the Prefect laughed when I suggested, upon our first interview, that it was just possible this mystery troubled him so much on account of its being so *very* self-evident.'

'Yes,' said I, 'I remember his merriment well. I really thought he would have fallen into convulsions.'

'The material world,' continued Dupin, 'abounds with very strict analogies to the immaterial; and thus some color of truth has been given to the rhetorical dogma, that metaphor, or simile, may be made to strengthen an argument, as well as to embellish a description. The principle of the *vis inertiæ*, for example, seems to be identical in physics and metaphysics. It is not more true in the former, that a large body is with more difficulty set in motion than a smaller one, and that its subsequent *momentum* is commensurate with this difficulty, than it is, in the latter, that intellects of the vaster capacity, while more forcible, more constant, and more eventful in their movements than those of inferior grade, are yet the less readily moved, and more embarrassed and full of hesitation in the first few steps of their progress. Again: have you ever noticed which of the street signs, over the shop doors, are the most attractive of attention?'

'I have never given the matter a thought,' I said.

'There is a game of puzzles,' he resumed, 'which is played upon a map. One party requires another to find a given word – the name of town, river, state or empire – any word, in short, upon the motley and perplexed surface of the chart. A novice in the game generally seeks to embarrass his opponents by giving them the most minutely lettered names; but the adept selects such words as stretch, in large characters, from one end of the chart to the other. These, like the over-largely lettered signs and placards of the street, escape observation by dint of being excessively obvious; and here the physical oversight is precisely analogous with the moral inapprehension by which the intellect suffers to pass unnoticed those considerations which are too obtrusively and too palpably self-evident. But this is a point, it appears, somewhat above or beneath the understanding of the Prefect. He never once thought it probable, or possible, that the Minister had deposited the letter immediately beneath the nose of the whole world, by way of best preventing any portion of that world from perceiving it.

'But the more I reflected upon the daring, dashing, and discriminating ingenuity of D—; upon the fact that the document must always have been *at hand*, if he intended to use it to good purpose; and upon the decisive evidence, obtained by the Prefect, that it was not hidden within the limits of that dignitary's ordinary search – the more satisfied I became that, to conceal this letter, the Minister had resorted to the comprehensive and sagacious expedient of not attempting to conceal it at all.

'Full of these ideas, I prepared myself with a pair of green spectacles, and called one fine morning, quite by accident, at the

Ministerial hotel. I found D— at home, yawning, lounging, and dawdling, as usual, and pretending to be in the last extremity of *ennui*. He is, perhaps, the most really energetic human being now alive – but that is only when nobody sees him.

'To be even with him, I complained of my weak eyes, and lamented the necessity of the spectacles, under cover of which I cautiously and thoroughly surveyed the apartment, while seemingly intent only upon the conversation of my host.

'I paid special attention to a large writing-table near which he sat, and upon which lay confusedly, some miscellaneous letters and other papers, with one or two musical instruments and a few books. Here, however, after a long and very deliberate scrutiny, I saw nothing to excite particular suspicion.

'At length my eyes, in going the circuit of the room, fell upon a trumpery fillagree card-rack of pasteboard, that hung dangling by a dirty blue ribbon, from a little brass knob just beneath the middle of the mantelpiece. In this rack, which had three or four compartments, were five or six visiting cards and a solitary letter. This last was much soiled and crumpled. It was torn nearly in two, across the middle – as if a design, in the first instance, to tear it entirely up as worthless, had been altered, or stayed, in the second. It had a large black seal, bearing the D— cipher *very* conspicuously, and was addressed, in a diminutive female hand, to D—, the minister, himself. It was thrust carelessly, and even, as it seemed, contemptuously, into one of the upper divisions of the rack.

'No sooner had I glanced at this letter, than I concluded it to be that of which I was in search. To be sure, it was, to all appearance, radically different from the one of which the Prefect had read us so minute a description. Here the seal was large and black, with the D— cipher; there it was small and red, with the ducal arms of the S— family. Here, the address, to the Minister, was diminutive and feminine; there the superscription, to a certain royal personage, was markedly bold and decided; the size alone formed a point of correspondence. But, then, the *radicalness* of these differences, which was excessive; the dirt; the soiled and torn condition of the paper, so inconsistent with the *true* methodical habits of D—, and so suggestive of a design to delude the beholder into an idea of the worthlessness of the document; these things, together with the hyperobtrusive situation of this document, full in the view of every visiter, and thus exactly in accordance with the conclusions to which I had previously arrived; these things, I say, were strongly corroborative of suspicion, in one who came with the intention to suspect.

'I protracted my visit as long as possible, and, while I maintained a most animated discussion with the Minister, on a topic which I knew well had never failed to interest and excite him, I kept my attention really riveted upon the letter. In this examination, I committed to memory its external appearance and arrangement in the rack; and also fell, at length, upon a discovery which set at rest whatever trivial doubt I might have entertained. In scrutinizing the edges of the paper, I observed them to be more *chafed* than seemed necessary. They presented the *broken* appearance which is manifested when a stiff paper, having been folded and pressed with a folder, is refolded in a reversed direction, in the same creases or edges which had formed the original fold. This discovery was sufficient. It was clear to me that the letter had been turned, as a glove, inside out, re-directed, and re-sealed. I bade the Minister good morning, and took my departure at once, leaving a gold snuff-box upon the table.

The next morning I called for the snuff-box, when we resumed, quite eagerly, the conversation of the preceding day. While thus engaged, however, a loud report, as if of a pistol, was heard immediately beneath the windows of the hotel, and was succeeded by a series of fearful screams, and the shoutings of a mob. D— rushed to a casement, threw it open, and looked out. In the meantime, I stepped to the card-rack, took the letter, put it in my pocket, and replaced it by a *fac-simile*, (so far as regards externals,) which I had carefully prepared at my lodgings; imitating the D— cipher, very readily, by means of a seal formed of bread.

'The disturbance in the street had been occasioned by the frantic behavior of a man with a musket. He had fired it among a crowd of women and children. It proved, however, to have been without ball, and the fellow was suffered to go his way as a lunatic or a drunkard. When he had gone, D— came from the window, whither I had followed him immediately upon securing the object in view. Soon afterwards I bade him farewell. The pretended lunatic was a man in my own pay.'

'But what purpose had you,' I asked, 'in replacing the letter by a *fac-simile*? Would it not have been better, at the first visit, to have seized it openly, and departed?'

'D—,' replied Dupin, 'is a desperate man, and a man of nerve. His hotel, too, is not without attendants devoted to his interests. Had I made the wild attempt you suggest, I might never have left the Ministerial presence alive. The good people of Paris might have heard of me no more. But I had an object apart from these considerations. You know my political prepossessions. In this matter, I act as a partisan of the lady concerned. For eighteen months the Minister has had her in his power. She has now him in hers; since, being unaware that the letter is not in his possession, he will proceed with his exactions as if it was. Thus will he inevitably commit himself, at once, to his political destruction. His downfall, too, will not be more precipitate than awkward. It is all very well to talk about the *facilis descensus Averni*; but in all kinds of climbing, as Catalani said of singing, it is far more easy to get up than to come down. In the present instance I have no sympathy – at least no pity – for him who descends. He is that *monstrum horrendum*, an unprincipled man of genius. I confess, however, that I should like very well to know the precise character of his thoughts, when, being defied by her whom the Prefect terms "a certain personage," he is reduced to opening the letter which I left for him in the card-rack.'

'How? did you put any thing particular in it?'

'Why – it did not seem altogether right to leave the interior blank – that would have been insulting. D—, at Vienna once, did me an evil turn, which I told him, quite good-humoredly, that I should remember. So, as I knew he would feel some curiosity in regard to the identity of the person who had outwitted him, I thought it a pity not to give him a clue. He is well acquainted with my MS., and I just copied into the middle of the blank sheet the words –

―― Un dessein si funeste,
S'il n'est digne d'Atrée, est digne de Thyeste.[2]

They are to be found in Crébillon's "Atrée." '

The Facts in the Case of M. Valdemar

OF course I shall not pretend to consider it any matter for wonder, that the extraordinary case of M. Valdemar has excited discussion. It would have been a miracle had it not – especially under the circumstances. Through the desire of all parties concerned, to keep the affair from the public, at least for the present, or until we had farther opportunities for investigation – through our endeavors to effect this – a garbled or exaggerated account made its way into society, and became the source of many unpleasant misrepresentations, and, very naturally, of a great deal of disbelief.

It is now rendered necessary that I give the *facts* – as far as I comprehend them myself. They are, succinctly, these :

My attention, for the last three years, had been repeatedly drawn to the subject of Mesmerism; and, about nine months ago, it occurred to me, quite suddenly, that in the series of experiments made hitherto, there had been a very remarkable and most unaccountable omission : – no person had as yet been mesmerized *in articulo mortis*. It remained to be seen, first, whether, in such condition, there existed in the patient any susceptibility to the magnetic influence; secondly, whether, if any existed, it was impaired or increased by the condition; thirdly, to what extent, or for how long a period, the encroachments of Death might be arrested by the process. There were other points to be ascertained, but these most excited my curiosity – the last in especial, from the immensely important character of its consequences.

In looking around me for some subject by whose means I might test these particulars, I was brought to think of my friend, M. Ernest Valdemar, the well-known compiler of the 'Bibliotheca Forensica,' and author (under the *nom de plume* of Issachar Marx) of the Polish versions of 'Wallenstein' and 'Gargantua.' M. Valdemar, who has resided principally at Harlaem, N.Y., since the year 1839, is (or was) particularly noticeable for the extreme spareness of his person – his lower limbs much resembling those of John Randolph; and, also, for the whiteness of his whiskers, in violent contrast to the blackness of his hair – the latter, in consequence, being very generally mistaken for a wig. His temperament was markedly nervous, and rendered him a good subject for mesmeric experiment. On two or three occasions I had put him to sleep with little difficulty, but was disappointed in other results which his peculiar constitution had naturally led me to anticipate. His will was at no period positively, or thoroughly, under my control, and in regard to *clairvoyance*, I could accomplish with him nothing to be relied upon. I always attributed my failure at these points to the disordered state of his health. For some months previous to my becoming acquainted with him, his physicians had declared him in a confirmed phthisis. It was his custom, indeed, to speak calmly of his approaching dissolution, as a matter neither to be avoided nor regretted.

When the ideas to which I had alluded first occurred to me, it was of course very natural that I should think of M. Valdemar. I knew the steady philosophy of the man too well to apprehend any scruples from *him*; and he had no relatives in America who would be likely to interfere. I spoke to him frankly upon the subject; and, to my surprise, his interest seemed vividly excited. I say to my surprise; for, although he had always yielded his person freely to my experiments, he had never before given me any tokens of sympathy with what I did. His disease was of that character which would admit of exact calculation in respect to the epoch of its termination in death; and it was finally arranged between us that he would send for me about twenty-four hours before the period announced by his physicians as that of his decease.

It is now rather more than seven months since I received, from M. Valdemar himself, the subjoined note:

MY DEAR P—,

You may as well come *now*. D— and F— are agreed that I cannot hold out beyond tomorrow mid-night; and I think they have hit the time very nearly.   VALDEMAR.

I received this note within half an hour after it was written, and in fifteen minutes more I was in the dying man's chamber. I had not seen him for ten days, and was appalled by the fearful alteration which the brief interval had wrought in him. His face wore a leaden hue; the eyes were utterly lustreless; and the emaciation was so extreme that the skin had been broken through by the cheek-bones. His expectoration was excessive. The pulse was barely perceptible. He retained, nevertheless, in a very remarkable manner, both his mental power and a certain degree of physical strength. He spoke with distinctness – took some palliative medicines without aid – and, when I entered the room, was occupied in penciling memoranda in a pocket-book. He was propped up in the bed by pillows. Doctors D— and F— were in attendance.

After pressing Valdemar's hand, I took these gentlemen aside, and obtained from them a minute account of the patient's condition. The left lung had been for eighteen months in a semi-osseous or cartilaginous state, and was, of course, entirely useless for all purposes of vitality. The right, in its upper portion, was also partially, if not thoroughly, ossified, while the lower region was merely a mass of purulent tubercles, running one into another. Several extensive perforations existed; and, at one point, permanent adhesion to the ribs had taken place. These appearances in the right lobe were of comparatively recent date. The ossification had proceeded with very unusual rapidity; no sign of it had been discovered a month before, and the adhesion had only been observed during the three previous days. Independently of the phthisis, the patient was suspected of aneurism of the aorta; but on this point the osseous symptoms rendered an exact diagnosis impossible. It was the opinion of both physicians that M. Valdemar would die about midnight on the morrow (Sunday). It was then seven o'clock on Saturday evening.

On quitting the invalid's bed-side to hold conversation with myself, Doctors D— and F— had bidden him a final farewell. It had not been their intention to return; but, at my request, they agreed to look in upon the patient about ten the next night.

When they had gone, I spoke freely with M. Valdemar on the

subject of his approaching dissolution, as well as, more particularly, of the experiment proposed. He still professed himself quite willing and even anxious to have it made, and urged me to commence it at once. A male and a female nurse were in attendance; but I did not feel myself altogether at liberty to engage in a task of this character with no more reliable witnesses than these people, in case of sudden accident, might prove. I therefore postponed operations until about eight the next night, when the arrival of a medical student with whom I had some acquaintance, (Mr Theodore L—l,) relieved me from farther embarrassment. It had been my design, originally, to wait for the physicians; but I was induced to proceed, first, by the urgent entreaties of M. Valdemar, and secondly, by my conviction that I had not a moment to lose, as he was evidently sinking fast.

Mr L—l was so kind as to accede to my desire that he would take notes of all that occurred; and it is from his memoranda that what I now have to relate is, for the most part, either condensed or copied *verbatim*.

It wanted about five minutes of eight when, taking the patient's hand, I begged him to state, as distinctly as he could, to Mr L—l, whether he (M. Valdemar) was entirely willing that I should make the experiment of mesmerizing him in his then condition.

He replied feebly, yet quite audibly, 'Yes, I wish to be mesmerized' – adding immediately afterwards, 'I fear you have deferred it too long.'

While he spoke thus, I commenced the passes which I had already found most effectual in subduing him. He was evidently influenced with the first lateral stroke of my hand across his forehead; but although I exerted all my powers, no farther perceptible effect was induced until some minutes after ten o'clock, when Doctors D— and F— called, according to appointment. I explained to them, in a few words, what I designed, and as they opposed no objection, saying that the patient was already in the death agony, I proceeded without hesitation – exchanging, however, the lateral passes for downward ones, and directing my gaze entirely into the right eye of the sufferer.

By this time his pulse was imperceptible and his breathing was stertorous, and at intervals of half a minute.

This condition was nearly unaltered for a quarter of an hour. At the expiration of this period, however, a natural although a very deep sigh escaped the bosom of the dying man, and the stertorous breathing ceased – that is to say, its stertorousness was no longer apparent; the intervals were undiminished. The patient's extremities were of an icy coldness.

At five minutes before eleven I perceived unequivocal signs of the mesmeric influence. The glassy roll of the eye was changed for that expression of uneasy *inward* examination which is never seen except in cases of sleep-waking, and which it is quite impossible to mistake. With a few rapid lateral passes I made the lids quiver, as in incipient sleep, and with a few more I closed them altogether. I was not satisfied, however, with this, but continued the manipulations vigorously, and with the fullest exertion of the will, until I had completely stiffened the limbs of the slumberer, after placing them in a seemingly easy position. The legs were at full length; the arms were nearly so, and reposed on the bed at a moderate distance from the loins. The head was very slightly elevated.

When I had accomplished this, it was fully midnight, and I requested the gentlemen present to examine M. Valdemar's condition. After a few experiments, they admitted him to be in an unusually perfect state of mesmeric trance. The curiosity of both the physicians was greatly excited. Dr D — resolved at once to remain with the patient all night, while Dr F— took leave with a promise to return at daybreak. Mr L—l and the nurses remained.

We left M. Valdemar entirely undisturbed until about three o'clock in the morning, when I approached him and found him in precisely the same condition as when Dr F— went away – that is to say, he lay in the same position; the pulse was imperceptible; the breathing was gentle (scarcely noticeable, unless through the application of a mirror to the lips); the eyes were closed naturally; and the limbs were as rigid and as cold as marble. Still, the general appearance was certainly not that of death.

As I approached M. Valdemar I made a kind of half effort to influence his right arm into pursuit of my own, as I passed the latter gently to and fro above his person. In such experiments with this patient I had never perfectly succeeded before, and assuredly I had little thought of succeeding now; but to my astonishment, his arm very readily, although feebly, followed every direction I assigned it with mine. I determined to hazard a few words of conversation.

'M. Valdemar,' I said, 'are you asleep?' He made no answer, but I perceived a tremor about the lips, and was thus induced to repeat the question, again and again. At its third repetition, his whole frame was agitated by a very slight shivering; the eyelids unclosed themselves so far as to display a white line of the ball; the lips moved sluggishly, and from between them, in a barely audible whisper, issued the words:

'Yes; – asleep now. Do not wake me! – let me die so!'

I here felt the limbs and found them as rigid as ever. The right arm, as before, obeyed the direction of my hand. I questioned the sleep-waker again:

'Do you still feel pain in the breast, M. Valdemar?'

The answer now was immediate, but even less audible than before:

'No pain – I am dying.'

I did not think it advisable to disturb him farther just then, and nothing more was said or done until the arrival of Dr F—, who came a little before sunrise, and expressed unbounded astonishment at finding the patient still alive. After feeling the pulse and applying a mirror to the lips, he requested me to speak to the sleep-waker again. I did so, saying:

'M. Valdemar, do you still sleep?'

As before, some minutes elapsed ere a reply was made; and during the interval the dying man seemed to be collecting his energies to speak. At my fourth repetition of the question, he said very faintly, almost inaudibly:

'Yes; still asleep – dying.'

It was now the opinion, or rather the wish, of the physicians, that M. Valdemar should be suffered to remain undisturbed in his present apparently tranquil condition, until death should supervene – and this, it was generally agreed, must now take place within a few minutes. I concluded, however, to speak to him once more, and merely repeated my previous question.

While I spoke, there came a marked change over the countenance of the sleep-walker. The eyes rolled themselves slowly open, the pupils disappearing upwardly; the skin generally assumed a cadaverous hue, resembling not so much parchment as white paper; and the circular hectic spots which, hitherto, had been strongly defined in the centre of each cheek, *went out* at once. I use this expression, because the suddenness of their departure put me in mind of nothing so much as the extinguishment of a candle by a puff of the breath. The upper lip, at the same time, writhed itself away from the teeth, which it had previously covered completely; while the lower jaw fell with an audible jerk, leaving the mouth widely extended, and disclosing in full view the swollen and blackened tongue. I presume that no member of the party then present had been unaccustomed to death-bed horrors; but so hideous beyond conception was the appearance of M. Valdemar at this moment, that there was a general shrinking back from the region of the bed.

I now feel that I have reached a point of this narrative at which every reader will be startled into positive disbelief. It is my business, however, simply to proceed.

There was no longer the faintest sign of vitality in M. Valdemar; and concluding him to be dead, we were consigning him to the charge of the nurses, when a strong vibratory motion was observable in the tongue. This continued for perhaps a minute. At the expiration of this period, there issued from the distended and motionless jaws a voice – such as it would be madness in me to attempt describing. There are, indeed, two or three epithets which might be considered as applicable to it in part; I might say, for example, that the sound was harsh, and broken and hollow; but the hideous whole is indescribable, for the simple reason that no similar sounds have ever jarred upon the ear of humanity. There were two particulars, nevertheless, which I thought then, and still think, might fairly be stated as characteristic of the intonation – as well adapted to convey some idea of its unearthly peculiarity. In the first place, the voice seemed to reach our ears – at least mine – from a vast distance, or from some deep cavern within the earth. In the second place, it impressed me (I fear, indeed, that it will be impossible to make myself comprehended) as gelatinous or glutinous matters impress the sense of touch.

I have spoken both of 'sound' and of 'voice.' I mean to say that the sound was one of distinct – of even wonderfully, thrillingly distinct – syllabification. M. Valdemar *spoke* – obviously in reply to the question I had propounded to him a few minutes before. I had asked him, it will be remembered, if he still slept. He now said:

'Yes; – no; – I *have been* sleeping – and now – now – I *am dead.*'

No person present even affected to deny, or attempted to repress, the unutterable, shuddering horror which these few words, thus uttered, were so well calculated to convey. Mr L—l (the student) swooned. The nurses immediately left the chamber, and could not be induced to return. My own impressions I would not pretend to render intelligible to the reader. For nearly an hour, we busied ourselves, silently – without the utterance of a word – in endeavors to revive Mr L—l. When he came to himself, we addressed ourselves again to an investigation of M. Valdemar's condition.

It remained in all respects as I have last described it, with the exception that the mirror no longer afforded evidence of respiration. An attempt to draw blood from the arm failed. I should mention, too, that this limb was no farther subject to my will. I endeavored in vain to make it follow the direction of my hand. The only real indication, indeed, of the mesmeric influence, was now found in the vibratory movement of the tongue, whenever I addressed M. Valdemar a question. He seemed to be making an effort to reply, but had no longer sufficient volition. To queries put to him by any other person than myself he seemed utterly insensible – although I endeavored to place each member of the company in mesmeric *rapport* with him. I believe that I have now related all that is necessary to an understanding of the sleep-waker's state at this epoch. Other nurses were procured; and at ten o'clock I left the house in company with the two physicians and Mr L——l.

In the afternoon we all called again to see the patient. His condition remained precisely the same. We had now some discussion as to the propriety and feasibility of awakening him; but we had little difficulty in agreeing that no good purpose would be served by so doing. It was evident that, so far, death (or what is usually termed death) had been arrested by the mesmeric process. It seemed clear to us all that to awaken M. Valdemar would be merely to insure his instant, or at least his speedy dissolution.

From this period until the close of last week – *an interval of nearly seven months* – we continued to make daily calls at M. Valdemar's house, accompanied, now and then, by medical and other friends. All this time the sleep-waker remained *exactly* as I have last described him. The nurses' attentions were continual.

It was on Friday last that we finally resolved to make the experiment of awakening, or attempting to awaken him; and it is the (perhaps) unfortunate result of this latter experiment which has given rise to so much discussion in private circles – to so much of what I cannot help thinking unwarranted popular feeling.

For the purpose of relieving M. Valdemar from the mesmeric trance, I made use of the customary passes. These, for a time, were unsuccessful. The first indication of revival was afforded by a partial descent of the iris. It was observed, as especially remarkable, that this lowering of the pupil was accompanied by the profuse out-flowing of a yellowish ichor (from beneath the lids) of a pungent and highly offensive odor.

It was now suggested that I should attempt to influence the patient's arm, as heretofore. I made the attempt and failed. Dr F— then intimated a desire to have me put a question. I did so, as follows :

'M. Valdemar, can you explain to us what are your feelings or wishes now?'

There was an instant return of the hectic circles on the cheeks; the tongue quivered, or rather rolled violently in the mouth (although the jaws and lips remained rigid as before;) and at length the same hideous voice which I have already described, broke forth:

'For God's sake! – quick! – quick! – put me to sleep – or, quick! – waken me! – quick ! – *I say to you that I am dead!*'

I was thoroughly unnerved, and for an instant remained undecided what to do. At first I made an endeavor to re-compose the patient; but, failing in this through total abeyance of the will, I retraced my steps and as earnestly struggled to awaken him. In this attempt I soon saw that I should be successful – or at least I soon fancied that my success would be complete – and I am sure that all in the room were prepared to see the patient awaken.

For what really occurred, however, it is quite impossible that any human being could have been prepared.

As I rapidly made the mesmeric passes, amid ejaculations of 'dead! dead!' absolutely *bursting* from the tongue and not from the lips of the sufferer, his whole frame at once – within the space of a single minute, or even less, shrunk – crumbled – absolutely *rotted* away beneath my hands. Upon the bed, before that whole company, there lay a nearly liquid mass of loathsome – of detestable putridity.

The Cask of Amontillado

THE thousand injuries of Fortunato I had borne as I best could, but when he ventured upon insult I vowed revenge. You, who so well know the nature of my soul, will not suppose, however, that I gave utterance to a threat. At *length* I would be avenged; this was a point definitely settled – but the very definitiveness with which it was resolved precluded the idea of risk. I must not only punish but punish with impunity. A wrong is unredressed when retribution overtakes its redresser. It is equally unredressed when the avenger fails to make himself felt as such to him who has done the wrong.

It must be understood that neither by word nor deed had I given Fortunato cause to doubt my good will. I continued, as was my wont, to smile in his face, and he did not perceive that my smile *now* was at the thought of his immolation.

He had a weak point – this Fortunato – although in other regards he was a man to be respected and even feared. He prided himself on his connoisseurship in wine. Few Italians have the true virtuoso spirit. For the most part their enthusiasm is adopted to suit the time and opportunity, to practise imposture upon the British and Austrian *millionaires*. In painting and gemmary, Fortunato, like his countrymen, was a quack, but in the matter of old wines he was sincere. In this respect I did not differ from him materially; – I was skilful in the Italian vintages myself, and bought largely whenever I could.

It was about dusk, one evening during the supreme madness of the carnival season, that I encountered my friend. He accosted me with excessive warmth, for he had been drinking much. The man wore motley. He had on a tight-fitting parti-striped dress, and his head was surmounted by the conical cap and bells. I was so pleased to see him that I thought I should never have done wringing his hand.

I said to him – 'My dear Fortunato, you are luckily met. How remarkably well you are looking today. But I have received a pipe of what passes for Amontillado, and I have my doubts.'

'How?' said he. 'Amontillado? A pipe? Impossible! And in the middle of the carnival!'

'I have my doubts,' I replied; 'and I was silly enough to pay the full Amontillado price without consulting you in the matter. You were not to be found, and I was fearful of losing a bargain.'

'Amontillado!'

'I have my doubts.'

'Amontillado!'

'And I must satisfy them.'

'Amontillado!'

'As you are engaged, I am on my way to Luchresi. If any one has a critical turn it is he. He will tell me –'

'Luchresi cannot tell Amontillado from Sherry.'

'And yet some fools will have it that his taste is a match for your own.'

'Come, let us go.'

'Whither?'

'To your vaults.'

'My friend, no; I will not impose upon your good nature. I perceive you have an engagement. Luchresi –'

'I have no engagement; – come.'

'My friend, no. It is not the engagement, but the severe cold with which I perceive you are afflicted. The vaults are insufferably damp. They are encrusted with nitre.'

'Let us go, nevertheless. The cold is merely nothing. Amontillado! You have been imposed upon. And as for Luchresi, he cannot distinguish Sherry from Amontillado.'

Thus speaking, Fortunato possessed himself of my arm; and putting on a mask of black silk and drawing a *roquelaire* closely about my person, I suffered him to hurry me to my palazzo.

There were no attendants at home; they had absconded to make merry in honour of the time. I had told them that I should not return until the morning, and had given them explicit orders not to stir from the house. These orders were sufficient, I well knew, to insure their immediate disappearance, one and all, as soon as my back was turned.

I took from their sconces two flambeaux, and giving one to Fortunato, bowed him through several suites of rooms to the archway that led into the vaults. I passed down a long and winding staircase, requesting him to be cautious as he followed. We came at length to the foot of the descent, and stood together upon the damp ground of the catacombs of the Montresors.

The gait of my friend was unsteady, and the bells upon his cap jingled as he strode.

'The pipe,' he said.

'It is farther on,' said I; 'but observe the white web-work which gleams from these cavern walls.'

He turned towards me, and looked into my eyes with two filmy orbs that distilled the rheum of intoxication.

'Nitre?' he asked, at length.

'Nitre,' I replied. 'How long have you had that cough?'

'Ugh! ugh! ugh! – ugh! ugh! ugh! – ugh! ugh! ugh! – ugh! ugh! ugh! – ugh! ugh! ugh!'

My poor friend found it impossible to reply for many minutes.

'It is nothing,' he said, at last.

'Come,' I said, with decision, 'we will go back; your health is precious. You are rich, respected, admired, beloved; you are happy, as once I was. You are a man to be missed. For me it is no matter. We will go back; you will be ill, and I cannot be responsible. Besides, there is Luchresi –'

'Enough,' he said; 'the cough is a mere nothing; it will not kill me. I shall not die of a cough.'

'True – true,' I replied; 'and, indeed, I had no intention of alarming you unnecessarily – but you should use all proper caution. A draught of this Medoc will defend us from the damps.'

Here I knocked off the neck of a bottle which I drew from a long row of its fellows that lay upon the mould.

'Drink,' I said, presenting him the wine.

He raised it to his lips with a leer. He paused and nodded to me familiarly, while his bells jingled.

'I drink,' he said, 'to the buried that repose around us.'

'And I to your long life.'

He again took my arm, and we proceeded.

'These vaults,' he said, 'are extensive.'

'The Montresors,' I replied, 'were a great and numerous family.'

'I forget your arms.'

'A huge human foot d'or, in a field azure; the foot crushes a serpent rampant whose fangs are imbedded in the heel.'

'And the motto?'

'Nemo me impune lacessit.'

'Good!' he said.

The wine sparkled in his eyes and the bells jingled. My own fancy grew warm with the Medoc. We had passed through long walls of piled skeletons, with casks and puncheons intermingling, into the inmost recesses of the catacombs. I paused again, and this time I made bold to seize Fortunato by an arm above the elbow.

'The nitre!' I said; 'see, it increases. It hangs like moss upon the vaults. We are below the river's bed. The drops of moisture trickle among the bones. Come, we will go back ere it is too late. Your cough –'

'It is nothing,' he said; 'let us go on. But first, another draught of the Medoc.'

I broke and reached him a flagon of De Grâve. He emptied it at a breath. His eyes flashed with a fierce light. He laughed and threw the bottle upwards with a gesticulation I did not understand.

I looked at him in surprise. He repeated the movement – a grotesque one.

'You do not comprehend?' he said.

'Not I,' I replied.

'Then you are not of the brotherhood.'

'How?'

'You are not of the masons.'

'Yes, yes,' I said; 'yes, yes.'

'You? Impossible! A mason?'

'A mason,' I replied.

'A sign,' he said, 'a sign.'

'It is this,' I answered, producing from beneath the folds of my *roquelaire* a trowel.

'You jest,' he exclaimed, recoiling a few paces. 'But let us proceed to the Amontillado.'

'Be it so,' I said, replacing the tool beneath the cloak and again offering him my arm. He leaned upon it heavily. We continued our route in search of the Amontillado. We passed through a range of low arches, descended, passed on, and descending again, arrived at a deep crypt, in which the foulness of the air caused our flambeaux rather to glow than flame.

At the most remote end of the crypt there appeared another less spacious. Its walls had been lined with human remains, piled to the vault overhead, in the fashion of the great catacombs of Paris. Three sides of this interior crypt were still ornamented in this manner. From the fourth side the bones had been thrown down, and lay promiscuously upon the earth, forming at one point a mound of some size. Within the wall thus exposed by the displacing of the bones, we perceived a still interior crypt or recess, in depth about four feet, in width three, in height six or seven. It seemed to have been constructed for no especial use within itself, but formed merely the interval between two of the colossal supports of the roof of the catacombs, and was backed by one of their circumscribing walls of solid granite.

It was in vain that Fortunato, uplifting his dull torch, endeavoured to pry into the depth of the recess. Its termination the feeble light did not enable us to see.

'Proceed,' I said; 'herein is the Amontillado. As for Luchresi –'

'He is an ignoramus,' interrupted my friend, as he stepped unsteadily forward, while I followed immediately at his heels. In an instant he had reached the extremity of the niche, and finding his progress arrested by the rock, stood stupidly bewildered. A moment more and I had fettered him to the granite. In its surface were two iron staples, distant from each other about two feet, horizontally. From one of these depended a short chain, from the other a padlock. Throwing the links about his waist, it was but the work of a few seconds to secure it. He was too much astounded to resist. Withdrawing the key I stepped back from the recess.

'Pass your hand,' I said, 'over the wall; you cannot help feeling the nitre. Indeed, it is *very* damp. Once more let me *implore* you to return. No? Then I must positively leave you. But I must first render you all the little attentions in my power.'

'The Amontillado!' ejaculated my friend, not yet recovered from his astonishment.

'True,' I replied; 'the Amontillado.'

As I said these words I busied myself among the pile of bones of which I have before spoken. Throwing them aside, I soon uncovered a quantity of building stone and mortar. With these materials and with the aid of my trowel, I began vigorously to wall up the entrance of the niche.

I had scarcely laid the first tier of the masonry when I discovered that the intoxication of Fortunato had in a great measure worn off. The earliest indication I had of this was a low moaning cry from the depth of the recess. It was *not* the cry of a drunken man. There was then a long and obstinate silence. I laid the second tier, and the third, and the fourth; and then I heard the furious vibrations of the chain. The noise lasted for several minutes, during which, that I might hearken to it with the more satisfaction, I ceased my labours and sat down upon the bones. When at last the clanking subsided, I resumed the trowel, and finished without interruption the fifth, the sixth, and the seventh tier. The wall was now nearly upon a level with my breast. I again paused, and holding the flambeaux over the mason-work, threw a few feeble rays upon the figure within.

A succession of loud and shrill screams, bursting suddenly from the throat of the chained form, seemed to thrust me violently back. For a brief moment I hesitated, I trembled. Unsheathing my rapier, I began to grope with it about the recess; but the thought of an instant reassured me. I placed my hand upon the solid fabric of the catacombs, and felt satisfied. I reapproached the wall; I replied to the yells of him who clamoured.

I re-echoed, I aided, I surpassed them in volume and in strength. I did this, and the clamourer grew still.

It was now midnight, and my task was drawing to a close. I had completed the eighth, the ninth and the tenth tier. I had finished a portion of the last and the eleventh; there remained but a single stone to be fitted and plastered in. I struggled with its weight; I placed it partially in its destined position. But now there came from out the niche a low laugh that erected the hairs upon my head. It was succeeded by a sad voice, which I had difficulty in recognizing as that of the noble Fortunato. The voice said –

'Ha! ha! ha! – he! he! he! – a very good joke, indeed – an excellent jest. We will have many a rich laugh about it at the palazzo – he! he! he! – over our wine – he! he! he!'

'The Amontillado'! I said.

'He! he! he! – he! he! he! – yes, the Amontillado. But is it not getting late? Will not they be awaiting us at the palazzo, the Lady Fortunato and the rest? Let us be gone.'

'Yes,' I said, 'let us be gone.'

'*For the love of God, Montresor!*'

'Yes,' I said, 'for the love of God!'

But to these words I hearkened in vain for a reply. I grew impatient. I called aloud –

'Fortunato!'

No answer. I called again –

'Fortunato!'

No answer still. I thrust a torch through the remaining aperture and let it fall within. There came forth in return only a jingling of the bells. My heart grew sick; it was the dampness of the catacombs that made it so. I hastened to make an end of my labour. I forced the last stone into its position; I plastered it up. Against the new masonry I re-erected the old rampart of bones. For the half of a century no mortal has disturbed them. *In pace requiescat!*

[handwritten: May he rest in peace.]

Hop-Frog

I NEVER knew any one so keenly alive to a joke as the king was. He seemed to live only for joking. To tell a good story of the joke kind, and to tell it well, was the surest road to his favor. Thus it happened that his seven ministers were all noted for their accomplishments as jokers. They all took after the king, too, in being large, corpulent, oily men, as well as inimitable jokers. Whether people grow fat by joking, or whether there is something in fat itself which predisposes to a joke, I have never been quite able to determine; but certain it is that a lean joker is a *rara avis in terris.*

About the refinements, or, as he called them, the 'ghosts' of wit, the king troubled himself very little. He had an especial admiration for *breadth* in a jest, and would often put up with *length*, for the sake of it. Over-niceties wearied him. He would have preferred Rabelais's 'Gargantua', to the 'Zadig' of Voltaire: and, upon the whole, practical jokes suited his taste far better than verbal ones.

At the date of my narrative, professing jesters had not altogether gone out of fashion at court. Several of the great continental 'powers' still retained their 'fools,' who wore motley, with caps and bells, and who were expected to be always ready with sharp witticisms, at a moment's notice, in consideration of the crumbs that fell from the royal table.

Our king, as a matter of course, retained his 'fool.' The fact is, he *required* something in the way of folly if only to counterbalance the heavy wisdom of the seven wise men who were his ministers – not to mention himself.

His fool, or professional jester, was not *only* a fool, however. His value was trebled in the eyes of the king, by the fact of his being also a dwarf and a cripple. Dwarfs were as common at court, in those days, as fools; and many monarchs would have found it difficult to get through their days (days are rather longer

367

at court than elsewhere) without both a jester to laugh *with*, and a dwarf to laugh *at*. But, as I have already observed, your jesters, in ninety-nine cases out of a hundred, are fat, round and unwieldy – so that it was no small source of self-gratulation with our king that, in Hop-Frog (this was the fool's name,) he possessed a triplicate treasure in one person.

I believe the name 'Hop-Frog' was *not* that given to the dwarf by his sponsors at baptism, but it was conferred upon him, by general consent of the seven ministers, on account of his inability to walk as other men do. In fact, Hop-Frog could only get along by a sort of interjectional gait – something between a leap and a wriggle – a movement that afforded illimitable amusement, and of course consolation, to the king, for (notwithstanding the protuberance of his stomach and a constitutional swelling of the head) the king, by his whole court, was accounted a capital figure.

But although Hop-Frog, through the distortion of his legs, could move only with great pain and difficulty along a road or floor, the prodigious muscular power which nature seemed to have bestowed upon his arms, by way of compensation for deficiency in the lower limbs, enabled him to perform many feats of wonderful dexterity, where trees or ropes were in question, or anything else to climb. At such exercises he certainly much more resembled a squirrel, or a small monkey, than a frog.

I am not able to say, with precision, from what country Hop-Frog originally came. It was from some barbarous region, however, that no person ever heard of – a vast distance from the court of our king. Hop-Frog, and a young girl very little less dwarfish than himself (although of exquisite proportions, and a marvellous dancer,) had been forcibly carried off from their respective homes in adjoining provinces, and sent as presents to the king, by one of his ever-victorious generals.

Under these circumstances, it is not to be wondered at that a close intimacy arose between the two little captives. Indeed, they soon became sworn friends. Hop-Frog, who, although he made a great deal of sport, was by no means popular, had it not in his power to render Trippetta many services; but *she*, on account of her grace and exquisite beauty (although a dwarf,) was universally admired and petted: so she possessed much influence; and never failed to use it, whenever she could, for the benefit of Hop-Frog.

On some grand state occasion – I forget what – the king determined to have a masquerade; and whenever a masquerade, or anything of that kind, occurred at our court, then the talents both of Hop-Frog and Trippetta were sure to be called in play. Hop-Frog, in especial, was so inventive in the way of getting up pageants, suggesting novel characters, and arranging costume, for masked balls, that nothing could be done, it seems, without his assistance.

The night appointed for the *fête* had arrived. A gorgeous hall had been fitted up, under Trippetta's eye, with every kind of device which could possibly give *éclat* to a masquerade. The whole court was in a fever of expectation. As for costumes and characters, it might well be supposed that everybody had come to a decision on such points. Many had made up their minds (as to what *rôles* they should assume) a week, or even a month, in advance; and, in fact, there was not a particle of indecision anywhere – except in the case of the king and his seven ministers. Why *they* hesitated I never could tell, unless they did it by way of a joke. More probably, they found it difficult, on account of being so fat, to make up their minds. At all events, time flew; and, as a last resource, they sent for Trippetta and Hop-Frog.

When the two little friends obeyed the summons of the king, they found him sitting at his wine with the seven members of his cabinet council; but the monarch appeared to be in a very ill humor. He knew that Hop-Frog was not fond of wine; for it excited the poor cripple almost to madness; and madness is no comfortable feeling. But the king loved his practical jokes, and took pleasure in forcing Hop-Frog to drink and (as the king called it) 'to be merry.'

'Come here, Hop-Frog,' said he, as the jester and his friend entered the room: 'swallow this bumper to the health of your absent friends [here Hop-Frog sighed,] and then let us have the benefit of your invention. We want characters – *characters*, man – something novel – out of the way. We are wearied with this everlasting sameness. Come, drink! the wine will brighten your wits.'

Hop-Frog endeavored, as usual, to get up a jest in reply to these advances from the king; but the effort was too much. It happened to be the poor dwarf's birthday, and the command to drink to his 'absent friends' forced the tears to his eyes. Many large, bitter drops fell into the goblet as he took it, humbly, from the hand of the tyrant.

'Ah! ha! ha! ha!' roared the latter, as the dwarf reluctantly drained the beaker. 'See what a glass of good wine can do! Why, your eyes are shining already!'

Poor fellow! his large eyes *gleamed*, rather than shone; for the effect of wine on his excitable brain was not more powerful than instantaneous. He placed the goblet nervously on the table, and looked round upon the company with a half-insane stare. They all seemed highly amused at the success of the king's '*joke*.'

'And now to business,' said the prime minister, a *very* fat man.

'Yes,' said the king; 'come, Hop-Frog, lend us your assistance. Characters, my fine fellow; we stand in need of characters – all of us – ha! ha! ha!' and as this was seriously meant for a joke, his laugh was chorused by the seven.

Hop-Frog also laughed, although feebly and somewhat vacantly.

'Come, come,' said the king, impatiently, 'have you nothing to suggest?'

'I am endeavoring to think of something *novel*,' replied the dwarf, abstractedly, for he was quite bewildered by the wine.

'Endeavoring!' cried the tyrant, fiercely; 'what do you mean by *that*? Ah, I perceive. You are sulky, and want more wine. Here, drink this!' and he poured out another goblet full and offered it to the cripple, who merely gazed at it, gasping for breath.

'Drink, I say!' shouted the monster, 'or by the fiends –'

The dwarf hesitated. The king grew purple with rage. The

courtiers smirked. Trippetta, pale as a corpse, advanced to the monarch's seat, and, falling on her knees before him, implored him to spare her friend.

The tyrant regarded her, for some moments, in evident wonder at her audacity. He seemed quite at a loss what to do or say – how most becomingly to express his indignation. At last, without uttering a syllable, he pushed her violently from him, and threw the contents of the brimming goblet in her face.

The poor girl got up as best she could, and, not daring even to sigh, resumed her position at the foot of the table.

There was a dead silence for about a half a minute, during which the falling of a leaf, or of a feather might have been heard. It was interrupted by a low, but harsh and protracted *grating* sound which seemed to come at once from every corner of the room.

'What – what – *what* are you making that noise for?' demanded the king, turning furiously to the dwarf.

The latter seemed to have recovered, in great measure, from his intoxication, and looking fixedly but quietly into the tyrant's face, merely ejaculated :

'I – I? How could it have been me?'

'The sound appeared to come from without,' observed one of the courtiers. 'I fancy it was the parrot at the window, whetting his bill upon his cage-wires.'

'True,' replied the monarch, as if much relieved by the suggestion; 'but, on the honor of a knight, I could have sworn that it was the gritting of this vagabond's teeth.'

Hereupon the dwarf laughed (the king was too confirmed a joker to object to any one's laughing), and displayed a set of large, powerful, and very repulsive teeth. Moreover, he avowed his perfect willingness to swallow as much wine as desired. The monarch was pacified; and having drained another bumper with no very perceptible ill effect, Hop-Frog entered at once, and with spirit, into the plans for the masquerade.

'I cannot tell what was the association of idea,' observed he, very tranquilly, and as if he had never tasted wine in his life, 'but *just after* your majesty had struck the girl and thrown the wine in her face – *just after* your majesty had done this, and while the parrot was making that odd noise outside the window, there came into my mind a capital diversion – one of my own country frolics – often enacted among us, at our masquerades: but here it will be new altogether. Unfortunately, however, it requires a company of eight persons, and –'

'Here we *are*!' cried the king, laughing at his acute discovery of the coincidence; 'eight to a fraction – I and my seven ministers. Come! what is the diversion?'

'We call it,' replied the cripple, 'the Eight Chained Ourang-Outangs, and it really is excellent sport if well enacted.'

'We will enact it,' remarked the king, drawing himself up, and lowering his eyelids.

'The beauty of the game,' continued Hop-Frog, 'lies in the fright it occasions among the women.'

'Capital!' roared in chorus the monarch and his ministry.

'I will equip you as ourang-outangs,' proceeded the dwarf; 'leave all that to me. The resemblance shall be so striking, that the company of masqueraders will take you for real beasts – and, of course, they will be as much terrified as astonished.'

'O, this is exquisite!' exclaimed the king. 'Hop-Frog! I will make a man of you.'

'The chains are for the purpose of increasing the confusion by their jangling. You are supposed to have escaped, *en masse*, from your keepers. Your majesty cannot conceive the *effect* produced, at a masquerade, by eight chained ourang-outangs, imagined to be real ones by most of the company; and rushing in with savage cries, among the crowd of delicately and gorgeously habited men and women. The *contrast* is inimitable.'

'It *must* be,' said the king: and the council arose hurriedly (as it was growing late), to put in execution the scheme of Hop-Frog.

His mode of equipping the party as ourang-outangs was very simple, but effective enough for his purposes. The animals in question had, at the epoch of my story, very rarely been seen in any part of the civilized world; and as the imitations made by the dwarf were sufficiently beast-like and more than sufficiently hideous, their truthfulness to nature was thus thought to be secured.

The king and his ministers were first encased in tight-fitting stockinet shirts and drawers. They were then saturated with tar. At this stage of the process, some one of the party suggested feathers; but the suggestion was at once overruled by the dwarf, who soon convinced the eight, by ocular demonstration, that the hair of such a brute as the ourang-outang was much more efficiently represented by *flax*. A thick coating of the latter was accordingly plastered upon the coating of tar. A long chain was now procured. First, it was passed about the waist of the king, *and tied*; then about another of the party, and also tied; then about all successively, in the same manner. When this chaining arrangement was complete, and the party stood as far apart from each other as possible, they formed a circle; and to make all things appear natural, Hop-Frog passed the residue of the chain, in two diameters, at right angles, across the circle, after the fashion adopted, at the present day, by those who capture Chimpanzees, or other large apes, in Borneo.

The grand saloon in which the masquerade was to take place, was a circular room, very lofty, and receiving the light of the sun only through a single window at top. At night (the season for which the apartment was especially designed,) it was illuminated principally by a large chandelier, depending by a chain from the centre of the sky-light, and lowered, or elevated, by means of a counter-balance as usual; but (in order not to look unsightly) this latter passed outside the cupola and over the roof.

The arrangements of the room had been left to Trippetta's superintendence; but, in some particulars, it seems, she had been guided by the calmer judgment of her friend the dwarf. At his suggestion it was that, on this occasion, the chandelier was removed. Its waxen drippings (which, in weather so warm, it was quite impossible to prevent,) would have been seriously detrimental to the rich dresses of the guests, who, on account of the crowded state of the saloon, could not *all* be expected to keep from out its centre – that is to say, from under the chandelier. Additional sconces were set in various parts of the hall, out of the way; and a flambeau, emitting sweet odor, was placed in the right hand of each of the Caryatides that stood against the wall – some fifty or sixty altogether.

The eight ourang-outangs, taking Hop-Frog's advice, waited patiently until midnight (when the room was thoroughly filled with masqueraders) before making their appearance. No sooner had the clock ceased striking, however, than they rushed, or rather rolled in, all together – for the impediment of their chains caused most of the party to fall, and all to stumble as they entered.

The excitement among the masqueraders was prodigious, and filled the heart of the king with glee. As had been anticipated, there were not a few of the guests who supposed the ferocious-looking creatures to be beasts of *some* kind in reality, if not precisely ourang-outangs. Many of the women swooned with affright; and had not the king taken the precaution to exclude all weapons from the saloon, his party might soon have expiated their frolic in their blood. As it was, a general rush was made for the doors; but the king had ordered them to be locked immediately upon his entrance; and, at the dwarf's suggestion, the keys had been deposited with *him*.

While the tumult was at its height, and each masquerader attentive only to his own safety – (for, in fact, there was much *real* danger from the pressure of the excited crowd,) – the chain by which the chandelier ordinarily hung, and which had been drawn up on its removal, might have been seen very gradually to descend, until its hooked extremity came within three feet of the floor.

Soon after this, the king and his seven friends, having reeled about the hall in all directions, found themselves, at length, in its centre, and, of course, in immediate contact with the chain. While they were thus situated, the dwarf, who had followed closely at their heels, inciting them to keep up the commotion, took hold of their own chain at the intersection of the two portions which crossed the circle diametrically and at right angles. Here, with the rapidity of thought, he inserted the hook from which the chandelier had been wont to depend; and, in an instant, by some unseen agency, the chandelier-chain was drawn so far upward as to take the hook out of reach, and, as an inevitable consequence, to drag the ourang-outangs together in close connection, and face to face.

The masqueraders, by this time, had recovered, in some measure, from their alarm; and, beginning to regard the whole matter as a well-contrived pleasantry, set up a loud shout of laughter at the predicament of the apes.

'Leave them to *me*!' now screamed Hop-Frog, his shrill voice making itself easily heard through all the din. 'Leave them to *me*. I fancy I know them. If I can only get a good look at them, I can soon tell who they are.'

Here, scrambling over the heads of the crowd, he managed to get to the wall; when, seizing a flambeau from one of the Caryatides, he returned, as he went, to the centre of the room – leaped, with the agility of a monkey, upon the king's head – and thence clambered a few feet up the chain – holding down the torch to examine the group of ourang-outangs, and still screaming, 'I shall soon find out who they are!'

And now, while the whole assembly (the apes included) were convulsed with laughter, the jester suddenly uttered a shrill whistle; when the chain flew violently up for about thirty feet – dragging with it the dismayed and struggling ourang-outangs, and leaving them suspended in mid-air between the sky-light and the floor. Hop-Frog, clinging to the chain as it rose, still maintained his relative position in respect to the eight maskers, and still (as if nothing were the matter) continued to thrust his torch down towards them, as though endeavoring to discover who they were.

So thoroughly astonished were the whole company at this ascent, that a dead silence, of about a minute's duration, ensued. It was broken by just such a low, harsh, *grating* sound, as had before attracted the attention of the king and his councillors, when the former threw the wine in the face of Trippetta. But, on the present occasion, there could be no question as to *whence* the sound issued. It came from the fang-like teeth of the dwarf, who ground them and gnashed them as he foamed at the mouth, and glared, with an expression of maniacal rage, into the upturned countenances of the king and his seven companions.

'Ah, ha!' said at length the infuriated jester. 'Ah, ha! I begin to see who these people *are*, now!' Here, pretending to scrutinize the king more closely, he held the flambeau to the flaxen coat which enveloped him, and which instantly burst into a sheet of vivid flame. In less than half a minute the whole eight ourang-outangs were blazing fiercely, amid the shrieks of the multitude who gazed at them from below, horror-stricken, and without the power to render them the slightest assistance.

At length the flames, suddenly increasing in virulence, forced the jester to climb higher up the chain, to be out of their reach; and, as he made this movement, the crowd again sank, for a brief instant, into silence. The dwarf seized his opportunity, and once more spoke:

'I now see *distinctly*,' he said, 'what manner of people these maskers are. They are a great king and his seven privy-councillors – a king who does not scruple to strike a defenceless girl, and his seven councillors who abet him in the outrage. As for myself, I am simply Hop-Frog, the jester – and *this is my last jest*.'

Owing to the high combustibility of both the flax and the tar to which it adhered, the dwarf had scarcely made an end of his brief speech before the work of vengeance was complete. The eight corpses swung in their chains, a fetid, blackened, hideous, and indistinguishable mass. The cripple hurled his torch at them, clambered leisurely to the ceiling, and disappeared through the sky-light.

It is supposed that Trippetta, stationed on the roof of the saloon, had been the accomplice of her friend in his fiery revenge, and that, together, they effected their escape to their own country: for neither was seen again.

3. Essays and Reviews

Letter to B—

It has been said that a good critique on a poem may be written by one who is no poet himself. This, according to *your* idea and *mine* of poetry, I feel to be false – the less poetical the critic, the less just the critique, and the converse. On this account, and because there are but few B—'s in the world, I would be as much ashamed of the world's good opinion as proud of your own. Another than yourself might here observe, Shakespeare is in possession of the world's good opinion, and yet Shakespeare is the greatest of poets. It appears then that the world judge correctly, why should you be ashamed of their favorable judgment? The difficulty lies in the interpretation of the word 'judgment' or 'opinion.' The opinion is the world's, truly, but it may be called theirs as a man would call a book his, having bought it; he did not write the book, but it is his; they did not originate the opinion, but it is theirs. A fool, for example, thinks Shakespeare a great poet – yet the fool has never read Shakespeare. But the fool's neighbor, who is a step higher on the Andes of the mind, whose head (that is to say, his more exalted thought) is too far above the fool to be seen or understood, but whose feet (by which I mean his every-day actions) are sufficiently near to be discerned, and by means of which that superiority is ascertained, which *but* for them would never have been discovered – this neighbor asserts that Shakespeare is a great poet – the fool believes him, and it is henceforward his *opinion*. This neighbor's opinion has, in like manner, been adopted from one above *him*, and so, ascendingly, to a few gifted individuals who kneel around the summit, beholding, face to face, the master spirit who stands upon the pinnacle. . . .

You are aware of the great barrier in the path of an American writer. He is read, if at all, in preference to the combined and established wit of the world. I say established; for it is with literature as with law or empire – an established name is an estate in tenure, or a throne in possession. Besides, one might suppose that books, like their authors, improve by travel – their having crossed the sea is, with us, so great a distinction. Our antiquaries abandon time for distance; our very fops glance from the binding to the bottom of the title-page, where the mystic characters which spell London, Paris, or Genoa, are precisely so many letters of recommendation. . . .

I mentioned just now a vulgar error as regards criticism. I think the notion that no poet can form a correct estimate of his own writings is another. I remarked before, that in proportion to the poetical talent, would be the justice of a critique upon poetry. Therefore, a bad poet would, I grant, make a false critique, and his self-love would infallibly bias his little judgment in his favor; but a poet, who is indeed a poet, could not, I think, fail of making a just critique. Whatever should be deducted on the score of self-love, might be replaced on account of his intimate acquaintance with the subject; in short, we have more instances of false criticism than of just, where one's own writings are the test, simply because we have more bad poets than good. There are of course many objections to what I say : Milton is a great example of the contrary; but his opinion with respect to the Paradise Regained, is by no means fairly ascertained. By what trivial circumstances men are often led to assert what they do not really believe ! Perhaps an inadvertent word has descended to posterity. But, in fact, the Paradise Regained is little, if at all, inferior to the Paradise Lost, and is only supposed so to be, because men do not like epics, whatever they may say to the contrary, and reading those of Milton in their natural order, are too much wearied with the first to derive any pleasure from the second.

I dare say Milton preferred Comus to either – if so – justly. . . .[1]

As I am speaking of poetry, it will not be amiss to touch slightly upon the most singular heresy in its modern history – the heresy of what is called very foolishly, the Lake School. Some years ago I might have been induced, by an occasion like the present, to attempt a formal refutation of their doctrine; at present it would be a work of supererogation. The wise must bow to the wisdom of such men as Coleridge and Southey, but being wise, have laughed at poetical theories so prosaically exemplified.

Aristotle, with singular assurance, has declared poetry the most philosophical of all writings[2] – but it required a Wordsworth to pronounce it the most metaphysical. He seems to think that the end of poetry is, or should be, instruction – yet it is a truism that the end of our existence is happiness; if so, the end of every separate part of our existence – every thing connected with our existence should be still happiness. Therefore the end of instruction should be happiness; and happiness is another name for pleasure; – therefore the end of instruction should be pleasure: yet we see the above mentioned opinion implies precisely the reverse.

To proceed: ceteris paribus, he who pleases, is of more importance to his fellow men than he who instructs, since utility is happiness, and pleasure is the end already obtained which instruction is merely the means of obtaining.

I see no reason, then, why our metaphysical poets should plume themselves so much on the utility of their works, unless indeed they refer to instruction with eternity in view; in which case, sincere respect for their piety would not allow me to express my contempt for their judgment; contempt which it would be difficult to conceal, since their writings are professedly to be understood by the few, and it is the many who stand in need of salvation. In such case I should no doubt be tempted to think of the devil in Melmoth,[3] who labors indefatigably through three octavo volumes, to accomplish the destruction of one or two souls, while any common devil would have demolished one or two thousand. . . .

Against the subtleties which would make poetry a study – not a passion – it becomes the metaphysician to reason – but the poet to protest. Yet Wordsworth and Coleridge are men in years; the one imbued in contemplation from his childhood, the other a giant in intellect and learning. The diffidence, then, with which I venture to dispute their authority, would be overwhelming, did I not feel, from the bottom of my heart, that learning has little to do with the imagination – intellect with the passions – or age with poetry. . . .

> 'Trifles, like straws, upon the surface flow,
> He who would search for pearls must dive below,'[4]

are lines which have done much mischief. As regards the greater truths, men oftener err by seeking them at the bottom than at the top; the depth lies in the huge abysses where wisdom is sought – not in the palpable places where she is found. The ancients were not always right in hiding the goddess in a well: witness the light which Bacon has thrown upon philosophy; witness the principles of our divine faith – that moral mechanism by which the simplicity of a child may overbalance the wisdom of a man.

We see an instance of Coleridge's liability to err, in his Biographia Literaria – professedly his literary life and opinions, but, in fact, a treatise *de omni scibili et quibusdam aliis.*[5] He goes wrong by reason of his very profundity, and of his error we have a natural type in the contemplation of a star. He who regards it directly and intensely sees, it is true, the star, but it is the star without a ray – while he who surveys it less inquisitively is conscious of all for which the star is useful to us below – its brilliancy and its beauty. . . .

As to Wordsworth, I have no faith in him. That he had, in youth, the feelings of a poet I believe – for there are glimpses of extreme delicacy in his writings – (and delicacy is the poet's own kingdom – his *El Dorado*) – but they have the appearance of a better day recollected; and glimpses, at best, are little evidence of present poetic fire – we know that a few straggling flowers spring up daily in the crevices of the glacier.

He was to blame in wearing away his youth in contemplation with the end of poetizing in his manhood. With the increase of his judgment the light which should make it apparent has faded away. His judgment consequently is too correct. This may not be understood, – but the old Goths of Germany would have understood it, who used to debate matters of importance to their State twice, once when drunk, and once when sober – sober that they might not be deficient in formality – drunk lest they should be destitute of vigor.

The long wordy discussions by which he tries to reason us into admiration of his poetry, speak very little in his favor: they are full of such assertions as this – (I have opened one of his volumes at random) 'Of genius the only proof is the act of doing well what is worthy to be done, and what was never done before' – indeed! then it follows that in doing what is *unworthy* to be done, or what *has* been done before, no genius can be evinced; yet the picking of pockets is an unworthy act, pockets have been picked time immemorial, and Barrington, the pick-pocket, in point of genius, would have thought hard of a comparison with William Wordsworth, the poet.

Again – in estimating the merit of certain poems, whether they be Ossian's or M'Pherson's, can surely be of little consequence, yet, in order to prove their worthlessness, Mr W. has expended many pages in the controversy. *Tantæne animis?* Can great minds descend to such absurdity? But worse still: that he may bear down every argument in favor of these poems, he triumphantly drags forward a passage, in his abomination of which he expects the reader to sympathize. It is the beginning of the epic poem '*Temora*.' 'The blue waves of Ullin roll in light; the green hills are covered with day; trees shake their dusky heads in the breeze.' And this – this gorgeous, yet simple imagery, where all is alive and panting with immortality – this, William Wordsworth, the author of 'Peter Bell,' has *selected* for his contempt. We shall see what better he, in his own person, has to offer. Imprimis:

> 'And now she's at the pony's head,
> And now she's at the pony's tail,
> On that side now, and now on this,
> And almost stifled her with bliss –
> A few sad tears does Betty shed,
> She pats the pony where or when
> She knows not: happy Betty Foy!
> O, Johnny! never mind the Doctor!'

Secondly:

> 'The dew was falling fast, the – stars began to blink,
> I heard a voice; it said – drink, pretty creature, drink;
> And, looking o'er the hedge, be – fore me I espied
> A snow-white mountain lamb, with a – maiden at its side.
> No other sheep were near, the lamb was all alone,
> And by a slender cord was – tether'd to a stone.'[6]

Now, we have no doubt this is all true; we *will* believe it, indeed, we will, Mr W. Is it sympathy for the sheep you wish to excite? I love a sheep from the bottom of my heart....

But there *are* occasions, dear B—, there are occasions when even Wordsworth is reasonable. Even Stamboul, it is said, shall have an end, and the most unlucky blunders must come to a conclusion. Here is an extract from his preface –

'Those who have been accustomed to the phraseology of modern writers, if they persist in reading this book to a conclusion (*impossible!*) will, no doubt, have to struggle with feelings of awkwardness; (ha ! ha ! ha !) they will look round for poetry (ha ! ha ! ha ! ha !) and will be induced to inquire by what species of courtesy these attempts have been permitted to assume that title.' Ha ! ha ! ha ! ha ! ha !

Yet let not Mr W. despair; he has given immortality to a wagon, and the bee Sophocles has transmitted to eternity a sore toe, and dignified a tragedy with a chorus of turkeys....

Of Coleridge I cannot speak but with reverence. His towering intellect ! his gigantic power ! He is one more evidence of the fact 'que la plupart des sectes ont raison dans une bonne partie de ce qu'elles avancent, mais non pas en ce qu'elles nient.'[7] He has imprisoned his own conceptions by the barrier he has erected against those of others. It is lamentable to think that such a mind should be buried in metaphysics, and, like the Nyctanthes, waste its perfume upon the night alone. In reading his poetry, I tremble, like one who stands upon a volcano, conscious, from the very darkness bursting from the crater, of the fire and the light that are weltering below.

． ． ． ． ． ． ． ．

What is Poetry? – Poetry! that Proteus-like idea, with as many appellations as the nine-titled Corcyra! Give me, I demanded of a scholar some time ago, give me a definition of poetry. 'Très-volontiers,' and he proceeded to his library, brought me a Dr Johnson, and overwhelmed me with a definition. Shade of the immortal Shakespeare! I imagine to myself the scowl of your spiritual eye upon the profanity of that scurrilous Ursa Major. Think of poetry, dear B—, think of poetry, and then think of – Dr Samuel Johnson! Think of all that is airy and fairy-like, and then of all that is hideous and unwieldly; think of his huge bulk, the Elephant! and then – and then think of the Tempest – the Midsummer Night's Dream – Prospero – Oberon – and Titania! ...

A poem, in my opinion, is opposed to a work of science by having, for its *immediate* object, pleasure, not truth; to romance, by having for its object an *indefinite* instead of a *definite* pleasure, being a poem only so far as this object is attained; romance presenting perceptible images with definite, poetry with indefinite sensations, to which end music is an *essential*, since the comprehension of sweet sound is our most indefinite conception. Music, when combined with a pleasurable idea, is poetry; music without the idea is simply music; the idea without the music is prose from its very definitiveness.

What was meant by the invective against him who had no music in his soul? ...

To sum up this long rigmarole, I have, dear B—, what you no doubt perceive, for the metaphysical poets, *as* poets, the most sovereign contempt. That they have followers proves nothing –

> The Indian prince has to his palace
> More followers than a thief to the gallows.[8]

Georgia Scenes

GEORGIA SCENES, CHARACTERS, INCIDENTS, &C. IN
THE FIRST HALF CENTURY OF THE REPUBLIC. BY
A NATIVE GEORGIAN. AUGUSTA, GEORGIA.

THIS book has reached us anonymously – not to say anomalously
– yet it is most heartily welcome. The author, whoever he is, is a
clever fellow, imbued with a spirit of the truest humor, and endowed, moreover, with an exquisitely discriminative and penetrating understanding of *character* in general, and of Southern
character in particular. And we do not mean to speak of *human*
character exclusively. To be sure, our Georgian is *au fait* here too
– he is learned in all things appertaining to the biped without
feathers. In regard, especially, to that class of southwestern mammalia who come under the generic appellation of 'savagerous wild
cats,' he is a very Theophrastus in duodecimo. But he is not the
less at home in other matters. Of geese and ganders he is the La
Bruyère, and of good-for-nothing horses the Rochefoucault.

Seriously – if this book were printed in England it would make
the fortune of its author. We positively mean what we say – and
are quite sure of being sustained in our opinion by all proper judges
who may be so fortunate as to obtain a copy of the '*Georgia
Scenes*,' and who will be at the trouble of sifting their peculiar
merits from amid the *gaucheries* of a Southern publication. Seldom
– perhaps never in our lives – have we laughed as immoderately
over any book as over the one now before us. If these *scenes* have
produced such effect upon *our* cachinnatory nerves – upon *us* who
are not 'of the merry mood,' and, moreover, have not been used to
the perusal of somewhat similar things – we are at no loss to
imagine what a hubbub they would occasion in the uninitiated
regions of Cockaigne. And what would Christopher North say to
them? – ah, what would Christopher North say? that is the ques-

tion. Certainly not a word. But we can fancy the pursing up of his lips, and the long, loud, and jovial resonation of his wicked, uproarious ha ! ha's !

From the Preface to the Sketches before us we learn that although they are, generally, nothing more than fanciful combinations of real incidents and characters, still, in some instances, the narratives are literally true. We are told also that the publication of these pieces was commenced, rather more than a year ago, in one of the Gazettes of the State, and that they were favorably received. 'For the last six months,' says the author, 'I have been importuned by persons from all quarters of the State to give them to the public in the present form.' This speaks well for the Georgian taste. But that the publication will *succeed*, in the bookselling sense of the word, is problematical. Thanks to the long-indulged literary supineness of the South, her presses are not as apt in putting forth a *saleable* book as her sons are in concocting a wise one.

From a desire of concealing the author's name, two different signatures, Baldwin and Hall, were used in the original *Sketches*, and, to save trouble, as preserved in the present volume. With the exception, however, of one scene, 'The Company Drill,' all the book is the production of the same pen. The first article in the list is 'Georgia Theatrics.' Our friend *Hall*, in this piece, represents himself as ascending, about eleven o'clock in the forenoon of a June day, 'a long and gentle slope in what was called the Dark Corner of Lincoln County, Georgia.' Suddenly his ears are assailed by loud, profane, and boisterous voices, proceeding, apparently, from a large company of ragamuffins, concealed in a thick covert of undergrowth about a hundred yards from the road.

•   •   •   •   •   •   •   •

And now the sounds assume all the discordant intonations inseparable from a Georgia 'rough and tumble' fight. Our traveller listens in dismay to the indications of a quick, violent, and deadly struggle. With the intention of acting as pacificator, he dismounts in haste, and hurries to the scene of action. Presently, through a gap in the thicket, he obtains a glimpse of one, at least, of the combatants. This one appears to have his antagonist beneath him on the ground, and to be dealing on the prostrate wretch the most unmerciful blows. Having overcome about half the space which separated him from the combatants, our friend Hall is horror-stricken at seeing 'the uppermost make a heavy plunge with both his thumbs, and hearing, at the same instant, a cry in the accent of keenest torture, "Enough! my eye's out!" ' ·

Rushing to the rescue of the mutilated wretch the traveller is surprised at finding that all the accomplices in the hellish deed have fled at his approach – at least so he supposes, for none of them are to be seen.

*   *   *   *   *   *   *   *

All that had been seen or heard was nothing more nor less than a Lincoln rehearsal; in which all the parts of all the characters of a Georgian Court-House fight had been sustained by the youth of the plough *solus*. The whole anecdote is told with a raciness and vigor which would do honor to the pages of Blackwood.

The second Article is 'The Dance, a Personal Adventure of the Author' in which the oddities of a backwood reel are depicted with inimitable force, fidelity and picturesque effect. 'The Horse-swap' is a vivid narration of an encounter between the wits of two Georgian horse-jockies. This is most excellent in every respect – but especially so in its delineations of Southern bravado, and the keen sense of the ludicrous evinced in the portraiture of the steeds. We think the following free and easy sketch of a *hoss* superior, in joint humor and verisimilitude, to any thing of the kind we have ever seen.

*   *   *   *   *   *   *   *

'The character of a Native Georgian' is amusing, but not so good as the scenes which precede and succeed it. Moreover the character described (a practical humorist) is neither very original, nor appertaining exclusively to Georgia.

'The Fight' although involving some horrible and disgusting details of southern barbarity is a sketch unsurpassed in dramatic vigor, and in the vivid truth to nature of one or two of the personages introduced. *Uncle Tommy Loggins*, in particular, an oracle in 'rough and tumbles,' and Ransy Sniffle, a misshapen urchin 'who in his earlier days had fed copiously upon red clay and blackberries,' and all the pleasures of whose life concentre in a love of fisticuffs – are both forcible, accurate and original generic delineations of real existences to be found sparsely in Georgia, Mississippi and Louisiana, and very plentifully in our more remote settlements and territories. This article would positively make the fortune of any British periodical.

'The Song' is a burlesque somewhat overdone, but upon the whole a good caricature of Italian bravura singing. The following account of Miss Aurelia Emma Theodosia Augusta Crump's execution on the piano is inimitable.

·   ·   ·   ·   ·   ·   ·   ·

The *'Turn Out'* is an excellent – a second edition of Miss Edgeworth's 'Barring Out,' and full of fine touches of the truest humor. The scene is laid in Georgia, and in the good old days of *fescues*, *abbiselfas*, and *anpersants* – terms in very common use, but whose derivation we have always been at a loss to understand. Our author thus learnedly explains the riddle.

'The *fescue* was a sharpened wire, or other instrument, used by the preceptor, to point out the letters to the children. *Abbiselfa* is a contraction of the words "a, by itself, a." It was usual, when either of the vowels constituted a syllable of a word, to pronounce it, and denote its independent character, by the words first mentioned, thus: "a by itself *a*, c-o-r-n corn, *acorn*" – *e* by itself *e*, v-i-l, evil. The character which stands for the word *and* (&) was probably pronounced with the same accompaniments, but in terms borrowed from the Latin language, thus: "& *per se* (by itself) &." Hence *"anpersant."* '

This whole story forms an admirable picture of school-boy democracy in the woods. The *master* refuses his pupils an Easter holiday; and upon repairing, at the usual hour of the fatal day, to his school house, 'a log pen about twenty feet square,' finds every avenue to his ingress fortified and barricadoed. He advances, and is assailed by a whole wilderness of sticks from the cracks.

Growing desperate, he seizes a fence rail, and finally succeeds in effecting an entrance by demolishing the door. He is soundly flogged however for his pains, and the triumphant urchins suffer him to escape with his life, solely upon condition of their being allowed to do what they please as long as they shall think proper.

'The Charming Creature as a Wife,' is a very striking narrative of the evils attendant upon an ill-arranged marriage – but as it has nothing about it peculiarly Georgian, we pass it over without further comment.

'The Gander Pulling' is a gem worthy, in every respect, of the writer of 'The Fight,' and 'The Horse Swap.' What a 'Gander Pulling' is, however, may probably not be known by a great majority of our readers. We will therefore tell them. It is a piece of unprincipled barbarity not infrequently practised in the South and West. A circular horse path is formed of about forty or fifty yards in diameter. Over this path, and between two posts about ten feet apart, is extended a rope which, swinging loosely, vibrates in an arc of five or six feet. From the middle of this rope, lying directly over the middle of the path, a gander, whose neck and head are well greased, is suspended by the feet. The distance of the fowl from the ground is generally about ten feet – and its neck is consequently just within reach of a man on horseback. Matters being thus arranged, and the mob of vagabonds assembled, who are desirous of entering the chivalrous lists of the 'Gander Pulling,' a hat is handed round, into which a quarter or half dollar, as the case may be, is thrown by each competitor. The money thus collected is the prize of the victor in the game – and the game is thus conducted. The ragamuffins mounted on horseback, gallop round the circle in Indian file. At a word of command, given by the proprietor of the gander, the pulling, properly so called, commences. Each villain as he passes under the rope, makes a grab at the throat of the devoted bird – the end and object of the tourney being to pull off his head. This of course is an end not easily accomplished. The fowl is obstinately bent upon retaining his caput if possible – in which determination he finds a powerful adjunct in the grease. The rope, moreover, by the efforts of the human devils, is kept in a troublesome and tantalizing state of vibration, while two assistants of the proprietor, one at each pole, are provided with a tough cowhide, for the purpose of preventing any horse from making too long a sojourn beneath the gander. Many hours, therefore, not unfrequently elapse before the contest is decided.

'The Ball' – a Georgia ball – is done to the life. Some passages, in a certain species of sly humor, wherein intense observation of character is disguised by simplicity of relation, put us forcibly in mind of the Spectator. For example.

.   .   .   .

'The Mother and her Child,' we have seen before – but read it a second time with zest. It is a laughable burlesque of the baby gibberish so frequently made use of by mothers in speaking to their children. This sketch evinces, like all the rest of the Georgia scenes – a fine dramatic talent.

'The Debating Society' is the best thing in the book – and indeed one among the best things of the kind we have ever read. It has all the force and freedom of some similar articles in the Diary of a Physician – without the evident straining for effect which so disfigures that otherwise admirable series. We will need no apology for copying The Debating Society entire.

.   .   .   .

'The Militia Company Drill,' is not by the author of the other pieces but has a strong family resemblance, and is very well executed. Among the innumerable descriptions of Militia musters which are so rife in the land, we have met with nothing at all equal to this in the matter of broad farce.

'The Turf' is also capital, and bears with it a kind of dry and sarcastic morality which will recommend it to many readers.

'An Interesting Interview' is another specimen of exquisite dramatic talent. It consists of nothing more than a facsimile of the speech, actions, and thoughts of two drunken old men – but its air of truth is perfectly inimitable.

'The Fox-Hunt,' 'The Wax Works,' and 'A Sage Conversation,'

are all good – but neither *as* good as many other articles in the book.

'*The Shooting Match*,' which concludes the volume, may rank with the best of the Tales which precede it. As a portraiture of the manners of our South-Western peasantry, in especial, it is perhaps better than any.

Altogether this very humorous, and very clever book forms an æra in our reading. It has reached us per mail, and without a cover. We will have it bound forthwith, and give it a niche in our library as a sure omen of better days for the literature of the South.

The Drake—Halleck Review (excerpts)

THE CULPRIT FAY, AND OTHER POEMS, BY JOSEPH
RODMAN DRAKE. NEW YORK: GEORGE DEARBORN.

ALNWICK CASTLE, WITH OTHER POEMS, BY FITZ
GREENE HALLECK. NEW YORK: GEORGE DEARBORN.

BEFORE entering upon the detailed notice which we propose of
the volumes before us, we wish to speak a few words in regard to
the present state of American criticism. It must be visible to all
who meddle with literary matters, that of late years a thorough
revolution has been effected in the censorship of our press. That
this revolution is infinitely for the worse we believe. There was
a time, it is true, when we cringed to foreign opinion – let us
even say when we paid a most servile deference to British critical
dicta. That an American book could, by any possibility, be
worthy perusal, was an idea by no means extensively prevalent in
the land; and if we were induced to read at all the productions
of our native writers, it was only after repeated assurances from
England that such productions were not altogether contemptible. But there was, at all events, a shadow of excuse, and
a slight basis of reason for a subserviency so grotesque. Even now,
perhaps, it would not be far wrong to assert that such basis of
reason may still exist. Let us grant that in many of the abstract
sciences – that even in Theology, in Medicine, in Law, in
Oratory, in the Mechanical Arts, we have no competitors whatever, still nothing but the most egregious national vanity would
assign us a place, in the matter of Polite Literature, upon a level
with the elder and riper climes of Europe, the earliest steps of
whose children are among the groves of magnificently endowed
Academies, and whose innumerable men of leisure, and of consequent learning, drink daily from those august fountains of

inspiration which burst around them everywhere from out the tombs of their immortal dead, and from out their hoary and trophied monuments of chivalry and song. In paying then, as a nation, a respectful and not undue deference to a supremacy rarely questioned but by prejudice or ignorance, we should, of course, be doing nothing more than acting in a rational manner. The *excess* of our subserviency was blamable – but, as we have before said, this very excess might have found a shadow of excuse in the strict justice, if properly regulated, of the principle from which it issued. Not so, however, with our present follies. We are becoming boisterous and arrogant in the pride of a too speedily assumed literary freedom. We throw off, with the most presumptuous and unmeaning hauteur, *all* deference whatever to foreign opinion – we forget, in the puerile inflation of vanity, that *the world* is the true theatre of the biblical histrio – we get up a hue and cry about the necessity of encouraging native writers of merit – we blindly fancy that we can accomplish this by indiscriminate puffing of good, bad, and indifferent, without taking the trouble to consider that what we choose to denominate encouragement is thus, by its general application, rendered precisely the reverse. In a word, so far from being ashamed of the many disgraceful literary failures to which our own inordinate vanities and misapplied patriotism have lately given birth, and so far from deeply lamenting that these daily puerilities are of home manufacture, we adhere pertinaciously to our original blindly conceived idea, and thus often find ourselves involved in the gross paradox of liking a stupid book the better, because, sure enough, its stupidity is American.[1] . . .

Who will deny that in regard to individual poems no definitive opinions can exist, so long as to Poetry in the abstract we attach no definitive idea? Yet it is a common thing to hear our critics, day after day, pronounce, with a positive air, laudatory or condemnatory sentences, *en masse*, upon material works of whose merits or demerits they have, in the first place, virtually confessed an utter ignorance, in confessing ignorance of all determinate principles by which to regulate a decision. Poetry has never been defined to the satisfaction of all parties: Perhaps, in the present condition of language it never will be. Words cannot hem it in. Its intangible and purely spiritual nature refuses to be bound down within the widest horizon of mere sounds. But it is not, therefore, misunderstood – at least, not by all men is it misunderstood. Very far from it. If, indeed, there be any one circle of thought distinctly and palpably marked out from amid the jarring and tumultuous chaos of human intelligence, it is that evergreen and radiant Paradise which the true poet knows, and knows alone, as the limited realm of his authority – as the circumscribed Eden of his dreams. But a definition is a thing of words – a conception of ideas. And thus while we readily believe that Poesy, the term, it will be troublesome, if not impossible to define – still, with its image vividly existing in the world, we apprehend no difficulty in so describing Poesy, the Sentiment, as to imbue even the most obtuse intellect with a comprehension of it sufficiently distinct for all the purposes of practical analysis.

To look upwards from any existence, material or immaterial, to its *design*, is, perhaps, the most direct, and the most unerring method of attaining a just notion of the nature of the existence itself. Nor is the principle at fault when we turn our eyes from Nature even to Nature's God. We find certain faculties, implanted within us, and arrive at a more plausible conception of the character and attributes of those faculties, by considering, with what finite judgment we possess, the *intention* of the Deity in so implanting them within us, than by any actual investigation of their powers, or any speculative deductions from their visible and material effects. Thus, for example, we discover in all men a disposition to look with reverence upon superiority, whether real or supposititious. In some, this disposition is to be recognized with difficulty, and, in very peculiar cases, we are occasionally even led to doubt its existence altogether, until circumstances beyond the common routine bring it accidentally into development. In others again it forms a prominent and distinctive feature of character, and is rendered palpably evident in its excesses. But in all human beings it is, in a greater or less degree, finally perceptible. It has been, therefore, justly considered a primitive sentiment. Phrenologists call it Veneration. It is, indeed, the instinct given to man by God as security for his own worship. And although, preserving its nature, it becomes perverted from its principal purpose, and although swerving from that purpose, it serves to modify the relations of human society – the relations of father and child, of master and slave, of the ruler and the ruled – its primitive essence is nevertheless the same, and by a reference to primal causes, may at any moment be determined.

Very nearly akin to this feeling, and liable to the same analysis, is the Faculty of Ideality – which is the sentiment of Poesy. This sentiment is the sense of the beautiful, of the sublime, and of the mystical.[2] Thence spring immediately admiration of the fair flowers, the fairer forests, the bright valleys and rivers and mountains of the Earth – and love of the gleaming stars and other burning glories of Heaven – and, mingled up inextricably with this love and this admiration of Heaven and of Earth, the unconquerable desire – *to know*. Poesy is the sentiment of Intellectual Happiness here, and the Hope of a higher Intellectual Happiness hereafter.[3]

Imagination is its soul.[4] With the *passions* of mankind – although it may modify them greatly – although it may exalt, or inflame, or purify, or control them – it would require little ingenuity to prove that it has no inevitable, and indeed no necessary co-existence. We have hitherto spoken of poetry in the abstract: we come now to speak of it in its every-day acceptation – that is to say, of the practical result arising from the sentiment we have considered.

And now it appears evident, that since Poetry, in this new sense, *is* the practical result, expressed in language, of this Poetic Sentiment in certain individuals, the only proper method of testing the merits of a poem is by measuring its capabilities of exciting the Poetic Sentiment in others.

And to this end we have many aids – in observation, in experience, in ethical analysis, and in the dictates of common sense. Hence the *Poeta nascitur*, which is indisputably true if we consider the Poetic Sentiment, becomes the merest of absurdities when we regard it in reference to the practical result. We do not hesitate to say that a man highly endowed with the powers of Causality – that is to say, a man of metaphysical acumen – will, even with a very deficient share of Ideality, compose a finer poem (if we test it, as we should, by its measure of exciting the Poetic Sentiment) than one who, without such metaphysical acumen, shall be gifted, in the most extraordinary degree, with the faculty of Ideality. For a poem is not the Poetic faculty, but the *means* of exciting it in mankind. Now these means the metaphysician may discover by analysis of their effects in other cases than his own, without even conceiving the nature of these effects – thus arriving at a result which the unaided Ideality of his competitor would be utterly unable, except by accident, to attain. It is more than possible that the man who, of all writers, living or dead, has been most successful in writing the purest of all poems – that is to say, poems which excite most purely, most exclusively, and most powerfully the imaginative faculties in men – owed his extraordinary and almost magical pre-eminence rather to metaphysical than poetical powers. We allude to the author of Christabel, of the Rime of the Auncient Mariner, and of Love – to Coleridge – whose head, if we mistake not its character, gave no great phrenological tokens of Ideality, while the organs of Causality and Comparison were most singularly developed.

Perhaps at this particular moment there are no American poems held in so high estimation by our countrymen, as the poems of Drake, and of Halleck. The exertions of Mr George Dearborn have no doubt a far greater share in creating this feeling than the lovers of literature for its own sake and spiritual uses would be willing to admit. We have indeed seldom seen more beautiful volumes than the volumes now before us. But an adventitious interest of a loftier nature – the interest of the living in the memory of the beloved dead – attaches itself to the few literary remains of Drake. The poems which are now given to us with his name are nineteen in number; and whether all, or whether even the best of his writings, it is our present purpose to speak of these alone, since upon this edition his poetical reputation to all time will most probably depend.

It is only lately that we have read *The Culprit Fay*. This is a poem of six hundred and forty irregular lines, generally iambic, and divided into thirty-six stanzas of unequal length. The scene of the narrative, as we ascertain from the single line,

> The moon looks down on old *Cronest*,

is principally in the vicinity of West Point on the Hudson. . . .[5]

It is more than probable that from ten readers of the *Culprit Fay*, nine would immediately pronounce it a poem betokening the most extraordinary powers of imagination, and of these nine, perhaps five or six, poets themselves, and fully impressed with the truth of what we have already assumed, that Ideality is indeed the soul of the Poetic Sentiment, would feel embarrassed between a half-consciousness that they *ought* to admire the production, and a wonder that they *do not*. This embarrassment would then arise from an indistinct conception of the results in which Ideality is rendered manifest. Of these results some few are seen in the *Culprit Fay*, but the greater part of it is utterly destitute of any evidence of imagination whatever. The general character of the poem will, we think, be sufficiently understood by any one who may have taken the trouble to read our foregoing compendium of the narrative. It will be there seen that what is so frequently termed the imaginative power of this story, lies especially – we should have rather said is thought to lie – in the passages we have quoted, or in others of a precisely similar nature. These passages embody, principally, mere specifications of qualities, of habiliments, of punishments, of occupations, of circumstances &c., which the poet has believed in unison with the size, firstly, and secondly with the nature of his Fairies. To all which may be added specifications of other animal existences (such as the toad, the beetle, the lance-fly, the fire-fly and the like) supposed also to be in accordance. An example will best illustrate our meaning upon this point – we take it from page 20.

He put his acorn helmet on;
It was plumed of the silk of the thistle down:
The corslet plate that guarded his breast
Was once the wild bee's golden vest;
His cloak of a thousand mingled dyes,
Was formed of the wings of butterflies;
His shield was the shell of a lady-bug queen,
Studs of gold on a ground of green;[6]
And the quivering lance which he brandished bright
Was the sting of a wasp he had slain in fight.

We shall now be understood. Were any of the admirers of the *Culprit Fay* asked their opinion of these lines, they would most probably speak in high terms of the *imagination* they display. Yet let the most stolid and the most confessedly unpoetical of these admirers only try the experiment, and he will find, possibly to his extreme surprise, that he himself will have no difficulty whatever in substituting for the equipments of the Fairy, as assigned by the poet, other equipments equally comfortable, no doubt, and equally in unison with the pre-conceived size, character, and other qualities of the equipped. Why we could accoutre him as well ourselves – let us see.

His blue-bell helmet, we have heard
Was plumed with the down of the humming-bird,
The corslet on his bosom bold
Was once the locust's coat of gold,
His cloak, of a thousand mingled hues,
Was the velvet violet, wet with dews,
His target was the crescent shell
Of the small sea Sidrophel,
And a glittering beam from a maiden's eye
Was the lance which he proudly wav'd on high.

The truth is, that the only requisite for writing verses of this nature, *ad libitum*, is a tolerable acquaintance with the qualities of the objects to be detailed, and a very moderate endowment of the faculty of Comparison – which is the chief constituent of *Fancy* or the powers of combination. A thousand such lines may be composed without exercising in the least degree the Poetic Sentiment, which is Ideality, Imagination, or the creative ability. And, as we have before said, the greater portion of the *Culprit Fay* is occupied with these, or similar things, and upon such, depends very nearly, if not altogether, its reputation. We select another example from page 25.

> But oh ! how fair the shape that lay
>   Beneath a rainbow bending bright,
> She seem'd to the entranced Fay
>   The loveliest of the forms of light;
> Her mantle was the purple rolled
>   At twilight in the west afar;
> 'T was tied with threads of dawning gold,
>   And button'd with a sparkling star.
> Her face was like the lily roon
>   That veils the vestal planet's hue;
> Her eyes, two beamlets from the moon
>   Set floating in the welkin blue.
> Her hair is like the sunny beam,
> And the diamond gems which round it gleam
> Are the pure drops of dewy even,
> That ne'er have left their native heaven.

Here again the faculty of Comparison is alone exercised, and no mind possessing the faculty in any ordinary degree would find a difficulty in substituting for the materials employed by the poet other materials equally as good. But viewed as mere efforts of the Fancy and without reference to Ideality, the lines just quoted are much worse than those which were taken from page 20. A congruity was observable in the accoutrements of the Ouphe, and we had no trouble in forming a distinct conception of his appearance when so accoutred. But the most vivid powers of Comparison can attach no definitive idea to even 'the loveliest form of light,' when habited in a mantle of 'rolled purple tied with threads of dawn and buttoned with a star,' and sitting at the same time under a rainbow with 'beamlet' eyes and a visage of 'lily roon.'

But if these things evince no Ideality in their author, do they not excite it in others? – if so, we must conclude, that without being himself imbued with the Poetic Sentiment, he has still succeeded in writing a fine poem – a supposition as we have before endeavoured to show, not altogether paradoxical. Most assuredly we think not. In the case of a great majority of readers the only sentiment aroused by compositions of this order is a species of vague wonder at the writer's *ingenuity*, and it is this indeterminate sense of wonder which passes but too frequently current for the proper influence of the Poetic power. For our own part we plead guilty to a predominant sense of the ludicrous while occupied in the perusal of the poem before us – a sense whose promptings we sincerely and honestly endeavored to quell, perhaps not altogether successfully, while penning our compend of the narrative. That a feeling of this nature is utterly at war with the Poetic Sentiment, will not be disputed by those who comprehend the character of the sentiment itself. This character is finely shadowed out in that popular although vague idea so prevalent throughout all time, that a species of melancholy is inseparably connected with the higher manifestations of the beautiful. But with the numerous and seriously-adduced incongruities of the Culprit Fay, we find it generally impossible to connect other ideas than those of the ridiculous. We are bidden, in the first place, and in a tone of sentiment and language adapted to the loftiest breathings of the Muse, to imagine a race of Fairies in the vicinity of West Point. We are told, with a grave air, of their camp, of their king, and especially of their sentry, who is a wood-tick. We are informed that an Ouphe of about an inch in height has committed a deadly sin in falling in love with a mortal maiden, who may, very possibly, be six feet in her stockings. The consequence to the Ouphe is – what? Why, that he has 'dyed his wings,' 'broken his elfin chain,' and 'quenched his flame-wood lamp.' And he is therefore sentenced to what? To catch a spark from the tail of a falling star, and a drop of water from the belly of a sturgeon. What are his equipments for the first adventure? An acorn-helmet, a thistle-down plume, a butterfly cloak, a lady-bug shield, cockle-seed spurs, and a fire-fly horse. How does he ride to the second? On the back of a bull-frog. What are his opponents in the one? 'Drizzly-mists,' 'sulphur and smoke,' 'shadowy hands and flame-shot tongues.' What in the other? 'Mailed shrimps,' 'prickly prongs,' 'blood-red leeches,' 'jellied quarls,' 'stony star fishes,' 'lancing squabs' and 'soldier crabs.' Is that all? No – Although only an inch high he is in imminent danger of seduction from a 'sylphid queen,' dressed in a mantle of 'rolled purple,' 'tied with threads of dawning gold,' 'buttoned with a sparkling star,' and sitting under a rainbow with 'beamlet eyes' and a countenance of 'lily roon.' In our account of all this matter we have had reference to the book – and to the book alone. It will be difficult to prove us guilty in any degree of distortion or exaggeration. Yet such are the puerilities we daily find ourselves called upon to admire, as among the loftiest efforts of the human mind, and which was to assign a rank with the proud trophies of the matured and vigorous genius of England, is to prove ourselves at once a fool, a maligner, and no patriot.[7]

As an instance of what may be termed the sublimely ridiculous we quote the following lines from page 17.

> With sweeping tail and quivering fin,
>   Through the wave the sturgeon flew,
> And like the heaven-shot javelin,
>   He sprung above the waters blue.
>
> Instant as the star-fall light,
>   He plunged into the deep again,
> But left an arch of silver bright
>   The rainbow of the moony main.
>
> *It was a strange and lovely sight*
>   *To see the puny goblin there;*
> *He seemed an angel form of light*
>   *With azure wing and sunny hair,*
>   *Throned on a cloud of purple fair*
> *Circled with blue and edged with white*
>   *And sitting at the fall of even*
>   *Beneath the bow of summer heaven.*

The verses here italicized, if considered without their context, have a certain air of dignity, elegance, and chastity of thought. If however we apply the context, we are immediately over-whelmed with the grotesque. It is impossible to read without laughing, such expressions as 'It was a strange and lovely sight' – 'He seemed an angel form of light' – 'And sitting at the fall of even, beneath the bow of summer heaven' to a Fairy – a goblin – an Ouphe – half an inch high, dressed in an acorn helmet and butterfly-cloak, and sitting on the water in a muscle-shell, with a 'brown-backed sturgeon' turning somersets over his head.

In a world where evil is a mere consequence of good, and good a mere consequence of evil – in short where all of which we have any conception is good or bad only by comparison – we have never yet been fully able to appreciate the validity of that decision which would debar the critic from enforcing upon his readers the merits or demerits of a work by placing it in juxta-position with another. It seems to us that an adage based in the purest ignorance has had more to do with this popular feeling than any just reason founded upon common sense. Thinking thus, we shall have no scruple in illustrating our opinion in regard to what is not Ideality or the Poetic Power, by an example of what is.[8]

We have already given the description of the Sylphid Queen in the *Culprit Fay*. In the *Queen Mab* of Shelley a Fairy is thus introduced –

> Those who had looked upon the sight
> Passing all human glory,
> Saw not the yellow moon,
> Saw not the mortal scene,
> Heard not the night wind's rush,
> Heard not an earthy sound,
> Saw but the fairy pageant,
> Heard but the heavenly strains
> That filled the lonely dwelling –

and thus described –

The Fairy's frame was slight; yon fibrous cloud
That catches but the faintest tinge of even,
And which the straining eye can hardly seize
When melting into eastern twilight's shadow,
Were scarce so thin, so slight; but the fair star
That gems the glittering coronet of morn,
Sheds not a light so mild, so powerful,
As that which, bursting from the Fairy's form,
Spread a purpureal halo round the scene,
Yet with an undulating motion,
Swayed to her outline gracefully.

In these exquisite lines the Faculty of mere Comparison is but little exercised — that of Ideality in a wonderful degree. It is probable that in a similar case the poet we are now reviewing would have formed the face of the Fairy of the 'fibrous cloud,' her arms of the 'pale tinge of even,' her eyes of the 'fair stars,' and her body of the 'twilight shadow.' Having so done, his admirers would have congratulated him upon his *imagination*, not taking the trouble to think that they themselves could at any moment *imagine* a Fairy of materials equally as good, and conveying an equally distinct idea. Their mistake would be precisely analogous to that of many a school boy who admires the imagination displayed in *Jack the Giant-Killer*, and is finally rejoiced at discovering his own imagination to surpass that of the author, since the monsters destroyed by Jack are only about forty feet in height, and he himself has no trouble in imagining some of one hundred and forty. It will be seen that the Fairy of Shelley is not a mere compound of incongruous natural objects, inartificially put together, and unaccompanied by any *moral* sentiment — but a being, in the illustration of whose nature some physical elements are used collaterally as adjuncts, while the main conception springs immediately *or thus apparently springs*, from the brain of the poet, enveloped in the moral sentiments of grace, of color, of motion — of the beautiful, of the mystical, of the august — in short of *the ideal*.[9]

It is by no means our intention to deny that in the *Culprit Fay* are passages of a different order from those to which we have objected – passages evincing a degree of imagination not to be discovered in the plot, conception, or general execution of the poem. The opening stanza will afford us a tolerable example.

> 'Tis the middle watch of a summer's night –
> *The earth is dark but the heavens are bright*
> Naught is seen in the vault on high
> But the moon, and the stars, and the cloudless sky,
> And the flood which rolls its milky hue
> A river of light on the welkin blue.
> The moon looks down on old Cronest,
> She mellows the shades of his shaggy breast,
> And seems his huge grey form to throw
> In a silver cone on the wave below;
> His sides are broken by spots of shade,
> By the walnut bow and the cedar made,
> And through their clustering branches dark
> *Glimmers and dies* the fire-fly's spark –
> Like starry twinkles that momently break
> Through the rifts of the gathering tempest rack.

There is Ideality in these lines – but except in the case of the words italicised – it is Ideality *not of a high order*. We have, it is true, a collection of natural objects, each individually of great beauty, and, if actually seen as in nature, capable of exciting in any mind, through the means of the Poetic Sentiment more or less inherent in all, a certain sense of the beautiful. But to view such natural objects as they exist, and to behold them through the medium of words, are different things. Let us pursue the idea that such a collection as we have here will produce, of necessity, the Poetic Sentiment, and we may as well make up our minds to believe that a catalogue of such expressions as moon, sky, trees, rivers, mountains, &c, shall be capable of exciting it, – it is merely an extension of the principle. But in the line 'the earth is dark, *but* the heavens are bright' besides the simple mention of the 'dark earth' and 'the bright heaven,' we have, directly, the moral sentiment of the brightness of the sky compensating for the darkness of the earth – and thus, indirectly, of the happiness of a future state compensating for the miseries of the present.

All this is effected by the simple introduction of the word *but* between the 'dark earth' and the 'bright heaven' – this introduction, however, was prompted by the Poetic Sentiment, and by the Poetic Sentiment alone. The case is analogous in the expression 'glimmers and dies,' where the imagination is exalted by the moral sentiment of beauty heightened in dissolution.

In one or two shorter passages of the *Culprit Fay* the poet will recognize the purely ideal, and be able at a glance to distinguish it from that baser alloy upon which we have descanted. We give them without farther comment.

> The winds *are whist*, and the owl is still
>   The bat in the shelvy rock *is hid*
> And naught is heard on the *lonely* hill
> But the cricket's chirp and the answer *shrill*
>   Of the gauze-winged katy-did;
> And the plaint of the *wailing* whippoorwill
>   Who mourns *unseen*, and ceaseless sings
> Ever a note of wail and wo –

> Up to the vaulted firmament
> His path the fire-fly courser bent,
> And at every gallop on the wind
> *He flung a glittering spark behind.*

> He blessed the force of the charmed line
>   And he banned the water-goblins' spite,
> For he saw around in the *sweet moonshine,*
> *Their little wee faces above the brine,*
> *Giggling and laughing with all their might*
> At the piteous hap of the Fairy wight.

The poem 'To a Friend' consists of fourteen Spenserian stanzas. They are fine spirited verses, and probably were not supposed by their author to be more. Stanza the fourth, although beginning nobly, concludes with that very common exemplification of the bathos, the illustrating natural objects of beauty or grandeur by reference to the tinsel of artificiality.

Oh ! for a seat on Appalachia's brow,
That I might scan the glorious prospects round,
Wild waving woods, and rolling floods below,
Smooth level glades and fields with grain embrowned,
High heaving hills, with tufted forests crowned,
Rearing their tall tops to the heaven's blue dome,
And emerald isles, *like banners green unwound,*
Floating along the lake, while round them roam
Bright helms of billowy blue, and plumes of dancing foam.[10]

*

Halleck's poetical powers appear to us essentially inferior, upon the whole, to those of his friend Drake. He has written nothing at all comparable to *Bronx*. By the hackneyed phrase, *sportive elegance*, we might possibly designate at once the general character of his writings and the very loftiest praise to which he is justly entitled.

Alnwick Castle is an irregular poem of one hundred and twenty-eight lines – was written, as we are informed, in October 1822 – and is descriptive of a seat of the Duke of Northumberland, in Northumberlandshire, England. The effect of the first stanza is materially impaired by a defect in its grammatical arrangement. The fine lines,

> Home of the Percy's high-born race,
>   Home of their beautiful and brave,
> Alike their birth and burial place,
>   Their cradle and their grave !

are of the nature of an invocation, and thus require a continuation of the address to the 'Home, &c.' We are consequently disappointed when the stanza proceeds with –

> Still sternly o'er the castle gate
> *Their* house's Lion stands in state
>   As in *his* proud departed hours;
> And warriors frown in stone on high,
> And feudal banners "float the sky"
>   Above *his* princely towers.

The objects of allusion here vary, in an awkward manner, from the castle to the Lion, and from the Lion to the towers. By writing the verses thus the difficulty would be remedied.

> Still sternly o'er the castle gate
> *Thy* house's Lion stands in state,
>   As in his proud departed hours;
> And warriors frown in stone on high,
> And feudal banners "float the sky"
>   Above *thy* princely towers.

The second stanza, without evincing in any measure the loftier powers of a poet, has that quiet air of grace, both in thought and expression, which seems to be the prevailing feature of the Muse of Halleck.

> A gentle hill its side inclines,
>   Lovely in England's fadeless green,
> To meet the quiet stream which winds
>   Through this romantic scene
> As silently and sweetly still,
> As when, at evening, on that hill,
>   While summer's wind blew soft and low,
> Seated by gallant Hotspur's side
> His Katherine was a happy bride
>   A thousand years ago.

There are one or two brief passages in the poem evincing a degree of rich imagination not elsewhere perceptible throughout the book. For example –

> Gaze on the Abbey's ruined pile:
>   Does not the succoring Ivy keeping,
> Her watch around it seem to smile
>   As o'er a lov'd one sleeping?

and,

> One solitary turret gray
>   Still tells in melancholy glory
> The legend of the Cheviot day.

The commencement of the fourth stanza is of the highest order of Poetry, and partakes, in a happy manner, of that quaintness of expression so effective an adjunct to Ideality, when employed by the Shelleys, the Coleridges and the Tennysons, but so frequently debased, and rendered ridiculous, by the herd of brainless imitators.

> Wild roses by the abbey towers
>   Are gay in their young bud and bloom:
> *They were born of a race of funeral flowers,*
> That garlanded in long-gone hours,
>   A Templar's knightly tomb.

The tone employed in the concluding portions of Alnwick Castle, is, we sincerely think, reprehensible, and unworthy of Halleck. No true poet can unite in any manner the low burlesque with the ideal, and not be conscious of incongruity and of a profanation. Such verses as

> Men in the coal and cattle line
> From Teviot's bard and hero land,
> From royal Berwick's beach of sand,
> From Wooller, Morpeth, Hexham, and
>   Newcastle upon Tyne.

may lay claim to oddity – but no more. These things are the defects and not the beauties of *Don Juan*. They are totally out of keeping with the graceful and delicate manner of the initial portions of *Alnwick Castle*, and serve no better purpose than to deprive the entire poem of all unity of effect. If a poet must be farcical, let him be just that, and nothing else. To be drolly sentimental is bad enough, as we have just seen in certain passages of the *Culprit Fay*, but to be sentimentally droll is a thing intolerable to men, and Gods and columns.[11]

*

As a versifier Halleck is by no means equal to his friend, all of whose poems evince an ear finely attuned to the delicacies of melody. We seldom meet with more inharmonious lines than those, generally, of the author of *Alnwick Castle*. At every step such verses occur as,

> And *the* monk's hymn and minstrel's song –
> True *as* the steel of *their* tried blades –
> For him the joy of *her* young years –
> Where *the* Bard-peasant first drew breath –
> And withered *my* life's leaf like thine –

in which the proper course of the rhythm would demand an accent upon syllables too unimportant to sustain it. Not unfrequently, too, we meet with lines such as this,

> Like torn branch from death's leafless tree,

in which the multiplicity of consonants renders the pronunciation of the words at all, a matter of no inconsiderable difficulty.

But we must bring our notice to a close. It will be seen that while we are willing to admire in many respects the poems before us, we feel obliged to dissent materially from that public opinion (perhaps not fairly ascertained) which would assign them a very brilliant rank in the empire of Poesy. That we have among us poets of the loftiest order we believe – but we do *not* believe that these poets are Drake and Halleck.

Watkins Tottle

WATKINS TOTTLE, AND OTHER SKETCHES, ILLUSTRA-
TIVE OF EVERY-DAY LIFE, AND EVERY-DAY PEOPLE. BY
BOZ. PHILADELPHIA: CAREY, LEA AND BLANCHARD.

THIS book is a re-publication from the English original, and
many of its sketches are with us old and highly esteemed acquaintances. In regard to their author we know nothing more
than that he is a far more pungent, more witty, and better discip-
lined writer of sly articles, than nine-tenths of the Magazine
writers in Great Britain – which is saying much, it must be
allowed, when we consider the great variety of genuine talent,
and earnest application brought to bear upon the periodical
literature of the mother country.

The very first passage in the volume before us, will convince
any of our friends who are knowing in the requisites of 'a good
thing,' that we are doing our friend Boz no more than the
simplest pieces of justice. Hearken to what he says of Matrimony
and of Mr Watkins Tottle.

* * * * * * * *

It is not every one who can put 'a good thing' properly together, although, perhaps, when thus properly put together,
every tenth person you meet with may be capable of both conceiving and appreciating it. We cannot bring ourselves to believe
that less actual ability is required in the composition of a really
good 'brief article,' than in a fashionable novel of the usual
dimensions. The novel certainly requires what is denominated
a sustained effort – but this is a matter of mere perseverance,
and has but a collateral relation to talent. On the other hand –
unity of effect, a quality not easily appreciated or indeed comprehended by an ordinary mind, and a *desideratum* difficult of

attainment even by those who can conceive it – is indispensable in the 'brief article,' and not so in the common novel. The latter, if admired at all, is admired for its detached passages, without reference to the work as a whole – or without reference to any general design – which, if it even exist in some measure, will be found to have occupied but little of the writer's attention, and cannot, from the length of the narrative, be taken in at one view, by the reader.

The Sketches by Boz are all exceedingly well managed, and never fail to tell as the author intended. They are entitled, Passage in the Life of Mr Watkins Tottle – The Black Veil – Shabby Genteel People – Horatio Sparkins – The Pawnbroker's Shop – The Dancing Academy – Early Coaches – The River – Private Theatres – The Great Winglebury Duel – Omnibuses – Mrs Joseph Porter – The Steam Excursion – Sentiment – The Parish – Miss Evans and the Eagle – Shops and their Tenants – Thoughts about People – A Visit to Newgate – London Recreations – The Boarding-House – Hackney-Coach Stands – Brokers and Marine Store-Shops – The Bloomsbury Christening – Gin Shops – Public Dinners – Astley's – Greenwich Fair – The Prisoner's Van – and A Christmas Dinner. The reader who has been so fortunate as to have perused any one of these pieces, will be fully aware of how great a fund of racy entertainment is included in the Bill of Fare we have given. There are here some as well conceived and well written papers as can be found in any other collection of the kind – many of them we would especially recommend, as a study, to those who turn their attention to Magazine writing – a department in which, generally, the English as far excel us as Hyperion a Satyr.

The *Black Veil*, in the present series, is distinct in character from all the rest – an act of stirring tragedy, and evincing lofty powers in the writer. Broad humor is, however, the prevailing feature of the volumes. *The Dancing Academy* is a vivid sketch of Cockney low life, which may probably be considered as somewhat too *outré* by those who have no experience in the matter. *Watkins Tottle* is excellent. We should like very much to copy the whole of the article entitled *Pawnbroker's Shop*, with a view of contrasting its matter and manner with the insipidity of the passage we have just quoted on the same subject from the 'Ups and Downs' of Col. Stone, and by way of illustrating our remarks on the *Unity of effect* – but this would, perhaps, be giving too much of a good thing. It will be seen by those who peruse both these articles, that in that of the American, two or three anecdotes are told which have merely a relation – a very shadowy relation, to pawn-broking – in short, they are barely elicited by this theme, have no necessary dependence upon it, and might be introduced equally well in connection with any one of a million other subjects. In the sketch of the Englishman we have no anecdotes at all – the *Pawnbroker's Shop* engages and enchains our attention – we are enveloped in its atmosphere of wretchedness and extortion – we pause at every sentence, not to dwell upon the sentence, but to obtain a fuller view of the gradually perfecting picture – which is never at any moment any other matter than the *Pawnbroker's Shop*. To the illustration of this one end all the *groupings* and *fillings in* of the paintings are rendered subservient – and when our eyes are taken from the canvass, we remember the personages of the sketch not at all as independent existences, but as essentials of the one subject we have witnessed – as a part and portion of the *Pawnbroker's Shop*. So perfect, and never-to-be-forgotten a picture cannot be brought about by any such trumpery exertion, or still more trumpery talent, as we find employed in the ineffective daubing of Colonel Stone. The scratchings of a schoolboy with a slate pencil on a slate might as well be compared to the groupings of Buonarotti.

We conclude by strongly recommending the Sketches of Boz to the attention of American readers, and by copying the whole of his article on Gin Shops.

*   *   *   *   *

The Philosophy of Furniture

IN the internal decoration, if not in the external architecture of their residences, the English are supreme. The Italians have but little sentiment beyond marbles and colours. In France, *meliora probant, deteriora sequuntur* – the people are too much a race of gadabouts to maintain those household proprieties of which, indeed, they have a delicate appreciation, or at least the elements of a proper sense. The Chinese and most of the eastern races have a warm but inappropriate fancy. The Scotch are *poor* decorists. The Dutch have, perhaps, an indeterminate idea that a curtain is not a cabbage. In Spain they are *all* curtains – a nation of hangmen. The Russians do not furnish. The Hottentots and Kickapoos are very well in their way. The Yankees alone are preposterous.

How this happens, it is not difficult to see. We have no aristocracy of blood, and having therefore as a natural, and indeed as an inevitable thing, fashioned for ourselves an aristocracy of dollars, the *display of wealth* has here to take the place and perform the office of the heraldic display in monarchical countries. By a transition readily understood, and which might have been as readily foreseen, we have been brought to merge in simple *show* our notions of taste itself.

To speak less abstractly. In England, for example, no mere parade of costly appurtenances would be so likely as with us, to create an impression of the beautiful in respect to the appurtenances themselves – or of taste as regards the proprietor: – this for the reason, first, that wealth is not, in England, the loftiest object of ambition as constituting a nobility; and secondly, that there, the true nobility of blood, confining itself within the strict limits of legitimate taste, rather avoids than affects that mere costliness in which a *parvenu* rivalry may at any time be successfully attempted.

The people *will* imitate the nobles, and the result is a thorough diffusion of the proper feeling. But in America, the coins current being the sole arms of the aristocracy, their display may be said, in general, to be the sole means of the aristocratic distinction; and the populace, looking always upward for models, are insensibly led to confound the two entirely separate ideas of magnificence and beauty. In short, the cost of an article of furniture has at length come to be, with us, nearly the sole test of its merit in a decorative point of view – and this test, once established, has led the way to many analogous errors, readily traceable to the one primitive folly.

There could be nothing more directly offensive to the eye of an artist than the interior of what is termed in the United States – that is to say, in Appallachia – a well-furnished apartment. Its most usual defect is a want of keeping. We speak of the keeping of a room as we would of the keeping of a picture – for both the picture and the room are amenable to those undeviating principles which regulate all varieties of art; and very nearly the same laws by which we decide on the higher merits of a painting, suffice for decision on the adjustment of a chamber.

A want of keeping is observable sometimes in the character of the several pieces of furniture, but generally in their colours or modes of adaptation to use. Very often the eye is offended by their inartistic arrangement. Straight lines are too prevalent – too uninterruptedly continued – or clumsily interrupted at right angles. If curved lines occur, they are repeated into unpleasant uniformity. By undue precision, the appearance of many a fine apartment is utterly spoiled.

Curtains are rarely well disposed, or well chosen in respect to other decorations. With formal furniture, curtains are out of place; and an extensive volume of drapery of any kind is, under any circumstance, irreconcilable with good taste – the proper quantum, as well as the proper adjustment, depending upon the character of the general effect.

Carpets are better understood of late than of ancient days, but we still very frequently err in their patterns and colours. The soul of the apartment is the carpet. From it are deduced not only the hues but the forms of all objects incumbent. A judge at common law may be an ordinary man; a good judge of a carpet *must be* a genius. Yet we have heard discoursing of carpets, with the air *'d'un mouton qui rêve,'* fellows who should not and who could not be entrusted with the management of their own *moustaches*. Every one knows that a large floor *may* have a covering of large figures, and that a small one *must* have a covering of small – yet this is not all the knowledge in the world. As regards texture, the Saxony is alone admissible. Brussels is the preterpluperfect tense of fashion, and Turkey is taste in its dying agonies. Touching pattern – a carpet should *not* be bedizzened out like a Riccaree Indian – all red chalk, yellow ochre, and cock's feathers. In brief – distinct grounds, and vivid circular or cycloid figures, *of no meaning*, are here Median laws. The abomination of flowers, or representations of well-known objects of any kind, should not be endured within the limits of Christendom. Indeed, whether on carpets, or curtains, or tapestry, or ottoman coverings, all upholstery of this nature should be rigidly Arabesque. As for those antique floor-cloths still occasionally seen in the dwellings of the rabble – cloths of huge, sprawling, and radiating devises, stripe-interspersed, and glorious with all hues, among which no ground is intelligible – these are but the wicked invention of a race of time-servers and money-lovers – children of Baal and worshippers of Mammon – Benthams, who, to spare thought and economize fancy, first cruelly invented the Kaleidoscope, and then established joint-stock companies to twirl it by steam.

Glare is a leading error in the philosophy of American household decoration – an error easily recognised as deduced from the perversion of taste just specified. We are violently enamoured of gas and of glass. The former is totally inadmissible within doors. Its harsh and unsteady light offends. No one having both brains and eyes will use it. A mild, or what artists term a cool light, with its consequent warm shadows, will do wonders for even an ill-furnished apartment. Never was a more lovely thought than that of the astral lamp. We mean, of course, the astral lamp proper – the lamp of Argand, with its original plain ground-glass shade, and its tempered and uniform moonlight rays. The cut-glass shade is a weak invention of the enemy. The eagerness with which we have adopted it, partly on account of its *flashiness*, but principally on account of its *greater cost*, is a good commentary on the proposition with which we began. It is not too much to say, that the deliberate employer of a cut-glass shade, is either radically deficient in taste, or blindly subservient to the caprices of fashion. The light proceeding from one of these gaudy abominations is unequal, broken, and painful. It alone is sufficient to mar a world of good effect in the furniture subjected to its influence. Female loveliness, in especial, is more than one-half disenchanted beneath its evil eye.

In the matter of glass, generally, we proceed upon false principles. Its leading feature is *glitter* – and in that one word how much of all that is detestable do we express! Flickering, unquiet lights, are *sometimes* pleasing – to children and idiots always so – but in the embellishment of a room they should be scrupulously avoided. In truth, even strong *steady* lights are inadmissible. The huge and unmeaning glass chandeliers, prism-cut, gas-lighted, and without shade, which dangle in our most fashionable drawing-rooms, may be cited as the quintessence of all that is false in taste or preposterous in folly.

The rage for *glitter* – because its idea has become, as we before observed, confounded with that of magnificence in the abstract – has led us, also, to the exaggerated employment of mirrors. We line our dwellings with great British plates, and then imagine we have done a fine thing. Now the slightest thought will be sufficient to convince any one who has an eye at all, of the ill effect of numerous looking-glasses, and especially of large ones. Regarded apart from its reflection, the mirror presents a continuous, flat, colourless, unrelieved surface, – a thing always and obviously unpleasant. Considered as a reflector, it is potent in producing a monstrous and odious uniformity: and the evil is here aggravated, not in merely direct proportion with the augmentation of its sources, but in a ratio constantly increasing. In fact, a room with four or five mirrors arranged at random, is, for all purposes of artistic show, a room of no shape at all. If we add to this evil, the attendant glitter upon glitter, we have a perfect farrago of discordant and displeasing effects. The veriest bumpkin, on entering an apartment so bedizzened, would be instantly aware of something wrong, although he might be altogether unable to assign a cause for his dissatisfaction. But let the same person be led into a room tastefully furnished, and he would be startled into an exclamation of pleasure and surprise.

It is an evil growing out of our republican institutions, that here a man of large purse has usually a very little soul which he keeps in it. The corruption of taste is a portion or a pendant of the dollar-manufacture. As we grow rich, our ideas grow rusty. It is, therefore, not among *our* aristocracy that we must look (if at all, in Appallachia), for the spirituality of a British *boudoir*. But we have seen apartments in the tenure of Americans of modern means, which, in negative merit at least, might vie with any of the *or-molu'd* cabinets of our friends across the water. Even *now*, there is present to our mind's eye a small and not ostentatious chamber with whose decorations no fault can be found. The proprietor lies asleep on a sofa – the weather is cool – the time is near midnight: we will make a sketch of the room during his slumber.

It is oblong – some thirty feet in length and twenty-five in breadth – a shape affording the best (ordinary) opportunities for the adjustment of furniture. It has but one door – by no means a wide one – which is at one end of the parallelogram, and but two windows, which are at the other. These latter are large, reaching down to the floor – have deep recesses – and open on an Italian *veranda*. Their panes are of a crimson-tinted glass, set in rose-wood framings, more massive than usual. They are curtained within the recess, by a thick silver tissue adapted to the shape of the window, and hanging loosely in small volumes. Without the recess are curtains of an exceedingly rich crimson silk, fringed with a deep net-work of gold, and lined with silver tissue, which is the material of the exterior blind. There are no cornices; but the folds of the whole fabric (which are sharp rather than massive, and have an airy appearance), issue from beneath a broad entablature of rich giltwork, which encircles the room at the junction of the ceiling and walls. The drapery is thrown open also, or closed, by means of a thick rope of gold loosely enveloping it, and resolving itself readily into a knot; no pins or other such devices are apparent. The colours of the curtains and their fringe – the tints of crimson and gold – appear everywhere in profusion, and determine the *character* of the room. The carpet – of Saxony material – is quite half an inch thick, and is of the same crimson ground, relieved simply by the appearance of a gold cord (like that festooning the curtains) slightly relieved above the surface of the *ground*, and thrown upon it in such a manner as to form a succession of short irregular curves – one occasionally overlaying the other. The walls are prepared with a glossy paper of a silver gray tint, spotted with small Arabesque devices of a fainter hue of the prevalent crimson. Many paintings relieve the expanse of the paper. These are chiefly landscapes of an imaginative cast – such as the fairy grottoes of Stanfield, or the lake of the Dismal Swamp of Chapman. There are, nevertheless, three or four female heads, of an ethereal beauty – portraits in the manner of Sully. The tone of each picture is warm, but dark. There are no 'brilliant effects.' *Repose* speaks in all. Not one is of small size. Diminutive paintings give that *spotty* look to a room, which is the blemish of so many a fine work of Art overtouched. The frames are broad but not deep, and richly carved, without being *dulled* or filagreed. They have the whole lustre of burnished gold. They lie flat on the walls, and do not hang off with cords. The designs themselves are often seen to better advantage in this latter position, but the general appearance of the chamber is injured. But one mirror – and this not a very large one – is visible. In shape it is nearly circular – and it is hung so that a reflection of the person can be obtained from it in none of the ordinary sitting-places of the room. Two large low sofas of rosewood and crimson silk, gold-flowered, form the only seats, with the exception of two light conversation chairs, also of rose-wood. There is a pianoforte (rose-wood, also), without cover, and thrown open. An octagonal table, formed altogether of the richest gold-threaded marble, is placed near one of the sofas. This is also without cover – the drapery of the curtains has been thought sufficient. Four large and gorgeous Sèvres vases, in which bloom a profusion of sweet and vivid flowers, occupy the slightly rounded angles of the room. A tall candelabrum, bearing a small antique lamp with highly perfumed oil, is standing near the head of my sleeping friend. Some light and graceful hanging shelves, with golden edges and crimson silk cords with gold tassels, sustain two or three hundred magnificently bound books. Beyond these things, there is no furniture, if we except an Argand lamp, with a plain crimson-tinted ground-glass shade, which depends from the lofty vaulted ceiling by a single slender gold chain, and throws a tranquil but magical radiance over all.

Wyandotté

WYANDOTTÉ, OR THE HUTTED KNOLL. A TALE, BY THE
AUTHOR OF 'THE PATHFINDER,' 'DEERSLAYER,' 'LAST
OF THE MOHICANS,' 'PIONEERS,' 'PRAIRIE,' &c., &c. LEA
& BLANCHARD: PHILADELPHIA.

'WYANDOTTÉ, or The Hutted Knoll,' is, in its general features, precisely similar to the novels enumerated in the title. It
is a forest subject; and, when we say this, we give assurance
that the story is a good one; for Mr Cooper has never been
known to fail, either in the forest or upon the sea. The interest,
as usual, has no reference to *plot*, of which, indeed, our novelist
seems altogether regardless, or incapable, but depends, first upon
the nature of the theme; secondly, upon a Robinson-Crusoe-like
detail in its management; and thirdly, upon the frequently repeated portraiture of the half-civilized Indian. In saying that the
interest depends, *first*, upon the nature of the theme, we mean to
suggest that this theme – life in the Wilderness – is one of intrinsic and universal interest, appealing to the heart of man in
all phases; a theme, like that of life upon the ocean, so unfail-
ingly omniprevalent in its power of arresting and absorbing
attention, that while success or popularity is, with such a subject,
expected as a matter of course, a failure might be properly regarded as conclusive evidence of imbecility on the part of the
author. The two theses in question have been handled *usque ad
nauseam* – and this through the instinctive perception of the
universal interest which appertains to them. A writer, distrustful
of his powers, can scarcely do better than discuss either one or
the other. A man of genius will rarely, and should never, undertake either; first, because both are excessively hackneyed; and,
secondly, because the reader never fails, in forming his opinion of

a book, to make discount, either wittingly or unwittingly, for
that intrinsic interest which is inseparable from the subject and
independent of the manner in which it is treated. Very few and
very dull indeed are those who do not instantaneously perceive
the distinction; and thus there are two great classes of factions,
– a popular and widely circulated class, read with pleasure but
without admiration – in which the author is lost or forgotten;
or remembered, if at all, with something very nearly akin to
contempt; and then, a class not so popular, nor so widely diffused, in which, at every paragraph, arises a distinctive and
highly pleasurable interest, springing from our perception and
appreciation of the skill employed, or the genius evinced in the
composition. After perusal of the one class, we think solely of the
book – after reading the other, chiefly of the author. The former
class leads to popularity – the latter to fame. In the former case,
the books sometimes live, while the authors usually die; in the
latter, even when the works perish, the man survives. Among
American writers of the less generally circulated, but more
worthy and more artistical fictions, we may mention Mr Brock-
den Brown, Mr John Neal, Mr Simms, Mr Hawthorne; at the
head of the more popular division we may place Mr Cooper.

'The Hutted Knoll,' without pretending to detail facts, gives a
narrative of fictitious events, similar, in nearly all respects, to
occurrences which actually happened during the opening scenes
of the Revolution, and at other epochs of our history. It pictures
the dangers, difficulties, and distresses of a large family, living,
completely insulated, in the forest. The tale commences with a
description of the 'region which lies in the angle formed by the
junction of the Mohawk with the Hudson, extending as far
south as the line of Pennsylvania, and west to the verge of that
vast rolling plain which composes Western New York' – a region
of which the novelist has already frequently written, and the
whole of which, with a trivial exception, was a wilderness before
the Revolution. Within this district, and on a creek running into
the Unadilla, a certain Captain Willoughby purchases an estate,
or 'patent' and there retires, with his family and dependents, to
pass the close of his life in agricultural pursuits. He has been an

officer in the British army, but, after serving many years, has sold his commission, and purchased one for his only son, Robert, who alone does not accompany the party into the forest. This party consists of the captain himself; his wife; his daughter, Beulah; an adopted daughter, Maud Meredith; an invalid sergeant, Joyce, who had served under the captain; a Presbyterian preacher, Mr Woods; a Scotch mason, Jamie Allen; an Irish laborer, Michael O'Hearn; a Connecticut man, Joel Strides; four negroes, Old Plin and Young Plin, Big Smash and Little Smash; eight axe-men; a house-carpenter; a millwright, &c., &c. Besides these, a Tuscarora Indian called Nick, or Wyandotté, accompanies the expedition. This Indian, who figures largely in the story, and gives it its title, may be considered as the principal character – the one chiefly elaborated. He is an outcast from his tribe, has been known to Captain Willoughby for thirty years, and is a compound of all the good and bad qualities which make up the character of the half-civilized Indian. He does not remain with the settlers; but appears and re-appears at intervals upon the scene.

Nearly the whole of the first volume is occupied with a detailed account of the estate purchased, (which is termed 'The Hutted Knoll' from a natural mound upon which the principal house is built) and of the progressive arrangements and improvements. Toward the close of the volume the Revolution commences; and the party at the 'Knoll' are besieged by a band of savages and 'rebels,' with whom an understanding exists, on the part of Joel Strides, the Yankee. This traitor, instigated by the hope of possessing Captain Willoughby's estate, should it be confiscated, brings about a series of defections from the party of the settlers, and finally, deserting himself, reduces the whole number to six or seven, capable of bearing arms. Captain Willoughby resolves, however, to defend his post. His son, at this juncture, pays him a clandestine visit, and, endeavoring to reconnoitre the position of the Indians, is made captive. The captain, in an attempt at rescue, is murdered by Wyandotté, whose vindictive passions had been aroused by ill-timed allusions, on the part of Willoughby, to floggings previously inflicted, by his orders, upon the Indian. Wyandotté, however, having satisfied his personal vengeance, is still the ally of the settlers. He guides Maud, who is beloved by Robert, to the hut in which the latter is confined, and effects his escape. Aroused by this escape, the Indians precipitate their attack upon the Knoll, which, through the previous treachery of Strides in ill-hanging a gate, is immediately carried. Mrs Willoughby, Beulah, and others of the party, are killed. Maud is secreted and thus saved by Wyandotté. At the last moment, when all is apparently lost, a reinforcement appears, under command of Evert Beekman, the husband of Beulah; and the completion of the massacre is prevented. Woods, the preacher, had left the Knoll, and made his way through the enemy, to inform Beekman of the dilemma of his friends. Maud and Robert Willoughby are, of course, happily married. The concluding scene of the novel shows us Wyandotté repenting the murder of Willoughby, and converted to Christianity through the agency of Woods.

It will be at once seen that there is nothing *original* in this story. On the contrary, it is even excessively commonplace. The lover, for example, rescued from captivity by the mistress; the Knoll carried through the treachery of an inmate; and the salvation of the besieged, at the very last moment, by a reinforcement arriving, in consequence of a message borne to a friend by one of the besieged, without the cognizance of the others; these, we say, are incidents which have been the common property of every novelist since the invention of letters. And as for *plot*, there has been no attempt at anything of the kind. The tale is a mere succession of events, scarcely any one of which has any necessary dependence upon any one other. Plot, however, is at best, an artificial effect, requiring, like music, not only a natural bias, but long cultivation of taste for its full appreciation; some of the finest narratives in the world – 'Gil-Blas' and 'Robinson Crusoe,' for example – have been written without its employment; and 'The Hutted Knoll,' like all the sea and forest novels of Cooper, has been made deeply interesting, although depending upon this peculiar source of interest not at all. Thus the absence of plot can never be critically regarded as a *defect*;

although its judicious use, in all cases aiding and in no case in-injuring other effects, must be regarded as of a very high order of merit.

There are one or two points, however, in the mere *conduct* of the story now before us, which may, perhaps, be considered as defective. For instance, there is too much *obviousness* in all that appertains to the hanging of the large gate. In more than a dozen instances Mrs Willoughby is made to allude to the delay in the hanging; so that the reader is too positively and pointedly forced to perceive that this delay is to result in the capture of the Knoll. As we are never in doubt of the fact, we feel diminished interest when it actually happens. A single vague allusion, well managed, would have been in the true artistical spirit.

Again we see too plainly, from the first, that Beekman is to marry Beulah, and that Robert Willoughby is to marry Maud. The killing of Beulah, of Mrs Willoughby, and Jamie Allen, produces, too, a painful impression, which does not properly appertain to the right fiction. Their deaths affect us as revolting and supererogatory; since the purposes of the story are not thereby furthered in any regard. To Willoughby's murder, how-ever distressing, the reader makes no similar objection; merely because in his decease is fulfilled a species of poetical justice. We may observe here, nevertheless, that his repeated references to his flogging the Indian seem unnatural, because we have other-wise no reason to think him a fool, or a madman, and these references, under the circumstances, are absolutely insensate. We object, also, to the manner in which the general interest is dragged out, or suspended. The besieging party are kept before the Knoll so long, while so little is done, and so many oppor-tunities of action are lost, that the reader takes it for granted that nothing of consequence will occur – that the besieged will be finally delivered. He gets so accustomed to the presence of danger that its excitement, at length, departs. The action is not suffici-ently rapid. There is too much procrastination. There is too much mere talk for talk's sake. The interminable discussions be-tween Woods and Captain Willoughby are, perhaps, the worst feature of the book, for they have not even the merit of referring to the matters on hand. In general, there is quite too much colloquy for the purpose of manifesting character, and too little for the explanation of motive. The characters of the drama would have been better made out by action; while the motives to action, the reasons for the different courses of conduct adopted by the *dramatis personæ*, might have been made to proceed more satisfactorily from their own mouths, in casual conversations, than from that of the author in person. To conclude our remarks upon the head of ill-conduct in the story, we may mention occasional incidents of the merest melodramatic absurdity; as, for example, at page 156, of the second volume, where 'Willoughby had an arm round the waist of Maud, and bore her forward with a rapidity to which her own strength was entirely unequal.' We may be permitted to doubt whether a young lady of sound health and limbs, exists, within the limits of Christendom, who could not run faster, on her own proper feet, for any considerable distance, than she could be carried upon *one arm* of either the Cretan Milo or of the Hercules Farnese.

On the other hand, it would be easy to designate many particulars which are admirably handled. The love of Maud Meredith for Robert Willoughby is painted with exquisite skill and truth. The incident of the tress of hair and box is naturally and effectively conceived. A fine collateral interest is thrown over the whole narrative by the connexion of the theme with that of the Revolution; and, especially, there is an excellent dramatic point, at page 124 of the second volume, where Wyandotté, remembering the stripes inflicted upon him by Captain Willoughby, is about to betray him to his foes, when his purpose is arrested by a casual glimpse, through the forest, of the hut which contains Mrs Willoughby, who had preserved the life of the Indian, by inoculation for the small-pox.

In the depicting of character, Mr Cooper has been unusually successful in 'Wyandotté.' One or two of his personages, to be sure, must be regarded as little worth. Robert Willoughby, like most novel heroes, is a nobody; that is to say, there is nothing about him which may be looked upon as distinctive. Perhaps he is rather silly than otherwise; as, for instance, when he confuses all his father's arrangements for his concealment, and bursts into the room before Strides – afterward insisting upon accompanying that person to the Indian encampment, without any possible or impossible object. Woods, the parson, is a sad bore, upon the Dominie Sampson plan, and is, moreover, caricatured. Of Captain Willoughby we have already spoken – he is too often on stilts. Evert Beekman and Beulah are merely episodical. Joyce is nothing in the world but Corporal Trim – or, rather, Corporal Trim and water. Jamie Allen, with his prate about Catholicism, is insufferable. But Mrs Willoughby, the humble, shrinking, womanly wife, whose whole existence centres in her affections, is worthy of Mr Cooper. Maud Meredith is still better. In fact, we know no female portraiture, even in Scott, which surpasses her; and yet the world has been given to understand, by the enemies of the novelist, that he is incapable of depicting a woman. Joel Strides will be recognised by all who are conversant with his general prototypes of Connecticut. Michael O'Hearn, the County Leitrim man, is an Irishman all over, and his portraiture abounds in humor; as, for example, at page 31, of the first volume, where he has a difficulty with a skiff, not being able to account for its revolving upon its own axis, instead of moving forward! or, at page 132, where, during divine service, to exclude at least a portion of the heretical doctrine, he stops *one* of his ears with his thumb; or, at page 195, where a passage occurs so much to our purpose that we will be pardoned for quoting it in full. Captain Willoughby is drawing his son up through a window, from his enemies below. The assistants, placed at a distance from this window to avoid observation from without, are ignorant of what burthen is at the end of the rope:

The men did as ordered, raising their load from the ground a foot or two at a time. In this manner the burthen approached, yard after yard, until it was evidently drawing near the window.

'It's the captain hoisting up the big baste of a hog, for provisioning the hoose again a saige,' whispered Mike to the negroes, who grinned as they tugged; 'and, when the craitur squails, see to it, that ye do not squail yourselves.' At that moment the head and shoulders of a man appeared at the window. Mike let go the rope, seized a chair, and was about to knock the intruder upon the head; but the captain arrested the blow.

'It's one o' the vagabone Injins that has undermined the hog and come up in its stead,' roared Mike.

'It's my son,' said the captain; 'see that you are silent and secret.'

The negroes are, without exception, admirably drawn. The Indian, Wyandotté, however, is the great feature of the book, and is, in every respect, equal to the previous Indian creations of the author of 'The Pioneer.' Indeed, we think this 'forest gentleman' superior to the other noted heroes of his kind – the heroes which have been immortalized by our novelist. His keen sense of the distinction, in his own character, between the chief Wyandotté, and the drunken vagabond, Sassy Nick; his chivalrous delicacy toward Maud, in never disclosing to her that knowledge of her real feelings toward Robert Willoughby, which his own Indian intuition had discovered; his enduring animosity toward Captain Willoughby, softened, and for thirty years delayed, through his gratitude to the wife; and then, the vengeance consummated, his pity for that wife conflicting with his exultation at the deed – these, we say, are all traits of a lofty excellence indeed. Perhaps the most effective passage in the book, and that which, most distinctively, brings out the character of the Tuscarora, is to be found at pages 50, 51, 52 and 53 of the second volume, where, for some trivial misdemeanor, the captain threatens to make use of the whip. The manner in which the Indian *harps* upon the threat, returning to it again and again, in every variety of phrase, forms one of the finest pieces of mere character-painting with which we have any acquaintance.

The most obvious and most unaccountable faults of 'The Hutted Knoll,' are those which appertain to the *style* – to the mere grammatical construction; – for, in other and more important particulars of style, Mr Cooper, of late days, has made a very manifest improvement. His sentences, however, are arranged with an awkwardness so remarkable as to be matter of absolute astonishment, when we consider the education of the author, and his long and continual practice with the pen. In minute descriptions of localities, any verbal inaccuracy, or confusion, becomes a source of vexation and misunderstanding, detracting very much from the pleasure of perusal; and in these inaccuracies 'Wyandotté' abounds. Although, for instance, we carefully read and re-read that portion of the narrative which details the situation of the Knoll, and the construction of the buildings and walls about it, we were forced to proceed with the story without any exact or definite impressions upon the subject. Similar difficulties, from similar causes, occur *passim* throughout the book. For example, at page 31, vol. I. :

'The Indian gazed at the house, with that fierce intentness which sometimes glared, in a manner that had got to be, in its ordinary aspects, dull and besotted.' This it is utterly impossible to comprehend. We presume, however, the intention is to say that although the Indian's ordinary manner (of gazing) had 'got to be' dull and besotted, he occasionally gazed with an intentness that glared, and that he did so in the instance in question. The 'got to be' is atrocious – the whole sentence no less so.

Here at page 9, vol. I., is something excessively vague : 'Of the latter character is the face of most of that region which lies in the angle formed by the junction of the Mohawk with the Hudson,' &c., &c. The Mohawk, joining the Hudson, forms two angles, of course, – an acute and an obtuse one; and, without farther explanation, it is difficult to say which is intended.

At page 55, vol. I., we read : – 'The captain, owing to his English education, had avoided straight lines, and formal paths; giving to the little spot the improvement on nature which is a consequence of embellishing her works without destroying them. On each side of this lawn was an orchard, thrifty and young, and which *were* already beginning to show signs of putting forth their blossoms.' Here we are tautologically informed that improvement is a consequence of embellishment, and supererogatorily told that the rule holds good only where the embellishment is not accompanied by destruction. Upon the 'each orchard *were*' it is needless to comment.

At page 30, vol. I., is something similar, where Strides is represented as 'never doing anything that required a particle more than the exertion and strength that were absolutely necessary to affect his object.' Did Mr C. ever hear of any labor that *required* more exertion than was *necessary*? He means to say that Strides exerted himself no farther than was necessary – that's all.

At page 59, vol. I., we find this sentence – 'He was advancing by the only road that was ever travelled by the stranger as he approached the Hut; or, he came up the valley.' This is merely a vagueness of speech. 'Or' is intended to imply 'that is to say.' The whole would be clearer thus – 'He was advancing by the valley – the only road travelled by a stranger approaching the Hut.' We have here sixteen words, instead of Mr Cooper's twenty-five.

At page 8, vol. II., is an unpardonable awkwardness, although an awkwardness strictly grammatical. 'I was a favorite, I believe, with, certainly was much petted by, both.' Upon this we need make no farther observation. It speaks for itself.

We are aware, however, that there is a certain air of unfairness, in thus quoting detached passages, for animadversion of this kind; for, however strictly at random our quotations may really be, we have, of course, no means of proving the fact to our readers; and there are *no* authors, from whose works individual inaccurate sentences may not be culled. But we mean to say that Mr Cooper, no doubt through haste or neglect, is *remarkably* and *especially* inaccurate, as a general rule; and, by way of demonstrating this assertion, we will dismiss our extracts at random, and discuss some entire page of his composition. More than this: we will endeavor to select that particular page upon which it might naturally be supposed he would bestow the most careful attention. The reader will say at once – 'Let this be his *first* page – the first page of his Preface.' This page, then, shall be taken of course.

The history of the borders is filled with legends of the sufferings of isolated families, during the troubled scenes of colonial warfare. Those which we now offer to the reader, are distinctive in many of their leading facts, if not rigidly true in the details. The first alone is necessary to the legitimate objects of fiction.

'*Abounds* with legends,' would be better than 'is filled with legends;' for it is clear that if the history were *filled* with legends, it would be all legend and no history. The word 'off,' too, occurs, in the first sentence, with an unpleasant frequency. The '*those*' commencing the second sentence, grammatically refers to the noun 'scenes,' immediately preceding, but is intended for 'legends.' The adjective '*distinctive*' is vaguely and altogether improperly employed. Mr C. we believe means to say, merely, that although the details of his legends may not be strictly true, facts similar to his leading ones have actually occurred. By use of the word '*distinctive*,' however, he has contrived to convey a meaning nearly converse. In saying that his legend is '*distinctive*' in many of the leading facts, he has said what he, clearly, did not wish to say – viz.: that his legend contained facts which distinguished it from all other legends – in other words, facts never before discussed in other legends, and belonging peculiarly to his own. That Mr C. *did* mean what we suppose, is rendered evident by the third sentence – 'The first alone is necessary to the legitimate objects of fiction.' This third sentence itself, however, is very badly constructed. 'The first' can refer, grammatically, only to 'facts;' but no such reference is intended. If we ask the question – what is meant by 'the first?' – *what* 'alone is necessary to the legitimate objects of fiction?' – the natural reply is 'that facts similar to the leading ones have actually happened.' The circumstance is alone to be cared for – this consideration 'alone is necessary to the legitimate objects of fiction.'

'One of the misfortunes of a nation is to hear nothing besides its own praises.' This is the fourth sentence, and is by no means lucid. The design is to say that individuals composing a nation, and living altogether within the national bounds, hear from each other only praises of the nation, and that this is a misfortune to the individuals, since it misleads them in regard to the actual condition of the nation. Here it will be seen that, to convey the intended idea, we have been forced to make distinction between the nation and its individual members; for it is evident that a nation is considered as such only in reference to other nations; and thus *as a nation*, it hears *very* much 'besides its own praises;'

431

that is to say, it hears the detractions of other rival nations. In endeavoring to compel his meaning within the compass of a brief sentence, Mr Cooper has completely sacrificed its intelligibility.

The fifth sentence runs thus: – 'Although the American Revolution was probably as just an effort as was ever made by a people to resist the first inroads of oppression, the cause had its evil aspects, as well as all other human struggles.'

The American Revolution is here improperly called an 'effort.' The effort was the cause, of which the Revolution was the result. A rebellion is an 'effort' to effect a revolution. An 'inroad of oppression' involves an untrue metaphor; for 'inroad' appertains to aggression, to attack, to active assault. 'The cause had its evil aspects as well as all other human struggles,' implies that the cause had not only its evil aspects, but had, also, all other human struggles. If the words must be retained at all, they should be thus arranged – 'The cause like [or as well as] all other human struggles, had its evil aspects;' or better thus – 'The cause had its evil aspect, as have all human struggles.' 'Other' is superfluous.

The sixth sentence is thus written: – 'We have been so much accustomed to hear everything extolled, of late years, that could be dragged into the remotest connexion with that great event, and the principles which led to it, that there is danger of overlooking truth in a pseudo patriotism.' The 'of late years,' here, should follow the 'accustomed,' or precede the 'We have been;' and the Greek 'pseudo' is objectionable, since its exact equivalent is to be found in the English 'false.' 'Spurious' would have been better, perhaps, than either.

Inadvertences such as these sadly disfigure the style of 'The Hutted Knoll;' and every true friend of its author must regret his inattention to the minor morals of the Muse. But these 'minor morals,' it may be said, are trifles at best. Perhaps so. At all events, we should never have thought of dwelling so pertinaciously upon the unessential demerits of 'Wyandotté,' could we have discovered any more momentous upon which to comment.

Music

WHEN music affects us to tears, seemingly causeless, we weep
not, as Gravina supposes, from 'excess of pleasure'; but through
excess of an impatient, petulant sorrow that, as mere mortals,
we are as yet in no condition to banquet upon those supernal
ecstasies of which the music affords us merely a suggestive and
indefinite glimpse.

Time and Space

WE appreciate *time* by events alone. For this reason we define time (somewhat improperly) as the succession of events; but the fact itself – that events are our sole means of appreciating time – tends to the engendering of the erroneous idea that events *are* time – that the more numerous the events, the longer the time; and the converse. This erroneous idea there can be no doubt that we should absolutely entertain in all cases, but for our practical means of correcting the impression – such as clocks, and the movements of the heavenly bodies – whose revolutions, after all, we only *assume* to be regular.

Space is precisely analogous with time. By objects alone we estimate space; and we might as rationally define it 'the succession of objects' as time 'the succession of events.' But, as before. – The fact, that we have no other means of estimating space than objects afford us – tends to the false idea that objects *are* space – that the more numerous the objects the greater the space; and the converse; and this erroneous impression we should receive in all cases, but for our practical means of correcting it – such as yard measures, and other conventional measures, which resolve themselves, ultimately, into certain natural standards, such as barleycorns, which, after all, we only *assume* to be regular.

The mind can form *some* conception of the distance (however vast) between the sun and Uranus, because there are ten objects which (mentally) intervene – the planets Mercury, Venus, Earth, Mars, Ceres, Vesta, Juno, Pallas, Jupiter, and Saturn. These objects serve as stepping-stones to the mind; which, nevertheless, is utterly lost in the attempt at establishing a notion of the interval between Uranus and Sirius; lost – yet, clearly, not on account of the mere *distance* (for why should we not conceive the abstract idea of the distance, two miles, as readily as that of the distance, one?) but, simply, because between Uranus and Sirius we happen to know that all is void. And, from what I have

434

already said, it follows that this vacuity – this want of intervening points – will cause *to fall short* of the truth any notion we shall endeavor to form. In fact, having once passed the limits of absolutely practical admeasurement, by means of intervening objects, our ideas of distances are *one*; they have no variation. Thus, in truth, we think of the interval between Uranus and Sirius precisely as of that between Saturn and Uranus, or of that between any one planet and its immediate neighbor. We fancy, indeed, that we form different conceptions of the different intervals; but we mistake the mathematical knowledge of the fact of the interval, for an idea of the interval itself.

It is the principle for which I contend that instinctively leads the artist, in painting what he technically calls distances, to introduce a succession of objects between the 'distance' and the foreground. Here it will be said that the intention is the perspective comparison of *the size* of the objects. Several men, for example, are painted, one beyond the other, and it is the diminution of apparent size by which the idea of distance is conveyed; – this, I say, will be asserted. But here is mere confusion of the two notions of abstract and comparative distance. By this process of diminishing figures, we are, it is true, made to feel that one is at a *greater* distance than the other, but the idea we thence glean of abstract distance, is gleaned altogether from the mere succession of the figures, independently of magnitude. To prove this, let the men be painted out, and *rocks* put in their stead. A rock may be of any size. The farthest may be, for all we know, really, and not merely optically, the least. The effect of absolute distance will remain untouched, and the sole result will be confusion of idea respecting the comparative distances from rock to rock. But the thing is clear: if the artist's intention is really, as supposed, to convey the notion of great distance by perspective comparison of the *size* of men at different intervals, we must, at least, grant that he puts himself to unnecessary trouble in the multiplication of his men. *Two* would answer all the purposes of two thousand; – one in the foreground as a standard, and one in the background, of a size corresponding with the artist's conception of the distance.

In looking at the setting sun in a mountainous region, or with a city between the eye and the orb, we see it of a certain seeming magnitude, as we do not perceive that this seeming magnitude varies when we look at the same sun setting on the horizon of the ocean. In either case we have a chain of objects by which to appreciate a certain distance; – in the former case this chain is formed of mountains and towers – in the latter, of ripples, or specks of foam; but the result does not present any difference. In each case we get the same idea of the distance, and consequently of the size. This size we have in our mind when we look at the sun in his meridian place; but this distance we have *not* – for no objects intervene. That is to say, the distance falls short, while the size remains. The consequence is, that, to accord with the diminished distance, the mind instantaneously diminishes the size. The conversed experiment gives, of course, a conversed result.

Dr Lardner's 'so it is' is amusing to say no more. In general, the mere natural philosophers have the same exaggerated notions of the perplexity of metaphysics. And, perhaps, it is this *looming* of the latter science which has brought about the vulgar derivation of its name from the supposed superiority to physics – as if μετὰ φυσικά had the force of *super* physical. The fact is, that Aristotle's Treatise on Morals is next in succession to his Book on Physics, and this he supposes the rational order of study. His Ethics, therefore, commence with the words Μετὰ τὰ φυσικά – whence we take the word, Metaphysics. That Leibnitz, who was fond of interweaving even his mathematical, with ethical speculations, making a medley rather to be wondered at than understood – that *he* made no attempt at amending the common explanation of the difference in the sun's apparent size – this, perhaps, is more really a matter for marvel than that Dr Lardner should look upon the common explanation as only too 'learned' and too 'metaphysical' for an audience in Yankee-Land.

Twice-Told Tales

TALE-WRITING – NATHANIEL HAWTHORNE. – TWICE-TOLD TALES. BY NATHANIEL HAWTHORNE. JAMES MUNROE & CO., BOSTON. 1842.

IN the preface to my sketches of New York Literati, while speaking of the broad distinction between the seeming public and real private opinion respecting our authors, I thus alluded to Nathaniel Hawthorne:

'For example, Mr Hawthorne, the author of "Twice-Told Tales," is scarcely recognized by the press or by the public, and when noticed at all, is noticed merely to be damned by faint praise. Now, my opinion of him is, that although his walk is limited and he is fairly to be charged with mannerism, treating all subjects in a similar tone of dreamy *innuendo*, yet in this walk he evinces extraordinary genius, having no rival either in America or elsewhere; and this opinion I have never heard gainsaid by any one literary person in the country. That this opinion, however, is a spoken and not a written one, is referable to the facts, first, that Mr Hawthorne is a poor man, and, secondly, that he *is not* an ubiquitous quack.'

The reputation of the author of 'Twice-Told Tales' has been confined, indeed, until very lately, to literary society; and I have not been wrong, perhaps, in citing him as *the* example, *par excellence*, in this country, of the privately-admired and publicly-unappreciated man of genius. Within the last year or two, it is true, an occasional critic has been urged, by honest indignation, into very warm approval. Mr Webber, for instance, (than whom no one has a keener relish for that kind of writing which Mr Hawthorne has best illustrated,) gave us, in a late number of 'The American Review,' a cordial and certainly a full tribute to his talents; and since the issue of the 'Mosses from an Old Manse,' criticisms of similar tone have been by no means infrequent in our more authoritative journals. I can call to mind few reviews of Hawthorne published *before* the 'Mosses.' One I remember in 'Arcturus' (edited by Matthews and Duyckinck) for May, 1841; another in the 'American Monthly' (edited by Hoffman and Herbert) for March, 1838; a third in the ninety-sixth number of the 'North American Review.' These criticisms, however, seemed to have little effect on the popular taste – at least, if we are to form any idea of the popular taste by reference to its expression in the newspapers, or by the sale of the author's book. It was never the fashion (until lately) to speak of him in any summary of our best authors. The daily critics would say, on such occasions, 'Is there not Irving and Cooper, and Bryant and Paulding, and – Smith?' or, 'Have we not Halleck and Dana, and Longfellow and – Thompson?' or, 'Can we not point triumphantly to our own Sprague, Willis, Channing, Bancroft, Prescott and – Jenkins?' but these unanswerable queries were never wound up by the name of Hawthorne.

Beyond doubt, this inappreciation of him on the part of the public arose chiefly from the two causes to which I have referred – from the facts that he is neither a man of wealth nor a quack; – but these are insufficient to account for the whole effect. No small portion of it is attributable to the very marked idiosyncrasy of Mr Hawthorne himself. In one sense, and in great measure, to be peculiar is to be original, and than the true originality there is no higher literary virtue. This true or commendable originality, however, implies not the uniform, but the continuous peculiarity – a peculiarity springing from ever-active vigor of fancy – better still if from ever-present force of imagination, giving its own hue, its own character to everything it touches, and, especially, *self impelled to touch everything.*

It is often said, inconsiderately, that very original writers always fail in popularity – that such and such persons are too original to be comprehended by the mass. 'Too peculiar,' should be the phrase, 'too idiosyncratic.' It is, in fact, the excitable, undisciplined and childlike popular mind which most keenly feels the original. The criticism of the conservatives, of the hackneys, of the cultivated old clergymen of the 'North American Review,' is precisely the criticism which condemns and alone condemns it. 'It becometh not a divine,' saith Lord Coke, 'to be of a fiery and salamandrine spirit.' Their conscience allowing them to move nothing themselves, these dignitaries have a holy horror of being moved. 'Give us *quietude*,' they say. Opening their mouths with proper caution, they sign forth the word '*Repose*.' And this is, indeed, the one thing they should be permitted to enjoy, if only upon the Christian principle of give and take.

The fact is, that if Mr Hawthorne were really original, he could not fail of making himself felt by the public. But the fact is, he is *not* original in any sense. Those who speak of him as original, mean nothing more than that he differs in his manner of tone, and in his choice of subjects, from any author of their acquaintance – their acquaintance not extending to the German Tieck, whose manner, in *some* of his works, is absolutely identical with that *habitual* to Hawthorne. But it is clear that the element of the literary originality is novelty. The element of its appreciation by the reader is the reader's sense of the new. Whatever gives him a new and insomuch a pleasurable emotion, he considers original, and whoever frequently gives him such emotion, he considers an original writer. In a word, it is by the sum total of these emotions that he decides upon the writer's claim to originality. I may observe here, however, that there is clearly a point at which even novelty itself would cease to produce the legitimate originality, if we judge this originality, as we should, by the effect designed; this point is that at which *novelty becomes nothing novel*; and here the artist, *to preserve his originality* will subside into the commonplace. No one, I think, has noticed that, merely through inattention to this matter, Moore has comparatively failed in his 'Lalla Rookh.' Few readers, and indeed few critics, have commended this poem for originality – and, in fact, the effect, originality, is not produced by it – yet no work of equal size so abounds in the happiest originalities, individually considered. They are so excessive, as, in the end, to deaden in the reader all capacity for their appreciation.

These points properly understood, it will be seen that the critic (unacquainted with Tieck) who reads a single tale or essay by Hawthorne, may be justified in thinking him original; but the tone, or manner, or choice of subject, which induces in this critic the sense of the new, will – if not in a second tale, at least in a third and all subsequent ones – not only fail of inducing it, but bring about an exactly antagonistic impression. In concluding a volume, and more especially in concluding all the volumes of the author, the critic will abandon his first design of calling him 'original,' and content himself with styling him 'peculiar.'

With the vague opinion that to be original is to be popular, I could, indeed, agree, were I to adopt an understanding of originality which, to my surprise, I have known adopted by many who have a right to be called critical. They have limited, in a love for mere words, the literary to the metaphysical originality. They regard as original in letters, only such combinations of thought, of incident, and so forth, as are, in fact, absolutely novel. It is clear, however, not only that it is the novelty of *effect* alone which is worth consideration, but that this effect is *best* wrought, for the end of all fictitious composition, pleasure, by shunning rather than by seeking the absolute novelty of combination. Originality, thus understood, tasks and startles the intellect, and so brings into undue action the faculties to which, in the lighter literature, we least appeal. And thus understood, it cannot fail to prove unpopular with the masses, who, seeking in this literature amusement, are positively offended by instruction. But the true originality – true in respect of its purposes – is that which, in bringing out the half-formed, the reluctant, or the unexpressed fancies of mankind, or in exciting the more delicate pulses of the heart's passion, or in giving birth to some universal sentiment or instinct in embryo, thus combines with the pleasurable effect of *apparent* novelty, a real egoistic delight. The reader, in the case first supposed, (that of the absolute novelty,) is excited, but embarrassed, disturbed, in some degree even pained at his own want of perception, at his own folly in not having himself hit upon the idea. In the second case, his pleasure is doubled. He is filled with an intrinsic and extrinsic delight. He feels and intensely enjoys the seeming novelty of the thought, enjoys it as really novel, as absolutely original with the writer – *and himself*. They two, he fancies, have, alone of all men, thought thus. They two have, together, created this thing. Henceforward there is a bond of sympathy between them, a sympathy which irradiates every subsequent page of the book.

There is a species of writing which, with some difficulty, may be admitted as a lower degree of what I have called the true original. In its perusal, we say to ourselves, not 'how original this is!' nor 'here is an idea which I and the author have alone entertained,' but 'here is a charmingly obvious fancy,' or sometimes even, 'here is a thought which I am not sure has ever occurred to myself, but which, of course, has occurred to all the rest of the world.' This kind of composition (which still appertains to a high order) is usually designated as 'the natural.' It has little external resemblance, but strong internal affinity to the true original, if, indeed, as I have suggested, it is not of this latter an inferior degree. It is best exemplified, among English writers, in Addison, Irving and *Hawthorne*. The 'ease' which is so often spoken of as its distinguishing feature, it has been the fashion to regard as ease in appearance alone, as a point of really difficult attainment. This idea, however, must be received with some reservation. The natural style is difficult only to those who should never intermeddle with it – to the unnatural. It is but the result of writing with the understanding, or with the instinct, that the *tone*, in composition, should be that which, at any given point or upon any given topic, would be the tone of the great mass of humanity. The author who, after the manner of the North Americans, is merely at *all* times *quiet*, is, of course, upon *most* occasions, merely silly or stupid, and has no more right to be thought 'easy' or 'natural' than has a cockney exquisite or the sleeping beauty in the wax-works.

The 'peculiarity' or sameness, or monotone of Hawthorne, would, in its mere character of 'peculiarity,' and without reference to what *is* the peculiarity, suffice to deprive him of all chance of popular appreciation. But at his failure to be appreciated, we can, *of course,* no longer wonder, when we find him monotonous at decidedly the worst of all possible points – at that point which, having the least concern with Nature, is the farthest removed from the popular intellect, from the popular sentiment and from the popular taste. I allude to the strain of allegory which completely overwhelms the greater number of his subjects, and which in some measure interferes with the direct conduct of absolutely all.

In defence of allegory, (however, or for whatever object, employed,) there is scarcely one respectable word to be said. Its best appeals are made to the fancy – that is to say, to our sense of adaptation, not of matters proper, but of matters improper for the purpose, of the real with the unreal; having never more of intelligible connection than has something with nothing, never half so much of effective affinity as has the substance for the shadow. The deepest emotion aroused within us by the happiest allegory, *as* allegory, is a very, very imperfectly satisfied sense of the writer's ingenuity in overcoming a difficulty we should have preferred his not having attempted to overcome. The fallacy of the idea that allegory, in any of its moods, can be made to enforce a truth – that metaphor, for example, may illustrate as well as embellish an argument – could be promptly demonstrated : the converse of the supposed fact might be shown, indeed, with very little trouble – but these are topics foreign to my present purpose. One thing is clear, that if allegory ever establishes a fact, it is by dint of overturning a fiction. Where the suggested meaning runs through the obvious one in a *very* profound under-current so as never to interfere with the upper one without our own volition, so as never to show itself unless *called* to the surface, there only, for the proper uses of fictitious narrative, is it available at all. Under the best circumstances, it must always interfere with that unity of effect which to the artist, is worth all the allegory in the world. Its vital injury, however, is rendered to the most vitally important point in fiction – that of earnestness or verisimilitude. That 'The Pilgrim's Progress' is a ludicrously over-rated book, owing its seeming popularity to one or two of those accidents in critical literature which by the critical are sufficiently well understood, is a matter upon which no two thinking people disagree; but the pleasure derivable from it, in any sense, will be found in the direct ratio of the reader's capacity to smother its true purpose, in the direct ratio of his ability to keep the allegory out of sight, or of his inability to comprehend it. Of allegory properly handled, judiciously subdued, seen only as a shadow or by suggestive glimpses, and making its nearest approach to truth in a not obtrusive and therefore not unpleasant *appositeness*, the 'Undine' of De La Motte Fouqué is the best, and undoubtedly a very remarkable specimen.

The obvious causes, however, which have prevented Mr Hawthorne's *popularity*, do not suffice to condemn him in the eyes of the few who belong properly to books, and to whom books, perhaps, do not quite so properly belong. These few estimate an author, not as do the public, altogether by what he does, but in great measure – indeed, even in the greatest measure – by what he evinces a capability of doing. In this view, Hawthorne stands among literary people in America much in the same light as did Coleridge in England. The few, also, through a certain warping of the taste, which long pondering upon books as books merely never fails to induce, are not in condition to view the errors of a scholar as errors altogether. At any time these gentlemen are prone to think the public not right rather than an educated author wrong. But the simple truth is that the writer who aims at impressing the people, is *always* wrong when he fails in forcing that people to receive the impression. How far Mr Hawthorne has addressed the people at all, is, of course, not a question for me to decide. His books afford strong internal evidence of having been written to himself and his particular friends alone.

There has long existed in literature a fatal and unfounded prejudice, which it will be the office of this age to overthrow – the idea that the mere bulk of a work must enter largely into our estimate of its merit. I do not suppose even the weakest of the quarterly reviewers weak enough to maintain that in a book's size or mass, abstractly considered, there is anything which especially calls for our admiration. A mountain, simply through the sensation of physical magnitude which it conveys, does, indeed, affect us with a sense of the sublime, but we cannot admit any such influence in the contemplation even of 'The Columbiad.' The Quarterlies themselves will not admit it. And yet, what else are we to understand by their continual prating about 'sustained effort?' Granted that this sustained effort has accomplished an epic – let us then admire the effort, (if this be a thing admirable,) but certainly not the epic on the effort's account. Common sense, in the time to come, may possibly insist upon measuring a work of art rather by the object it fulfils, by the impression it makes, than by the time it took to fulfil the object, or by the extent of 'sustained effort' which became necessary to produce the impression. The fact is, that perseverance is one thing and genius quite another; nor can all the transcendentalists in Heathendom confound them.

Full of its bulky ideas, the last number of the 'North American Review,' in what it imagines a criticism on Simms, 'honestly avows that it has little opinion of the mere tale;' and the honesty of the avowal is in no slight degree guaranteed by the fact that this Review has never yet been known to put forth an opinion which was *not* a very little one indeed.

The tale proper affords the fairest field which can be afforded by the wide domains of mere prose, for the exercise of the highest genius. Were I bidden to say how this genius could be most advantageously employed for the best display of its powers, I should answer, without hesitation, 'in the composition of a rhymed poem not to exceed in length what might be perused in an hour.' Within this limit alone can the noblest order of poetry exist. I have discussed this topic elsewhere, and need here repeat only that the phrase 'a long poem' embodies a paradox. A poem must intensely excite. Excitement is its province, its essentiality. Its value is in the ratio of its (elevating) excitement. But all excitement is, from a psychal necessity, transient. It cannot be sustained through a poem of great length. In the course of an hour's reading, at most, it flags, fails; and then the poem is, in effect, no longer such. Men admire, but are wearied with the 'Paradise

Lost;' for platitude follows platitude, *inevitably*, at regular interspaces, (the depressions between the waves of excitement,) until the poem, (which, properly considered, is but a succession of brief poems,) having been brought to an end, we discover that the sums of our pleasure and of displeasure have been very nearly equal. The absolute, ultimate or aggregate effect of any epic under the sun is, for these reasons, a nullity. 'The Iliad,' in its form of epic, has but an imaginary existence; granting it real, however, I can only say of it that it is based on a primitive sense of Art. Of the modern epic nothing can be so well said as that it is a blindfold imitation of a 'come-by-chance.' By and by these propositions will be understood as self-evident, and in the meantime will not be essentially damaged as truths by being generally condemned as falsities.

A poem *too* brief, on the other hand, may produce a sharp or vivid, but never a profound or enduring impression. Without a certain continuity, without a certain duration or repetition of the cause, the soul is seldom moved to the effect. There must be the dropping of the water on the rock. There must be the pressing steadily down of the stamp upon the wax. De Béranger has wrought brilliant things, pungent and spirit-stirring, but most of them are too immassive to have *momentum*, and, as so many feathers of fancy, have been blown aloft only to be whistled down the wind. Brevity, indeed, may degenerate into epigrammatism, but this danger does not prevent extreme length from being the one unpardonable sin.

Were I called upon, however, to designate that class of composition which, next to such a poem as I have suggested, should best fulfil the demands and serve the purposes of ambitious genius, should offer it the most advantageous field of exertion, and afford it the fairest opportunity of display, I should speak at once of the brief prose tale. History, philosophy, and other matters of that kind, we leave out of the question, of course. *Of course*, I say, and in spite of the gray-beards. These grave topics, to the end of time, will be best illustrated by what a discriminating world, turning up its nose at the drab pamphlets, has agreed to understand as *talent*. The ordinary novel is objectionable, from its length, for reasons analogous to those which render length objectionable in the poem. As the novel cannot be read at one sitting, it cannot avail itself of the immense benefit of *totality*. Worldly interests, intervening during the pauses of perusal, modify, counteract and annul the impressions intended. But simple cessation in reading would, of itself, be sufficient to destroy the true unity. In the brief tale, however, the author is enabled to carry out his full design without interruption. During the hour of perusal, the soul of the reader is at the writer's control.

A skilful artist has constructed a tale. He has not fashioned his thoughts to accommodate his incidents, but having deliberately conceived a certain *single effect* to be wrought, he then invents such incidents, he then combines such events, and discusses them in such tone as may best serve him in establishing this preconceived effect. If his very first sentence tend not to the outbringing of this effect, then in his very first step has he committed a blunder. In the whole composition there should be no word written of which the tendency, direct or indirect, is not to the one pre-established design. And by such means, with such care and skill, a picture is at length painted which leaves in the mind of him who contemplates it with a kindred art, a sense of the fullest satisfaction. The idea of the tale, its thesis, has been presented unblemished, because undisturbed – an end absolutely demanded, yet, in the novel, altogether unattainable.

Of skillfully-constructed tales – I speak now without reference to other points, some of them more important than construction – there are very few American specimens. I am acquainted with no better one, upon the whole, than the 'Murder Will Out' of Mr Simms, and this has some glaring defects. The 'Tales of a Traveler,' by Irving, are graceful and impressive narratives – 'The Young Italian' is especially good – but there is not one of the series which can be commended as a whole. In many of them the interest is subdivided and frittered away, and their conclusions are insufficiently *climactic*. In the higher requisites of composition, John Neal's magazine stories excel – I mean in vigor of thought, picturesque combination of incident, and so forth –

but they ramble too much, and invariably break down just before coming to an end, as if the writer had received a sudden and irresistible summons to dinner, and thought it incumbent upon him to make a finish of his story before going. One of the happiest and best-sustained tales I have seen is 'Jack Long; or, The Shot in the Eye,' by Charles W. Webber, the assistant editor of Mr Colton's 'American Review.' But in general skill of construction, the tales of Willis, I think, surpass those of any American writer – with the exception of Mr Hawthorne.

I must defer to the better opportunity of a volume now in hand, a full discussion of his individual pieces, and hasten to conclude this paper with a summary of his merits and demerits.

He is peculiar and *not* original – unless in those detailed fancies and detached thoughts which his want of general originality will deprive of the appreciation due to them, in preventing them forever reaching the *public eye*. He is infinitely too fond of allegory, and can never hope for popularity so long as he persists in it. This he will not do, for allegory is at war with the whole tone of his nature, which disports itself never so well as when escaping from the mysticism of his Goodman Browns and White Old Maids into the hearty, genial, but still Indian-summer sunshine of his Wakefields and Little Annie's Rambles. Indeed, *his* spirit of 'metaphor run-mad' is clearly imbibed from the phalanx and phalanstery atmosphere in which he has been so long struggling for breath. He has not half the material for the exclusiveness of authorship that he possesses for its universality. He has the purest style, the finest taste, the most available scholarship, the most delicate humor, the most touching pathos, the most radiant imagination, the most consummate ingenuity; and with these varied good qualites he has done *well* as a mystic. But is there any one of these qualities which should prevent his doing doubly as well in a career of honest, upright, sensible, prehensible and comprehensible things? Let him mend his pen, get a bottle of visible ink, come out from the Old Manse, cut Mr Alcott, hang (if possible) the editor of 'The Dial,' and throw out of the window to the pigs all his odd numbers of 'The North American Review.'

The American Drama (excerpts)

A BIOGRAPHIST of Berryer[1] calls him *'l'homme qui dans ses description, demande la plus grande quantité possible d'antithèse';*[2] – but that ever recurring topic, the decline of the drama, seems to have consumed, of late, more of the material in question than would have sufficed for a dozen prime ministers – even admitting them to be French. Every trick of thought and every harlequinade of phrase have been put in operation for the purpose *'de nier ce qui est, et d'expliquer ce qui n'est pas.'*[3]

Ce qui n'est pas: – for the drama has *not declined*. The facts and the philosophy of the case seem to be these. The great opponent to Progress is Conservatism. In other words – the great adversary of Invention is Imitation: – the propositions are in spirit identical. Just as an art is imitative, is it stationary. The most imitative arts are the most prone to repose – and the converse. Upon the utilitarian – upon the business arts, where necessity impels, Invention, Necessity's well-understood off-spring, is ever in attendance. And the less we see of the Mother the less we behold of the child. No one complains of the decline of the art of Engineering. Here the Reason, which never retrogrades, or reposes, is called into play. But let us glance at Sculpture. We are not *worse*, here, than the ancients, let pedantry say what it may, (the Venus of Canova is worth at any time two of that of Cleomenes), but it is equally certain that we have made, in general, no advances; and Sculpture, properly considered, is perhaps the *most* imitative of all arts which have a right to the title of Art at all. Looking next at Painting we find that we have to boast of progress only in the ratio of the inferior imitativeness of painting, when compared with Sculpture. As far indeed as we have any means of judging, our improvement has been exceedingly little, and did we know anything of ancient Art in this department, we might be astonished at discovering that

448

we had advanced even far less than we suppose. As regards Architecture, whatever progress we have made, has been precisely in those particulars which have no reference to imitation : – that is to say we have improved the utilitarian and not the ornamental provinces of the art. Where Reason predominated, we advanced; where mere Feeling or Taste was the guide, we remained as we were.

Coming to the Drama, we shall see that in its mechanisms we have made progress, while in its spirituality we have done little or nothing for centuries certainly – and, perhaps, little or nothing for thousands of years. And this is because what we term the spirituality of the drama is precisely its imitative portion – is exactly that portion which distinguishes it as one of the principal of the imitative arts.

Sculptors, painters, dramatists, are, from the very nature of their material, – their spiritual material – imitators – conservatists – prone to repose in old Feeling and in antique Taste. For this reason – and for this reason only – the arts of Sculpture, Painting and the Drama have not advanced – or have advanced feebly, and inversely in the ratio of their imitativeness.

But it by no means follows that either has *declined*. All *seem* to have declined, because they have remained stationary while the multitudinous other arts (of reason) have flitted so rapidly by them. In the same manner the traveller by railroad can imagine that the trees by the wayside are retrograding. The trees in this case are absolutely stationary – but the Drama has not been altogether so, although its progress has been so slight as not to interfere with the general effect – that of seeming retrogradation or decline.

This seeming retrogradation, however, is to all practical intents an absolute one. Whether the drama has declined, or whether it has merely remained stationary, is a point of no importance, so far as concerns the public encouragement of the drama. It is unsupported, in either case, because it does not deserve support.

But if this stagnation, or deterioration, grows out of the very idiosyncrasy of the drama itself, as one of the principal of the imitative arts, how is it possible that a remedy shall be applied – since it is clearly impossible to alter the nature of the art, and yet leave it the art which it now is?

We have already spoken of the improvements effected, in Architecture, in all its utilitarian departments, and in the Drama, at all the points of its mechanism. 'Wherever Reason predominates we advance; where mere Feeling or Taste is the guide, we remain as we are.' We wish now to suggest that, by the engrafting of Reason upon Feeling and Taste, we shall be able, and thus alone shall be able, to force the modern Drama into the production of any profitable fruit.

At present, what is it we do? We are content if, with Feeling and Taste, a dramatist does *as other dramatists have done*. The most successful of the more immediately modern playwrights has been Sheridan Knowles[4] and to play Sheridan Knowles seems to be the highest ambition of our writers for the stage. Now the author of 'The Hunchback,' possesses what we are weak enough to term the true 'dramatic feeling,' and this true dramatic feeling he has manifested in the most preposterous series of imitations of the Elizabethan drama, by which ever mankind were insulted and begulled. Not only did he adhere to the old plots, the old characters, the old stage conventionalities throughout; but, he went even so far as to persist in the obsolete phraseologies of the Elizabethan period – and just in proportion to his obstinacy and absurdity at all points, did we pretend to like him the better, and pretend to consider him a great dramatist.

Pretend – for every particle of it was pretence. Never was enthusiasm more utterly false than that which so many 'respectable audiences' endeavored to get up for these plays – endeavored to get up, first, because there was a general desire to see the drama revive, and secondly, because we had been all along entertaining the fancy that 'the decline of the drama' meant little, if anything, else than its deviation from the Elizabethan routine – and that, consequently, the return to the Elizabethan routine was, and of necessity must be, the revival of the drama.

But if the principles we have been at some trouble in explaining, are true – and most profoundly do we feel them to be so – if the spirit of imitation is, in fact, the real source of the drama's stagnation – and if it is so because of the tendency in all imitation to render Reason subservient to Feeling and to Taste – it is clear that only by deliberate counteracting of the spirit, and of the tendency of the spirit, we can hope to succeed in the drama's revival.

The first thing necessary is to burn or bury the 'old models,' and to forget, as quickly as possible, that ever a play has been penned. The second thing is to consider *de novo* what are the *capabilities* of the drama – not merely what hitherto have been its conventional purposes. The third and last point has reference to the composition of a play (showing to the fullest extent these capabilities), conceived and constructed with Feeling and with Taste, but with Feeling and Taste guided and controlled in every particular by the details of Reason – of Common Sense – in a word, of a Natural Art.

It is obvious, in the meantime, that towards the good end in view, much may be effected by discriminative criticism on what has already been done. The field, thus stated, is of course, practically illimitable – and to Americans the American drama is the special point of interest. We propose, therefore, in a series of papers, to take a somewhat deliberate survey of some few of the most noticeable American plays. We shall do this without reference either to the date of the composition, or its adaptation for the closet or the stage. We shall speak with absolute frankness both of merits and defects – our principal object being understood not as that of mere commentary on the individual play – but on the drama in general, and on the American drama in especial, of which each individual play is a constituent part. We will commence at once with

TORTESA, THE USURER.

This is the third dramatic attempt of Mr Willis,[5] and may be regarded as particularly successful, since it has received, both on the stage and in the closet, no stinted measure of commendation. This success, as well as the high reputation of the author, will justify us in a more extended notice of the play than might, under other circumstances, be desirable.

The story runs thus: – Tortesa, an usurer of Florence, and whose character is a mingled web of good and evil feelings, gets into his possession the palace and lands of a certain Count Falcone. The usurer would wed the daughter (Isabella) of Falcone – not through love, but, in his own words,

'To please a devil that inhabits him –'

in fact to mortify the pride of the nobility, and avenge himself of their scorn. He therefore bargains with Falcone [a narrow-souled villain] for the hand of Isabella. The deed of the Falcone property is restored to the Count, upon an agreement that the lady shall marry the usurer – this contract being invalid should Falcone change his mind in regard to the marriage, or should the maiden demur – but valid should the wedding be prevented through any fault of Tortesa, or through any accident not springing from the will of the father or child. The first Scene makes us aware of this bargain, and introduces us to Zippa, a glover's daughter, who resolves, with a view of befriending Isabella, to feign a love for Tortesa, [which, in fact, she partially feels] hoping thus to break off the match.

The second Scene makes us acquainted with a young painter, (Angelo) poor, but of high talents and ambition, and with his servant, (Tomaso) an old bottle-loving rascal, entertaining no very exalted opinion of his master's abilities. Tomaso does some injury to a picture, and Angelo is about to run him through the body, when he is interrupted by a sudden visit from the Duke of Florence, attended by Falcone. The Duke is enraged at the murderous attempt, but admires the paintings in the studio. Finding that the rage of the great man will prevent his patronage if he knows the aggressor as the artist, Angelo passes off Tomaso as himself, (Angelo) making an exchange of names. This is a point of some importance, as it introduces the true Angelo to a job which he had long coveted – the painting of a portrait of Isabella, of whose beauty he had become enamoured through report. The Duke wishes the portrait painted. Falcone, however, on account of a promise to Tortesa, would have objected to admit to his daughter's presence the handsome Angelo, but in regard to Tomaso, has no scruple. Supposing Tomaso to be Angelo and the artist, the count writes a note to Isabella, requiring her 'to admit the painter Angelo.' The real Angelo is thus admitted. He and the lady love at first sight, (much in the manner of Romeo and Juliet,) each ignorant of the other's attachment.

The third Scene of the Second Act is occupied with a conversation between Falcone and Tortesa, during which a letter arrives from the Duke, who, having heard of the intended sacrifice of Isabella, offers to redeem the Count's lands and palace, and desires him to preserve his daughter for a certain Count Julian. But Isabella, – who, before seeing Angelo, had been willing to sacrifice herself for her father's sake, and who, since seeing him, had entertained hopes of escaping the hateful match through means of a plot entered into her by herself and Zippa – Isabella, we say, is now in despair. To gain time, she at once feigns a love for the usurer, and indignantly rejects the proposal of the Duke. The hour for the wedding draws near. The lady has prepared a sleeping potion, whose effects resemble those of death. (Romeo and Juliet.) She swallows it – knowing that her supposed corpse would lie at night, pursuant to an old custom, in the sanctuary of the cathedral; and believing that Angelo – whose love for herself she has elicited, by a stratagem, from his own lips – will watch by the body, in the strength of his devotion. Her ultimate design (we may suppose, for it is not told,) is to confess all to her lover, on her revival, and throw herself upon his protection – their marriage being concealed, and herself regarded as dead by the world. Zippa, who *really* loves Angelo – (her love for Tortesa, it must be understood, is a very equivocal feeling, for the fact cannot be denied that Mr Willis makes her love both at the same time) – Zippa, who really loves Angelo – who has discovered his passion for Isabella – and who, as well as that lady, believes that the painter will watch the corpse in the cathedral, – determines, through jealousy, to prevent his so doing, and with this view informs Tortesa that she has learned it to be Angelo's design to steal the body, *for artistical purposes*, – in short as a model to be used in his studio. The usurer, in consequence, sets a guard at the doors of the cathedral. This guard does, in fact, prevent the lover from watching the corpse, but, it appears, does *not* prevent the lady, on her revival and disappointment in not seeing the one she sought, from passing unperceived from the church. Weakened by her long sleep, she wanders aimlessly through the streets, and at length finds herself, when just sinking with exhaustion, at the door of her father. She has no resource but to knock. The Count — who here, we must say, acts very much as Thimble of old – the knight, we mean, of the 'scolding wife' – maintains that she is dead, and shuts the door in her face. In other words, he supposes it to be the ghost of his daughter who speaks; and so the lady is left to perish on the steps. Meantime Angelo is absent from home, attempting to get access to the cathedral; and his servant Tomaso, takes the opportunity of absenting himself also, and of indulging his bibulous propensities while perambulating the town. He finds Isabella as we left her; and through motives which we will leave Mr Willis to explain, conducts her unresistingly to Angelo's residence, and – *deposits her in Angelo's bed*. The artist now returns – Tomaso is kicked out of doors – and we are not told, but left to presume, that a full explanation and perfect understanding are brought about between the lady and her lover.

We find them, next morning, in the studio, where stands leaning against an easel, the portrait (a full length) of Isabella, with curtains adjusted before it. The stage-directions, moreover, inform us that 'the back wall of the room is such as to form a natural ground for the picture.' While Angelo is occupied in retouching it, he is interrupted by the arrival of Tortesa with a guard, and is accused of having stolen the corpse from the sanctuary – the lady, meanwhile, having stepped behind the curtain. The usurer insists upon seeing the painting, with a view of ascertaining whether any new touches had been put upon it, which would argue an examination, *post mortem*, of those charms of neck and bosom which the living Isabella would not have unveiled. Resistance is vain – the curtain is torn down; but, to the surprise of Angelo, the lady herself is discovered, 'with her hands crossed on her breast, and her eyes fixed on the ground, standing motionless in the frame which had contained the picture.' The *tableau*, we are to believe, deceives Tortesa, who steps back to contemplate what he supposes to be the portrait of his betrothed. In the meantime the guards, having searched the house, find the veil which had been thrown over the imagined corpse in the sanctuary; and, upon this evidence, the artist is carried before the Duke. Here he is accused, not only of sacrilege, but of the murder of Isabella, and is about to be condemned to death, when his mistress comes forward in person; thus resigning herself to the usurer to save the life of her lover. But the nobler nature of Tortesa now breaks forth; and, smitten with admiration of the lady's conduct, as well as convinced that her love for himself was feigned, he resigns her to Angelo – although now feeling and acknowledging for the first time that a fervent love has, in his own bosom, assumed the place of this misanthropic ambition which, hitherto, had alone actuated him in seeking her hand. Moreover, he endows Isabella with the lands of her father Falcone. The lovers are thus made happy. The usurer weds Zippa; and the curtain drops upon the promise of the Duke to honor the double nuptials with his presence.

This story, as we have given it, hangs better together (Mr Willis will pardon our modesty) and is altogether more easily comprehended, than in the words of the play itself. We have really put the best face upon the matter, and presented the whole in the simplest and clearest light in our power. We mean to say that 'Tortesa' (partaking largely, in this respect, of the drama of Cervantes and Calderon) is over-clouded – rendered misty – by a world of unnecessary and impertinent *intrigue*. This folly was adopted by the Spanish comedy, and is imitated by us, with the idea of imparting 'action,' 'business,' 'vivacity.' But vivacity, however desirable, can be attained in many other ways, and is dearly purchased, indeed, when the price is intelligibility.

The truth is that *cant* has never attained a more owl-like dignity than in the discussion of dramatic principle. A modern stage critic is nothing, if not a lofty contemner of all things simple and direct. He delights in mystery – revels in mystification – has transcendental notions concerning P. S. and O. P., and talks about 'stage business and stage effect,' as if he were discussing the differential calculus. For much of all this, we are indebted to the somewhat over-profound criticisms of Augustus William Schlegel.

But the *dicta* of common sense are of universal application, and, touching this matter of *intrigue*, if, from its superabundance, we are compelled, even in the quiet and critical *perusal* of a play, to pause frequently and reflect long – to re-read passages over and over again, for the purpose of gathering their bearing upon the whole – of maintaining in our mind a general connexion – what but fatigue can result from the exertion? How then when we come to the representation? – when these passages – trifling, perhaps, in themselves, but important when considered in relation to the plot – are hurried and blurred over in the stuttering enunciation of some miserable rantipole, or omitted altogether through the constitutional lapse of memory so peculiar to those lights of the age and stage, bedight (from being of no conceivable use) supernumeraries? For it must be borne in mind that these bits of *intrigue* (we use the term in the sense of the German critics) appertain generally, indeed altogether, to the after-thoughts of the drama – to the underplots – are met with, consequently, in the mouth of the lacquies and chamber-maids – and are thus consigned to the tender mercies of the *stellæ minores*. Of course we get but an imperfect idea of what is going on before our eyes. Action after action ensues whose mystery we cannot unlock without the little key which these barbarians have thrown away and lost. Our weariness increases in proportion to the number of these embarrassments, and if the play escape damnation at all, it escapes *in spite* of that intrigue to which, in nine cases out of ten, the author attributes his success, and which he will persist in valuing exactly in proportion to the misapplied labor it has cost him.

But dramas of this kind are said, in our customary parlance, to 'abound in *plot*.' We have never yet met any one, however, who could tell us what precise ideas he connected with the phrase. A mere succession of incidents, even the most spirited, will no more constitute a plot, than a multiplication of zeros, even the most infinite, will result in the production of a unit. This all will admit – but few trouble themselves to think farther. The common notion seems to be in favor of mere *complexity*; but a plot, properly understood, is perfect only inasmuch as we shall find ourselves unable to detach from it *or disarrange* any single incident involved, without *destruction* to the mass. This we say is the point of perfection – a point never yet attained, but not on that account unattainable. Practically, we may consider a plot as of high excellence, when no one of its component parts shall be susceptible of *removal* without *detriment* to the whole. Here, indeed, is a vast lowering of the demand – and with less than this no writer of refined taste should content himself.

As this subject is not only in itself of great importance, but will have at all points a bearing upon what we shall say hereafter, in the examination of various plays, we shall be pardoned for quoting from the 'Democratic Review' some passages (of our own) which enter more particularly into the rationale of the subject:

'All the Bridgewater treatises have failed in noticing the *great* idiosyncrasy in the Divine system of adaptation: – that idiosyncrasy which stamps the adaptation as divine, in distinction from that which is the work of merely human constructiveness. I speak of the complete *mutuality* of adaptation. For example: – in human constructions, a particular cause has a particular effect – a particular purpose brings about a particular object; but we see no reciprocity. The effect does not re-act upon the cause – the object does not change relations with the purpose. In Divine constructions, the object is either object or purpose as we choose to regard it, while the purpose is either purpose or object; so that we can never (abstractly – without concretion – without reference to facts of the moment) decide which is which.

'For secondary example: – In polar climates, the human frame, to maintain its animal heat, requires, for combustion in the capillary system, an abundant supply of highly azotized food, such as train oil. Again: – in polar climates nearly the sole food afforded man is the oil of abundant seals and whales. Now whether is oil at hand because imperatively demanded? or whether is it the only thing demanded because the only thing to be obtained? It is impossible to say – there is an absolute reciprocity of adaptation for which we seek in vain among the works of man.

'The Bridgewater tractists may have avoided this point, on

account of its apparent tendency to overthrow the idea of *cause* in general – consequently of a First Cause – of God. But it is more probable that they have failed to perceive what no one preceding them has, to my knowledge, perceived.

'The pleasure which we derive from any exertion of human ingenuity, is in the direct ratio of the *approach* to this species of reciprocity between cause and effect. In the construction of *plot*, for example, in fictitious literature, we should aim at so arranging the points, or incidents, that we cannot distinctly see, in respect to any one of them, whether that one depends from any one other or upholds it. In this sense, of course, perfection of plot is unattainable *in fact* – because Man is the constructor. The plots of God are perfect. The Universe is a plot of God.'

The pleasure derived from the contemplation of the unity resulting from plot, is far more intense than is ordinarily supposed, and, as in Nature we meet with no such combination of *incident*, appertains to a very lofty region of the ideal. In speaking thus we have not said that plot is more than an adjunct to the drama – more than a perfectly distinct and separable source of pleasure. It is *not* an essential. In its intense artificiality it may even be conceived injurious in a certain degree (unless constructed with consummate skill) to that real *life-likeness* which is the soul of the drama of character. Good dramas have been written with very little plot – capital dramas might be written with none at all. Some plays of high merit, having plot, abound in irrelevant incident – in incident, we mean, which could be displaced or removed altogether without effect upon the plot itself, and yet are by no means objectionable as dramas; and for this reason – that the incidents are *evidently* irrelevant – *obviously* episodical. Of their digressive nature the spectator is so immediately aware, that he views them, as they arise, in the simple light of interlude, and does not fatigue his attention by attempting to establish for them a connexion, or more than an illustrative connexion, with the great interests of the subject. Such are the plays of Shakespeare. But all this is very different from *that* irrelevancy of intrigue which disfigures and very usually damns the work of the unskilful artist. With him the great error lies in *inconsequence*. Underplot is piled upon underplot, (the very word is a paradox,) and all to no purpose – *to no end*. The interposed incidents have no ultimate effect upon the main ones. They may hang upon the mass – they may even coalesce with it, or, as in some intricate cases, they may be so intimately blended as to be lost amid the chaos which they have been instrumental in bringing about – but still they have no portion in the plot, which exists, if at all, independently of their influence. Yet the *attempt* is made by the author to establish and demonstrate a dependence – an identity; and it is the *obviousness of this attempt* which is the cause of weariness in the spectator, who, of course, cannot at once see that his attention is challenged to no purpose – that intrigues so obtrusively forced upon it, are to be found, in the end, without effect upon the leading interests of the play.

'Tortesa' will afford us plentiful examples of this irrelevancy of intrigue – of this misconception of the nature and of the capacities of plot. We have said that our digest of the story is more easy of comprehension than the detail of Mr Willis. If so, it is because we have forborne to give such portions as had no influence upon the whole. These served but to embarrass the narrative and fatigue the attention. How much was irrelevant is shown by the brevity of the space in which we have recorded, somewhat at length, all the influential incidents of a drama of five acts. There is scarcely a scene in which is not to be found the germ of an underplot – a germ, however, which seldom proceeds beyond the condition of a bud, or, if so fortunate as to swell into a flower, arrives, in no single instance, at the dignity of fruit. Zippa, a lady altogether without character (dramatic) is the most pertinacious of all conceivable concoctors of plans never to be matured – of vast designs that terminate in nothing – of *cul-de-sac* machinations. She plots in one page and counterplots in the next. She schemes her way from P. S. to O. P., and intrigues perseveringly from the footlights to the slips. A very singular instance of the inconsequence of her manœuvres is found towards the conclusion of the play. The whole of the second scene, (occupying five pages,) in the fifth act, is obviously introduced for the purpose of giving her information, through Tomaso's means of Angelo's arrest for the murder of

Isabella. Upon learning his danger she rushes from the stage to be present at the trial, exclaiming that her evidence can save his life. We, the audience, of course applaud, and now look with interest to her movements in the scene of the judgment hall. She, Zippa, we think, is somebody after all; she will be the means of Angelo's salvation; she will thus be the chief unraveller of the plot. All eyes are bent, therefore, upon Zippa – but alas, upon the point at issue, Zippa does not so much as open her mouth. It is scarcely too much to say that not a single action of this impertinent little busy-body has any real influence upon the play : – yet she appears upon every occasion – appearing only to perplex.

Similar things abound; we should not have space even to allude to them all. The whole conclusion of the play is supererogatory. The immensity of pure *fuss* with which it is overloaded, forces us to the reflection that all of it might have been avoided by one word of explanation to the duke – an amiable man who admires the talent of Angelo, and who, to prevent *Isabella's marrying against her will*, had *previously* offered to free Falcone of his bonds to the usurer. That he would free him *now*, and thus set all matters straight, the spectator cannot doubt for an instant, and he can conceive no better reason why explanations are *not* made, than that Mr Willis does not think proper they should be. In fact, the whole drama is exceedingly ill *motivirt*.

We have already mentioned in inadvertence, in the fourth Act, where Isabella is made to escape from the sanctuary through the midst of guards who prevented the ingress of Angelo. Another occurs where Falcone's conscience is made to reprove him, upon the appearance of his daughter's supposed ghost, for having occasioned her death by forcing her to marry against her will. The author had forgotten that Falcone submitted to the wedding, after the duke's interposition, only upon Isabella's assurance *that she really loved the usurer*. In the third Scene, too, of the first Act, the imagination of the spectator is no doubt a little taxed, when he finds Angelo, in the first moment of his introduction to the palace of Isabella, commencing her portrait by laying on color after color, before he has made any attempt at an outline. In the last Act, moreover, Tortesa gives to Isabella a deed.

'Of the Falcone palaces and lands,
And all the money forfeit by Falcone.'

This is a terrible blunder, and the more important as upon this act of the usurer depends the development of his new-born sentiments of honor and virtue – depends, in fact, the most salient point of the play. Tortesa, we say, gives to Isabella the lands forfeited by Falcone; but Tortesa was surely not very generous in giving what, clearly, was not his own to give. Falcone had *not forfeited* the deed, which had been restored to him by the usurer, and which was then in his (Falcone's) possession. Hear Tortesa:

'He put it in the bond,
That if, by any humor of my own,
Or accident that came not from himself,
Or from his daughter's will, the match were marred,
His tenure stood intact.'

Now Falcone is still resolute for the match; but this new generous 'humor' of Tortesa induces him (Tortesa) to decline it. Falcone's tenure is then intact; he retains the deed, the usurer is giving away property not his own.

As a drama of character, 'Tortesa' is by no means open to so many objections as when we view it in the light of its plot; but it is still faulty. The merits are so exceedingly negative, that it is difficult to say anything about them. The Duke is nobody; Falcone, nothing; Zippa, less than nothing. Angelo may be regarded simply as the medium through which Mr Willis conveys to the reader his own glowing feelings – his own refined and delicate fancy – (delicate, yet bold) – his own rich voluptuousness of sentiment – a voluptuousness which would offend in almost any other language than that in which it is so skilfully apparelled. Isabella is – the heroine of the Hunchback. The revolution in the character of Tortesa – or rather the final triumph of his innate virtue – is a dramatic point far older than the hills. It may be observed, too, that although the representation of no human character should be quarrelled with for its inconsistency, we yet require that the inconsistencies be not absolute antagonisms to the extent of neutralization: they may be permitted to be oils and waters, but they must not be alkalies and acids. When, in the course of the *dénouement*, the usurer bursts forth into an eloquence virtue-inspired, we cannot sympathize very heartily in his fine speeches, since they proceed from the mouth of the self-same egotist who, urged by a disgusting vanity, uttered so many sotticisms (about his fine legs, &c.) in the earlier passages of the play. Tomaso is, upon the whole, the best personage. We recognise some originality in his conception, and conception was seldom more admirably carried out.

One or two observations at random. In the third scene of the fifth Act, Tomaso, the buffoon, is made to assume paternal authority over Isabella, (as usual, without sufficient purpose,) by virtue of a law which Tortesa thus expounds:

> 'My gracious liege, there is a law in Florence,
> That if a father, for no guilt or shame,
> Disown and shut his door upon his daughter,
> She is the child of him who succors her,
> Who, by the shelter of a single night,
> Becomes endowed with the authority
> Lost by the other.'

No one, of course, can be made to believe that any such stupid law as this ever existed either in Florence or Timbuctoo; but, on the ground *que le vrai n'est pas toujours le vraisemblable*,[6] we say that even its real existence would be no justification of Mr Willis. It has an air of the far-fetched – of the desperate – which a fine taste will avoid as a pestilence. Very much of the same nature is the attempt of Tortesa to extort a second bond from Falcone. The evidence which convicts Angelo of murder is ridiculously frail. The idea of Isabella's assuming the place of the portrait, and so deceiving the usurer, is not only glaringly improbable, but seems adopted from the 'Winter's Tale.' But in this latter play, the deception is at least possible, for the human figure but imitates a statue. What, however, are we to make of Mr W.'s stage direction about the back wall's being 'so arranged as to form a natural ground for the picture?' Of course, the very slightest movement of Tortesa (and he makes many) would have annihilated the illusion by disarranging the perspective; and in no manner could this latter have been arranged at all for more than one particular point of view – in other words, for more than one particular person in the whole audience. The 'asides,' moreover, are unjustifiably frequent. The prevalence of this folly (of speaking aside) detracts as much from the acting merit of our drama generally, as any other inartistic-ality. It utterly destroys veri-similitude. People are not in the habit of soliloquizing aloud – at least, not to any positive extent; and why should an author have to be told, what the slightest reflec-tion would teach him, that an audience, by dint of no imagination, can or will conceive that what is sonorous in their own ears at the distance of fifty feet, cannot be heard by an actor at the distance of one or two?

Having spoken thus of 'Tortesa' – in terms of nearly unmiti-gated censure – our readers may be surprised to hear us say that we think highly of the drama as a whole – and have little hesita-tion in ranking it before most of the dramas of Sheridan Knowles. Its leading faults are those of the modern drama generally – they are not peculiar to itself – while its great merits *are*. If in support of our opinion, we do not cite points of commendation, it is be-cause those form the mass of the work. And were we to speak of fine passages, we should speak of the entire play. Nor by 'fine passages' do we mean passages of merely fine language, embody-ing fine sentiment, but such as are replete with truthfulness, and teem with the loftiest qualities of the dramatic art. *Points* – capital points abound; and these have far more to do with the general excellence of a play, than a too speculative criticism has been willing to admit. Upon the whole, we are proud of 'Tortesa' – and here again, for the fiftieth time at least, record our warm admira-tion of the abilities of Mr Willis.

We proceed now to Mr Longfellow's

SPANISH STUDENT.

The reputation of its author as a poet, and as a graceful writer of prose, is, of course, long and deservedly established – but as a dramatist he was unknown before the publication of this play. Upon its original appearance, in 'Graham's Magazine,' the general opinion was greatly in favor – if not exactly of 'The Spanish Student' – at all events of the writer of Outre-Mer. But this general opinion is the most equivocal thing in the world. It is never self-formed. It has very seldom indeed an original development. In regard to the work of an already famous or infamous author it decides, to be sure, with a laudable promptitude; making up all the mind that it has, by reference to the reception of the author's immediately previous publication; – making up thus the ghost of a mind *pro tem.* – a species of critical shadow, that fully answers, nevertheless, all the purposes of a substance itself, until the substance itself shall be forthcoming. But, beyond this point, the general opinion can only be considered that of the public, as a man may call a book *his*, having bought it. When a new writer arises, the shop of the true, thoughtful, or critical opinion, is not simultaneously thrown away – is not immediately set up. Some weeks elapse; and, during this interval, the public, at a loss where to procure an opinion of the *débutant*, have necessarily no opinion of him at all, for the nonce.

The popular voice, then, which ran so much in favor of 'The Spanish Student,' upon its original issue, should be looked upon as merely the ghost *pro tem.* – as based upon critical decisions respecting the previous works of the author – as having reference in no manner to 'The Spanish Student' itself – and thus as utterly meaningless and valueless *per se*.

The few – by which we mean those who think, in contradistinction from the many who think they think – the few who think at first hand, and thus twice before speaking at all – these received the play with a commendation somewhat less *prononcée* – somewhat more guardedly qualified – than Professor Longfellow might have desired, or may have been taught to expect. Still the composition was approved upon the whole. The few words of censure were very far, indeed, from amounting to condemnation. The chief defect insisted upon, was the feebleness of the *dénouement*, and, generally, of the concluding scenes, as compared with the opening passages. We are not sure, however, that anything like detailed criticism has been attempted in the case – nor do we propose now to attempt it. Nevertheless, the work has interest, not only within itself, but as the first dramatic effort of an author who has remarkably succeeded in almost every other department of light literature than that of the drama. . . .[7]

The 'Spanish Student' has an unfortunate beginning, in a most unpardonable, and yet, to render the matter worse, in a most indispensable 'Preface:'

'The subject of the following play,' says Mr Longfellow, 'is taken in part from the beautiful play of Cervantes, La Gitanilla. To this source, however, I am indebted for the main incident only, the love of a Spanish student for a Gypsy girl, and the name of the heroine, Preciosa. I have not followed the story in any of its details. In Spain this subject has been twice handled dramatically; first by Juan Perez de Montalvan, in La Gitanilla, and afterwards by Antonio de Solís y Rivadeneira in La Gitanilla de Madrid. The same subject has also been made use of by Thomas Middleton, an English dramatist of the seventeenth century. His play is called The Spanish Gypsy. The main plot is the same as in the Spanish pieces; but there runs through it a tragic underplot of the loves of Rodrigo and Doña Clara, which is taken from another tale of Cervantes, La Fuerza de la Sangre. The reader who is acquainted with La Gitanilla of Cervantes, and the plays of Montalvan, Solis, and Middleton, will perceive that my treatment of the subject differs entirely from theirs.'

Now the authorial originality, properly considered, is threefold. There is, first, the originality of the general thesis; secondly, that of the several incidents, or thoughts, by which the thesis is developed; and, thirdly, that of manner, or tone, by which means alone, an old subject, even when developed through hackneyed incidents, or thoughts, may be made to produce a fully original effect – which, after all, is the end truly in view.

But originality, as it is one of the highest, is also one of the rarest of merits. In America it is especially, and very remarkably rare: – this through causes sufficiently well understood. We are content per force, therefore, as a general thing, with either of the lower branches of originality mentioned above, and would regard with high favor indeed any author who should supply the great desideratum in combining the three. Still the three should be combined; and from whom, if not from such men as Professor

Longfellow – if not from those who occupy the chief niches in our Literary Temple – shall we expect the combination? But in the present instance, what has Professor Longfellow accomplished? Is he original at any one point? Is he original in respect to the first and most important of our three divisions? 'The *subject* of the following play,' he says himself, 'is taken *in part* from the beautiful play of Cervantes, La Gitanilla.' 'To this source, however, I am indebted for the main incident *only*, the love of the Spanish student for a Gipsy girl, and the name of the heroine, Preciosa.'

The Italics are our own, and the words Italicized involve an obvious contradiction. We cannot understand how 'the love of the Spanish student for the Gipsy girl' can be called an 'incident,' or even a 'main incident,' at all. In fact, this love – this discordant and therefore eventful or incidentful love – is the true *thesis* of the drama of Cervantes. It is this anomalous 'love' which originates the incidents by means of which, itself, this 'love,' the thesis, is developed. Having based his play, then, upon this 'love,' we cannot admit his claim to originality upon our first count; nor has he any right to say that he has adopted his 'subject' 'in part.' It is clear that he has adopted it altogether. Nor would he have been entitled to claim originality of subject, even had he based his story upon *any variety* of love arising between parties naturally separated by prejudices of *caste* – such, for example, as those which divide the Brahmin from the Pariah, the Ammonite from the African, or even the Christian from the Jew. For here in its ultimate analysis, is the real thesis of the Spaniard. But when the drama is founded, not merely upon this general thesis, but upon this general thesis in the identical application given it by Cervantes – that is to say, upon the prejudice of *caste* exemplified in the case of the Catholic, and this Catholic a Spaniard, and this Spaniard a student, and this student loving a Gipsy, and this Gipsy a dancing-girl, and this dancing-girl bearing the name Preciosa – we are not altogether prepared to be informed by Professor Longfellow that he is indebted for an 'incident only' to the 'beautiful Gitanilla of Cervantes.'

Whether our author is original upon our second and third

points – in the true incidents of his story, or in the manner and *tone* of their handling – will be more distinctly seen as we proceed.

It is to be regretted that 'The Spanish Student' was not sub-entitled 'A Dramatic Poem,' rather than 'A Play.' The former title would have more fully conveyed the intention of the poet; for, of course, we shall not do Mr Longfellow the injustice to suppose that his design has been, in any respect, *a play*, in the ordinary acceptation of the term. Whatever may be its merits in a merely poetical view, 'The Spanish Student' could not be endured upon the stage.

Its plot runs thus: – Preciosa, the daughter of a Spanish gentleman, is stolen, while an infant, by Gipsies; brought up as his own daughter, and as a dancing-girl, by a gipsy leader, Crusado; and by him betrothed to a young Gipsy, Bartolomé. At Madrid, Preciosa loves and is beloved by Victorian, a student of Alcalá, who resolves to marry her, notwithstanding her *caste*, rumors involving her purity, the dissuasions of his friends, and his betrothal to an heiress of Madrid. Preciosa is also sought by the Count of Lara, a *roué*. She rejects him. He forces his way into her chamber, and is there seen by Victorian, who, misin-terpreting some words overheard, doubts the fidelity of his mis-tress, and leaves her in anger, after challenging the Count of Lara. In the duel, the Count receives his life at the hands of Victorian; declares his ignorance of the understanding between Victorian and Preciosa; boasts of favors received from the latter; and, to make good his words, produces a ring which she gave him, he asserts, as a pledge of her love. This ring is a duplicate of one previously given the girl by Victorian, and known to have been so given, by the Count. Victorian mistakes it for his own, be-lieves all that has been said, and abandons the field to his rival, who, immediately afterwards, while attempting to procure access to the Gipsy, is assassinated by Bartolomé. Meanwhile, Victorian, wandering through the country, reaches Guadarrama. Here he receives a letter from Madrid, disclosing the treachery practised by Lara, and telling that Preciosa, rejecting his addresses, had been, through his instrumentality hissed from the stage, and now again roamed with the Gipsies. He goes in search of her; finds her in a wood near Guadarrama; approaches her, disguising his voice; she recognises him, pretending she does not, and unaware that he knows her innocence; a conversation of *équivoques* ensues; he sees his ring upon her finger; offers to purchase it; she refuses to part with it; a full *éclaircissement* takes place at this juncture, a servant of Victorian's arrives with 'news from court,' giving the first intimation of the true parentage of Preciosa. The lovers set out, forthwith, for Madrid, to see the newly-discovered father. On the route, Bartolomé dogs their steps; fires at Preciosa; misses her; the shot is returned; he falls; and 'The Spanish Student' is concluded.

This plot, however, like that of 'Tortesa,' looks better in our naked digest than amidst the details which develope only to disfigure it. The reader of the play itself will be astonished, when he remembers the name of the author, at the inconsequence of the incidents – at the utter want of skill – of art – manifested in their conception and introduction. In dramatic writing, no principle is more clear than that nothing should be said or done which has not a tendency to develope the catastrophe, or the characters. But Mr Longfellow's play abounds in events and conversations that have no ostensible purpose, and certainly answer no end. In what light, for example, since we cannot suppose this drama intended for the stage, are we to regard the second scene of the second act, where a long dialogue between an Archbishop and a Cardinal is wound up by a dance from Preciosa? The Pope thinks of abolishing public dances in Spain, and the priests in question have been delegated to examine, personally, the proprieties or improprieties of such exhibitions. With this view, Preciosa is summoned and required to give a specimen of her skill. Now this, in a mere spectacle, would do very well; for here all that is demanded is an occasion or an excuse for a dance; but what business has it in a pure drama? or in what regard does it further the end of a dramatic poem, intended only to be read? In the same manner, the whole of Scene the eighth, in the same act, is occupied with six lines of stage directions, as follows:

The Theatre. The orchestra plays the Cachuca. Sound of castanets behind the scenes. The curtain rises and discovers Preciosa in the attitude of commencing the dance. The Cachuca. Tumult. Hisses. Cries of Brava! and Aguera! She falters and pauses. The music stops. General confusion. Preciosa faints.

But the *inconsequence* of which we complain will be best exemplified by an entire scene. We take Scene the Fourth, Act the First:

An inn on the road to Alcalá. BALTASAR *asleep on a bench. Enter* CHISPA.

Chispa. And here we are, half way to Alcalá, between cocks and midnight. Body o' me! what an inn this is! The light out and the landlord asleep! Holá! ancient Baltasar!

Baltasar [*waking*]. Here I am.

Chispa. Yes, there you are, like a one-eyed alcade in a town without inhabitants. Bring a light, and let me have supper.

Baltasar. Where is your master?

Chispa. Do not trouble yourself about him. We have stopped a moment to breathe our horses; and if he chooses to walk up and down in the open air, looking into the sky as one who hears it rain, that does not satisfy my hunger, you know. But be quick, for I am in a hurry, and every one stretches his legs according to the length of his coverlet. What have we here?

Baltasar [*setting a light on the table*]. Stewed rabbit.

Chispa [*eating*]. Conscience of Portalegre! stewed kitten, you mean!

Baltasar. And a pitcher of Pedro Ximenes, with a roasted pear in it.

Chispa [*drinking*]. Ancient Baltasar, amigo! you know how to cry wine and sell vinegar. I tell you this is nothing but vino tinto of La Mancha, with a tang of the swine-skin.

Baltasar. I swear to you by Saint Simon and Judas, it is all as I say.

Chispa. And I swear to you by Saint Peter and Saint Paul, that it is no such thing. Moreover, your supper is like the hidalgo's dinner – very little meat and a great deal of table-cloth.

Baltasar. Ha! ha! ha!

Chispa. And more noise than nuts.

Baltasar. Ha! ha! ha! You must have your joke, Master Chispa. But shall I not ask Don Victorian in to take a draught of the Pedro Ximenes?

Chispa. No; you might as well say, 'Don't you want some?' to a dead man.

Baltasar. Why does he go so often to Madrid?

Chispa. For the same reason that he eats no supper. He is in love. Were you ever in love, Baltasar?

Baltasar. I was never out of it, good Chispa. It has been the torment of my life.

Chispa. What! are you on fire, too, old hay-stack? Why, we shall never be able to put you out.

Victorian [*without*]. Chispa!

Chispa. Go to bed, Pero Grullo, for the cocks are crowing.

Victorian. Ea! Chispa! Chispa!

Chispa. Ea! Señor. Come with me, ancient Baltasar, and bring water for the horses. I will pay for the supper to-morrow.

[*Exeunt.*]

Now here the question occurs – what is accomplished? – how has the subject been forwarded? We did not need to learn that Victorian was in love – that was known before; and all that we glean is that a stupid imitation of Sancho Panza drinks, in the course of two minutes, (the time occupied in the perusal of the scene,) a bottle of vino tinto, by way of Pedro Ximenes, and devours a stewed kitten in place of a rabbit.

In the beginning of the play this Chispa is the valet of Victorian; subsequently we find him the servant of another; and near the *dénouement,* he returns to his original master. No cause is assigned, and not even the shadow of an object is attained; the whole tergiversation being but another instance of the gross inconsequence which abounds in the play.

The author's deficiency of skill is especially evinced in the scene of the *éclaircissement* between Victorian and Preciosa. The former having been enlightened respecting the true character of the latter, by means of *a letter* received at Guadarrama, from a friend at Madrid, (how wofully inartistical is this!) resolves to go in search of her forthwith, and forthwith, also, discovers her in a wood close at hand. Whereupon he approaches, disguising *his voice*: – yes, we are required to believe that a lover may so disguise his voice from his mistress, as even to render his person

470

in full view, irrecognisable! He approaches, and each knowing the other, a conversation ensues under the hypothesis that each to the other is unknown – a very unoriginal, and, of course, a very silly source of *équivoque*, fit only for the gum-elastic imagination of an infant. But what we especially complain of here, is that our poet should have taken so many and so obvious pains to bring about this position of *équivoque*, when it was impossible that it could have served any other purpose than that of injuring his intended effect! Read, for example this passage:

> *Victorian.* I never loved a maid;
> For she I loved was then a maid no more.
> *Preciosa.* How know you that?
> *Victorian.* A little bird in the air
> Whispered the secret.
> *Preciosa.* There take back your gold!
> Your hand is cold like a deceiver's hand!
> There is no blessing in its charity!
> Make her your wife, for you have been abused;
> And you shall mend your fortunes mending hers.
> *Victorian.* How like an angel's speaks the tongue of woman,
> When pleading in another's cause her own!

Now here it is clear that if we understood Preciosa to be really ignorant of Victorian's identity, the 'pleading in another's cause her own,' would create a favorable impression upon the reader, or spectator. But the advice, – 'Make her your wife,' &c., takes an interested and selfish turn when we remember that she knows to whom she speaks.

Again when Victorian says,

> That is a pretty ring upon your finger,
> Pray give it me!

And when she replies:

> No, never from my hand
> Shall that be taken,

we are inclined to think her only an artful coquette, knowing, as we do, the extent of her knowledge; on the other hand, we should have applauded her constancy (as the author intended) had she been represented ignorant of Victorian's presence. The effect upon the audience, in a word, would be pleasant in place of disagreeable were the case altered as we suggest, while the effect upon Victorian would remain altogether untouched.

A still more remarkable instance of deficiency in the dramatic *tact* is to be found in the mode of bringing about the discovery of Preciosa's parentage. In the very moment of the *éclaircissement* between the lovers, Chispa arrives almost as a matter of course, and settles the point in a sentence:

> Good news from Court; Good news! Beltran Cruzado,
> The Count of the Calés is not your father,
> But your true father has returned to Spain
> Laden with wealth. You are no more a Gipsy.

Now here are three points: – first, the extreme baldness, platitude, and *independence* of the incident narrated by Chispa. The *opportune* return of the father (we are tempted to say the *excessively* opportune) stands by itself – has no relation to any other event in the play – does not appear to arise, in the way of *result*, from any incident or incidents that have arisen before. It has the air of a happy chance, of a God-send, of an ultra-accident, invented by the playwright by way of compromise for his lack of invention. *Nec Deus intersit*, &c. – but here the God has interposed, and the knot is laughably unworthy of the God.

The second point concerns the return of the father 'laden with wealth.' The lover has abandoned his mistress in her poverty, and while yet the words of his proffered reconciliation hang upon his lips, comes his own servant with the news that the mistress' father has returned 'laden with wealth.' Now, so far as regards the audience, who are behind the scenes and know the fidelity of the lover – so far as regards the audience, all is right; but the poet had no business to place his heroine in the sad predicament of being forced, provided she is not a fool, to suspect both the ignorance and the disinterestedness of the hero.

The third point has reference to the words – 'You are now no more a Gipsy.' The thesis of this drama, as we have already said, is love disregarding the prejudices of *caste*, and in the development of this thesis, the powers of the dramatist have been engaged, or should have been engaged, during the whole of the three Acts of the play. The interest excited lies in our admiration of the sacrifice, and of the love that could make it; but this interest immediately and disagreeably subsides when we find that the sacrifice has been made to no purpose. 'You are no more a Gipsy' dissolves the charm, and obliterates the whole impression which the author has been at so much labor to convey. Our romantic sense of the hero's chivalry declines into a complacent satisfaction with his fate.

We drop our enthusiasm, with the enthusiast, and jovially shake by the hand the mere man of good luck. But is not the latter feeling the more comfortable of the two? Perhaps so; but 'comfortable' is not exactly the word Mr Longfellow might wish applied to the end of his drama, and then why be at the trouble of building up an effect through a hundred and eighty pages, merely to knock it down at the end of the hundred and eighty-first?

We have already given, at some length, our conceptions of the nature of *plot* – and of that of 'The Spanish Student,' it seems almost superfluous to speak at all. It has nothing of construction about it. Indeed there is scarcely a single incident which has any necessary dependence upon any one other. Not only might we take away two-thirds of the whole without ruin – but without detriment – indeed with a positive benefit to the mass. And, even as regards the mere order of arrangement, we might with a very decided *chance* of improvement, put the scenes in a bag, give them a shake or two by way of shuffle, and tumble them out. The whole mode of collocation – not to speak of the feebleness of the incidents in themselves – evinces, on the part of the author, an utter and radical want of the adapting or constructive power which the drama so imperatively demands.

Of the unoriginality of the thesis we have already spoken; and now, to the unoriginality of the events by which the thesis is developed, we need do little more than allude. What, indeed, *could* we say of such incidents as the child stolen by gipsies – as her education as a *danseuse* – as her betrothal to a Gipsy – as her preference for a gentleman – as the rumors against her purity – as her persecution by a *roué* – as the inruption of the *roué* into her chamber – as the consequent misunderstanding between her and her lover – as the duel – as the defeat of the *roué* – as the receipt of his life from the hero – as his boasts of success with the girl – as her *ruse* of the duplicate ring – as the field, in consequence, abandoned by the lover – as the assassination of Lara while scaling the girl's bed-chamber – as the disconsolate peregrination of Victorian – as the *équivoque* scene with Preciosa – as the offering to purchase the ring and the refusal to part with it – as the 'news from court' telling of the Gipsy's true parentage – what *could* we say of all these ridiculous things, except that we have met them, each and all, some two or three hundred times before, and that they have formed, in a greater or less degree, the staple material of every Hop O'My Thumb tragedy since the flood? There is not an incident, from the first page of 'The Spanish Student' to the last and most satisfactory, which we would not undertake to find boldly, at ten minutes' notice, in some one of the thousand and one comedies of intrigue attributed to Calderon and Lope de Vega.

But if our poet is grossly unoriginal in his subject, and in the events which evolve it, may he not be original in his handling of *tone*? We really grieve to say that he is not, unless, indeed, we grant him the meed of originality for the peculiar manner in which he has jumbled together the quaint and stilted tone of the old English dramatists with the *dégagée* air of Cervantes. But this is a point upon which, through want of space, we must necessarily permit the reader to judge altogether for himself. We quote, however, a passage from the Second Scene of the first Act, by way of showing how very easy a matter it is to make a man discourse Sancho Panza:

Chispa. Albernuncio Satanas! and a plague upon all lovers who ramble about at night, drinking the elements, instead of sleeping

quietly in their beds. Every dead man to his cemetery, say I; and
every friar to his monastery. Now, here's my master Victorian, yesterday a cow-keeper and to-day a gentleman; yesterday a student
and to-day a lover; and I must be up later than the nightingale, for
as the abbot sings so must the sacristan respond. God grant he may
soon be married, for then shall all this serenading cease. Ay, marry,
marry, marry! Mother, what does marry mean? It means to spin,
to bear children, and to weep, my daughter! And, of a truth, there
is something more in matrimony than the wedding-ring. And now,
gentlemen, Pax vobiscum! as the ass said to the cabbages!

And, we might add, as an ass *only* should say.

In fact throughout 'The Spanish Student,' as well as throughout other compositions of its author, there runs a very obvious
vein of *imitation*. We are perpetually reminded of something we
have seen before – some old acquaintance in manner or matter;
and even where the similarity cannot be said to amount to
plagiarism, it is still injurious to the poet in the good opinion of
him who reads.

Among the minor defects of the play, we may mention the
frequent allusion to book incidents not generally known, and
requiring each a Note by way of explanation. The drama demands that everything be so instantaneously evident that he
who runs may read; and the only impression effected by these
Notes to a play is, that the author is desirous of showing his
reading.

We may mention, also, occasional tautologies – such as:

> 'Never did I behold thee so *attired*
> And *garmented* in beauty as to-night!'

Or –

> 'What we need
> Is the celestial fire to change the fruit
> Into *transparent* crystal, *bright and clear!*'

We may speak, too, of more than occasional errors of grammar.
For example, p. 23:

Did no one see thee? None, my love, but *thou.*

Here 'but' is not a conjunction, but a preposition, and governs *thee* in the objective. 'None but *thee*' would be right; meaning none *except* thee, *saving* thee.

At page 27, 'mayst' is somewhat incorrectly written 'may'st.'

At page 34 we have:

I have no other saint than *thou* to pray to.

Here authority and analogy are both against Mr Longfellow. 'Than' also is here a preposition governing the objective, and meaning *save*, or *except*. 'I have none other God than thee,' &c. See Horne Tooke. The Latin '*quam te*' is exactly equivalent. At page 80 we read:

'*Like thee* I am a captive, and *like thee*,
I have a gentle gaoler.'

Here 'like thee' (although grammatical of course) does not convey the idea. Mr L. does not mean that the speaker is *like* the bird itself, but that his *condition* resembles it. The true reading would thus be:

As *thou* I am a captive, and, *as thou*,
I have a gentle gaoler:

That is to say, *as thou art*, and *as thou hast*.

Upon the whole, we regret that Professor Longfellow has written this work, and feel especially vexed that he has committed himself by its republication. Only when regarded as a mere poem, can it be said to have merit of any kind. For, in fact, it is only when we separate the poem from the drama, that the passages we have commended as beautiful can be understood to have beauty. We are not too sure, indeed, that a 'dramatic poem' is not a flat contradiction in terms. At all events a man of true genius, (and such Mr L. unquestionably is,) has no business with these hybrid and paradoxical compositions. Let a poem be a poem only; let a play be a play and nothing more. As for 'The Spanish Student,' its thesis is unoriginal; its incidents are antique; its plot is no plot; its characters have no character: in short, it is little better than a play upon words, to style it 'A Play' at all.

Hazlitt

WILEY & PUTNAM'S LIBRARY OF CHOICE READING. NO.
XVII. THE CHARACTERS OF SHAKSPEARE. BY WILLIAM
HAZLITT.

THIS is one of the most interesting numbers of 'The Library'
yet issued. If anything *could* induce us to read anything more in
the way of commentary on Shakspeare, it would be the name of
Hazlitt prefixed. With his hackneyed theme he has done wonders,
and those wonders well. He is emphatically a critic, brilliant,
epigrammatic, startling, paradoxical, and suggestive, rather than
accurate, luminous, or profound. For purposes of mere amusement, he is the best commentator who ever wrote in English. At
all points, except, perhaps in fancy, he is superior to Leigh Hunt,
whom nevertheless he remarkably resembles. It is folly to compare him with Macaulay for there is scarcely a single point of
approximation, and Macaulay is by much the greater man.
The author of 'The Lays of Ancient Rome' has an intellect so
well balanced and so thoroughly proportioned, as to appear, in
the eyes of the multitude, much smaller than it really is. He
needs a few foibles to purchase him *éclat*. Now, take away the
innumerable foibles of Hunt and Hazlitt, and we should have
the anomaly of finding them more diminutive than we fancy
them while the foibles remain. Nevertheless, they are men of
genius still.

In all commentating upon Shakspeare, there has been a radical
error, never yet mentioned. It is the error of attempting to expound his characters – to account for their actions – to reconcile
his inconsistencies – not as if they were the coinage of a human
brain, but as if they had been actual existences upon earth. We
talk of Hamlet the man, instead of Hamlet the *dramatis persona*
– of Hamlet that God, in place of Hamlet that Shakspeare

created. If Hamlet had really lived, and if the tragedy were an accurate record of his deeds, from this record (with some trouble) we might, it is true, reconcile his inconsistences and settle to our satisfaction his true character. But the task becomes the purest absurdity when we deal only with a phantom. It is not (then) the inconsistencies of the acting man which we have as a subject of discussion – (although we proceed as if it were, and thus *inevitably* err,) but the whims and vacillations – the conflicting energies and indolences of the poet. It seems to us little less than a miracle, that this obvious point should have been overlooked.

While on this topic we may as well offer an ill-considered opinion of our own as to the *intention of the poet* in the delineation of the Dane. It must have been well known to Shakspeare, that a leading feature in certain more intense classes of intoxication, (from whatever cause,) is an almost irresistible impulse to counterfeit a farther degree of excitement than actually exists. Analogy would lead any thoughtful person to suspect the same impulse in madness – where beyond doubt it is manifest. This, Shakspeare *felt* – not thought. He felt it through his marvellous power of *identification* with humanity at large – the ultimate source of his magical influence upon mankind. He wrote of Hamlet as if Hamlet he were; and having, in the first instance, imagined his hero excited to partial insanity by the disclosures of the ghost – he (the poet) *felt* that it was natural he should be impelled to exaggerate the insanity.

The Philosophy of Composition

CHARLES DICKENS, in a note now lying before me, alluding to an examination I once made of the mechanism of 'Barnaby Rudge,' says – 'By the way, are you aware that Godwin wrote his "Caleb Williams" backwards? He first involved his hero in a web of difficulties, forming the second volume, and then, for the first, cast about him for some mode of accounting for what had been done.'

I cannot think this the *precise* mode of procedure on the part of Godwin – and indeed what he himself acknowledges, is not altogether in accordance with Mr Dickens' idea – but the author of 'Caleb Williams' was too good an artist not to perceive the advantage derivable from at least a somewhat similar process. Nothing is more clear than that every plot, worth the name, must be elaborated to its *dénouement* before anything be attempted with the pen. It is only with the *dénouement* constantly in view that we can give a plot its indispensable air of consequence, or causation, by making the incidents, and especially the tone at all points, tend to the development of the intention.

There is a radical error, I think, in the usual mode of constructing a story. Either history affords a thesis – or one is suggested by an incident of the day – or, at best, the author sets himself to work in the combination of striking events to form merely the basis of his narrative – designing, generally, to fill in with description, dialogue, or autorial comment, whatever crevices of fact, or action, may, from page to page, render themselves apparent.

I prefer commencing with the consideration of an *effect*. Keeping originality *always* in view – for he is false to himself who ventures to dispense with so obvious and so easily attainable a source of interest – I say to myself, in the first place, 'Of the innumerable effects, or impressions, of which the heart, the intellect, or (more generally) the soul is susceptible, what one shall I, on the present occasion, select?' Having chosen a novel, first, and secondly a vivid effect, I consider whether it can be best wrought by incident or tone – whether by ordinary incidents and peculiar tone, or the converse, or by peculiarity both of incident and tone – afterward looking about me (or rather within) for such combinations of event, or tone, as shall best aid me in the construction of the effect.

I have often thought how interesting a magazine paper might be written by any author who would – that is to say who could – detail, step by step, the processes by which any one of his compositions attained its ultimate point of completion. Why such a paper has never been given to the world, I am much at a loss to say – but, perhaps, the autorial vanity has had more to do with the omission than any one other cause. Most writers – poets in especial – prefer having it understood that they compose by a species of fine frenzy – an ecstatic intuition – and would positively shudder at letting the public take a peep behind the scenes, at the elaborate and vacillating crudities of thought – at the true purposes seized only at the last moment – at the innumerable glimpses of idea that arrived not at the maturity of full view – at the fully matured fancies discarded in despair as unmanageable – at the cautious selections and rejections – at the painful erasures and interpolations – in a word, at the wheels and pinions – the tackle for scene-shifting – the step-ladders and demon-traps – the cock's feathers, the red paint and the black patches, which, in ninety-nine cases out of the hundred, constitute the properties of the literary *histrio*.

I am aware, on the other hand, that the case is by no means common, in which an author is at all in condition to retrace the steps by which his conclusions have been attained. In general, suggestions, having arisen pell-mell, are pursued and forgotten in a similar manner.

For my own part, I have neither sympathy with the repugnance alluded to, nor, at any time the least difficulty in recalling to mind the progressive steps of any of my compositions; and, since the interest of an analysis, or reconstruction, such as I have considered a *desideratum*, is quite independent of any real or fancied interest in the thing analyzed, it will not be regarded as a breach of decorum on my part to show the *modus operandi* by which some one of my own works was put together. I select 'The Raven,' as most generally known. It is my design to render it manifest that no one point in its composition is referrible either to accident or intuition – that the work proceeded, step by step, to its completion with the precision and rigid consequence of a mathematical problem.

Let us dismiss, as irrelevant to the poem, *per se*, the circumstance – or say the necessity – which, in the first place, gave rise to the intention of composing *a* poem that should suit at once the popular and the critical taste.

We commence, then, with this intention.

The initial consideration was that of extent. If any literary work is too long to be read at one sitting, we must be content to dispense with the immensely important effect derivable from unity of impression – for, if two sittings be required, the affairs of the world interfere, and every thing like totality is at once destroyed. But since, *ceteris paribus*, no poet can afford to dispense with *any thing* that may advance his design, it but remains to be seen whether there is, in extent, any advantage to counterbalance the loss of unity which attends it. Here I say no, at once. What we term a long poem is, in fact, merely a succession of brief ones – that is to say, of brief poetical effects. It is needless to demonstrate that a poem is such, only inasmuch as it intensely excites, by elevating, the soul; and all intense excitements are, through a psychal necessity, brief. For this reason, at least one half of the 'Paradise Lost' is essentially prose – a succession of poetical excitements interspersed, *inevitably*, with corresponding depressions – the whole being deprived, through the extremeness of its length, of the vastly important artistic element, totality, or unity, of effect.

– It appears evident, then, that there is a distinct limit, as regards length, to all works of literary art – the limit of a single sitting – and that, although in certain classes of prose composition, such as 'Robinson Crusoe,' (demanding no unity,) this limit may be advantageously overpassed, it can never properly be overpassed in a poem. Within this limit, the extent of a poem may be made to bear mathematical relation to its merit – in other words, to the excitement or elevation – again in other words, to the degree of the true poetical effect which it is capable of inducing; for it is clear that the brevity must be in direct ratio of the intensity of the intended effect: – this, with one proviso – that a certain degree of duration is absolutely requisite for the production of any effect at all.

Holding in view these considerations, as well as that degree of excitement which I deemed not above the popular, while not below the critical, taste, I reached at once what I conceived the proper *length* for my intended poem – a length of about one hundred lines. It is, in fact, a hundred and eight.

My next thought concerned the choice of an impression, or effect, to be conveyed: and here I may as well observe that, throughout the construction, I kept steadily in view the design of rendering the work *universally* appreciable. I should be carried too far out of my immediate topic were I to demonstrate a point upon which I have repeatedly insisted, and which, with the poetical, stands not in the slightest need of demonstration – the point, I mean, that Beauty is the sole legitimate province of the poem. A few words, however, in elucidation of my real meaning, which some of my friends have evinced a disposition to misrepresent. That pleasure which is at once the most intense, the most elevating, and the most pure, is, I believe, found in the contemplation of the beautiful. When, indeed, men speak of Beauty, they mean, precisely, not a quality, as is supposed, but an effect – they refer, in short, just to that intense and pure elevation of *soul* – *not* of intellect, or of heart – upon which I have commented, and which is experienced in consequence of contemplating 'the beautiful.' Now I designate Beauty as the province of the poem, merely because it is an obvious rule of Art that effects should be made to spring from direct causes – that objects should be attained through means best adapted for their attainment – no one as yet having been weak enough to deny that the peculiar elevation alluded to is *most readily* attained in the poem. Now the object, Truth, or the satisfaction of the intellect, and the object Passion, or the excitement of the heart, are, although attainable, to a certain extent, in poetry, far more readily attainable in prose. Truth, in fact, demands a precision, and Passion a *homeliness* (the truly passionate will comprehend me) which are absolutely antagonistic to that Beauty which, I maintain, is the excitement, or pleasurable elevation, of the soul. It by no means follows from any thing here said, that passion, or even truth, may not be introduced, and even profitably introduced, into a poem – for they may serve in elucidation, or aid the general effect, as do discords in music, by contrast – but the true artist will always contrive first, to tone them into proper subservience to the predominant aim, and, secondly, to enveil them, as far as possible, in that Beauty which is the atmosphere and the essence of the poem.

⸺ Regarding, then, Beauty as my province, my next question referred to the *tone* of its highest manifestation – and all experience has shown that this tone is one of *sadness*. Beauty of whatever kind, in its supreme development, invariably excites the sensitive soul to tears. Melancholy is thus the most legitimate of all the poetical tones.

—The length, the province, and the tone, being thus determined, I betook myself to ordinary induction, with the view of obtaining some artistic piquancy which might serve me as a key-note in the construction of the poem – some pivot upon which the whole structure might turn. In carefully thinking over all the usual artistic effects – or more properly *points*, in the theatrical sense – I did not fail to perceive immediately that no one had been so universally employed as that of the *refrain*. The universality of its employment sufficed to assure me of its intrinsic value, and spared me the necessity of submitting it to analysis. I considered it, however, with regard to its susceptibility of improvement, and soon saw it to be in a primitive condition. As commonly used, the *refrain*, or burden, not only is limited to lyric verse, but depends for its impression upon the force of monotone – both in sound and thought. The pleasure is deduced solely from the sense of identity – of repetition. I resolved to diversify, and so heighten, the effect, by adhering, in general, to the monotone of sound, while I continually varied that of thought: that is to say, I determined to produce continuously novel effects, by the variation of *the application* of the *refrain* – the *refrain* itself remaining, for the most part, unvaried.

These points being settled, I next bethought me of the *nature* of my *refrain*. Since its application was to be repeatedly varied, it was clear that the *refrain* itself must be brief, for there would have been an insurmountable difficulty in frequent variations of application in any sentence of length. In proportion to the brevity of the sentence, would, of course, be the facility of the variation. This led me at once to a single word as the best *refrain*. –

The question now arose as to the *character* of the word. Having made up my mind to a *refrain*, the division of the poem into stanzas was, of course, a corollary: the *refrain* forming the close of each stanza. That such a close, to have force, must be sonorous and susceptible of protracted emphasis, admitted no doubt: and these considerations inevitably led me to the long *o* as the most sonorous vowel, in connection with *r* as the most producible consonant.

The sound of the *refrain* being thus determined, it became necessary to select a word embodying this sound, and at the same time in the fullest possible keeping with that melancholy which I had predetermined as the tone of the poem. In such a search it would have been absolutely impossible to overlook the word 'Nevermore.' In fact, it was the very first which presented itself.

The next *desideratum* was a pretext for the continuous use of the one word 'nevermore.' In observing the difficulty which I at once found in inventing a sufficiently plausible reason for its continuous repetition, I did not fail to perceive that this difficulty arose solely from the pre-assumption that the word was to be so continuously or monotonously spoken by *a human* being – I did not fail to perceive, in short, that the difficulty lay in the reconciliation of this monotony with the exercise of reason on the part of the creature repeating the word. Here, then, immediately arose the idea of a *non*-reasoning creature capable of speech; and, very naturally, a parrot, in the first instance, suggested itself, but was superseded forthwith by a Raven, as equally capable of speech, and infinitely more in keeping with the intended tone.

I had now gone so far as the conception of a Raven – the bird of ill omen – monotonously repeating the one word, 'Nevermore,' at the conclusion of each stanza, in a poem of melancholy tone, and in length about one hundred lines. Now, never losing sight of the object supremeness, or perfection, at all points, I asked myself – 'Of all melancholy topics, what, according to the universal understanding of mankind, is the most melancholy?' Death – was the obvious reply. 'And when,' I said, 'is this most melancholy of topics most poetical?' From what I have already explained at some length, the answer, here also, is obvious – 'When it most closely allies itself to Beauty: the death, then, of a beautiful woman is, unquestionably, the most poetical topic in the world – and equally is it beyond doubt that the lips best suited for such topic are those of a bereaved lover.'

I had now to combine the two ideas, of a lover lamenting his deceased mistress and a Raven continuously repeating the word 'Nevermore.' – I had to combine these, bearing in mind my design of varying, at every turn, the application of the word repeated; but the only intelligible mode of such combination is that of imagining the Raven employing the word in answer to the queries of the lover. And here it was that I saw at once the opportunity afforded for the effect on which I had been depending – that is to say, the effect of the variation of application. I saw that I could make the first query propounded by the lover – the first query to which the Raven should reply 'Nevermore' – that I could make this first query a commonplace one – the second less so – the third still less, and so on – until at length the lover, startled from his original nonchalance by the melancholy character of the word itself – by its frequent repetition – and by a consideration of the ominous reputation of the fowl that uttered it – is at length excited to superstition, and wildly propounds queries of a far different character – queries whose solution he has passionately at heart – propounds them half in superstition and half in that species of despair which delights in self-torture – propounds them not altogether because he believes in the prophetic or demoniac character of the bird (which, reason assures him, is merely repeating a lesson learned by rote) but because he experiences a phrenzied pleasure in so modeling his questions as to receive from the *expected* 'Nevermore' the most delicious because the most intolerable of sorrow. Perceiving the opportunity thus afforded me – or, more strictly, thus forced upon me in the progress of the construction – I first established in mind the climax, or concluding query – that query to which 'Nevermore' should be in the last place an answer – that in reply to which this word 'Nevermore' should involve the utmost conceivable amount of sorrow and despair.

Here then the poem may be said to have its beginning – at the end, where all works of art should begin – for it was here, at this point of my preconsiderations, that I first put pen to paper in the composition of the stanza :

'Prophet,' said I, 'thing of evil ! prophet still if bird or devil !
By that heaven that bends above us – by that God we both adore,
Tell this soul with sorrow laden, if within the distant Aidenn,
It shall clasp a sainted maiden whom the angels name Lenore –
Clasp a rare and radiant maiden whom the angels name Lenore.'
    Quoth the raven 'Nevermore.'

I composed this stanza, at this point, first that, by establishing the climax, I might the better vary and graduate, as regards seriousness and importance, the preceding queries of the lover – and, secondly, that I might definitely settle the rhythm, the metre, and the length and general arrangement of the stanza – as well as graduate the stanzas which were to precede, so that none of them might surpass this in rhythmical effect. Had I been able, in the subsequent composition, to construct more vigorous stanzas, I should, without scruple, have purposely enfeebled them, so as not to interfere with the climacteric effect.

And here I may as well say a few words of the versification. My first object (as usual) was originality. The extent to which this has been neglected, in versification, is one of the most unaccountable things in the world. Admitting that there is little possibility of variety in mere *rhythm*, it is still clear that the possible varieties of metre and stanza are absolutely infinite – and yet, *for centuries, no man, in verse, has ever done, or ever seemed to think of doing, an original thing.* The fact is, that originality (unless in minds of very unusual force) is by no means a matter, as some suppose, of impulse or intuition. In general, to be found, it must be elaborately sought, and although a positive merit of the highest class, demands in its attainment less of invention than negation.

Of course, I pretend to no originality in either the rhythm or metre of the 'Raven.' The former is trochaic – the latter is octameter acatalectic, alternating with heptameter catalectic repeated in the *refrain* of the fifth verse, and terminating with tetrameter catalectic. Less pedantically – the feet employed throughout (trochees) consist of a long syllable followed by a short: the first line of the stanza consists of eight of these feet – the second of seven and a half (in effect two-thirds) – the third of eight – the fourth of seven and a half – the fifth the same – the sixth three and a half. Now, each of these lines, taken individually, has been employed before, and what originality the 'Raven' has, is in their *combination into stanza*; nothing even remotely approaching this combination has ever been attempted. The effect of this originality of combination is aided by other unusual, and some altogether novel effects, arising from an extension of the application of the principles of rhyme and alliteration.

The next point to be considered was the mode of bringing together the lover and the Raven – and the first branch of this consideration was the *locale*. For this the most natural suggestion might seem to be a forest, or the fields – but it has always appeared to me that a close *circumscription of space* is absolutely necessary to the effect of insulated incident: – it has the force of a frame to a picture. It has an indisputable moral power in keeping concentrated the attention, and, of course, must not be confounded with mere unity of place.

I determined, then, to place the lover in his chamber – in a chamber rendered sacred to him by memories of her who had frequented it. The room is represented as richly furnished – this in mere pursuance of the ideas I have already explained on the subject of Beauty, as the sole true poetical thesis.

The *locale* being thus determined, I had now to introduce the bird – and the thought of introducing him through the window, was inevitable. The idea of making the lover suppose, in the first instance, that the flapping of the wings of the bird against the shutter, is a 'tapping' at the door, originated in a wish to increase, by prolonging, the reader's curiosity, and in a desire to admit the incidental effect arising from the lover's throwing open the door, finding all dark, and thence adopting the half-fancy that it was the spirit of his mistress that knocked.

I made the night tempestuous, first, to account for the Raven's seeking admission, and secondly, for the effects of contrast with the (physical) serenity within the chamber.

I made the bird alight on the bust of Pallas, also for the effect of contrast between the marble and the plumage – it being understood that the bust was absolutely *suggested* by the bird – the bust of *Pallas* being chosen, first, as most in keeping with the scholarship of the lover, and, secondly, for the sonorousness of the word, Pallas, itself.

About the middle of the poem, also, I have availed myself of the force of contrast, with a view of deepening the ultimate impression. For example, an air of the fantastic – approaching as nearly to the ludicrous as was admissible – is given to the Raven's entrance. He comes in 'with many a flirt and flutter.'

Not the *least obeisance made he* – not a moment stopped or stayed he,
But with *mien of lord or lady*, perched above my chamber door.

In the two stanzas which follow, the design is more obviously carried out: –

Then this ebony bird beguiling my sad fancy into smiling
By the *grave and stern decorum of the countenance it wore*,
'Though thy *crest be shorn and shaven* thou,' I said, 'art sure no craven,

Ghastly grim and ancient Raven wandering from the nightly shore –
Tell me what thy lordly name is on the Night's Plutonian shore?'
                    Quoth the Raven 'Nevermore.'

Much I marvelled *this ungainly fowl* to hear discourse so plainly
Though its answer little meaning – little relevancy bore;
For we cannot help agreeing that no living human being
Ever yet was blessed with seeing bird above his chamber door –
Bird or beast upon the sculptured bust above his chamber door,
                    With such name as 'Nevermore.'

The effect of the *dénouement* being thus provided for, I immediately drop the fantastic for a tone of the most profound seriousness : – this tone commencing in the stanza directly following the one last quoted, with the line,

But the Raven, sitting lonely on that placid bust, spoke only, etc.

From this epoch the lover no longer jests – no longer sees any thing even of the fantastic in the Raven's demeanor. He speaks of him as a 'grim, ungainly, ghastly, gaunt, and ominous bird of yore,' and feels the 'fiery eyes' burning into his 'bosom's core.' This revolution of thought, or fancy, on the lover's part, is intended to induce a similar one on the part of the reader – to bring the mind into a proper frame for the *dénouement* – which is now brought about as rapidly and as *directly* as possible.

With the *dénouement* proper – with the Raven's reply, 'Nevermore,' to the lover's final demand if he shall meet his mistress in another world – the poem, in its obvious phase, that of a simple narrative, may be said to have its completion. So far, every thing is within the limits of the accountable – of the real. A raven, having learned by rote the single word 'Nevermore,' and having escaped from the custody of its owner, is driven at midnight, through the violence of a storm, to seek admission at a window from which a light still gleams – the chamber-window of a student, occupied half in poring over a volume, half in dreaming of a beloved mistress deceased. The casement being thrown open at the fluttering of the bird's wings, the bird itself perches on the most convenient seat out of the immediate reach of the student, who, amused by the incident and the oddity of the visitor's demeanor, demands of it, in jest and without looking for a reply, its name. The raven addressed, answers with its customary word, 'Nevermore' – a word which finds immediate echo in the melancholy heart of the student, who, giving utterance aloud to certain thoughts suggested by the occasion, is again startled by the fowl's repetition of 'Nevermore.' The student now guesses the state of the case, but is impelled, as I have before explained, by the human thirst for self-torture, and in part by superstition, to propound such queries to the bird as will bring him, the lover, the most of the luxury of sorrow, through the anticipated answer 'Nevermore.' With the indulgence, to the extreme, of this self-torture, the narration, in what I have termed its first or obvious phase, has a natural termination, and so far there has been no overstepping of the limits of the real.

But in subjects so handled, however skilfully, or with however vivid an array of incident, there is always a certain hardness or nakedness, which repels the artistical eye. Two things are invariably required – first, some amount of complexity, or more properly, adaptation; and, secondly, some amount of suggestiveness – some under-current, however indefinite, of meaning. It is this latter, in especial, which imparts to a work of art so much of that *richness* (to borrow from colloquy a forcible term) which we are too fond of confounding with *the ideal*. It is the *excess* of the suggested meaning – it is the rendering this the upper instead of the under current of the theme – which turns into prose (and that of the very flattest kind) the so called poetry of the so called transcendentalists.

Holding these opinions, I added the two concluding stanzas of the poem – their suggestiveness being thus made to pervade all the narrative which has preceded them. The under-current of meaning is rendered first apparent in the lines –

'Take thy beak from out *my heart*, and take thy form from off
    my door !'
        Quoth the Raven 'Nevermore !'

It will be observed that the words, 'from out my heart,' involve the first metaphorical expression in the poem. They, with the answer, 'Nevermore,' dispose the mind to seek a moral in all that has been previously narrated. The reader begins now to regard the Raven as emblematical – but it is not until the very last line of the very last stanza, that the intention of making him emblematical of *Mournful and Never-ending Remembrance* is permitted distinctly to be seen:

And the Raven, never flitting, still is sitting, still is sitting,
On the pallid bust of Pallas, just above my chamber door;
And his eyes have all the seeming of a demon's that is dreaming,
And the lamplight o'er him streaming throws his shadow on the
    floor;
And my soul *from out that shadow* that lies floating on the floor
                 Shall be lifted – nevermore.

raven symbollic of never-ending yearning.

Song-writing

THERE are few cases in which mere popularity should be considered a proper test of merit; but the case of song-writing is, I think, one of the few. In speaking of song-writing, I mean, of course, the composition of brief poems with an eye to their adaptation for music in the vulgar sense. In this ultimate destination of the song proper, lies its essence – its genius. It is the strict reference to music – it is the dependence upon modulated expression – which gives to this branch of letters a character altogether *unique*, and separates it, in great measure and in a manner not sufficiently considered, from ordinary literature; rendering it independent of merely ordinary proprieties; allowing it, and in fact demanding for it, a wide latitude of Law; absolutely, insisting upon a certain wild license and *indefinitiveness* – an indefinitiveness recognized by every musician who is not a mere fiddler, as an important point in the philosophy of his science – as the *soul*, indeed, of the sensations derivable from its practice – sensations which bewilder while they enthral – and which would *not* so enthral if they did not so bewilder.

The sentiments deducible from the conception of sweet sound simply, are out of the reach of analysis – although referable, possibly, in their last result, to that merely mathematical recognition of *equality* which seems to be *the root of all Beauty*. Our impressions of harmony and melody in conjunction, are more readily analyzed; but one thing is certain – that the *sentimental* pleasure derivable from music, is nearly in the ratio of its indefinitiveness. Give to music any undue *decision* – imbue it with any very *determinate* tone – and you deprive it, at once, of its ethereal, its ideal, and, I sincerely believe, of its intrinsic and essential character. You dispel its dream-like luxury: – you dissolve the atmosphere of the mystic in which its whole nature is bound up: – you exhaust it of its breath of faëry. It then becomes a tangible and easily appreciable thing – a conception of the earth, earthy. It will not, to be sure, lose *all* its power to please, but all that I consider the *distinctiveness* of that power. And to the *over*-cultivated talent, or to the unimaginative apprehension, this deprivation of its more delicate *nare* will be, not unfrequently, a recommendation. A *determinateness* of expression is sought – and sometimes by composers who should know better – is sought as a beauty, rather than rejected as a blemish. Thus we have, even from high authorities, attempts at absolute *imitation* in musical sounds. Who can forget, or cease to regret, the many errors of this kind into which some great minds have fallen, simply through over-estimating the triumphs of *skill.* Who can help lamenting the Battles of Prague? What man of taste is not ready to laugh, or to weep, over their 'guns, drums, trumpets, blunderbusses and thunder'? 'Vocal music,' says L'Abbate Gravina, 'ought to imitate the natural language of the human feelings and passions, rather than the warblings of Canary birds, which our singers, now-a-days, affect so vastly to mimic with their quaverings and boasted cadences.' This is true only so far as the 'rather' is concerned. If *any* music must imitate *any thing*, it were, undoubtedly, better that the imitation should be limited as Gravina suggests.

That *indefinitiveness* which is, at least, *one* of the essentials of true music, must, of course, be kept in view by the song-writer; while, by the critic, it should always be considered in his estimate of the *song*. It is, in the author, a consciousness – sometimes merely an instinctive appreciation, of this necessity for the indefinite, which imparts to all songs, rightly conceived, that free, affluent, and *hearty* manner, little scrupulous about niceties of phrase, which cannot be better expressed than by the hackneyed French word *abandonnement*, and which is so strikingly exemplified in both the serious and joyous ballads and carols of our old English progenitors. Wherever verse has been found most strictly married to music, this feature prevails. It is thus the essence of all antique song. It is the soul of Homer. It is the spirit of Anacreon. It is even the genius of Æschylus. Coming down to our own times, it is the vital principle in De

Béranger. Wanting this quality, no song-writer was ever truly popular, and, for the reasons assigned, no song-writer need ever expect to be so.

These views properly understood, it will be seen how baseless are the ordinary objections to songs proper, on the score of 'conceit,' (to use Johnson's word,) or of hyperbole, or on various other grounds tenable enough in respect to poetry not designed for music. The 'conceit,' for example, which some envious rivals of *Morris* have so much objected to –

> Her heart and morning broke together
> In the storm –

this 'conceit' is merely in keeping with the essential spirit of the song proper. To all reasonable persons it will be sufficient to say that the fervid, hearty, free-spoken songs of Cowley and of Donne – more especially of Cunningham, of Harrington and of Carew – abound in precisely similar things; and that they are to be met with, plentifully, in the polished pages of Moore and of Béranger, who introduce them with thought and retain them after mature deliberation.

Morris is, very decidedly, our best writer of songs – and, in saying this, I mean to assign him a high rank as *poet*. For my own part, I would much rather have written the best *song* of a nation than its noblest *epic*. One or two of Hoffman's songs have merit – but they are sad echoes of Moore, and even if this were not so (everybody knows that it *is* so) they are totally deficient in the real song-essence. *'Woodman spare that Tree'* and *'By the Lake where droops the Willow'* are compositions of which any poet, living or dead, might justly be proud. By these, if by nothing else, Morris is *immortal*. It is quite impossible to put down such things by sneers. The affectation of contemning them is of no avail – unless to render manifest the envy of those who affect the contempt. As mere *poems*, there are several of Morris's compositions equal, if not superior, to either of those just mentioned, but as *songs* I much doubt whether these latter have ever been surpassed. In quiet grace and unaffected tenderness, I know no American poem which excels the following:

Where Hudson's wave o'er silvery sand
   Winds through the hills afar,
Old Crow-nest like a monarch stands,
   Crowned with a single star.
And there, amid the billowy swells
   Of rock-ribbed, cloud-capped earth,
My fair and gentle Ida dwells,
   A nymph of mountain birth.

The snow-flake that the cliff receives –
   The diamonds of the showers –
Spring's tender blossoms, buds and leaves –
   The sisterhood of flowers –
Morn's early beam – eve's balmy breeze –
   Her purity define : –
But Ida's dearer far than these
   To this fond breast of mine.

My heart is on the hills; the shades
   Of night are on my brow.
Ye pleasant haunts and silent glades
   My soul is with you now.
I bless the star-crowned Highlands where
   My Ida's footsteps roam : –
Oh, for a falcon's wing to bear –
   To bear me to my home.

On Imagination

THE *pure Imagination* chooses, from *either Beauty or Deformity*, only the most combinable things hitherto uncombined; the compound, as a general rule, partaking, in character, of beauty, or sublimity, in the ratio of the respective beauty or sublimity of the things combined – which are themselves still to be considered as atomic – that is to say, as previous combinations. But, as often analogously happens in physical chemistry, so not unfrequently does it occur in this chemistry of the intellect, that the admixture of two elements results in a something that has nothing of the qualities of one of them, or even nothing of the qualities of either. . . . Thus, the range of Imagination is unlimited. Its materials extend throughout the universe. Even out of deformities it fabricates that *Beauty* which is at once its sole object and its inevitable test. But, in general, the richness or force of the matters combined; the facility of discovering combinable novelties worth combining; and, especially the absolute 'chemical combination' of the completed mass – are the particulars to be regarded in our estimate of Imagination. It is this thorough harmony of an imaginative work which so often causes it to be undervalued by the thoughtless, through the character of *obviousness* which is superinduced. We are apt to find ourselves asking *why* it is that these combinations have never been imagined before.

The Veil of the Soul

WERE I called on to define, very briefly, the term 'Art,' I should call it 'the reproduction of what the Senses perceive in Nature through the veil of the soul.' The mere imitation, however accurate, of what is in Nature, entitles no man to the sacred name of 'Artist.' Denner was no artist. The grapes of Zeuxis were inartistic – unless in a bird's-eye view; and not even the curtain of Parrhasius could conceal his deficiency in point of genius. I have mentioned 'the veil of the soul.' Something of the kind appears indispensable in Art. We can, at any time, double the true beauty of an actual landscape by half closing our eyes as we look at it. The naked Senses sometimes see too little – but then *always* they see too much.

The Poetic Principle (excerpts)

IN speaking of the Poetic Principle, I have no design to be either thorough or profound. While discussing, very much at random, the essentiality of what we call Poetry, my principal purpose will be to cite for consideration, some few of those minor English or American poems which best suit my own taste, or which, upon my own fancy, have left the most definite impression. By 'minor poems' I mean, of course, poems of little length. And here, in the beginning, permit me to say a few words in regard to a somewhat peculiar principle, which, whether rightfully or wrongfully, has always had its influence in my own critical estimate of the poem. I hold that a long poem does not exist. I maintain that the phrase, 'a long poem,' is simply a flat contradiction in terms.

I need scarcely observe that a poem deserves its title only inasmuch as it excites, by elevating the soul. The value of the poem is in the ratio of this elevating excitement. But all excitements are, through a psychal necessity, transient. That degree of excitement which would entitle a poem to be so called at all, cannot be sustained throughout a composition of any great length. After the lapse of half an hour, at the very utmost, it flags – fails – a revulsion ensues – and then the poem is, in effect, and in fact, no longer such.

There are, no doubt, many who have found difficulty in reconciling the critical dictum that the 'Paradise Lost' is to be devoutly admired throughout, with the absolute impossibility of maintaining for it, during perusal, the amount of enthusiasm which that critical dictum would demand. This great work, in fact, is to be regarded as poetical, only when, losing sight of that vital requisite in all works of Art, Unity, we view it merely as a series of minor poems. If, to preserve its Unity – its totality of effect or impression – we read it (as would be necessary) at a single sitting, the result is but a constant alternation of excitement and depression. After a passage of what we feel to be true poetry, there follows, inevitably, a passage of platitude which no critical pre-judgment can force us to admire; but if, upon completing the work, we read it again; omitting the first book – that is to say, commencing with the second – we shall be surprised at now finding that admirable which we before condemned – that damnable which we had previously so much admired. It follows from all this that the ultimate, aggregate, or absolute effect of even the best epic under the sun, is a nullity: – and this is precisely the fact.

In regard to the Iliad, we have, if not positive proof, at least very good reason, for believing it intended as a series of lyrics; but, granting the epic intention, I can say only that the work is based in an imperfect sense of art. The modern epic is, of the supposititious ancient model, but an inconsiderate and blindfold imitation. But the day of these artistic anomalies is over. If, at any time, any very long poem *were* popular in reality, which I doubt, it is at least clear that no very long poem will ever be popular again.

That the extent of a poetical work is, *ceteris paribus*, the measure of its merit, seems undoubtedly, when we thus state it, a proposition sufficiently absurd – yet we are indebted for it to the Quarterly Reviews. Surely there can be nothing in mere *size*, abstractly considered – there can be nothing in mere *bulk*, so far as a volume is concerned, which has so continuously elicited admiration from these saturnine pamphlets! A mountain, to be sure, by the mere sentiment of physical magnitude which it conveys, *does* impress us with a sense of the sublime – but no man is impressed after *this* fashion by the material grandeur of even 'The Columbiad.'[1] Even the Quarterlies have not instructed us to be so impressed by it. As *yet*, they have not *insisted* on our estimating Lamartine[2] by the cubic foot, or Pollok[3] by the pound – but what else are we to *infer* from their continual prating about 'sustained effort?' If, by 'sustained effort,' any little gentleman has accomplished an epic, let us frankly commend him for the effort – if this indeed be a thing commendable

– but let us forbear praising the epic on the effort's account. It is to be hoped that common sense, in the time to come, will prefer deciding upon a work of art, rather by the impression it makes, by the effect it produces, than by the time it took to impress the effect or by the amount of 'sustained effort' which had been found necessary in effecting the impression. The fact is, that perseverance is one thing, and genius quite another – nor can all the Quarterlies in Christendom confound them. By-and-by, this proposition, with many which I have been just urging, will be received as self-evident. In the meantime, by being generally condemned as falsities, they will not be essentially damaged as truths.

On the other hand, it is clear that a poem may be improperly brief. Undue brevity degenerates into mere epigrammatism. A *very* short poem, while now and then producing a brilliant or vivid, never produces a profound or enduring effect. There must be the steady pressing down of the stamp upon the wax. De Béranger has wrought innumerable things, pungent and spirit-stirring; but, in general, they have been too imponderous to stamp themselves deeply into the public attention; and thus, as so many feathers of fancy, have been blown aloft only to be whistled down the wind.

A remarkable instance of the effect of undue brevity in depressing a poem – in keeping it out of the popular view – is afforded by the following exquisite little Serenade:

> I arise from dreams of thee
>   In the first sweet sleep of night,
> When the winds are breathing low,
>   And the stars are shining bright;
> I arise from dreams of thee,
>   And a spirit in my feet
> Hath led me – who knows how? –
>   To thy chamber-window, sweet!
>
> The wandering airs, they faint
>   On the dark, the silent stream –
> The champak odours fail
>   Like sweet thoughts in a dream;

The nightingale's complaint,
    It dies upon her heart,
As I must die on thine,
    O, beloved as thou art!

O, lift me from the grass!
    I die, I faint, I fail!
Let thy love in kisses rain
    On my lips and eyelids pale.
My cheek is cold and white, alas!
    My heart beats loud and fast:
Oh! press it close to thine again,
    Where it will break at last!

Very few, perhaps, are familiar with these lines – yet no less a poet than Shelley is their author. Their warm, yet delicate and ethereal imagination will be appreciated by all – but by none so thoroughly as by him who has himself arisen from sweet dreams of one beloved to bathe in the aromatic air of a southern midsummer night.

One of the finest poems by Willis [4] – the very best, in my opinion, which he has ever written – has, no doubt, through this same defect of undue brevity, been kept back from its proper position not less in the critical than in the popular view.

THE shadows lay along Broadway,
    'Twas near the twilight-tide –
And slowly there a lady fair
    Was walking in her pride.
Alone walk'd she; but, viewlessly,
    Walk'd spirits at her side.

Peace charm'd the street beneath her feet,
    And Honour charm'd the air;
And all astir looked kind on her,
    And call'd her good and fair –
For all God ever gave to her
    She kept with chary care.

She kept with care her beauties rare
  From lovers warm and true –
For her heart was cold to all but gold,
  And the rich came not to woo –
But honour'd well are charms to sell,
  If priests the selling do.

Now walking there was one more fair –
  A slight girl, lily-pale;
And she had unseen company
  To make the spirit quail –
'Twixt Want and Scorn she walk'd forlorn,
  And nothing could avail.

No mercy now can clear her brow
  For this world's peace to pray;
For, as love's wild prayer dissolved in air,
  Her woman's heart gave way ! –
But the sin forgiven by Christ in Heaven
  By man is cursed alway !

In this composition we find it difficult to recognise the Willis who has written so many mere 'verses of society.' The lines are not only richly ideal, but full of energy; while they breathe an earnestness – an evident sincerity of sentiment – for which we look in vain throughout all the other works of this author.

While the epic mania – while the idea that, to merit in poetry, prolixity is indispensable – has, for some years past, been gradually dying out of the public mind, by mere dint of its own absurdity – we find it succeeded by a heresy too palpably false to be long tolerated, but one which, in the brief period it has already endured, may be said to have accomplished more in the corruption of our Poetical Literature than all its other enemies combined. I allude to the heresy of *The Didactic*. It has been assumed, tacitly and avowedly, directly and indirectly, that the ultimate object of all Poetry is Truth. Every poem, it is said, should inculcate a moral; and by this moral is the poetical merit of the work to be adjudged. We Americans especially have patronised this happy idea; and we Bostonians, very especially, have developed it in full. We have taken it into our heads that to write a poem simply for the poem's sake, and to acknowledge such to have been our design, would be to confess ourselves radically wanting in the true Poetic dignity and force : – but the simple fact is, that, would we but permit ourselves to look into our own souls, we should immediately there discover that under the sun there neither exists nor *can* exist any work more thoroughly dignified – more supremely noble than this very poem – this poem *per se* – this poem which is a poem and nothing more – this poem written solely for the poem's sake.

With as deep a reverence for the True as ever inspired the bosom of man, I would, nevertheless, limit, in some measure, its modes of inculcation. I would limit to enforce them. I would not enfeeble them by dissipation. The demands of Truth are severe. She has no sympathy with the myrtles. All *that* which is so indispensable in Song, is precisely all *that* with which *she* has nothing whatever to do. It is but making her a flaunting paradox, to wreathe her in gems and flowers. In enforcing a truth, we need severity rather than efflorescence of language. We must be simple, precise, terse. We must be cool, calm, unimpassioned. In a word, we must be in that mood which, as nearly as possible, is the exact converse of the poetical. He must be blind, indeed, who does not perceive the radical and chasmal differences between the truthful and the poetical modes of inculcation. He must be theory-mad beyond redemption who, in spite of these differences, shall still persist in attempting to reconcile the obstinate oils and waters of Poetry and Truth.

Dividing the world of mind into its three most immediately obvious distinctions, we have the Pure Intellect, Taste, and the Moral Sense. I place Taste in the middle, because it is just this position which, in the mind, it occupies. It holds intimate relations with either extreme; but from the Moral Sense is separated by so faint a difference that Aristotle has not hesitated to place some of its operations among the virtues themselves. Nevertheless, we find the *offices* of the trio marked with a sufficient distinction. Just as the Intellect concerns itself with Truth, so Taste informs us of the Beautiful while the Moral Sense is regardful of Duty. Of this latter, while Conscience teaches the obligation, and Reason the expediency, Taste contents herself with displaying the charms : – waging war upon Vice solely on the ground of her deformity – her disproportion – her animosity to the fitting, to the appropriate, to the harmonious – in a word, to Beauty.

An immortal instinct, deep within the spirit of man, is thus, plainly, a sense of the Beautiful. This it is which administers to his delight in the manifold forms, and sounds, and odours, and sentiments amid which he exists. And just as the lily is repeated in the lake, or the eyes of Amaryllis in the mirror, so is the mere oral or written repetition of these forms, and sounds, and colours, and odours, and sentiments, a duplicate source of delight. But this mere repetition is not poetry. He who shall simply sing, with however glowing enthusiasm, or with however vivid a truth of description, of the sights, and sounds, and odours, and colours, and sentiments, which greet *him* in common with all mankind – he, I say, has yet failed to prove his divine title. There is still a something in the distance which he has been unable to attain. We have still a thirst unquenchable, to allay which he has not shown us the crystal springs. This thirst belongs to the immortality of Man. It is at once a consequence and an indication of his perennial existence. It is the desire of the moth for the star. It is no mere appreciation of the Beauty before us – but a wild effort to reach the Beauty above. Inspired by an ecstatic prescience of the glories beyond the grave, we struggle, by multiform combinations among the things and thoughts of Time, to attain a portion of that Loveliness whose very elements, perhaps, appertain to eternity alone. And thus when by Poetry – or when by Music, the most entrancing of the Poetic moods – we find ourselves melted into tears – we weep then – not as the Abbate Gravina supposes – through excess of pleasure, but through a certain, petulant, impatient sorrow at our inability to grasp *now*, wholly, here on earth, at once and for ever, those divine and rapturous joys, of which *through* the poem, or *through* the music, we attain to but brief and indeterminate glimpses.

The struggle to apprehend the supernal Loveliness – this

struggle, on the part of souls fittingly constituted – has given to the world all *that* which it (the world) has ever been enabled at once to understand and to *feel* as poetic.

The Poetic Sentiment, of course, may develope itself in various modes – in Painting, in Sculpture, in Architecture, in the Dance – very especially in Music – and very peculiarly, and with a wide field, in the composition of the Landscape Garden. Our present theme, however, has regard only to its manifestation in words. And here let me speak briefly on the topic of rhythm. Contenting myself with the certainty that Music, in its various modes of metre, rhythm, and rhyme, is of so vast a moment in Poetry as never to be wisely rejected – is so vitally important an adjunct, that he is simply silly who declines its assistance, I will not now pause to maintain its absolute essentiality. It is in Music, perhaps, that the soul most nearly attains the great end for which, when inspired by the Poetic Sentiment, it struggles – the creation of supernal Beauty. It *may* be, indeed, that here this sublime end is, now and then, attained *in fact*. We are often made to feel, with a shivering delight, that from an earthly harp are stricken notes which *cannot* have been unfamiliar to the angels. And thus there can be little doubt that in the union of Poetry with Music in its popular sense, we shall find the widest field for the Poetic development. The old Bards and Minnesingers had advantages which we do not possess – and Thomas Moore,[5] singing his own songs, was, in the most legitimate manner, perfecting them as poems.

To recapitulate, then: – I would define, in brief, the Poetry of words as *The Rhythmical Creation of Beauty. Its* sole arbiter is Taste. With the Intellect or with the Conscience, it has only collateral relations. Unless incidentally, it has no concern whatever either with Duty or with Truth.

A few words, however, in explanation. *That* pleasure which is at once the most pure, the most elevating, and the most intense, is derived, I maintain, from the contemplation of the Beautiful. In the contemplation of Beauty we alone find it possible to attain that pleasurable elevation, or excitement, *of the soul*, which we recognise as the Poetic Sentiment, and which is so easily distinguished from Truth, which is the satisfaction of the Reason, or from Passion, which is the excitement of the heart. I make Beauty, therefore – using the word as inclusive of the sublime – I make Beauty the province of the poem, simply because it is an obvious rule of Art that effects should be made to spring as directly as possible from their causes: – no one as yet having been weak enough to deny that the peculiar elevation in question is at least *most readily* attainable in the poem. It by no means follows, however, that the incitements of Passion, or the precepts of Duty, or even the lessons of Truth, may not be introduced into a poem, and with advantage; for they may subserve, incidentally, in various ways, the general purposes of the work: – but the true artist will always contrive to tone them down in proper subjection to that *Beauty* which is the atmosphere and the real essence of the poem.

I cannot better introduce the few poems which I shall present for your consideration, than by the citation of the Proem to Mr Longfellow's 'Waif':

> The day is done, and the darkness
>   Falls from the wings of Night,
> As a feather is wafted downward
>   From an Eagle in his flight.
>
> I see the lights of the village
>   Gleam through the rain and the mist,
> And a feeling of sadness comes o'er me,
>   That my soul cannot resist;
>
> A feeling of sadness and longing,
>   That is not akin to pain,
> And resembles sorrow only
>   As the mist resembles the rain.
>
> Come, read to me some poem,
>   Some simple and heartfelt lay,
> That shall soothe this restless feeling,
>   And banish the thoughts of day.
>
> Not from the grand old masters,
>   Not from the bards sublime,

Whose distant footsteps echo
   Through the corridors of Time.

For, like strains of martial music,
   Their mighty thoughts suggest
Life's endless toil and endeavour;
   And to-night I long for rest.

Read from some humbler poet,
   Whose songs gushed from his heart,
As showers from the clouds of summer,
   Or tears from the eyelids start;

Who through long days of labour,
   And nights devoid of ease,
Still heard in his soul the music
   Of wonderful melodies.

Such songs have power to quiet
   The restless pulse of care,
And come like the benediction
   That follows after prayer.

Then read from the treasured volume
   The poem of thy choice,
And lend to the rhyme of the poet
   The beauty of thy voice.

And the night shall be filled with music,
   And the cares that infest the day,
Shall fold their tents, like the Arabs,
   And as silently steal away.

With no great range of imagination, these lines have been justly admired for their delicacy of expression. Some of the images are very effective. Nothing can be better than—

      – The bards sublime,
   Whose distant footsteps echo
   Down the corridors of Time.[6]

The idea of the last quatrain is also very effective. The poem, on the whole, however, is chiefly to be admired for the graceful *insouciance* of its metre, so well in accordance with the character of the sentiments, and especially for the *ease* of the general manner. This 'ease,' or naturalness, in a literary style, it has long been the fashion to regard as ease in appearance alone – as a point of really difficult attainment. But not so : – a natural manner is difficult only to him who should never meddle with it – to the unnatural. It is but the result of writing with the understanding, or with the instinct, that *the tone*, in composition, should always be that which the mass of mankind would adopt – and must perpetually vary, of course, with the occasion. The author who, after the fashion of 'The North American Review,' should be, upon *all* occasions, merely 'quiet,' must necessarily upon *many* occasions, be simply silly, or stupid; and has no more right to be considered 'easy,' or 'natural,' than a Cockney exquisite, or than the sleeping Beauty in the wax-works.

Among the minor poems of Bryant, none has so much impressed me as the one which he entitles 'June.' I quote only a portion of it :

> There, through the long, long summer hours,
>   The golden light should lie,
> And thick young herbs and groups of flowers
>   Stand in their beauty by.
> The oriole should build and tell
> His love-tale, close beside my cell;
>   The idle butterfly
> Should rest him there, and there be heard
> The housewife-bee and humming-bird.
>
> And what if cheerful shouts, at noon,
>   Come, from the village sent,
> Or songs of maids, beneath the moon,
>   With fairy laughter blent?
> And what, if in the evening light,
> Betrothed lovers walk in sight
>   Of my low monument?
> I would the lovely scene around
> Might know no sadder sight nor sound.

I know, I know I should not see
    The season's glorious show,
Nor would its brightness shine for me,
    Nor its wild music flow;
But if, around my place of sleep,
The friends I love should come to weep,
    They might not haste to go.
Soft airs, and song, and light, and bloom
Should keep them lingering by my tomb.

These to their softened hearts should bear
    The thought of what has been,
And speak of one who cannot share
    The gladness of the scene;
Whose part, in all the pomp that fills
The circuit of the summer hills,
    Is – that his grave is green;
And deeply would their hearts rejoice
To hear again his living voice.

The rhythmical flow, here, is even voluptuous – nothing could be more melodious. The poem has always affected me in a remarkable manner. The intense melancholy which seems to well up, perforce, to the surface of all the poet's cheerful sayings about his grave, we find thrilling us to the soul – while there is the truest poetic elevation in the thrill. The impression left is one of a pleasurable sadness. And if, in the remaining compositions which I shall introduce to you, there be more or less of a similar tone always apparent, let me remind you that (how or why we know not) this certain taint of sadness is inseparably connected with all the higher manifestations of true Beauty. ....[7]

From Alfred Tennyson – although in perfect sincerity I regard him as the noblest poet that ever lived – I have left myself time to cite only a very brief specimen. I call him, and *think* him the noblest of poets – *not* because the impressions he produces are, at *all* times, the most profound – *not* because the poetical excitement which he induces is, at *all* times, the most intense – but because it *is*, at all times, the most ethereal – in other words, the most elevating and the most pure. No poet is so little of the earth, earthy. What I am about to read is from his last long poem, 'The Princess':

> Tears, idle tears, I know not what they mean,
> Tears from the depth of some divine despair
> Rise in the heart, and gather to the eyes,
> In looking on the happy Autumn-fields,
> And thinking of the days that are no more.
>
> Fresh as the first beam glittering on a sail,
> That brings our friends up from the underworld,
> Sad as the last which reddens over one
> That sinks with all we love below the verge;
> So sad, so fresh, the days that are no more.
>
> Ah, sad and strange as in dark summer dawns
> The earliest pipe of half-awaken'd birds
> To dying ears, when unto dying eyes
> The casement slowly grows a glimmering square;
> So sad, so strange, the days that are no more.
>
> Dear as remember'd kisses after death,
> And sweet as those by hopeless fancy feign'd
> On lips that are for others; deep as love,
> Deep as first love, and wild with all regret;
> O Death in Life, the days that are no more.

Thus, although in a very cursory and imperfect manner, I have endeavoured to convey to you my conception of the Poetic Principle. It has been my purpose to suggest that, while this Principle itself is, strictly and simply, the Human Aspiration for Supernal Beauty, the manifestation of the Principle is always found in *an elevating excitement of the Soul* – quite independent of that passion which is the intoxication of the Heart – or of that Truth which is the satisfaction of the Reason. For, in regard to Passion, alas! its tendency is to degrade, rather than to elevate the Soul. Love, on the contrary – Love – the true, the divine Eros – the Uranian, as distinguished from the Dionæan Venus – is unquestionably the purest and truest of all poetical themes. And in regard to Truth – if, to be sure, through the attainment of a truth, we are led to perceive a harmony where none was apparent before, we experience, at once, the true poetical effect – but this effect is referable to the harmony alone, and not in the least degree to the truth which merely served to render the harmony manifest.

We shall reach, however, more immediately a distinct conception of what the true Poetry is, by mere reference to a few of the simple elements which induce in the Poet himself the true poetical effect. He recognises the ambrosia which nourishes his soul, in the bright orbs that shine in Heaven – in the volutes of the flower – in the clustering of low shrubberies – in the waving of the grain-fields – in the slanting of tall, Eastern trees – in the blue distance of mountains – in the grouping of clouds – in the twinkling of half-hidden brooks – in the gleaming of silver rivers – in the repose of sequestered lakes – in the star-mirroring depths of lonely wells. He perceives it in the songs of birds – in the harp of Æolus – in the sighing of the night-wind – in the repining voice of the forest – in the surf that complains to the shore – in the fresh breath of the woods – in the scent of the violet – in the voluptuous perfume of the hyacinth – in the suggestive odour that comes to him, at eventide, from far-distant, undiscovered islands, over dim oceans, illimitable and unexplored. He owns it in all noble thoughts – in all unworldly motives – in all holy impulses – in all chivalrous, generous, and self-sacrificing deeds. He feels it in the beauty of woman – in the grace of her step – in the lustre of her eye – in the melody of her voice – in her soft laughter – in her sigh – in the harmony of the rustling of her robes. He deeply feels it in her winning endearments – in her burning enthusiasms – in her gentle charities – in her meek and devotional endurances – but above all – ah, far above all – he kneels to it – he worships it in the faith, in the purity, in the strength, in the altogether divine majesty – of her *love*.

Let me conclude – by the recitation of yet another brief poem – one very different in character from any that I have before quoted. It is by Motherwell,[8] and is called 'The Song of the Cavalier.' With our modern and altogether rational ideas of the absurdity and impiety of warfare, we are not precisely in that frame of mind best adapted to sympathise with the sentiments, and thus to appreciate the real excellence of the poem. To do this fully, we must identify ourselves, in fancy, with the soul of the old cavalier.

> Then mounte! then mounte, brave gallants, all,
>   And don your helmes amaine:
> Deathe's couriers, Fame and Honour, call
>   Us to the field againe.
> No shrewish teares shall fill our eye
>   When the sword-hilt 's in our hand, –
> Heart-whole we 'll part, and no whit sighe
>   For the fayrest of the land;
> Let piping swaine, and craven wight,
>   Thus weepe and puling crye,
> Our business is like men to fight,
>   And hero-like to die!

Notes

As generations of enthusiastic readers attest, Poe's work can stand very well without notes. His topical allusions are few; literary references, like foreign words and phrases, generally make themselves clear in context; and Poe is sufficiently close to us in time to seem modern in his spelling, vocabulary, and punctuation. In the following notes, therefore, I have drawn attention only to passages whose meanings are not immediately available to the reader through context, or where Poe's own misquotations or faulty knowledge of foreign languages is likely to create misunderstanding. Mottos to his poems and stories are of sufficient significance to call for annotation in every case, but I have not glossed foreign words and phrases which are in common use, nor have I identified all of Poe's literary allusions. His erudition was often distinctly second-hand, but little if anything is contributed to our understanding of his work through detailed knowledge of the manner in which he came by his information, or the exact nature of his 'lapses'. References to works of the occult, the philosophical, and the pseudo-scientific in Poe's writing are often intended merely to create mood or credibility : to annotate all of them would result in notes of cumbersome length, and my aim in compiling this volume has been to allow Poe as much space as possible in which to speak for himself in the great variety of voices in which he spoke to his contemporaries. It is not, I think, an inappropriate way to treat the writings of a man who argued that the individual work of art should contain within itself 'everything necessary for its understanding'.

1. Poems

STANZAS

'STANZAS' was originally published without title in *Tamerlane and Other Poems* (1827), revised for the 1829 edition of the poems, and reprinted in that form in the *Broadway Journal* in 1845. Poe's epigraph is from Lord Byron's 'The Island'.

SONNET – TO SCIENCE

First published in *Al Aaraaf, Tamerlane, and Minor Poems* (1829), 'Sonnet – To Science' was revised for the 1831 edition, again for publication in the *Southern Literary Messenger* in 1836, and achieved its final form in the version Poe published in the *Broadway Journal* in 1845.

p. 53, 1. a tree nymph whose life was associated with an individual tree, and ended when the tree died.

p. 53, 2. a nymph associated with springs, rivers, and lakes.

AL AARAAF

'Al Aaraaf' is here printed in the 1845 version; it was first published in the poems of 1829, extensively revised for the 1831 edition, and published in the present form in *The Raven and Other Poems*. Poe completed only two of the four projected parts of the poem.

PART 1

p. 54, 1. 'A star was discovered by Tycho Brahe which appeared suddenly in the heavens – attained, in a few days, a brilliancy surpassing that of Jupiter – then as suddenly disappeared, and has never been seen since' (Poe). Poe derived his idea of the wandering star from Sale's translation of the Mohammedan Koran. 'Al Aaraaf' was the Mohammedan conception of the region between heaven and hell; appropriately, for Poe's purpose, it was also the name assigned by Arabian astronomers to the star discovered by Tycho Brahe in November 1572.

p. 54, 2. Nesace, the ruler of Al Aaraaf, personifies beauty in the poem; she has the power of penetrating infinity with her vision, and has been ordered by God to spread the powers of imaginative perception not only through her own realm, but throughout the lower orders as well.

p. 55, 3. 'On Santa Maura – olim Deucadia' (Poe). In this and succeeding references, Poe is quoting from the notes in Thomas Moore's Evenings in Greece.

p. 55, 4. 'Sappho' (Poe).

p. 55, 5. 'This flower is much noticed by Lewenhoeck and Tournefort. The bee, feeding upon its blossom, becomes intoxicated' (Poe). Poe's knowledge of botany – much of it of questionable validity – was derived almost entirely from secondary sources and is an excellent example of the delight he took in sporting borrowed 'erudition'.

p. 56, 6. 'The Chrysanthemum Peruvianum, or, to employ a better-known term, the turnsol – which turns continually towards the sun, covers itself, like Peru, the country from which it comes, with dewy clouds which cool and refresh its flowers during the most violent heat of the day. – B. De St. Pierre' (Poe).

p. 56, 7. 'There is cultivated in the king's garden at Paris, a species of serpentine aloes without prickles, whose large and beautiful flower exhales a strong odour of the vanilla, during the time of its expansion, which is very short. It does not blow till towards the month of July – you then perceive it gradually open its petals – expand them – fade and die. – St. Pierre' (Poe).

p. 56, 8. 'There is found, in the Rhone, a beautiful Lily of the Valisnerian kind. Its stem will stretch to the length of three or four feet – thus preserving its head above water in the dwellings of the river' (Poe).

p. 56, 9. 'The Hyacinth' (Poe).

p. 56, 10. 'It is a fiction of the Indians, that Cupid was first seen floating down the river Ganges – and that he still loves the cradle of his childhood' (Poe).

p. 56, 11. 'And golden vials full of odors which are the prayers of the saints. – *Rev. St. John*' (Poe).

p. 57, 12. 'The humanitarians held that God was to be understood as having a human form. – V*ide Clarke's Sermons*, vol. I, page 26, fol. edit.

'The drift of Milton's argument leads him to employ language which would appear, at first sight, to verge upon their doctrine; but it will be seen immediately, that he guards himself against the charge of having adopted one of the most ignorant errors of the dark ages of the church. – *Dr. Sumner's Notes on Milton's Christian Doctrine.*

'This opinion, in spite of many testimonies to the contrary, could never have been very general. Andeus, a Syrian of Mesopotamia, was condemned for the opinion, as heretical. He lived in the beginning of the fourth century. His disciples were called Anthropomorphites. – V*ide Du Pin.*

'Among Milton's minor Poems are these lines : –

> Dicite sacrorum præsides nemorum Deæ, &c.
> Quis ille primus cujus ex imagine
> Natura solers finxit humanum genus?
> Eternus, incorruptus, æquævus polo,
> Unusque et universus exemplar Dei. –

And afterwards

> Non cui profundum Cæcitas lumen dedit
> Dircæus augur vidit hunc alto sinu, &c.'

(Poe),

p. 57, 13.
> 'Seltsamen Tochter Jovis
> Seinem Schosskinde
> Der Phantasie.
>   – *Goethe*' (Poe).

Poe later used this quotation from Goethe's *Meine Göttin* as the motto for his *Tales of the Grotesque and Arabesque*. It translates,

> Strange daughter of Jove
> His darling
> Fantasy.

p. 57, 14. 'Sightless – too small to be seen. – Legge' (Poe).

p. 58, 15. 'I have often noticed a peculiar movement of the fireflies; – they will collect in a body and fly off, from a common centre, into innumerable radii' (Poe).

p. 58, 16. 'Therasæa, the island mentioned by Seneca, which in a moment arose from the sea to the eyes of astonished mariners' (Poe).

PART 2

p. 59, 1. 'Some star which, from the ruin'd roof
Of shak'd Olympus, by mischance, did fall.
– *Milton'* (Poe).

Poe has taken some liberties with Milton's text, 'On the Death of a Fair Infant Dying of a Cough'.

p. 59, 2. 'Voltaire, in speaking of Persepolis, says, "Je connois bien l'admiration qu'inspirent ces ruines – mais un palais érigé au pied d'une chaine des rochers stérils – peut-il être un chef d'œuvre des arts !" ' (Poe).

p. 59, 3. ' "Oh, the wave" – Ula Deguisi is the Turkish appellation, but, on its own shores, it is called Bahar Loth, or Almotanah. There were undoubtedly more than two cities engulfed in the "dead sea." In the valley of Siddim were five – Adrah, Zeboin, Zoar, Sodom and Gomorrah. Stephen of Byzantium mentions eight, and Strabo thirteen, (engulphed) – but the last is out of all reason.

'It is said (Tacitus, Strabo, Josephus, Daniel of St. Saba, Nau, Mandrell, Troilo, D'Arvieux) that after an excessive drought, the vestiges of columns, walls, &c. are seen above the surface. At *any* season, such remains may be discovered by looking down into the transparent lake, and at such distances as would argue the existence of many settlements in the space now usurped by the "Asphalites" ' (Poe).

p. 59, 4. 'Eyraco – Chaldea' (Poe).

p. 59, 5. 'I have often thought I could distinctly hear the sound of darkness as it stole over the horizon' (Poe).

NOTES

p. 60, 6. 'Fairies use flowers for their charactery. – *Merry Wives of Windsor*' (Poe).

p. 60, 7. 'In Scripture is this passage – "The sun shall not harm thee by day, nor the moon by night." It is perhaps not generally known that the moon, in Egypt, has the effect of producing blindness to those who sleep with the face exposed to its rays, to which circumstances the passage evidently alludes' (Poe).

p. 61, 8. This is the first use which Poe makes of this favourite name; here Ligeia is the goddess of harmony, invoked by Nesace as an emissary to the lower orders of creation.

p. 61, 9. 'The albatross is said to sleep on the wing' (Poe).

p. 62, 10. 'I met with this idea in an old English tale, which I am now unable to obtain and quote from memory: – "The verie essence and, as it were, springheade and origine of all musiche is the verie pleasaunte sounde which the trees of the forest do make when they growe"' (Poe).

p. 62, 11. 'The wild bee will not sleep in the shade if there be moonlight.

'The rhyme in this verse, as in one about sixty lines before, has an appearance of affectation. It is, however, imitated from Sir W. Scott, or rather from Claud Halero – in whose mouth I admired its effect:

> O! were there an island,
> Tho' ever so wild
> Where woman might smile, and
> No man be beguil'd, &c.'
>
> (Poe).

p. 63, 12. 'With the Arabians there is a medium between Heaven and Hell, where men suffer no punishment, but yet do not attain that tranquil and even happiness which they suppose to be characteristic of heavenly enjoyment.

> Un no rompido sueno –
> Un dia puro – allegre – libre
> Quiera –
> Libre de amor – de zelo –
> De odio – de esperanza – de rezelo.
> – *Luis Ponce de Leon*.

'Sorrow is not excluded from "Al Aaraaf," but it is that sorrow which the living love to cherish for the dead, and which, in some minds, resembles the delirium of opium. The passionate excitement of Love and the buoyancy of spirit attendant upon intoxication are its less holy pleasures – the price of which, to those souls who make choice of "Al Aaraaf" as their residence after life, is final death and annihilation' (Poe).

p. 63, 13.

> 'There be tears of perfect moan
> Wept for thee in Helicon.
> – *Milton*' (Poe).

The lines are quoted from Milton's 'Epitaph on the Marchioness of Winchester'.

p. 63, 14. In the figures of Angelo and Ianthe, Poe is recasting a common mythological story, in which a mortal falls in love with an immortal. Angelo is united with the nymph Ianthe through willing his own death; Ianthe, however, must suffer the pains and perils of earthly beings. The surrender to sensuous temptation thus brings disharmony to the world of Al Aaraaf, as it did to the Garden of Eden.

p. 64, 15. 'It [the Parthenon] was entire in 1687 – the most elevated spot in Athens' (Poe).

p. 64; 16.

> 'Shadowing more beauty in their airy brows
> Than have the white breasts of the Queen of Love.
> – *Marlowe*' (Poe).

The quotation is from *Doctor Faustus*.

p. 65, 17. 'Pennon – for pinion. –*Milton*' (Poe).

ROMANCE

'Romance' was first published as the 'Preface' to *Tamerlane and Other Poems* (1829) and, in considerably expanded form, as 'Introduction' to *Poems: Second Edition* (1831). In 1845, when the poem appeared in the *Broadway Journal*, Poe returned to the shorter text of 1829, with some slight revisions. Some of Poe's additions to the poem may have seemed to him too personal, but are of interest to the reader for precisely this reason. The additions of 1831 incorporated a number of striking phrases, but the total impact of the poem is more direct in the simplified early version. In 1831 the first stanza concluded:

> Succeeding years, too wild for song,
> Then roll'd like tropic storms along,
> Where, thro' the garish lights that fly,
> Dying along the troubled sky
> Lay bare, thro' vistas thunder-riven,
> The blackness of the general Heaven,
> That very blackness yet doth fling
> Light on the lightning's silver sing [? wing].

Following this was an entirely new stanza:

> For, being an idle boy lang syne,
> Who read Anacreon, and drank wine,
> I early found Anacreon rhymes
> Were almost passionate sometimes –
> And by a strange alchemy of brain
> His pleasure always turn'd to pain –
> His naivete to wild desire –
> His wit to love – his wine to fire –
> And so, being young and dipt in folly
> I fell in love with melancholy,
> And used to throw my earthly rest
> And quiet all away in jest –
> I could not love except where Death
> Was mingling his with Beauty's breath –
> Or Hymen, Time, and Destiny
> Were stalking between her and me.

Poe added the following lines to the conclusion of the poem:

> But *now* my soul hath too much room –
> Gone are the glory and the gloom –
> The Black hath mellow'd into gray,
> And all the fires are fading away.
>
> My draught of passion hath been deep –
> I revell'd, and I now would sleep –

And after-drunkenness of soul
Succeeds the glories of the bowl –
An idle longing night and day
To dream my very life away.

But dreams – of those who dream as I,
Aspiringly, are damned, and die:
Yet should I swear I mean alone,
By notes so very shrilly blown,
To break upon Time's monotone,
While yet my vapid joy and grief
Are tintless of the yellow leaf –
Why not an imp the graybeard hath
Will shake his shadow in my path –
And even the graybeard will o'erlook
Connivingly my dreaming-book.

TO HELEN

One of Poe's most famous poems, 'To Helen' was possibly inspired by Mrs Jane Stith Stannard, a beautiful woman who befriended Poe when he was a boy in Richmond. The 'Helen' of the poem is, of course, an idealized figure, whose name always conveyed for Poe associations of the beauty and the power of woman. Poe's claim that he wrote the poem before the age of fourteen is questionable. It first appeared in the 1831 *Poems*, and was revised before its 'rededication' to Mrs Helen Whitman in 1845; the version printed here appeared in *The Raven and Other Poems* (1845).

p. 68, 1. The word Nicean has been variously interpreted as referring to the seacoast of Nicea (Asia Minor); to the nymph Nicaea; and as a derivative of the Greek form NIKH, meaning 'victorious. There is no more excellent example of the unnecessary obfuscation which so often characterizes criticism of Poe's work: the word is clearly intended to impress by its musical qualities, and to evoke the splendour of the ancient world; its precise origin is, within the context of the poem, triumphantly irrelevant.

ISRAFEL

First published in the 1831 *Poems*, 'Israfel' was revised on several occasions before it achieved the final form printed in the *Broadway Journal* in 1845.

p. 69, 1. 'And the angel Israfel, whose heart-strings are a lute, and who has the sweetest voice of all God's creatures. – KORAN' (Poe). Poe's version of this sentence from George Sale's translation of the Koran is slightly garbled, and he has interpolated the phrase 'whose heart-strings are a lute'. The phrase could have been derived from either Thomas Moore's *Lalla Rookh* or De Béranger's 'Le Refus', which provides the similar epigram to 'The Fall of the House of Usher'. Through the figure of Israfel, a symbol of poetic inspiration, Poe advances some of his own major theories of the art of poetry.

p. 69, 2. The reference is not to the Pleiad, the seven most eminent Greek poets of the reign of Ptolemy II, but to the Pleiades (from whom the name of the Pleiad was derived) – the seven daughters of Atlas who were pursued by Orion and turned into constellations.

p. 69, 3. A nymph of the Mohammedan paradise.

THE CITY IN THE SEA

The first known version of 'The City in the Sea' appeared in the *Poems* of 1831; the text used here includes Poe's final manuscript revisions of 1845.

THE SLEEPER

First published in the *Poems* of 1831, 'The Sleeper' was later revised and is printed here as it appeared in 1845 in the *Philadelphia Saturday Museum*, with corrections by Lorimer Graham.

LENORE

First published in 1831, 'Lenore' was extensively revised in subsequent years, and may at one time have been published under the title 'Helen', as a tribute to Mrs Whitman; the text used here dates from 1843. The revised text of 1845 joins lines of this version to produce a poem composed of improbable and rather irritating heptameter lines.

THE VALLEY OF UNREST

'The Valley of Unrest' was originally published, in the *Poems* of 1831, as 'The Valley of Nis'; the final version, used here, was published in the *American Whig Review* (April 1845) and incorporated extensive revisions.

THE RAVEN

Various myths surround the composition of Poe's most famous poem, which he probably began in 1842 or 1843. With considerable editorial fanfare, it appeared anonymously in the *New York Evening Mirror* on 29 January 1845, and was reprinted the following month over Poe's name in the *American Whig Review*. During Poe's lifetime the poem appeared in eleven periodicals, and sixteen manuscript versions survive. The text used here is that included in *The Raven and Other Poems* (1845), with Poe's own corrections and variations collated by Lorimer Graham.

p. 79, 1. Poe plays on the obscure secondary meaning of 'gloated': 'to refract light from'.

p. 79, 2. In classical mythology, nepenthe was a potion with the power to banish sorrow.

ULALUME

'Ulalume' first appeared in the *American Review* (December 1847), and contained a tenth stanza which Poe omitted in the subsequent revised printings of the poem, which was published in four other magazines before his death. The version followed here is that of Griswold's edition of the *Works*, which agrees with the final manuscript revisions. The title 'Ulalume' is perhaps intended to suggest wailing – from the Latin *ululare*.

p. 81, 1. Perhaps a reference to Daniel François Auber, whose *Le Lac des Fées* was a very popular ballet in America.

p. 81, 2. Like 'Auber', Weir might well be a word of Poe's own invention, or one which he borrowed because of its musical properties. If the name was derived from a specific source, the most likely claimant is Robert Walter Weir, a nineteenth-century landscape painter of the romantically 'misty' school.

p. 81, 3. A recently discovered Antarctic volcano, rather obscurely invoked at this point in the poem.

FOR ANNIE

Addressed to Mrs 'Annie' Richmond, the poem appeared shortly before Poe's death in both the *Flag of our Union* and *Home Journal* (28 April 1849); the latter text is used here.

A VALENTINE

The poem is an acrostic: by taking the first letter of the first line, the second letter of the second line, etc., the reader discovers the name Frances Sargent Osgood, to whom the poem is dedicated. Poe's Valentine address was written in 1846 and published in the *New York Evening Mirror* on 21 February of that year. In his first version of the poem Poe misspelled 'Sargent' as Sergeant', so that he was later compelled to rewrite the latter half of the poem; the concluding four lines are entirely different. The revised poem was published in 1849 in the *Flag of our Union* and *Sartain's Union Magazine* (February 1849); the latter text is used here.

ANNABEL LEE

By one of those recurrent ironies with which Poe's life is marked, 'Annabel Lee' was published in the *New York Tribune* on the day Poe died (9 October 1849). Although Mrs Whitman imagined, like various other ladies of the day, that the poem referred to herself, there is no reason to doubt that of the various events in his own life which might have provided inspiration for the poem, the death of Virginia is the most probable. After its initial publication the poem was reprinted in the *Southern Literary Messenger* and *Sartain's Union Magazine*; the *Tribune* text is used here.

THE BELLS

First published in April 1849, 'The Bells' may have been written at the suggestion of Mary Louise Shew, who gave the Poes so much assistance during Virginia's final illness, and at whose house Poe was a guest following his wife's death. Though no doubt written a year or two before, the poem was first published in April 1849, in *Home Journal*. An ingenious example of the use of onomatopoeia, this was Poe's last major poem. In the *Home Journal* version it was only eighteen lines in length; in its expanded and revised form it appeared posthumously in *Sartain's Union Magazine* in November of 1850.

ELDORADO

'Eldorado' was first printed in the *Flag of our Union* on 21 April 1849. The text used here is from the Griswold edition.

2. Tales

MS. FOUND IN A BOTTLE

'MS. Found in a Bottle' was awarded the *Baltimore Saturday Visitor* fiction prize in 1833, and was a major event in Poe's literary career; the story was subsequently reprinted in *The Gift*, the *Southern Literary Messenger*, and the *Broadway Journal* of 1845, which provides the version printed here. The asterisks appear in the original, and do not indicate emendation.

p. 99, 1. The epigraph translates,

> He who has but a moment to live,
> No longer has anything to dissimulate.

p. 109, 2. 'NOTE. – The "MS. Found in a Bottle," was originally published in 1831, and it was not until many years afterwards that I became acquainted with the maps of Mercator, in which the ocean is represented as rushing, by four mouths, into the (northern) Polar Gulf, to be absorbed into the bowels of the earth; the Pole itself being represented by a black rock, towering to a prodigious height' (Poe). The date of publication is incorrect.

LIGEIA

'Ligeia', which Poe once asserted to be his best tale, was first published in the *Baltimore American·Museum* (18 September 1838), included in *Tales of the Grotesque and Arabesque*, and extensively revised for the *Broadway Journal* publication (27 September 1845).

p. 110, 1. Poe's attribution of the epigram to Joseph Glanvill has never been substantiated. If the quotation is apocryphal, Poe nonetheless attributed it to a highly probable source, since Glanvill was one of the Cambridge Platonists whose idealism partially embraced ancient Hebrew cabbalism, emphasizing spiritualistic manifestations of the immortality of the soul.

p. 111, 2. Poe would seem to have invented this deity, as he may have invented his epigram; the word suggests both Ashtoreth, the Phoenician and Egyptian fertility goddess, and Tophet, a version of hell associated in the Old Testament with Egyptian worship of Moloch, a Semitic deity to whom children were burned in sacrifice.

p. 112, 3. Frances Sheridan's oriental romance, *The History of Nourjahad* (1767), was no doubt familiar to Poe.

p. 116, 4. The poem did not appear in the first published version of 'Ligeia', but was published separately in *Graham's Magazine* (January 1843) as 'The Conqueror Worm' and incorporated in the *Broadway Journal* version of the tale.

THE MAN THAT WAS USED UP

First published in *Burton's Gentleman's Magazine* when Poe was editor, the tale was slightly revised for publication in *Tales of the Grotesque and Arabesque, The Prose Romances of Edgar A. Poe*, and the *Broadway Journal*, which provides the final text. In the subtitle Poe may have been playing on the 'Tippecanoe and Tyler Too' slogan of the 1840 presidential election, when General Harrison's victory over Tecumseh at Tippecanoe (1811) was celebrated as part of the coon-skin and log-cabin ethos with which the Whigs sought to remake their fading national image into that of the party of the people.

p. 127, 1. The epigraph, from Corneille's *Le Cid*, translates,

Weep, weep, my eyes, and dissolve in water!
The better half of my life has placed the other in the tomb.

THE FALL OF THE HOUSE OF USHER

'The Fall of the House of Usher' was first published in *Burton's Gentleman's Magazine* in 1839. The final text – heavily revised – is provided by the *Tales* of 1845.

p. 138, 1. Poe's motto, from Pierre Jean de Béranger's 'Le Refus', translates,

His heart is a suspended lute;
Whenever one touches it, it resounds.

cf. 'Israfel'.

p. 147, 2. 'The Haunted Palace' was published separately in the *Baltimore Museum* (April 1839) before it appeared as part of the story.

p. 149, 3. All the works in Usher's library of the occult and exotic are real works with the possible exception of the *Vigiliæ Mortuorum secundum Chorum Ecclesiæ Maguntinæ*, which has not been positively identified.

p. 153, 4. *The Mad Trist* of Sir Launcelot Canning is almost certainly of Poe's own invention.

WILLIAM WILSON

First published in *Burton's Gentleman's Magazine* in 1839, 'William Wilson' draws in a highly figurative manner on Poe's own schooldays in England; the Reverend John Bransby conducted the Manor House School which Poe attended, and his name has been retained in the story. Poe revised 'William Wilson' for publication in the *Broadway Journal* (30 August 1845), and this provides the final text. The plot of the story was suggested by Washington Irving's 'Unwritten Drama of Lord Byron'.

p. 158, 1. The quotation is not to be found in Chamberlayne's *Pharronida*, and has not otherwise been identified.

THE MAN OF THE CROWD

'The Man of the Crowd' was first published in *Burton's Gentleman's Magazine* in 1840 and revised for the 1845 edition of the *Tales*, which provides the final text.

p. 179, 1. The motto translates, 'This great misfortune – not being able to be alone.'

p. 188, 2. 'The *Hortulus Animæ cum Oratiunculis Aliquibus Superadditis* [of Grüninger]' (Poe).

THE MURDERS IN THE RUE MORGUE

Poe's first detective story, 'The Murders in the Rue Morgue', was published in *Graham's Magazine* in 1841; the *Tales* of 1845 provides the final version, meticulously revised. The name Dupin may have been suggested by R. M. Walsh's *Conspicuous Living Char-*

acters of France, which Poe reviewed for *Graham's Magazine* the same month the story appeared.

p. 196, 1. 'The first letter destroys the antique sound.'

p. 224, 2. 'Rousseau, *Nouvelle Héloïse*' (Poe). The phrase translates, 'of denying that which does exist, and explaining that which does not.'

A DESCENT INTO THE MAELSTRÖM

'A Descent into the Maelström' was published in *Graham's Magazine* in 1841 and slightly revised for the *Tales* of 1845, which provides the final text.

p. 225, 1. Poe slightly misquotes from Glanvill's *Essays on Several Important Subjects in Philosophy and Religion*.

p. 226, 2. The Lofoden Islands and the maelström to which Poe refers in the story are actual, although he exaggerates the latter's size and power and alters some of the Norwegian place names.

p. 240, 3. 'See Archimedes, "*De Incidentibus in Fluido*"' (Poe).

ELEONORA

First published in *The Gift* for 1842, 'Eleonora' was extensively revised for publication in the *Broadway Journal* in 1845. The asterisks appear in the original and do not denote emendation.

p. 243, 1. The epigram translates, 'The soul is saved by the preservation of the specific form.'

p. 243, 2. The Nubian geographer referred to is Claudius Ptolemaeus (Ptolemy) of Alexandria, the founder of the Ptolemaic system of geography and astronomy. Poe also invokes his authority in 'A Descent into the Maelström'. The Latin translates, 'They faced a sea of shadows with the idea of exploring what it contained.'

THE OVAL PORTRAIT

'The Oval Portrait' was first published in *Graham's Magazine* and slightly revised for publication in the *Broadway Journal* (26 April 1845), which provides the final text.

THE MASQUE OF THE RED DEATH

First published in *Graham's Magazine* in 1842, 'The Masque of the Red Death' appeared in final form in the *Broadway Journal* (19 July 1845).

THE PIT AND THE PENDULUM

'The Pit and the Pendulum' was published in *The Gift* for 1843 and considerably revised for the *Broadway Journal* publication in 1845.

p. 261, 1. The Latin motto, from a quatrain composed for the gates of a market to be erected on the site of the Jacobin club house in Paris, translates, 'The unholy gang of torturers fed its long furies from the blood of the innocent and was not satisfied. Now that the fatherland is safe, the cave of death is broken; where terrible death was, life and health appear.'

THE TELL-TALE HEART

One of Poe's most terrifying stories, 'The Tell-Tale Heart' was first published in James Russell Lowell's *Pioneer* in 1843 and carefully revised for publication in 1845, in the *Broadway Journal*, which provides the final text.

THE GOLD-BUG

'The Gold-Bug' was the prize-winning story in a competition sponsored by the *Philadelphia Dollar Newspaper*, where it appeared in 1843; the revised version included in the *Tales* of 1845, with Poe's own corrections, is followed here.

p. 283, 1. The epigram is quoted from Charles Dibdin's *All in the Wrong* (1822).

THE BLACK CAT

Originally published in the *United States Saturday Post* in 1843, 'The Black Cat' appeared in slightly revised form in the *Tales* of 1854, which provides the present text.

THE PURLOINED LETTER

The third of Poe's detective stories, 'The Purloined Letter' was published in *The Gift* for 1845, and shortly thereafter in the *Tales* of 1845; the version printed here incorporates Poe's own later corrections.

p. 330, 1. The epigraph, not to be found in Seneca, translates, 'Nothing is more detestable to wisdom than too much subtlety.'

p. 349, 2. The lines from Prosper Jolyot de Crébillon's *Atrée* translate,

A design so deadly,
If not worthy of Atreus, is worthy of Thyestes.

The reference is to the revenge of King Atreus of Mycenae against his brother Thyestes; the latter had seduced King Atreus's wife, and the king retaliated by killing his brother's sons and serving them to Thyestes at a banquet.

THE FACTS IN THE CASE OF M. VALDEMAR

Certainly Poe's most horrific story, 'The Facts in the Case of M. Valdemar' was first published in the *American Whig Review* for December 1845; the final text is taken from the *Broadway Journal* of 1845, incorporating Poe's own later corrections. In Poe's lifetime the tale was reprinted in England in *The Popular Record of Modern Science* as 'The Last Conversation of a Somnambule' and as a pamphlet entitled *Mesmerism, In Articulo Mortis*; it was generally accepted as the scientific description of a real event.

THE CASK OF AMONTILLADO

The only known text of 'The Cask of Amontillado' is that published in *Godey's Lady's Book* in November 1846. In his edition of Poe's work, Griswold made various alterations on the basis of manuscript revisions theoretically in his possession, but these cannot be authenticated.

HOP-FROG

This story originally appeared in the *Flag of our Union* (17 March 1849) as 'Hop-Frog; or, The Eight Chained Ourang-outangs', and was perhaps inspired by Froissart's account of the accidental burning of several French aristocrats during a masquerade party – if not by the original, then by the passages which E. A. Duyckinck had cited in *Barbarities of the Theatre*, in conjunction with the story of a young dancer who burned to death when her costume caught fire. 'Hop-Frog' was the last story to be published during Poe's lifetime, and is often seen as an allegory in which the writer takes revenge on his critics.

3. Essays and Reviews

LETTER TO B—

First published under the title 'Letter to Mr. —— —' as a preface to the *Poems* of 1831, the essay was corrected and slightly revised before its publication under the present title in the *Southern Literary Messenger* of July 1836. At that time Poe appended the note, 'These detached passages form part of the preface to a small volume printed some years ago for private circulation. They have vigor and much originality – but of course we shall not be called upon to endorse all the writer's opinions'. 'B' may well have been Elam Bliss, the publisher of Poe's first volume of poetry.

p. 380, 1. The punctuation is as it appeared in the original, and does not denote emendation here or elsewhere in the essay.

p. 381, 2. '*Spoudaiotaton kai philosophikotaton genos*' (Poe). The phrase is from Aristotle's *Poetics*, though Poe may have derived it from Wordsworth's Preface to the *Lyrical Ballads*.

p. 381, 3. The reference is to Charles Robert Maturin's Gothic romance, *Melmoth the Wanderer* (1820).

p. 382, 4. Poe has slightly misquoted from the Preface to Dryden's *All for Love* : for 'Trifles' read 'Errors'.

p. 382, 5. 'concerning all that can be known, and certain other things as well.'

p. 384, 6. Poe introduced the dashes into Wordsworth's 'The Pet Lamb' in order to emphasize what he considered the triteness of the poet's sentiments.

p. 384, 7. Poe's faulty French translates 'that most sects are correct, for the most part, in what they advocate, but not in those things which they deny.' The author quoted by Coleridge and misquoted by Poe is Leibnitz (*Trois Lettres à M. Redmond de Mont-Mort*).

p. 385, 8. The quotation is from Samuel Butler's *Hudibras*.

GEORGIA SCENES

Poe's review of *Georgia Scenes* appeared in the *Southern Literary Messenger* in March 1836. The anonymous author was Augustus Baldwin Longstreet (1790–1870). Poe shows his astuteness as a reviewer in recognizing the authenticity and artistic validity of the southwestern or frontier humour and vernacular which characterize the book, and since Longstreet can be seen as a direct forerunner of Mark Twain, much credit must be given the young reviewer who regards the book as 'a sure omen of better days for the literature of the South'. The punctuation in the review nowhere denotes emendation.

THE DRAKE–HALLECK REVIEW (excerpts)

'The Drake–Halleck Review' was Poe's first major attack on literary provincialism. It appeared in the *Southern Literary Messenger* in April 1836.

p. 394, 1. 'The charge of indiscriminate puffing will, of course, only apply to the *general* character of our criticism – there are some notable exceptions. We wish also especially to discriminate between those *notices* of new works which are intended merely to call public attention to them, and deliberate criticism of the works themselves' (Poe). There follows a lengthy discussion in which Poe quotes from various attacks on the *Messenger* and defends his own editorial policies.

p. 396, 2. 'We separate the sublime and the mystical – for, despite of high authorities, we are firmly convinced that the latter *may* exist, in the most vivid degree, without giving rise to the sense of the former' (Poe).

p. 396, 3. 'The consciousness of this truth was possessed by no mortal more than by Shelley, although he has only once specifically alluded to it' (Poe). Poe substantiates this assertion by quoting stanzas 5 and 6 from Shelley's 'Hymn to Intellectual Beauty'.

p. 396, 4. 'Imagination is, possibly in man, a lesser degree of the creative power of God. What the Deity imagines, is, but was also. The mind of man cannot imagine what is not. This latter point may be demonstrated. – See *Les Premiers Traits de L'Erudition Universelle, par M. Le Baron de Bielfield, 1767'* (Poe).

p. 398, 5. At this point Poe summarizes the plot of the poem and quotes a number of characteristic passages.

p. 399, 6.

> 'Chestnut color, or more slack,
> Gold upon a ground of black.
>   Ben Johnson' (Poe).

p. 402, 7. 'A review of Drake's poems, emanating from one of our proudest Universities, does not scruple to make use of the following language in relation to the *Culprit Fay*. "It is, to say the least, an elegant production, the purest specimen of Ideality we have ever met with, sustaining in each incident a most bewitching interest. Its very title is enough,"* &c. &c. We quote these expressions as a fair specimen of the general unphilosophical and adulatory tenor of our criticism' (Poe).

p. 403, 8. 'As examples of entire poems of the purest ideality, we would cite the *Prometheus Vinctus* of Aeschylus, the *Inferno* of Dante, Cervantes' *Destruction of Numantia*, the *Comus* of Milton, Pope's *Rape of the Lock*, Burns' *Tam O'Shanter*, the *Ancient Mariner*, the *Christabel*, and the *Kubla Khan* of Coleridge; and most especially the *Sensitive Plant* of Shelley, and the *Nightingale* of Keats. We have seen American poems evincing the faculty in the highest degree' (Poe).

p. 404, 9. 'Among things, which not only in our opinion, but in the opinion of far wiser and better men, are to be ranked with the mere prettiness of the Muse, are the positive similes so abundant in the writings of antiquity, and so much insisted upon by the critics of the reign of Queen Anne' (Poe).

p. 407, 10. At this point in the review Poe discusses a number of the shorter poems in Drake's volume.

p. 409, 11. Poe continues the review with a discussion of several of Halleck's shorter poems, which he attacks primarily for their artificiality.

WATKINS TOTTLE

Poe's review of *Watkins Tottle* marks an important stage in the establishment of Dickens's reputation in America; the review appeared in the *Southern Literary Messenger* for June 1836. The punctuation nowhere denotes emendation.

THE PHILOSOPHY OF FURNITURE

First published in *Burton's Gentleman's Magazine* in May 1840, 'The Philosophy of Furniture' was only slightly revised for publication in the *Broadway Journal* in 1845. This description of the 'ideal' chamber bears close comparison with descriptions of the haunted chambers in which so many of Poe's characters find themselves.

WYANDOTTÉ

Poe's review of James Fenimore Cooper's *Wyandotté* was published in *Graham's Magazine* in November 1843.

MUSIC

This piece is one of the 'Marginalia' which Poe wrote over a period of five years; some of the ideas expressed in these notebook pieces were later developed more fully in longer essays and reviews, but others were left to stand. In 1836 Poe began to sell them as 'fillers' to various magazines. 'Music' was published in the *Democratic Review* of 1844.

TIME AND SPACE

One of the 'Marginalia', 'Time and Space' foreshadows some of the scientific and philosophical questions with which Poe was to concern himself in *Eureka*. It appeared in the *Democratic Review* of 1844.

TWICE-TOLD TALES

Important not only for its early recognition of Hawthorne's genius, but more significantly as a statement of Poe's own theories of the short story, the review of *Twice-Told Tales* was published in *Graham's Magazine* in May 1842, and in revised form as 'Tale-Writing' in *Godey's Lady's Book* in November 1847.

THE AMERICAN DRAMA

One of several essays in which Poe considers the state of contemporary American drama, this one was published in the *American Whig Review* for August 1845, and carries forward some of the ideas advanced in a similar essay published in *Burton's Gentleman's Magazine* in 1839.

p. 448, 1. Pierre Antoine Berryer (1790–1868), French advocate and parliamentarian, won distinction for his championship of legitimism and defense of freedom of the press. By an irony of which Poe may have been conscious, Berryer and his father, in defending Marshall Ney in the trial of 1816, were assisted by an advocate named André Dupin.

p. 448, 2. 'the man who, in his description(s), demands the greatest possible quantity of antithesis.'

p. 448, 3. 'of denying that which does exist, and explaining that which does not.'

p. 450, 4. James Sheridan Knowles (1784–1862), poet and popular dramatist, gave up the stage in 1843 to become a Baptist preacher.

p. 451, 5. Nathaniel Parker Willis (1806–1867), American poet, journalist, editor and dramatist, began to write for the stage only under pressure of financial need; in 1845 he became co-editor of the *Home Journal*, to which Poe was an occasional contributor.

p. 462, 6. 'that the true is not always the credible'.

p. 465, 7. At this point in his review Poe quotes at length, and virtually without comment, from the play, in order to demonstrate the 'graceful, well-expressed, imaginative' quality of the verse itself.

HAZLITT

Poe's review of *The Characters of Shakespeare*, by William Hazlitt, appeared in the *Broadway Journal* on 16 August 1845.

THE PHILOSOPHY OF COMPOSITION

Poe's famous essay on poetry was first published in *Graham's Magazine* in April 1846, and purported to be an analysis of the techniques the poet had observed in writing 'The Raven'. The piece was originally written as a lecture, intended to take advantage of the poem's considerable popularity.

SONG-WRITING

'Song-Writing', one of the 'Marginalia', was published in the *Southern Literary Messenger* in April 1849.

ON IMAGINATION

One of the 'Marginalia', 'On Imagination' appeared in the *Southern Literary Messenger* in May 1849.

THE VEIL OF THE SOUL

This brief but revealing definition of art, from the 'Marginalia', appeared in the *Southern Literary Messenger* in June 1849.

THE POETIC PRINCIPLE (excerpts)

This final statement of Poe's theory of verse embodies ideas which had already been stated in earlier essays and reviews, but never so forcefully or cohesively. 'The Poetic Principle', which Poe delivered many times as a lecture during the last years of his life, was published after his death in the *Home Journal* (31 August 1850) and in *Sartain's Union Magazine* (October 1850).

p. 500, 1. Joel Barlow's *Columbiad*, published in 1807, was a vast and cumbersome attempt to create a national American epic.

p. 500, 2. The popular and highly prolific French romantic poet, Alphonse de Lamartine (1790–1869).

p. 500, 3. The Scottish poet Robert Pollock (1798–1827) had composed a pretentious and ponderous verse essay entitled *The Course of Time*, whose apocalyptic visions won him a high reputation among the devout.

p. 502, 4. Nathaniel Parker Willis (1806–67): see 'The American Drama' above, and also note 5 to that essay.

p. 506, 5. The Irish poet-composer Thomas Moore (1779–1852) found his real vocation when he composed the *Irish Melodies*, which guaranteed his recognition as the national song-writer of Ireland. In Poe's admiration for Moore one sees a further instance of his belief in the necessary relationship between poetry and music, cf. 'Song-Writing'.

p. 508, 6. At this point Poe misquotes from the poem, given above in its correct form, 'Through the corridors of Time'.

p. 510, 7. At this point Poe quotes at length from the work of Edward Coote Pinkney, Thomas Moore, Thomas Hood, and Byron. Since he does not, in the process, add constructively to his argument, and was obviously playing upon the popular tastes of his own day, this section of the lecture has been omitted.

p. 512, 8. William Motherwell (1797–1877) was a Scottish poet and antiquarian very much in vogue in America.

READ MORE IN PENGUIN

In every corner of the world, on every subject under the sun, Penguin represents quality and variety – the very best in publishing today.

For complete information about books available from Penguin – including Puffins, Penguin Classics and Arkana – and how to order them, write to us at the appropriate address below. Please note that for copyright reasons the selection of books varies from country to country.

In the United Kingdom: Please write to *Dept. EP, Penguin Books Ltd, Bath Road, Harmondsworth, West Drayton, Middlesex UB7 ODA*

In the United States: Please write to *Consumer Sales, Penguin Putnam Inc., P.O. Box 12289 Dept. B, Newark, New Jersey 07101-5289*. VISA and MasterCard holders call 1-800-788-6262 to order Penguin titles

In Canada: Please write to *Penguin Books Canada Ltd, 10 Alcorn Avenue, Suite 300, Toronto, Ontario M4V 3B2*

In Australia: Please write to *Penguin Books Australia Ltd, P.O. Box 257, Ringwood, Victoria 3134*

In New Zealand: Please write to *Penguin Books (NZ) Ltd, Private Bag 102902, North Shore Mail Centre, Auckland 10*

In India: Please write to *Penguin Books India Pvt Ltd, 11 Community Centre, Panchsheel Park, New Delhi 110017*

In the Netherlands: Please write to *Penguin Books Netherlands bv, Postbus 3507, NL-1001 AH Amsterdam*

In Germany: Please write to *Penguin Books Deutschland GmbH, Metzlerstrasse 26, 60594 Frankfurt am Main*

In Spain: Please write to *Penguin Books S. A., Bravo Murillo 19, 1° B, 28015 Madrid*

In Italy: Please write to *Penguin Italia s.r.l., Via Benedetto Croce 2, 20094 Corsico, Milano*

In France: Please write to *Penguin France, Le Carré Wilson, 62 rue Benjamin Baillaud, 31500 Toulouse*

In Japan: Please write to *Penguin Books Japan Ltd, Kaneko Building, 2-3-25 Koraku, Bunkyo-Ku, Tokyo 112*

In South Africa: Please write to *Penguin Books South Africa (Pty) Ltd, Private Bag X14, Parkview, 2122 Johannesburg*

READ MORE IN PENGUIN

A CHOICE OF CLASSICS